The "Unknown" Reality:
A Seth Book

Volume 2

Books by Jane Roberts

The Coming of Seth
    (Original title: How to Develop Your ESP Power)
The Seth Material
Seth Speaks: The Eternal Validity of the Soul
The Education of Oversoul Seven
The Nature of Personal Reality: A Seth Book
Adventures in Consciousness: An Introduction to Aspect Psychology
Dialogues of the Soul and Mortal Self in Time
Psychic Politics: An Aspect Psychology Book
The "Unknown" Reality: A Seth Book (in two volumes)
The World View of Paul Cézanne: A Psychic Interpretation
The Afterdeath Journal of an American Philosopher: The World
    View of William James
The Further Education of Oversoul Seven
Emir's Education in the Proper Use of Magical Powers
The Nature of the Psyche: Its Human Expression (A Seth Book)

The "Unknown" Reality:
A Seth Book
Volume 2

by Jane Roberts

notes and introduction by Robert F. Butts

Prentice-Hall, Inc., Englewood Cliffs, New Jersey

Printed in the United States of America

Prentice-Hall International, Inc., London
Prentice-Hall of Australia, Pty. Ltd., Sydney
Prentice-Hall of Canada, Ltd., Toronto
Prentice-Hall of India Private Ltd., New Delhi
Prentice-Hall of Japan, Inc., Tokyo
Prentice-Hall of Southeast Asia Pte. Ltd., Singapore
Whitehall Books Limited, Wellington, New Zealand
10 9 8 7 6 5

Library of Congress Cataloging in Publication Data
Roberts, Jane
    The "unknown" reality

    Includes indexes.
    1. Psychical Research.   I. Seth.   II. Title.
BF1031.R634 1977   133.9   77-1092
ISBN 0-13-938704-8 (v. 1)
ISBN 0-13-938779-X (v. 1) pbk.
ISBN 0-13-938696-3 (v. 2)
ISBN 0-13-938852-4 (v. 2) pbk.

TO ROB

Contents

SECTION 6: Reincarnation and Counterparts: The "Past" Seen Through the Mosaics of Consciousness 515

"Nature, without nature's source, would not last a moment."

Seth
September 19, 1977

With Winged

With winged brains
We swoop and swirl
Inside the blue bell
Of the outer world.

Birds of curved dimensions
Have their neighborhood
Limited by ceiling's
Weight of bone and blood.

But time and space are one to us.
The infinite skull
Opens skies all curled within,
Miniature world on world.

(A note by R.F.B.: Jane was 32 years old when she wrote this poem in April 1961. It clearly foreshadows certain ideas in the Seth material, which she was to begin delivering 19 months later. With Winged also makes interesting reading along with the verse from her much earlier poem, Summer Is Winter; *see page 1 of Volume 1 of* "Unknown" Reality.)

Introductory Notes
by Robert F. Butts

The two volumes making up *The "Unknown" Reality: A Seth Book*, were dictated by my wife, Jane Roberts, in cooperation with Seth, the nonphysical "energy personality essence" for whom she speaks when she's in trance. I wrote in the Introductory Notes for Volume 1 that Jane began delivering *"Unknown" Reality* (as we soon came to call it) in the 679th session for February 4, 1974, and finished it with the 744th session for April 23, 1975. She produced the two books in an accumulated trance time of about 90 hours—an accomplishment that I think quite remarkable.

Let me quickly recap a few more facts about the production of this work. Seth himself always referred to *"Unknown" Reality* as one unit until we reached the last session. He divided the manuscript into six sections of varying lengths. There are no chapters *per se*. As Seth explained in the 743rd session: "This book had no chapters [in order] to further disrupt your accepted notions of what a book should be. There are different kinds of organization present, however, and in any given section of the book, several levels of consciousness are appealed to at once."

Seth also presented the entire work in such a way that the events of our daily lives were intimately connected with his material, serving as personal examples of how his theories actually work in everyday experience. He hadn't been delivering *"Unknown" Reality* for long, then, before I realized that I'd have to devise a system of presentation that would handle his material, my own notes (which I could see were going to be considerably longer than they are in Seth's other books, *Seth Speaks* and *The Nature of Personal Reality*), excerpts from Jane's ESP classes, appendixes, and anything else that might be included.

As Seth continued dictation I was fired by *his* purpose to make the unknown elements of human life at least partially visible—an audacious goal, I thought—and I tried to do my part in recording all such disclosures as they appeared in our lives and were reflected in the experiences of our friends and students.

The accumulated material further added to the length of the work, which was considerable. Finally we chose to divide *"Unknown" Reality* into two volumes. This meant that our readers could have access to part of the manuscript while I was preparing the rest. Seth agreed with our decision.

It isn't necessary to repeat many more of the Introductory Notes for Volume 1 here, although I'll ask the reader to review them in connection with the material presented below. But the most important thing about those notes, I think, is Jane's own account of her subjective relationship with Seth.

Seth's Preface is in Volume 1, of course, and it too should be studied again; to me, such acts of referral between the two volumes help the reader mentally unite them.

After I touch upon the contents of Volume 1, I'll have the freedom to move into some other topics that occurred to Jane and me as I put Volume 2 together—subjects regarding the Seth phenomenon itself, for example. I also want to present a few passages from both regular and private (or "deleted") sessions that were held before, during, or after Seth-Jane's actual production of *"Unknown" Reality* in its entirety. At least some of Jane's other books will be mentioned occasionally.

Seth often advances his ideas by weaving together several themes into a complex pattern in any given session, or throughout a body of material. This process can also result in a similar approach on my part when I discuss his dictation, so I'll initiate a summary of

Volume 1 by using four sources presented by Seth himself: a key passage from his Preface; the headings he gave for the three sections that comprise Volume 1, along with a few elaborations of my own; a brief description of the appendixes which I assembled over a period of time; and a passage from the 762nd session, in which, eight months after he'd finished *"Unknown" Reality*, Seth speaks further about his purposes in producing it.

First, though, I'll explain that in sessions Seth refers to Jane by her male entity name, Ruburt—and that he does so (as I quote him in Appendix 18) simply because "the given entity identifies itself more with the so-called male characteristics than with the female." He also addresses me by my entity name, which is Joseph.

Now these quotations are from Seth's Preface (for Volume 1):

"Jane Roberts's experience to some extent hints at the multidimensional nature of the human psyche and gives clues as to the abilities that lie within each individual. These are part of your racial heritage. They give notice of psychic bridges connecting the known and 'unknown' realities in which you dwell.

"In my other books I used many accepted ideas as a springboard to lead readers into other levels of understanding. Here, I wish to make it clear that *["Unknown" Reality]* will initiate a journey in which it may <u>seem</u> that the familiar is left far behind. Yet when I am finished, I hope you will discover that the known reality is even more precious, more 'real,' because you will find it illuminated both within and without by the rich fabric of an 'unknown' reality now seen emerging from the most intimate portions of daily life. . . . Your concepts of personhood are now limiting you personally and *en masse*, and yet your religions, metaphysics, histories, and even your sciences are hinged upon your ideas of who and what you are. Your psychologies do not explain your own reality to you. They cannot contain your experience. Your religions do not explain your greater reality, and your sciences leave you just as ignorant about the nature of the universe in which you dwell.

"These institutions and disciplines are composed of individuals, each restrained by limiting ideas about their own private reality; and so it is with private reality that we will begin and always return. Period. The ideas in this book are meant to expand the <u>private reality</u> of each reader. They may appear esoteric or complicated, yet they are not beyond the reach of any person who is determined to understand the nature of the unknown elements of the self, and its greater world."

Where do the events of our lives begin or end? Where do

we fit into them, individually and as members of the species? These questions, with Seth's explanations, are the heart of Volume 1. Because *"Unknown" Reality* is organized along intuitive rather than consecutive lines, though, it's difficult to provide a brief résumé. Jane probably described Volume 1 as simply as possible, however, when she said: "Volume 1 provides the general background and information upon which the exercises and methods in Volume 2 depend." I quoted that statement in Volume 1's Epilogue, and now, after finishing my own work on the entire manuscript, I realize how truly apropos it is.

The first volume, like this one, defies easy description, then, since it leaps over many definitions we usually take for granted; and with its lack of chapter divisions it even confounds our ideas of what a book is. Yet it certainly contains a most intriguing, multi-dimensional view of the nature of probabilities, a view in which our ideas of a "simple, single event" must vanish; at least we can never again look at any event as being concrete, finished, or absolute. Seth stresses the importance of probabilities as they exist in relationship to a thought, an ordinary physical event, or the mass event of *Homo sapiens* as a species, and emphasizes the existence of probable realities as the understructure of free will.

His headings for the three sections of Volume 1 do give some indication of its contents.

Section 1: "You and the 'Unknown' Reality"—Nine sessions describing how probabilities merge with the events of our private lives.

Section 2: "Parallel Man, Alternate Man, and Probable Man: The Reflection of These in the Present, Private Psyche. Your Multidimensional Reality in the Now of Your Being"—Eight sessions dealing with the vast unknown origin of our species in a psychological past that by contrast makes evolutionary time look like yesterday.

Section 3: "The Private Probable Man, the Private Probable Woman, the Species in Probabilities, and Blueprints for Realities"—Nine sessions devoted to the importance of dreams in the creation of "concrete" events from probable ones. This section also includes discussions on the True Dream-Art Scientist, the True Mental Physicist, and the Complete Physician, as well as material on subatomic particles and the spin of electrons in relationship to perceived reality.

Volume 1 of *"Unknown" Reality* concludes with 11 appendixes compiled from Seth sessions related to the book's subject matter. These are supplemented by notes regarding the relationship involving Seth, Jane, and myself, and by other pertinent material that throws light upon the larger framework in which these sessions take place. I also provided a certain number of cross references, directing the reader to connected passages in Seth's and/or Jane's other books.

To me, some of the most important material in Volume 1 is Jane's information on her sensing of other neurological pulses as they're connected with probable events, and how she picked up those pulses by bypassing her direct, or ordinary neurological impact. See her work in appendixes 4 and 5. Seth also discussed such neurological changeovers in Session 685, among others. I think this kind of material offers a rich source for future scientific investigation.

This present book, Volume 2, goes on from there as Seth creates an intriguing thematic framework, and then invites us to "play along," to join in and to discover the unknown reality for ourselves through a series of exercises geared to illuminate the inner structures upon which our exterior ones depend.

In the 762nd session for December 15, 1975, mentioned earlier, Seth explained how *"Unknown" Reality* fit into the larger body of his material:

"In *Seth Speaks* I tried to describe certain extensions of your own reality in terms that my readers could understand. In *The Nature of Personal Reality*, I tried to extend the boundaries of individual existence as it is usually experienced . . . to give the reader hints that would increase practical, spiritual and physical enjoyment and fulfillment in daily life. Those books were dictated by me in a more or less straight narrative style. In *'Unknown' Reality* I went further, showing how the experiences of the psyche splash outward into the daylight, so to speak. I hope that [in those two books] through my dictation and through Ruburt's and Joseph's experiences, the reader can see the greater dimensions that touch ordinary living, and sense the psyche's greater magic. *'Unknown' Reality* required much more work on Joseph's part, and that additional effort in itself was a demonstration that the psyche's events are very difficult to pin down in time. Seemingly its action goes out in all directions. . . . As Joseph did his notes, it became apparent that some events . . . seemed to have no beginning or end."

Later in these notes I plan to return to Seth's point about the psyche's events and time. In any case, I finished preparing Volume 1 for publication in January 1977, and it appeared in print later that year. We were delighted that the public could take advantage of part of the material while I made the second volume ready. The days and weeks I spent working on my notes for Volume

2 began to pile up into months, however, and I became more and more concerned.

It seemed that I should have finished my part of both books long ago, even though simultaneously I was working on several other projects with Jane, as well as painting a few hours a day. Finally, the disparity between the time Seth-Jane had spent producing Volume 1 alone (around 45 hours), and my own commitment in ordinary time, became so great in my mind as to be almost overwhelming.

I also felt that the chronology of presentation for both Seth's and Jane's books was being distorted: Because I was so slow in finishing my work on Volume 2 of *"Unknown" Reality*, Jane published her *Psychic Politics* first, for example, when the reverse order should have prevailed. After all, I told myself innumerable times, these were Seth's and Jane's books, not mine. I wasn't hesitant about recognizing my own role in helping Jane's psychic abilities show themselves in a consistent way (as, say, in intuitively devising the session format for the presentation of the Seth material). But that recognition didn't make me feel any better.

Jane insisted that the notes were important, as a constant reminder to the reader that psychic or inner events happen in the context of daily life. Sometimes I thought she was simply being kind in so reassuring me. Seth too agreed that the notes, appendixes, and other additions were pertinent. He also stressed that our plan to divide the work was intuitively correct, and based on legitimate inner knowledge. This cheered me considerably, of course. (However, the decision to publish in two volumes, made when *"Unknown" Reality* was almost finished, caused me to rewrite most of my original notes for it with that new presentation in mind.)

The whole adventure has certainly been a learning experience, one demanding a kind of forbearance that neither Jane nor I could have really anticipated. If the waiting until I finished with Volume 2 has been difficult for me, it's been doubly so for Jane, since by nature she's much more spontaneous and quick than I am. Yet the wait itself was creative. As I show below, putting this Volume 2 together has represented a process of discovery for me—just as I hope studying it will for the reader.

It seemed that each time I searched through all of those unpublished sessions (covering well over a decade) for just the right supplementary material, I found something new. More often than not, this made me redo my own notes in unanticipated ways—always a creative challenge that was most enjoyable, and yet, paradoxically, one that at times was very frustrating. Such episodes often caused me to take much longer to produce finished work. I learned a patience that I hadn't suspected was possible for me. For this patience, employed in conjuring up thoughts and images through words, was objectively and subjectively quite different in quality from that which I was so used to using in producing painted images. I could feel my mind and abilities, using either words *or* pictures, stretch as a result.

Seth himself helped me out more than once—and others can find his material here useful in many situations. From the 751st session for June 30, 1975, which was held a couple of months after he'd finished his part of the long project:

"Now: You need not worry about *'Unknown' Reality*. You have already done the books in another probable reality, and completed them very well.

"The model for them and your notes already exists within your mind. Scan any paragraph of your notes, then turn your mind gently a half notch aside. As you do so you will be able to sense your own completed version, and any word that does not fit will be instantly sensed, while another will at once slip to mind.

"Your final paragraphs are already there in the probability, now, that you have chosen. That probability belongs with the present you have now—yet you chose it from an infinite number of other realities. The books arose from probabilities, both yours and mine as well as Ruburt's.

"In some we did not meet. Even those, however, contain the probability that we will, since here we do."

I used that information of Seth's many times while working with *"Unknown" Reality*. Even so, I learned that on such a long-term project it's easy to lose that acute sense of what one really wants to do and show—but I also learned how to constantly renew my focus. This presented me with what seemed like an endless series of challenges, yet I discovered again and again that I enjoyed them: Each time I sat down to work, whether on the most routine short note or the most complicated appendix, I searched for that particular, personal sense of intense concentration on the matter at hand. And each time I achieved it I experienced once more that complete inner and outer, mental and physical involvement in which time was often significantly negated. These were actual, felt episodes during which I rose above those frustrations mentioned earlier. (I've often wondered how much one's ordinary bodily aging processes are either slowed or superseded during such periods of great focus.)

Now, Jane and I also see much more clearly how our respective characteristics contribute to our joint work. Without

Jane's psychic ability and spontaneity there would be no Seth sessions or books, as I tell her often. Then she tells me that without my persistence and diligence, the Seth material might not have been recorded or correlated, or might exist in a different form entirely. I wonder.

Questions, questions, questions—why do Jane and I have so many of them? First, the very nature of her abilities leads to hosts of them, in ways that would have been entirely unexpected earlier in our lives. A second group stems from what Seth *says*, and what we've come to believe about what he tells us. A third set arises from the reactions of others to the first two, through the letters and calls we receive and the questions of people knocking on our doors. In spite of all this, we've found that any one group of questions amplifies or adds to those related to the other two categories—i.e., like energy regenerating itself, the questions automatically proliferate. Many times I've had the idea that a good analogy here is furnished by Seth's concept of the "moment point." As he told us in the 681st session for Volume 1 of *"Unknown" Reality*:

"In your terms —the phrase is necessary—the moment point, the present, is the point of interaction between all existences and reality. All probabilities flow through it, though one of your moment points may be experienced <u>as centuries, or as a breath</u>, in other probable realities of which you are a part." Thus, just as a moment point can be explored indefinitely, so each newly arising question results in an ever-widening pool of inquiry.

In my notes introducing Volume 1, I wrote about placing the basic "artistic ideas" embodied in the Seth material at our conscious, aesthetic, and practical service in daily life. That's really what Seth's work is all about, in my opinion. Such an endeavor essentially involves the pursuit of an ideal, and represents our attempts to give physical and mental shape to the great inner, creative commotion of the universe that each person intuitively feels. Of course Jane and I want Seth's ideas and our own to touch responsive reflexes within others; then each individual can use the material in his or her own expression of that useful ideal, letting it serve to stimulate inner perceptions.

In Jane's case, at least, the role of the "medium" (or of the investigator or initiator) is extremely challenging. It's also arduous: In our Western societies it's much more comforting to grapple with chemistry, say, or farming or salesmanship, or with any of numerous other "practical" jobs or disciplines, than it is to confront the inner senses.

What Jane has to offer results from the study of consciousness itself, as it's expressed through her own experience and abilities. By choice, she has no buffers between herself and the exterior world—no assured status, for example. She doesn't enjoy the protection a scientist does, who probes into a particular subject in depth, then makes a learned report on it from an "objective" position that's safely outside the field of study. At the same time, I know that Jane feels a responsibility to "publish her results," and make them available to others. She's tough in ways that science, for instance, doesn't understand at all.

Still, her work has met with a great deal of understanding from many people, if hardly from everyone who's heard of it. It's interesting to ask how even extensive accepted credentials would help her respond to the extremes of feeling with which she and Seth are sometimes greeted: the outright rejection or the sheer adulation—or the threats she receives on occasion from those who say they'll commit suicide if Seth doesn't come through with a session for them immediately.

In important ways, Jane's work *is* outside of society's accepted frameworks—scientific, "occult," philosophical, or whatever. Not that we dwell upon that comparative isolation much, but we are aware of it. And I know that Jane sometimes misses the kind of camaraderie enjoyed by professionals who fit more comfortably into accepted structures. Actually, though, we consider many of our correspondents as friends, even though we never meet most of them, and despite the fact that Jane can only reply to their cheering communications with Seth's dictated letter (as well as our own), or with notes scribbled quickly on postcards. We've become quite aware of *that* kind of support, for which we're very grateful. Many such people are somewhat like us—refusing to accept any kind of dogma.

But some others, according to Seth, are uneasy with Jane's mental independence. In a personal session given for us in 1977, he said: "Some [people] do not want my authority questioned. *(Humorously:)* They think that if they had their own Supersoul, they would have far better sense than Ruburt; and they would use me as if I were a magic genie. They are afraid that Ruburt might question me out of existence. . . ." He went on to say that such individuals didn't understand that Jane's questioning nature fired the sessions' onset to begin with, and is somewhat responsible for the production of his work and books, as well as her own.

And in one form or another, Jane carries all of those books

with her from reality to reality. During an ESP class, Seth called them her "beloved paraphernalia," or symbols, then continued:

"They are more than symbols, however. They are means of recognition that stand for something else, a reality; signs that stand for words, spoken before the birth of words; words imprinted in molecules; words that were imprinted in other ways before the birth of molecules; and yet (*to class members*) words that echo within your own individual psyches. In one way or another these words, like pebbles, are left along the beach of your [collective] reality.

"Some will pick them up and say, 'What lovely stones,' and gaze upon them and see what they mean, and others will kick them aside. But in one way or another . . . those words continue to be spoken, whether through these lips, or through the sound of leaves, or through the invisible music of your own cells. So do they exist. And that is the meaning behind the books and the symbols."

Certainly Seth is saying that Jane's books (and his) represent her acknowledgment of and search for an ideal. So do my own efforts in life. (See Seth's material on "ideals set in the heart of man" in sessions 696–97 for Volume 1 of *"Unknown" Reality*.) Apropos of such concepts, I'll close these introductory notes by quoting from a personal session Seth gave for Jane and me, in which he reiterates the importance of the individual and the pursuit of the ideal. Seth initiated the following passages by talking to me about "the safe universe" that each person can create, and live within. Although his words were directed to me, they have a broad general application:

"In your mind you creatively envision the ideal—the sanity of some future culture that, you hope, our work and [that of] others will bring about. If not tomorrow, then sometime.

"When you thoroughly understand what is meant by the entire safe-universe concept, then the physical, cultural climate is seen as a medium through which the ideal can be expressed. The ideal is meaningless if it is not physically manifest to one degree or another. The ideal seeks expression. In so doing, it often seems to change or alter in ways that are not understood. Yet those distortions may be the very openings that allow others to perceive.

"In a way, with [this] book and with your art, your purpose is the expression of the ideal, and that expression must be physically materialized, obviously. Your joy, your challenge, should be in the manifestation of the ideal as you see it, whether or not you can in your terms count the consequences or the impediments—whether or not the expression comes to fulfillment in your terms—and even if it seems to fall on ground on which it will not grow.

"As an artist alone your purpose is expression, which involves disclosures, the difference between the ideal and the actual. Be reckless in the expression of the ideal, and it will never betray you. Treat it with kid gloves and you are in the middle of a battle."

To be truly reckless in the sense of Seth's definition—how daring! I'd say that attaining such a state represents quite an achievement. For most of us, including myself, it means shedding many encrusted and limiting personal beliefs. I do get glimpses of that condition of inner and outer freedom; just enough to understand some of the many practical benefits that can flow from it. I can't think of a better goal.

I hope these Introductory Notes have prepared the reader to take up *"Unknown" Reality* in the middle, more or less, with the 705th session. But as I wrote in introducing Volume 1, whatever comments I make along the way will explain Jane's trance performances from my view, as best I can offer them—her behavior while she's "under," the varied, powerful or muted use of her voice as she speaks for Seth, her stamina and humor in sessions, the speed or slowness of her delivery. But above all I try to help the reader appreciate the uncanny feeling of energy and/or intelligence—of *personality*—in the sessions, as exemplified by and through Seth; conscious energy, then, taking a guise that's at least somewhat comprehensible to us, in our terms of reality, so that we can understand what's happening.

As in Volume 1, notes are presented at session break times as always, but I've indicated the points of origin of what would ordinarily be footnotes by using consecutive (superscription) numbers within the text of each session. Then, I've grouped the actual notes at the end of the individual sessions for quick consultation. All such reference numbers are printed in the same small type throughout both volumes. Footnotes will be found "in place" only when they're used to call attention to a specific appendix in the same book. For the most part, then, these approaches keep the body of each session free of interruptions between break designations.

The appendix idea worked out well in *The Seth Material* and in *Seth Speaks*, and in both volumes of *"Unknown" Reality* each excerpt or session in an appendix, with whatever notes *it* might carry, is usually fairly complete in itself. These pieces can be read at any time, but I'd rather the reader went over each one when it's first mentioned in a footnote; just as he or she ought to check out all other reference material in order throughout both volumes. I think it especially informative to compare Jane's *Psychic Politics* with Volume

2 of *"Unknown" Reality*, for she produced large sections of both works concurrently; there are many interesting exchanges of viewpoint between the two.

Section 4

EXPLORATIONS. A STUDY OF THE PSYCHE AS IT IS
RELATED TO PRIVATE LIFE AND THE EXPERIENCE OF
THE SPECIES. PROBABLE REALITIES AS A COURSE OF
PERSONAL EXPERIENCE. PERSONAL EXPERIENCE AS IT
IS RELATED TO "PAST" AND "FUTURE"
CIVILIZATIONS OF MAN

Session 705
June 24, 1974
9:09 P.M. Monday

(The 704th session was held a week ago. In it Seth gave the heading for Section 4, just before finishing his evening's work with a few minutes of personal information for Jane and me. He's remarked more than once that he'll close a session by dictating the heading for the next chapter, or whatever, "so that Ruburt [Jane] knows what I am doing. It gives him confidence." But I'd say his procedure also helps satisfy Jane's spontaneous impatience about learning what's coming next in the material.

(In this case, though, too much time passed between sessions. The regularly scheduled session for last Wednesday night wasn't held while we made ready for several approaching events, and as the days went by Jane [and I] simply forgot about what was coming up in "Unknown" Reality. I read her the heading for Section 4 now, while we waited for Seth to come through. "I haven't the vaguest idea, even, of what all that means," she said. Usually a certain kind of serene existence makes the best kind of day-by-day framework for these sessions and our other creative work, even while those days may contain within them points of unusual interest or excitement [such as Jane's weekly ESP

class]. But given that right kind of equanimity, time—our ordinary time— slides by; then, looking back periodically, we discover that we've accomplished at least something of what we wanted to do.

(One of the events we've been preparing for is the visit tomorrow of Tam Mossman, Jane's editor at Prentice-Hall, Inc. He plans to attend ESP class tomorrow night, then stay over Wednesday to read and discuss the two works Jane has in progress, Adventures in Consciousness: An Introduction to Aspect Psychology, *and* "Unknown" Reality. *Tam will also look at my first rough sketches for Jane's book of poetry,* Dialogues of the Soul and Mortal Self in Time.[1] *Then on Wednesday night he'll witness the scheduled 706th session. If Seth comes through with material for* "Unknown" Reality, *Tam will be the first "outsider" to sit in on a session for this work. Almost always Jane dictates book material without witnesses other than myself, and uses the framework of ESP class for emotional interactions involving herself, Seth, and others. That rather formal division in her trance activities suits us well; we enjoy doing most of our work by ourselves, no matter what kind it may be.*

(The atmosphere in our second-story living room was very pleasant and prosaic this evening. We had lights on in the approaching dusk. From the busy intersection just west of our apartment house the sounds of traffic rose up through the open windows. Jane smoked a cigarette and sipped a beer as she waited for the session to start; she was in the process of turning her consciousness inward, actually, on her way to meet Seth in a nonphysical journey that had nothing to do with our ordinary concepts of space or distance.

(When that meeting took place, Jane was in trance; off came her glasses; once again she'd met Seth on the psychological bridge the two of them had established when these sessions began, over a decade ago. Seth has explained such a connective as "a psychological extension, a projection of characteristics on both of our parts, and this I use for our communications . . . it is like a road that must be kept clear of debris."[2]

(As is usually the case in our private sessions, Jane's Seth voice was only a little deeper than her own regular one. Her Seth accent, however, was quite unique. I often think it bears traces of a European heritage—but one that's impossible to pinpoint by country. Her eyes in trance were much darker, and seemingly without highlights.)

Good evening.

("Good evening, Seth.")

Dictation: Let us begin this section with a brief discussion concerning "evolution."

For now think of it as you usually do, in a time context. It has been fashionable in the past to believe that each species was oriented selfishly toward its own survival. Period. Each was seen in competition with all other species. In that framework cooperation was simply a by-product of a primary drive toward survival. One species might use another, for instance. Species were thought to change, and "mutants" form, because of a previous alteration in the environment, to which any given species had to adjust or disappear. The motivating power was always projected outside* (underlined).

All of this presented a quite erroneous picture. Physically speaking, earth itself has its own kind of gestalt consciousness. If you must, then think of that earth consciousness as grading (*spelled*) upward in great slopes of awareness from relatively "inert" particles of dust and stone through the mineral, vegetable, and animal kingdoms. Even then, remember that those kingdoms are not so separate after all. Each one is highly related to each of the others. Nothing happens in one such kingdom that does not affect the others. A great, gracious cooperation exists between those seemingly separate systems, however. If you will remember that even atoms and molecules have consciousness, then it will be easier for you to understand that there is indeed a certain kind of awareness that unites these kingdoms.

In your terms, consciousness of self did not develop because of any exterior circumstances in which your species won out, so to speak. In fact, that consciousness of self in any person is dependent upon the constant, miraculous cooperations that exist between the mineral, vegetable, and animal worlds.[3] The inner intent always forms any exterior alteration. This applies on any scale you use. Consciousness forms the environment. The environment itself is conscious (*forcefully*). Atoms and molecules themselves operate in their own fields of probabilities. In their own ways, they "yearn" toward all probable developments. When they form living creatures they become a physical basis for species alteration. The body's adaptability is not simply an adjusting mechanism or quality. The cells have inner capabilities that you have not discovered. They contain within themselves memory of all the "previous" forms they have been a part of.

I would like to make an aside here: In certain terms, you cannot destroy life by a nuclear disaster. You would of course destroy life as you know it, and in your terms bring to an end, if the conditions were right (or wrong), life forms with which you are familiar. In greater terms, however, mutant life would emerge— mutant only by your standards—but life quite natural to itself.

(*9:38.*) To return to our main subject of the moment: The fact is that the so-called process of evolution is highly dependent upon the cooperative tendencies inherent in all properties of life and

*See Appendix 12.

in all species. There is no transmigration of souls, in which the entire personality of a person "comes back" as an animal. Yet in the physical framework there is a constant intermixing, so that the cells of a man or a woman may become the cells of a plant or an animal,[4] and of course vice versa. The cells that have been a part of a human brain know this in their way. Those cells that now compose your own bodies have combined and discombined many times to form other portions of the natural environment.

This inner and yet physical transmigration of consciousness has always been extremely important, and represents a natural method of communication, uniting all species and all physical life. Inside all physical organisms, therefore, there is a thrust for development and change, even as there is also a pattern of stability within which such alterations can take place.

Give us a moment . . . Historically, of course, you follow a one-line pattern of thought, so you see a picture in which fish left the oceans and became reptiles; from these mammals eventually appeared, and apes and men. That is, I admit, a simple statement, but it is the way most people think evolution occurred. The terms of "progression" are tricky. You never imagine the situation being reversed, for example. Few of you ever imagine a conscious reptilian man. It seems to you that the direction you took is the only direction that could have been taken.

Give us a moment . . . You identify a highly evolved self-consciousness with your own species development, and with your own kind of perceptive mechanisms. You apply these as rules or conditions whenever you examine any other kind of life. In your system of probabilities there are no reptilian men or women, yet in other probabilities they do indeed exist. I mention this only to show you that the evolutionary system you recognize is but one such system. *(Intently:)* The physical basis rests latently within your own cellular structure, however. You think that evolution is finished. Its impetus, however, comes from within the nature of consciousness itself. It always has. In some quarters it is fashionable these days to say that man's consciousness is now an element in a new kind of evolution—but that "new consciousness" has always been inherent. You are only now beginning to recognize its existence. Every consciousness is aware of itself as itself.[5] Each consciousness, then, is self-aware. It may not be self-aware in the same way that you are. It may not reflect upon its own condition. On the other hand, it may have no need to.

(10:02.) Give us a moment . . . So-called future developments of your species are now dependent upon your ideas and

beliefs. This applies genetically in personal terms. For instance, if you believe that you can live to a healthy and happy old age, well into your nineties, then even in Western civilization you will do so. Your emotional intent and your belief will direct the functioning of your cells and (*emphatically*) bring out in them those properties and inherent abilities that will ensure such a condition. There are groups of people in isolated places who hold such beliefs, and in all such cases the body responds. The same applies to the race—or the species, to be more exact. There is an inexhaustible creativity within the cells themselves, that you are not using as a species because your beliefs lag so far behind your innate biological spirituality and wisdom. Your ideas are beginning to change. But unless you alter your framework you will continue to emphasize medical and technological manipulation. Period. In isolated cases this will show you some of the results possible on a physical basis alone. However, such techniques will not work in mass terms, or allow you, say, to prolong effective, productive life unless you change your beliefs in other areas also, and learn the inner dynamics of the psyche.

(The telephone started to ring. I jumped. Once again, I'd forgotten to turn off the bell before the session began. As Seth, Jane stared up at me.)

Take your break.

(10:14. The call was from out of town. A young man had finished reading The Seth Material *this evening. He had many questions—and was too impatient to finish the letter to Jane that he'd just started. His enthusiastic response was one we'd experienced many times before. I talked to him for a few minutes while Jane rested after coming out of trance, and suggested that he call her later in the week. Resume at 10:36.)*

Now: It is true, then, that the cells do operate on the one hand apart from time, and on the other with a firm basis in time, so that the body's integrity as a time-space organism results.

It is true that on a conscious level you do not as yet operate outside of time, but are bound by it. When you learn to free yourselves from those dimensions to some extent, you are not simply duplicating or "returning" to some vaster condition, but adding a new element to that condition. The kind of self-awareness you have is unique, but all kinds are unique. Each triumph you make as an individual is reflected in your species and in its cellular knowledge.

Give us a moment... In a way you are all your own mutants, creatively altering cellular formations. Period. When your fate seems dependent upon heredity, for example, then the transmission of ideas and beliefs operates; these give signals to the chromosomes. They cause miniature self-images, so to speak, that are mirrored in the cells. In many cases these images can be altered, but not with the technology that you have.

(*Long pause at 10:48.*) Give us a moment . . . (*Over a one-minute pause. Then quietly:*) Basically, cellular comprehension straddles time. There is, then, a way of introducing "new" genetic information to a so-called damaged cell in the present.[6] This involves the manipulation of consciousness, basically, and not that of gadgets, as well as a time-reversal principle. First the undesirable information must be erased. It must be erased in the "past" in your terms. Some, but very few, psychic healers do this automatically without realizing what they are doing. The body on its own performs this service often, when it automatically rights certain conditions, even though they were genetically imprinted. The imprints become regressive. In your terms, they fade into a probable series of events that do not physically affect you.

> End of dictation.

> (*Pause at 10:57. After delivering material on several other subjects, Seth said good night at 11:20 P.M.*)

NOTES: Session 705

1. For those who are interested in publishing matters: Like counterpoint endeavors, Jane's *Dialogues* and *Adventures* have become interwound with her Seth books. She discussed her "own" works in her Introduction to *Personal Reality*. I mention them in various notes in that book, and selections of poetry from *Dialogues* itself are presented in chapters 10 and 11; in the latter chapter Seth used one of those excerpts in connection with his own material. Then in Volume 1 of *"Unknown" Reality*, Seth refers to *Adventures* on occasion, while I give information about it in Note 3 for his Preface, and Note 5 for Session 680, among others.

Jane finished *Dialogues* last year (in March 1973), and now (in June 1974) is halfway through the final draft of *Adventures*. I'm to finish illustrations for each of them by the end of this year, if possible, since Prentice-Hall will publish both books in 1975. Therefore, I have much work to do on the 40 pen-and-ink drawings for *Dialogues*, and on a series of diagrams for *Adventures*.

Throughout this volume, as in the first one, I'll be referring to Jane's other books. They're listed in the front matter.

2. The quotes are from *Seth Speaks*: see Chapter 1 at 9:35. In this present volume, perhaps in an appendix, I hope to add excerpts from some of Seth's unpublished observations on the psychological bridge linking Jane and himself. Right now, however, see Jane's essay on her relationship with Seth as given in the Introductory Notes for Volume 1 of *"Unknown" Reality*.

3. A note added five months later: Diagram 11 in Chapter 19 of Jane's *Adventures* is relevant to Seth's material here. It schematically shows the relationship of the individual birth-to-death cycle (including probable events), to the other, successively less differentiated kingdoms or realities that help make up the world. See Note 1.

4. Jane and I understand Seth's point when he tells us that "the cells of a man or woman may become the cells of a plant or an animal." However, for the reasons given in Note 3 for Session 687, in Volume 1, we'd rather think of the molecular *components* of cells as participating in the structures of a variety of forms. (And I can note a week later that at the end of Session 707, Seth makes his own comment about cells surviving changes of form.)

For additional material on cellular life and death as mediated by Seth's CU's, or units of consciousness, see the 688th session between 10:26 and 10:59: "When the cell dies physically, its inviolate nature is not betrayed. It is simply no longer physical."

5. Seth's statement here reminded me of my question about the consciousness of our species, as noted at the end of Session 699, in Volume 1.

6. Session 654, in Chapter 14 of *Personal Reality*, contains information on the changing cellular memory, genetic codes, and neuronal patterns. Then, in Volume 1 of *"Unknown" Reality*, see the 690th session to 10:16 for material on biological precognition.

Session 707
July 1, 1974
9:21 P.M. Monday

(The 706th session was held as scheduled last Wednesday night, and our guest, Tam Mossman, did witness it—but since Seth didn't come through with any dictation for "Unknown" Reality during the session, it's hereby deleted.

(Earlier this evening I reminded Jane of the conversation about cells, versus their components, that we'd had because of Seth's material at 9:38 in Session 705. Some of tonight's book work refers to the questions growing out of our talk, I think, as does Seth's brief clarification near the end of the session.)

Now: Good evening.

("Good evening, Seth.")

Dictation . . . The cells of course are changing. The atoms and molecules within them are always in a state of flux. The CU's[1] that are within all matter have a memory bank that would far surpass any computer's. As cellular components, the atoms and molecules, therefore, carry memory of all the forms of which they have been part.

At deep levels the cells are always working with probabilities, and comparing probable actions and developments in the light of genetic information. The most intricate behavior is involved and calculations instantly made, for instance, before you can take one step or lift your finger. This does not involve only the predictive behavior of the physical organism alone, however. At these deeper levels the cellular activity includes making predictive judgments about the environment outside of the body. The body obviously does not operate alone, but in relationship with everything about it. When you want to walk across the room, the body must not only operate using hindsight and "prediction" as far as its own behavior is concerned, but it must take into consideration the predictive activity of all of the other elements in that room.

Give us a moment... At basic levels, of course, the motion of a muscle involves the motion of cells and of cellular components. Here I am saying that the atoms and molecules themselves, because of their characteristics, not only deal with probabilities within the body's cellular structure, but also help the body make predictive judgments about entities or objects outside of itself.

(Pause, then humorously:) You "know" that a chair is not going to chase you around the room, for instance—at least the odds are against it. You know this because you have a reasoning mind, but that particular kind of reasoning mind knows what it knows because at deep levels the cells are aware of the nature of probable action. The beliefs of the conscious mind, however, set your goals and purposes. "You" are the one who decides to walk across the floor, and then all of these inner calculations take place to help you achieve your goal. The conscious intent, therefore, activates the inner mechanisms and changes the behavior of the cells and their components.

In far greater terms, the goals set consciously by your species also set into operation the same kind of inner biological activity. The goals of the species do not exist apart from individual goals. As you go about your life, therefore, you are very effectively taking part in the "future" developments of your species. Period. Let us look for a moment at the private psyche.

(9:48.) The "private psyche" sounds like a fine term, but it is meaningless unless you apply it to your psyche. A small amount of self-examination should show you that in a very simple way you are always thinking about probabilities. You are always making choices between probable actions and alternate courses. A choice presupposes probable acts, each possible, each capable of actualization within your system of reality. Your private experience is far more filled with such decisions than you usually realize. There are tiny innocuous instances that come up daily: "Shall I go to the movies, or bowling?" "Shall I brush my teeth now or later?" "Should I write to my friend today or tomorrow?" There are also more pertinent questions having to do with careers, ways of life, or other deeper involvements. In your terms, each decision you make alters the reality that you know to one degree or another.

PRACTICE ELEMENT 9

For an exercise, keep notes for a day or so of all the times you find yourself thinking of probable actions,[2] large or small. In your mind, try to follow "what might have happened" had you taken the course you did not take. Then imagine what might happen as a result of your chosen decisions. You are a member of the species. Any choice you make privately affects it biologically and psychically.

You can literally choose between health and illness; between a concentration upon the mental more than the physical, or upon the physical more than the mental. Such private decisions affect the genetic heritage of the species. Your intent is all-important —for you can alter your own genetic messages[3] within certain limits. You can cause a cell, or a group of cells, to change their self-image, for example; and again, you do this often—as you healed yourselves of diseases because of your intent to become well. The intent will be conscious, though the means may not be. Period. In such a case, however, the self-healing qualities of the cells are reinforced, and the self-healing abilities of the species are also strengthened.

Take your break.

(10:05 to 10:32.)

Now: Your private psyche is intimately concerned with your earthly existence, and in your dream state you deal with probable actions, and often work out in that condition the solutions to problems or questions that arise having to do with probable sequences of events.[4]

On many occasions then you set yourself a problem— "Shall I do this or that?"—and form a dream in which you follow through the probable futures that would "result" from the courses available. While you are sleeping and dreaming, your chemical and hormonal activity faithfully follows the courses of the dreams. Even in your accepted reality, then, to that extent in such a dream you react to probable events as well as to the events chosen for waking physical experience. Your daily life is affected, because in such a dream you deal with probable predictabilities. You are hardly alone, however, so each individual alive also has his and her private dreams, and these help form the accepted probability sequence of the following day, and of "time to come." The personal decisions all add up to the global happenings on any given day.

Give us a moment . . . *(Long pause, eyes closed.)* There are lands of the mind.[5] That is, the mind has its own "civilizations," its own personal culture and geography, its own history and inclinations. But the mind is connected with the physical brain, and so hidden in its [the brain's] folds there is an archaeological memory. To some extent what you know now is dependent upon what will be known, and what has been known, in your terms. The "past" races of men live to that extent within your Now, as do those who will seemingly come after. So, ideally speaking, the history of your species can be discovered quite clearly within the psyche; and true archaeological events are found not only by uncovering rocks and relics, but by bringing to light, so to speak, the memories that dwell within the psyche.

Now that is the end of dictation.

(10:45. Next, Seth came through with a page of information for Jane and me. In it were these lines: "I believe, incidentally, that I cleared up your question for you. Cells, as entities, do not drop off [the physical form] like apples. I was using, I suppose, a kind of shorthand I believed was clear in the context given."

(End at 11:01 P.M.)

NOTES: Session 707

1. See Note 3 for Appendix 12, in this volume.

2. In Volume 1 of *"Unknown" Reality*, Seth designed all but two of his eight exercises, or practice elements, to help the reader directly explore some of the aspects of probable realities—although even the exceptions (numbers 6 and 8) aren't far removed from probability concepts. His first practice element grew out of Jane's projection into a probable past in her hometown of Saratoga Springs, N.Y.

3. See the 705th session at 10:48.

4. In Volume 1, see Session 687 at 10:01: Seth discussed how the dreamer and his or her probable selves, having "the same psychic roots," can share in working out a given challenge in a probable reality.

I also suggest a rereading of the material on dreams and probable realities in chapters 14 and 15 of *The Seth Material*.

5. Jane herself first mentioned "lands of the mind" during break in the 703rd session, which was held some three weeks ago—but she'd picked up the phrase from Seth. See the notes at the close of that session, in Volume 1.

Session 708
September 30, 1974
8:58 P.M. Monday

(Jane and I hadn't realized it at first, but we were to take a long rest from work on "Unknown" Reality following the 707th session, for July 1. We were busy during the next 14 weeks, of course; there follow a few notes about some of our activities, grouped together by subject matter rather than chronology.

(We did have a few "deleted" sessions for ourselves. Jane also kept her ESP class going, and within that spontaneous format she often spoke for Seth, or sang in Sumari,[1] her trance language. The break in book dictation gave me time to begin attending class regularly, and I plan to continue doing so. And when I began sitting in on class, I discovered anew that its loose structure served as a catalyst for certain little psychic events that I find most enjoyable: Tuesday night is class night, and often such an experience takes place as I rest for half an hour late that afternoon. I record each episode [no matter when I have it]. Sometimes I make a drawing also, and use that to supplement my description of the event in class.

(Following the conference with her editor late in June, Jane has devoted herself to finishing her manuscript for Adventures, *while I've worked*

steadily on the diagrams for it, as well as on the drawings for Dialogues. *I completed the detailed pencil guides for both sets of art this week. Next comes the finished work for publication, which I'll produce by placing a sheet of clear acetate over each guide, then rendering on that untouched surface the final version in "line," or pen and ink. This is my own system; the acetate, riding above the penciled outlines, leaves me free to search for various spontaneous effects that are quite inhibited if I try to follow those preliminary images too literally. Then in late August, long before I had the 16 diagrams [plus two other pieces of art] done for* Adventures, *I mailed to Prentice-Hall Jane's completed manuscript for that book.* Adventures *is scheduled for publication in mid-1975, but I'll continue referring to it in these notes.*

(In the meantime, on Saturday morning, July 27, Jane received her first copy of The Nature of Personal Reality: A Seth Book, *from her publisher. She was delighted. So was I. The book's physical appearance was most pleasing to us. As an artist, I'm very conscious of whether I think the "package" equals its contents, though since she is verbally oriented this is less important to Jane.*

(However, the emergence of Personal Reality *into the marketplace soon resulted in an increase in the number of letters and calls that we'd been receiving. Requests for personal appearances also mounted. We're no longer into that activity for a number of reasons; yet when the host for a Miami, Florida, radio show called Jane early this morning [September 30] about the possibility of a taped interview, she impulsively suggested to that rather startled individual that the tape be made then—and so for half an hour she exchanged with him a free, unrehearsed dialogue about her work for later airing.*

(Just as I had some small psychic adventures during our time off from "Unknown" Reality, Jane did too. One of hers that I'll mention here is related to published material. During the night following the arrival of that first copy of Personal Reality, *while lying quietly beside me in an altered state of consciousness, Jane received information of how "the ancients paralyzed the air." It could then be walked upon and manipulated in various other ways. She woke me up to tell me about the experience, and to remind her to write an account of it the next day. She couldn't identify its source, except to say that she hadn't been dreaming. At the breakfast table, I told her I thought the material was connected to the sessions in* Personal Reality *on the interior sound, light, and electromagnetic values "around or from which" the physical image forms. Involved here also, I added, were certain ideas in her novel,* The Education of Oversoul Seven.[2]*

(I haven't read "Unknown" Reality since I finished typing the last session for it over three months ago; Jane had reviewed all of Seth's material on the book last week, yet still had to remind herself today of the contents of that [707th] session. While we went over it this afternoon I became aware of a familiar, though infrequent, sound: the honking of geese. It was the kind of

transient commotion I could listen to indefinitely. The southbound flight was soon out of sight in the rainy sky, and in another few moments it was out of hearing.

(I took the sign of migration as a good omen, though, for the circumstances of the flight were strongly reminiscent of those described at the beginning of the 687th session, in Volume 1 of "Unknown" Reality. It had been raining then, too, on that day last March—and as I wrote at the time, in some half-romantic fashion I've hooked up the flights of geese with Jane's and my work on the Seth books. I'm still surprised that I've done so, for whatever reasons; but we're ready to dig in for a winter's work.

(As we sat waiting for the session at 8:50 Jane felt a little nervous; she often does after a layoff from book dictation. But she laughed, as she has before in such cases: "I just want to get it—the beginning—over with." At 8:55, moving closer to that familiar dissociated state, approaching that psychological bridge which serves as a common meeting ground for Seth and herself, she announced that she felt "a rather generalized idea of what Seth will say on the book stuff." Less clear were some data about herself, but she thought Seth would cover all of that along with his material on "Unknown" Reality. "I guess we'll start out with the book. . . ."

(Jane's delivery as Seth was good. Indeed, it was often fast, with no sense of the three-month break that had ensued since the 707th session.)

Good evening.

("Good evening, Seth.")

Now, dictation: Consciousness operates with what you may call code *(spelled)* systems. These are beyond count. Consciousness differentiates itself, therefore, by operating within certain code systems that help direct particular kinds of focus, bringing in certain kinds of significances[3] while blocking out other data.

These other data, of course, might well be significant in <u>different</u> code systems. In their way, however, these systems are interrelated, so that at other levels there is communication between them—secondary data, you might say, that is supportive but not primarily concentrated upon.

These code systems involve molecular constructions and light values,[4] and in certain ways the light values are as precisely and effectively used as your alphabet is. For example, certain kinds of life obviously respond to spectrums with which you are not familiar—but beyond that there are electromagnetic ranges, or rather <u>extensions</u> of electromagnetic ranges, completely unknown to you, to which other life forms respond.

Again, all of these code systems[5] <u>are</u> interrelated. In the same way, the private psyche contains within it hints and glimpses of other alternate realities. These operate as secondary codes, so to speak, beneath the existence that you officially recognize. Such secondary systems can tell you much about the potentials of human reality, those that are latent but can at any time be "raised" to primary importance. Such secondary systems also point toward the probable developments possible for individuals or species.

All of the probabilities practically possible in human development are therefore present to some extent or another in each individual. Any biological or spiritual advancement that you might imagine will of course not come from any outside agency, but from within the heritage of consciousness made flesh. Generally, those alive in this century chose a particular kind of orientation. The species chose to specialize in certain kinds of physical manipulation, to devote its energies in certain directions. Those directions have brought forth a reality unique in its own fashion. Man has not driven himself down a blind alley, in other words. He has been studying the nature of his consciousness—using it as if it were apart from the rest of nature, and therefore seeing nature and the world in a particular light.[6] That light has finally made him feel isolated, alone, and to some extent relatively powerless *(intently)*.

(Rapidly:) He is learning how to use the light of his own consciousness, and discovering how far one particular method of using it can be counted upon. He is studying what he can do and not do with that particular focus. He is now discovering that he needs other lights also, in other words—that he has been relying upon only a small portion of an entire inner searchlight that can be used in many directions. Let us look at some of those other directions that are native to man's consciousness, still waiting to be used effectively.

I am speaking in your historical terms because before the historical system that you recognize, man had indeed experimented with these other directions, and with some success. This does not mean that man in the present has fallen from some higher spiritual achievement to his current state.

(Pause at 9:16.) There are cycles in which consciousness forms earthly experience, and maps out historical sequences. So there have been other species of mankind beside your own, each handling physical data in its own way. Some have taken other directions, therefore, than the one that you have chosen. Even those paths are latent or secondary, however, within your own private and mass experience. They reside within you, presenting you with alternate realities[7] that you may or may not choose privately or *en masse*, as you prefer.

Each system, of course, brings forth its own culture, "technology," art, and science. The physical body is basically equipped to maintain itself as a healthy long-living organism far beyond your present understanding, medically speaking. The cellular comprehension[8] provides all kinds of inner therapeutics that operate quite naturally. There is a physical give-and-take between the body and environment beyond that which you recognize; an inner dynamics here that escapes you, that unites the health of plants, animals, and men. In the most simple and mundane of examples, if you are living in a fairly well-balanced, healthy environment, your houseplants and your animals will also be well. You form your environment and you are a part of it. You react to it, often forgetting that relationship. Ideally, the body has the capacity to keep itself in excellent health—but beyond that, to maintain itself at the highest levels of physical achievement. The exploits of your greatest athletes give you a hint of the body's true capacity. In your system of beliefs, however, those athletes must train and focus all of their attention in that direction, often at the expense of other portions of their own experience. But their performances show you what the body is capable of.

The body is equipped, ideally again now, to rid itself of any diseases, and to maintain its stability into what you would call advanced old age, with only a gradual overall change. At its best, however, the change would bring about spiritual alterations. When you leave for a vacation, for example, you close down your house. In these ideal terms, death would involve a closing down of your [physical] house; it would not be crumbling about you.

(Pause at 9:34.) Now, certain individuals glimpse this great natural healing ability of the body, and use it. Doctors sometimes encounter it when a patient with a so-called incurable disease suddenly recovers. "Miraculous" healings are simply instances of nature unhampered. Complete physicians, as mentioned earlier,[9] would be persons who understood the true nature of the body and its own potentials—persons who would therefore transmit such ideas to others and encourage them to trust the validity of the body. Some of the body's abilities will seem impossible to you, for you have no evidence to support them. Many organs can completely replace themselves; diseased portions can be replaced by new tissue.

(Pause, in a slower delivery.) Many people, without knowing it, have developed cancer and rid themselves of it. Appendixes removed by operations have grown back. These powers of the body are biologically quite achievable in practical terms, but only by a

complete change of focus and belief. Your insistence upon separating yourselves <u>from</u> nature automatically prevented you from
trusting the biological aspects of the body, and your religious
concepts further alienated you from the body's spirituality.

In your reality, your consciousness is usually identified
with the body, on the other hand—that is, you think of your
consciousness as being always within your flesh. Yet many individuals have found themselves outside of the body, fully conscious and
aware *(including Jane and me)*.

*(9:45. Jane left her trance state very easily, as she usually does.
"Well," I asked her, "how do you feel now?"*

("It's good to be back with the book sessions," she replied, smiling.

*(We sat quietly. We could hear the automobiles swooshing across the
new Walnut Street Bridge that lifted gracefully over the Chemung River, less
than a quarter of a block from our apartment house; it had been raining earlier
this evening and the traffic noise was softened. Incidentally, in a brief ceremony,
the four-lane span had been opened to the public just this morning. Its old-
fashioned predecessor had been destroyed by Tropical Storm Agnes in June
1972; see my notes for the 613th session in Chapter 1 of* Personal Reality.

(Resume at a slower pace at 9:56.)

Under certain conditions, therefore, the body can maintain itself while the "main consciousness" is away from it. The body
consciousness is quite able, then, to provide the overall equilibrium.
At certain levels of the sleep state this does in fact happen. In
sleepwalking the body is active, but the main consciousness is not
"awake." It is not manipulating the body. The main consciousness is
elsewhere. Under such conditions the body <u>can</u> perform tasks and
often maneuver with an amazing sense of balance. This finesse,
again, hints at physical abilities not ordinarily used. The main
consciousness, because of its beliefs, often hampers such manipu-
lability in normal waking life.

Let us look for a moment at the body consciousness.

It is equipped, as an animal is, to perform beautifully in its
environment. You would call it mindless, since it would seem not to
reason. For the purpose of this discussion alone, imagine a body
with a fully operating body consciousness, not diseased for any
reason or defective by birth, but one without the overriding ego-
directed consciousness that you have. There have been species of
such a nature. In your terms they would seem to be like sleepwalkers, yet their physical abilities surpassed yours. They were
indeed as agile as animals—nor were they <u>un</u>conscious.[10] They
simply dealt with a different kind of awareness.

In your terms they did not have [an overall] purpose, yet their purpose was simply to be. Their main points of consciousness were elsewhere, in another kind of reality, while their physical manifestations were separate. Their primary focuses of consciousness were scarcely aware of the bodies they had created. Yet even those bodies learned, in quotes now, "through experience," and began to "awaken," to become aware of themselves, to discover time, or to create it. Period.

(Pause.) The sleepwalkers, as we will call them, were not asleep to themselves, and would seem so only from your viewpoint. There were several such races of human beings. Their [overall] primary experience was outside of the body. The physical corporal existence was a secondary effect. To them the real was the dream life, which contained the highest stimuli, the most focused experience, the most maintained purpose, the most meaningful activity, and the most organized social and cultural behavior. Now this is the other side of your own experience, so to speak. Such races left the physical earth much as they found it. The main activity, then, involved consciousness apart from the body. In your terms, physical culture was rudimentary.

Now the physical organism as such is capable of that kind of reality system. It is not better or worse than your own. It is simply alternate behavior, biologically and spiritually possible. No complicated physical transportation systems were set up. In the physical state, in what you would call the waking state, these individuals slept. To you, comparatively speaking, their waking activities would seem dreamlike, and yet they behaved with great natural physical grace, allowing the body to function to capacity. They did not saddle it with negative beliefs of disease or limitation. Such bodies did not age to the extent, now, that yours do, and enjoyed the greatest ease and sense of belonging with the environment.

(10:24.) Consciousness connected with the flesh, then, has great leeway spiritually and biologically, and can focus itself in many ways with and through the flesh, beside your own particular orientation. There have been highly sophisticated, developed civilizations that would not be apparent to you because the main orientation was mental or psychic, while the physical race itself would seem to be highly undeveloped.

In some of their own private dreams, many of my readers will have discovered a reality quite as vivid as the normal one, and sometimes more so. These experiences can give you some vague hint of the kind of existence I am speaking of.[11] There are also physical apparatuses connected with the hibernation abilities of

some animals that can give further clues as to the possible relationships of consciousness to the body. Under certain conditions, for
example, consciousness can leave the corporal mechanism while it
remains intact—functioning, but at a maintenance level. When
optimum conditions return, then the consciousness reactivates the
body. Such behavior is possible not only with the animals. In
systems different from your own, there are realities in which physical
organisms are activated after what would seem to you to be centuries
of inactivity[12]—again, when the conditions are right. To some extent
your own life-and-death cycles are simply another aspect of the
hibernation principle as you understand it. Your own consciousness
leaves the body almost in the same way that messages leap the nerve
ends.[13] The consciousness is not destroyed in the meantime.

     Now in the case of an animal who hibernates, the body is
in the same state. But in the greater hibernation of your own
experience, the body as a whole becomes inoperable. The cells
within you obviously die constantly. The body that you have now is
not the one that you had 10 years ago; its physical composition has
died completely many times since your birth, but, again, your
consciousness bridges those gaps *(with gestures)*. They could be
accepted instead, in which case it would seem to you that you were,
say, a reincarnated self at age 7 *(intently)*, or 14 or 21. The particular
sequence of your own awareness follows through, however. In basic
terms the body dies often, and as surely as you think it dies but once
in the death you recognize. On numerous occasions it physically
breaks apart, but your consciousness rides beyond those "deaths."
You do not perceive them. The stuff of your body literally falls into
the earth many times, as you think it does only at the "end of your
life."

     Again, your own consciousness triumphantly rides above
those deaths that you do not recognize as such. In your chosen
three-dimensional existence, however, and in those terms, your
consciousness finally recognizes a death. From the outside it is
nearly impossible to pinpoint that intersection of consciousness and
the seeming separation from the body. There is a time when you, as a
consciousness, decide that death will happen, when in your terms
you no longer bridge the gap of minute deaths not accepted.

    (Pause at 10:43, during a strong delivery.) Here consciousness
decides to leave the flesh, to accept an official[14] death. You have
already chosen a context, however, and it seems that that context is
inevitable. It appears, then, that the body will last so long and no
longer. The fact remains that you have chosen the kind of consciousness that identifies with the flesh for a certain period of time.

Other species of consciousness—of a different order entirely, and with a different rhythm of experience—would think of a life in your terms as a day, and have no trouble bridging that gap between apparent life, death, and new life.

Some individuals find themselves with memories of other lives, which are other days to the soul. Such persons then become aware of a greater consciousness reaching over those gaps, and realize that earthly experience can contain [among other things] a knowledge of existence in more than one body. Inherently then consciousness, affiliated with the flesh, can indeed carry such comprehensions. The mind of man as you know it shows at least the potential ability for handling a kind of memory with which you are usually not acquainted. This means that even biologically the species is equipped to deal with different sequences of time, while still manipulating within one particular time scheme. This also implies a far greater psychological richness—quite possible, again, within corporal reality—in which many levels of relationships can be handled. Such inner knowledge is inherent in the cells, and in ordinary terms of evolution is quite possible as a "future" development.

Knowledge is usually passed down through the ages in your reality, through books and historic writings, yet each individual contains within himself or herself a vast repository: direct knowledge of the past, in your terms, through unconscious comprehension.

The unknown reality: Much of that reality is unknown simply because your beliefs close you off from your own knowledge. The reaches of your own consciousness are not limited. Because you accept the idea of a straight-line movement of time, you cannot see before or after what you think of as your birth or death,* yet your greater consciousness is quite aware of such experience. Ideally it is possible not only to remember "past" lives, but to plan future ones now. In greater terms, all such lives happen at once. Your present neurological structure makes this seem impossible, yet your inner consciousness is not so impeded.

(Louder:) Take your break, or end the session as you prefer.
("We'll take the break.")

(11:00. Jane's trance had been excellent. She vaguely remembered that Seth had talked about "sleepwalkers." I described the material briefly, then added, "It would be a joke if that information applied to our own ancestors, our cavemen, as we think of them." Whereupon Jane said she thought it did at one level, but she didn't elaborate.

*See Appendix 13.

(She wanted Seth to discuss a couple of her own questions, now that he had "Unknown" Reality underway again, so I suggested we ask for that material now. Jane hesitated. "I sense stuff on both the book and me; I don't know what to do. Wait—there's a practice element involved. . . ."
(Resume at 11:25.)
Now:

PRACTICE ELEMENT 10

You can hold within your conscious attention far more data than you realize. You have hypnotized yourselves into believing that your awareness is highly limited.

Think back to yesterday. Try to remember what you did when you got up; what you wore. Attempt to follow the sequence of your activities from the time you awakened until you went to sleep. Then flesh in the details. Try to recall your feelings at all of those times. Most of you will be lucky to get this far. Those who do, go even further and try to recall the daydreams you might have had also. Try to remember what stray thoughts came into your mind.

At first, doing this will take all of your attention. You might do the exercise sitting quietly, or riding a bus or waiting for someone in an office. Some of you might be able to do the exercise while performing a more or less automatic series of actions—but do not try to carry it out while driving your car, for example.

As you become more expert at it, then purposely do something else at the same time—a physical activity, for instance. When most of you begin this exercise it will almost seem as if you were a sleepwalker yesterday. The precise, fine alignment of senses with physical activity will seem simply lost; yet as you progress the details will become clear, and you will find that you can at least hold within your mind certain aspects of yesterday's reality while maintaining your hold in today.

In larger terms there are other entire lives, which for you are forgotten essentially as yesterday is. These too, however, are a secondary series of activities, riding beneath your present primary concern. They are as unconsciously a part of your present, and as connected with it, as yesterday is.

Now: the second part of the exercise.

Imagine vividly what you will do tomorrow, and in detail plan a probable day that will rise naturally from your present experience, behavior, and purposes. Follow through as you did with the first part of the exercise. *(Pause.)* That day's reality is already anticipated by your cells. Your body has prepared for it, all of its functions precognitively projecting their own existences into it. Your "future" life exists in the same manner, and in your terms grows as much out of your present as tomorrow grows out of your today.

Doing the exercise will simply acquaint your normal consciousness with the sense of its own flexibility. You will be exercising the invisible muscles of your consciousness as certainly as you might exercise your body with gymnastics.

To other portions of yourself you would seem to be a sleepwalker. Full creative participation in any moment, however, awakens you to your own potentials, and therefore allows you to experience a unity between your own consciousness and the comprehension of your physical cells. Those cells are as spiritual as your soul is.

(11:40.) Now give me a moment. A good one . . . This is not dictation.

(What followed were three and a half pages of material for Jane and me. Here are a few condensed, more generalized excerpts:)

To one extent or another in your society, you are taught to not trust yourself. There are various schools and religions that try to express the self's validity, but their distortions have smothered the basic authenticity of the teachings.

In those terms, Ruburt started from scratch as a member of your society who finally threw aside, as you did [Joseph], the current frameworks of belief. For some time he was simply between belief systems, discarding some entirely, accepting portions of others; but mainly he was a pioneer—and this while carrying the largely unrealized, basic belief of society that you cannot trust the self . . .

While that emotionally invisible belief is carried, then anything the self does must be scrutinized, put to the test; in the meantime beliefs that have sustained others are suspended. The development of Ruburt's abilities would, therefore, lead him away from comforting structures while he searched for others to sustain him . . .

He has put to the test much of what he has learned. His own personality has blossomed in all aspects, especially in terms of relating with others and in personal creativity . . . He has been testing out our information in the world that he knows. He felt that it was necessary . . . For how could the self, taught that it was bad, bring forth good?

There were frameworks that could have offered help, but he saw that they were not intrinsically valid, and so did not depend upon them. . . .

(Seth said good night at 12:18 A.M. Jane's deliveries had been very energetic throughout the session.

(In his material above, concerning Jane's search for newer, larger frameworks of belief once she began to dispense with her old "comforting" ideas, Seth very lucidly dealt with certain aspects of the role she's chosen for this life. However, I want to emphasize here the emotional terms of Jane's search— and state that at times those qualities have been very difficult for her to contend with. To some degree I've been involved in many changes of belief also, but I'm a participator in the development of the Seth material, not its originator; the pressures and challenges weren't—aren't—as demanding. [With a humor born out of many a struggle, however, I note that it isn't easy to give up certain cherished old beliefs, even when they're demonstrably wrong; they may fit the personality all too well. . . .]

(In connection with these notes, and Seth's excerpts after 11:40, then, I recommend a review of the following in Volume 1:

(1. The material on Jane, religion, and mysticism in the Introductory Notes, the 679th session, and Appendix 1 for that session.

(2. Note 8 for the 679th session, on Jane's beliefs and physical symptoms.

(3. Appendix 10 [for Session 692], on Jane's efforts to make a "middle ground" between the extremes of society's reactions to her psychic abilities: rejection by the conventionally closed-minded at one end, and gullible acceptance at the other.

(And added the next day: Now see Appendix 14 for the little episode that developed on Jane's part as we retired for the evening.)

NOTES: Session 708

1. See chapters 7 and 8 in *Adventures*.

2. In *Personal Reality*, see sessions 623–25 in Chapter 5. In *Oversoul Seven*, see the material in Chapter 12, for example, wherein Jane described not only the airborne movement of objects—rocks—but an "extra tension" in the air itself, "as if a million vowels and syllables rose into the air, all glittering, all . . . alive; like animals of sound. . . ."

3. In Volume 1 of *"Unknown" Reality*, see the 681st session from 11:47, and the 682nd session from 10:21.

4. The sessions in Chapter 5 of *Personal Reality*, referred to in Note 2, contain information on the functions of the body's inner sound, light, and electromagnetic values. Session 625 especially mentions those attributes on atomic and molecular levels.

5. See Appendix 4 (for Session 685) in Volume 1.

6. In Volume 1, all of the material in Session 686, including that for Practice Element 1, can apply here.

7. All in Volume 1: Seth refers to some varieties of ancient man in Session 689 (also see Note 4), and in Session 691 after 10:30. Then see Appendix 6 for Jane's material on parallel man, alternate man, and probable man.

In addition, the reader might review Seth's information on ancient civilizations, as presented in Chapter 15 of *Seth Speaks*.

8. See the 705th session after 10:36.

9. See sessions 703–4 in Volume 1.

10. This material immediately reminded me that before the session tonight Jane and I had discussed Seth's promise to answer the two questions I'd posed for him before sessions 698–99, in Volume 1. The question of interest here (I summarized them both in the notes following the 699th session) had to do with my inability to comprehend an "unconscious" species state. Not that I thought Seth was going out of his way to deal with such concepts tonight, but by the time he was through with his material on the sleepwalkers, I thought he'd considered at least one possible facet of my inquiry.

11. See Note 4 for Session 707.

The 699th session, in Volume 1, dealt in part with dream images and subjective dream "photographs." I used Note 1 for that session to insert one of my favorite Jane poems: *My Dreaming Self*. She wrote it in 1965, a year and a half or so after beginning the Seth material. Now I can add that at the time Jane actually wrote two poems on dreaming; I've been saving the second one for use in Volume 2.

In Midnight Thickets

In midnight thickets
Dreamers plunge
While the moon
Shines calmly on.
The town is sleeping.
Bodies lie
Neat and empty,
Side by side.

But every self
Sneaks out alone
In darkness with
No image on,
And travels freely,
All alert,
Roads unlisted
On a map.

No man can find
Where he has been,

Or follow in flesh
Where the self tread,
Or keep the self in
Though doors are closed,
For the self moves through
Wood and stone.

No man can find
The post or sign
That led the self
Through such strange land.
The way is gone.
The self returns
To slip its smooth-skinned
Image on.

12. And added two weeks or so later: I see connections between the "centuries of inactivity" that Seth describes in this (708th) session, and certain unique psychic abilities of Jane's—namely, those involving "massiveness" and "long sound." In Volume 1, see not only Session 681 between 10:22 and 11:47 for data on one of her massive experiences, but that session's accompanying Appendix 3. Then in this section of Volume 2, see both Note 9 and Appendix 19 for the 712th session, concerning material on Jane's long-sound trances; during one of these it could theoretically take her a week—or a century—of our time to pronounce just one syllable of one word.

13. By "nerve ends" Seth means the synapses, which are the minute sites where neurons, or nerve cells, contact each other.

14. In Volume 1, see Note 2 for Session 695.

Session 709
October 2, 1974
9:21 P.M. Wednesday

(At 9:18 Jane said, "I feel him around." Then: "I have an idea of what he's going to talk about—but I haven't quite got it yet so I have to wait. . . ." Then, very quietly:)

Good evening.

("Good evening, Seth.")

Now: Dictation: Everything that is apparent three-dimensionally has an inside source, out of which its appearance springs. Some of this, again, is difficult to explain—not because Ruburt does not have the vocabulary, but because serial-word language automatically prepackages ideas into certain patterns, and to escape prepackaging can be a task. We will try our best, however.

The cell as you understand it is but the cell's three-dimensional face. The idea of tachyons[1] as currently understood is basically legitimate, though highly distorted. Before a cell as such makes its physical appearance there are "disturbances" in the spot in

340

which the cell will later show itself. Those disturbances are the result of a slowing down of prior effects of faster-than-light activity, and represent the emergence into your space-time system of energy that can then be effectively used and formed into the cellular pattern.

The very slowing-down process itself helps "freeze" the activity into a form. At the death of a cell a reverse process occurs—the death is the escape of that energy from the cell form, its release, the release itself triggering certain stages of acceleration. There is what might be called a residue, or debris energy, "coating" the cell, that stays within this system. None of this can be ascertained from within the system—that is, the initial faster-than-light activity or the deceleration afterward. Such faster-than-light behavior, then, helps form the basis for the physical universe. This characteristic is an attribute of the CU's, which have already slowed down to some extent when they form EE units.[2]

(Pause, one of many, at 9:37.) While operating through the body structures, consciousnesses such as your own focus largely upon the three-dimensional orientation. In out-of-body states, however, consciousness can travel faster than light—often, in fact, instantaneously.

This frequently happens in the dream state, although such a performance can be achieved in varying altered states of consciousness. At such times consciousness simply puts itself in a different relationship with time and space. The physical body cannot follow, however. It is by altering its own relationship with the physical universe that consciousness can best understand its own properties, and glimpse from another vantage point that physical universe, where it will be seen in a different light. Operating outside the body, consciousness can better perceive the properties of matter. It cannot (intently) experience matter, however, in the same fashion as it can when it is physically oriented.

From your ordinary point of view the traveling consciousness is off-focus, not locked into physical coordinates in the designated fashion. The so-called inner world can be at least theoretically explored, however, in just such a way. Consciousness "unlocks" itself for a while from its usual coordinates. When this happens the out-of-body traveler is not simply out of his or her corporal form. The person steps out of usual context. Even if an individual leaves the body and wanders about the room no more than a few feet away from where the body is located,[3] there are alterations, dash—the relationship of consciousness to the room is different. The relationship of the individual to time and space has altered. Time out of the body is "free time" by your standards. You do not age, for example, although this effect varies according to certain principles. I will mention these later.[4]

(9:48.) Such a traveling consciousness may journey within physical reality, colon: While not relating to that system in the usual manner, it may still be allied with it. From that viewpoint matter itself will seem to appear differently than it does ordinarily. On the other hand, an out-of-body consciousness may also enter other physically attuned realities: those operating "at different frequencies than your own." The basically independent nature of consciousness allows for such disentanglement.[5] The body consciousness maintains its own equilibrium, and acts somewhat like a maintenance station.

Any discussion of the unknown reality must necessarily involve certain usually dismissed hypotheses about the characteristics of consciousness itself. The world as you know it is the result of a complicated set of "codes" (as given at the beginning of the last session), each locked in one to the other, each one in those terms dependent upon the others. Your precise perceived universe in all of its parts, then, results from coded patterns, each one fitting perfectly into the next. Alter one of these and to some extent you step out of that context (underlined). Any event of any kind that does not directly, immaculately intersect with your space-time continuum, does not happen, in your terms, but falls away. It becomes probable in your system but seeks its own "level," and becomes actualized as it falls into place in another reality whose "coded sequence" fits its own. Period.

(Pause at 10:10.) When consciousness leaves the body, therefore, it alters some of the coordinates. There are various questions involving the nature of perception that then occur, and these will be discussed somewhat later (but see Note 4). Consciousness is equipped to focus its main energy, in your terms at least, generally within the body, or to stray from it for varying amounts of time. Theoretically, your human consciousness can take many different roads while still maintaining its physical base. In far-past historical times, different kinds of orientation were experimented with (as by the "sleepwalkers" described in the last session, for instance). Your own present private experience can give hints and clues about such other cultures, for those abilities reside within the natural framework, now, but are underdeveloped.

To one extent or another, therefore, all of the potentials of the species are now latent within each individual. Often these spring to the surface through events that may seem bizarre. The "unknown" reality is unknown only because you have not looked for its aspects in yourself. You have been taught to pay almost exclusive attention to your exterior behavior. Privately, then, much of your inner life escapes you. You often structure your life according to that exterior pattern of events. These, while important, are the result of your own inner world of activity. That inner world is your only real connection with the exterior events, and the objective details make sense only because of the subjectivity that gave them birth.[6]

In the same way, when you look at the current state of the world, or at history, you often structure your perceptions so that only the topmost surfaces of events are seen. Using the same kind of reasoning, you are apt to judge the historic past of your species in very limited terms, and to overlook great clues in your history because they seem to make no sense.

(Long pause, eyes closed.) While you believe, for example, that technology as you understand it (underlined) alone means progress, and that progress necessarily requires overriding physical manipulation of the environment that must forever continue, you will judge past civilizations in that light. This will blind you to certain accomplishments and other orientations to such an extent that you will not be able to see evidence of achievement when it appears before your eyes.

(Well over a one-minute pause at 10:30, eyes closed.) Give us a moment . . . You have not worked with the power of thought or feeling, but only with its physical effects. Therefore, to you only physically materialized events are obvious. You do not accept your dreams as real, for example, but as a rule you consider them fantasies—imaginative happenings. Until very recently you generally believed that all information came to the body through the outer senses, and ignored all evidence to the contrary. It was impossible to imagine civilizations built upon data that were mentally received, consciously accepted, and creatively used.[7] Under such circumstances scientists could hardly look for precognition in cells.[8] They did not believe it existed to begin with.

The human body itself has limitless potentials, and great variations that allow for different kinds of orientation. Probable man represents alternate man from your viewpoint, alternate versions of the species. The same applies individually. In out-of-body states many people have encountered probable selves and probable realities. They have also journeyed into the past and the future as you think of them. The private psyche contains within itself the knowledge of its own probabilities, and it contains a mirror in which the experience of the species can at least be glimpsed.

You are used to a particular kind of orientation, accustomed to using your consciousness in one particular manner. In order to study the "unknown" reality, however, you must try to see what else your consciousness can do. This really means that you must learn to regain the true feeling of yourself.

There are two main ways of trying to find out about the nature of reality—an exterior method and an interior one. The methods can be used together, of course, and from your vantage point must be for the greatest efficiency. You are well acquainted with the exterior means, that involve studying the objective universe and collecting facts upon which certain deductions are made. In this book, therefore, we will be stressing interior ways of attaining, not necessarily facts, but knowledge and wisdom. Now, facts may or may not give you wisdom. They can, if they are slavishly followed, even lead you away from true knowledge. Wisdom shows you the insides of facts, so to speak, and the realities from which facts emerge.

Much of the remainder of *"Unknown" Reality*, then, will deal with an inside look at the nature of reality, and with some exercises that will allow you to see yourself and your world from another perspective. Later I intend to say far more about some civilizations that, in your terms, came before your own *(but see the last sentence in Note 4)*. Before you can understand their orientation, we will have to speak about various alternate kinds of consciousness and out-of-body experience. These will help you to understand how other kinds of cultures could operate in ways so alien to your own.

(Louder:) You may take a break or end the session as you prefer.

("We'll take the break."

(10:55: Jane's delivery had become somewhat faster and very absorbed as it progressed. Just as they had before our three-month layoff from book work [after Session 707], her trances for "Unknown" *Reality were proving to be more "difficult" to initiate than those for the previous Seth books.[9] She often had to wait for just the right moment to get back into dictation following a break, too; so tonight, after we'd shared an apple, she sat rather impatiently anticipating Seth's return. Resume, finally, at 11:25.)*

Dictation: We will be discussing alternate methods of orientation that consciousness can take when allied with flesh, trying to give the reader some personal experience with such altered conditions, along with a brief history of some civilizations that utilized these unofficial orientations as their predominant method of focus.

To become familiar with the "unknown" reality you must

to some extent grant that it exists, then, and be willing to step aside from your usual behavior. All of the methods given are quite natural, inherent in the body structure, and even biologically anticipated. Your consciousness could not leave your body and return to it again unless there were biological mechanisms that allowed for such a performance.

I have said *(as at 9:48)* that the body can indeed carry on, performing necessary maintenance activities while the main consciousness is detached from it. To some extent it can even perform simple chores. *(Pause.)* In sleep, in fact, it is not at all necessary that the main consciousness be alert in the body. Only in certain kinds of civilizations, for that matter, is such a close body-and-main-consciousness relationship necessary. There are other situations, therefore, in which consciousness ordinarily strays much further, returning to the body as a home station and basis of operation, relying upon it for certain kinds of perception only, but not depending upon it for the entire picture of reality. Physical life alone does not necessarily require the <u>kind</u> of identification of self with flesh that is your own.

This does not mean that an alienation results in those realities simply a relationship in which the body and consciousness relate to other events. Only your beliefs, training, and neurological indoctrination prevent you from recognizing the true nature of your consciousness while you sleep. You close out those data. In that period, however, at an inner order of events, you are highly active and do much of the interior mental work that will later appear as physical experience.

(Slowly at 11:43:) While your consciousness is so engaged, your body consciousness performs many functions that are impossible for it during your waking hours. The greatest biological creativity takes place while you sleep, for example, and certain cellular functions[10] are accelerated. Some such disengagement of your main consciousness and the body is therefore obviously necessary, or it would not occur. Sleeping is not a by-product of waking life.

In greater terms you are just as awake when you are asleep, but the focus of your awareness is turned in other directions. As you know, you can live for years while in a coma, but you could not live for years without ever sleeping. Even in a coma there is mental activity, though it may be impossible to ascertain it from the outside. A certain kind of free conscious behavior is possible when you are <u>not</u> physically oriented as you are in the waking state, and that activity is necessary even for physical survival.

This also has to do with pulsations of energy in which consciousness as you know it, now, exercises itself, using native abilities that cannot be expressed through physical orientation alone.

Your own main consciousness has the ability to travel faster than light *(as noted at 9:37),* but those perceptions are too fast, and the neurologically structured patterns that you accept cannot capture them. For that matter, cellular comprehension and reaction are too fast for you to follow. The poised framework of physical existence requires a particular platform of experience that you accept as valid and real. At that level only is the universe that you know experienced. That platform or focus is the result of the finest cooperation. Your own free consciousness and your body consciousness form an alliance that makes this possible.

(With many pauses:) Give us a moment . . . Such a performance actually means that physical reality clicks off and on.[11] In your terms, it exists only in your waking hours. The inner work that makes it possible is largely done in the sleep state. The meeting of body consciousness and your main consciousness requires an intense focus, in which the greatest manipulations are necessary. Perceptions must be precise in physical terms. To some extent, however, that exquisite concentration means that certain limitations occur. Cellular comprehension is not tuned into by the normally conscious self, which is equally unaware of its own free-wheeling nature at "higher" levels. So a disengagement process must happen that allows each to regenerate. The consciousness then leaves the body. The body consciousness stays with it.

Give us a moment . . . We are about to end the session after a few remarks.

(Pause at 12:07. Seth's comments were for Jane, and took up another page of notes. End at 12:19 A.M.

(After the session we had something more to eat, then relaxed by playing with our cat, Willy. When we did get to bed Jane fell asleep at once. As I lay beside her in a most pleasant daze, I heard quite clearly in the cool night air the honking of geese as they flew south. Drowsily I remembered the flight I'd listened to in the rain the day before yesterday. . . .)

NOTES: Session 709

1. Tachyons, or meta-particles, are supposed faster-than-light particles that are thought to be possible within the context of Einstein's special theory of relativity. Physicists are still trying to experimentally

discover them. As I interpret Seth here, then, tachyons or something much like them will be found.

In Volume 1 of *"Unknown" Reality*, see Note 4 for Session 682.

2. For material on CU and EE units in Volume 1, see sessions 682 (with notes 3 and 4), 683–84, and 688. The last two sessions also contain some of Seth's comments on cellular consciousness.

3. One of the most unique out-of-body experiences, or projections, I've had was much like that which Seth describes here. It took place in April 1971, and I wrote about it in Chapter 20 of *Seth Speaks*. See the notes for the 583rd session. My consciousness didn't travel more than 10 feet from my body that time, but the little journey, so vivid and pleasant, did much to reinforce the enlarged view of reality that I'd gradually begun to adopt after Jane started delivering the Seth material late in 1963. I've never forgotten the sense of freedom that that modest projection engendered within me—and during it, my temporal relationships *were* different.

In Note 12 for Appendix 12, I wrote about out-of-body travel and naïve realism.

4. A note added some eight months later: Once in a great while Seth refers to the slower rate of physical aging connected with the out-of-body state, and notes the "certain principles" involved, as he does here. Jane and I have always felt that he has some very interesting material on the subject, and that we'll get it someday. But it didn't come through before *"Unknown" Reality* was finished, in April 1975.

5. "Disentanglement" immediately reminded me of the inner senses—those qualities and abilities which the personality uses to apprehend its physical (or camouflage) world. Seth began describing the inner senses early in 1964. His "Disentanglement From Camouflage" happened to be number eight on a list of nine, although the order is unimportant. Jane devoted Chapter 19 of *The Seth Material* to the inner senses.

"With disentanglement," Seth stated in the 43rd session, "the inner self disengages itself from one particular camouflage before it either adopts another set smoothly or dispenses with camouflage entirely. This is accomplished through what you might call a changing of frequencies or vibrations . . . In some ways, your dream world gives you a closer experience with basic inner reality than does your waking world, where the inner senses are so shielded from your awareness."

A note: Just as he periodically reminds us of his material-to-come on physical aging and out-of-body states (see Note 4, above), Seth mentions that there are more inner senses he'll tell us about someday—then adds that many of them are so far removed from reality as we understand it that our comprehension will be intellectual at best; in such cases we won't be able to identify with them emotionally. And then other groups of inner senses, Seth continues, are truly "beyond verbalization."

6. Much of the material in Appendix 12 (including the notes), deals with connections between our inner and outer worlds.

7. In Volume 1, see the 689th session. In Volume 2, see the references in Note 7 for Session 708.

8. So far in the two volumes of *"Unknown" Reality*, Seth has discussed the freedom of cells from time, along with a number of their other attributes, in well over a dozen sessions. In Session 684 (in Volume 1) he said at 10:07: "Your body's condition at any time is not so much the result of its own comprehension of its 'past history' as it is of its own comprehension of future probabilities. The cells precognate."

9. Appendixes 4 and 5, in Volume 1, show the insights Jane herself has gained so far about the more complicated trances she experiences while delivering the sessions for *"Unknown" Reality*. As noted in Appendix 4, she waits for that "certain clear focus" she needs before taking up the challenges of "translating multidimensional experience into linear terms and thought patterns." And from Appendix 5: "It's as though my consciousness is trying to use a new kind of organization—for me, for it—and so there's a kind of unfamiliarity."

10. Perhaps I should have asked Seth to be more specific about those "certain cellular functions" that are accelerated in the sleep state, but I didn't; I was tiring. It's well known that parts of the brain are much more active when we sleep than when we're awake, for instance, but I doubt that Seth was referring to such phenomena here.

The brain itself never sleeps, of course, since it's endlessly involved in running the vastly complicated physiological functions of the body. Sleep for the conscious mind results when neural activity in the reticular activating system (the RAS), which screens the sensory information reaching consciousness, falls below a minimum level.

11. In Volume 1, see sessions 681 and 684.

Session 710
October 7, 1974
9:31 P.M. Monday

(We have two compositions, both of them by Jane, to add to this session. She produced the first very short one, given below, yesterday. Seth briefly mentions it in the excerpted material at the end of tonight's session, with a promise to say more later.

(Those excerpts, in turn, came from his remarks about Jane's second composition, which she wrote late this afternoon after we'd finished reading certain material. Since this [second] piece is much longer, it's presented as Appendix 15. I suggest that it be read now, or at least before reaching the end of this session.

(From Jane's dream journal, then, for Sunday, October 6, 1974:

("I heard Seth's voice, very loud and powerful, as I lay asleep in bed last night [Saturday]. This was the first time I've had such an experience. The voice was coming from the area of the room next door or just beyond, but also from above; like out of the sky or something. It wasn't speaking through anyone—that is, it wasn't coming from inside my head or through me as it always has so far, even in the dream state. I tried to understand what was said.

The words didn't seem to be directed at me, particularly, but just to be there. It seemed that Seth was really laying it on somebody. At first I thought he was angry, but then I realized I was interpreting the power of the voice that way. This wasn't part of a dream, but I awakened almost at once as I tried to make out the words. Subjectively, I wasn't aware of Seth's presence in any way. The sound was like a supervoice; maybe like Nature speaking, or something; not the way a person would speak.")

Now, good evening.

("Good evening, Seth.")

Dictation *(quietly)*: To explore the unknown reality you must venture within your own psyche, travel inward through invisible roads as you journey outward on physical ones.

Your material reality is formed through joint cooperation. Period. Your own ideas, objectified, become a part of the physical environment. In this vast cooperative venture the thoughts and feelings of each living being take root, so to speak, springing up as objectified data. I said *(in the 708th session)* that each system of reality uses its own codified system. This effectively provides a sort of framework. Generally speaking, then, you agree to objectify certain inner data privately and *en masse* at any given "time." In those terms the airplane objectified the inner idea of flying in "your" time, and not in A.D. 1500, for example.

You may have heard people say of an idea: "Its time has not yet come." This simply means that there is not enough energy connected with the idea to propel it outward into the world of physical experience as an objective mass-experienced event.

In the dream state and in certain other levels of reality, ideas and their symbols are immediately experienced. There is no time lag, then, between a feeling and its "exteriorized" condition. It is automatically experienced in whatever form is familiar and natural to the one who holds it. The psyche is presented with its own concepts, which are instantly reflected in dream situations and other events that will be explained shortly. If you dream of or yearn for a new house in physical life, for instance, it may take some time before that ideal is realized, even though such a strong intent <u>will</u> most certainly bring about its physical fulfillment. The same desire in the dreaming state, however, may lead to the instant creation of such a house as far as your dream experience is concerned. Again, there is no time lag there between desire and its materialization.

(Pause, one of many, at 9:49.) There are levels within dreams, highly pertinent but mainly personal, in that they reflect your own private intents and purposes. There are other levels, further away in your terms, that involve mass behavior on a psychic level, where

together the inhabitants of the physical world plan out future events. Here probabilities are recognized and utilized. Symbolism is used. There is such an interweaving of intent that this is difficult to explain. Private desires here are magnified as they are felt by others, or minimized accordingly, so that in the overall, large general plans are made having to do with the species at any given "time." Here again, these desires and intents must fit into the codified system as it exists.

(Pause, in a quiet but intent delivery.) At these levels you are still close to home. Beyond, there are layers of actuality in which your psyche is also highly involved, and these may or may not appear to have anything to do with the world that you know.

When you travel into such realms you usually do so from the dream state, still carrying your private symbols with you. Even here, these are automatically translated into experience. This is not your own codified system, however. You may journey through such a reality, perceiving it opaquely, layering it over with your own perceived symbols, and taking those for the "real" environment. In these terms the real environment will be that which was generally perceived by the natural inhabitants of the system.

To begin with, your own symbols rise from deep levels of the psyche, and in certain terms you are a part of any reality that you experience—but you may have difficulty in the interpretation of events.

If you are in a world not yours, with your consciousness drifting, you are in free gear, so to speak, your feelings and thoughts flowing into experience. You have to learn how to distinguish your psychological state from the reality in which you find yourself, if you want to maintain your alertness and explore that environment. Many of my readers find themselves in just such situations while they are sleeping. While still dreaming they seem to come suddenly awake in an environment that appears to make no sense. Demons may be chasing them. The world may seem topsy-turvy. The dead and the living may meet and speak.

(10:16.) Now: In almost all instances, demons in dreams represent the dreamer's belief in evil, instantly materialized. They are not the inhabitants of some nether world, then, or underground. We will be giving some instructions that will enable readers to experiment with the projection of consciousness at least to some extent. It is very important for you to realize that even in dreams you form your own reality. Your state of mind, freed from its usual physical focus, creatively expresses itself in all of its power and brilliance. The state of mind itself serves as an intent, propelling you into realities of like conditions.

(Pause.) In your world you travel from one country to another, and you do not expect them to be all alike. Instead, you visit various parts of the world precisely because of the differences among them—so all out-of-body journeys do not lead to the same locale.

Instinctively you leave your body for varying amounts of time each night while you sleep, but those journeys are not "programmed." You plan your own tours, in other words. As many people with the same interests may decide to visit the same country together, on tour, so in the out-of-body condition you may travel alone or with companions. If you are alert you may even take snapshots—only as far as inner tours are concerned, the snapshots consist of clear pictures of the environment taken at the time, developed in the unconscious, and then presented to the waking mind.

There are techniques for using cameras,[1] and a camera left at home will do you little good abroad. So it is the conscious alert mind that must take these pictures if you hope to later make sense of your inner journeys. That conscious reasoning mind must <u>therefore</u> be taken along. There are many ways of doing this, methods not really difficult to follow. Certain techniques will help you pack your conscious mind for your journey as you would pack your camera. It will be there when you need it, to take the pictures that will be your conscious memories of your journey.

Do you want to rest your hand?

(10:22. "No," I said, although I'd been writing pretty steadily for the better part of an hour. Jane, in trance, held up a fresh bottle of beer. I opened it for her. Then:)

You must remember that the objective world <u>also</u> is a projection from the psyche.[2] Because you focus in it primarily, you understand its rules well enough to get along. A trip in the physical world merely represents the decision to walk or to choose a particular kind of vehicle—a car will not carry you across the ocean, so you take a ship or a plane. You are not astonished to see that the land suddenly gives way to water. You find that natural alteration quite normal. <u>You expect time to stay in its place, however.</u> The land may change to water, for example, but today must not change into yesterday in the same fashion, or into tomorrow in the beginning of today's afternoon.

Walking down the avenue, you expect the trees to stay in their places, and not transform themselves into buildings. All of these assumptions are taken for granted in your physical journeys. You may find different customs and languages, yet even these will be accepted in the vast, overall, basic assumptions within whose boundaries physical life occurs. You are most certainly traveling through the private and mass psyche when you so much as walk down the street. The physical world seems objective and outside of yourself, however. The idea of such outsideness is one of the assumptions upon which you build that existence. Interior traveling is no more subjective, then, than a journey from New York to San Francisco. You are used to projecting all destinations outside of yourself. Period. The idea of varied inward destinations, involving motion through time and space, therefore appears strange.

Now take your break.

(10:36. Jane's delivery had remained quiet and steady. "Boy, he was going strong," she said. "He kept me under a good long time because of the noise [in the apartment] upstairs—and because of those phone calls, too, I'll bet. . . ." Here she referred to a number of out-of-state calls she'd taken after supper this evening; she'd found two of them in particular to be rather upsetting.

(Resume in the same manner at 10:58.)

Generally speaking, you have explored the physical planet enough so that you have a good idea of what to expect as you travel from country to country.

Before a trip, you can produce travel folders that outline the attractions and characteristics of a certain locale. You are not traveling blind, therefore, and while any given journey may be new to you, you are not really a pioneer: The land has been mapped and there are few basic surprises.

The inner lands have not been as well explored. To say the least, they lie in virgin territory as far as your conscious mind is concerned. Others have journeyed to some of these interior locales, but since they were indeed explorers they had to learn as they went along. Some, returning, provided guidebooks or travel folders, telling us what could be expected. You make your own reality. If you were from a foreign land and asked one person to give you a description of New York City, you might take his or her description for reality. The person might say: "New York City is a frightful place in which crime is rampant, gangs roam the streets, murders and rapes are the norm, and people are not only impolite but ready to attack you at a moment's notice. There are no trees. The air is polluted, and you can expect only violence." If you asked someone else, this individual might say instead: "New York City has the finest of museums, open-air concerts in some of the parks, fine sculpture, theater, and probably the greatest collection of books outside of the Vatican. It has a good overall climate, a great mixture of cultures. In it, millions of people go their way daily in freedom." Period. Both people would be speaking about the same locale. Their descriptions would vary because of their private beliefs, and would be colored by the individual focus from which each of them viewed that city.

One person might be able to give you the city's precise location in terms of latitude and longitude. The other might have no such knowledge, and say instead: "I take a plane at such-and-such a place, at such-and-such a time, giving New York City as my destination, and if I take the proper plane I always arrive there."

(Pause at 11:13.) Explorers traveling into inner reality, however, do not have the same kind of landmarks to begin with. Many have been so excited with their discoveries that they wrote guidebooks long before they even began to explore the inner landscape. They did not understand that they found what they wanted to find, or that the seemingly objective phenomena originated in the reflections of the psyche.

You may, for example, have read books numbering the "inner realms," and telling you what you can expect to encounter in each. Many of these speak of lords or gods of the realm, or of demons. In a strange way these books do provide a service, for at certain levels you will find your own ideas materialized; and if you believe in demons then in those terms you will encounter them. The authors, however, suppose that the devils have a reality outside of your belief in them, and such is not the case. The demons simply represent a state of your own mind that is seemingly out there, objectified. Therefore, whatever methods the authors used to triumph over these demons is often given as proof not only of the demons' reality, but of each method's effectiveness.

Now if you read such books you may often program your activity along those lines, in the same way that a visitor to New York City might program experience of the city in terms of what he or she had been told existed there.

That kind of structuring also does a disservice, however, for it prevents you from coming in contact with your own original concepts. There is no reason, for example, to encounter any demons or devils in any trance or out-of-body condition.[3] *(Pause.)* In such cases your own hallucinations blind you to the environment within which they are projected. When your consciousness is not directly focused in physical reality, then, the great creativity of the psyche is given fuller play. All of its dimensions are faithfully and instantly produced as experience when you learn to take your "normally alert" conscious mind with you; and when you are free of such limiting ideas, then at those levels you can glimpse the inner powers of your own psyche, and watch the interplay of beliefs and symbols as they are manifested before your eyes. Until you learn to do this you will most certainly have difficulty, for you will not be able to tell the difference between your projections and what is happening in the inner environment.

Any exploration of inner reality must necessarily involve a journey through the psyche, and these effects can be thought of as atmospheric conditions, natural at a certain stage, through which you pass as you continue. Period.

(Louder at 11:31:) Now give us a moment. . . .

("I'm in between," Jane said after a pause, and in her "own" voice. "I don't know what's coming. I'm sort of half in trance and half out. . . ." She lit a cigarette.

("Do you want me to get you some more beer?")

("I don't think it'll last that long," she said. Seth returned—and stayed longer, probably, than she'd anticipated he would. His material was for Jane, and grew out of the paper she wrote this afternoon on Eastern religious thought [see Appendix 15]. The more personal parts of Seth's delivery aren't given here, yet enough remains to show Jane's main challenges some 11 years after she began speaking for him.

(The quotations also indicate how pervasive the regular Western view of "reality" is in our society, and what an undertaking it is to step outside of that framework, or just to enlarge upon it. Jane is still in the process of that objective, intellectual—and yet very emotional—movement of her psyche [as I am], but she's made considerable progress. In each of her books she tries to more clearly communicate the details and developments of her journey. [I note also that neither one of us is trying to get rid of our Western orientation, or to desert it—but to understand *it more fully.]*

(Now Seth said in part, beginning at 11:33:)

Ruburt is working through the philosophical problems that were really only questions not completely asked. All of the writing he did today is important. He is preparing to go ahead in all directions.

There are too many levels here to discuss all at once . . . One such level reinforces a trust in himself. The trust is accepted, however, because he is finally ready to work through the issues. As given *[at various times over the years, mostly in personal material]*, they involve cultural training and religious indoctrinations.[4] He is challenging, finally, the old beliefs that say that the self's spontaneity is not to be trusted. He is challenging those ideas emotionally and philosophically, uniting physical action and inner mobility. In the past he was still afraid to touch those beliefs with any but the slightest of hands.

Give us a moment . . . What he wrote is pertinent. Before he could go fully ahead he had to accept the challenges of the past, and this meant he had to examine those old beliefs. He is only now really beginning to do so. . . .

They were not only his <u>private</u> religious beliefs, but those of his contemporaries generally—and *(loudly:)* <u>the foundations upon which your present civilization was made.</u> He had to find the courage to encounter those old beliefs boldly, and he is finally doing so. I will have more to say to him in the dream state this evening, and I will shortly explain his experience with my voice.

In a way, then, the session will continue at another level of communication. It will all be down in black and white for you before too long, however.

My heartiest wishes to you both, and a fond good evening.

("Thank you, Seth, and the same to you. Good night."

(11:46 P.M. All Jane could say the next morning was that she had no conscious memory of any contact Seth might have made with her in the dream state. Looking ahead a bit: In tomorrow night's session, though, Seth does explain her weekend sleep-state encounter with his voice.)

NOTES: Session 710

1. A note added six weeks later: Seth further "develops" his camera analogy (as dream photography, for instance), in Section 5. See sessions 719–20.

2. Is there really an objective world—"something out there"— for each of us to perceive? See my passage on naive realism in Appendix 12, along with Seth's own material on the question in Note 13 for that appendix.

3. In Chapter 14 of *The Seth Material*, Jane and Seth gave a humorous-serious account of her out-of-body encounter with a demon, or "black thing," of her own creation.

4. See the notes (at 12:18 A.M.) concluding the 708th session.

Session 711
October 9, 1974
9:17 P.M. Wednesday

(ESP class had really jumped last night. The 32 people crowded into our living room enjoyed rich, active, loud, and even profane exchanges among themselves, with Jane, and with Seth. "Fuck you, Seth!" one girl screamed—which daunted that worthy not at all: Class members hardly agree with Seth or anyone else all of the time. As usual, Jane found herself learning along with her students. She also took time to sing very delicately in Sumari, in contrast to Seth's powerful deliveries. All was recorded, of course. Class lasted from 7 P.M. until after midnight, and by the time it was over everyone involved was, if not exhausted, certainly well exercised emotionally. We're to get a transcript of the evening's Seth material at next week's class.*)

Good evening *(whispering.*

("Good evening, Seth.")

Now: Dictation *(still whispering)*. Never as dramatic as our noisy class sessions.

*See Appendix 16.

Your world, again, is the result of a certain focus of consciousness, without which that world cannot be perceived. Period. The range of consciousness involved is obviously physically oriented, yet within it there are great varieties of consciousness, each experiencing that seemingly objective world from a private perspective. The physical environment is real in different terms to an animal, a fish, a man, or a rock, for example, and different portions of that environment are correspondingly unreal [to each of those forms]. This is highly important.

If an inhabitant from another reality outside of your own physical system entirely were to visit it, and if "his" intelligence was roughly of the same degree as your own, he would still have to learn to focus his consciousness in the same way that you do, more or less, in order to perceive your world. He would have to alter his native focus and turn it in a direction that was foreign to him. In this way he could "pick up your station."[1] There would be distortions, because even though he managed such manipulations he might not have the same kind of native physical structure as your own, of course, through which to receive and interpret those data his altered consciousness perceived.

Your visitor would then be forced to translate that information as best he could through his own native structure, if it were to make any sense to his consciousness in its usual orientation. All realities are the result of certain unique focuses taken by consciousness, therefore. In those terms, there is no outside. The effects of objectivity are caused as the psyche projects its experience into inner dimensions that it has itself created.

(9:35.) Within, those frameworks are ever expanding, so that in your terms at least it seems that greater and greater distances are involved. Travel to any other land of physical reality must then involve alterations of consciousness.[2]

New paragraph. While all of your own thoughts and feelings are "somewhere" materialized, only some of them become physical in your terms. They are then accepted as physical reality. They provide the basis for the physical events, objects, and phenomena upon which you all agree. Therefore your world has a stability that you accept, a certain order and predictability[3] that works well enough for daily concerns. At that point you are tuned in precisely on your "home station." You ignore the ghost symbols or voices, the probable actions that also occur, but that are muffled in the clear tones of your accepted reality. When you begin to travel away from that home station, you become more aware of the other frequencies[4] that are buried within it. You move through other frequencies, but to do this you must alter your own consciousness.*

The probable realities connected with your own system are like the suburbs, say, surrounding a main city. If for simplicity's sake you think of other realities as different cities, then after you leave your own you would pass through the suburbs, then into the country, then after a time into other suburbs until you reached another metropolis. Here each metropolis would represent a conglomeration of consciousnesses operating within an overall general frequency of clearest focus, a high point of psychic communication and exquisite focus in the given kind of reality. Unless you are tuned in to those particular frequencies, however, you could not pick up that reality. You might instead perceive the equivalent of jumbled sound or meaningless static *(as Jane has done)*, or jigsaw images *(as I have done)*. You might simply realize that some kind of activity was there, but without being able to pinpoint it.

Now all consciousness, including your own, is highly mobile. While you focus your attention primarily in your own world, certain portions of your consciousness are always straying. When you are sleeping, then, your consciousness often ventures into other realities, usually in a wandering fashion without tuning itself in to any precise frequencies. Beneath many seemingly chaotic dreams there are often valid experiences in which your consciousness "lights" in another reality, without being attuned to it with the necessary precision that would allow for clear perception. The information cannot be sifted or used effectively and is translated into dream images, as your consciousness returns toward your own home station. Therefore, it has been difficult to achieve any kind of clear picture of such other realities.

(Pause at 9:59.) Certain particular focuses then bring in different worlds, but unless your consciousness is tuned in with exquisite precision you will not be able to perceive clearly. You will instead pick up at best the ghost images, probabilities, and private data that are not officially recognized as part of the main reality's official structure of events.

New paragraph. Basically, however, consciousness is freewheeling. Such realities therefore always exist—in your own psyche—outside of your "home station," and some portion of your own consciousness is always involved in them. Period. There are bleedthroughs, so to speak, in the form of unofficial perceptions that often

*See Appendix 17.

occur, or "impossible" events that are seemingly beyond explanation. *(Pause.)* For now think of your own psyche, which is a con-
sciousized identity, as a kind of "supernatural radio." All of the
stations exist at once within the psyche. These do not come through
with sound alone, but with all the living paraphernalia of the world.
The "you" that you recognize is but one signal on one such station,
tuned in to a certain frequency, experiencing that station's overall
reality from your own viewpoint—one that is unique and like no
other, and yet contributing to the whole life of the station.

    (Smile:) The supernatural radio that is your entire psyche
contains many such stations, however. These are all playing at the
same time. It would be highly confusing in this analogy to experience or hear all of these at once, however, so different portions of the
psyche tune in to different stations, concentrate upon them, and
tune out the others for immediate practical purposes. Because these
stations all operate within the same psyche or supernatural radio, the
overall quality of the programs will have much to do with the nature
of the psyche itself. Radios are wired and contain transformers and
transistors. The overall reception is dependent upon the wiring and
the inner workings of the radio—and *(intently)* those workings exist
apart from the stations they are meant to pick up. In the same way,
the "supernatural psyche" exists apart from the stations of consciousness that it contains. In this case indeed the psyche itself makes
the radio, adding ever-new connections and stations.

    (10:18.) New paragraph. Pretend that you have a radio
with which you can clearly pick up 10 stations. First imagine that
during the daily programming there are three soap operas, four
news programs, several excellent dramas, a few operas, some popular music, several religious sermons, and some sports programs.
Each of these has its own commercials or messages, which may or
may not have anything to do with the programs given.

    First of all, it would be nearly impossible for you to sample
all of these programs with any effectiveness while going about your
own affairs. To make matters more complicated, again, these programs do not involve only sound. Each one has its own dimensional
realities. Beside that, there is a give-and-take between programs.

    For example: Say that you have a certain Wilford Jones,
who is a character in one of the soap operas. This Wilford, while
carrying on within his own drama as, say, a sickly grocer in Iowa,
with a mistress he cannot support, and a wife that he must support
(with amusement)—this poor, besieged man on station KYU is also
aware of all the other programs going on at the other stations. All of
the other characters in all of the other plays are also aware of our

grocer. There is a constant, creative give-and-take between the day's various programs. Period.

When our Wilford dramatically cries out to his mistress: "I am afraid my wife will learn of our affair," then the symphony playing on another station becomes melodramatic, and the sports program shows that a hero fumbles the football. Yet each character has its own free will. The football player, unconsciously picking up the grocer's problem, for example, may use it as a challenge and say: "No, I will not fumble the ball." The crowds then cheer, and our grocer in his soap opera may smile and say: "But it will all work out after all."

In other words, there is in the psyche constant interaction between all of the stations, and marvelous, literally unlimited creativity—in which, in your terms, all actions in one station affect all others in the other stations.

Now take a break.

(10:34. Jane's trance had been excellent, her delivery steady and rather quiet for the most part. "I knew what Seth was talking about," she said, "because I had the images to go along with what he was saying. Not that I could repeat him now, word for word. . . ."

(I reminded Jane that during Monday's session, the 710th, Seth had promised to "shortly explain" her hearing his booming voice in her sleep state last Saturday night. See Jane's description of the event preceding that session.

(Resume at 10:54.)

Now: Dictation: Still using the same analogy: As he falls asleep some night our grocer, Wilford, might suddenly hear the full strains of a symphony in his head, or instead catch a quick glimpse of a football player; or on the other hand one of the musicians in the symphony orchestra may suddenly find himself thinking about how difficult it would be to have a mistress and a wife at the same time.

From the point of view of the perceiver these would be unofficial events, and yet they could serve as important clues to the nature of reality. The separate programs existing at once each have their own schedules, and from your reality you could not play them all at once. It seems to you that you are outside of the psyche, so you think of someone as yourself operating this radio from that external position. From your point of view you could not pick up the grocer's escapades and the symphony, for instance, if both came through at 8 o'clock in the evening, without switching from one to the other: You would have to choose which program you wanted.

It is very easy of course to expand our analogy, changing the radio to a television set. In this case the projections on the screen would be fully dimensional, aware of each viewer in each living room. *(Pause.)* Not only this, but the screen people would understand the relationship between you the viewer, and, say, the other viewers in the same town. Behind the scenes not only would the performers, as performers in all of the programs, all know each other, but the characters portrayed by them would know each other and be aware of each other's roles in the programs, and even now and then stray into one another's dramas.

At levels beyond the comprehension of the viewer, all of the dramas and programs would be related. Again, because of the specific poise of your consciousness, it seems to you that you are outside of all these programs. You tune in to them, making choices, for example, if more than one favorite plays at the same hour.

In greater terms you are a part of the same "set," and at another level someone sees you as a character in a living room turning on a television set. Intrinsically the psyche, the private psyche, contains all such programs and realities. Certain portions of it, however, choose to take different focuses in order to bring those aspects in more clearly.

(Pause at 11:13.) To some extent, signals from all of the other stations are always in the background of any given program, and by momentarily altering the direction of your own attention you can learn how to bring other stations into focus. Psychically and psychologically, those other stations upon which you do not concentrate form the structure of the psyche as you understand it, from which your earthly experience springs into focus. Studying yourself and the nature of your own consciousness, then, will automatically lead you to some extent to an understanding of the "unknown" reality. The unknown reality is composed of those blocked-out portions of your own psyche, and the corresponding frameworks of experience they form.

(Long pause.) New paragraph. For the sake of imagery, you can imagine your normal consciousness as your connection with this home planet—the familiar station that you tune in to every day. When you project your consciousness away from it, then you will encounter various kinds of atmospheric conditions. Once you understand what these are, and what effects can be expected, such journeys can be undertaken consciously, with the conscious mind that you know acting as the astronaut, for example, and the rest of your consciousness acting as the vehicle. Such journeys lead to quite valid realities, but as an astronaut must know the best landing conditions, so you must learn how to "come in" at the most auspicious time and under the best conditions.

Such journeys take you through the nature of the psyche

itself, as well as to those other realities that exist as the result of the psyche's concentration within particular frequencies.

Projecting your consciousness out of your body, therefore, provides at the same time an inner probing of consciousness itself, as well as experience of its manifestations. There are then inner lands of the mind, and other worlds quite as legitimate as your own. They are intimately connected, however, with mental states which are then materialized, and so your own mental processes are highly involved.

Take your break.

(11:28. "He's really going, though, I'm telling you," Jane said, after remarking upon the shorter delivery. "I'm hoping he says something about when I heard his voice in my sleep." Resume at a faster pace at 11:40.)

Now: First of all, I have been speaking of the psyche as if it were a completed thing, with definite boundaries. The private psyche is ever creative, actually—expansive and literally without beginning or end.

Your experience of yourself marks the seeming boundaries of yourself. In a manner of speaking, I am one personality and one program or station. Ruburt is another. We have learned to be aware of each other,* to communicate between stations, to affect each other's programs and to change each other's worlds. I do not speak alone to Ruburt and Joseph, for example, but my words go out to the world that you know. Still within your framework, Ruburt tunes in to another station, translates it and broadcasts the information. To do this, however, he has to alter his own consciousness, withdraw momentarily from the official station to bring in this one. That means tuning in to other portions of the psyche, as well as another kind of reality. The final translation of my material has to come through his organism, however, or it would be meaningless to you.

Through him I am aware of the nature and condition of your world, and offer from my viewpoint comments meant to help you. Through Ruburt, then, I am permitted to view the earth "again" in your terms. I exist apart from him, as he exists apart from me, yet we are together a part of the same entity—and that simply carries the idea of the psyche further.

The other [Saturday] evening while he was in bed Ruburt had a somewhat surprising experience. He was not dreaming. His body was asleep but his consciousness was drifting. He clearly heard my voice. It seemed to come literally from out of the sky, down into another room outside of *(next-door to, actually)* the one in which his

*See Appendix 18.

body slept. For a moment the power frightened him, for it sounded like a radio turned up to an incredible degree—louder than thunder. At the time words were clearly distinguishable, though later he forgot what they said. For an instant he was tempted to interpret the power as anger, for in your world when someone is shouting they are usually angry. He realized, however, that something else was involved. He did not sense my presence, but only heard the thunder of the voice. It shocked him because he is used to hearing my words from within his head—he had never before been aware of my voice as existing apart from him. In the dream state he has heard me giving him information. In these instances, however, he was the channel through which my voice came. He has often wondered about the nature of my own independence, and the kind of reality in which I exist.

He was also aware at the time that while the voice literally boomed out, no one else would have heard it. Yet the voice definitely came from outside of himself, and he certainly seemed to hear it with his physical ears.

("Can you tell us what the voice said?")

(Whispering:) Let me continue . . .

Ruburt acts as a receiver when I speak, and so I must make certain adjustments so that my message can be channeled under conditions that involve, among other things, his nervous system and physical apparatus. That evening, through using what I call interior sound,[5] I let Ruburt become acquainted with the power at my disposal so that he could realize that it did, basically now, come from beyond his personality as he understands it.

(12:02.) In regular sessions, as now, he and I again both make adjustments, and so in sessions I am what I call a bridge personality, composed of a composite self—Ruburt and I meeting and merging to form a personality that is not truly either of us, but a new one that exists between dimensions. Beyond that is my real identity.

Ruburt does extremely well with interior sound, and so I use that method rather than, say, an image to make my independent existence known. Now Ruburt called me originally (last Saturday night) at unconscious levels because he was upset with "earth programming." He thought that you needed some help from the outside, so to speak. That intent set up certain signals that reached into other realities or stations, and I answered. I was not speaking to Ruburt personally when he heard me, but addressing myself to the world at large in a program that was indeed picked up by others.

This program spread out and was translated by others in dream states. In physical terms, however, the message given that evening is still to be presented through these books.

Give us a moment . . . End of dictation.

(12:09. And so in his own way Seth answered my question of a few minutes ago. Now Jane paused, then came partially out of trance. "I know he said that was the end of book work," she told me, "but I think there's more on it. So if you'll get me a new pack of cigarettes. . . ." Then:)

Continue dictation: Now: In your local programming you have hosts of familiar characters, and at different times, in your terms, you have them play different roles. They <u>take</u> different roles. These often represent strong idealizations alive in the private and mass psyche. *(Humorously:)* Let me give you a brief example that will also show you how well I have learned your culture.

(Seth proceeded to name three currently famous television detectives.)

In their own ways, these are heroes representing the detective who is out to protect good against evil, to set things right. Now these characters exist <u>more</u> vividly in the minds of television viewers than the actors do who play those roles. The actors know themselves as apart from the roles. The viewers, however, identify with the characters. They may even dream about the characters. These have their own kind of superlife because they so clearly represent certain living aspects within each psyche.

The aspects are personified in the character. Through the centuries, in your terms, there have been different personalities, some physical and some not, with whom the species identified. Christ is one of these: in some respects the most ideal detective—in a different context, however—out to save the good and to protect the world from harm. In certain ways man also projected outward the idea of a devil or devils, and for somewhat the same reasons, so that he could identify with what he thought of as the unsavory portions of the psyche as he understood them at any given time. In between there are a multitude of such personalities, all vividly portraying parts of the psyche.

(12:21.) These characters become portions of the <u>inner</u> literature of the mind. Suppose an inhabitant from another reality saw [one of those three programs] and realized that people were watching it. Pretend he wanted to add more depth to the show. He might then come on himself in the guise of [the hero detective], but enlarging upon the characterization, adding more dimension to the plot. So, often when some personality from another station wants to help change the programming, he comes on in the form of a

personality already known in fact or fiction. However, you must realize that that personality is larger than fact or fiction. "It" is independent at its own level, yet it is also a part of the portion of the private and mass psyche that is so represented.

I am Seth in those terms.

There are many myths connected with my name.[6] They all represent portions of the psyche as they were understood at various times in man's history. Those portions were originally projected out of the psyche as it began to understand itself, and personified its abilities and characteristics, forming superheroic characters of one kind or another, to which the psyche could then correspond and relate.

End of dictation.

(12:29. Then, after producing a couple of paragraphs on another matter:)

End of session—

("Okay.")

—and a fond good evening. I stop to give you a rest.

("I'm all right."

(With much amusement:) It shows you that I have concern.

("Yes. Well, thank you, Seth. Good night."

(End at 12:35 A.M. As we ate breakfast several hours later, Jane told me that during the night she'd kept waking up with ideas she thought were connected to "Unknown" Reality. When I asked her to write down what she could remember of them, she produced these items, with whatever distortions they may contain:)

"1. Some of the (hypnagogic) images you see in your mind prior to sleeping, and those at other times, are alternates—that is, you could see those pictures physically if you opened your eyes, instead of the ordinary reality you 'know' is there. Inner vision evolves physical sight, lining up exterior data into the kinds of images that correlate.

"2. Each reality is surrounded by its probabilities, but this is obviously relative . . .

"3. Our experience of the present is enriched by our memory of past perceptions. In some systems it works *the other way:* Inhabitants are aware of the future as we are of the past. On the other hand their 'memory' of the past fades almost at once.

"4. Again I received information on Atlantis, only to forget it right away. I'd wanted to tell Rob about it this morning. . . ."

(Jane also came through with material about Atlantis right after the 708th session was held, less than two weeks ago; see Appendix 14. We'd described that episode briefly in ESP class the night before this [711th] session was held—so had our doing so caused her second Atlantis pickup? But it's also

quite interesting to note that on both occasions Jane tuned in to data on Atlantis within hours after Seth had discussed ideas involving alternate realities.)

NOTES: Session 711

1. A note added later: Seth puts the "home station of consciousness" analogy to good use in several more sessions for this volume. See the 716th session in Section 5, for instance.

2. In Note 4 for Session 702, in Volume 1, Seth briefly discussed "space travel" into another probability.

3. Refer to Seth's material on the basic unpredictability of consciousness, and on probabilities, in the 681st session in Volume 1 of *"Unknown" Reality*.

4. In Volume 1, see sessions 685–86, and Appendix 4.

5. See Note 4 for the 708th session.

6. About Seth's reference to the myths connected with his name: Set, or Seth, was an Egyptian god of evil (with an animal's head) whose complicated origins could, it's thought, reach back in antiquity to at least 7500 B.C. In Judaism, of course, Seth was the third son of Adam and Eve, after Cain and Abel (Genesis 4 & 5). (As one correspondent wrote us: "Seth is also a Hebrew name meaning 'appointed'—i.e., the appointed one.") However, some very early priestly genealogies omit Cain and Abel, and consider Seth as the oldest son of Adam; in the second century A.D., for instance, the Sethites, who were members of a little-known Gnostic sect, thought of Seth, the son of Adam, as the Messiah. Seth also shows up in writings of the ancient occult religious philosophy, the cabala, which was originated by certain Jewish rabbis who sought to interpret the scriptures through numerical values; the soul of Seth is seen as infusing Moses; he was to reappear as the Messiah. . . .

Perhaps it's been remiss on our parts, but Jane and I haven't concerned ourselves with any connections *her* Seth may have with ancient Seths. We don't believe such relationships exist on any kind of personalized basis, although someday we'll ask Seth to comment here. We think the name of Jane's Seth came about through much more pragmatic needs. In Chapter 1 of *The Seth Material*, Jane quoted Seth-to-be from the 4th session for December 8, 1963, as that personality came through on the Ouija board (which we'd used to initiate these sessions): "You may call me whatever you choose. I call myself Seth. It fits the me of me. . . ." Reincarnation had been mentioned by the 2nd session, but since the concept meant little to us we hardly considered the many names that would be involved. Once Seth gave us a name by which to call him, we simply began using it. I'm sure that at the time Jane had no conscious knowledge about Egyptian, Hebrew, or even Christian origins or uses connected with the name, Seth.

Now I present Seth in part from the ESP class session for April 17, 1973, as he answered students' questions:

"So I ask you: 'What is your name, each of you?' My name is

nameless. I have no name. I give you the name of Seth because it is a name and you want names. You give yourselves names . . . because you believe they are important.

"Your existence is nameless. It is not voiceless, but it is nameless. The names you take are structures upon which you hang your images . . . What you are cannot be uttered, and no letter or alphabet can contain it. Yet, now you need words and letters, and names and objects. You want magic that will tell you what you are.

"You believe that you cannot speak to me unless I have a name, so I am Seth . . . I told Ruburt from our earliest sessions that he could call me Seth. I never said, 'My name is Seth,' (but 'I call myself Seth'—my emphasis), for I am nameless. I have had too many identities to cling to one name!"

Seth treats his own reincarnational background both generally and specifically, if rather briefly on both counts, in Chapter 22 of *Seth Speaks*. For the names of three of his past personalities as given in that chapter, see sessions 588–89. A fourth name (as well as names for Jane and me) can be found in the 595th session in the Appendix of *Seth Speaks*.

Session 712
October 16, 1974
9:13 P.M. Wednesday

(No session was held Monday night, October 14, as scheduled. Jane was busy instead doing a program for a radio station in a western state, live, via telephone from our living room in Elmira. She sat at her desk and was interviewed by the program's host, then answered questions from listeners. The show went well. In Volume 1, see the notes leading off the 702nd session.

(After supper this evening Jane received from Seth [without subjectively hearing his voice] information that the session would contain material about "probability clusters." We liked the term. But not until Seth began discussing the subject did I realize that Jane had tuned in to it herself following last Wednesday night's session. It appears at the end of that [711th] session as item No. 2 on the list of topics she came up with during the sleep state.

(In ESP class yesterday evening Jane engaged in one of her periodic and unusual "long-sound experiences," as we call them. Seth goes into her adventure in consciousness after first break.)

Good evening.

("Good evening, Seth.")

Now: Dictation: As per Ruburt's notes, each system of reality is indeed surrounded by its probable realities, though any one of those "probable realities" can be used as the hub, or core reality; in which case all of the others will then be seen as probable. In other words, relativity certainly applies here.

The rockbed reality is the one in which the perceiver is focused. From that standpoint all others would seem peripheral. Taking that for granted, however, any given reality system will be surrounded by its probability clusters. These can almost be thought of as satellites. Time and space need not be connected, however—that is, the attractions that exist between a reality and any given probability cluster may have nothing to do with time and space at all. The closest probability satellite to any given reality may, for example, be in an entirely different universe altogether. *(Pause.)* In that regard, you may find brethren more or less like yourselves outside of your own universe—as you think of it—rather than inside it. You imagine your universe as extending outward in space (and backwards in time). You think of it as an exteriorized manifestation, expanding perhaps, but in an exterior rather than an interior fashion.[1]

(Slowly:) Your idea of space travel, for example, is to journey over the "skin of your universe." You do not understand that your system is indeed expanding within itself, bringing forth new creativity and energy (underlined).

Give us time . . . Your universe is only one of many. Each one creates probable versions of itself. When you journey on the earth you move around the outside of it. So far, your ideas of space travel involve that kind of surface navigation. Earth trips, however, are made with the recognition of their surface nature.[2] When you think in terms of traveling to other planets or to other galaxies, though, the same kind of surface travel is involved. As closely as I can explain it in your terms, your concepts of space travel have you going around space rather than directly through it.

(9:40.) Give us time . . . You are also viewing your solar system through your own time perspective, which is relative. You "look backward into time," you say, when you stare outward into the universe. You could as well look into the future, of course. Your own coordinates[3] close you off from recognizing that there are indeed other intelligences alive even within your own solar system. You will never meet them in your exterior reality, however, for you are not focused in the time period of their existence. You may physically visit the "very same planet" on which they reside, but to you the planet will appear barren, or not able to support life.

In the same way, others can visit your planet with the same results. There is then a whole great inner dimension even to the space that you know, that you do not perceive. There are intelligent beings outside of your own galaxy, "adjacent" to you. Theoretically, you can visit them with some vast improvements in your technology, but great amounts of time would be involved. Others have visited your own planet in that particular fashion. Yours is still a linear technology. Some intelligent beings have visited your planet, finding not the world you know but a probable one.[4] There are always feedbacks between probable systems. A dominant species in one may appear as a bizarre trace species in another. More will be said about this and your planet later in the book.[5] The closest equivalent to your own kind of intelligence and being can actually be found not by following the outer skin of space, but by going through it, so to speak.

Give us time . . . There are, again, inner coordinates having to do with the inner behavior of electrons. If you understood these, then such travel could be relatively instantaneous. The coordinates that link you with others who are more or less of your kind have to do with psychic and psychological intersections that result in a like space-time framework.

Here I would like to give a very simple example, evocative of what I mean. The other day Ruburt received a telephone call from a woman in California who was in difficulty. Ruburt promised to send [healing] energy. Hanging up, he closed his eyes and imagined energy being sent out from a universal source through his own body, and directed toward the person in need. When he did so, Ruburt mentally saw a long "heavy" beam extending straight to the west from a point between his eyes. It reached without impediment. He felt that this extension was composed of energy, and it seemed so strong that a person could walk upon it without difficulty. Subjectively he felt that this beam of energy reached its destination. And so it did.[6]

Energy was almost instantly transmitted across the continent from one specific individual to another. When you are dealing with that kind of energy, and particularly when you believe in it, space does not matter. Emotional connections are set up and form their own set of coordinates. (Pause.) That beam of energy is as strong and real as a beam of steel, though it moves faster than a beam of light.

(10:09.) If Ruburt had tried to visit the woman by plane he would have followed the curve of the earth, but in those terms the energy went through in the "straightest" way.[7]

("But not through the earth?" I asked. Whereupon Seth repeated his last sentence three times. That was the answer he wanted to give.)

The psychic and emotional communication, then, cut

through physical coordinates. Ruburt was momentarily allied with the woman.

Now: In the same way you can be allied and in tune with other probabilities that do not coincide with your space-time axis. The exterior universe with its galaxies—as you understand it, and on that level of activity—can be encountered on certain rigid space-time coordinates. You can visit other planets only in your present (underlined). Your present may be the past or the future as far as inhabitants of a given planet are concerned. Your physical senses will only operate in their and your present.

"Effective" space travel, creative space travel on your part, will not occur until you learn that your space-time system is one focus. Otherwise you will seem to visit one dead world after another, blind to civilizations that may exist on any of them. Some of these difficulties could be transcended if you learned to understand the miraculous multidimensionality of even your own physical structure, and allowed your consciousness some of its greater freedom.

To some extent you have neurologically blinded yourselves. You accept only a certain range of neurological impulses as "reality."[8] You have biologically prejudiced yourselves. The physical structure is innately aware of many more valid versions of reality than you allow it to be.

Theoretically, a thoroughly educated space traveler in your time, landing upon a strange planet, would be able to adjust his own consciousness so that he could perceive the planet in various "sequences" of time. If you land upon a planet in a spaceship and find volcanos, you would, perhaps, realize that other portions of that planet might show different faces. You have confidence in your ability to move through space, so you might then explore the terrain that you could not see from your original landing point. If you did not understand the change in qualities of space, you might imagine that the whole planet was a giant volcano.

You do not understand as yet, however, that in a way you can move through time as you move through space—and until you understand that, you will not know the meaning of a true journey, or be able to thoroughly explore any planet—or any reality, including your own.

You imagine that your own earth is mapped out, and all frontiers known, but the linear aspects of your planet's life represent a most minute portion of its reality.

Take your break.

(10:24. Jane told me that Seth had been "really there," although

her delivery hadn't seemed to be any stronger or faster, say, than it usually is when she's under. She added that the material had appeared to be endless, and that Seth had called for a break now only so that we could rest before he launched into the next block of data—for that too was already "there."

(Rain had fallen in a fine drizzle throughout most of the day; and now, I saw from our second-story living room windows, a heavy fog lay over the street corner below and the newly finished Walnut Street Bridge just south of the intersection. The whole area had a warm dispersed glow from the bridge's lights.

(Resume in the same manner at 10:45.)

The portions of the psyche reflect and create the portions of the universe from its most minute to its greatest part. You identify with one small section of your psyche, and so you name as reality only one small aspect of the universe.

New paragraph. In class last evening Ruburt "picked up" messages that <u>seemed</u> to be too slow for his neurological structure. He was convinced that it would take many hours of your time in order to translate perhaps a simple clear paragraph of what he was receiving. He experienced some strain, feeling that each vowel and syllable was so drawn out, in your terms of time, that he must either slow down his own neurological workings to try to make some suitable adjustments. He chose the latter. Messages, therefore, perceptions, "came through" at one speed, so to speak, and he managed to receive them while translating them into a more comfortable, neurologically familiar speed.

One part of Ruburt accepted the "slow" [or "long"] perceptions, while another part quickened them into something like normal speech patterns. Some communication did result.[9]

What he was sensing, however, was an entirely different kind of reality. He was beginning to recognize another synapse [neuronal] pattern not "native"; he was familiarizing himself with perceptions at a different set of coordinate points. Such activity automatically alters the nature of time in your experience, and is indicative of intersections of your consciousness with another kind of consciousness. That particular type of consciousness operates "at different speeds" than your own. Biologically, your own physical structures are quite able to operate at those same speeds, though as a species you have disciplined yourselves to a different kind of neurological reaction. By altering such neurological prejudice,[10] however, you can indeed learn to become aware of other realities that coincide with yours. Period.

Now: Electrons themselves operate at different "speeds." The structure of the atom that you recognize, and its activity, is in larger terms one probable version of an atom.[11] Your consciousness, as it is allied with the flesh, follows the activity of atoms as far as it is reflected in your system of reality.

Ruburt is learning to minutely experience—change that—Ruburt is learning to minutely alter his experience with the probable atomic correlations that exist quite as validly as does the particular kind of atomic integrity that you generally recognize. When he does so, in your terms, he alters atomic receptivity. This automatically brings probabilities to the forefront. To perceive other realities you alter your own coordinates, tuning them in to other systems and attracting those into your focus.

Now take a break or end the session as you prefer.

("We'll take the break.")

(11:08 to 11:26.)

Now: To some extent or another there are counterparts[12] of all realities within your psyche. When you slow down, or quicken your thoughts or your perceptions, you automatically begin to alter your focus, to step aside from your officially recognized existence. This is highly important, for in certain terms you are indeed transcending the time framework that you imagine to be so real.

In other terms, certain portions of your own reality have long since "vanished" in the unrecognized death that your own sense of continuity has so nicely straddled. Your personal cluster of probable realities surrounds you, again, on a cellular basis, and biologically your physical body steers its own line, finding its balance operating in a cluster of probabilities while maintaining the focus that is your own. You can even learn to tune in to the cellular comprehension. It will help you realize that your consciousness is not as limited as you suppose. All realities emerge from the psyche, and from the CU's *(the units of consciousness)* that compose it.

(Heartily:) End of dictation. Give us a moment. . . .

(11:38. Now Jane came through with several pages of material for herself. Some of it was quite personal, but one part consisted of Seth's response to an assessment she'd written after supper tonight, wherein she examined her progress since the inauguration of her psychic abilities late in 1963. Seth, here, adds to our understanding of Jane's reactions to some of the challenges she took up 11 years ago. His material is also an extension of much that he gave in the 679th session for Volume 1 of "Unknown" Reality, when he discussed the early background of the probable Jane who chose to live in this physical reality, and how that Jane began to contend with her strongly mystical nature. See especially Note 8 for Session 679, and Appendix 1.)

The paper Ruburt wrote this evening is pertinent, and

highly significant. Have him show it to you. Indeed, though he dislikes the word, he is finishing the first portion of his "apprenticeship"—in which he became acquainted with a different kind of reality, and had to learn how to equate it with the "normal" one.

Certain strains were involved that in one way were as natural as growing pains. This has nothing to do with so-called psychic phenomena, but the natural growth and development of a personality whenever it tries to go beyond its space and time context, and takes on challenges of such a nature.

In one way, on one level, such a personality seems to be operating "blind," while in another it is aware of its accomplishments and challenges. Often a situation of unbalance is set up that would not exist had the personality not accepted the challenges and, hence, the potentials for an even greater development.

The more prosaic elements of the personality then take whatever measures seem necessary at the time, while new orientation is tried out. These methods may seem to lead to great distortions, particularly in contrast with the sensed possibilities of development. In one way or another, however, they still provide a framework in which the personality feels itself free to pursue its goals. The built-in impetuses provide clue points. When the new sensed reality is strong enough to provide not only greater comprehensions but also to construct a new framework, then the old framework is seen as limiting, and discarded.

Elements in your lives were experienced as negative simply because Ruburt was not sure of himself. Pleas for help (directed to Jane as well as Seth) were seen as demands—not as opportunities to use abilities—so he felt hounded. He was not sure enough of his new world; he was still enough a part of the old one so that he often saw his life and abilities through the eyes of the "old world inhabitants"—the others who might scorn him, or set him up for ridicule.[13] They represented portions of his own psyche still at that level of consciousness, not having quite assimilated the greater knowledge or experience, so he felt he needed protection—the protection that would ... cleverly ... serve all of his purposes, allowing him to go ahead as he wanted to ... that would keep him at home working, and yet also serve as a control against too much inner spontaneity until he learned that he could indeed trust the new world of experience.

(Then later:) There is far more I could say. The time this evening does not permit it, though I can talk as long as you can write.

My consciousness does not normally operate at the same

speeds as yours, either *(see Note 9)*, so in my terms what I am saying has long ago been said, while in your present it is new, or just reaching you.

(And later yet:) Ruburt should have another experience involving me or my voice . . .

And <u>now</u> *(emphatically, but with a smile)* I bid you a fond— and indeed the <u>most</u> fond of good evenings.

("Thank you, Seth. Good night."

(End at 12:01 A.M.

(A note added after Seth had completed his dictation for "Unknown" Reality in April 1975: the 712th session was held on October 16, 1974. In her notes at the beginning of the 710th session, Jane described how she'd heard Seth's very powerful voice in her sleep state during the night of October 5. I can write now that she has yet to have any subsequent, similar kind of encounter with Seth or his voice.)

NOTES: Session 712

1. Jane delivered this material for Seth in the 42nd session for April 8, 1964: "The universe is continually being created . . . as <u>all</u> universes are . . . and the appearance of expansion seen by your scientists is distortive for many reasons.

"Their time measurements, based on camouflage [physical information] to begin with, are almost riotously inadequate and bound to give distortive data, since the universe simply cannot be measured in those terms. The universe was not created at any particular time, but neither is it expanding into nowhere like an inflated balloon that grows forever larger— at least not along the lines now being considered. The expansion is an illusion, based among other things upon inadequate time measurements, and cause-and-effect theories; and yet in some manners the universe <u>could</u> be said to be expanding, but with entirely different connotations than are usually used."

From the 43rd session: "The universe is expanding in the way that a dream does . . . this in a most basic manner is more like the growth of an idea."

At the beginning of Appendix 12, see the longer presentation from the 44th session for Seth's discussion of "the value climate of psychological reality"—the "medium" that spontaneously contains within it all of our camouflage constructions of space, time, growth, and durability. Note 2 for Appendix 12 also fits in here, especially Seth's references within it to our endless questions about the beginning and ending of the physical universe.

From the 250th session for April 11, 1966: "The atom you 'see' does not grow larger in mass, or expand outward in your space, and neither does your universe."

Seth's material in those early sessions, given well over a decade ago for the most part, reflected of course his reactions to current astronomical theory about the state—and fate—of our physical (camouflage) universe. The idea of an infinitely expanding universe, with all of its stars ultimately burned out and all life extinct, is still the view largely accepted today; it's based on the red shift measurements of some of the supposedly receding galaxies, their apparent brightnesses, the "missing mass" of the universe, and other very technical data. Yet I find it most interesting to note that now some astrophysicists and mathematicians believe our universe may be destined to contract—indeed, to collapse in upon itself—after all. But again, these ideas aren't based on the kind of thinking Seth espouses (that consciousness comes first, that its creations are continuous), but upon other quite complicated camouflage observations and measurements. One of these is the discovery of at least some of that missing mass, thus indicating that gravitational fields may exist among the galaxies, and galactic clusters, strong enough not only to halt the expansion of the universe but to pull all matter back together again.

In scientific terms, it doesn't seem likely that the conflict between the two views will ever be resolved, or any decision reached that our universe may be an oscillating one, forever contracting and expanding. There are too many variables in measurement and interpretation, including the difficulties the human mind encounters when it attempts to grasp the enormous spans of time and space involved.

I hasten to add that it's only of academic interest to us, though, whether the universe disperses itself through an eternity of frozen expansion or compresses itself into a cosmic fireball of unbelievable proportions. Our scientists have projected either ending many billions of years into the future, although in the meantime, "only" an estimated five billion years from now, our own aging, exploding sun will have consumed the inner planets of the solar system—including the earth.

2. Just as he talks here about the surface nature of our travel, in Volume 1 of *"Unknown" Reality* Seth had a similar observation to make about our ideas of time; see the 688th session after 10:26: "Again, you live on the surface of the moments, with no understanding of the unrecognized and unofficial realities that lie beneath."

3. Seth began discussing coordinate points in Chapter 5 of *Seth Speaks.* See the 524th session: "Other kinds of consciousness coexist within the same 'space' that your world inhabits. They do not perceive your physical objects, for their reality is composed of a different camouflage structure. This is a general statement, however, for various points of your realities can and do coincide ... points of what you would call double reality, containing great energy potential ... where realities merge."

4. For one instance when Seth discussed our coming attempts at space travel, see Note 4 for Session 702, in Volume 1. Here's part of the

material I quoted from the 40th session: "It is very possible that you might end up in what you intend as a space venture only to discover that you have 'traveled' to another plane [probability]. But at first you will not know the difference."

Then, in the Appendix of *Seth Speaks,* see the transcript of the ESP class session for January 12, 1971. Certain sightings of UFO's (unidentified flying objects), Seth told class members, represented the appearance of visitors from other *realities,* rather than from elsewhere in our own universe.

5. But, regrettably, it isn't. . . .

6. In this particular case, subsequent correspondence seemed to confirm that the energy sent out by Jane had indeed been on target; its recipient reported quite beneficial results. I write "seemed to confirm" because we made no attempt to verify any results here except to check the time elements involved. Jane and I do our thing by ourselves. It would take a considerable organization of trained investigators, and much time, to thoroughly study the results of such projections of energy. There could be many reasons why the receiver would benefit from attempts to give that kind of assistance, though; one of them being the simple knowledge that someone else—the "sender," Jane—cared enough to try to help. But we do think that more than just suggestion is involved.

7. Of the books on astronomy that I've read (and I'm way short of scanning any great number of them, obviously), only one contains a brief mention of a similar notion in connection with space travel—that is, journeying almost instantaneously in a straight line between planets instead of following the relativistic *curve* of space. The volume's learned author treats the idea as just an idea, however, and a pretty far-out one at that—while here Jane demonstrated her version of the same principle in a practical way. See Note 2 for Session 709.

(An aside: As I wrote this note I asked Jane if she'd seen the appropriate passage in the astronomical text. She wasn't sure. She'd skimmed the whole thing one day recently without trying to read it. "Well," I said, joking, "you've just about lost your chance. The book's overdue at the library and I'm taking it back tomorrow. . . ." But she didn't look at it again.)

A few days after the episode Seth describes in this session had taken place, Jane had another experience with such a beam of energy. This time she lay on her side facing north after we'd retired, for she wanted to send help to a very ill person in a small town in Canada. She felt the transmission go out from her forehead in a straight line toward its destination. She was physically uncomfortable as she lay on her left side, however, so after a few moments she turned over. The movement shut off the beam. After she'd settled down on her *right* side, she felt it go out again—but from the *back* of her head now, and still traveling truly north to its Canadian goal.

Jane is often aware of her "beam of energy," or variations of it, when she's reaching out to others. There's at least an evocative analogy here with the behavior of neutrinos, which are fundamental subatomic "particles." Generated by the nuclear reactions in the cores of stars, neutrinos travel at the speed of light. They have practically no mass, no electric charge, and hardly ever interact with matter. Not only can they pass through the earth, they can traverse the universe itself without losing much of their energy.

8. See Appendix 4 in Volume 1.

9. With some wonder I can write that our average-sized living room had been more than crowded last night: Well over 30 people were present for ESP class. Very few of them had witnessed one of Jane's infrequent "long sound" sessions, as we call them, although a fair number had heard us describe the phenomenon at one time or another. Seth had also referred to it. I seldom take notes in class or use a tape recorder, preferring to be free to engage in the class's spontaneous development. Usually quite a few people will tape a class, yet last night it happened that only two did so. The results were unfortunate, as I'll explain later.

These notes deal with Jane's experiences in this week's class (held in October 1974). I made a verbatim record of her first encounter with slow, or long, sound in the 612th session for September 6, 1972, just about a year after she'd finished *Seth Speaks*. Since the material in that session wasn't covered in *Personal Reality* or *Adventures,* we're publishing most of it as an appendix for this volume.* Not only will it illuminate these notes; it will also link, if loosely, Seth's reality, Seth Two, and some other "rapid" effects. There's much to be learned here, and perhaps eventually we'll be able to do something about that.

Chapter 2 of *Seth Speaks* contains two short passages from Seth that I find very reminiscent of Jane's expression of long sound. See Session 514 for February 9, 1970: 1. "We can follow a consciousness through all of its forms, for example, and in your terms, within the flicker of an eye." 2. ". . . for we can spend a century as a tree or as an uncomplicated life form in another reality."

After she'd grappled with her reception of some long-sound material last night, Jane spoke a few words for Seth. It was then that we began to glimpse what we could call a "source" of the long material—for Jane told class that from our physical viewpoint "Seth's true reality had sounded like a mountain" to her. It had been "that slow, that massive, that powerful. I slow down . . . like a mountain, and feel trees grow." By making a strong effort she'd speeded up her reception of him so that he came through sounding like the familiar Seth. Thus she gained new insights into Seth and his home environment. And from that much larger, more encompassing reality, Seth could follow a consciousness in our camouflage world through all of its forms "within the flicker of an eye."

Jane had to renew her very strict control each time she tried to transmit long data, however; I could see that otherwise she'd slide into an extremely slow delivery. That happened often. Then it would take her

*See Appendix 19.

many minutes to contend with a single syllable; her tongue worked persistently at the "sal" in "universal," for example, but even so all that issued from her was an elongated hissing sound based upon the "s" alone.

As the evening passed Jane told class that she'd keep Seth's "true reality rhythm-speed" to her left and, she hoped, would speak an understandable translation of it, speeded up for our cognition, to her right. "But I keep getting pulled back into a more true expression of Seth's reality. . . ." She could manage only a few words at a time from the Seth we were used to.

Now for the unfortunate results I mentioned near the beginning of this note: Of the two cassette tape recorders that had been operated by class members last night, one malfunctioned throughout the evening, unknown to its owner, and so recorded no class material at all. The other recorder's tape snapped just before Jane finally succeeded in consistently uniting Seth's slow, or long, reality with the accelerated version we ordinarily hear. For a few minutes, then, she was able to speak for Seth about his home environment—but since the information wasn't recorded I have nothing to quote here. By then class was nearly over. I don't want to try reconstructing Seth from memory, but will note that his material took off from some of that in the 612th session (see Appendix 19).

From its owner Jane and I borrowed the one incomplete class tape that had been made. As we'd expected, her long-sound experiences hadn't recorded well at all. The key episodes had been more visible than verbal. While Jane had been straining to compress a long syllable into something recognizable, the tape picked up little except distracting background noises: class people coughing, or moving about or shuffling papers; the sounds of traffic . . . But Jane and I take class events as they come. Otherwise we'd be continually involved in note-taking, making tapes, and so forth.

A note added later: Of course, nowhere in the 712th session did Seth come right out and say that in class the night before Jane had tried to express her version of his "own true reality." Strange it may be, but I didn't catch this during the session, nor did either of us notice it for some time afterward. And for whatever reasons, with the exception of one rather oblique reference at the end of this (712th) session, Seth himself chose to discuss the whole class adventure from quite a detached viewpoint.

10. In Chapter 6 of *Adventures,* see Jane's discussion of "prejudiced perception," which in "our reality is characterized as much by the kind of events it excludes as by those it embraces."

In Volume 1 of *"Unknown" Reality,* see Session 686 at 12:19 for Seth's account of Jane's "Saratoga experience," with its altered neurological connotations.

11. In Volume 1, see these two sessions: the 694th to 10:00 P.M., and the 702nd, with Note 6. In Volume 2, see Note 24 for Appendix 18.

12. A note added later: See the 721st session, with its Appendix 21.

13. See Appendix 10 in Volume 1. In Volume 2, see the 708th session after 11:40, and (added a few days later) the opening notes for Session 713. All of these passages show Jane's attempts to understand her abilities and beliefs, and to relate them to herself and to the world in general.

Session 713
October 21, 1974
9:28 P.M. Monday

(*"The truth is,"* Jane said to me the other evening, *"I'm alone in this psychic thing. I'm the one who's got to do it. . . ."* We were discussing the material Seth had given after 11:38 in the last [712th] session; he'd talked about some of the strains Jane had experienced while serving "the first portion of her apprenticeship" in the development of her psychic abilities. I've heard her say the same thing before, of course; see Note 13 for the 712th session. Basically, her examination of her inner dimensions must be a solitary one. When she began the sessions over 11 years ago, we requested advice and help from a few people,[1] but as we slowly began to understand the very personal nature of her gifts we realized that she'd have to find her own answers as she went along, with whatever help I could learn to offer.

(*Those circumstances might have acted as a leavening factor in the early years, perhaps to a mild degree helping determine the direction of some of Jane's psychic explorations, with and without Seth. Much more important is that she's always wanted to do her own thing. Besides, how would she ask advice from another about such an individual, intuitive quality as, say, the next step to*

*take in her psychic growth? These notes make her quest appear to be much
simpler than it actually was—and is.* [2]

    *(This afternoon Jane told me that in her sleep last night she'd had
bleed-throughs from Seth about the material to come next in his book. She
described it to me—and tonight Seth followed that subject matter very closely in
the first part of the session. I suggest the reader review the 711th session in
connection with this evening's data to 11:26.)*

    Good evening.

    ("Good evening, Seth.")

    Dictation. Give us a moment. . . .

    (Long pause.) It might help here if you imagine the psyche
again as some multidimensional living television set. In what seems
to be the small space of the screen many programs are going on,
though you can tune in to only one at a time.

    In a manner of speaking, however, all of the other pro-
grams are "latent" in the one you are watching. There are coordinates that unite them all. There is a give-and-take quite invisible to
you between one program and another, and action within one,
again, affects the action within each of the others.

    Like this imaginary multidimensional television, the
psyche contains within it other programs than the one in which you
are acting—other plots, environments, and world situations. Theoretically you can indeed momentarily "walk out of" your program
into another as easily, when you know how, as you now move from
one room to another. You must know that the other programs exist
or the possibility of such action will not occur to you. In larger terms
all of the programs are but portions of <u>one</u>, colon: The various sets
are real, however, and the characters quite alive.

    Now: Actors playing parts are obviously <u>alive</u>, as actors,
but in a fictional play, for example, the characters portrayed by the
actors are not alive, in your terms, in the same fashion that the actors
are. In the psyche, however, and in its greater reality, the characters
have their own lives—quite as real as those of the actors.

    Think again of the psyche in the manner mentioned,
taking it for granted that the program now on the screen is a fully
dimensioned reality, and that hidden somehow in its very elements
are all of the other programs not showing. These are not lined up in
space behind the "front" program, but in a completely different way
contained within it. The point of any image at any given time in the
picture showing might represent, for example, a top hat on a table.
Everyone acting in that scene would view the hat and the table, and
react accordingly with their own individual characteristics.

Give us a moment ... The hat on the table, while possessing all of the necessary paraphernalia of reality for that scene, might also, however, serve as a different kind of reference point for one of the other programs simultaneously occurring. In that reality, say program two, the entire configuration of hat and table may be meaningless, while still being interpreted in an entirely different way from a quite different perspective. There in program two the table might be a flat natural plain, and the hat an oddly shaped structure upon it—a <u>natural</u> rather than a manufactured one. Objects in your reality have an entirely different aspect in another. Any of the objects shown in the program you are watching, then, may be used as a different kind of reference point in another reality, in which those objects appear as something else.

(9:50.) We are trying to make an analogy here on two levels, so please bear with me. In terms of your psyche, each of your own thoughts and actions exist not only in the manner with which you are familiar with them, but also in many other forms that you do not perceive, colon: forms that may appear as natural events in a different dimension than your own, as dream images, and even as self-propelling energy. No energy is ever lost. The energy within your own thoughts, then, does not dissipate even when you yourself have finished with them. Their energy has reality in other worlds.[3]

Now imagine that the picture on the television screen shows your own universe. Your idea of space travel would be to send a ship from one planet, earth, outward into the rest of space that you perceive on that "flat" screen. Even with your projected technology, this would involve great elements of time. Imagine here, now, that the screen's picture is off-center to begin with, so that everything is distorted to some extent, and going out into space seems to be going backward into time.

(Pause.) If the picture were magically centered, then all "time" would be seen to flow out from the instant moment[4] of perception, the private now; and in many ways the mass now, or mass perception, represents the overall now-point of your planet. From that now, "time" goes out in all probable directions. Actually it also goes <u>inward</u> in all probable directions.

(Slowly:) The simple picture of the universe that you see on our screen, therefore, represents a view from your own now-perspective—but each star, planet, galaxy or whatever is made up of other reference points in which, to put it simply, the same patterns have different kinds of reality. True space travel would of course be time-space travel,[5] in which you learned how to use points in your own universe as "dimensional clues" that would serve as entry points into other worlds. Otherwise you are simply flying like an insect around the outside of the television set, trying to light on the fruit, say, that is shown upon the screen—and wondering, like a poor bemused fly, why you cannot. You use one main focus in your reality. In the outside world this means that you have a "clear picture." *(Humorously:)* There is no snow! That physical program is the one you are acting in, alive in, and it is the one shown on the screen. The screen is the part of your psyche upon which you are concentrating. You not only tune in the picture but you also create the props, the entire history of the life and times, hyphen—but in living three-dimensional terms, and "you" are within that picture.

The kind of reality thus created by that portion of your consciousness forms a given kind of experience. It is valid and real. When you want to travel, you do so within the dimensions of the reality thus created. If you drive or fly from one city to another, you do not consider the journey imaginary. You are exploring the dimensions given.

(10:18.) Now: If you alter that picture a little so that the images are somewhat scrambled—and you do this by altering the focus of your consciousness—then the familiar coordination is gone. Objects may appear blurred, ordinary sounds distorted. It seems as if you are on the outskirts of your own reality. In such a state, however, it is easy to see that your usual orientation may be but one of many frames of reference. *(Pause.)* If you did change the focus of your consciousness still further, you might then "bring in" another picture entirely. On the outside this would give you another reality. *(Intently:)* In it your "old" reality might still be somewhat per-ceivable as a ghost image,[6] if you knew what to look for and remembered your former coordinates. On the inside, however, you would be traveling not around or about, but through one portion of the psyche with its reality, into another portion of the psyche with its reality. That kind of journey would not be any more imaginary than a trip from one city to another.

There are space-time coordinates that operate from your viewpoint—and space travel from the standpoint of your time, made along the axis of your space, will be a relatively sterile procedure. (In parentheses: Some reported instances of UFO's happened in the past as far as the visitors were concerned, but appeared as images or realities in your present. This involves craft sightings only.*)

Give us time . . . When you change your ordinary tele-vision set from one station to another you may encounter snow or

*See Appendix 20.

distortion. If something is wrong with the set you may simply tune in patterns that seem meaningless and carry no particular program. You may have sound without a picture, and sometimes even a picture but sound from another program. So when you begin to experiment with states of altered consciousness you often run into the same kind of phenomena, when nothing seems to make sense.

(10:32.) Currently, physicists have made some important breakthroughs, but they do not recognize their significance. The universe that you know is full of microscopic black holes and white holes,[7] for example. Since your scientists have themselves given these labels, then using those terms I will say *(with much gentle humor)* that there are red, green, orange and purple holes—that is, the so-called black holes and white holes only represent what physicists have so far deduced about the deeper properties of your universe, and the way that certain coordinate points in one world operate, as providing feed-through into another.

Nothing exists outside the psyche, however, that does not exist within it, and there is no unknown world that does not have its psychological or psychic counterpart. Man learned to fly as he tried to exteriorize inner experience, for in out-of-body states in dreams he had long been familiar with flight. All excursions into outer reality come as the psyche attempts to reproduce in any given "exterior" world the inner freedom of its being.

Men have also visited other worlds through the ages. Others have visited your world. In dreams, and in altered states through history as you accept it, men have been taken upon such journeys. On their return they almost always interpreted their experiences in terms of their home programs, intertwining what happened into what ended up as great myths and stories—real but not real.

Take your break.

(10:45. "Man," Jane said after quickly leaving an excellent dissociated state, "is he going to town. There's just tons of material there, all ready and waiting. . . ." I could tell that this was the case: Her delivery had reached a steady, quiet yet driving level that she seemed capable of maintaining indefinitely.

(Jane commented here on something I'd also become aware of in recent sessions. For whatever reasons since holding the 709th session, she hasn't had to wait for that certain, more "difficult" kind of trance to develop before launching into Seth's book material; see the note at 10:55 for that session. In some fashion she can't describe, Jane is now able to reach the "right" trance state, or to arrive at it, much more easily. For other contrasting examples, in Volume 1 see the notes closing out sessions 688 and 703, as well as related

material in Appendix 4, wherein I wrote about the translation challenges she's often faced since beginning "Unknown" Reality: "—hence her talk before many of these sessions . . . about attaining that 'certain clear focus,' or 'the one clearest place in consciousness,' before she began speaking for Seth."

("I get the strangest feeling of 'folded time' during the sessions," Jane continued. "I'm caught. I can get more on the book, or some on me. I don't know what to do. I know the book stuff is all right there—but it takes time to get it. It's too bad I can't get it instantaneously.[8] *I really want both sets of material, so I guess I'll wait and see what happens. . . ."*

(Resume in the same manner at 11:01.)

While all of this may sound quite esoteric, it is highly practical, and we are dealing with the nature of creativity itself.

Your thoughts, for example, and your intents, have their own validity and force. You set them into motion, but then they follow their own laws and realities. All creativity comes from the psyche. I [recently] suggested a project to Ruburt's class—one that will ultimately illuminate many of the points I am making in *"Unknown" Reality.* I suggested that Ruburt's students create a "city"[9] at another level of reality. This is not to be a pie-in-the-sky sort of thing, or some "heaven" hanging suspended above, but a very valid meeting place between worlds. A psychic marketplace, for example, where ideas are exchanged, a place of psychic commerce, a pleasant environment with quite definite coordinates, established as an "orbiting satellite" on the outskirts of your world.

Initially, all worlds are created in just that fashion.

In certain terms, then, this involves in a very small way the creation and colonization of a different kind of reality—consciously accepted, however, from your perspective. On an unconscious level, the world as you know it expands in just such a fashion.[10] Several students have had dreams involving their participation in such a project. Ruburt found himself in an out-of-body state, looking at a jacket. It had four rectangular pockets. It was giant-sized. As he looked at it the front flap was open. In the dream he flew through this flap literally into another dimension, where the point of the flap was a hill upon which he landed. From that second perspective, the pockets of the jacket in the first perspective became the windows of a building that existed in a still-further, third dimension beyond the hill. Standing on the hill, he knew that in Perspective One the windows of the building in Perspective Three were jacket pockets, but he could no longer perceive them as such. Looking out from the hill in Perspective Two, Perspective One was invisibly behind him, and Perspective Three was still "ahead" of him, separated from him by a gulf he did not understand.

(11:15) He knew, however, that if the shades were pulled in the windows in Perspective Three, then the jacket-pocket flaps would appear to be closed in Perspective One. He also realized he had been directing the erection of the building in Perspective Three by making the jacket *(in Perspective One)*.

When he approached the hill in Perspective Two, he spoke to the contractor who was there before him. Ruburt said that he wanted to change the design. The contractor agreed, and shouted orders to people who were working in Perspective Three, where the building stood.

Now: Ruburt <u>was</u> validly involved in the erection of that building, and he did indeed travel through various dimensions in which the objects in one represented something entirely different in another. He used the particular symbols, however, simply to bring the theory home to him, but it represented the fact that any given object in one dimension has its own reality in another. You cannot move through time and space without altering the focus of your psyche. *(Intently:)* <u>When you so alter that focus</u>, however, you also change the exterior reality that you then experience.

Give us a moment. Rest your hand . . . Later you will realize the startling nature of what has been given this evening.

(Still in trance, Jane poured herself more beer. As Seth, she'd recited without hesitation all of the difficult, complicated material connected with her own dream.)

The following is for Ruburt, yet also for others, and can serve as a brief essay on the nature of will.

(11:26. But in our opinions a lot of what Seth had to say was pretty personal—so much so that only certain parts of it are given below, along with a few bracketed changes I've made to help tie it together. These excerpts still furnish characteristic insights into aspects of Jane's personality, as well as my own, and I might add that the deleted portions are even more meaningful to us. We're making good use of all of this material.)

Ruburt directed his will in certain areas. Your will is your intent. All of the power of your being is mobilized by your will, which makes its deductions according to your beliefs about reality. Each of you use your will in your own way. Each of you have your own way of dealing with challenges. Ruburt used his will to solve [a series of] challenges.

He was determined to find the kind of mate that would best suit him and his own unique characteristics. That intent was in his mind. When that challenge was met he used his will and mobilized all of his power to fulfill his abilities, and to bring about conditions in which he hoped Joseph *(as Seth calls me)* could also fulfill his. The will, again, operates according to the personality's beliefs about reality, so its desires are sometimes tempered as those beliefs change. In his own way Ruburt always concentrated upon one challenge at a time—boring in, so to speak, and ignoring anything else that might distract him.

He wanted to write, to use his creative and psychic abilities to the fullest, and so he cut down all distractions. His literal mind led him to . . . a rich diet of creativity and psychic experience, and to a situation in which Joseph and he could finally be financially free [to some extent], and not in that way threatened.

To his way of thinking he cut out all excess baggage, so he had a spare diet, physically speaking . . . The power of his will is amazingly strong. He is not one to work in many areas at once. Each person lives by their intent, which springs up about the force of their being. In all of this probabilities are involved, so in all moments of the past he touched points of probable healings.[11] No one can be healed against his or her will. There is no such coercion.

Ruburt does not like [some personal aspects] of his plan on the one hand. On the other it was part of his method, a way of intensifying focus, increasing perception in a small area while also ensuring safety, so that inner excursions would be balanced by [conditions in his exterior environment] . . . He sees that the challenge has been won, and now it is time to take up the next one, to apply the power of the will to certain physical areas.

Now many people never learn to apply the power of the will at all.

You [Joseph] were determined to find the kind of relationship you have with Ruburt, the kind of bond your parents never had,[12] and you applied the power of your will in that direction. At the same time you were determined to set yourself apart from the world to some extent, while still maintaining and developing an emotional contact with a mate that would be unlike any in your earlier experience. Creativity would have to be involved. You were also intrigued, determined to travel into the nature of reality, and at least glimpse a vague picture of what it could be. In this probability you provided yourself with a background that included sports and the love of the body, knowing [those qualities] would sustain you.

One of your beliefs, then, was a strong joint one that you had to protect your energy at all costs, and block out worldly distractions. Ruburt with his practical mind interpreted this more literally than you did, and physical restriction was a part of his natural early environment [because of his mother's chronic illness], as it was not in yours. But he is amazingly resilient . . . The power of his will is indeed awesome, and he is just now beginning to feel it. With that awareness, it can be used in a new physically oriented directive. The altered directive is all that is necessary. The rest will unconsciously follow . . . The point of power is in the present[13]; this kind of material and its understanding [by Ruburt and others] is more important than "past" causes.

There has been a series of challenges that Ruburt has met through using the power of his will, and this [physical one] is simply the next one to be conquered. Again, many people are not even familiar with that power.

I bid you a fond good evening.

(*End at 12:23 A.M. At the breakfast table some hours later, Jane told me that once again she'd "worked on Seth's book all night."*

(*And added a year later: Seth also discussed the will in a personal session that was held just six months after he'd finished dictating* "Unknown" Reality *in April 1975. As soon as Jane came through with the material, I thought of adding some of its more generalized portions to this session. Seth:*)

. . . you cannot equivocate. You have a will for a reason. When you are born, that will is directed toward growth and development. You literally will yourselves alive. That will-to-be triggers all bodily activity, which then operates automatically, with the same power from which the will itself emerged.

In infancy and childhood the will singleheartedly directs the body to go full thrust ahead, sweeping aside obstacles in the great impetus toward growth and development. The will is meant to assess the conditions into which the organism grows, however—to also seek out the best areas for expansion.

There are times in history when the species deals with different kinds of challenges. In programmed societies where "each man or woman knows his or her place," then the will knows which directions to follow, though other conditions and prerogatives might be ignored. Actually, in your own society there are many prerogatives . . .

Ruburt wanted to go in one particular direction, but with no clear-cut known ways of getting there. He wanted to pursue a course that was unconventional. He felt he needed protection while he learned, and until he attained enough wisdom.[14] The search itself would lead to a completely different set of values and a new belief system.

You see about you others dealing with life's challenges, following the old beliefs. They must see for themselves that those beliefs do not work.

The universe is with you and not against you. Your fellow

men are with you and not against you. When [each of] you realize
that, then you reach those portions of your fellows that are with you.
You meet them at a different level that is illuminating to them also,
and starts them developing . . . The will's power is impressive, and it
is "distributed" throughout the body. The body depends upon it for
direction. The will's beliefs, again, activate the body's automatic
resources.

     End of session.

NOTES: Session 713

     1. See the references to the Dr. Instream material (for 1965–67)
in Appendix 18 with its Note 18. In chapters 5 and 6 of *The Seth Material,*
Jane described other contacts we made as we sought to understand her
psychic growth.

     2. A note added six months later: These lines are from a
personal session Seth delivered on April 29, 1975, just five days after
finishing dictation on *"Unknown" Reality* (in the 744th session): "Our books,
and I am including Ruburt's, fall into no neat category . . . In the beginning, particularly, and for that matter now, Ruburt had no accepted
credentials. He is not a doctor of anything, for there is no one alive who
could give him a degree in his particular line of research, or in yours . . . He
hides behind no credentials, or social system, or dogma. . . ."

     3. The 453rd session, for December 4, 1968, is printed in its
entirety in the Appendix of *The Seth Material.* In that session, I think, Seth
came through with one of his most evocative conceptions: "You do not
understand the dimensions into which your own thoughts drop, for they
continue their own existences, and others look up to them and view them
like stars. I am telling you that your own dreams and thoughts and mental
actions appear to the inhabitants of other systems like the stars and planets
within your own; and those inhabitants do not perceive what lies within and
behind the stars in their own heavens."

     Seth continued the session by expressing his concern lest this
kind of material lead to feelings of insignificance on our parts. (In Volume 1
of *"Unknown" Reality,* see Session 681 at 10:00, with Note 2.) However, in a
poem she wrote for me a few years later—at Christmastime 1973—Jane
herself dealt equally well with the idea of simultaneous interactions between
realities:

     Dear Love

     Dear love,
     what time unmanifest
     in our lives resides

beneath our nights and days?
What counterparts break
within our smiles,
what cracks appear in other skies
as we talk and drink coffee
in quiet domestic grace?

Does the smallest wrinkle
spreading on my face
peal like thunder
to molecular identities
who study tissue heavens
with a worried air,
and dwell in cells, each
private, yet connected?
And when I frown—
or you reading the news,
throw down the paper in disgust—
do storms break out
in miniature worlds inside;
taking precautions
to protect their cellular
heavens, do minute inhabitants
save us, rushing with their
tiny antibodies to repair
punctures in a universe
we share?
And when we make love
do their crops grow?

4. For a definition of the moment point, see Note 11 for Appendix 12.

5. See the 712th session to first break, with its appropriate notes.

6. In Volume 1, see Practice Element 1 (in the 686th session) for Seth's description of Jane's projection into a probable past of her own—her "Saratoga experience," as we call it.

7. In Appendix 19, see the 612th session after 10:50, and Note 11.

8. Jane has had strong yearnings before to instantaneously receive book material that was "immediately available." See the closing notes for Appendix 7 in Volume 1, in which are described her feelings of intense frustration at her inability to speak all at once the contents of a potential book, *The Way Toward Health*.

9. See Appendix 16 for Session 711.

10. See Note 1 for the 712th session.

11. See Seth on Jane, her will, her relationship with me, and her physical symptoms in Session 679 for Volume 1. I discussed her symptoms in Note 8 for that session also, besides referring the reader to appropriate material in *Personal Reality*.

12. For some material on the kind of relationship my parents *did* have (one obviously involving their children in the most intimate ways, of course), see the first two sessions in Volume 1: the 679th from 11:37, with Note 9, and the 680th from 9:44, with notes 1–3.

13. In *Personal Reality*, see especially the 657th session in Chapter 15.

14. See the opening notes for this (713th) session.

Session 714
October 23, 1974
9:36 P.M. Wednesday

(This afternoon Jane called Tam Mossman, her editor at Prentice-Hall, and told him: "I've got my next book." She's calling it Psychic Politics. *Already she thinks of it as another aspect psychology book, a sequel to* Adventures in Consciousness.[1]

(Jane, in an obvious state of altered or enhanced consciousness, not only outlined all of Politics *today, but wrote four manuscript pages that will either go into its Introduction or Chapter 1. All of the material poured out of her in a most remarkable, unimpeded way— ".... as though it was already finished somewhere else, just waiting for me to get it down. But I had to do it just so, right to the last word," she said, then added enthusiastically, "I think it's a classic." Involved with* Politics *is her perception of another version of herself in a psychic "library," from which, evidently, she is to acquire a significant portion of her new book.*

(There were clear-cut connections between her creative performance today and her reception of the outline for The Way Toward Health *last March; see the notes at 10:45, as well as Note 8, for Session 713; and in*

394

Volume 1, see Appendix 7. But there was even more creative expression to come through Jane this evening; not only in the session itself, of course, but after it, as I try to explain in the concluding notes.

(As we sat waiting at 9:32, Jane reported that she was getting her "pyramid" or "cone" effect. At such times she feels that subjective shape come down just over her head—always pointed upward, symbolically perhaps, toward other realities. She also thought she might go into her "massive" feelings at any moment. "But I don't think any of this has to do with Seth Two,"[2] she said. She was still exhilarated from her work on Politics. *"I'm getting two things: The sessions's going to be book dictation, which surprises me, but it's also going to be on what's happening to me now ... And I am getting the massive thing. ..."*

(She had something of a cold, but had told me earlier in the evening that she wanted to hold the session. She fell quiet now after reassuring me that she was all right. The evening was quite warm; we had a window open; the traffic noises rushed up to our second-floor living room. Using many pauses, Jane began speaking very softly for Seth.[3])

Good evening.

("Good evening, Seth.")

This is somewhat of a momentous evening for Ruburt ... As I speak he is experiencing certain sensations, in which his body feels drastically elongated *(pause)*, the head reaching out beyond the stars, the whole form straddling realities.

Now in a sense the physical body does this always—that is, it sits astride realities, containing within itself dimensions of time and being that cannot be even verbally described. The cells themselves are "eternal," though they exist in your world only "for a time."

The unknown reality and the psyche's greater existence cannot be separated from the intimate knowledge of the flesh, however, for the life of the flesh takes place within that framework. As earlier mentioned,[4] the conscious self generally focuses in but one small dimension. Period. That dimension is experienced as fully as possible, its clear brilliance and exquisite focus possible only because you tune in to it and bring it to the forefront of your attention. In your terms, when you understand how to do this, then you can begin to tune in to other "stations" as well.

You know where physical reality is, then, on the dial of your multidimensional television set. While focused within that living scene you can learn to travel through it, leaving the "surface" picture intact and whole. In a way you program yourself, going about your daily duties as conscientiously and effectively as usual— but at the same time you discover an additional portion of your own reality. This does not diminish the physical self. Instead, in fact, it enriches it. You discover that the psyche has many aspects. While fully enjoying the physical aspect you find that there is some part of you left over, so to speak; and that part can travel into other realities. It can also then return, bringing the physically oriented self "snapshots" of its journeys. These snapshots are usually interpreted in terms of your home program. Otherwise, they might make no sense to the physical self.

Throughout the ages people have taken such journeys. The snapshots[5] are developed in the "darkroom" that exists between your world and those visited. The people who have journeyed into the unknown reality have always been adventurous. Yet many had already seen the snapshots sent to your world by others, and so they began to clothe their own original visions of their journeys in the guise of those other pictures. A group of handy ideas, concepts, and images then formed. The clear vision of such explorers became lost. Those travelers no longer tried to make their own original snapshots of the strange environments and realities through which they passed. It was easier to interpret their experiences through the psychic penny postcards.

(Pause at 9:59.) At one time these postcards represented initial original visions and individual interpretations. Later, however, they began to serve as guidebooks consulted ahead of time. For instance: If you plan to travel to a distant country in your own world, you can find such publications to tell you what to expect. When you journey into other realities, or when your consciousness leaves your body, you can also rely upon guidebooks that program your activities ahead of time. Period.

Instead of telling you that you take an airplane from a certain airport at a certain time for a particular earthly destination, leaving one latitude and longitude and arriving at another set; instead of telling you that you leave your country for another ruled by a dictator, or a president, or by anarchy, they will tell you that you leave this astral plane for any one of a number of others, ruled as the case may be by lords or masters, gods and goddesses. Instead of pointing out to you, as in earthly travel booklets, the locations of art galleries and museums, they will direct you to the Akashic Records.[6] Instead of leading you to the archaeological sites of your world *(intently)*, and its great ruins of previous civilizations, they will tell you how to find Atlantis and Mu[7] and other times in your past.

So you take a psychic guided tour into other realities; the unknown seems known, so that you are not an explorer after all, but a tourist, taking with you the paraphernalia of your own civilization, and beliefs that are quite conventional.

There are inner conventions, then, as there are outer ones. As the exterior mores try to force you to conform to the generally accepted ideas, so the interior conventions try to force you to make your inner experience conform to preconceived packaging.

There are good reasons for conventions. Generally, they help organize experience. If they are lightly held to and accepted, they can serve well as guidelines. Applied with a heavy hand they become unnecessary dogma, rigidly limiting experience. This applies to inner and outer activity. Conventions are the results of stratified and rigid "spontaneity." At one time, in your terms, each custom had a meaning. Each represented a spontaneous gesture, an individual reaction. When these become a system of order, however, the original spontaneity is lost, and you project an artificial order that serves to stratify behavior rather than to express it. So there are psychic customs as there are physical ones, religious and psychic dogmas, guided tours of consciousness in which you are told to follow a certain line or a certain program. You become afraid of your private interpretation of whatever reality you find yourself experiencing.

Ruburt has thus far insisted upon his private vision and his unique expression of the unknown reality as he experiences it, and so he brings back bulletins that do not agree with the conventional psychic line.

Take your break.

(10:18. Jane's trance had been good, her delivery quiet and rather fast; her voice had become a little rough because of her cold, though. When Seth talked about Jane's private psychic vision he reminded me of her own remarks on the same subject; see the notes opening the 713th session.

(Jane was aware of the elongated, giant-sized feeling now, as she had been just before the session began. "Everything's in proportion, though," she said. "It's crazy, but I feel that when I stand up my head could go through the ceiling." But she looked quite normal to me, and of course nothing out of character happened when she stood up.

(Resume at 10:25.)

The psychic postcards and travel folders are handy and colorful. They are also highly misleading.

(Long pause.) Once individual travelers took those snapshots, and they represented original interpretations of other realities. They stood for individual versions of certain travelers taking brief glimpses of strange worlds, and interpreting their experiences to the

best of their abilities. As such they were very valid. *(Louder:)* They were as valid as any snapshot that you might take of your backyard in the morning. That picture, however, would vary considerably from one taken by an inhabitant of your planet in a different part of the world, and in a different environment.

If there were discrepancies among the snapshots, however, people worried. While you expect pictures of your own reality to be diverse, those who journeyed into the unknown reality became concerned if their snapshots did not agree, so they tried desperately to make all of the pictures look alike. They touched them up, in other words.

First of all, in your own world those travelers into unknown realms were considered outcasts, so to speak, as if they were picking up television programs that no one else saw.[8] If their stories of their experiences did not jibe, who would believe them? They felt threatened. They felt that they had to tell the same story or they would be considered insane, so they made a tacit agreement, interpreting their experiences in the terms used by those who had gone "before."

You make your own reality. So, programmed ahead of time, they perceived [data] according to the psychic conventions that had been established. There are tigers in Asia, but you can travel through Asia and if you do not want to you'll never see a tiger. It's according to where you go. In the unknown reality your thoughts are instantly made apparent and real, materialized according to your beliefs. There, if you believe in demons, you will see them— without ever realizing that they are part of the environment of your psyche, formed by your beliefs, and thrown out as mirages over a very real environment that you do not perceive. You will believe the psychic tour books and go hunting for demons instead of tigers.

Give us a moment . . . Individually and *en masse*, you form the world that you know, yet it has an overall individual and mass basis so that some things are agreed upon. You view those things through your own unique vision. You form the reality. It is a valid one. It is experience. It is not therefore unreal, but one of the appearances that reality takes. It has a valid basis—an environment that you all accept, in which certain experiences are possible.

The same applies to other realities. You know there is a difference between, say, the picture before your eyes and a postcard, "artificial," rendition of it. So there is a difference between the unknown reality and the postcards that have been given to you to depict it.

In your terms, Ruburt has been out for the real thing—to

experience the unknown reality directly through his own perceptions, as divorced from the scenes given him by the postcards.
Period.

Give us a moment. . . .

*(10:47. "I'm out of it," Jane said abruptly, coughing. Then: "I'm
on to something. Wait a minute. I don't know if I can get it, or what. . . ." She
coughed again and again; her voice had become very hoarse since break, so much
so that a few minutes ago I'd been on the verge of asking her to end the session.
Now, over my protests, she wanted a fresh pack of cigarettes. See Note 3 in
connection with the following material.)*

"If I can get this it'll be something, I'll tell you," Jane said,
lighting up. She sipped her beer. "Bob—what I'm getting is something like it would be in real fast, quick beautiful sounds that I can't
duplicate—very quick, very musical—connected with the spin of
electrons[9] and cellular composition.

"The spin of electrons is faster than the cellular composition. The faster speed of the electrons somehow gives the cells their
boundaries. And there's something that's in a trance, say, in crystals,
that's alive in the cells.

"Wait a minute," Jane exclaimed again. "What I'm getting
is a fantastic sound that's imprisoned in a crystal, that *speaks* through
light, that's the essence of personality. I'm getting almost jewel-like
colored sounds . . . I'll see what I can do with it. I want to get it in
verbal stuff—and I'm getting it fast." Pause.

"—and we're speaking of personality now," Jane said,
coughing again. "As the seed falls, blown by the wind in any
environment, so there's a seed of personality that rides on the wings
of itself and falls into the worlds of many times and places. Falling
with a sound that is its own *true tone*, struck in different chords."

(10:58.) "Sounds are aware of their own separateness,
gloriously unique, yet each one merging into a symphony. Each
sound recognizes itself as itself, striking the dimensional medium in
which it finds its expression; yet it's aware of the infinite other
multitudinous sounds it makes in other realities—the instruments
through which it so grandly plays. Each cell, c-e-l-l, strikes in the
same fashion, *and so does each self*, s-e-l-f, in a kaleidoscope in which
each slightest variation has meaning and affects the individual notes
made by all.

"So we strike in more realities than one, and *I hear* those
notes together yet separately, perhaps as raindrops, and attempt to
put them together and yet hear each separate note . . .

"Seth—or somebody's saying—maybe it's just me—
relates to the people in our time. I've tried to do the same thing, but I

suddenly heard my own true tone, which I'm bound to follow . . . to go beyond the conventionalized postcards . . . I'm done, Bob."

(11:03 P.M. "Wow, I'm out, I'm telling you," Jane said rather groggily after a few moments. "I don't know how you're going to put this together with the Seth stuff. It's like a note that finds its own true tone, and when it does nothing else makes sense. That's all I can say. But once you strike it, you know that's it."

(Except for a few instances in which I eliminated repetitive phrases, all of the material Jane gave after 10:47 is unchanged here. At times, because her delivery had become so steady, even precise, I'd wondered if she had entered into a Seth trance, but one without Seth's usual voice effects. I had also been concerned lest she speak so rapidly that I wouldn't be able to keep up with her in my notes, but that hadn't happened. Nor had she spoken for Seth, I realized by the time she finished. Her enhanced state of consciousness had been her "own."

("I know there's a universe between my chair here [in the living room] and the kitchen floor," Jane said as she got up, "but I can walk it okay. When you strike your own true tone, you recognize it and you've got it made. You know your own meaning in the universe, even if you can't verbalize it. . . ."

(Jane told me that her feelings of massiveness had left her by the time she began her own dissertation. I was surprised to suddenly notice that her voice was much clearer now, cold or no. She did feel unsettled. She didn't quite know what to do. She let our cat, Willy, into the living room from the second apartment we rent across the hall. I suggested she eat something. "It's strange," she commented. "I feel that no matter which way I turn, there's a path laid out for me—and I never felt that way before." Then she announced that she was going to bed. "But as soon as I get over there [in the other apartment] I'll turn around and come back here, I'll bet." She left. I decided to have a snack myself, and to work on these notes while waiting to see if she would return.

(Now here's how I "put this together with the Seth stuff," meaning that from my viewpoint I'll briefly discuss the various states of consciousness Jane enjoyed today, as well as her massive sensations and her psychic perceptions of sound in connection with tonight's session. [The session itself, of course, embodied yet another altered state.] At the same time, the reader can make his or her own intuitive connections in assembling such materials, even if "only" in unconscious ways.

(Much of Jane's day had been made up of a series of altered, and at times even near-ecstatic states of consciousness, each one expressing a unique and creative facet of her essentially mystical nature.[10] Even though not at her best, she'd been able to draw upon lavish amounts of energy. I think that her experience with inner sound after the session represented her interpretation of the information Seth gave on feeling-tones, some two years ago; see the 613th session for Chapter 1 of Personal Reality. *There are certainly deep connections between Jane's apprehension of her true tone, and Seth's statement in that*

session that each of us possesses certain qualities of feeling uniquely our own, ". . . that are like deep musical chords." He went on to say at 10:06: "These feeling-tones, then, pervade your being. They are the form your spirit takes when combined with flesh." I also think that Jane's sensing of her true path reflects her understanding of Seth's subsequent remark at 10:16 [in that 613th session]: "The feeling-tone is the motion and fiber—and timbre—of your energy devoted to your physical experience.[11]

(So, given Jane's satisfying yet exhilarating expressions of consciousness throughout the day, I hardly regard it as surprising that she plunged into additional excellent states this evening. Paradoxically, her inspired reception of the material for Psychic Politics *came about not only because of her innate knowledge of feeling-tones, but because she gave that basic creative phenomenon expression in* Politics.

(And she's quite conscious of the fact that her massive sensations are one of the ways by which, as she has written, she tries to "view our three-dimensional existence and this universe from outside this framework," or to travel beyond the conventionalized psychic postcards.

(A note in closing out the evening's work: Jane didn't come back to join me in the living room while I ate and wrote. I found her sleeping deeply . . . .)

NOTES: Session 714

1. *Adventures* itself won't be published until next summer. See notes 1 and 3 for Session 705, and the opening notes for Session 708. Right now I'm finishing Diagram 11 of the 16 planned for *Adventures.*

2. In Appendix 19, see the 612th session for material on both Seth Two and Jane's feelings of massiveness.

3. A note added later: Jane used certain portions of the 714th session in Chapter 1 of *Politics*, while making her own points there. Since it's obviously part of *"Unknown" Reality* too, however, the entire session is presented in place in Volume 2. The same reasoning applies to the material each of us contributed at session's end.

4. See the 712th session, for instance.

5. Seth offered an analogy involving the camera and the traveling conscious mind in the 710th session after 10:16.

6. In her work on *Politics* today, Jane had already begun writing about the Akashic Records. Her inspiration had been the result of her quite unexpected, humorous, appalling—yet finally illuminating—encounter this morning with a visitor who'd attended her ESP class last night.

In occult terms, the Akashic Records are supposed to contain the complete cosmic account of every action, thought, and feeling that has transpired since creation "began."

"I don't believe in them," Jane said in answer to my question.

"At least not in that fashion—so what am I doing tuning in to a psychic library?" She laughed. "I'm having enough trouble explaining my own ideas. I've got to figure it all out."

But see Note 1 (with *its* references) for Session 697 in Volume 1; it contains some of Seth's material on the consciousness connected with any information.

7. Just as legend has it that the continent of Atlantis lay in the Atlantic Ocean between Europe/Africa and the Americas, so the great land of Mu (the Motherland) is said to have existed in the vast Pacific Ocean between the Americas and Asia. Each of those mythical domains eventually sank beneath the waters in a great cataclysm; each perished more than 10,000 years ago. For some Atlantis material and references in Volume 2 of *"Unknown" Reality*, see Appendix 14.

8. And "those travelers into unknown worlds" can still be called outcasts, strange, weird—or worse. Jane has had her share of such reactions from others (as have I). When combined with her own natural-enough questions about her psychic abilities, as sometimes happens, such episodes aren't any fun. In accidental ways that would be quite humorous if they weren't so personal, we've also learned what negative ideas others can have about us: A person will inadvertently reveal to us, during a conversation, or in a letter or over the telephone, the unflattering opinions his or her mate, or parents, or friends, really have of Jane and me and the work we're engaged in with the Seth material.

Occasionally we'll meet one or more of our secondhand detractors. Then of course we're greeted with polite smiles; the conversation may touch upon the weather, but hardly ever upon matters psychic. Sometimes we'll discover that the "knowledge" of us held by the skeptic(s) in question is so far removed from our actual beliefs and activities that it would take us a very long time to establish any real understanding among all involved—if it would be possible to begin with, that is. We always elect to pass up such "opportunities."

Even as I wrote this note Jane received a letter: "Do what I ask for me, if you are not a fraud. . . ." I threw the letter away. At the same time I remembered, as I do every so often, the prophetic and amused remarks Seth made way back in the 20th session for January 29, 1964: "As far as publishing this material is concerned, I have no objections. I didn't give it to you, and I'm not giving it to you, simply for your [collective] edification. Because of its source you will probably be called crackpots, but I imagine you know this by now."

Yes . . . And in the face of such skepticism or misunderstanding, Jane and I may at times find ourselves wondering why psychic attributes even exist *in* nature, in those terms, if they're denied any application within that framework. "You [each] must have a basic approval of yourself," Seth told us recently in a personal session. "This is information not only for the two of you, of course, but for others: You must trust your basic being, with its characteristics and abilities. You have them for a reason, in all of their unique combinations. You should also avoid labels, for these can stereotype your perception of yourself."

9. Presented as they are in Appendix 19, both that portion of Session 612 and its notes contain material on the kinds of fast (and slow) sounds that Jane has been able to perceive so far. See especially notes 7 and 10 there; chromoesthesia, or colored hearing, is defined in the latter. Information on electrons, including electron spin, is either given or referred to in notes 8 and 9 for the 612th session.

10. See the material on Jane and mysticism in Appendix 1 for Volume 1.

11. Of interest here are a few excerpts from a personal session held just a year later, in October 1975. During the session Seth discussed inner sound in connection with Jane's own physical symptoms. (In Volume 1 of *"Unknown" Reality*, see the 679th session before 10:31, and Note 8. The quotations below are also related to the material on inner sound, light, and electromagnetic values in Chapter 5 of *Personal Reality*.) Seth, at 11:07 P.M.:

"Give us a moment . . . The movement of the joints makes sound. The sounds are messages. When hormones are released they make sounds. Those sounds are messages.

"I say 'sounds'—yet these inner body sounds can only be compared to an interior body situation where sound operates as light. You are used to thinking in terms of opaque or transparent color. In those terms there is opaque light, and transparent light as well. Sound has light value, and light has sound value. These operate within the body.

"Each frequency, so to speak, functions as a messenger, triggering body response before an actual reaction is apparent . . . In any body difficulty, the light and sound frequencies become out of tune, you might say. The overall 'true tone' is muddied. When Ruburt began *Politics* he experienced his 'true tone' mentally and psychically. Though he did not realize it, this gave him something to go by, so that now . . . he is unconsciously [still] bringing about the physical equivalent of that true tone."

Session 715
October 28, 1974
9:25 P.M. Monday

(See Note 1 for descriptions of the [two] unusual mental events I experienced Sunday and today: I may have seen myself as a Roman military officer in the first century A.D.

(In the opening notes for last Wednesday's session I described how Jane had started her new book, Psychic Politics, that same day while she had been immersed in a state of high creativity; I added that at the same time she'd become aware of a slightly different Jane in a psychic library from which, it seemed, she was to get much of the material for Politics. Jane visited her library several times on Thursday, without actually transcribing anything from it. Then on Friday morning she received another, shorter passage of library material. I quote in part: "There are ever-changing models for physical reality, transforming themselves constantly in line with new equations instantly set up with each new stabilization . . . We tune in to these models, and our intersections with them alter them at any given point, causing new dimensions of actuality that then reach out from that new focus."[2]

(Jane didn't really understand what she'd written. Neither of us

404

realized it at the time, but she was to soon embark upon one of the key episodes[3] of her psychic life: "My later experiences that day were a practical lesson in how models work," she wrote after it was all over.

(At noontime that Friday, then, Jane told me that she was going into another altered or enhanced state of consciousness. We were eating lunch. She compared her feelings with those heightened perceptions she'd enjoyed so much yesterday and Wednesday in connection with the birth of Politics. Even though her state of awareness was still growing, Jane decided that she wanted to ride downtown with me after we'd finished eating; I planned to pick up one of our typewriters at a repair shop, then buy some groceries. Already she was so "loose" that she noticed an unsteadiness in her walking. "It's as though the floor's rising up beneath my feet, supporting my weight, but in a way that I'm not used to," she said. She was enchanted.

("Watch it when we go out to the car," I joked. "If people see you staggering around they'll think you're loaded."

(As I drove east on Water Street, heading for the center of Elmira, Jane exclaimed again and again over the new beauty she was discovering in her world. A bit later I plan to quote from her own notes some of the details of her transcendent perceptions; but by the time I'd secured the typewriter, then driven over to the supermarket at Langdon Plaza, she didn't think she could get out of the car. Nor did she want to try doing anything that might interrupt the magnificence of her greatly expanded state of consciousness. For all the while she was having the most profound group of experiences in seeing, feeling, and knowing the ordinary physical world about her.

(We searched the glove compartment of the car for paper and a pencil or pen, so that Jane could make notes about some of her perceptual changes—but to my amazement we could find nothing to use in spite of our efforts to keep writing tools in that very place. Among other papers I finally turned up half a sheet of blank paper, and gave Jane the pen I usually used to cross out items on the grocery list. We were parked in front of a drugstore; I hurried in there to buy pens and a notepad for her. So, while I busied myself in the familiar market next door, she sat in the car writing—looking quite ordinary, a small black-haired woman with her head bent forward . . . When I'd finished shopping perhaps 30 minutes later she was still writing. She had covered half a dozen pages.

(Now here are some excerpts from Jane's notes, as I've put them together. [And added later: I remind the reader to see her own much-longer account of the whole experience in Chapter 2 of Politics.])

"Then, between one moment and the next, the world literally changed for me. I'm viewing it from an entirely different perspective. It's like the old world but infinitely richer, more 'now,' built better, and with much greater depth.

"Words aren't describing this at all. Each person who passes the car is more than three-dimensional, super-real in this time, but part of a 'model' of a greater self . . . and each person's reality is obviously and clearly more than three-dimensional. I know I'm repeating myself here, but it's as if before I've seen only a part of people or things. The world is so much more solid right now[4] that by contrast my earlier experience of it is like a shoddy version, made up of disconnected dots or blurred focus. . . ."

And: "Qualitatively, the [supermarket plaza] was so different than usual that I could hardly believe it. While Rob did the shopping I kept looking—and looking—and looking. I knew that each person I saw had free will, and yet each motion was inevitable and somehow there was no contradiction. I could look at each person and sense his or her 'model' and all the variations, and see how the model was here and now in the person. I saw these people as True People in the meaning of a whole people. These people were 'more here,' fuller somehow, more complete. People seemed to be classics of themselves.

"I faced a group of shops and saw these also as models and their variations. The same applied to everything I looked at. I thought: 'I'm being filled to the brim'; and for a moment I wondered if I'd been fitted with a spectacular new pair of glasses. It was an effort to write these notes to begin with. I wanted to just look forever."

(Jane was still deeply within her great experience during our ride back to the apartment house. "Wow," she exclaimed, "I wouldn't touch acid [LSD] for anything after this. Who needs to?" I laughed: "How to go on your own free trip, huh?" She does not use hallucinogenic drugs of any kind.

("What would happen if you opened your eyes and really *saw the world?" Jane mused. "It's indescribable. . . ." And later today she wrote: "Driving home with Rob, for example, I felt the earth support the road which supported the tires and the car. I felt this physically, in the same way that we sense, say, temperature; a positive support or pressure that held the road up and almost seemed to push up of its own accord in a long powerful arch, like a giant animal's back."*

(Jane's "adventure in consciousness" was so rich,[5] even from my observor's viewpoint, that my attempts to describe it seem terribly inadequate by comparison. In this session Seth discusses to some extent the whole subject of her psychic growth.)

Good evening.

("Good evening, Seth.")

Give us a moment for dictation.

I said at our last session that the evening was momentous for Ruburt, and that is true for many reasons. This book[6] deals with the unknown reality, and Ruburt began a different excursion into other dimensions last week.

I hope in these sessions to show the indivisible connections between the experience of the psyche at various levels and the resulting experience in terms of varying systems—each valid, each to some extent or another bearing on the life you know.

Ruburt has allowed a portion of his this-life consciousness to go off on a tangent, so to speak, on another path into another system of actuality *(i.e., into his psychic library)*. His life there is as valid as his existence in your world. In the waking state he is able, now, to alter the direction of his focus precisely enough to bring about a condition in which he perceives both realities simultaneously. He is just beginning, so as yet he is only occasionally conscious of that other experience. He is, however, aware of it now in the back of his mind more or less constantly. It does not intrude upon the world that he knows, but enriches it.

The concepts in *"Unknown" Reality* will help expand the consciousness of each of its readers, and the work itself is presented in such a manner that it automatically pulls your awareness out of its usual grooves, so that it bounces back and forth between the standardized version of the world you accept, and the unofficial[7] versions that are sensed but generally unknown to you.

Now as Ruburt delivers this material, the same thing happens in a different way to him, so that in some respects he has been snapping back and forth between dimensions, practicing with the elasticity of his consciousness; and in this book more than in previous ones his consciousness has been sent out further, so to speak. The delivery of the material itself has helped him to develop the necessary flexibility for his latest pursuits.

Clear understanding or effective exploration of the unknown reality can be achieved only when you are able to leave behind you many "facts" that you have accepted as criteria of experience. *"Unknown" Reality* is also written in such a way that it will, I hope, bring many of your cherished beliefs about existence into question. Then you will be able to look even at this existence with new eyes.

Ruburt is taking this new step from your perspective, and from that standpoint he is doing two things.

(At a slower pace:) He is consciously entering into another room of the psyche, and also entering into the reality that corresponds to it. This brings the two experiences together so that they coincide. They are held, however, both separately and in joint focus. As a rule you use one particular level of awareness, and this correlates all of your conscious activities. I told you that the physical body itself was able to pick up other neurological messages beside

those to which you usually react.[8] Now let me add that when a certain proficiency is reached in alterations of consciousness, this allows you to become practically familiar with some of these other neurological messages. In such a way Ruburt is able to physically perceive what he is doing in his "library."

He first saw this library from the inside last Wednesday. He was simultaneously himself here in this living room, watching the image of himself in a library room, and he was the self in the library. Period. Before him he saw a wall of books, and the self in the living room suddenly knew that his purpose here in <u>this</u> reality was to re-create some of those books. He knew that he was working at both levels. The unknown and the known realities merged, clicked in, and were seen as the opposite sides of each other.

He has been working with me for some time, in your terms, yet I do not "control" his subjective reality in any way. I have certainly been a teacher to him.[9] Yet his progress is always his own challenge and responsibility, and basically what he does with my teaching is up to him. *(Humorously:)* In parentheses: (Right now I give him an "A.")

(Pause at 10:01.) Like many, however, he was brought up to believe that the intellect's function was <u>mainly</u> to dissect, criticize, and analyze, rather than for instance to creatively unite and build, colon: and analysis was thought of as separating the elements of a concept rather than restricting original concepts. New concepts were thought of as intuitional or psychic, as opposed to the conventional duties of the intellect, so the two seemed separate. Therefore, Ruburt felt duty-bound to question any intuitive construct most vigorously as a matter of principle. This actually provided an excellent transitory working method, for what he thought of as intuitions would instantly come up with a new psychic construct in answer to what he thought of as intellectual scrutiny and skepticism. Period.

Actually, the intellect and intuitions go hand in hand. In Ruburt's experience,[10] the two finally began to work together as they should. What I call the high intellect then took over, a superb blend of intuitional and intellectual abilities working together so that they almost seem to form a new faculty *(intently)*.

The development freed Ruburt from many old limitations, and allowed him to at last have practical experience with the unknown reality in intimate terms. Ruburt's library <u>does</u> exist as surely as this room does. It also exists as <u>unsurely</u> as this room. It is one thing to be theoretically convinced that other worlds exist, and to take a certain comfort and joy from the idea. It is <u>quite another thing</u> to find yourself in such an environment, and to feel the worlds coincide. Reality is above all practical, so when you <u>expand</u> your concepts concerning the nature of reality, you are apt then to find yourselves scandalized, appalled, or simply disoriented. So in this work I am presenting you not only with probabilities as conjecture, but, often, showing you how such probabilities affect your daily lives, and giving examples of the ways in which Ruburt's and Joseph's lives have been so touched.

For a while, many of you will play with the concepts while avoiding all direct encounters with any other experience, save that already acceptable. Yet the immensities of your own abilities speak in your dreams, in your private moments, as even inaudibly in the knowledge of your own molecules.

There are <u>civilizations of the psyche</u>,[11] and only by learning about these will you <u>discover</u> the truth about the "lost" civilizations of your planet, for each such physical culture coincided with and emerged from a corresponding portion of the psyche that you even now possess.

Take your break.

(10:19 to 10:43.)

Many of you are fascinated by theories or concepts that hint at the multidimensionality of your beings, and yet you are scandalized by any evidence that supports it.

Often you interpret such evidence in terms of the dogmas with which you are already familiar. This makes them more acceptable. Ruburt <u>was</u> often almost indignant when presented with such evidence, but he also refused to cast it in conventionalized guise, and his own curiosity and creative abilities kept him flexible enough so that learning could take place while he maintained normal contact with the world you know.[12]

He has had many experiences in which he glimpsed momentarily the rich <u>otherness</u> within physical reality. He has known heightened perceptions of a unique nature. Never before, however, has he stepped firmly, while awake, into another level of reality, where he allowed himself to sense the continual vivid connection between worlds. He hid his own purpose from himself, as many of <u>you</u> do. At the same time he was pursuing it, of course, as all of you <u>are</u> working toward your own goals.

To admit his purpose, however, to bring it out into the open, would mean for Ruburt a private and public statement of affiliation such as he was not able to make earlier. The goals of each of you differ. Some of you are embarked upon adventures that deal with intimate family contact, deep personal involvement with children, or with other careers that meet "vertically" with physical experience. So journeys into unknown realities may be highly intriguing, and represent important sidelights to your current preoccupations. These interests will be like an avocation to you, adding great understanding and depth to your experience.

Ruburt and Joseph chose to specialize, so to speak, in precisely those excursions or explorations that are secondary to others. The focus of each of their consciousnesses therefore was made up of a certain kind of mixture that made such probabilities, in your terms, possible as prime incentives.

(Long pause, eyes closed, at 10:56.) Each person is at his place or her place. You are where you are because your consciousness formed that kind of reality. Your whole physical situation will be geared to it, and your neurological structure will follow the habitual pattern. As you learn to throw aside old concepts you will begin to experience the evidence for other levels of reality, and become aware of other "messages" that you have previously blocked. A certain portion of Ruburt's training period is over. The entire focus of his personality now accepts the validity of many worlds—and this means in practical terms.

I have told you many times that your consciousness is not stationary, but ever-moving and creative, so that each of you through your life moves through your psyche. Your physical experience is correspondingly altered.

During these years, then, Ruburt's position within his psyche has gradually shifted until he found a new, for him better, firmer point of basis. From this new framework he can more effectively handle different kinds of stimuli, and form these together to construct an understandable model of other realities. I will continue to speak from my own unique viewpoint, but in your terms Ruburt is one of you, and his explorations, taken from your perspective, can be most valuable.

Give us moment... These books, those written and not yet written, of his and mine, will provide frameworks for others to follow if they wish, as they wish.

End of dictation.

(11:08.) Give us a moment...

(Seth discussed another matter involving Jane; after delivering about a page of material he ended the session at 11:19 P.M.)

NOTES: Session 715

1. Yesterday afternoon, Sunday, I lay down for a nap. Just before I drifted into the sleep state I had three little experiences involving

internal vision. My eyes were closed. In the episode of interest here, I saw myself back in the first century A.D.: I was an officer of rather high rank in a Roman legion, and I was aboard a small galley in the Mediterranean Sea. I knew that I was on official military business for a land-based armed force, even though I was on ship. I didn't much like the blunt, unfeeling "I" that I saw. Briefly through those eyes I looked out upon twin rows of galley slaves . . . I described the scene and my feelings about it to Jane, and made small, full-face and profile pen-and-ink drawings of myself as the officer. I had no name for that other self. Given Seth's concept of simultaneous time, I thought I might have glimpsed another existence—whether a reincarnational one or a probable one—that I was living now.

This afternoon, Monday, I decided upon a nap once again, and once again I was aware of myself as the Roman officer; at least I thought I was that individual. I entered into a sequel to the first vision: I felt myself floating face down in the Mediterranean with my hands tied behind my back. I knew that I'd been deliberately thrown into the sea. I cut off my awareness of the experience right there, possibly to avoid undergoing my own death in that life. From the safety of the cot in my studio, I didn't panic as that other me faced such a life-threatening situation, yet I was disturbed by it—enough so that I repressed conscious recall of the whole episode until the evening after this (715th) session was held. I'm citing it here so that I can present my "first and second Romans," as I call them, together.

No sooner had I described this second adventure to Jane than she surprised me by saying she might use both of the Roman experiences in *Politics*. She thought she could tie them in with her material on the "everchanging models for physical reality" that she'd obtained from her psychic library last Friday morning.

After my first Roman, I speculated about whether I might have touched upon a reincarnational self or a probable one. See, therefore, Seth's material on reincarnation in Chapter 4 (among others) of *Seth Speaks*; then see his material on probable selves in Chapter 16 of that book, and in Session 680 for Volume 1 of *"Unknown" Reality*.

For myself, I think of reincarnational selves as having their roots in the physical reality we know (whether in simultaneous or linear terms of time), but of probable selves as having much wider and more complicated ranges of existence: I believe that even though we create them on an individual basis, our probable selves can reach into a multitude of other realities, both physical and nonphysical. I don't remember Seth discussing such "probable" possibilities in just that way, especially, and they would be much too involved to go into here, but I've often felt that some of our probable selves move into realms of being that are literally incomprehensible to us, so different—alien—are they and their environments from our usual conceptions of "solid" physical existence.

2. In Chapter 2 for *Psychic Politics* Jane presents not only her library material, but quotations from the 715th session for *"Unknown" Reality* itself. I wrote this note a month after Session 715 was held in October 1974. By late November, in other words, Jane had signed a contract with

Prentice-Hall for the publication of *Politics* in 1976, and had also had time to do considerable work on its early chapters. We already knew that she would initiate some transposition of material from Volume 2 of *"Unknown" Reality* into *Politics*, since she was so intimately and enthusiastically involved in producing both works at the same time: I first wrote about such an exchange in Note 3 for Session 714 (when indicating that she'd used portions of *that* session in Chapter 1 of *Politics*).

But although for *Politics* Jane drew upon the same transcendent experience I described in the opening notes for the 715th session, she did so in her own subjective way; in *"Unknown" Reality* I present my version of the event from an observor's viewpoint. The interested reader might compare the two accounts. I think they're both well worth having on record, since Jane's experience was a profound one—and, in my opinion, very revealing for what it tells us about how we ordinarily view our mundane physical reality, and about the much more powerful versions, or "models," for that reality that exist behind it.

3. In *Dialogues*, her book of poetry, Jane explored several other "key" episodes in her psychic development; see her Preface, then these selections in Part Two: "The Paper and Trips Through an Inner Garden," and "Single-Double Worlds, the Rain Creature, and the Light." She also wrote about those transcendent experiences in *Adventures*; see Chapter 9 for her "paper" perceptions (in March 1972), and Chapter 15 for her encounters with the rain creature and the light (in February 1973). Both Jane and Seth had things to say about the rain creature and the light in *Personal Reality*; see the 639th session for Chapter 10.

4. Jane's declaration of the "super-real" aspects of her ecstatic state, that "The world is so much more solid right now," soon had me hunting for relevant material I remembered Seth giving, but couldn't place. I found two sources in *Seth Speaks*. In Chapter 7, see the 530th session for May 20, 1970, at 10:02: "There are realities that are 'relatively more valid' than your own... your physical table [for example] would appear as shadowy in contrast... You would have a sort of 'supertable' in those terms. Yours is not a system of reality formed by the most intense concentration of energy... Other portions of yourself, therefore, of which you are not consciously aware, do inhabit what you could call a super-system of reality in which consciousness learns to handle and perceive much stronger concentrations of energy..."

In Chapter 16, see the 567th session for February 17, 1971, at 9:24: "You understand that there are spectrums of light. So there are spectrums of matter. Your system of physical reality is not dense in comparison with some others. The dimensions that you give to physical matter barely begin to hint at the varieties of dimensions possible. Some systems are far heavier or lighter than your own..."

5. So far in Volume 2, I've mentioned the inner senses (as described by Seth) in Note 5 for Session 709, and Note 6 for Appendix 18. Seth came through with No. 6, *Innate Knowledge of Basic Reality*, in the 40th

session for April 1, 1964: "This is an extremely rudimentary sense. It is concerned with the entity's working knowledge of the basic vitality of the universe . . . Without this sixth sense and its constant use by the inner self, you could not construct the physical camouflage universe. You can compare this sense with instinct, although it is concerned with the innate knowledge of the entire universe."

At least to some degree, Jane's exploration last Friday afternoon of those super-real models for our world represented her use of the sixth inner sense—the same one, she wrote in Chapter 19 of *The Seth Material*, that ". . . also shows itself in inspirations, and episodes of spontaneous 'knowing.' Surely this sense was partially responsible for my *Idea Construction* manuscript." In Volume 1, see Note 7 for Session 679.

6. A note added six months later: When Seth referred to "this book" in the 715th session, he meant a one-volume edition of *"Unknown" Reality*, of course. Jane and I didn't decide to publish the work in two volumes until just before the 741st session (for Section 6) was held, in April 1975. See the early Introductory Notes for Volume 2.

7. For contrast, in Volume 1 see the references to "official" reality that are given in Note 2 for Session 695.

8. See the 686th session in Volume 1; then see Jane's material on other-than-usual neurological messages and speeds in appendixes 4 and 5. And (later) I add here a paragraph from the private session Seth held for us on May 1, 1974—10 days after he'd finished his work on *"Unknown" Reality*:

"He [Ruburt-Jane] has an ability to identify with others, and communicate. He has always been mentally quick and intellectually agile. As a youngster he received the messages from others so quickly that he was diagnosed as having an overactive thyroid gland. Actually, he was receiving "unofficial" messages that are usually neurologically censored. He could not allow them to become conscious in that world . . ."

9. See Appendix 18.

In the 4th session, for December 8, 1963, Seth announced his presence to Jane and me through the Ouija board. In the 6th session he told Jane, in connection with our questions: "Begin training." In the 12th session, for January 2, 1964, he informed us that we were his "first lesson class," then added: "At one time or another all of us on my plane give such lessons, but psychic bonds between teacher and pupils are necessary. This means that we must wait until personalities in your reality have progressed sufficiently for lessons to begin . . . although reason is extremely important, and I do not mean to minimize its value, nevertheless what you call emotion or feeling is the connective between us, and it is the connective that most clearly represents the life force on any plane and under any circumstances."

Later, we were to learn about the distortions that could happen as Jane relayed some of Seth's material; given the open-ended nature of time, and considering the idea of probable realities, we came to realize that simultaneously we could and could not be Seth's "first lesson class." But in those early sessions we had no background knowledge out of which to ask meaningful questions. In the 15th session Seth told Jane and me: "I am giving you what may be considered a broad outline to be filled in."

10. See the opening notes for the 713th session.

11. In Note 5 for Session 692, in Volume 1, I refer to Seth's term, "species of consciousness," and the links between his material in that session and this one.

12. Note 25 for Appendix 18 contains information on *The Coming of Seth*, in which Jane described her burgeoning psychic abilities.

Section 5

HOW TO JOURNEY INTO THE "UNKNOWN" REALITY:
TINY STEPS AND GIANT STEPS.
GLIMPSES AND DIRECT ENCOUNTERS

Session 716
October 30, 1974
9:33 P.M. Wednesday

(In Note 1, I described my third "Roman," which took place this afternoon.

("I guess I'm confused," Jane said as we waited for the session to begin. "I think Seth's going to start another section tonight—but I don't think he's quite finished with the last one. . . ." However, Section 4 was finished after all.)

Good evening.

("Good evening, Seth.")

Dictation. The next section *(5):* "How to Journey Into the 'Unknown' Reality," colon: "Tiny Steps and Giant Steps. Glimpses and Direct Encounters."

This section will deal with various methods that will allow you to come in contact with the unknown reality to one extent or another. We have spoken of probable man, hinted at probable civilizations, and mentioned alternate systems of actuality.[2] Yet these do not exist completely apart from the world that you know, or

417

entirely cut off from the psyche. If you have no experience with such realities, then their existence remains delightful or speculative conjecture.

(Pause.) The unknown reality is a variation of the one that you know, so that many of its features are latent rather than predominant in your own private and mass experience. Any encounter with such phenomena will then include a bringing-into-focus of elements that are usually not concentrated upon. Your consciousness must learn to organize itself in more than one fashion—or rather, you must be willing to allow your consciousness to use itself more fully. It is not necessarily a matter of trying to ignore the contents of the world, or to deny your physical perception. Instead, the trick is to view the contents of the world in different fashions, to free your physical senses from the restraints that your mental conventions have placed upon them.

Each particular "station" of consciousness perceives in a different kind of reality, and as mentioned earlier (in Session 711, for instance), you usually tune in to your home station most of the time. If you turn your focus only slightly away, the world appears differently; and if that slightly altered focus were the predominant one, then that is how the world would seem to be. Each aspect of the psyche perceives the reality upon which it is focused, and that reality is also the materialization of a particular state of the psyche projected outward. You can learn to encounter other realities by altering your position within your own psyche.

In order to begin, you must first become familiar with the working of your own consciousness as it is directed toward the physical world. You cannot know when you are in focus with another reality if you do not even realize what it feels like to be in full focus with your own. Many people phase in and out of that state without being aware of it, and others are able to keep track of their own "inner drifting." Here, simple daydreaming represents a slight shift of awareness out of directly given sense data.

If you listen to an FM radio station, there is a handy lock-in gadget that automatically keeps the station in clear focus; it stops the program from "drifting." In the same way, when you daydream you drift away from your home station, while still relating to it, generally speaking. You also have the mental equivalent, however, of the FM's lock-in mechanism. On your part this is the result of training, so that if your thoughts or experience stray too far this mental gadget brings them back into line. Usually this is automatic—a learned response that by now appears to be almost instinctive. Period.

You must learn to use this mechanism consciously for your own purposes, for it is extremely handy. Many of you do not pay attention to your own experience, subjectively speaking, so you drift in and out of clear focus in this reality, barely realizing it. Often your daily program is not nearly as clear or well-focused as it should be, but full of static; and while this may annoy you, you often put up with it or even become so used to the lack of harmony that you forget what a clear reception is like. However, in this world you are surrounded by familiar objects, details, and ideas, and your main orientation is physical so that you can operate through habit alone even when you are not as well focused within your reality as you should be.

(9:56.) When you go traveling off into other systems, however, you cannot depend upon your habits. Indeed, often they can only add to your mental clutter, turning into "static"—so you must learn first of all what a clear focus is.

You will not learn it by trying to escape your own reality, or by attempting to dull your senses. This can only teach you what it means not to focus, and in whatever reality you visit the ability to focus clearly and well is a prerequisite. Once you learn how to really tune in, then you will understand what it means to change the direction of your focus.

One of the simplest exercises is hardly an original one, but it is of great benefit.

PRACTICE ELEMENT 11

Try to experience all of your present sense data as fully as you can. This tones your entire physical and psychic organism, bringing all of your perceptions together so that your awareness opens fully. Body and mind operate together. You experience an immediate sense of power because your abilities are directed to the fullest of their capacities. In a physical moment you can act directly on the spot, so to speak.

Sit with your eyes open easily, letting your vision take in whatever is before you. Do not strain. On the other hand, do explore the entire field of vision simultaneously. Listen to everything. Identify all the sounds if you can, mentally placing them with the objects to which they correspond even though the objects may be invisible. Sit comfortably but make no great attempt to relax. Instead, feel your body in an alert manner—not in a sleepy distant fashion. Be aware of its pressure against the chair, for example, and of its temperature, of variations: Your hands may be warm and your feet cold, or your belly hot and your head cold. Consciously, then, feel your body's sensations. Is there any taste in your mouth? What odors do you perceive?

Take as much time as you want to with this exercise. It places you in your universe clearly. This is an excellent exercise to use before you begin—and after you finish with—any experiment involving an alteration of consciousness.

Take a brief break.

(10:19. Jane's delivery had been quite a bit faster than usual— which means she'd kept me writing at a steady pace even though I was recording the material with my homemade "shorthand." She said she felt that in this section Seth would have a series of exercises related to the one he'd just given; these would help people glimpse at least some of the alternate or probable realities discussed in Section 4.

(Break, though, was hardly brief. Resume in the same manner at 10:42.)

Now: Bring all of those sensations together. Try to be aware of all of them at once, so that one adds to the others. If you find yourself being more concerned with one particular perception, then make an attempt to bring the ignored ones to the same clear focus. Let all of them together form a brilliant awareness of the moment.

When you are using this exercise following any experiment with an alteration of consciousness, then end it here and go about your other concerns. You may also utilize it as an initial step that will help you get the feeling of your own inner mobility. To do this proceed as given, and when you have the moment's perception as clearly as possible, then willfully let it go.

Let the unity disappear as far as your conscious thought is concerned. No longer connect up the sounds you hear with their corresponding objects. Make no attempt to unify vision and hearing. Drop the package, as it were, as a unified group of perceptions. The previous clarity of the moment will have changed into something else. Take one sound if you want to, say of a passing car, and with your eyes closed follow the sound in your mind. Keep your eyes closed. Become aware of whatever perceptions reach you, but this time do not judge or evaluate. Then in a flash open your eyes, alert your body, and try to bring all of your perceptions together again as brilliantly and clearly as possible.

When you have the sense world before you this time, let it climax, so to speak, then again close your eyes and let it fall away. Do not focus. In fact, unfocus. Period.

When you have done this often enough so that you are intimately aware of the contrast, you will have a subjective feeling, a point of knowing within yourself, that will clearly indicate to you how your consciousness feels when it is at its finest point of focus in physical reality.

As you go about your day, try now and then to recapture that point and to bring all data into the clearest possible brilliance. You will find that this practice, continued, will vastly enrich your normal experience. You find it much easier to concentrate, to attend. To attend is to pay attention and take care of. So this exercise will allow you to attend—to focus your awareness to the matters at hand as clearly and vividly as possible. The subjective knowledge of your own point of finest focus will also serve as a reference point for many other exercises.

(Pause at 10:58.)

PRACTICE ELEMENT 12

Exercise two [in the session]. For your benefit, Joseph, this entire section will be made up of practice elements, with comments and directions.

You must work from your own subjective experience, so when you find your own finest focus point, that is your clearest reception for your own home station. You may feel that it has a certain position in your inner vision, or in your head, or you may find that you have your own symbol to represent it. You might imagine it, if you want to, as a station indicator on your own radio or television set, but your subjective recognition of it is your own cue.

In our just-previous exercise, when I spoke of having you let your clear perception drop away, and told you to disconnect vision from hearing, you were drifting in terms of your own home station. Your consciousness was straying. This time begin with the point of your own finest focus, which you have established, then let your consciousness stray as given. Only let it stray in a particular direction—to the right or the left, whichever seems most natural to you. In this way you are still directing it and learning to orient yourself. In the beginning, 15 minutes at most for this exercise; but let your awareness drift in whatever direction you have chosen.

Each person will have his or her own private experience here, but gradually certain kinds of physical data will seem to disappear while others may take prominence. For example, you might mentally hear sounds, while knowing they have no physical origin. You may see nothing in your mind, or you may see images that seem to have no exterior correlation, but you may hear nothing. For a while ordinary physical data may continue to intrude. When it does, recognize it as your home station, and mentally let yourself drift further away from it. What is important is your own sensation as you experience the mobility of your consciousness. If ever you grow concerned simply return to your home station, back to the left or right according to the direction you have chosen. I do not suggest that you use "higher" or "lower" as directions, because of the interpretations that you may have placed upon them through your beliefs.

Do not be impatient. As you continue with this exercise over a period of time you will be able to go further away, orienting yourself as you grow more familiar with the feeling of your mind. Gradually you will discover that this inner sense data will become clearer and clearer as you move toward another "station." It will represent reality as perceived from a different state of consciousness.

The first journey from one home station to another, unfamiliar one may bring you in contact with various kinds of bleed-throughs, distortions, or static. These can be expected. They are simply the result of not yet learning how to tune your own consciousness clearly in to other kinds of focus. Before you can pick up the "next" station, for example, you may see ghost images in your mind, or pick up distorted versions from your own home station. You have momentarily dispensed with the usual, habitual organizational process by which you unite regular physical sense perceptions, so while you are "between stations," you may well encounter mixed signals from each. When you alter your conscious focus in such a fashion, you are also moving away from the part of your psyche that you consider its center. You are journeying through your own psyche, in other words, for different realities are different states of the psyche—materialized, projected outward and experienced. That applies to your home station or physical world as well.

Are you tired?

(11:20. "No," I said. Seth-Jane's pace had been good, though—quiet yet forceful.)

Even your home station has many programs, and you have usually tuned in to one main one and ignored others. Characters in your "favorite program" at home may appear in far different guises when you are between stations, and elements of other programs that you have ignored at home may suddenly become apparent to you.

(Pause.) I will give you a simple example. At home you may tune in to religious programs. That means that you might organize your daily existence about highly idealistic principles. You may try to ignore what you consider other programs dealing with hatred, fear, or violence. You might do such a good job of organizing

your physical data about your ideal that you shut out any emotions that involve fear, violence, or hatred. When you alter your consciousness, again, you automatically begin to let old organizations of data drop away. You may have tuned out what you think of as negative feelings or programming. These, however, may have been present but ignored, and when you dispense with your usual method of organizing physical data they may suddenly become apparent.

If you tell yourself that sexual feeling is wrong, and organize your daily programming in that fashion, then when you "meditate," or dispense with that orientation, you may suddenly find yourself presented with material that you consider unsavory. You cannot deny the reality of the psyche, or those natural feelings that you experience in the flesh. When you begin to alter your perception, then, and your habitual picture of reality drops away, you may well find yourself encountering in distorted fashion elements of your own reality that you have up to then studiously denied or ignored.

This is most apparent with those who use the Ouija board or automatic writing as methods to alter consciousness.

Do you want a break?

(11:34. "No," I said again, in answer to Seth-Jane's obvious concern. It was a warm night for the end of October, and we had the windows open; the traffic noise from the busy intersection just one house removed was bothering me more than anything else.)

In your home station, events are encountered clearly in space and time. When you move away, however, you may meet events in time but not in space, and reality that you have tried to deny may then appear vividly. If you understand this you can gain immeasurably, for as you move your focus away from your organized reality, other portions of it upon which you have not concentrated will come into view.

This can show you what was missing from your home station if you know how to read the clues. You form your home station according to your beliefs. If you firmly believe, again, that sex is wrong, then your home station may involve you in a life "programming" in which you constantly try to deny the vitality of the flesh. The sight of a nude body might upset you. You might undress in the dark, or think, if you are married, of the sexual act of intercourse as dirty. If you are a man, you might be ashamed of what you consider to be your need.

I have an example in point. A young man I will call Joe wrote Ruburt a letter. He left his home in San Francisco to travel to

India to study with a guru. He has been told that sexual desire mitigates against spiritual illumination. His home program involves him with no sex whatsoever. Joe tries desperately to abstain. At the same time, when he meditates and alters his consciousness, he immediately finds himself with a blinding headache, images of nude women, and fantasies of female goddesses out to tempt him from his celibate state.

Joe thinks of such images as very wrong. Instead, they are telling him something—that his home program is impoverished, for he has been denying the reality of his being.[3] If he ignores the advice of his psyche, then his journeys into the unknown reality will be highly distorted. Seductive goddesses will follow him wherever he goes.

Take your break or end the session as you prefer.

(11:46 P.M. Break turned out to mark the end of the session, though Jane was surprised at the time; she'd been in trance for over an hour. "My God—he's got the whole thing all laid out," she exclaimed. She too had been bothered by the rush and clatter of traffic, even in trance, and we talked about moving to quieter surroundings before next summer.[4]

(Jane wanted to continue the session, but she was also hungry. "I feel guilty," she laughed. "I want a nice big snack, but I feel all this stuff that Seth's got ready, right on the line . . . Oh, to hell with it—let's eat!")

NOTES: Session 716

1. In Note 1 for Session 715, I described my "first and second Romans"—internal visions or perceptions that had come to me as I lay down for afternoon naps last Sunday and Monday. Each time I'd evidently seen myself as a Roman military officer living early in the first century A.D. In the first episode I was aboard a galley in the Mediterranean; in the second, I floated face down in that sea with my hands bound behind me.

As I prepared to sleep this afternoon I had my third vision in the series. Presumably this will be the last one—for now, closely following upon my precarious circumstance in the water, I saw myself as dead. When I woke up I made another little drawing: I showed my Roman-captain self still face down in the water, but entangled with the branches projecting from a waterlogged tree trunk—I'd been caught that way for a while, before a group of fishermen on a North American beach hauled body and tree ashore in their net. At least, I thought as I described the experience to Jane, I dared face my death in that life *after* the fact of its happening, even if I didn't care to undergo the actual process.

And added later: Jane did use my three Roman experiences in her *Psychic Politics*: she'd mentioned doing so after the second one had taken place, and ended up quoting my own accounts of them in Chapter 4. (As I wrote up my third vision, incidentally, I called myself "captain," automatically using present-day terminology to denote a certain military rank. Then I began to wonder if such a classification had even existed in the Roman armed forces in those ancient times. I learned that it had: A captain was called a "centurio.")

  2. Seth discussed probable man and probable civilizations, and mentioned alternate systems of actuality, in various portions of Volume 1. See the 687th session (which bridges sections 1 and 2), for instance, and Appendix 6 for that session.

  3. Later, in Chapter 10 of *Politics*, Jane elaborated upon Seth's "Joe" material. She also related Joe's limited model of his nature to some of her own ideas about disciplining her "writing self."

  4. A note added four and a half months later: And we did!

Session 718
November 6, 1974
9:50 P.M. Wednesday

(On Monday, November 4, I mailed to Jane's publisher all of the art due for her Adventures in Consciousness: An Introduction to Aspect Psychology: *the 16 diagrams I'd just finished, plus two older pieces of work. All are in "line," or pen-and-ink. I thought it interesting that as I was completing work for Jane's first book on aspect psychology, she was starting* Psychic Politics, *the second one in the series. But now I can return to my longer project—the 40 line drawings for Jane's book of poetry,* Dialogues of the Soul and Mortal Self in Time. Adventures *and* Dialogues *are to be published by Prentice-Hall in the spring and fall, respectively, of 1975. Other references to both books can be found in Note 1 for Session 714.*

(Our last session, the 717th, is deleted from "Unknown" Reality. *For it was and wasn't a Seth session, and it was and wasn't book dictation, as the following notes will show.*

(Before what we expected to be our regular session for Monday evening, Jane told me that she'd awakened in the middle of the previous night with insights about two practice elements[1] Seth would discuss—but we didn't

hear from Seth even though she felt him "around" as we prepared for the session.

(Instead a development took place that left us puzzled, intrigued, and more than a little upset. Yet at this writing [immediately following the 718th session], I can note that we've been somewhat relieved by subsequent events. Now, in fact, I'm veering toward the idea that Monday night's session marked a distinct step in the further development of Jane's abilities. She may also use some of that new material in Politics.[2]

(It seems that a combination of factors led to those oddly disturbing yet challenging events in the 717th session. One is probably just the state of Jane's recent exceptional psychic receptivity. Another is my own longtime interest in the American psychologist and philosopher, William James [1842–1910]; he wrote the classic The Varieties of Religious Experience.[3] *A third is a letter received last week from a Jungian psychologist who had been inspired by Seth's material on the Swiss psychologist and psychiatrist, Carl Jung [1875–1961], in Chapter 13 of* Seth Speaks. *And a fourth factor would be a most evocative experience Jane had Monday afternoon, in which she found herself experiencing consciousness as an ordinary housefly[4]: From that minute but enthralling viewpoint she knew "herself" crawling up a giant-sized blade of grass. She was exploring the "world view" of a fly. This adventure was certainly a preparation for developments in the 717th session.*

(Other reasons must enter in, of course. But for now let's say that Jane knows of James and his work; she's read parts of his Varieties, *for instance, but seemed rather put off by it, where I reread passages from it frequently.*

(The letter from the Jungian psychologist evidently provided the immediate impetus for the fly episode and for Monday evening's events, though. The author requested additional material from Seth on Jung or his works. I hardly think it accidental now that such an inquiry came just when Jane's abilities seemed about to ripen in the particular way they did that night.

(We were discussing the letter and half-facetiously wondering whether Seth might respond in any way, when Jane suddenly told me that she was picking up material on the "essence" of William James. Because of his own persistent melancholy, she said, James had been able to understand others with the same kind of disposition. As she continued to give her impressions, though, I wondered: Why James? He wasn't mentioned in the psychologist's letter, for instance. Why this picking up on, and identifying with, a famous dead personality? Most likely my own interest in James's work exerted some kind of influence upon Jane's newly developing abilities, I thought; but still, that didn't answer my questions.

(What had happened to Seth? That individual would have to wait. "I was getting just now," *Jane said at 8:58,* "that James called his melancholy 'a cast of soul.' " *Her eyes were closed.* "Now I'm getting a book. Why, it's a paperback. I see this printed material, only it's very small, almost microscopic,

and oddly enough the whole thing is printed on grayish-type paper. I see it really small, in my mind."

(And with that, in an altered state of consciousness, Jane began delivering last Monday evening the material from the book she mentally saw. Before I fully realized what was happening, I was taking her words down verbatim.

(The material itself was beautifully done, rather quaint in expression but of excellent quality. When I typed it the next day [yesterday], there were over 10 pages of double-spaced prose. Here's a small quotation from it, dealing with part of a vision "James" had following his physical death:

("There was a procession, a procession of the gods that went before my very eyes. I wondered and watched silently. Each god or goddess had a poet who went in company, and the poets sang that they gave reason voice. They sang gibberish, yet as I listened the gibberish turned into a philosophical dialogue. The words struck at my soul. A strange mirror-image type of action followed, for when I spoke the poets' words backwards, to my intellect they made perfect sense."

(At one of our breaks Jane said that she had picked up the title of the James book from which she'd been "reading": The Varieties of Religious States—*with only* States *differing from* Experience *in the name of James's book in our physical reality. She'd also felt Seth around, like a supervisor, perhaps. She added: "I felt as if the James stuff was coming from a person who was very intent about trying to say something."*

(Which pointed up our dilemma, I thought at the time. I said little to Jane, but I was most uneasy that she was delivering material supposedly from a member of the famous dead. Actually, we'd always thought that such performances were somehow suspect. Not that mediums, or others, couldn't communicate with the "dead"—but to us, anyhow, exhibitions involving well-known personages usually seem . . . psychologically tainted. So our feelings about the night's affair weren't of the best at that point.

(The events to come didn't help matters any, either. No sooner had Jane finished with the lengthy James material than she promptly began to get impressions from "Carl Jung." This time she was almost apologetic. We decided to go ahead, though. Jane didn't see a book or have any visual data. The words just came to her along with strong emotional feelings that she connected with Jung.

(The material seemed endless. It was a few minutes before midnight when Jane just stopped, saying that she'd more or less "had it" for the evening. The Jung material felt much more animated, she added, with a lot of vitality and energy to it: " 'He' really seemed excitable." Neither of us found the Jung passages as evocative as the James material, however. This is a brief Jungian excerpt:

("Numbers have an emotional equivalent, in that their symbols

*originally arose from the libido that always identifies itself with the number 1,
and feels all other numbers originating out of itself. The libido knows itself as
God, and therefore all fractions fly out of the self-structure of its own reality."*

(*Jane said she had the impression of someone very compact, loaded
with energy, almost wildly adolescent in a way, going off in too many directions
at once.*

(*We both wondered right then if Jane was going off in too many
directions at once. She'd always refused to try to "reach the dead" in this way
before. Both of us were more than a little troubled—but as usual, we were
intrigued even as we questioned our own reactions. We were also quite aware of
the humorous aspects of the situation, since Jane does speak for at least one of
the "dead": Seth. And of course, as we sat for tonight's session we wondered if
Seth would discuss what had happened Monday night.*

(*I'd just begun typing the "James and Jung" material, so from my
original notes I read the rest of it to Jane as we waited for Seth to come through. I
also thought she discussed an excellent idea of her own, saying that she believed
the James-Jung episode itself was an exercise in making the unknown reality
known. She'd already done some writing yesterday, for Psychic Politics,
leading toward this view ⁵; so whatever we learned through Seth this evening,
we already felt reasonably sure that in usual trite terms Jane hadn't been
communicating directly with two such famous personalities. Instead, she was
involved in something quite a bit different—and much more believable.*)

Good evening.

(*"Good evening, Seth."*)

Now. This section [of *"Unknown" Reality*] deals with the
various exercises that will, I hope, provide you with your own
intimate glimpses into previously unknown realities.

I said *(in sessions 711 and 716, for instance)* that your normal
focus of consciousness can be compared to your home station. So
far, exercises have been described that will gently lead you away
from concentration upon this home base, even while its structure is
strengthened at the same time. You can also call this home station or
local program your world view, since from it you perceive your
reality. To some extent it represents your personal focus, through
which you interpret most of your experience. As I mentioned *(in
Session 715, for instance)*, when you begin to move away from that
particular organization, strange things may start to happen. You
may be filled with wonder, excitement, or perplexity. You may be
delighted or appalled, according to whether or not your new
perceptions agree or disagree with your established world view.

Instead of a regular session *(last Monday night)*, the framework of the session was used in a new kind of exercise. It was meant
as an example of what <u>can</u> happen under the best of circumstances,

when someone leaves a native world view and tunes in to another, quite different from the original.

You always form your own experience. Ruburt picked up on the world view of a man known dead. He was not directly in communication with William James.

(Slowly:) He was aware, however, of the universe through William James's world view. Period. As you might dial a program on a television set, Ruburt tuned in to the view of reality now held in the mind of William James. Because that view necessarily involved emotions, Ruburt felt some sense of emotional contact—but only with the validity of the emotions. Each person has such a world view, whether living or dead in your terms, and that "living picture" exists despite time or space. It can be perceived by others.

(Pause, one of many.) Each world view exists at its own particular "frequency," and can only be tuned in to by those who are more or less within the same range. However, the frequencies themselves have to be adjusted properly to be brought into focus, and those adjustments necessitate certain intents and sympathies. It is not possible to move in to such a world view if you are basically at odds with it, for example. You simply will not be able to make the proper adjustments.

Ruburt has been working with alterations of consciousness *(for Psychic Politics)*, and wondering about the basic validity of religion. He has been trying to reconcile intellectual and emotional knowledge. James is far from one of his favorite writers, yet Ruburt's interests, intent, and desire were close enough so that under certain conditions he could experience the world view held by James. The unknown reality is unknown only because you believe it must be hidden. Once that belief is annihilated, then other quite-as-legitimate views of reality can appear to your consciousness, and worlds just as valid as your own swim into view.

To do this, you must have faith in yourself, and in the framework of your known reality. Otherwise you will be too afraid to abandon even briefly the habitual, organized view of the world that is your own.

Even in your life as you understand it, if you are insecure or frightened, you cannot properly see your family or your neighbors. If you are afraid, then your own fear stands between yourself and others. You do not dare take your eyes off yourself for a second. You cannot afford to be friendly, for instance, because you are terrified of being rebuffed.

In the same way, if you are overly concerned about the nature of your own reality, and if you are looking to others to justify your existence, you will not be able to abandon your own world view successfully, for you will feel too threatened. Or, traveling in psychic exercises even slightly away from your own home station, you will still try to take your familiar paraphernalia with you, and interpret even entirely new situations of consciousness in the light of your own world view. You will transpose your own set of assumptions, then, into conditions in which they may not really fit at all.

(10:22.) Ruburt picked up on William James's world view because their interests coincided. A letter from a Jungian psychologist helped serve as a stimulus. The psychologist asked me *(deeper and with humor)* to comment about Jung. Ruburt felt little correspondence with Jung. In the back of his mind he wondered about James, mainly because he knew that Joseph *(Rob)* enjoyed one of James's books.

It is quite possible to tune in to the world view of any person, living or dead in your terms. The world view of any individual, even not yet born from your standpoint, exists nevertheless. Ruburt's experience simply serves as an example of what is possible.

Quite rightly, he did not interpret the event in conventional terms, and Joseph did not suppose that James himself was communicating in the way usually imagined *(but see the opening notes for this session)*. Joseph did recognize the excellence of the material. James was not aware of the situation. For that matter, James himself is embarked upon other adventures. Ruburt picked up on James's world view, however, as in your terms at least it "existed" perhaps 10 years ago.[6] Then, in his mind, James playfully thought of a book that he would write were he "living," called *The Varieties of Religious States*—an altered version of a book he wrote in life.

He felt that the soul chooses states of emotion as you would choose, say, a state to live in. He felt that the chosen emotional state was then used as a framework through which to view experience. He began to see a conglomeration of what he loosely called religious states, each different and yet each serving to unify experience in the light of its particular "natural features." These natural features would appear as the ordinary temperaments and inclinations of the soul.

Ruburt tuned in to that unwritten book. It carried the stamp of James's own emotional state at that "time," when he was viewing his earthly experience, in your terms, from the standpoint of one who had died, could look back, and see where he thought his ideas were valid and where they were not. At that point in his existence, there were changes. The plan for the book existed, and still does. In Ruburt's "present," he was able to see this world view as expressed within James's immortal mind.

To do this, Ruburt had to be free enough to accept the view of reality as perceived by someone else. To accomplish this, Ruburt allowed one portion of his consciousness to remain securely anchored in its own reality while letting another portion soak up, so to speak, a reality not its own.

(Pause.) The unknown reality, colon: Again, because of your precise orientation you are often theoretically intrigued by the contemplation of worlds not your own. And while you may often yearn for some evidence of those other realities, you are just as apt to become scandalized[7] by the very evidence that you have so earnestly requested.

Ruburt has embarked upon his own journeys into the unknown reality. I cannot do that for him. I can only point out the way, as I do for each reader. In his own new book (Politics) Ruburt has his personal way of explaining what he is experiencing, and since he shares the same reality with you, then you will be able to relate— perhaps better, even—to his explanations than to mine.

However, it is quite possible for him to tune in to James's complete book if he desires to, for that work is indeed a psychic reality, a plan or a model existing in the inward order of activity (as Jane had explained to me in similar terms this afternoon).

Such creative "architect's plans" are often unknowingly picked up by others, altered or changed, ending up as entirely new productions. Most writers do not examine their sources that closely. The same applies, of course, to any field of endeavor. Many quite modern and sophisticated developments have existed in what you think of now as past civilizations. The plans, as models, were picked up by inventors, scientists, and the like, and altered to their own specific directions, so that they emerged in your world not as copies but as something new. Many so-called archaeological discoveries were made when individuals suddenly tuned in to a world view of another person not of your space or time. Before you have the confidence to leave your own particular home station, however, you must be secure within it. You must know it will "be there" when you get back.

Take your break.

(10:52. Jane's trance had been deep, her delivery for the most part just about as fast as I could write. I told her that Seth's material was excellent, that it backed up her ideas as to the nature of the James-Jung "communications," and added more data as well.

("I felt out of the James thing until you read it to me before the session," she said, "then a lot of aspects about it came back. We won't bother doing that book of his, I know, but I could get it—the whole thing. It's right there in the library. . . ." We talked about what an interesting product The Varieties of Religious States *would be, and the many implications involved, without intending to do anything more about such a work.*

(We also discussed the parallels—and differences—revolving around Jane's perception of the James book this week, and her development eight months ago of the outline and chapter headings for the possible book, The Way Toward Health. *Two months later, in May, she produced the summary for* The Wonderworks, *which would be a shorter dissertation on her own dreams, Seth, and the dream-formation of the universe as we know it. [See appendixes 7 and 11 in Volume 1 of "Unknown" Reality.] Jane hasn't taken the time to concentrate upon either of those projects, interesting as they are, although she would if one—or both—of them "caught fire" for her. Neither Jane nor Seth had delivered their respective world-view ideas when she came through with* Health *and* Wonderworks, *so another significant aspect of her abilities has since become conscious. Once more questions arise. For instance: Whose world view was Jane tuning in to for the health book? Her own? In turn, of course, all three potential endeavors—Religious States, Health, and Wonderworks—must have origins that are closely related to the source of information behind the "psychic library" Jane tells of visiting in* Politics.

(Resume in the same manner at 11:14.)

Now: Ruburt has trained himself to deal with words as a writer. When he picks up a world view that belongs to someone else, he can quite automatically translate it faithfully enough in that idiom of language. Many artists do the same thing, translating inner "models" into paint, lines, and form.

So do scientists and inventors often tune in to the world views of others—living or dead, in your terms—that correlate with their own intents, talents, and purposes.[8]

These "other," reinterpreted world views form a matrix from which new creativity emerges. The same thing applies in more mundane endeavors in ordinary life. For example: You may be in a predicament that seems beyond solving. It may be highly individual, since it is yours. It is unique, and has happened in no other way before. No one else has viewed your particular dilemma through your eyes, yet others have been in similar situations, solved the challenges involved, and gone on to greater creativity and fulfillment. If you can momentarily abandon your private world view, that focus from which you experience reality, then you can allow the experience of others who have had similar challenges to color your perception. You can tune in to their solutions and apply them to your particular circumstances. You often do this unconsciously. I do not want you to think, then, that such occurrences work only in esoteric terms.

Many people working with the Ouija board or automatic writing receive messages that seem, or purport, to come from historic personages. Often, however, the material is vastly inferior to that which could have been produced by the person in question during his or her existence. Any comparison with the material received to the written books or accounts already existing would immediately show glaring discrepancies.

Yet in many such instances, the Ouija board operator or the automatic writer is to some extent or another tuning in to a world view, struggling to open roads of perception free enough to perceive an altered version of reality, but not equipped enough through training and temperament, perhaps, to express it.

(Long pause at 11:30.) The most legitimate instances of communication between the living and the dead occur in an intimate personal framework, in which a dead parent makes contact with its offspring[9]: or a husband or wife freshly out of physical reality appears to his or her mate. But very seldom do historic personages make contact, except with their own intimate circles.

(Emphatically:) There is great energy, however, in those who have persevered enough to become generally known in their time, and the great impetus of that psychic and mental energy does not cease at death, but continues. In their way others may tune in to that continuing world view; and, picking it up, can be convinced that they are in contact with the physical personality who held it.

Give us a moment . . . You are so used to your own private interpretation of reality that when you allow yourselves to stray from it, you immediately want to interpret your new experience in terms that make sense to your familiar orientation. You are also highly involved with symbols. In ordinary life you often hamper your own creativity. When you use the Ouija board or trance procedures, you frequently free philosophical areas of your mind that have been frozen. The resulting information then definitely seems to come from outside of yourself, and because you are literal-minded you try to interpret such experiences in a literal way. The material must come from a philosopher, therefore (amused), and since it certainly seems profound to your usual mudane organization, then it appears that such information must originate with a profound mind certainly not your own.

You may signify this to yourself symbolically, so that the board or the automatic writing designates its origin as being Socrates[10] or Plato. If you are spiritualistically oriented, the information may come from a famous psychic recently dead. Instead, you yourself have momentarily escaped from your accustomed world view, or home program; you are reaching out into other levels of reality, but still interpreting your experience in old terms. Therefore much of its creativity escapes you.

You are each as valid as Socrates or Plato. Your influences reach through the entire framework of actuality in ways that you do not understand. Socrates and Plato—and William James (note that I smiled)—specialized in certain fashions. You know those individuals as names of people that existed—but in your terms, and in your terms only, those existences represented the flowering aspects of their personalities. (Louder:) They often dwelled nameless upon the face of the earth, as many of you do, in your terms only, now, before reaching what you think of as those summits.

Wait a moment. End of dictation—though I will have something to say about Ruburt's experience as a fly.

(11:49. Jane rested a minute or so, still in trance. Her fly experience of last Monday afternoon is mentioned in the opening notes for this session. When Seth returned, he delivered half a page of material for Jane and me, including this passage: "He [Ruburt] has made an extraordinary leap into his [psychic] library, and it is freeing him physically. You have made as vital a leap, and it is freeing you artistically. The library is valid, and in the most legitimate of terms it is far more important, for example, than a physical library. . . ." Seth finished his personal material at 12:10 A.M., and we thought the session was over. Jane was very tired, much more so than she usually is after a session. She wanted only to sleep.

(We keep our typewritten transcripts of the sessions in a series of three-ring binders. I not only record the current session in the latest one, of course, but have in there a page or two of comments and questions so that from time to time I can ask Seth to clear them up. In closing the notebook tonight, I noticed the query I'd written following the 697th session for May 13, 1974, in Volume 1. In that session Seth told us: "Because you are now a conscious species, in your terms, there are racial idealizations that you can accept or deny."

(I've never really forgotten that statement of almost six months ago, nor Seth's saying at the end of the 699th session that he'd go into my questions about it "when your material will fit."

("What," I wrote at the time, "would a state other than a conscious one be? I have difficulty conceiving of such a situation—which, perhaps, is more revealing of the way I think than of anything else. But how could the species, or *its individual members,* not *be 'conscious'? Since I think our collective and individual actions are self-consciously designed for survival, in the best meaning of that word, I'm curious to know in what other state these functions could be performed, for existence's sake . . . There are many ramifications here, as I discovered when I started making notes about this concept, so I'm purposely keeping them short."*

(When Jane first read my question after she'd held the 697th session, she told me that she "didn't get it"—that perhaps I was drawing inferences from Seth's material that weren't intended. I tried to explain the point at issue to her on several different occasions, and discovered each time that it was an oddly elusive one to put into words.

(Idly now, not intending that Jane do any more work this evening, I read my question aloud. She raised a hand in dismay. "I'm tired," she said, but wait a minute—I've got the answer. Seth's all ready. Get me a pack of cigarettes, and I'll do it. . . ."

(12:14.) Now: I have been using your terms as I understood your meaning of them.

There are, in those terms, gradations. When I used the word "conscious" (or "consciousness"), I meant it as I thought you understood it. I thought that you meant: conscious of being conscious, or placing yourself on the one hand outside of a portion of your own consciousness—viewing it *(intently)* and then saying, "I am conscious of my consciousness."

Consciousness is always conscious of itself, and of its validity and integrity, and in those terms there is no unconsciousness.

When I use the term time-wise, I refer it to the formation of a structure from which one kind of consciousness then views itself, sees itself as unique, and then tries to form other kinds of conscious structures. A fly is conscious of itself, fulfilled within that reality, and feels no need to form an "extension" of that awareness from which to view its own existence.

In your terms, time considerations involved extensions of that kind of consciousness, in which separations could occur and divisions could be made. In terms of an <u>organic</u> structure, this could be likened to developing another arm or leg, or protrusion or filament—another method of locomotion through another kind of dimension.

The fly is intensely conscious, at every moment engrossed in itself and its environment, precisely tuned to elements of which <u>you</u> are "unconscious." There are simply different kinds of consciousness, and you cannot basically compare one to the other any more than you can compare, say, a toad to a star to an apple to a thought to a woman to a child to a native to a suburbanite to a spider to a cat. They are <u>varieties</u> of consciousness, each focused upon its own view of reality, each containing experience that others exclude.

(Louder, humorously:) End of explanation.

(With a laugh: "Thank you very much." 12:19 A.M. And so it turned out that I brought up my questions about self-consciousness, and Seth answered them, when that material did fit.

(A note added in December 1977: The 718th session on world views proved to be a cornerstone in Jane's own development, and in Seth's thematic structure as well. Jane's The World View of Paul Cézanne: A Psychic Interpretation, *was published earlier this year, and as I type this final manuscript for Volume 2 of* "Unknown" Reality *I can add that she's also completed* The Afterdeath Journal of an American Philosopher: The World View of William James. *It came out in 1978.*

(In a sense, both world-view books were "born" in the 718th session and the odd previous one that took place under Seth's auspices. I write this although Jane had no idea of producing such works when those two sessions were held [but see my speculations in Note 6]. Nothing has been forthcoming on any additional material concerning Carl Jung, however—nor has Jane tried for this.

(The entire world-view concept is extremely interesting, of course, and worthy of continuous investigation.

(Oddly enough, the original pages of the James material that Jane saw mentally during the 717th session [and later presented in Chapter 6 of Psychic Politics] *never appeared in* Afterdeath Journal. *There were two different James books in her "library," Jane said. She transcribed only one of them.)*

NOTES: Session 718

1. Jane remembered part of one of the two practice elements she'd tuned in to Sunday night; perhaps we'll get them later. She said that Seth had designed them to follow those he'd given in the 716th session. At the moment, even the fragment she recalled is well worth trying: Seth instructed the reader to immerse himself or herself in an old photograph of a person—and then to look out at our current physical reality through that individual's eyes. An interesting way to gain a fresh perspective on our present time.

2. A note added several months later: I see now that I should enlarge upon Note 2 for the 715th session, in which I wrote that Jane "would initiate the transposition of material from Volume 2 of *'Unknown' Reality* into *Politics*, since she was so intimately and enthusiastically involved in producing both books at the same time." For her to work this way is entirely in keeping with her spontaneous nature; she intuitively seeks to use whatever sources of information—including Seth himself—she has at hand

for whatever project she may be engaged in. In the early chapters of *Politics* especially, then, she both quotes and paraphrases material from Volume 2, beginning with the 714th session, which contains her account of her original inspiration for that work.

However, Jane's use of material in this manner is quite natural in another way also: for *Politics* represents her personal exploration of the unknown reality that Seth has been so graphically describing in his own work.

I always indicate in Volume 2 when such a movement of material into *Politics* has taken place. Yet Jane did no blind copying, and almost always she quoted an excerpt rather than a complete passage from a session, for instance. Jane and Seth each say what they want to say from their unique, respective viewpoints—and it becomes obvious that her book should be read as an adjunct to Seth's.

For example, Jane began *Politics* by describing how impatient she was, how "disconnected" she felt, because she hadn't been inspired since finishing *Adventures* two months previously. Indeed, she was very upset over this, and quite serious in her feeling, as she later wrote in her new book, of being abandoned by her inner self. In Volume 2, now, the reader can note the many events Jane was actually involved in before she began *Politics* (on October 23), and see just how objective her perception of her activities was—or see, really, the demanding standards of creativity against which she constantly judges herself.

In my own notes, of course, I described those events dealt with by Jane and Seth from my own perspective, as I watched them happen. "In *'Unknown' Reality* the reader should focus upon the material from Seth's viewpoint," Jane said. "Yet it might be fun now and then to look at the daily events in our lives *first*, as recorded in Rob's notes—and see the dictation in the sessions as emerging from those humble sources. What I've said in *Psychic Politics* should certainly add a lot of insight there."

3. Longmans, Green and Co., London, 1908.

4. The contents of this note flow out of what I wrote in Note 2: Seth mentions Jane's fly experience in this (718th) session, and Jane discussed it in more detail in Chapter 5 of *Politics*. Then in Chapter 6 of her book she presented long excerpts from the James-Jung material as it developed in the 717th session.

5. See Jane's "library" material at the beginning of Chapter 7 of *Politics*. And again: For her own purposes she quoted in the same chapter the appropriate Seth material from the 718th session.

6. Since William James died in 1910, this means that in our terms Jane picked up on his world view as it existed some 54 years after his physical death. We could easily ask Seth a dozen questions about the ideas he's given in just this one paragraph of material. Very lengthy answers could result, leading to more queries. A book on world views could even develop. But the questions always pile up ahead of us; often they're never

voiced, no matter how interesting they may be. Whether Seth will ever deal with this latest batch, implied as they are, is very problematical.

7. See the 715th session after 10:43.

8. Seth's information here, that scientists and inventors often tune in to the world views of other such individuals, at once reminded me that a similar long-term situation could have existed within the Butts family.

In Volume 1, see Session 680, with notes 1–3. My father, Robert Sr., who died in 1971, was very gifted mechanically. According to Seth, a still-living probable self of Robert Butts, Sr., is "a well-known inventor, who never married but used his mechanically creative abilities to the fullest while avoiding emotional commitment." Although my father's "sole intent" was the very challenging one of raising a family in this reality, still he may have often exchanged ideas about automobiles, motorcycles, welding torches, cameras, and so forth, with that other inventor-self.

Do probable selves actually communicate with each other through their world-view frameworks, then, or can such an interchange of idea or emotion take place more "directly" at times—simply between the probable personalities involved? Either situation can apply, it seems to me, or the two methods may merge at any given "time." We plan to ask Seth to elaborate.

9. Nine months ago, in February 1974, Seth mentioned the few tentative contacts I'd evidently made with my deceased mother through dreams; see the 683rd session after 11:30, then see my account of one such dream in Note 5 for that session. Two months later, in the 693rd session, Seth described how I reacted (on a cellular, or "unconscious" level) to communications from my mother as Jane and I considered buying a certain house in my childhood neighborhood in Sayre, Pennsylvania. So far, Jane has nothing to report about meetings of any kind with her late mother or father. (All of our parents died between February 1971 and November 1973.)

10. I'd like to dwell a bit upon a point I made in the opening notes for this (718th) session, when I wrote about mediums, or others, contacting the well-known dead. I mean it kindly—but Jane and I have never believed that a living individual could be in contact with a famous dead person, especially through the Ouija board or automatic writing. Although we haven't scoffed at such instances when we heard of them, we've certainly regarded those encounters through very skeptical eyes. The gist of our attitudes is that we find it most difficult to believe that "Socrates"—wherever he is and whatever he may be doing, in our terms—is willing to drop everything to give very garbled information to a well-intentioned, really innocent person living in, say, a small town in Virginia. There must be other things he wants to do! Seth's world-view concept, and Jane's own experiences with it, make the accounts of such happenings much more understandable.

Session 719
November 11, 1974
9:36 P.M. Monday

(Jane was so relaxed and "floppy" before the session that I asked her if she'd rather not have it. She decided that she wanted to try. She's been experiencing many muscular changes and releases in recent days. I read parts of the last session to her, to remind us both of what Seth had discussed. At 9:30 Jane said: "There—I'm just beginning to feel him around. . . .")

Now: Good evening—

("Good evening, Seth.")

—and dictation. I consider my own book, *The Nature of Personal Reality: A Seth Book*, as a prerequisite for the exercises given here in this volume.

In that previous book I discussed the ways in which you form your private experience through your beliefs. You have certain pet ideas, therefore, and you use them to structure your own world view of the reality you know. It is important that you understand what your own beliefs are. Many of them might work quite well "at home," but when you begin to journey away from that home station you may find that those same ideas impede your progress.

Other concepts are really not basically workable even in your own physical reality. A rigid, dogmatic concept of good and evil will force you to perceive physical existence as a battleground of opposing forces, with the poor unwary soul almost as a buffer. Or you will think of the poor soul as a blackboard eraser, slapped between two hands—one good and one evil.

Upon the blackboard, in this homey analogy, would be written the soul's earthly experiences. With the eraser the "evil hand" would try to rub out all of the good, and at the same time the "good hand" would be trying to erase all of the evil. In such a case all of your experience becomes suspect. You will have a tendency to consider the body with its natural appetites wrong, and deny them, while at the same time the physical part of you will look upon your "good intents" as wrong, and infringements upon its own existence.

If you do not understand the natural grace of your being,[1] then when you try some of the exercises given here you may automatically translate them into a quite limiting set of beliefs.

You are familiar with your own view of the world. As you leave your usual orientation, however, altering the focus of your consciousness, you may very well structure your new experience just as you do your physical one. At the same time, you _are_ more free. You have greater leeway. You are used to projecting your beliefs onto physical objects and events. When you leave your home station, those objects and events no longer present themselves in the same fashion.

(*Intently:*) You often find yourself encountering your own structures, no longer hidden in the kind of experience with which you are familiar. These may then appear in quite a different light. You may be convinced that you are evil simply because you are physical. You may believe that the soul "descends" into the body, and therefore that the body is lower, inferior, and a degraded version of "what you really are." At the same time your own physical being knows better, and basically cannot accept such a concept.[2] So in daily life you may project this idea of unworth outward onto another person, who seems then to be your enemy; or upon another nation. In general, you might select animals to play the part of the enemy, or members of another religion, or political parties.

In any case, in your _private_ life you may hardly ever encounter your belief in your own unworth, or evil. You will not realize that you actually consider _yourself_ the enemy. You will be so convinced that your projection (onto others) is the enemy that there will be no slack to take up, for all of your feelings of self-hate or self-fear will be directed outward.

When you begin to leave your home station and alter your focus, however, you leave behind you the particular familiar receptors for your projections. Using the Ouija board or automatic writing, you may find yourself immediately confronted with this material that you have suppressed in the past. When it surfaces you may then project it outward from yourself again, but in a different fashion. Instead of thinking you are in contact with a great philosopher or "ancient soul," you may believe that you are instead visiting with a demon or a devil, or that you are possessed of an evil spirit.

In such a case, you will have already been convinced of the power of evil. Your natural feelings, denied, will also carry the great charge of repression. You may be filled with the feeling that you are in the midst of a great cosmic struggle between the forces of good and evil—and indeed, this often represents a valid picture of your own view of the world.

(Long pause.) None of this is necessary. There is no danger in the exercises I suggest. You are in far greater danger the longer you inhibit your natural feelings, and alterations of consciousness often present you with the framework in which these come to light. If they do not in one way or another come to your attention, then it is very possible that the denied energy behind them will erupt in ruptured relationships or illnesses.

(Long pause at 10:11.) "Psychic explorations" never cause such difficulties, nor do they ever compound original problems. On the contrary, they are often highly therapeutic, and they present the personality with an alternative—an alternative to continued repression that would be literally unbearable.

If you are normally capable of dealing with physical reality, you will encounter no difficulties in alterations of consciousness, or leaving your home station. Be reasonable, however: If you have difficulties in New York City, you are most apt to encounter them in a different form no matter where else you might travel. A change of environment might help clear your head by altering your usual orientation, so that you can see yourself more clearly, and benefit. The same applies when you leave your home station. Here the possible benefits are far greater than in usual life and travel, but you are still yourself. It is impossible not to structure reality in some fashion. Reality implies a structuring.

If you take your own world view with you all of the time, however, as you travel, even in your own world, then you never see the "naked culture." You are always a tourist, taking your homey paraphernalia with you and afraid to give it up. If you are American or English, or European, then when you visit other areas of the world you stay at cosmopolitan hotels. You always see other cultures through your own eyes.

Now when you leave your home station and alter your consciousness, you are always a tourist if you take your own baggage of ideas along with you, and interpret your experiences through your own personal, cultural beliefs. There is nothing unconventional about gods and demons, good spirits or bad spirits. These are quite conventional interpretations of experience, with religious overtones. Cults simply represent counter-conventions, and they are as dogmatic in their way as the systems they reject. Underline that sentence.

Give us a moment... When you try these exercises, therefore, make an honest attempt to leave your conventional ideas behind you. Step out of your own world view. There is an exercise that will help you.

PRACTICE ELEMENT 13

Close your eyes. Imagine a photograph of yourself (in parentheses: Yes, we are finally back to photographs).[3] In your mind's eye see the photograph of yourself on a table or desk. If you are working mentally with a particular snapshot, then note the other items in the picture. If the photograph is strictly imaginary, then create an environment about the image of yourself.

Look at the image in your mind as it exists in the snapshot, and see it as being aware only of those other objects that surround it. Its world is bounded by the four edges of the picture. Try to put your consciousness into that image of yourself. Your world view is limited to the photograph itself. Now in your mind see that image walking out of the snapshot, onto the desk or table. *(Pause.)* The environment of the physical room will seem gigantic to that small self. The scale and proportion alone will be far different. Imagine that miniature image navigating in the physical room, then going outside, and quite an expanded world view will result.

Take your break.

(10:37. Jane's delivery had been rather fast throughout, except for an occasional long pause. She felt more alert now, she said, but still wasn't as wide-awake as usual. She'd been taking a little wine during her trance. At her request I got her a glass of milk—which she didn't finish before Seth returned.

(During break I saw a certain look pass across Jane's tired face. I couldn't describe the expression, but it reminded me of the internal "vision" I'd

had this afternoon when I lay down to sleep: I found myself looking at a very old,
very probable future manifestation of myself in this life, who rested quietly in
bed. Just before supper tonight I finished writing an account of what I'd seen,
and Jane read it while we ate. See Note 4. Now as we discussed the event in a
little more detail, I made a quick sketch of that possible self of mine.

(Resume at 11:01.)

Dictation: Many of you do not really want to step out of
the photograph, or leave your world view, yet in the dream state you
are far freer. You can pretend that dreams are not "real," however, so
you can have your cake and eat it too, so to speak.

Different varieties of dreams often provide frameworks
that allow you to leave your own world view under "cushioned
conditions." You step out of the normal picture that you have made
of reality.

(As Seth, Jane took a swallow of milk. She promptly made a most
disapproving face. Her features wrinkled up, her lips drew back distastefully.
She held the half-empty glass of milk up to me, her Seth voice booming out:)

This is far different from any milk that I ever drank! It is
like a chalk with chemicals, far divorced from any cow!

(Still in trance, Jane set the milk aside. She didn't return to it, but
sipped her wine for the rest of the session. I was tempted to ask Seth to explain his
idea of what good milk was like, and in what life [or lives] he'd enjoyed such a
potion, but I didn't want to interrupt the flow of the material. While tasting the
milk during break, however, Jane "herself" had had no such reaction.)

Your alterations of consciousness frequently occur in the
dream state, therefore, where it seems to you at least that your
experiences do not have any practical application. You imagine that
only hallucinations are involved. Many of your best snapshots of
other realities are taken in your dreams.[5] They may be over-or-
underdeveloped, and the focus may be blurred, but your dreams
present you with far more information about the unknown reality
than you suppose. In the most intimate of terms your body is your
home station, so when you leave it you often hide this fact from
yourselves.

In your sleep, however, your consciousness slips out of
your body and returns to it frequently. You dream when you are out
of your body, even as you dream inside it. You may therefore form
dream stories about your own out-of-body travel, while your physical image rests soundly in bed. The unknown reality, you see, is not
really that mysterious to you. You only pretend that it is. Sometimes
you have quite clear perceptions of your journeys, but the actual
native territories that you visit are so different from your own world
that you try to interpret them as best you can in the light of usual
conditions. If you remember such an episode at all it may well seem

very confusing, for you will have superimposed your own world view where it does not belong.

(11:16.) In dream travel it is quite possible to journey to other civilizations—those in your past or future, or even to worlds whose reality exists in other probable systems. There is even a kind of "cross-breeding," for you affect any system of reality with which you have experience. There are no closed realities, only apparent boundaries that seem to separate them.[6] The more parochial your own world view, however, the less you will recall of their dreams or their activities, or the more distorted your "dream snapshots" will be.

Now here is another brief but potent exercise.

PRACTICE ELEMENT 14

Before you go to sleep, tell yourself that you will mentally take a dream snapshot[7] of the most significant dream of the night. Tell yourself that you will even be aware of doing this while asleep, and imagine that you have a camera with you. You mentally take this into the dream state. You will use the camera at the point of your clearest perceptions, snap your picture, and—mentally again—take it back with you so that it will be the first mental picture that you see when you awaken.

You will, of course, try to snap as good a picture as possible. Varying results can be expected. Some of you will awaken with a dream picture that presents itself immediately. Others may find such a picture suddenly appearing later in the day, in the middle of ordinary activities. If you perform this exercise often, however, many of you will find yourselves able to use the camera consciously even while sleeping, so that it becomes an element of your dream travels; you will be able to bring more and more pictures back with you.

These will be relatively meaningless, however, if you do not learn how to examine them. They are not to be simply filed away and forgotten. You should write down a description of each scene and what you remember of it, including your feelings both at the time of the dream, and later when you record it. The very effort to take this camera with you makes you more of a conscious explorer, and automatically helps you to expand your own awareness while you are in the dream state. Each picture will serve as just one small glimpse of a different kind of reality. You cannot make any valid judgment on the basis of one or two pictures alone.

Now this is a mental camera we are using. There is a knack about being a good dream photographer, and you must learn how to operate the camera. In physical life, for example, a photographer knows that many conditions affect the picture he takes. Exterior situations then are important: You might get a very poor picture on a dark day, for instance. With our dream camera, however, the conditions themselves are mental. If you are in a dark mood, for example, then your picture of inner reality might be dim, poorly outlined, or foreboding. This would not necessarily mean that the dream itself had tragic overtones, simply that it was taken in the "poor light" of the psyche's mood.

(Pause at 11:40.) Inner weather changes constantly, even as the exterior weather does. One dream picture with a dreary cast, therefore, is not much different from a physical photograph taken on a rainy afternoon.

Many people, however, remembering a dark dream, become frightened. You even structure your dreams, of course. For that matter, your dream world is as varied as the physical one. Each physical photographer has an idea of what he wants to capture on film, and so to that extent he structures his picture and his view. The same applies to the dream state. You have all kinds of dreams. You can take what you want, so to speak, from dream reality, as basically you take what you want from waking life. For that reason, your dream snapshots will show you the kind of experience that you are choosing from inner reality.

(Pause at 11:46.) Give us a moment . . . End dictation.

(Seth spent the next six minutes or so giving some personal material for Jane. Then, as he was about to wind up the session:

("Can I ask a question?")

You may indeed.

("What about my little view of myself this afternoon, as a very old man?")

Now: It represented two things: an association with a definite past old-age sensation, and a "precognitive" moment in this life that you have not as yet encountered. Because you were [psychically] open, the position of your body and head acted as the associative bridge between the two events. You were not senile in either.

My heartiest regards and a fond good evening.

("Thank you very much, Seth. Good night.")

(11:56 P.M. Seth's comments on my experience certainly illustrate his notions of simultaneous time to some extent, since from my "present" I perceived aspects of myself in the reincarnational "past" as well as in the "future" in this life. See Note 4.

(In ordinary terms I can only wait, of course, to see if I decide to create that distant probable moment in this reality. In the meantime, I have no

conscious memory of being an old man, let alone one in the specific, dependent situation in which I saw myself. However, aside from the idea of simultaneous time, I do believe that an individual can touch upon at least some of his or her earlier lives, provided enough long-term effort is given to the endeavor. Since through my internal vision I evidently looked in upon a particular past life of my own, however unaware I was of what I was doing, it seems that the knowledge of that existence may not be too deeply buried within my psyche. I might try jogging my memory through suggestion, to see what else about that life I can recall. It would also be interesting to see whether the same technique could help me tune in to my future in this life.

(But the big thing is finding the physical time to try everything I'd like to do—just as it is with Jane.)

NOTES: Session 719

1. In *Personal Reality*, see the 636th session in Chapter 9, and much of the material in the four sessions making up Chapter 12.

2. When I come across material that puts down the physical body, I sometimes try to counter such negative projections by turning to one of the technological accomplishments of our "degraded" species: I study photographs of minute portions of the human body, taken with a scanning electron microscope. Then I experience a series of steps in thinking—not all of them good, I'm afraid—and I'd like to mention each one in turn.

At this writing, an electron microscope can magnify the surfaces of tissue samples from 20,000 to 60,000 times. Always the resulting photographs obtained leave me groping as I try to appreciate the beauty, order, and complexity of the human organism at just the greatly enlarged levels shown. (If we could plunge "down" into the body's molecular and atomic stages, and *see* those, we'd find intricacies that are even more unbelievable.)

Next, I ask myself how such a marvelously structured being can think of its image as inferior to *anything*, especially since we're far from understanding it even on a "mere" physical basis, let alone from any sort of nonphysical standpoint. Jane's own abilities, for instance, raise questions about certain biological attributes as well as mental ones; in large part our society still doesn't want to contend with such challenges at this time.

Yet, the awe I invariably feel when I study a microphotograph of the retina of the eye, magnified "only" 20,000 times, is hardly an unalloyed blessing. For next I wonder how the human creature, whose bodily components each possess such a ceaseless, rational integrity, can often function so *ir*rationally as a whole, through the creation of war, poverty, pollution, disease, and so forth. Jane and I hope that her work with Seth is offering insights into these enormous questions about our species' individual and collective behavior. Surely we don't think that atoms or cells, or livers or eyeballs, are irrational.

Finally, the incredibly complex physical assemblage of the human being—or of any organism, to confine ourselves to just "living" entities—always reminds me that according to evolutionary theory life on earth arose by chance alone. We must remember that through Darwinism or Neo-Darwinism science tells us that life has no creative design, or any purpose, behind it; and that, moreover, this ineffable quality called "life" originated (more than 3.4 billion years ago) in a *single* fortuitous chance combination of certain atoms and molecules in a tidal pool, say, somewhere on the face of the planet. . . .

Aside from whatever difficulties I may have about resolving the internal beauties of our physical construction with our external behavior, I hope my deep skepticism about this little "official" scenario on evolution is apparent here. See Appendix 12.

3. In Volume 1 of *"Unknown" Reality*, Seth incorporated the use of photographs in practice elements 3–5 and 7.

After tonight's session, Jane told me that his Practice Element 13 was one of the two she'd had insights on during the night preceding the deleted 717th (James-Jung) session. Practice Element 14 didn't seem at all familiar to her, though. See Note 1 for Session 718.

4. I lay down for a nap as usual at 4:30 this afternoon (Monday, November 11). As I started drifting toward sleep I became aware that I was looking at my own head; the image lasted for several seconds and was quite clear, without being needle-sharp. My view was from my right side as I lay face up on the cot. This is a bit difficult to describe, but the glimpse of my own head came from a point usually invisible to me—centered perhaps two inches or so above and behind my right ear.

I saw the head of a very old man, in his late 80's or early 90's. I had no doubt that this was a definitely probable version of myself in this reality. How strange to peek at the curve of my own skull from that odd viewpoint. I saw short, almost wispy white hair, but I wasn't bald. Through the hair I could see the pulsing bluish veins in the skin as it lay over the bone—and in some fashion this sight alone was most evocative of the very young and the very old. I lay face up, bony arms folded across my chest, just as my present "me" did. I knew that I was resting, and that I wasn't senile. I don't believe I was bedridden, but that I was being cared for somehow.

My eyes were closed, and something about my bearing or pose reminded the present me of my father in *his* old age. When he lay dying, early in February 1971, I stood so that I had a view of him similar to the one I'd just experienced of myself. I was sure that this old man was me, though, and no one else. I was very thin beneath the blanket, which I believe was an ivory color.

The whole experience had a hard-to-define childlike or naive quality, as several members of Jane's ESP class remarked the next night when I read this account to them, and showed the sketch around.

5. All in Volume 1: Note 1 for Session 698 contains quotations from the dream material Seth gave in the 92nd session for September 28, 1964. Then see the equally interesting information on dreams in Session 699; I especially like Seth's statement that "In a way, one remembered dream can be compared to a psychological photograph. . . ." Jane's poem, *My Dreaming Self*, is presented in the notes following that session, along with references to other dream material.

6. See Note 2 for Session 688, in Volume 1.

7. See the 710th session for Seth's material on dreams, and the "snapshots" the conscious mind can learn to take during out-of-body travel.

Session 720
November 13, 1974
9:55 P.M. Wednesday

(Just as she had this afternoon, Jane "picked up" a little material from Seth at 9:00 this evening. I'll cover both episodes in the notes at the end of the session.)

Good evening.

("Good evening, Seth.")

Dictation *(whispering)*. Now, if you take a physical camera with you today and snap pictures as you go about your chores, walk, or talk with friends, then you will have preserved scenes from the day's activities.

Your film, however, will only take pictures today, of today. No yesterday or tomorrow will suddenly appear in the snapshots of the present. The photographer in the dream world, though, will find an entirely different situation, for there consciousness can capture scenes from entirely different times as easily as the waking photographer can take pictures of different places. Unless you realize this, some of your "dream albums" will make no sense to you.

In waking life you experience certain events as real, and generally these are the only ones that can be captured by an ordinary photographer. The dream world,[1] however, presents a much larger category of events. Many [events] may later appear as physical ones, while others just as valid will not. The dream camera, therefore, will capture probable events also.

When you awaken with a dream photograph in mind, it may appear meaningless because it does not seem to correlate with the official order of activities you recognize. You may make one particular decision in physical and waking consciousness, and that decision may bring forth certain events. Using your dream camera, you can with practice discover the history of your own psyche, and find the many probable decisions experienced in dreams. These served as a basis from which you made your physical decision. There is some finesse required as you learn to interpret the individual pictures within your dream album. This should be easy to grasp, for if you tried to understand physical life having only a group of snapshots taken at different places and in different times, then it would be rather difficult to form a clear idea of the nature of the physical world.

The same applies to dream reality, for the dreams that you recall are indeed like quick pictures snapped under varying conditions. No one picture alone tells the entire story. You should write down your description of each dream picture, therefore, and keep a continuing record, for each one provides more knowledge about the nature of your own psyche and the unknown reality in which it has its existence.

Give us a moment... When you take a physical photograph you have to know how your camera works. You must learn how to focus, how to emphasize those particular qualities you want to record, and how to cut out distracting influences. You know the difference between shadows, for example, and solid objects. Sometimes shadows themselves make fascinating photographic studies. You might utilize them in the background, but as a photographer you would not confuse the shadows with, say, the solid objects. No one would deny that shadows are real, however.

Now, using an analogy only, let me explain that your thoughts and feelings also give off shadows *(intently)* that we will here call hallucinations.[2] They are quite valid. They have as strong a part to play in dream reality as shadows do in the physical world. They are beautiful in themselves. They add to the entire picture. A shadow of a tree cools the ground. It affects the environment. So hallucinations alter the environment, but in a different way and at another level of reality. In the dream world hallucinations are like conscious shadows. They are not passive, nor is their shape dependent upon their origin. They have their own abilities.

Physically, an oak tree may cast a rich deep shadow upon the ground. It will move, faithfully mirroring the tiniest motion of the smallest leaf, but its freedom to move will be dictated by the motion of the oak. Not one oak leaf shadow will move unless its counterpart does.

Following our analogy, in the dream world the shadow of the oak tree, once cast, would then be free to pursue its own direction. Not only that, but there would be a creative give-and-take between it and the tree that gave it birth. Anyone fully accustomed to inner reality would have no difficulty in telling the dream oak tree from its frisky shadow, however *(humorously)*, any more than a waking photographer would have trouble distinguishing the physical oak tree from its counterpart upon the grass.

When you, a dream tourist, wander about the inner landscape with your mental camera, however, it may take a while before you are able to tell the difference between dream events and their shadows or hallucinations. So you may take pictures of the shadows instead of the trees, and end up with a fine composition indeed—but one that would give you somewhat of a distorted version of inner reality. So you must learn how to aim and focus your dream camera.

(Pause.) In your daily world objects have shadows, and thoughts or feelings do not, so in your dream travels simply remember that there "objects" do not possess shadows, but thoughts and feelings do.

Since these are far more lively than ordinary shadows, and are definitely more colorful, they may be more difficult to distinguish at first. You must remember that you are wandering through a mental or psychic landscape. You can stand before the shadow of a friend in the afternoon, in waking reality, and snap your fingers all you want to, but your friend's shadow will not move one whit. It will certainly not disappear because you tell it to. In the dream world, however, any hallucination will vanish immediately as soon as you recognize it as such, and tell it to go away. It was cast originally by your own thought or feeling, and when you withdraw that source, then its "shadow" is automatically gone.

Do you want a break?

(10:40. "No," I said, although Seth's pace had been good.)

Give us a moment...A stone's physical shadow will

faithfully mirror its form. In those terms, little creativity is allowed it. Far greater leeway exists, however, as a thought or feeling in the dream world casts its greater shadow out upon the landscape of the mind.

Moods obviously exist when you are dreaming as well as when you are waking. Physically the day may be brilliant, but if you are in a blue mood you may automatically close yourself off from the day's natural light, not notice it—or even use that natural beauty as counterpoint that only makes you feel more disconsolate. Then you might look outward at the day through your mood and see its beauty as a meaningless or even cruel façade. Your mood, therefore, will alter your perception.

The same applies in the dream state; but there, the shadows of your thoughts may be projected outward into scenes of darkest desolation. In the physical world you have mass sense data about you. Each individual helps form that exterior environment. No matter how dark your mood on any given sunny day, your individual thoughts alone will not suddenly turn the blue skies into rainy ones. You alone do not have that kind of control over your fellows' environment. In the dream world, however, such thoughts will definitely form your environment.

Stormy dream landscapes are on the one hand hallucinations, cast upon the inner world by your thoughts or feelings. On the other hand, they are valid representations of your inner climate at the time of any given dream. Such scenes can be changed in the dream state itself if you recognize their origin. You might choose instead to learn from such hallucinations by allowing them to continue, while realizing that they are indeed shadows cast by your own mind.

Take your break.

(10:52 to 11:12.)

Now: If you are honest with your thoughts and feelings, then you will express them in your waking life, and they will not cast disturbing shadows in your dreams.

You may be afraid that a beloved child or mate will die suddenly, yet you may never want to admit such a fear. The feeling itself may be generated because of your own doubts about yourself, however. You may be depending upon another such person too strongly, trying to live your own life secondhandedly through the life of another. Your own fear, admitted, would lead you to other feelings behind it, and to a greater understanding of yourself.

Unencountered in waking life, however, the fear might

cast its dim shadow, so that you dream of your child's death, or of the death of another close to you. The dream experience would be cast into the dream landscape and encountered there. Period.

If you remembered such a dream, therefore, you might think that it was precognitive, and that the event would become physical. Instead, the whole portent of the dream event would be an educational one, bringing your fear into clear focus. In such cases you should think of the dire dream situation as a shadow, and look for its source within your mind.

Shadows can be pleasant and luxurious, and on a hot sunny day you are certainly aware of their beneficial nature. So some dream hallucinations are beautiful, comforting, refreshing. They can bring great peace and be sought after for themselves. You may believe that God exists as a kindly father, or you might personify him as Christ or Buddha. In your dreams you might then encounter such personages. They are quite valid, but they are also hallucinations cast by your own thoughts and feelings. Dreams of Heaven and Hell alike fall into the same category, in those terms, as hallucinations.

Now: The physical shadow of a tree bears witness to the existence of a tree, even if you see only the shadow; so your hallucinations appearing in dreams also bear witness to their origin, and give testimony to a valid "objective" dream object that is as "solid" *(slowly)* in that reality as the tree is in your world.

(Long pause at 11:32.) In physical reality there is a time lag that exists between the conception of an idea, say, and its materialization. Beside that, other conditions operate that can slow down an idea's physical actualization, or even impede it altogether. If not physically expressed, the thought will be actualized in another reality. An idea must have certain characteristics, for example, that agree with physical assumptions before it turns into a recognizable event. It must appear within your time context.

In the dream world, however, each feeling or idea can be immediately expressed and experienced. The physical world has buildings in it that you manufacture—that is, they do not spring up naturally from the ground itself. In the same way, your thoughts are "manufactured products" in the dream world. They are a part of the environment and appear within its reality, though they change shape and form constantly, as physically manufactured objects do not.

The earth has its own natural given data, however, and you must use this body of material to form all of your manufactured products. The dream world also possesses its own natural environment. You form your dreams from it *(long pause)*, and use its natural products to manufacture dream images. Few view this natural inner environment, however.

Give us a moment . . . End of dictation.

(11:44. Speaking as Seth, Jane now delivered two pages of material for herself and me. Embedded within it were these lines: "Ruburt's idea did come from me, about your reincarnational episodes involving the Roman officer, and your personal experience illustrates what I am saying in "Unknown" Reality—the individual's history is written in the psyche, and can indeed be uncovered." Note Seth's heading for this Section 5, for example.

(Twice today Jane had tuned in to very similar concepts while going about her daily business. "I'm sure I got that from Seth," she told me after the first such instance had taken place this afternoon. "Not only about your reincarnational stuff, but your thing as the old man [as described in Note 4 for the 719th session]. And the history of the species is written in the mass psyche in just the same way. . . ."

(My "three Romans" are presented in the first notes for sessions 715–16. I'm quite concerned by some of the questions these experiences have raised—especially the possible time contradictions with some of my other supposed past lives. [I plan to soon explain these rather cryptic references.] In the meantime, my little psychic adventures continue to flow. I regret that I seldom seem to find the physical time for more than very quick sketches relative to any of them.

(Tonight's session ended, then, at 12:04 A.M.)

NOTES: Session 720

1. The reader can also refer to Seth's material on dreams in chapters 8 and 10 in *Seth Speaks*, and chapters 10 and 20 in *Personal Reality*.

2. Seth's creative use of "hallucinations" here is certainly at variance with the concepts ordinarily associated with the word. In a dictionary, for instance, hallucinations may be described as sights and sounds *apparently* perceived. Hallucinations are tied in with some mental disorders; with objects not actually present. Logically enough, then, in the dictionary one of the synonyms for hallucination will be a word like "delusion": a belief not true, a persistent opinion without corresponding physical evidence.

Session 721
November 25, 1974
9:14 P.M. Monday

(At the conclusion of the 720th session I mentioned the Roman-soldier visions I'd had near the end of October, and added that I would soon go into my questions about them. Before I could do so, however, I had another experience with psychic perceptions three days later—on November 16—that led to more questions. This one wasn't a "Roman," though, but a series of very vivid impressions of myself as a black woman on the island of Jamaica, in the Caribbean Sea. The time period was—is—the 19th century. See Note 1.

("Jamaica" took place on a Saturday, and Seth referred to it briefly in the next session, on Monday night. That session turned out to be private, rather than one for book dictation. Seth came back to Jamaica in Jane's ESP class the next evening [on November 19]; at the same time he began discussing his concept of "counterparts," which he formally introduces in tonight's [721st] session for "Unknown" Reality. His material enhances my Roman and Jamaican visions [and others]—which saves me considerable effort in figuring them out for myself, of course. And, obviously, Seth does a much better job of putting them all together than I could.

(I'd like to add that I hardly think it a coincidence, however, that within less than a month from my "first Roman," Seth was to initiate a body of information in which he began to clarify many of the questions I had about certain of my own psychic adventures. I don't think those events directly led Seth into beginning his new material, but in retrospect Jane and I agree that they certainly played some considerable part in establishing a foundation, or impetus, for such a development.

(Last Wednesday night's scheduled session wasn't held, giving Jane some rest the day after class. Then yesterday, Sunday, she gave a very long session on her own for a visiting scientist. When I write "on her own," I not only mean that Seth didn't come through, but that Jane wasn't aware of his presence even though she didn't give voice to it.

(Yesterday's "Jane" session seemed to run itself, to take place outside of time as we usually think of that quality. It lasted from 2:00 P.M. until after 12:30 A.M., with interruptions only for a casual supper of scrambled eggs, and an occasional short break. We estimate, then, that in a slightly altered state of consciousness Jane gave impressions for something like nine hours out of the actual ten and a half involved.

(She enjoyed the exchange a great deal; she made sketches while speaking on such subjects as the many facets of the electron and its behavior; time and its variations; gravity, its changes with motion, and its attributes in the past, present, and future; the velocities of light; mathematical equations; astronomy, including perceptions by telescope of the future as well as of the past; the structure of the earth's core; earthquakes and "black" sound/light; language, including glossolalia and her own Sumari; pyramids, coordination points, and so forth. Our guest recorded it all and is to send us a transcript [which he did]. Jane plans to quote parts of it in Psychic Politics.[2] These bits are from her material about gravity and age: "There is a different kind of gravity that surrounds older objects than that which surrounds younger ones, but we don't perceive this at the level of our instruments. We can pick it up, however, if we know where to look. Age affects gravity . . . Older objects are heavier. This is ordinary gravity—not some new kind."

(I asked Jane to write a paragraph about the predominant mode of consciousness she'd experienced during the long session, and here's what she produced:)

"It seems to be an easy natural state for me to take; I go into it 'like a duck takes to water,' I guess, but it's difficult to explain. It's a state in which hardly any resistance is encountered; answers are 'just there.' The only problem is in getting the information across to another person in terms of his or her vocabulary. I enjoy this particular 'alteration of consciousness,' although I don't really recognize it as alien to my regular one; it's just different. It's an accelerated condition mixed with passivity; poised. If [our scientist's] attitude had been critical, I probably wouldn't have done as well, though."

(I'll finish the references to yesterday's session by quoting the comments Seth made at the end of some material we've deleted from the 712th session in Section 4. A few weeks ago, through a magazine we subscribe to, Jane joined a science club. Now each month she receives a little kit to be assembled; this in turn is used to carry out the scientific experiment for the month. Seth: "Ruburt's science kit is something picked up, in your terms, from another probability—in which he learned all there is to know about science as you know it. That is why he can enter into the reality of electrons so easily."[3]

(And separately: Over the weekend Jane remarked more than once that "Unknown" Reality might prove to be so long that it could go into two volumes—a probable development I hardly took seriously. [Her statements turned out to be exactly prophetic, of course, as I noted five months later in the 741st session. Also see the beginning of the Introductory Notes for Volume 1.])

Good evening.

("Good evening, Seth.")

Now: Dictation: When you look into a mirror you see your reflection, but it does not talk back to you. In the dream state you are looking into the mirror of the psyche, so to speak, and seeing the reflections of your own thoughts, fears, and desires.

Here, however, the "reflections" do indeed speak, and take their own form. In a certain sense they are freewheeling, in that they have their own kind of reality. In the dream state your joys and fears talk back to you, perform, and act out the role in which you have cast them.

If, for example, you believe that you are possessed of great inner wealth, you may have a dream about a king in a fine palace. The king actually need not look like you at all, nor need you identify with him in the dream. Symbolically, however, this would represent one way of expressing your feelings. Inner wealth would be interpreted here in the same terms as worldly luxury. The dream, once created, would go its own way. If you have conflicts over the ideas connected with good and evil, or wealth and poverty, then the king might lose his lands or goods, or some catastrophe might befall him.

If you suspect that abundance is somehow spiritually dangerous,[4] then the king might be captured and punished. All kinds of other events might be involved: groups of people, for example, representing bands of "rampaging" desires. The entire drama would involve the "evolution" of an emotion or belief. In the dream state you set it free and see what will happen to it, how it will develop, where it will go.

The reflections of your ideas and intimate emotions are

then projected outward in a rich drama. You can observe the play, take a role in it, or move in and out of its acts as you prefer. You will use your own private symbols. These represent your psychic shorthand. They are connected with your personal creativity, so dream books will not help you in deciphering those meanings if they attach a specific significance to any given symbol. Symbols themselves change. If you had before you your entire dream history and could read—as in a book—the story of all of your dreams from birth, you would discover that you changed the meaning of your symbols as you went along, or as it suited your purposes. The content of a dream itself has much to do with the way you employ any given symbol.

The king, for example, may be at one time the symbol of great inner wealth. He may be kingly but poor, signifying the idea that wealth does not necessarily involve physical goods. He might at another time appear as a dictator, cruel and overbearing, where he would represent an entirely different framework of feeling and belief. He might show himself as a young monarch, signaling a belief that "youth is king." At various times in history the same image has been used quite differently. When people are fighting dictatorial monarchs then often the king appears in dreams as a despicable character, to be booted and routed out.

Give us a moment... Whether or not you remember your dreams, you are educating yourself as they happen. You may suddenly "awaken" while still within the dream state, however, and recognize the drama that you have yourself created. At this point you will understand the fact that the play, while seeming quite real, is to a certain extent hallucinatory. If you prefer, you can clear the stage at once by saying, "I do not like this play, and so I will create it no longer." You may then find yourself facing an empty stage, become momentarily disoriented at the sudden lack of activity, and promptly begin to form another dream play more to your liking.

If, however, you pause first and wait a moment, you can begin to glimpse the environment that serves as a stage: the natural landscape of the dream reality. In waking life, if you want to disconnect yourself from an event or place, you try to move away from it in space. In dream reality events occur in a different fashion, and places spring up about you. If you meet with people or events not of your liking, then you must simply move your attention away from them, and they will disappear as far as your experience is concerned. In physical reality you can move fairly freely through space, but you do not travel from one city to another, for example, unless you want to. Intent is involved. This is so obvious that its significance escapes you: but it is intent that moves you through space, and that is behind all of your physical locomotion. You utilize ships, automobiles, trains, airplanes, because you want to go to another place, and certain vehicles work best under certain conditions.

(9:53.) In the waking state you travel to places. They do not come to you. In dream reality, however, your intent causes places to spring up about you. They come to you, instead of the other way around. You form and attract "places," or a kind of inner space in which you then have certain experiences.

This inner space does not "displace" normal space, or knock it aside. Yet the creation of a definite inner environment or location is concerned.

Those of you who are curious, try this experiment.

PRACTICE ELEMENT 15

In a dream, attempt to expand whatever space you find yourself in. If you are in a room, move from it into another one. If you are on a street, follow it as far as you can, or turn a corner. Unless you are working out ideas of limitations for your own reasons, you will find that you can indeed expand inner space. There is no point where an end to it need appear.

(Long pause.) The properties of inner space, therefore, are endless. Most people are not this proficient in dream manipulation, but surely some of my readers will be able to remember what I am saying, while they are dreaming. To those people I say: "Look around you in the dream state. Try to expand any location in which you find yourself. If you are in a house, remember to look out the window. And once you walk to that window, a scene will appear. You can walk out of that dream house into another environment; and theoretically at least you can explore that world, and the space within it will expand. There will be no spot in the dream where the environment will cease."

Now: What you think of as exterior space expands in precisely the same manner. In this respect, dream reality faithfully mirrors what you refer to as the nature of the exterior world.

Earth experience, even in your terms, is far more varied than you ever consciously imagine. The intimate life of a person in one country, with its culture, is far different from that of an individual who comes from another kind of culture, with its own ideas of art, history, politics or religion or law. Because you focus upon similarities of necessity, then the physical world possesses its coherence.[5]

There are unknown gulfs that separate the private experience of a poor Indian, a rich Indian, a native in New Guinea, an American tailor, an African nationalist, a Chinese aristocrat, an Irish housewife. These differences cannot be objectively stated. They bring about qualitative differences, however, in the experience of space and time.

There are jet travelers and those who have never seen a train, so your own system of reality contains vast contrasts. The dream state, however, involves you with a kind of communication that is not physically practical, for there *(intently)* no man or woman is caught without a given role; no individual's ideas in the dream state are limited by his or her cultural background, or physical experience.

Even those who have never seen an airplane can travel from place to place in the twinkling of an eye, and the poor are fed, the ignorant are wise, the sick are well. The creativity that may be physically hampered is expressed. It is true that the hungry man, awakening, is still hungry. The ill may awaken no healthier than they were before. In deeper terms, however, in the dream state each person will be working out his or her own problems or challenges. Dreaming, a person can cure himself or herself of a disease, working through the problems that caused it. Dreaming, the hungry individual can discover ways to find food, or to procure the money to buy it. Dreaming is a practical activity. If it were understood as such, it would be even more practical in your terms.

Animals also dream, for example, and whole herds of starving animals will be led by their dreams to find better feeding grounds. In the same way, the dreams of starving people point toward the solution of the problem. Such data are largely ignored, however. *(With emphasis:)* In the dream state any individual can find the solution to whatever challenge exists.

The great natural cooperation that exists between the waking and the dreaming self has been mostly set aside. The conscious mind is quite equipped to interpret dream information.

You may take your break.

(10:26 to 10:39.

(Humorously:) You forget that dreaming is a part of life. You have disconnected it in your thoughts, at least, from your daily experience, so that dreams seem to have no practical application.

You live in a waking and dreaming mental environment, however. In both environments you are conscious.

Give us a moment . . . Your dream experience represents a pivotal reality, like the center of a wheel. Your physical world is one spoke. You are united with all of your other simultaneous existences through the nature of the dream state. The unknown reality is there presented to your view, and there is no biological, mental, or psychic reason why you cannot learn to use and understand your own dreaming reality.

In your dreams, in your terms, you find your personal past appearing in the present, so in those terms the past of the species also occurs. *(Long pause.)* Future probabilities are worked out there also so that individually and *en masse* the species decides upon its probable future. There is a feeling, held by many, that a study of dream reality will lead you further away from the world you know. Instead, it would connect you with that world in most practical terms.

I said *(in connection with Practice Element 15)* that inner space expands, but so does inner <u>time</u>. Those of you who can remember, try the following experiment.

PRACTICE ELEMENT 16

When you find yourself within a dream, tell yourself <u>you will know what happened before you entered it</u>, and the past will grow outward from that moment. Again, there will be no place where time will stop. The time in a dream does not "displace" physical time. It opens up from it. Exterior time, again, operates in the same fashion, though you do not realize it.

(Pause at 10:52.) Give us a moment . . . Now *(with a smile)*:

The following material may be used here in our book, or in your own book.[6] There will be no gap in <u>this</u> book if you do not use it here.[7]

Time expands in all directions, and away from any given point.[8] The past is never done and finished, and the future is never concretely <u>formed</u>. You choose to experience certain versions of events. You then organize these, nibbling at them, so to speak, a bit "at a time."

The creativity of any given entity is endless, and yet all of the potentials for experience will be explored. The poor man may dream he is a king. A queen, weary of her role, may dream of being a peasant girl. In the physical time that <u>you</u> recognize, the king is still a king, and the queen a queen. Yet their dreams are not as uncharacteristic or apart from their experiences as it might appear. In greater terms, the king has been a pauper and the queen a peasant. You follow in terms of continuity one <u>version</u> of yourself at any given "time."

Many people realize intuitively that the self is multitudinous and not singular. The realization is usually put in reincarnational terms, so that the self is seen as traveling through the centuries, moving through doors of death and life into other times and places.

The fact is that the basic nature of reality shows itself in the nature of the dream state quite clearly, where in any given night you may find yourself undertaking many roles simultaneously. You may change sex, social position, national or religious alliance, age, and yet know yourself as yourself.

Lately Joseph has found himself embarked upon a series of episodes that seem to involve reincarnational existences. There was a catch, however. He saw himself as a woman—black. Last month he also saw himself as a Roman soldier aboard a slave ship. He previously had experience that convinced him that he was a man called Nebene.[9] All of this could have been accepted quite easily in conventional terms of reincarnation, but Joseph felt that Nebene and the Roman soldier had existed during the same general time period, and he was not sure where to place the woman *(but see Note 1)*.

In all of these episodes definite emotional experience was involved. Also connected was an indefinable but unmistakable sense of familiarity. Space and time continually expand, and all probabilities of any given action are actualized in one reality or another. All of the potentials of the entity are also actualized.

(11:11.) Give us a moment... Quite literally, you live more than one life at a time. You do not experience your century simply from one separate vantage point, and the individuals alive in any given century have far deeper connections than you realize. *(Intently:)* You do not experience your space-time world, then, from one but from many viewpoints.

(Pause at 11:13.) If you are glutted—sated—with a steak dinner, for example, in America or Europe, then you are also famished in another portion of the world, experiencing life from an entirely different viewpoint. You speak of races of men. You do not understand how consciousness is distributed in that regard. You have counterparts[10] of yourself.

Give us a moment... Generally speaking, the people living within any given century are related in terms of consciousness and identity. This is true biologically and spiritually, through inter-relationships you do not understand.

Joseph was "picking up" on lives that "he" lived in the same time scheme. In this way and in your terms, he was beginning to recognize the familyship that exists between individuals who share your earth at any given time.

(11:20.) Give us a moment... because this is difficult to explain....

Each identity has free will, and chooses its environment as

a physical <u>stance</u> in space and time. Those involved in a given century are working on particular problems and challenges. Various races do not simply "happen," and diverse cultures do not just appear. The greater self "divides" itself, materializing in flesh as several individuals, with entirely different backgrounds—yet with each embarked upon the same kind of creative challenge.

The black man is somewhere a white man or woman <u>in your time</u>. The white man or woman is somewhere black. The oppressor is somewhere the oppressed. The conqueror is somewhere the conquered. The primitive is somewhere sophisticated— and, in your terms, somewhere on the face of the same earth in your general time. The murderer is somewhere the victim, and the other way around—and again, in <u>your</u> terms of space and time.

Each will choose his or her own framework, according to the intents of the consciousness of which each of you is an independent part. In such a fashion are the challenges and opportunities inherent in a given "time" worked out.

You are counterparts of yourselves, but as Ruburt would say *(amused)*, living "eccentric"[11] counterparts, each with your own abilities. So Joseph "was" Nebene, a scholarly man, not adventurous, obsessed with copying ancient truths, and afraid that creativity was error; authoritative and demanding. He feared sexual encounter, and he taught rich Roman children.

At the same time, in the same world and in the same century, Joseph was an aggressive, adventurous, relatively insensitive Roman officer, who would have little understanding of manuscripts or records—yet who also followed authority without question.[12]

In your terms, Joseph is now a man who questions authority, stamps upon it and throws it aside, who rips apart the very idea structures to which he "once" gave such service.

In greater terms, these experiences all occur at once. The black woman followed nothing but her own instincts *(and very vividly, too)*. I do not want to give too much background here, and hence rob our Joseph of discoveries that he will certainly make on his own— but *(louder)* the woman bowed only to the authority of her own emotions, and those emotions automatically put her in conflict with the [British colonial] politics of the times.

Give us a moment . . . Joseph's focus of identity is his own. He will follow it. He was <u>not</u> Nebene, or the Roman officer or the woman. Yet they are versions of what he <u>is</u>, and he is a version of what they "were," and at certain levels each is aware of the others. There is constant interaction.[13]

The Roman soldier dreams of the black woman, and of Joseph. There is a reminiscence that appears even in the knowledge of the cells, and a certain correspondence.[14] There are connections then as far as cellular recollection is concerned, and dreams. Now the Roman soldier and Nebene and the woman went their separate ways after death, colon: They contributed to the world as it existed, in those terms, and then followed their own lines of development, elsewhere, in other realities. So each of you exists in many times and places, and versions of yourselves exist in the world and time that you recognize. As you are part of a physical species, so you are a part of a species of consciousness. That species forms the races of mankind that you recognize.

Now: Give us a moment . . . and shortly we will end. This material is indeed endless *(as Jane had remarked at break).*

(11:44. Seth proceeded to deliver a block of material for Jane and me, which is deleted from this record. At 12:06 he presumably closed out the session, after remarking that I had access to as much energy as he did. I said good night. Then Jane told me that Seth could "continue forever"—whereupon he returned to touch upon Jane's and my reincarnational "history" from another angle:)

Now: In your terms only, [neither of] you . . . has a reincarnational future. Give us a moment . . . You have accepted this as your breaking-off point. In other terms there are three future lives, but your greater intents, as of now, break you off from this system of reality, and you have already journeyed, both of you, into another; and from that other reality I speak. In those terms I am a part of both of your realities. Think of this in terms of other information given this evening, and you may see what I mean.[15]

(End at 12:08 A.M. Jane's trances had been excellent.

("Well," I said after discussing the session with her, "it's my understanding that our whole self or entity experiences a group of simultaneous physical lives in various historical periods, and that in ordinary terms we think of those lives as following one after another. That includes so-called future lives, too. But each of those incarnations will have its cluster of counterpart lives, revolving around it like planets around a sun. Within that context, of course, each counterpart personality thinks of itself as being the sun, or the center of things. . . ."[16] Yawning, Jane agreed.

(I fell asleep almost at once when we went to bed. Sitting up beside me, though, smoking a cigarette, Jane got more material on reincarnation and counterparts. "In fact," she told me the next morning, "I was getting stuff on 'Unknown' Reality each time I woke up during the night. I was also reading solid copy in the dream state." In those cases she received the material "herself," while knowing that it came from Seth.

(Jane's own counterpart material included variations of Seth's basic concept. Here's one of her examples as she described it to me: "We can span a period like a century if we want to. We can be a child at one end of it and an old man or woman at the other . . . Michelangelo [who lived for 89 years, from 1475 to 1564] decided to span a century himself, instead of as three counterparts, say. Since there aren't any laws about all of this, a great man could choose to do it that way in order to affect our world more with his gifts, from his own personal angles. He wouldn't necessarily want or need the counterparts, at least for those purposes. He'd have more than enough to offer on his own."

(This session on counterparts represents a key point in Seth's discussion of the unknown reality. The reader is directed to Appendix 21 for related material from the recent past, which anticipated tonight's new concept. Some earlier intimations of the counterpart concept are also briefly discussed there.)

NOTES: Session 721

1. The series of visions that made up my overall perception of the black woman in Jamaica were the most vivid I've experienced yet. For me they had a most unique, thrilling, immediate quality, and strong emotional involvement. As I sat at the typewriter in my studio, I was flooded with perceptions of myself as such a woman: Pursued by an armed English military officer, she ran for her life down a hilly village street. She wasn't especially young. Her—my—name? Maumee, or Mawmee—an illiterate but shrewd, very strong personality who was acting in rebellion against the colonial authority of England in the early 1800's. She escaped that time, and lived to struggle often against such forces on the island.

After the experience was over I wrote a description of it, and made two pen-and-ink drawings—full-face self-portraits that hardly look like the me I know. One of the drawings is very successful, and I plan to do an oil painting from it.

I'm most gratified that some of the Jamaican visions were externalized, that I didn't see all of them within as I did for the Roman series. That is, with open eyes I *saw* fleeting hectic images in the studio. I *felt* emotions. I was exhilarated by the whole thing.

And added later: Jane presented my account of the Maumee episode, as well as portions of the 721st session itself, in Chapter 12 of *Politics*.

2. And eventually Jane did describe her day's work in *Politics*. See the opening pages of Chapter 11.

3. Both Jane and I think Seth's statement, that in another probability "Ruburt . . . learned all there is to know about science . . ." is pretty strong, but since it came through that way we let it stand. However, as Jane wrote later in Chapter 11 of *Politics*: "Finding out what's happening

to electrons, say, is something I really enjoy. I admit I feel much more free than I do when I have people's emotions to deal with. I'd rather 'find' a lost electron than a lost person any day, for example."

In Volume 1 of *"Unknown" Reality*, see her material on electron spin in the 702nd session after 10:22.

4. See the first two sessions in Chapter 13 of *Personal Reality*.

5. See Appendix 12. In it I quote Seth from the class session for June 23, 1970, as excerpted in the Appendix for *Seth Speaks*: "In this reality, [each of] you very nicely emphasize all the similarities which bind you together; you make a pattern of them, and you very nicely ignore all the dissimilarities . . . If you were able to focus your attention on the dissimilarities, merely those that you can perceive but do not, then you would be amazed that mankind can form any idea of an organized reality."

6. Here Seth refers to *Through My Eyes*—the book he suggested (in December 1972) that I write on the Seth phenomenon and other subjects. In Volume 1, see item No. 3 at 11:35, in Session 683. Replying to all of those who have asked: So far I haven't had the time to do more than short essays on art, Seth, the fairly recent deaths of my parents, and a few other topics for *Through My Eyes*. Certainly I won't be able to work steadily on the project until Volume 2 of *"Unknown" Reality* is ready for publication.

7. A note added later: Considering what was to come in *"Unknown" Reality*, though, I'm very glad I *did* decide to present "the following material" here.

8. See the quotations from Seth about the moment point in Note 11 for Appendix 12. One of the references also included in that note can be traced back to his material on reincarnation, moment points, and dreams in the 668th session for Chapter 19 of *Personal Reality*.

9. In those terms, my supposed "Nebene" life took place in Greece, Palestine, Rome, and other locations in the Middle East during the earlier part of the first century A.D. See Chapter 5 of Jane's *Adventures in Consciousness*.

10. This note is as much for my own edification as it is for anyone else's. The definitions are from *Webster's New World Dictionary of the American Language*, Second College Edition, © 1970 by The World Publishing Company, New York and Cleveland:

counterpart 1. a person or thing that corresponds to or closely resembles another, as in form or function 2. a thing which, when added to another, completes or complements it 3. a copy or duplicate, as of a lease

11. With some humor, Seth borrowed the word "eccentric" from Jane's own *Psychic Politics*. In her book she uses the term in connection with personality, to mean that each physical self is a creative—and unpredictable—version of an inner "heroic" model.

12. My Roman-soldier self might have "followed authority without question," as Seth states in this (721st) session, yet he must have behaved with more than a little guile. In a private session held some time after he'd finished *"Unknown" Reality*, Seth again referred to the Roman—

doing so because of additional material I'd produced about that first-
century personality. Seth:

"As a Roman, you pretended to be a follower while you were a
man of rank in the military. You had no belief in the conventional gods, yet
you were supposed to be conquering lands in their names. You traveled
even to Africa. You had a disdain for leaders as liars, and of the masses as
followers, and so you were always in one kind of dispute or another with
your fellows, and even with the authorities. You were of a querulous nature,
yet highly curious, and, again, physically involved.

"Your curiosity did not concern philosophies, but had to do
with the physical world, and particularly with its water passageways. . . ."

I've also accumulated more graphic information about my
other first-century counterpart, Nebene. Eventually I hope to discuss all of
my reincarnational data in *Through My Eyes*. (See Note 6.)

13. The "constant interaction" that Seth mentioned as involving
myself, Nebene, the Roman soldier, and the black woman, Maumee,
obviously takes place on other-than-usual conscious levels—at least in my
case, that is. For while I was having experience as the Roman, for instance, I
had no feeling for Nebene, or Maumee—no idea of reincarnation, or of
counterparts either. Each "time" I tuned in to one of those personalities I was
too caught up in that particular role to be aware of any of the others. Now,
however, as I write this I can at least feel ideas about them in the back of my
mind. . . .

14. For one example of Jane and Seth on cellular memory
(among other subjects), see the 653rd session as it bridges chapters 13 and
14 in *Personal Reality*. Jane also discussed some of the material in that session
in Chapter 17 of *Adventures*.

15. In Appendix 18 I discussed to some extent the relationships involving Jane, Seth, and me. I chose not to study this paragraph of
material in Appendix 18 because in it Seth mentions what I take to be
probable lives involving Jane and me (when he speaks of our future lives),
rather than reincarnational involvements we've had with Seth that "actually
happened."

Seth refers to evocative situations here, though—one of them
possibly being a kind of counterpart relationship among the three of us in
another reality.

16. As Jane wrote in Chapter 16 of *Adventures*: "In one way,
each person *is* at the center of the universe and at the center of the psyche."

Session 722
November 27, 1974
9:18 P.M. Wednesday

("C'mon, Seth," Jane said impatiently at 9:15; we'd been waiting since 9:00 for the session to begin. "I feel stuff there, but I haven't got it clear yet. . . ." Then:)

Good evening.

("Good evening, Seth.")

(Quietly:) I told you to take a moment while you were within a particular dream, and to use it to try to discover what had been happening within the dream before you experienced it.[1]

(Still quietly:) It is true that you create your own dreams, but it is also true that you only focus upon certain portions of your dream creations. Even in the dream state, any present expands into its own version of past and future; so in those terms the dream possesses its own background, its <u>own kind</u> (underlined) of historic past, the moment you construct it.

You need not experience those past dream events, although if you just turn your attention in that direction then the dream's past will become apparent. Mental impressions of any kind therefore are not simply imprinted, or written, as it were, in a medium of space and time. They have a greater dimensionality. The past and future ripple outward from any event, making it "thicker" than it appears to be.

In greater terms, the past is definitely created from the present. In your system of reality this does not seem to be the case at all, since your senses project a forward kind of motion outward upon events. "Subatomic particles," however, appear in your present, rippling into your system's dimensions, creating their own "tracks," which scientists then try to observe. In some cases, unknowingly, your scientists are close to observing the birth of time effects within your system. (Pause.) Since your brains are composed of cells with their atoms and molecules, and since these are themselves made of certain invisible particles,[2] then your memories are already structured by the biological mechanisms that make them possible in your terms. (In parentheses: After death, for example, you still possess a memory, though it does not operate through the physical organism as you understand it.)

Psychologically, then, while you are living your memories follow a pattern of past into present. It seems, therefore, quite inconceivable that in certain terms any present event can bring about a memory of a similar event that occurred before, while instead each actually occurs at once.

Give us a moment ... In the dream state, the freedom of events from time as you understand it can be more apparent. If you are alert and curious while dreaming (and you can learn to be), then you can catch yourself in the act of creating a dream's past and future at once.

Give us a moment ... Physicists know that waves can appear as particles upon certain conditions, and that particles can behave like waves.[3] So moments as you understand them are like waves experienced as "particles"—as small bubbles, for example, each one breaking and another forming. Subatomic particles also behave like waves sometimes; in fact, it is usually only when they act like particles that they are perceived at all.

(9:42.) Physicists think of atoms as particles. Their wave-like characteristics are not observed. At other levels of reality, atoms behave in a wavelike manner ... Give us a moment ... Subjectively, you will think of your own thoughts as waves rather than as particles. Yet in the dream level of reality those waves "break" into particles, so to speak. They form pseudo-objects from your viewpoint. While dreaming you accept that reality as real. Only upon awakening do the dream objects seem not-real, or imaginary. The nervous system itself is biologically equipped to perceive various gradations of physical matter, and there are "in-between" impulse passageways that are utilized while dreaming. From your point of view these are alternate passageways, but in the dream state they allow you to perceive as physical matter objects that in the waking state would not be observable.

Again, from the waking standpoint these other neurological recognitions could be thought of as ghost or trace methods of perception. Waking, you do not usually use them. They are utilized to some extent in daydreaming, however, and in certain alterations of consciousness while you perceive as real, or nearly real, events that are not immediately happening within your space-time structure.

Give us a moment . . . The dream world is as organized as your own, but from the waking state you do not focus upon that inner organization. Your dream images exist. They are quite as real as a table or a chair. They are built up from particles, invisible only from the waking situation.

Physicists are beginning to study the characteristics of "invisible" particles.[4] They seem to defy space and time principles. This is precisely why they form the basis for dream reality, semicolon; why objects in a dream can appear and disappear.

In your physical universe such particles are invisible components, deduced but never directly encountered. To a certain extent they are latent. In some other realities, however, their characteristics rule rather than the attributes of the visible particles that you see. Dream images, therefore, exist at a different range of matter.

You may take your break.

(10:01. Jane's trance had been good, but still she'd been bothered by the sounds of traffic rising up from the busy intersection close by our living room windows. Someone had made considerable noise while cleaning the halls of the apartment house, also — ". . . all while Seth wanted me to get that material just right," Jane said a bit ruefully. "Maybe I can get better at it, but you need such a fine control. . . ." Finally she laughed. "I don't know who's going to read this book, but they'll sure find a lot in it to study."

(Resume in a slower manner at 10:26.)

Now: Many of these invisible particles *(CU's)* can be in more than one place at a time—a fact that quite confounds the physically tuned brain perceiving a world in which objects stay where they are supposed to be.

(Pause.) Basically, however, each "appearance" of such a particle is a self-version, for it is altered to some extent by its

"location." Period. So can the human self appear in several places at once,[5] each such appearance subtly altering the "human" particle, so that each appearance is a version of an "original" self that <u>as</u> itself never appears in those terms.[6] When you look at an electron— figuratively speaking—you are observing a trace or a track of something else entirely, and that appearance is termed an electron. So the self that you know is a physical trace or intrusion into space and time of an "original" self that never appears. In a way, then, you are as ghostly as an electron.

  The unknown self, the "original self," <u>straddles</u> realities, dipping in and out of them in creative versions of itself, taking on the properties of the system in which it appears, and the characteristics native to that environment. Waves and particles are versions of other kinds of behavior taken by energy. Using that analogy, you flow in wavelike fashion into the physical particleized versions that you call corporal existences.

  Give us a moment... I am putting this as simply as possible; but when your "original self" enters [part of] itself into three-dimensional life from an inner reality, the energy waves carrying it break—not simply into one particle, following our analogy, but into a number of conscious particles. In certain terms these are built up using the medium at hand—the biological properties of the earth. They spread out from the "point of contact," forming individual lives. In your conception of the centuries, then, there are other counterparts of yourself living at the same time and in different places—all creative versions of the original self. There is a great intimate cooperation that exists biologically and spiritually between all of the beings on your planet "at any given time." You are all connected psychically in terms of inner and outer structures. A certain identity and cohesiveness is also maintained because of these inner connections.

  (10:51.) There are psychic structures quite as effective as physical ones, and these underlie the reality of your objective world. They merge together beautifully to form an inner picture of the world at any given "time," even while that picture is ever-changing. In greater terms, the picture of your world at any given time can be compared to the position, behavior, and characteristics of an invisible particle as it is "caught" intruding into your reality.

  Your dream adventures, however exciting, remain "invisible" from your waking standpoint. Within dreams space and time expand, again, as I have mentioned,[7] but in a way that you cannot physically pinpoint. Your own exterior space exists in precisely the same manner from the standpoint of <u>any other reality</u> (emphatically). For that matter, you yourself are so richly creative that your own thoughts give birth to other quite legitimate systems of which you have no knowledge.

Take the break.

(11:00. Seth's words just above, ". . . your own thoughts give birth . . ." reminded me of one of my favorite passages from Seth Speaks. *While discussing probabilities in the 565th session for Chapter 16 of that book, he said: "Each mental act opens up a new dimension of actuality. In a manner of speaking, your slightest thought gives birth to worlds."*[8] *I also found an opportunity to insert the same lines in Chapter 10 of* Personal Reality; *see the 641st session.*

(Resume at 11:17.)

Now: You are each members of a particular race, and you do not feel any the less individualistic because of that affiliation.

You consider yourselves, further, members of a species. The races are alive together at any given time on your earth in varying proportions, so there are physical organizations, biologically speaking, that you recognize. You do not feel threatened because you do not have your particular race to yourself. So there are inner psychic "races" to which you belong, or psychic <u>stocks</u>, so to speak, each providing physical variations.[9]

In those terms each living person has other counterparts of himself or herself alive, generally speaking, at the same time, sharing the physical face of the earth. There are psychic pools of identity, therefore; and generally speaking those alive in any given century are as much a part of that inner pool as they are a part of the particular race to which they may belong. Each member of the species is an individual, and each member of a psychic pool of identity is an individual.

Again, your idea of personhood limits you when you think of these concepts. You imagine personhood to be a kind of mental particle that must have definite boundaries, or it will lose its identity. The identity of even the smallest consciousness is always maintained—but not limited. If you can think of your present idea of identity as if it were but one shape or one motion of a moving particle, a shape or a motion that never loses its <u>imprint</u> or meaning, then you could also see how you could follow it forward or backward to the shape or motion taken "before or afterward."

You could retain the identity of yourself as you know yourself, and yet flow into a greater field or wave of reality that allowed you to perceive your own other motions or shapes or versions. You could become aware of a larger structure in which you also have your own validity, and therefore add to your own knowledge and to the dimensions of your experience.[10]

You can do this the easiest way, perhaps, by observing

yourself in the dream state, for there you create versions of yourself constantly. In the morning you are enriched, not diminished.

Give us a moment... *(Humorously, to me:)* You are the living version of yourself in space and time, around which your world revolves.[11] The great potentiality that exists in the unknown self, however, also actualizes other such focuses, and in the same space-time framework. They are not you, any more than you are the black man, or the white woman, or the Indian woman, or the Chinese man.

(Intently:) As certain races possess their own characteristics and shared biological background, and come from the same biological pool, however, so these counterparts come from the same psychic pool, and physically seed the members of the races at any given "time." In such a way mental abilities and propensities are given a greater range, and distributed about the earth.

(Heartily:) End of dictation. And end of session, unless you have questions.

("No, I guess not.")

I answered some of them.

("Yes." Here Seth referred to some comments about reincarnation and counterparts that I'd made to Jane this evening at the supper table.)

I bid you then a fond good evening. My heartiest wishes... Have him *(Jane)* read the latest material I gave for him *(which we'd deleted from its spot at 11:44 in the last session)* every day until our next one.

("Okay, Seth. Thank you very much. Good night."

(11:43 P.M. An aside: Lately I'd delayed typing these sessions from my notes because I've been so busy doing the finished pen-and-ink drawings for Jane's Dialogues. *Currently I'm working on the 12th one out of the 40 planned. Jane hasn't had a book session to read since the 718th, for November 6, was held almost four weeks ago. Now she reminded me that she misses keeping up with Seth's dictation—that she has trouble deciphering my personal shorthand, and that not knowing what Seth has been saying makes her feel "uneasy." This even though she and Seth have demonstrated often by now that as a team they're most capable of producing a work "blind," as it were, and on a continuing basis. But I'd become so involved with artwork that I hadn't appreciated her own interests and concerns.*

(During the whole of last month [October] Jane also had to go without reading a block of sessions [708–15] in Section 4; I used the time I'd have spent typing them to complete the diagrams for Adventures. *Tonight we decided, then, that from my notes I'd begin reading to her the four sessions following the 718th. Once we were caught up, I'd read her the Seth material received each week on the succeeding Saturday or Sunday until I got back to the*

twice-weekly routine of transcribing, early next year; I expect to do the last of the Dialogues *illustrations late in January 1975.)*

NOTES: Session 722

1. See Practice Element 16 in the 721st session.

2. For some background information on Seth's basic units of consciousness (CU's), cells, probabilities, time structures and other material in connection with his delivery here, I suggest reviewing these sessions in Volume 1 of *"Unknown" Reality:* 682–84, 688, and 694.

3. A number of subjects related to Seth's discussion of waves and particles can be found in the following sources (some of which contain their own references) in Appendix 18: the quotations from the 755th session (Seth: "My own psychological reality is not particleized"), and notes 24 and 35. Then see Note 9 for Appendix 19.

4. I doubt if by his statement Seth means that physicists are attempting to study his CU's (see Note 2)—certainly not yet, although a few scientists who have written us thereby show that they're familiar with Seth's thinking here. Rather, some "modern" physicists are searching for nonmaterial "particles" that certain theories (one of them having to do with "quarks," for example) say should exist if the theories are valid. Such pseudoparticles, then, are mathematical entities that can affect the actions of physical objects.

5. In Volume 1, see Seth's first delivery for the 681st session: "I told you once that there were pulses of activity in which you blinked off and on—this applying even to atomic and subatomic particles." The full session should be reviewed, especially those parts dealing with the "great inner unpredictability of any molecule, atom, or wave. . . ." Also see notes 1 and 2.

6. Several of my drawings in Part Two of *Adventures* relate visually to the idea of an "original self" (or "source self," in Jane's vocabulary) that never appears in physical reality. See diagrams 1, 8, and 14, for instance.

7. See practice elements 15 and 16, plus related material, in the 721st session.

8. Also see Note 3 for Session 713.

9. A note added two months later: In retrospect it's easy to see that while discussing his ideas of counterparts here, Seth was also preparing us for the families-of-consciousness material he was to start giving in January 1975. See the 732nd session in Section 6, for instance. In that session Seth was quickly at pains to say that belonging to a certain family of consciousness did not come first in our reality: "Your individuality comes first."

10. Material in many of the sessions in the first section of Volume 1 touches upon the contents of this paragraph. In the 687th

session, Seth stated: "I am saying that the individual self must become consciously aware of far more reality; that it must allow its recognition of identity to expand . . . move beyond the concepts of one god, one self, one body, one world, as those ideas are currently understood."

And Seth in his Preface for Volume 1: "Here, I wish to make it clear that this book will initiate a journey in which it may seem that the familiar is left far behind. Yet when I am finished, I hope you will discover that the known reality is even more precious, more 'real'. . . ."

11. As Seth, Jane spoke with a smile while staring at me, for I'd voiced the same sentence last night in ESP class.

Session 723
December 2, 1974
9:42 P.M. Monday

Good evening.

(*"Good evening, Seth."*)

Dictation: Your world view is your personalized interpretation of the physical universe.

Your home station[1] does not simply present programming for you to view. Instead you help create the program, of course, even while you are part of it. On any given afternoon certain elements of experience will be "given," roughly sketched in. There are certain cues to set the stage, colon: It may be a snowy, humid, or dry and sunny day, for instance; the location may be city or town. Yet within that loose framework you create the program of the day according to your own world view.

If that view is expansive, then you have far greater leeway in creating your experience. You can add greater depth, so to speak, to the characterization. You can, in other words, take advantage of the unknown reality by letting it add to your home station.

In the dream state you range beyond your waking world view. You are able to bring into focus other interests and activities. These can remain in the background during waking life—or you can decide to enlarge your world view by taking advantage of your dreaming activities. Many of the exercises given here are geared in that direction.

You are not alone in physical reality, so obviously your picture of the world is also affected by the world views of others, and you play a part in their experiences. There is a constant waking give-and-take. The same give-and-take occurs in the dream state, however. You affect your world through your dreams, then, as much as you do through your waking activities. In terms of time, lapses had to occur as various species physically matured and developed. They did so in response to inner impetus. The many languages that are now known originated in what you can call, from your point of view, nonwaking reality. Words, again, are related to the neurological structure, and languages follow that pattern. In the dream state many kinds of communication occur, and there are inner translations. Two people with different languages can speak together quite clearly in certain dreams, and understand each other perfectly. They may each translate the communication into their familiar language.

Undernearth this, however, there are basic inner sounds upon which all language is based, in which certain images give forth their own sound, and the two together portray clear, precise meaning.[2] A long time ago I said that language would be impossible were it not for its basis in telepathic communication[3]—and that communication is built up of microscopic images and sounds. These are translated into different languages.

Consciously, then, your world view is affected by the language of your culture or country. Certain sounds, inflections, and expressions, taken together, have a more or less precise meaning. The meaning is usually quite specific, and often directional. Words in a language function not only by defining what a specific object is, for example, but also by defining what it is not.[4]

(10:05.) To some extent in the dream state, you are freed of such cultural leanings. In the most effective of dreams experience is actually more direct, in that it is less limited by language concepts. Waking, you generally become familiar with your thoughts through words that are mental, automatically translating your thoughts into language. Your thoughts therefore fall, or flow, into prefabricated forms. In the dream state, however, thoughts are often experienced directly, colon: "You live" them out. You become what they are. They are projected instantly and in such a fashion. They escape the limitations that you often place upon them. That is why it is frequently difficult to remember your dreams in a verbal fashion, or squeeze them back into the expression of usual language. Period. Your language often purposely inhibits meaning.

Give us a moment... To some extent language <u>does</u> make the unknown known and recognizable. It sets up signposts that each person in a culture recognizes. To do this, however, it latches upon certain significances and ignores others. You might know the word for "rock," for instance. Knowing the word might actually prevent you from seeing any specific rock clearly as it is, or recognizing how it is different from all other rocks.

The play of sunlight or shadow upon any given rock may utterly escape you.[5] You will simply pass it by under the category of "rock." In the dream state you might find yourself sleeping on a sun-warmed rock, or climbing on icy ones. You might feel yourself encased in a rock, with your consciousness dispersed. You might have any number of different experiences involving rocks, all quite liberating. After such an experience you might look at rocks in an entirely different fashion, and see them in ways that escape your language. Rocks give forth sounds that you do not hear, for example, yet your language automatically limits your perception of what any rock is. To some extent words come between you and your direct expression. They should and can <u>express</u> that experience instead.

Take your break.

(10:22. Jane said her trance hadn't been good. "I was inhibited by all kinds of things—noises, mostly. I hope they didn't make me interfere with the material. Was there more noise than usual?"

(She has excellent hearing, so if her trance hadn't been as deep as usual, for whatever reasons, then even ordinary sounds might disrupt her. I told Jane that Seth's information was as penetrating as ever. I also reminded her that the house was actually quieter than it usually is. A wet snow had started after supper and we'd shut our windows, thus cutting down on the rumble and clatter of automobile traffic.

(Seth's remarks about inner sounds were quite interesting in view of an episode that had taken place 10 minutes or so before the session started. As we made ready for it in our living room, Jane became aware of a faint buzzing—a sound I couldn't hear. She repeatedly exclaimed over this noise until, investigating, we located its source high up in a far corner: a small insect moving among the leaves of our philodendron vines. We've encouraged the plants to grow up a set of poles that reach from the top of a bookcase to the ceiling. [The whole structure serves as a modest room divider, shielding the living room from the hall entrance to the apartment.]

("Well, I think it's going to be a short session," she finally laughed.

*"I feel restless—like going for a walk in the snow or something. . . ." But the
session hardly proved to be a short one. In connection with the practice element
that Seth gives below, plus the following two paragraphs of related information,
I'd like the reader to refer to chapters 7 and 8 in Jane's* Adventures in
Consciousness. *In them she discussed the development of her Sumari
"language."*

(Resume at 10:43.)

PRACTICE ELEMENT 17

Part of the unknown reality, then, is hidden beneath
language and the enforced pattern of accustomed words—so, for an
exercise, look about your environment. Make up new, different
"words" for the objects that you see about you. Pick up any object,
for example. Hold it for a few seconds, feel its texture, look at its
color, and spontaneously give it a new name by uttering the sounds
that come into your mind. See how the sounds bring out certain
aspects of the object that you may not have noticed before.

The new word will fit as much as the old one did. It may, in
fact, fit better. Do this with many objects, following the same procedure. You can instead say the name of any object backwards.[6] In
such ways you break up to some extent the automatic patterning of
familiar phrases, so that you can perceive the individuality that is
within each object.

To get in direct contact with your own feelings as they are,
comma, again make up your own spontaneous sounds sometimes.
Your emotions often cannot be expressed clearly in terms of language, and such unpatterning can allow them to flow freely.

The freshness of dream experience lies in its direct nature.
Your cultural world view does not have any clear understanding of
the nature of dreams, so that their direct, clear expression is not
recalled often in the morning. *(Pause.)* At night you tune in to
dreaming reality simply by closing out so-called waking reality, but
the same kind of dream experience continues beneath your focus in
waking life. Dreaming, you are still aware of your daily experience,
but it is seemingly peripheral. Waking, your dream experience is
peripheral also, but you are less aware of that condition. Both
together represent the dimensions of your consciousness, and they
exist simultaneously. You can and often do work out in dreams the
challenges of daily life. In waking life you are also working out
challenges set for yourselves in the dream state. Obviously, then,
your consciousness is equipped to function in the known and unknown realities, and the divisions that you have set up are quite
arbitrary.

(Pause at 11:01.) You may understand that many of your

dreams have a symbolic meaning. It may escape you, however, that the objects with which you surround yourself in physical life also have symbolic meanings—only these are three-dimensional. You may spend time trying to understand the nature of dreams and their implications, without ever realizing that your physical life is to some extent a three-dimensional dream. It will faithfully mirror your dream images at any given time.

Your physical life and your dreaming life are so intimately connected that it can be misleading to say what I am about to say, colon: that waking experience springs from the unknown dream reality. On the one hand the statement is indeed true. On the other hand, the intricate inner workings make it impossible to separate one from the other. "Reality" operates basically, however, in a way that is perceived more clearly in the dream state. Freedom from time and place, the wider kind of communication, the great mobility of consciousness—all of these experiences under dreaming conditions are characteristic of the basic nature of reality—whereas your waking experience provides limitations that are indicators of certain conditions only. Period.

To some extent the greater expression of consciousness can be experienced under usual waking conditions, but only when a personality is flexible enough and secure enough to alter the focus of consciousness. This way, other unperceived data become available. The unknown reality is not beyond your experience, therefore. Any of your scientific or religious disciplines could benefit from a study of the dreaming consciousness, for there the basic nature of reality exists as clearly as you can perceive it. The inner condition of dreaming is valid. You find yourselves in other times and places because basically neither time nor space exists as you suppose.[7]

There are no basic dangers involved in alterations of consciousness without drugs, but artificial dangers can occur because of your cultural beliefs. These result because such individuals find themselves with no acceptable framework in which to correlate or understand their experiences. They try to fall back upon religious or scientific or pseudoscientific explanations.[8]

In a way, the one-line kind of consciousness that you have developed can be correlated with your use of any one language. Experience is programmed, highly specialized, and attains a seemingly tight organization only because (intently) it limits so much of reality. In those terms, if you are bilingual you are somewhat better off, for your thoughts have a choice of two paths. Biologically, you are physically capable of speaking any language now in use on the face of the earth. You would consider it an achievement if you learned to speak many languages. You would not find it frightening or unnatural, though you would take it for granted that some training was involved. In the same way, your one-line kind of consciousness is but one of many "languages." The others are as native, as natural, as biologically feasible.

(11:18.) Ruburt has been involved with what he calls the Sumari language *(as referred to in the notes at break)*. This is an expression of the consciousness at a different focus. It is the native expression of a kind of experience that happens just outside of your official one-line focus of consciousness. First of all, it breaks up verbal patterning.[9] It is composed, however, of sounds and syllables Ruburt has heard before, made up of jumbled Romance languages.[10] These are "foreign" as far as he is concerned. At the same time those sounds are, in your terms, filled with the implications of antiquity, and bring up connotations of the species' and of the psyche's past.

(Pause.) They alter the usual physical response to meaningful sound. You may not realize it, but your language actually structures your <u>visual</u> perception of objects. Sumari breaks down the usual patterning, therefore, but it also releases the nervous system from its structured response to any particular stimulus. The sounds, however, while spontaneous, are not unstructured. They will present a sound equivalent of the emotion or object perceived, an equivalent that is very direct and immediate, and that bears legitimate correspondence with the object or emotion.

The fresh expression sets up a new kind of relationship between the so-called perceiver and the perceived. The Sumari then becomes a bridge between two different kinds of consciousness; and returning to his usual state, Ruburt can translate from the Sumari to English.

The English itself, however, then becomes charged, freshened with new concepts, carrying within a strangeness that itself alters the relationship of the words. This is a dream or trance language. It is as native to its level of consciousness as English is to your own—or Indian, or Chinese, or whatever. The various focuses of consciousness will have their own "languages." Ruburt has discovered that beneath the Sumari there are deeper meanings.[11] He has become aware of what he calls long and short sounds. Some come so quickly that he cannot keep track, or speak them quickly enough. Others are so slow that he feels a sentence would take a week to utter.[12] These are the signatures of different focuses of consciousness as they are transposed in your space-time system.

(Pause at 11:43.) Languages express certain kinds of reality, usually by organizing experience verbally and mentally. In your

case, again, a certain neurological prejudice occurs. If you experienced greater instances of out-of-body consciousness, for example, then your verbal expressions of space and time would automatically change. If you became aware of more of your dreaming experience, your language would automatically expand. Again automatically, you would also become aware of other neurological patterns than those you use. These *(intently)*, activated, would then be picked up by your scientific instruments, and therefore change your ideas in such fields.

(*Long pause.*) Many people find themselves singing "gibberish" when they are alone, and trying to free themselves from language structuring. Children often play by constructing their own languages; and speaking with tongues *(glossolalia)* is a beautiful example of the attempt to express a reality that escapes the tyranny of overly structured words.

Music is a language. Painting is a language. The senses have a language of their own—one that seeps into structured words but dimly.

Give us a moment... Other focuses of consciousness besides your own have different concepts of time, and are actually more biologically correct, in that they have greater knowledge of both cellular and spiritual realities. There is nothing "wrong" with your present habitual kind of consciousness, any more than there is anything wrong with speaking only one language. There is within you, however, the impetus to explore, to expand, to create, and that will automatically lead you to explore inner lands of consciousness; as, in your terms, it has led you to explore the other countries of the physical world.

(*Louder at 11:56:*) End of a very good session.

(*"Okay."*)

A small word to Ruburt. He is altering his world view. . . .

(*Seth postponed ending the session to make some comments on Jane's changing attitudes toward her physical environment, added a few remarks about the drawings I'm doing for* Dialogues, *then, in excellent humor, closed out the session at 12:01 A.M. Jane said her trance had been considerably deeper after break; certainly her delivery had been infused with more energy. And that energy lingered, for she felt much better now.*)

NOTES: Session 723

1. Seth began his "home station" and "world view" discussions in sessions 711 and 718, respectively.

2. In Chapter 5 of *Personal Reality,* sessions 623–25 all contain Seth material on inner sound, light, and electromagnetic structures of the body that ordinarily we do not perceive. From the 624th session, for example: "I told you that thoughts are translated into this inner sound, but thoughts always attempt to materialize themselves also. As such they are incipient images, collectors of energy."

3. Seth could be referring to his remark in the 34th session for March 11, 1964: "Telepathic comunications go on continually beneath consciousness, and without the aid of telepathy and of the inner senses, language itself would be meaningless. The hidden cues are the symbols that make language intelligible."

4. This material reminds me of Seth in the 681st session in Volume 1: "The deeper explanations, however [in this case of probabilities], demand a further expansion of ideas of consciousness . . . It is not so much a matter of Ruburt's vocabulary, incidentally, since even a specialized scientific one would only present these ideas in its own distorted fashion. It is more a problem of basic language itself, as you are acquainted with it. Words do not exist, for example, for some of the ideas I hope to convey. We will at any rate begin."

In conventional linear, evolutionary terms:

Many theories have been advanced throughout history to explain the origins of speech. Prior to the 17th century, extensive searches and studies were made for a "natural" or Adamic language, a basic form of human communication that was supposed to underlie all racial languages; no such universal protolanguage was ever isolated. As science now reaches back into human beginnings, the already scanty evidence gradually disappears, until finally it seems highly unlikely that the species will ever really know how or when its language and/or speech started.

Present linguistic thinking assigns the burgeoning of a "modern" language ability to late Neanderthal man, who existed across southern Europe and other lands in the Eastern Hemisphere during part of the last Ice Age glaciation (from about 70,000 to 10,000 years ago). Some 40,000 years ago, in Europe at least, Neanderthal man either evolved into or was supplanted by Cro-Magnon man *(Homo sapiens sapiens),* our immediate predecessor.

Numerous forms of vocal communication—whether "true" speech or not, in current opinion—undoubtedly existed among the ancestors of our species for many millennia before the appearance of late Neanderthal man, however; according to conservative estimates such methods could have been in use for well over two million years, perhaps beginning even with our prehuman or animal stages. Jane and I find certain other research claims inconceivable: that in some of those earlier times verbal exchanges between members of the species, whether they be called prehuman or human, could have been a *hindrance* rather than an asset. To us, even the potential for audible communication has always been as much a part of our creature states as arms and legs. I'm only noting that such abilities represent one more means, upon a vast time scale, by which consciousness inexhaustibly seeks to know itself in this camouflage reality.

Seth tells us, of course, that prehuman communication and human language and speech have originated in rhythmic patterns again and again, since in the far past our planet has seen the development of a number of presently unknown civilizations. See, for example, his material on reincarnational civilizations and the Lumanians in Chapter 15 of *Seth Speaks*. In Volume 1 of *"Unknown" Reality,* see his discussion on ancient man in the 702nd session, as well as Jane's own material on the "innumerable *species* of man-in-the making" in Appendix 6.

Certain presentations in Appendix 18 contain information from Seth about the distortive effects caused by words as he communicates through Jane. Review his excerpts from the 27th session for February 1964: "It is difficult for me to have to string out this material in words. . . ."

5. As an artist I'm so used to observing our physical world in terms of forms, colors, shadows, shapes, and "negative shapes"—the patterns formed by areas *between* and *around* shadows or objects–that I sometimes have to remind myself of the obvious: that each individual in the world perceives it from his or her own viewpoint. How strange, I've found myself thinking, that Joe, say, doesn't see our environment in artistic terms, since what I see is so plain to *me*. But then, I tell myself, Joe has a method of cognition that's quite natural to *him*. If he loves flowers, for instance, he may enjoy more of a sheer emotional reaction through the appreciation of a rose than I can.

6. Reading backward is something I've casually indulged in for many years. I don't think those actions inspired Seth's advice here, although my unconscious motivations for such a practice may coincide with it. I developed the habit as a teen-ager, reading signs and automobile license plates aloud and backward when my father would take my mother, my two younger brothers, and myself for Sunday rides in his 1932 Chevrolet. I found it to be great fun. I also taught myself to read upside-down print—an equally fascinating endeavor. In later years, working with others on a daily basis, I'd occasionally talk backward in a joking manner (ekil siht). The interesting thing here was that after a while my co-workers not only came to understand what I was saying, but joined in the game.

7. Seth has said all of this in various ways before, of course, since he began coming through Jane almost exactly 11 years ago—yet to my mind the four paragraphs just given contain some of his most important material in the two volumes of *"Unknown" Reality*. Certainly it buttresses any of his dream information in Volume 1.

8. Seth's material here can apply to the "case histories" Jane described in chapters 15 and 16 of *Adventures*.

9. Jane first came through with Sumari in her ESP class for November 23, 1971. Seth then devoted portions of the next five sessions to that development. From the 600th for December 13: "Each symbol in an alphabet stands for unutterable symbols beneath it . . . Sound itself, even without recognizable words, carries meaning. Oddly enough, sometimes the given meaning of the word does battle with the psychic and physical

meaning of the sounds that compose it . . . The [Sumari] word 'sham-balina' connotes the changing faces that the inner self adopts through its various experiences. Now this is a word that hints of relationships for which you have no word." And from the 602nd for January 5, 1972: "In your language there are words that sound like the reality they try to represent. These are called 'onomatopoeia' [in English]. 'Hush' is an example. . . ."

I recommend a rereading of Chapter 8 for *Adventures* in connection with the material in this note.

10. Such languages would be Italian, Spanish, French, and others stemming from Vulgar Latin.

11. In Chapter 8 of *Adventures,* Jane used her Sumari poem, *Song of the Pear Tree,* to present some examples of such layered, or deeper, meanings. In one instance she first translated the Sumari line, "Le lo terume," into "The pear tree stands." Later she came to understand that a more literal—and evocative—meaning is "Earth grows itself into a tree and becomes standing-earth-with-pear-faces."

12. See Appendix 19.

Session 724
December 4, 1974
9:45 P.M. Wednesday

(Yesterday afternoon, to my surprise, I had still another internal vision experience with a Roman counterpart self of mine in the first century A.D.; it was reminiscent of my three Romans of last October, yet perplexing, too—for this time I saw a different Roman counterpart. See Appendix 22 for my own material on the event, plus Seth's comments about it in ESP class last night, plus a quite unusual "confirmation" offered by class member Sue Watkins. My Jamaica experience of November 16 is also referred to by another student.

("I'm getting all this stuff," Jane said at 9:43, as we waited for Seth to come through, "but I can't verbalize it yet. It's like concepts that I have to unscramble. It's sort of frustrating . . . Strange . . . I'm getting images, too, but not clearly. One of them is about a world theater, made up of a particular century. I think we're going to get some great new material.

("That's funny," she continued, rather surprised. "It seems I can get the stuff either on my own, or go the Seth route. Well, it's easier to let Seth do it, so I guess I'll light a cigarette and go into the session. . . .")

Good evening.

("Good evening, Seth.")

This is not book dictation, in that it does not fit in with our section of exercises. You may, however, include portions of the session in *"Unknown" Reality* if you so choose. There are connections, of course.

Again, we come up against limited ideas of personhood. If I tell you that you are a part of a far greater personhood, then unfortunately you take this to mean that you are less than you are by contrast. I am not referring here to you specifically, Joseph, any more than I am to any reader or class member.

(Pause.) Each individual recognizes the existence of abilities or talents, leanings or propensities, that are largely unexpressed. In your system of reality you must operate in time. To develop as an athlete, for example, great training is required that automatically focuses energy and activity, and hence usually precludes deep concentration to the same degree in a different area. Similarly, to be a musician or an artist or a writer takes effort in time, and automatically focuses attention in specified directions that bar the same kind of work in other fields.

A person in time, then, can only do so much, and in your terms the great sources of the psyche are barely tapped in a given lifetime. That much is obvious. Earlier in this work I hinted at the hypothetical existence of a truly fulfilled earth-person—with a hyphen.[1] All of the spiritual, mental, and biological abilities would be actualized to whatever extent possible. Each physical body—in its own way, now, following its own individual peculiarities—would develop whatever skills it chose and found comfortable. Bodily abilities, however, would be freely expressed so that one woman might be a great runner, or a man excel at swimming. Physical endurance of the kind now considered extraordinary would be the norm. At the same time, all of the latent spiritual and mental qualities would be fulfilled in a like manner, so that all of the potentials of the species would find actualization in the most developed way in the experience of each individual. All aspects of the sciences and the arts would be explored.

(Pause at 10:02.) Again, in the terms of one lifetime such achievements are practically impossible. This does not mean that a different kind of education would not bring those ideals closer. It does mean that individuals choose to develop certain portions of their abilities, and that such a choice often necessitates ignoring other talents.

In its own way, the world at any given time is a unit of individuals with deep psychic and biological connections. Each of you take a hand at painting a combined world picture. Though each version is slightly different, and some appear strange within the whole context, still a world picture emerges at any given "time."

The people alive during any century are embarked upon certain overall challenges. These are the result of private challenges that can best be worked out within a certain kind of framework. Time as you understand it is utilized as a method of focus, a divider like a room divider, separating purposes instead of furniture. If you want a "Victorian room," you do not plank it down in the middle of a Spanish arrangement. Instead, you set it aside and frame it with its own decor, as you might in a museum that has separate rooms designating life in past centuries. The rooms in the museum exist at once. You may have to walk down a long corridor, go in a particular room and out the same door, before you can get to the next, adjoining room. The 18th-century drawing room may be next to a 12th-century chapel in this hypothetical museum, but you cannot move through one to the other. You have to go into the corridor first.

(Pause.) It is difficult to try to explain the creativity of the psyche when, as a species, you have such set ideas about it, but I shall try.

Physically you multiply. If you have a child, you are not diminished. You are not less yourself. You accept parents and grandparents, and see them as individuals, while you yourself are also you as an individual, and yet sprung from the same biological seeds.

Those seeds form the physical races, which are all variations on a theme, or as Ruburt would say, eccentricities[2] of an ever-changing model. You accept the fact that there are biological connections in terms of family, country, and race, between yourselves and the other individuals on your planet. The species divides itself up, so to speak, and the members of the different races at any given time distribute themselves in the various lands and continents. You are used to making organizations. You say: "This race is thus and so, and we can trace its history through the ages."* Or: "That race initiated language." Generally speaking, you see certain races as having their own characteristics. When you do this you often ignore other contradictory tendencies that are not as apparent. No one, however, feels less a person because of not being in a race by himself or herself.

(10:22.) Give us a moment . . . The children that spring from your loins are real. They have their own lives. They share a certain portion of your experience, but they use that experience as

*See Appendix 23.

they choose. In your terms, you exist in physical life before your children do. Now: In other terms, your own greater personhood exists before you do in the same way. That greater personhood gives birth to many "psychic children," who then become physical by being born into the races of men and women.

Each of those children wants to develop its abilities in a particular manner, translating them into earth experience in such a way that all other portions of the earth are also benefited.

Give us a moment . . . The world then is indeed like a theater at any given time, but the play is not preordained or laid out. It is instead a spontaneous happening in which overall themes are accepted beforehand. Each "greater personage" takes several parts, or brings forth several psychic children, who spring to life as individual human beings. These psychic children have as much say in their birth as you have in yours, physically speaking, and that is considerable.

You choose ahead of time your environment and purposes. This greater personage then has earthly counterparts, each individual alive taking part in the vital human drama of any given century. Each learns from the others, and the counterparts fit together like mosaics—except that these mosaics are fully endowed with independence and free will. So the individuals alive upon the body of the earth at any given time fit together as beautifully as the cells do within your individual body at a particular time (*most emphatically*).

Take your break.

(10:36 to 11:00.)

Now: I am not saying that the human personality is "as significant as a cell—no more and no less."

I am saying that in a way the people alive on the body of the earth have the same kind of relationship, one to another, as the cells have one to the other.

Psychically, you are made up of counterparts, as physically you come from various races. There are far more counterpart groupings than there are races, but then your definition of races is arbitrary. Period. Counterparts can be better related to physical families, for you might well have four or five counterparts alive in one century, as you might have four or five family members spanning the same amount of time. Basically, however, counterparts deal with fulfillments and developments that transcend races or countries.

Now remember: You are one earth version of your own greater personage. You are utterly yourself. That greater identity, however, is intrinsically your own, but is the part that cannot be physically expressed. Your experiences are your own. Through you they become a part of the experience of the greater identity, but its reality also "originally" gave you your physical existence, as you gave your children physical life. Your children are not you, yet once they were contained within the mother's womb. Yet they did not originate from the womb either, but from the seed and the egg.

Give us a moment... Your individual experience then becomes a part of your own greater personage, but at the same time you unconsciously draw upon the knowledge of that personage and use it for your purposes: You become an offshoot, so to speak. You are unconsciously aware of the experiences of "your" counterparts, as they are of yours, and you use that information to round out your own. Period.

Give us a moment... Certain abilities can be developed with much greater ease in particular time periods—in a highly industrialized technology, for example—and those interested in that kind of an environment did not generally appear in the eras of the cavemen, simply because those alive at that time were working with different challenges. So this hypothetical greater identity also chooses to be born in different time periods, historically speaking; and the same pattern appears in which counterparts are born as individuals, each biologically and spiritually connected, but with great intertwinings and variations, as with a physical family tree.

In its way, then, each century has its own integrity at all levels. The identity of each living person is always "brand new." Yet its rich psychic heritage connects it through memory and experience to those who will "come after," or those who have "gone before." You are closer to some family members than others, and you are closer to some counterparts than others.

Your parents have physical representations of their memories in terms of photos and letters—but take your break.

(11:27 to 11:38.)

Now: Those memories are not yours, and yet they are a very definite part of your heritage. In some cases your parents might tell you about events that happened in your own early childhood that you have forgotten. In a strange way, however, these are not your memories, but those of your parents about you. You take it on faith that particular events occurred even though you do not recall them.

New paragraph. Those incidents are recorded unconsciously, however, if they applied to your direct experience; and under hypnosis, for example, you could make them your own. So there are different kinds of memories. You share certain biological similarities with your parents, but there are other biological groupings not understood, uniting counterparts in any given century.

Organ transplants, for example, could be accepted more easily from counterparts, so that you have a kind of inner subspecies, or subfamily if you prefer, that operates within the regular physical divisions that you recognize.

Telepathic messages flash more quickly from one counterpart to another.

Give us a moment . . . Some of your counterpart's memories may appear in your dream states, where they show up as fantasies, perhaps, to you.

(A one-minute pause at 11:48.) These are like psychic snapshots rather than physical ones, involving instances that are a part of your heritage–yours but not yours. They add to what you are. They can give you correct information about the "past," even as your parents' photographs can tell you about a time in which you did not directly participate (in your terms). The old photographs will strike a chord within you, however, and so will the psychic memories.

(Pause.) You are always at the center of your life. Again, your being as you understand it is never annihilated, but continues to develop its own existence in other ways. A portion of you has lived many lives upon this planet, but the "you" that you know is freshly here, and will never again encounter space and time in precisely the same way. The same applies to each life lived either before or after. Biologically you rest upon a heritage, however, and psychically the same applies. The soul, or this greater personage, does not simply send out an old self in new clothes time and time again *(humorously)*, but each time a new, freshly-minted self that then develops and goes its own way. *(With much emphasis:)* That self rides firmly, however, in the great flight of experience, and feels within itself all of those other fully unique versions that also fling their way into existence.

So you, Joseph, were Nebene, and the black woman, and the Roman soldier,[3] and yet you were none of those. But their realities are also a part of your own greater alliance.

Now: Your friend Peter [Smith] shared the same earthly period.[4] You were not counterparts—or you are not counterparts, but closely enough allied so that in certain terms you "share" some of the same psychic memories, like cousins who speak about old dimly remembered brothers.

However, there are no coincidences in any groupings— biological or psychic or social. It is obvious that certain interests bring people together in any club meeting or gathering. Period. There are reasons, then, why people are born in any given century, and why they meet in space and time. So there are reasons why you and Peter met, and why certain people come to Ruburt's classes.

En d of that material for now.

(12:05. After adding a few sentences of personal information for Jane, Seth ended the session at 12:07 A.M. Jane had experienced internal images while delivering some of the book material, yet hadn't been able to get them clearly. One image had to do with an analogy involving plants and counterparts, she said; in it, the leaves of the plants "gave out" messages as counterparts did. But she couldn't elaborate upon this verbally.

(The next morning Jane told me that she'd been "getting stuff all night again" on "Unknown" Reality. As they have rather often recently, the phenomena had persisted in varying forms through her sleeping and waking states. They had been very creative phenomena, though. After breakfast Jane enthusiastically set to work writing about her new ideas; she plans to use them in Psychic Politics. *Here I can barely touch upon a couple of examples of what she experienced throughout the night, and wrote about today. She may revise her copy somewhat before it appears in* Politics, *but I prefer to quote from her original notes:*

(1. While asleep she'd been aware of many insights about receiving Seth material in that mode—some of it "at a preliminary stage, before it's ready." But all of it came through in a peculiar way, Jane continued, "as if I were equipped with mental earphones . . . This material is somehow being transmitted directly on to my brain waves; automatically; yet in a wild way without disturbing my own thinking. So is a different part of the brain being impressed than the part with which I do my usual thinking? Interesting . . ." She went on to develop an analogy involving two lines of music that eventually come together into one melody.[5]

(2. Once when Jane woke up she had the idea of "counterparts and four-fronted selves" in mind. As she wrote today: "There might be four counterparts alive in one general time period—a century—for example. These form a psychic 'block,' and any of the four can pick up information from this joint pool [of identity]. Each person is distinct, yet each is an added dimension of the others, so that on different levels the four [in this case] create an alliance and become a four-fronted counterpart self, covering a given century . . . This is a 'working alliance' that exists in potential form always. But the four-fronted counterpart self's own sense of continuity is not broken up; it persists outside of space and time, while its parts—the individual selves, or counterparts—live in space and time. . . ."[6]

(Now for two concluding paragraphs of commentary and reference: Jane's statement that the four-fronted counterpart self persists outside of space and time implies a contradiction, of course—but this situation is one that we, as physical creatures, will in some manner always have to contend with when we encounter certain of Jane's and Seth's concepts [including that of the four-fronted counterpart self]. Seth's own idea of "simultaneous time," that "all

exists at once, yet is not completed," has run throughout his material since its inception over a decade ago. As he quite humorously commented in the 14th session for January 8, 1964: ". . . for you have no idea of the difficulties involved in explaining time to someone who must take time to understand the explanation." Yet Seth's simultaneous time isn't an absolute, for, as he also told us in that session: "While I am not affected by time on your plane, I am affected by something resembling time on my plane . . . To me time can be manipulated, used at leisure and examined. To me your time is a vehicle, one of several by which I can enter your awareness. It is therefore still a reality of some kind to me [my emphasis]. Otherwise I could not utilize it in any way whatsoever." [7]

(Then, in the 44th session for April 15, 1964, Seth explained that in the inner universe, "Energy transformation and value fulfillment, both existing within the spacious present [or at once], add up to a durability that is at the same time spontaneous . . . and simultaneous." The durability being achieved through constant expansion in terms of value fulfillment. [8])

NOTES: Session 724

1. In Volume 1 of *"Unknown" Reality,* see the 683rd session just after 10:11. Seth commented: "You rarely find a person who is a great intellect, a great athlete, and also a person of deep emotional and spiritual understanding—an ideal prototype of what it seems mankind could produce."

2. See Chapter 3 (among others) of Jane's *Politics:* "Models and Beloved Eccentrics," as well as Note 11 for the 721st session in this Volume 2.

3. See the 721st session, as well as Note 11 for Appendix 22.

4. See Appendix 22.

5. Jane used an imaginary musical analogy in describing her sleep-state experience with "mental earphones"—but here are two psychic events of hers that can serve as real-life analogies: 1. Her reception 10 months ago, while asleep, of multidimensional data from Seth, which she followed the next day with her own material on neurological pulses; see Appendix 4 in Volume 1. 2. Her hearing Seth's thunderous voice in her sleep two months ago, as described in the opening notes for the 710th session.

6. A note added a few days later: In revised form, Jane did soon discuss her material on "counterparts and four-fronted selves" in *Politics.* See Chapter 12.

7. Because I think they contain some of Seth's most basic information, I also presented these quotations from the 14th session in my Introductory Notes for Volume 1. Additional material from the 14th session can be found in Appendix 13 (in Volume 2), and its Note 4.

8. For more thinking along these lines, I suggest the reader see the longer excerpts from the 44th session in Appendix 12, and also Chapter 18 of *The Seth Material.*

Session 725
December 11, 1974
9:17 P.M. Wednesday

(The regularly scheduled session for last Monday night was not held so that we could rest.

(Tonight Jane was so relaxed[1] that I didn't expect her to hold a session. But at 8:45 she wanted to try—especially since we hadn't done anything on Monday. "It might be a short one, though," she said. "Maybe Seth will talk about our own things instead of giving dictation—your material on your father [which I received this past Sunday evening], or what you got on your mother this afternoon. Or maybe he'll talk about what I got on your mother the other day, or my strands-of-consciousness stuff for Psychic Politics."

(Jane's material on strands of consciousness[2] had actually developed because of my experience involving my father while I was in an altered state of consciousness. That episode had upset me to some degree, but Jane's discussion of the subject in Politics, plus a few comments Seth made in ESP class last night, helped me put the affair in a more objective light.

(There's been a definite acceleration in Jane's and my own psychic adventures lately. In fact, we've had trouble keeping up with our experiences, and little time to study them. I am sure of one thing: I'm in contact with my

deceased parents in ways that I certainly didn't employ while they were physical
creatures. Nor did they in relation to me, of course. Yet certainly the use of such
inner abilities—or at least an awareness *of them—could greatly enhance*
communication between the members of a "living" family.)

Now: A quiet dictation *(but Jane's pace was almost fast.*
("Okay.")

This book is concerned with the nature of the unknown
reality, and the ways in which it can become known.

In this section, therefore, I have outlined various experiments or exercises for the reader. These will certainly lead you to
form your own versions of the exercises given, or will open your
mind so that spontaneously, in your own way, you become aware of
events that were literally invisible to you before.

You may find some of your most cherished conceptions to
be misconceptions in the light of your new experiences. Since
explorations are highly personal, you will most likely begin them
from the framework of your current beliefs. Symbols may be utilized, and these may change their meaning for you as you progress.
The symbols may evolve, therefore. In the beginning of this work I
"warned" the reader that here in these sessions we would go beyond
ideas of one god and one self.[3] I stated that your ideas of personhood
would be expanded. As *"Unknown" Reality* is being produced Ruburt
and Joseph are having their own experiences, and uncovering the
nature of the unknown reality as it applies to them.

Joseph recently had an experience that disturbed him,
simply because it was difficult to interpret even in the light of his
understanding about the nature of the self. You cannot explore the
nature of reality, hoping to discover its unknown aspects, if you insist
that those aspects correspond with the known ones. So Joseph
allowed himself some freedom—and then was almost scandalized
with the results.

His experience appeared to imply that his father's identity
had so much mobility, and so many possibilities for development,
that the very idea of identity seemed to lose its boundaries.[4]

First of all, in your terms "pure" identity has no form. You
speak of one self within one body because you are only familiar with
one portion of yourself. You suppose that all personhood in one way
or another must have an equivalent of a human form, spiritual or
otherwise, to "inhabit."

(9:34.) Identity itself is composed of pure energy. It takes
up no space. It takes up no time. I said that there are invisible
particles that can appear in more than one place simultaneously.[5] So

can identity. Atoms and molecules build blocks of matter, in your terms, even while the atoms and molecules remain separate. The table between Joseph and myself *(Jane, in trance, sat with her feet upon our long narrow coffee table)* does not feel invaded by the invisible particles that compose it. For that <u>matter</u> *(amused)*, if you will forgive me for that old pun, the atoms and molecules that form the table today did <u>not</u> have anything to do with the table five years ago—though the table appeared the same then as now.

(Pause.) In the same way, quite separate identities can merge with others in a give-and-take gestalt, in which the overall intent is as clear as the shape of the table. To some extent Joseph was perceiving that kind of inner psychic organization.

In your terms the earth at any given time represents the most exquisite physical, spiritual, and psychic cooperation, in which all consciousnesses are related and contribute to the overall reality. Physically, this is somewhat understood.

Give us a moment . . . *(Then slowly:)* It is difficult to explain on spiritual and psychic levels without speaking in terms of <u>gradations</u> of identity, for example, but in your terms even the smallest "particle" of identity <u>is inviolate</u>. It may <u>grow</u>, develop or expand, change alliances or organizations, and it does combine with others even as cells do. *(Long pause.)* Your body does not feel as if you invade it. Your consciousness and its consciousness are merged; yet it is composed of the multitudinous individual consciousnesses that form the tiniest physical particles within it. Those particles come and go, yet your body remains itself. What was physically a part of you last year is not today. Physically, you are a different person. Put simply, the stuff of the body is constantly returned to the earth,* where it forms again into physical actualization—but always differently.

(Long pause, eyes closed. Jane's delivery had slowed considerably.) In somewhat the same way your identity changes constantly, even while you retain your sense of permanence. <u>That</u> sense of permanence <u>rides</u> upon endless changes—it is actually dependent upon those physical, spiritual, and psychic changes. In your terms, for example, if they did not occur constantly your body would die. The cells, again, are not simply minute, handy, unseen particles that happen to compose your organs. They also possess consciousnesses of their own. That [kind of] consciousness unites all physical matter.

*See Appendix 24.

There is indeed a communication existing that joins all of nature, an inner webwork, so that each part of the earth knows what its other parts are doing. Cells are organizations, ever-changing, forming and unforming.

(10:00.) Give us a moment... Cells compose natural forms. An identity is not a thing of a certain size or shape that must always appear in one given way. It is a unit of consciousness ever itself and inviolate while still free to form other organizations, enter other combinations in which all other units also decide to play a part. As there are different shapes to physical objects, then, so identity can take different shapes—and basically those forms are far more rich and diverse than the variety of physical objects.

(Long pause.) You speak about the chromosomes. Your scientists write about heredity, buried and coded in the genes,[6] blueprints for an identity not yet formed. But there are psychic blueprints,[7] so to speak, wherein each identity knows of its "history"; and taking any given line of development, projects that history. The potential of such an identity is far greater, however, than can ever be expressed through any physical one-line kind of development *(forcefully).*

Identities, then, do send out "strands of consciousness" into as many realities as possible, so that all versions of any given identity have the potential to develop in as many ways as possible.

You, as you think of yourself, may have trouble following such concepts, just as you would have trouble trying to follow the "future" reality of the cells within your body at this moment. *(Long pause.)* You must understand that in greater terms there is no big or small. There is not a giant identity and a pygmy one. Each identity is inviolate. Each also unites with others while maintaining its individuality and developing its own potential.

A mountain exists. It is composed of rocks and trees, grass and hills, and in your terms of time you can look at it, see it as such, give it a name, and ignore its equally independent parts. Without those parts the mountain would not exist. It is not invaded by the trees or rocks that compose it, and while trees grow and die the mountain itself, at least in your terms of time, exists despite the changes. It is also dependent upon the changes. In a manner of speaking, your own identities as you think of them are dependent upon the same kinds of living organizations of consciousness.

(10:21.) Let us look at it differently. People who read so-called "occult" literature may consider me "an old soul," like a mountain. Period. In grand ancient fashion above other more homey villagelike souls, I have my own identity. Yet that identity is

composed of <u>other</u> identities, each independent, as the mountain is composed of its rocks and could not exist without them, even while it rises up so grandly above the plain. My understanding rests upon what I am, as the mountain's height rests upon what it is. I do not feel invaded by the selves or identities that compose me, nor do <u>they</u> feel invaded by me—any more than the trees, rocks, and grass would resent the mountain <u>shape</u> *(intently)* into which they have grown.

The top of the mountain can "see further," colon: Its view takes in the entire countryside. So I can look into your reality, as the top of the mountain can look down to the plain and the village. The mountain peak and the village are equally legitimate.

Let us look at this again in another way.

Your thinking mind, as you consider it, is the top of <u>your</u> mountain. In certain terms you can see "more" than your cells can, though they are also conscious of <u>their</u> realities. Were it not for their lives you would not be at the top of your psychological mountain. Even the trees at the highest tip of the hillside send sturdy roots into the ground, and receive from it nourishment and vitality—and there is a great give-and-take between the smallest sapling in the foothills and the most ancient pine. No single blade of grass dies but that it affects the entire mountain. The energy within the grass sinks into the earth, and in your terms is again reborn. Trees, rocks, and grass constantly exchange places as energy changes form *(very forcefully, leaning forward, eyes wide and dark)*.

Water rushes down the hillside into the valley, and there is a constant give-and-take between the village below, say, or the meadows, and the mountain. So there is the same kind of transformation, change, and cooperation between all identities. You can draw the lines where you will for convenience's sake, but each identity retains its individuality and inviolate nature even while it constantly changes.

Take your break.

(10:37. Jane's trance had been excellent, her delivery fast for much of the time. "And here I didn't even know if I could have a session," she said. "I got most of the mountain thing in images while I was giving it. I think it's a great concept and analogy. The whole thing comes from your father experience—the Miriam thing.

("Right now I think I'm getting that everything on the face of the earth is related—that your consciousness is in an ant, or a rock[8] or a tree, but that we're not used to thinking that way. Not that one is superior to another— just that we're all connected—that there's some kind of weird familiarity, biologically and psychically, that we've never gotten consciously . . . What I'm getting is that your father could do any of the things that you wrote about [in Note

*4], without invading anything or anyone. It's just that our ideas of personhood
and soul make it sound terrible, until you get used to those ideas. . . .*

*("Gee," Jane said enthusiastically, later, "I'm glad I decided to
have a session." Resume in the same manner at 11:05.)*

Now: Trees bear seeds. Some fall nearby. Others are
carried by the wind some distances into areas that the tree itself, for
all of its height, could not perceive.

The tree does not feel less, itself, because it brings forth
such seeds. So identities throw off seeds of themselves in somewhat
the same fashion. These may grow up in quite different environments. Their realities in no way threaten the identity of the "parent."
Identities have free choice, so they will pick their environments or
birthplaces.

(Long pause.) Because a tree is physical, physical properties
will be involved, and the seeds will mature following certain general
principles or characteristics. Atoms and molecules will sometimes
form trees; sometimes they will become parts of couches. They will
form people or ants or blades of grass, yet in each of these ventures
they will also retain their own sense of identity. They combine to
form cells and organs, and through all of these events they obtain
different kinds of experience.

Physically speaking, and generally, your body is composed of grasses and ants and rocks and beasts and birds, for in one
way or another all biological matter is related.[9] In certain terms,
through your experience, birds and rocks speak alphabets—and
certain portions of your own being fly or creep as birds or insects,[10]
forming the great gestalt of physical experience. It is fashionable to
say: "You are what you eat" semicolon; that, for example, "You
must not eat meat because you are killing the animals, and this is
wrong." But in deeper terms, physically and biologically, the animals are born from the body of the earth, which is composed of the
corpses of men and women as much as it is of other matter. The
animals consume you, then, as often as you consume them, and they
are as much a part of your humanity as you are a part of their so-
called animal nature.

*(Long pause at 11:21. Then Jane, speaking for Seth, delivered the
following material in a most emphatic manner. It was obvious that she was in a
deep trance.)*

The constant interchange that exists biologically means
that the same physical stuff that composes a man or a woman may be
dispersed, and later form a toad, a starfish, a dog or a flower. It may
be distributed into numberless different forms. That arithmetic[11] of
consciousness is not annihilated. It is multiplied and not divided.

Reminiscent within each form is the consciousness of all the other combinations, all of the other alliances, as identity continually forms new creative endeavors and gestalts of relatedness. There is no discrimination, no prejudice.

When you eat, you must eliminate through your bowels. That resulting matter eventually returns to the earth, where it helps form all other living things. The "dead" matter—the residue of a bird, the sloughed-off cells—these things are not then used by other birds (though they may be occasionally), but by men and women. There is no rule that says your discarded cellular material can be used only by your own species. Yet in your terms any identity, no matter how "minute," retains itself and its identity through many forms and alliances of organizations.

Through such strands of consciousness all of your world is related. Your own identity sends out strands of itself constantly, then. These mix psychically with other strands, as physically atoms and molecules are interchanged. So there are different organizations of identity in which you play a part.

Ruburt is connected with me in that manner. He is also connected with any ant in the backyard in the same way. Yet I retain my identity, the ant retains its identity, and Ruburt retains his.[12] But one could not exist without the other two—for in greater terms the reality of any one of the three presupposes the existence of the others.

(11:35.) Give us a moment... Not dictation: All of this should help you understand your own experience involving your father—and the later one with your mother; and, separately, Ruburt's with your mother, for [Stella Butts] was sending out strands of consciousness in the directions that interest her.

(After giving half a page of material for Jane, Seth closed out the session with this remark:)

His [Ruburt's] students are important, for as he is translating from the library, they are also translating.

End of session. A hearty good evening.

("Thank you, Seth. Good night.")

(End at 11:45 P.M. "He said that," Jane told me, laughing, "because I have to get something to eat. I'm starved. . . .")

(Seth's reference to the members of ESP class concerned the part many of them have begun playing in helping us answer the mail. With three Seth books on the market now, the number of letters Jane receives weekly has increased considerably, and evidently will continue to grow. A couple of months ago she thought of asking interested students to answer certain letters. The idea is working very well. It's one of those things that seem obvious once conceived.

There's also a rather unexpected bonus: Not only is the mail being answered much more quickly, but the students involved are gaining experience in dealing with a variety of intellectual and emotional questions posed by people they've never met. A series of very beneficial challenges has arisen for all concerned.[13])

NOTES: Session 725

1. Jane's relaxation tonight, while not a profound one, was similar to those effects she described in Note 6 for Appendix 19.

2. Jane originated the phrase, "strands of consciousness"—which she likes very much—some 10 months ago while describing her sleep-state reception of multidimensional material from Seth. See Appendix 4 for Volume 1 of *"Unknown" Reality.*

3. Here Seth referred to his material in the 687th session for Volume 1. After 11:07: "I am saying that the individual self must become consciously aware of far more reality; that it must allow its recognition of identity to expand so that it includes previously unconscious knowledge. To do this you must understand, again, that man must move beyond the concepts of one god, one self, one body, one world, as these ideas are currently understood."

Also see the Preface for Volume 1.

4. In this (725th) session Seth mentions two of my recent inner experiences and one of Jane's. Each one had to do with strands of consciousness, although in this note I'll stress only the very unsettling one I had with my "dead" father last Sunday night, December 11.

The event could have been triggered by my internal perception of just a month ago, the day the 719th session was held. In Note 4 for that session I described how I'd seen myself as a very old man, and made a quick sketch of that vision; I added that the episode had in turn reminded me of observing my father as he lay dying in February 1971, at the age of 81. In the 719th session itself, Seth remarked that the interior view of myself represented "a 'precognitive' moment" in my present life that (obviously!) I have yet to encounter.

Now last Sunday evening, as I studied that "old" drawing of myself, I thought once more of my father in his last days—then a whole block of information came to me regarding his present nonphysical circumstances and "plans." I wrote it all down immediately. I called it the "Miriam experience," and Jane presents it in Chapter 12 of *Politics.*

The material I picked up about my father's psychic intents was at first very bewildering. Hinted at was such a diffusion of consciousness that at the time individuality seemed to have little meaning. For I glimpsed Robert Butts, Sr. as he decided to disperse "himself" into a series of other personalities in both the past and the near future, so that I wondered how—in that mélange of identities—my father could possibly know himself. Seth's explanations in ESP class last night and in this evening's session helped clear my mind considerably, though: According to him, consciousness has no difficulty in making such alliances while maintaining continuity of identity, though its vast abilities are certainly almost impossible for us to grasp.

At 11:35 tonight Seth briefly referred to my second recent psychic experience, and to Jane's. Both involved more "conventional" ideas, and both involved perception of my deceased mother in her own nonphysical state. (Jane's happened on Monday afternoon, December 9, while mine took place this afternoon.) Jane's was especially clear, featuring a communication from Stella Butts—who was seemingly quite "herself." It isn't necessary to study those two events in detail here, however.

In class yesterday evening, Seth first came through with some very earthy material that's presented as Appendix 24. Then Jane read her notes on strands of consciousness, which—I can add later—also found their way into Chapter 12 of *Politics*. Seth soon returned in class with the following comments; he referred to Jane's ideas mainly, yet as he talked I began to understand my experience with my father and his after-death situation as I perceived it.

"There are no ceilings to the self, and no boundaries set about you. There is no place where identity need stop—yours or anyone else's. Now, if you want to rest for a while in the familiar privacy of your self-adopted selfhood, then that is all right. But if you discover paths or 'strands of consciousness' leading from yourself into other realities, then follow them . . .

"What selves do you encounter in time? And what makes you think that those selves exist in time as you understand it only? Why does it seem impossible that other strands of consciousness go to you and out from you constantly?"

A student asked: "What's the difference between a strand of consciousness and an identity?"

"That is for you to play with!" Seth replied. "To play with as you spook out the universe that spooks you out in return. Think of—my dear friend—the tiny weblike positions of the neurons within your skull. If they want to find you, where do they look? Where do they find your identity as apart from their own? Where do they draw the lines of identity? And where do their 'thoughts' break off so that they cannot follow, and yet they follow?

"That is your answer. It is one of my unanswers—and far more powerful than any other answer could be. . . ."

And added over a year later: Note 35 for Appendix 18 contains excerpts from the 775th session. See Seth's comments on the patterns of identity formed by consciousness, with their "particleized" and "wavelike" characteristics.

5. Seth meant his CU's, or basic units of consciousness, of course, which he discussed in sessions 682–84 in Volume 1. See the 682nd session after 9:47: "These units can indeed appear in several places at once. . . ."

6. In Volume 1, see the definitions of chromosomes and genes in Note 9 for Session 682.

7. Seth first discussed his blueprints for reality in Session 696 for Volume 1: "Each probability system has its own set of 'blueprints,' clearly defining its freedoms and boundaries, and setting forth the most favorable structures capable of fulfillment... As an individual you carry within you such a blueprint... The information is knit into the genes and chromosomes, but it exists apart... In the same fashion the species *en masse* holds within its vast inner mind such working plans or blueprints."

8. Strange—but recently I visually approached the idea of interrelated consciousnesses in two pen-and-ink drawings for Jane's book of poetry, *Dialogues of the Soul and Mortal Self in Time*: I incorporated humanoid features on large rocks. Resting in their natural outdoor world, these entities are subject to even the smallest change in their objective weather. But so are we—and might not both rock and human also respond to a uniting psychological weather?

I've completed finished art for only 15 of the 40 drawings planned for *Dialogues,* but have done extensive work on many of those remaining. I expect to be through with the whole job late next month (in January). See Note 1 for Session 705.

(And added 10 months later: The rock drawings referred to above are reproduced on pages 80 and 115 of *Dialogues.*)

9. See Note 3 for the 687th session in Volume 1. In that note Jane's poem, *Illumination,* is especially apropos of Seth's material here.

10. See the references in the 718th session to Jane's "fly experience" of last month—by myself in the opening notes and Note 4, and by Seth near the end of the session.

11. In 1959, some four and a half years before she began holding these sessions, Jane wrote a little poem about the arithmetic of her own being. She was 30 years old.

My Heart Knows No Arithmetic

My heart knows no arithmetic,
Yet one and one are two,
And the heart totals parts
That whisper sums their fibers through.

My brain is slow on calculus,
Yet its rules apply
To every cell my thoughts leap through
And everything I think or do.

I never knew equations,
But my atoms' chemistry
With precise calculation
Add up to me.

12. While reading those passages on identity, the reader might keep in mind the subject matter of Appendix 18: the complicated relationships involving Jane, Ruburt, and Seth.

13. But added a few weeks later: The idea, adopted so enthusiastically by so many class members, didn't work out after all. Jane and I came to realize that even her students tired of the unending process of writing letters (even about subjects they're interested in) week after week. "It turned into too much work," more than one student ruefully admitted. For the flow of letters is constant. Nor, we learned, did some of those who wrote Jane relish receiving a reply from someone else. The result of the experiment was that once more we were thrown back upon our own resources. We do what we can. Our latest attempts to handle the mail are described in the final passages of my Introductory Notes for Volume 1. Seth's most recent letter to correspondents is presented at the conclusion of those notes.

Session 726
December 16, 1974
9:43 P.M. Monday

("I'm beginning to get a cluster of images. They're of islands," Jane said at 9:40. "I don't know why, but I've been doing things that way lately. Then Seth uses what I get in the material . . . Okay: I guess I'm about ready." She lit a cigarette.)

Good evening.

("Good evening, Seth.")

Now: Dictation *(slowly and softly)*. The unknown reality: It cannot be expressed in the cozy terms of known knowledge, and so you must stretch your own imagination, <u>rouse</u> yourself from mental lethargy, and be bold enough to discard old dogmatic comfort blankets.

Imagine that you are a small sandy island with softly graded shores *(pause)*, some palm trees *(pause)*, and a haven for traveling birds. Pretend further that you are quite content, though sometimes lonely. A fine fog encircles you, though it does not

prevent the sun from shining directly down. You feel quite independent, and you think of the fog as a kind of cocoon that gently shields
you from the great expanse of an endless sea.

Then, however, you begin to wonder about the other
islands that you know exist beyond your vision. Are they like you?
Your wondering forms a tiny window in the fog, and you look
through. Astonished, you discover that a small coral path unites you
with the next island that is glimpsed, shimmering now through the
ever-growing window in the mist. Who is to say where you end and
the other island begins?

As you wonder, more astonished still, you discover other
coral paths extending from you in all directions. These lead to
further islands. "They are all me," you think, though each is very
different. One may have no trees at all, and another be the home of a
volcano. Some may be filled with soft grasses, innocent of sand.

Now this first island is very clever indeed, and so it sends
its spirit wandering to the closest counterpart, and says: "You are
myself, but without sand or palm trees."

Its neighbor responds: "I know. You are me without my
towering volcano, ignorant of the thundering magic of flowing lava,
calm and rather stupid *(emphatically)*, if the truth be known."

The spirits of the two islands join for a journey to a third
one, and there they discover a top-heavy land filled to the brim with
strange birds and insects and animals that neither knew at home.
The first island says to the third: "You are myself, only unbearably
social. How can you stand to nurture so many different kinds of life?"

The second island-spirit says, also to the third: "You are
myself, only my excitement, my joy and beauty, are concentrated in
the magic of my volcano, and you instead stand for the twittering
excitement of diverse species—birds and animals and insects—that
flow in far less grandiose fashion across the slopes of your uneasy
land."

(Pause.) The third island, startled, replies: "I am myself,
and you must be imperfect versions of my reality. I would no more
be a dull island of only sand and palms, or a neurotic landscape of
burning lava, any more than I would be a snail. My life is far the
better, and you two are only poor shadowy counterparts of me."

(Pause at 10:09.) The first island responds, in our hypothetical dialogue: "I suspect *(suddenly louder)* that each of us is quite
correct. And more, I wonder if we are really islands at all."

The second island says: "Suppose my spirit visits your
island for a while, to discover what it is like to possess palm trees, a

few birds, and a tranquil shore. I will give up my volcano for a while, and try to make an honest evaluation, if you will in turn come to my land and promise to view it without prejudice. Perhaps then you will understand the great majesty and explosive power of <u>my</u> exotic world."

The third island says: "I am myself too busy for such nonsense. The many species that roam my domain demand my attention, and if you two want to exchange your realities that is fine—but leave me out of it, please."

The spirit of the first island visits the second one, and finds itsclf amazed. It feels an ever-thrusting power, rushing up from beneath, that erupts in always-changing form. Yet it is always itself, comparing its experience to what it has known. When the volcano itself, ceaselessly erupting, wishes for peace, the spirit of the first island thinks of its own quiet home shores. The volcano learns a new lesson: It can direct its power in whatever way it chooses, shooting upward or lying quietly. It can indeed be dormant and dream for centuries. *(Slowly now:)* It can, if it chooses, allow soft sands to lie gracefully upon its cooling expanse.

In the meantime, the spirit of that volcanic island is visiting the first island, and finds itself enchanted by the still waters that lap against the shore, the gentle birds, and the few palm trees. However, it seems that the palm trees, and the birds and the sand, have dreamed for centuries.[1]

One day a bird flies out further from that first island than ever before, to another one, and comes back with a strange seed that falls from its beak. The seed grows. From it springs a completely new and unknown species of plant, as far as the island is concerned; and the plant in turn brings forth flowers with pollen, fruits, and scents *(spelled)* that have a different kind of creativity that is still its own. The spirit of the second island, then, brings forth elements in the first island that were not active earlier, but it becomes homesick, and so it finally returns to its own land.

(Heartily:) What a transformation! Its volcano, it finds, now gives birth to soil and pollen, its excitement roused in a million different ways. It meets the spirit of the first island that has been living there, and says: "What a change! I would like a still more spectacular display. The flowers are not nearly colorful or wild enough. It is, if you will forgive me, too <u>well-tamed</u>—yet all in all you've done wonders. Now, however, I'd like a cultural interchange with others still unknown; and if you don't mind I wish you'd go home. *(Whispering:)* This is, after all, me, and my land."

The spirit of Island One says: "I quite enjoyed my venture,

and I've learned that the great explosive thrusts of creativity are good—but, oh, I yearn for my own quiet, undisturbed shores; and so if you don't care I think I'll return there." And so it does—to find a land in some ways transformed. The sands still lie glittering, but the fog and mists are gone. The beloved birds have multiplied, and there is in the old familiar sameness a new, muted, but delightful refrain, colon: new species in keeping with the old, but more vigorous. The spirit of Island One realizes that it would find the old conditions quite boring now, and the new alterations fill it with pleasing excitement and challenge. What a delightful interchange. For the spirit is convinced that it definitely improved the condition of Island Two, and there is no doubt that the spirit of the second island improved Island One beyond degree.

(10:39.) In the meantime, Island Three's spirit has been thinking. The spirits of island One and Two did not appeal to it (or to him or her in any of these cases, if you prefer) at all. It was determined to retain its own identity. Yet it too has become lonely, and it has seen endless coral paths reaching out from itself.

Its spirit followed one such path and came upon a desert island upon which nothing grew. Figuratively, its image was appalled. "How can you stand such barrenness?" it calls to the spirit of this fourth island.

That island spirit responds: "Even the vigor of your questions sickens me. I sense that you come from a land so overcrowded and tumultuous that it makes my sands blanch even further, and the knuckles of my rocks turn white."

Island Three's spirit says: "You are myself, utterly devoid of feeling—dead and barren."

The spirit of the desert island replies: "I am myself. You must be some counterpart, drunken with sensation, not realizing the purity of my own stripped-down nothingness."

The two confront each other sideways, for neither can look in the other's eyes. What opposites, what contrasts, what fascinations! So they strike a bargain. The spirit of the desert island says: "You are all wrong. I will go to your land and prove it, and you can stay here and partake of the joys of my peaceful existence—and, I hope, learn the value of austerity."

So the spirit of Island Four journeys to that other reality, where all kinds of life swarm over shore and mountain, and the spirit of the third island visits a world of such peace that all motion seems stilled.

What peace! Yet in the peace, what power! And so little by little cacti grow where there were none, delicate buds opening, filled with water. The spirit of the third island immediately begins to transform the desert island. Great changes appear, and showers of power—quick bursts of rain, explosive inundations of energy.

In the meantime, the spirit of the desert island is almost overwhelmed by the teeming life forms on Island Three, so next it visits the volcanic one; and when the volcano becomes frightened of its own energy the spirit of the desert island says: "Peace. It is all right to sleep, all right to dream. You do not need to be so worried for your energy. It can flow swiftly, or slowly, in surges of dreams that take ages. Do as you will."

So the volcano throws its energy into the formation of still more new species, while the desert spirit sings its calmness through their tissues. But this new life confounds it also, and it yearns to return home to its old quietude. There, the spirit of the third island has quickened the desert's abilities so that it blooms with muted flowers not present before. The two spirits meet. Each island is changed. "We are counterparts, each of the other, yet inviolate."

And the spirit of the volcanic island says to the spirit of the first island: "My volcano knows, now, how best to use its energy. It can shoot into the heavens in great displays, or creep into the tiny crevices of earth, equally powerful."

And the spirit of the first island responds: "You have taught my island that life is not something to be afraid of, though still it is translated in my own familiar gentle terms."

This is the end of our analogy. The spirit of each of the four islands was itself intact, and the interchanges were chosen. You are not islands unto yourselves, except when you choose to be. Each counterpart views reality from its own viewpoint, and there is never any invasion.

Take your break.

(11:04. "I knew we weren't going to get a break until we finished that goddamn analogy," Jane laughed after she'd come out of a good trance. "I do think we're going to lose readers along the way, though—this book's getting too hard to follow. I also think it's going to be in two volumes. I haven't had the guts to see how much material we've gotten so far."

(Nor have I checked up on "Unknown" Reality's bulk. This was the second time in three weeks that Jane had mentioned a two-volume work; see the opening notes for the 721st session. I wondered aloud whether she might be getting herself used to such an idea. I added that I didn't think she need worry about readers following Seth's material—that certainly many others are just as curious as we are about where "Unknown" Reality is going.

(An aside: Jane said that toward the end of her delivery she'd been bothered by traffic noise. It was a warm if snowy night, and we had a kitchen

window open for fresh air; all through her delivery I'd been aware of the traffic ceaselessly negotiating the intersection just west of "our" apartment house, of course, and had asked her to repeat a number of words. We do intend to move out of our two apartments early next year, as soon as I finish the illustrations for Jane's Dialogues—*that is, we're going to start looking for a house we can buy.*

(The Seth material to come is presented for these reasons:

(1. It not only incorporates Seth's "island" analogy, but Jane's and his information in the last [725th] session on strands of consciousness.

(2. We think that many readers can more easily relate to "personalized" data.

(3. The material on my parents reaches back to the first two sessions, 679–80, in [added later] Volume 1 of "Unknown" Reality.

(4. The counterpart references are a good example of how Seth weaves such concepts into a discussion.

(5. I think the application of tonight's material to Jane and me is neatly summarized in the last paragraph of the session.

(6. At the same time, that paragraph contains very challenging ideas; they strongly remind me of the "Miriam" material I obtained about my father last week. See the last session, with its Note 4.

(Resume in a fast manner at 11:40.)

This is not dictation. But in the terms of our analogy, some island spirits are gamblers. So you and Ruburt are gamblers. You gambled above all that your instincts would lead you in the proper direction, and that you would "win out" despite the "odds" as you understood them.[2]

You are willing counterparts *(see the 721st session)* of each other, and have been in your terms before—each playing out "opposite" aspects of each other, yet merging for common purposes and goals.

So in one century you were Nebene, and Ruburt was indeed the "prostitute" priestess,[3] and so did you challenge each other, as in different ways you do now, with tendencies that appear to be opposites, but are instead different ways of approaching the same kind of challenge. If you could understand, it would help in many areas you do not as yet suspect.

(To me:) You viewed aspects—counterparts—of your father's reality. That reality invades no other. As in the analogy given this evening, the spirit of no island invaded any other, but looked momentarily and with permission through another's picture of reality.

Your mother and father are alive, as are Ruburt's parents,[4] but their realities are not pinpointed to any given island, and they are forming alliances, but always from the standpoints of their own unique identities. Your own private identities do not need fences. They are themselves. They can combine and unite with others, yet retain their uniqueness and experience. Only your concepts limit your understanding of that prime freedom.

One strand of your mother's consciousness—that one involved with you–is intertwined with your reality because of her interest in homes.[5] Another strand of hers is involved because of her interest in families—and hence with the children of your two brothers, Linden and Richard.

Now in a way your mother and Ruburt were counterparts; for Ruburt lives in a trust of individual abilities toward which your mother yearned; and Ruburt gives a love to you which your mother yearned to give—yet while retaining her identity—to a man. Your mother understood love's purpose and felt its presence in Ruburt. And at the same time she was actually annoyed when she felt that you were not following your [commercial] artistic ability through, despite her surface misunderstandings of it.[6]

She identified with you to some extent, and to some unrecognized degree was "only masculine, now," in her understanding of power. I hope you will recognize what I mean: but in the light of her understanding at the time, children were to be used as power, as a man might use weapons.[7]

Stella Butts changed and grew. But in certain terms she was the masculine center of the family, emotions or not; the aggressive one; and speaking conventionally now, your father (Robert Sr.) accepted the more passive creative role. This has meaning in terms of your [unpublished] information[8] involving the masculine and feminine aspects that united and separated your parents. Your father would have been more "comfortable" as a woman, and she as a male. Yet for their own purposes they each chose to experience the other side of the coin, so to speak.

This will make more sense to you later.

("I think it's very good information.")

Consciousness is not limited. Identities can mix and merge while retaining their inviolate nature and memories. This is all for now, but again, later, you will see where it relates, and how you can disperse your own characteristics into another and they can disperse theirs into you, with your consent and theirs, to form new aspects of reality and to cast new light on combined purposes and challenges.

End of session—

("Okay.")

—and a fond good evening.

("Thank you, Seth." 12:01 A.M.)

NOTES: Session 726

1. Seth's statement here is reminiscent of some of his material on moment points. See Note 11 for Appendix 12.

2. See the opening notes for the 713th session.

3. For material and references concerning my Nebene life in the first century A.D., see Session 721, with notes 9 and 12. Seth's remark here, that "Ruburt was indeed the 'prostitute' priestess," concerns unpublished material we plan to eventually study in depth.

4. Earlier in this decade of our camouflage reality, all four of our parents died within a period of less than three years. In Volume 1 of *"Unknown" Reality*, see Note 2 for Session 680, and the notes at the beginning of the 696th session.

5. In Volume 1 Seth described the role a nonphysical Stella Butts played in Jane's and my house-hunting activities in Sayre, Pennsylvania, last April: See the 693rd session, with notes.

6. From her viewpoint my mother was, indeed, quite baffled when I turned away from a well-paying career in commercial art toward a very risky one in "fine art," or painting. The year was 1953, and I'd just met Jane. My mother was 61 years old, I was 34, and Jane was 24. See the few additional details in Note 10 for the 679th session, in Volume 1.

7. And at various times through my early years, I understood how my mother used me (and my two brothers) as "weapons," or tools or objects, against my father. "Weapons," perhaps, is too strong a word, I think now, for I don't remember my mother blatantly encouraging "her" children to defy their father. Yet we would often end up being on *her* side. As I grew up I came to feel that my father was both strongly surprised and disappointed by the wife and children he'd chosen to be involved with.

I'd like to add that Seth's material tonight on the Butts family situation is, if brief, very acute.

8. Related material about my parents that *has* been published can be found in Volume 1. See Note 9 for the 679th session, and notes 2 and 3 for the 680th session.

Section 6

**REINCARNATION AND COUNTERPARTS: THE "PAST"
SEEN THROUGH THE MOSAICS OF CONSCIOUSNESS**

Session 727
January 6, 1975
9:11 P.M. Monday

(Jane held her last session for "Unknown" Reality three weeks ago. She came through with a private session two days later, on December 18, and we've been resting from psychic work—including ESP class—since then. All the time, we were unaware that Seth had finished Section 5.

(At the start of this same period my own inner adventures stopped completely, as though hidden by a curtain closing on a stage. They have yet to resume, and I miss them.

(Today I finished the 23rd drawing [out of 40] for Jane's Dialogues.)

Good evening.

("Good evening, Seth.")

Dictation. The next section *(6)* will be titled: "Reincarnation and Counterparts," colon: "The 'Past' Seen Through the Mosaics of Consciousness."

Give us a moment . . . In your terms, the land changes

through the ages. Mountains and islands arise, then disappear, to re-emerge in new form. The oceans rise and fall also, and in some cases the floor of the ocean becomes the surface of the planet, only to be covered again by water. Yet through all of these changes the earth retains a landscape, and at any given time the features of the land are quite dependable and permanent enough for your purposes.

(Pause.) So the islands that I spoke about in our last session rose up from beneath the sea. Even as the dialogue of those islands took place, the islands themselves were changing. In somewhat the same way the psyche sends up counterparts of itself, each with different features or characteristics. As the physical properties of the earth distribute themselves in a certain given fashion about the surface of the planet, so do the properties of the earth-tuned psyches distribute themselves. Period.

As all physical matter is connected in any particular time, or era, so the individual consciousness of each being is also connected with every other. This applies to all consciousnesses as you understand that term.

A mountain is composed of many layers of rock that serve, as you think of it, as its foundation. The top of the mountain represents the present to you, and the tiers of rock beneath stand for the past. The mountain itself is not any one of those rock layers that seemingly compose it, however. There is a relationship between the mountain and those strata, but the term "mountain" is one that you have applied. In greater terms the mountain and all of its components exist at once, of course. You can examine the various levels of rock structure. Geologists can tell when, in terms of time, certain sedimentary deposits formed. The rocks themselves still exist in the geologists' present time, or they could not make such an examination. The mountain would not be a mountain without that "foundation." Again, however, it is not any one of those rock layers.

Now: In somewhat the same manner, the self that you know is the mountain, and the rock layers forming it are past lives.

You are not any of those past selves, even though they are a part of the history of your being. They are themselves in their own space and time. They exist simultaneously with your own life, even as the strata of rock exist simultaneously with the mountain.

Your present existence, however, is highly related to those other levels of selfhood. Now what happens at the top of the mountain affects all that goes on below, and so everything that you do affects those other realms of selfhood, and there is an interchange that occurs constantly. Physical conditions may be quite different in the valley, in the foothills of the mountain, and at its top.

The very climate and vegetation may vary considerably, and yet all life and vegetation within the area are interrelated. Each layer of life that composes the mountain—

("Is 'life' the word you want used there?" This is one of the few times I've interrupted Seth during his presentation of "Unknown" Reality.)

Yes . . . life that composes the mountain is equally valid and important, and each concentrates upon its own reality at its own level.

Like the mountain, therefore, you have a history in terms of the present that is yours, and yet not yours. It does not control you, for you alter it with each thought and action, even as each motion at the mountain's top affects its base. The layers at the bottom, however, are also constantly changing, so that the whole area is a gestalt of relatedness.

(Pause at 9:43.) In the physical world, islands, valleys, plateaus, continents and oceans all have their place, and serve to form the physical basis of your reality. Each blade of grass helps form the life of the earth. So each consciousness, however minute, is indispensable in its place and time.

Each flower on a hillside looks out with its own unique vision of the world, and each consciousness does the same thing, fulfilling a position impossible for any other consciousness to fulfill.

(Most emphatically:) In terms of time only, there is an archaeological meaning that is hidden within your own nature. To discover it you look "down" through the levels of your own being, there to find the layers of selfhood that in your world represent the past history of yourself, from which you emerged. You are not those selves psychically, however, any more than you are your mother's or your father's in physical terms. You are as different from those reincarnational selves, therefore, as you are from your parents, though you share certain backgrounds and characteristics.

It is easy for you to see how you affect your parents in your lifetime, though they are older than you. In the same way, however, you affect your reincarnational family.

(Pause.) When it rains, water rushes in great exuberant gushes down the sides of the mountain, bringing life and vitality to all of its parts. In somewhat the same way, your own experiences flow down and into the cracks and crevices of all the other times and centuries that compose your present lifetime.

(With a smile:) I have a surprise for you, however, for I have been speaking of you as the top of our mountain—for it certainly seems to you that you are at the top, so to speak. Instead, your vantage point and your focus is such that you cannot turn your head

to look higher. Perhaps you are like a fine sunny cliff on the side of the mountain, jutting out, looking down to the valley beneath, not realizing that the mountain itself continues [up] beyond you. You are, then, in the position of any of the other levels "beneath," many also thinking themselves the top of the mountain, looking only downward.

You are convinced that you cannot see the future, and this means—in terms of our analogy, at least—that you cannot look upward beyond your own time. While that is the case, you will always think of reincarnation as occurring in the past.

(Very definitely at 10:02:) Think instead of strata of being, each simultaneously occurring. Physically the human fetus bears a memory of its "past."[1] In your terms, it travels through the stages of evolution before attaining its human form. It attains that form, however, because it responds to a future time,[2] a future self not as yet physically created.

The fetus itself, before its conception, responds to a self not yet physically apparent; and the future, in those terms, draws new life from the past. A reality of selfhood, an idea not yet materialized in the unformed future, reaches down into the past and brings that future into realization. The cells are imprinted with physical information in terms of space and time,[3] but those data came from a reality in which space and time are formed.

(And in answer to my second question of the evening, Seth told me that he wanted the word "formed" used in the last sentence, just as he'd given it.)

The knowledge of probabilities[4] brings forth present time and reality. Voices speak through the genes and chromosomes that connect the future and the past in a balance that you call the present form. The history of the private psyche and the mass experience of the species, again, resides in each individual. The archaeology of the past and the future alike is alive within the layers of consciousness that compose your being.

Take your break.

(10:13 to 10:31.)

Now . . . Give us a moment . . . In many ways your language[5] itself has a history that you do not understand.

The past is obviously built into words in terms of time. When you speak a given word you may not know the history of its changes through the years, yet you speak it perfectly. You seldom realize that the present state of your language, whatever it is, will for others someday seem to be an archaic version. In whatever terms, again, you think of yourselves as being at the top of the mountain. In your terms, language presupposes a particular kind of development of mind, and when you think of language you tie the two together.

There are languages that have nothing to do with words—or with thoughts as you understand them. Yet some of these communicate in a far more precise fashion.

Cellular transmission, for example, is indeed much more precise than any verbal language, communicating data so intricate that all of your languages together [6] would fall far short of matching such complexity. This kind of communication carries information that a thousand alphabets could not translate. In such a way, one part of the body knows what is happening in every other part, and the body as a whole knows its precise position on the surface of the planet. It is biologically aware of all the other life-forms around it to the most minute denominator.

This applies to the future as well as to the past. The body itself knows the source of water, for example, and food. Natives divorced from your technology do very well, as wild animals also do, in probing the life of the planet and their positions within it.

A simple tree deals with the nature of probabilities as it thrusts forward into new seeds. Computations go on constantly within it, and that communication involves an inner kind of language innocent of symbols and vowels. The tree knows its present and future history,[7] in your terms, but it understands a future that is not preordained. It feels its own power in the present as it constructs that future. In deeper terms the tree's seeds also realize that there is a future there—a variety of futures toward which they grope.

The fetus also understands that it can respond to a stimulus—to any stimulus it chooses—from a variety of probable futures. So do you unconsciously grope toward probable futures that to one extent or another beckon you onward.

(Long pause at 10:50.) Give us a moment . . .

(10:52.) You choose your futures, but you also choose your pasts. There is only so much that I can say, since I am using a verbal language that in itself makes a tyrant of time. This book is paced in such a way, however, that if you follow it an inner language will be initiated. This in itself annihilates your stereotyped concepts and releases you from time's dictatorship. Some of the exercises to be given in this section will be geared to that purpose.

An archaeologist or a geologist examining "old" rock strata will find dead fossils, just as from your viewpoint you will discover "dead" past lives as you look "downward" through your psyche. You will seem to view finished reincarnational existences, even as from his present the geologist will discover only inanimate fossils embedded in rock. Those fossils are still alive, however. The geologist is simply not tuned in to their life area. So reincarnational lives are still occurring, but they are a part of your being. They are not you, and you are not your reincarnational past.

To a future self no more illuminated than you are, you appear dead and lifeless—a dim memory. When you look out into the universe from your viewpoint, it seems as if you look into the past.[8] Scientists tell you that when the light from a very distant galaxy reaches you, the galaxy is already dead. In the same way, when you look "backward" into the psyche the life you may indistinctly view— the past life—is already vanished. Why is it that your scientists' instruments do not allow them to look into the future instead, into worlds not yet born, since they operate so well in discerning the past? And why is it, with all of your ideas about reincarnation, there is precious little said about future lives?[9]

The answer is that your language is limited. Your verbal language—for your biological communication is quite aware of probable future events, and the body constantly maintains itself amid a maze of probabilities.

(11:05.) Give us a moment, and rest your hand.

(Actually, this was the end of book dictation for the evening. After giving half a page of information about another matter, Seth closed out the session at 11:12 P.M.)

NOTES: Session 727

1. For Seth on the fetus—its astral and reincarnational attributes, its energy, its growth, its perceptions from inside the womb,—see the quotations from sessions 503–4 in the Appendix for *The Seth Material*. Those sessions were held in September 1969.

2. See the 683rd session in Volume 1 of *"Unknown" Reality*. As Seth told us: "All kinds of time—backward and forward—emerge from the basic unpredictable nature of consciousness, and are due to 'series' of significances . . . Memory operates backward and forward in time."

In Appendix 12 and its notes there are a number of passages from Seth (as well as a few of my own) that supplement his remarks, in this 727th session, on present form responding to a future time. See, for instance, the quotations from the 690th session in Volume 1; Seth discussed the ability of our species to precognitively alter the present from the future. Molecular biology and precognition are also referred to. Then see Note 17 for Appendix 12, wherein biological precognition and the cellular manipulation of probabilities are mentioned.

Other related material on reprogramming the past can be found in Chapter 14 of *Personal Reality*; see sessions 653–55.

3. In the 684th session for Volume 1, Seth came through with

one of my favorite statements (even if it is grammatically incorrect): "The cells precognate." Much of his material in that session applies here: "It is truer to say that heredity operates from the future backward into the past. . . ."

At 10:48 in the 705th session for Volume 2, see Seth's remarks on introducing "new" genetic information into a damaged cell; a time-reversal principle is involved.

4. I suggest reviewing Seth's excellent material on probabilities, cellular consciousness, the moment point, and related concepts in the 681st session for Volume 1.

5. Seth delivered much material on language in the 723rd session. Also see Note 4 for the same session.

6. Currently there are close to 6,000 languages and dialects in use around the world.

7. Seth's material on trees reminded me of his 18th session for January 22, 1964. It made a lasting impression upon me. It's full of evocative statements that were new to us at the time, since the sessions were barely underway: "As to Jane's feeling about trees having [a certain kind of] consciousness, of course this is the case . . . The tree is dissociated in one manner. It is in a state of drowsiness on the one hand, and on the other it focuses the useable portion of its energy into being a tree.

". . . the inner senses of the tree have a strong affinity with the properties of the earth itself. They feel their growing, as you listen to your heartbeat . . . They also experience pain [which] while definite, unpleasant, and sometimes agonizing, is not of an emotional nature in the same way that you might feel pain. It is as if your breath were to be suddenly cut off.

"A tree knows human beings also . . . by the vibrations in the air as they pass, which hit the tree's trunk from varying distances, and even by such things as voices. The tree does not build up an image of man, but a composite sensation which represents an individual. And the same tree will recognize the same person who passes it by each day. . . ."

Jane knows she wrote the following poem early in 1964, but isn't sure whether she did so before or after delivering the 18th session for Seth. As far as I'm concerned, at least, it hardly matters which came first; I like the poem as much as I do the session.

The Trees in the Forest

The trees in the forest
Stand secret and silent,
Their voices suspended
In lungs of leaves,
That only can whisper
Of dreams held dormant,
That breathe only once
In a million years.

Deep is the sleep
Of the moss and the pebble.

Long is the trance
Of the grass and the meadow.
Footfalls come
And footfalls pass,
But no sound can break
That green-eyed trance.

One might say that Seth continued his own tree data almost five years later, in the 453rd session for December 4, 1968. Jane presented that rather brief session in full in the Appendix for *The Seth Material*, but from it I'd like to quote these lines:

"To your way of thinking, some lives are lived in a twinkling *(in various systems)*, and others last for centuries. The perception of consciousness is not limited, however. I have told you, for example, that trees have their own consciousness. The consciousness of a tree is not as specifically focused as your own, yet to all intents and purposes, the tree is conscious of 50 years before its existence, and 50 years hence. Its sense of identity spontaneously goes beyond the change of its own form. It has no ego to cut the 'I' identification short. Creatures without the compartment of the ego can easily follow their own identity beyond any change of form."

The implications within that last sentence are, obviously, enormous.

8. See Seth's first delivery for the 712th session, with notes 1, 2, and 4, among others.

9. Seth's point, that "there is precious little said about future lives," is well taken. It's one that Jane and I feel pretty much alone with; others don't initiate the idea in discussions with us, for instance. In a very casual way lately I've been trying to tune in to a "future" existence so that I can do some writing and drawing about it, but haven't made any meaningful contact so far.

I've become quite interested in such an achievement in view of my recent but very limited successes in touching upon several personal "past" involvements: the two nameless Roman soldiers, and the woman called Maumee. The idea of trying to reach a future self has been with me for some three and a half years, though, or since I first encountered Nebene, that male personality who inhabits a distant niche in my psychic past.

One of the Roman soldiers, Maumee, and Nebene are mentioned in Appendix 21; see the excerpts there from the private session for November 18, 1974, as well as Note I. Then see the comments Seth made the next evening in ESP class: "There are, of course, future memories as well as past ones . . . As Joseph often says: 'When you think of reincarnation, you do so in terms of past lives.' You are afraid to consider future lives because then you have to face the death that must be met first, in your terms. And so you never think of future lives, or how you might benefit from knowing them. . . ."

Session 728
January 8, 1975
9:16 P.M. Wednesday

(Last night in ESP class Jane delivered a session that was long, forceful, dramatic, and humorous. Her energy was "up" for the whole evening. She also sang in Sumari, her trance language, after finishing with the session. Seth covered many interesting points, and [I can add later] Jane presents the entire session in slightly abbreviated form in Chapter 15 of Politics. *I suggest the reader review that material at this time.*

(In any event, here are short Seth quotations on five of the subjects he referred to that are of special interest to us. All are related, of course.

(1. "The individual is stronger than any system, and the individual always comes first."

(2. "The one thing about an ancient existence [like mine], if you will forgive the term, is that old hatreds do not last because you learn to have a sense of humor . . . Love, on the other hand, even with a sense of humor, becomes highly precious and large enough so that it can contain old hates very nicely."

(3. On his life as a minor pope in the fourth century A.D.: "I was a

525

petty, religious politician." And: ". . . our dear, politically minded, crooked old Pope. . . ." In Seth Speaks, *see sessions 588 and 590 for Chapter 22.*

(4. Seth also said that it would be "not practical" and "boring" for him to relive his life as a pope, then added: "In those terms, many people do choose to reexperience what you would think of as a past existence in order to change it as they go along." Yet this reexperiencing of a life is a different thing from the original one. Again in Seth Speaks, *see Seth's material at 10:07 in the 539th session for Chapter 10: "You may perfect [that past life], in other words, but you cannot again enter into that frame of reference as a completely participating consciousness—following, say, the historic trends of the time, joining into the mass-hallucinated existence that resulted from the applied consciousness of your self and your 'contemporaries.'"*

(5. To class members: "You are yourself. I am myself. I am not Ruburt. Ruburt is not me. Ruburt is me. I am myself . . . You are death and you are life . . . Ruburt can do many things that surprise me—that I did not do in my past, for remember that fresh creativity emerges from the past also, as in [Ruburt's novel] Oversoul Seven. *My memory does not include a predetermined past in which Ruburt exists. He can do things that did not happen in my memory of that existence, and did not, in fact, occur." [And added later: I quoted the last three lines in Appendix 18 for Volume 2 of* "Unknown" Reality.*]*

(We discussed points 4 and 5 while waiting for the session to begin this evening. Just before Seth came through Jane said she had information on them—but that she didn't have time to relay it to me. So I hoped her material would crop up in some form in the session itself.)

Now: Dictation.

("Yes.")

While mountains generally maintain a more or less permanent position, in your terms, the vegetation that grows on the different levels changes. New flowers come each spring. You may always find a patch of violets in the same general position in the foothills each year, for example; yet they are not the same violets that grew last season, or that will appear next season.

The pattern for those flowers serves to seed each new batch. All kinds of alterations also take place in the soil beneath the mountain's layers. So, while different ledges may appear more or less the same, this sameness is the result of minute changes, new growths and seasonal variations.

For our analogy, now, think of the various ledges or levels of the mountain as different time periods. It seems to you as if one reincarnational existence would be layered above the other. You may be able to see that those existences, like the mountain, would exist at once, but you might forget that there is endless creativity and change at all levels of the mountain. New vegetation grows at the bottom layers, for example, as well as at the top ones.

(Pause, one of many.) Time periods are natural and creative. They are like the levels of the mountain, bringing forth fresh life. They do not vanish when you are finished with your growth there, but serve as a growing media for other personalities.

Give us a moment . . . Time periods themselves, then, are somewhat like platforms—natural platforms—that serve "time and time again" to bring forth fresh life. Because of your viewpoint this is highly difficult [for you] to understand. Say you were born in 1940. It seems to you that 1940 is gone, though it was the time of your birth. Returning to our analogy, however: You are like one violet, born in one spring on one ledge, and we will call the ledge, here, 1940. Other people are being born in 1940 <u>now</u>, in a different "season."

You are only aware of your own position within time, or your own place on the "platform," or the ledge as you understand it.[1] Not only do these ledges or platforms of time exist simultaneously, but each one brings forth its own batches of personalities in its own different seasons. To that degree you are aware of your own season only, and we will call it the physical one—the particular probable reality that <u>you</u> accept as real.

(Intently:) The ledge of 1940, however, is still as immediate and now and present as it was when you were born.

Other personalities, again, are being born "there," but their season or reality is different than yours.

Psychically you are somewhat related, in the same way for instance that the violets that grow this year in one spot are related to all violets that have grown—or will ever grow—from (or on) the same spot. Each moment, each year, has other dimensions, therefore, that you do not comprehend as yet. To you, other people born <u>now</u> in 1940 would be born in a probable reality. Yet you share the same bed, so to speak. When you look at an object you see its exterior, and when you experience time you perceive its exterior.

(9:43.) Give us a moment . . . The year 1940, then, continues to exist as the mountain ledge continues to exist, and it brings forth new creativity "each season." The violets on our hypothetical mountainside contribute to the life of the mountain even while they have their own independent reality, and the overall cycle of the seasons regulates the growth and development of the mountain and all of its manifestations.

(Pause.) Time multiplies from within itself. When you think in terms of reincarnation, you are still dealing with very simple time concepts. You accept, if you were born in 1940, a particular

historical sequence: but others born in 1940 (in a different season than your own), are born into a different historical context, a different 1940, with its own probable events. You always think of being reincarnated in terms of being born backward into a history of which you have read. But any given year has its own variations.[2]

(Most emphatically:) In a way you seed yourself into time. But you could choose to be born five "times" in 1940, and each existence would be entirely separate, as you probed into the probable realities existing for you in the variations of that period.

As a physical being, your beliefs and concepts form your reality. The psyche from which your identity springs is free of the picture of reality that you have chosen. Period. You choose, in other words, to accept a given picture of the world, and you use that picture as a frame within which you form a life.

If you think in conventional terms about reincarnation, then you might examine a book in which each page is a life. You read the book from the beginning, so you think of one life or page following another. You should be able to see that the entire book exists at once. But in larger terms it is just one volume that you, the greater psyche, are reading, told in terms of serial time.

Instead, you are not only reading but writing many such books of living experience, that represent existences. Creativity is endless, and the psyche is the greatest source of creativity. Pretend that you are a writer of fiction, and you create a character. This character is so independent, alive and real, that it in turn forms other characters—and each writes its own book, or forms its own reality. That is a truer picture of your position.

Physically, the seeds of a plant fall onto the earth. They may be blown to some place distant from their birth, but the psyche's "seeds" fly into other realities also. Within all of this, however, there is the finest balance between spontaneity and order. Violets do not grow in wintertime. Their characteristics appear only when certain conditions are met. So if you were born in 1940 you have no trouble keeping track of your own time, and you fulfill your life under the same general conditions as those in which you were born.

Cells retain their shape and integrity, and their position more or less within your organs, although the atoms and molecules within them change. The overall pattern continues, however, so that your body retains its familiarity even as, in other terms, the mountain maintains its form. The cells serve as patterns of development on the one hand, through which atoms and molecules express their being. Each category is dependent upon the others. So your own consciousness follows a certain line of development that is its own, and that recognizes its own "seasons." Other offshoots of yourself, in your terms, operate following their own orders in times quite apart from your own.

Take your break.

(10:10. Jane's trance had been an excellent one, her delivery often forceful and rapid, her manner very animated. "I could feel him trying to get those ideas through just right," she said, "using as homey and everyday concepts as he could to make them clear. Mind-blowing . . . I don't know whether they've been expressed just like that before, or not. I had no idea of that material before the session."

(Finally, as we waited for Seth to return, Jane said: "Now I am confused—I can get material on three different subjects. . . ." One was "Unknown" Reality. The other two were points 4 and 5, as listed in the notes preceding this session; since Jane became consciously aware of material on them just before the session began, she'd had no time in which to give it. "Now I'll have to wait for things to sort themselves out," she mused. It didn't take long: Out of those very interesting ideas he'd mentioned in class last night, Seth ended up discussing the one I've noted as point 5.

(Resume at 10:35.)

Dictation: The roots of the tiniest plant know the best conditions for their growth, and they reach spontaneously toward the most fulfilling probabilities for development.

At each moment they sense their position. They are familiar with the most insignificant motion of the earth about them.[3] They grow downward even while the stem grows upward—and the flower has not yet seen the space into which it will grow. What knowledge then resides within those roots, and what precognitive ability, that the plant itself yearns toward fulfillment that is as yet not achieved?[4]

Is the psyche then any less miraculous? And does not each of my readers possess the same innate capacity? You have within yourselves the same yearning for your own greatest flowering. You are multidimensional, however, so you grow in different kinds of realities, sending petals of yourself into other times and places, and you have the ability to mature in environments that are quite different one from the others.

(Pause.) In terms of your reality only, however, you seem to come to bloom through the seasons of the earth, and in your terms only, through consecutive periods. You are like a flower bulb that each time gives birth to a different blossom, while still con- forming to certain overall patterns—but each blossom is entirely new. Because you think in terms of time sequences, it is natural for

you to think of your psychic lineage in the same way. Each flowering of the bulb, however, brings about a different expression. You were not your past "self," therefore, though you shared a certain relationship. Period.

You see the flower bulb as it exists from your own perspective. Yet, being multidimensional, you bloom in many other dimensions also. You have to walk around a plant on a table in order to see it from all sides. So, figuratively, walk around "time" to see yourself from all angles, and to perceive all of your manifestations.

(10:52.) Give us a moment . . . In certain terms, for instance, I am a future of Ruburt, but the "past" is always freshly creative. Ruburt's life as he knows it is not in my memory—because I did different things when I was Ruburt. And he is not bound by that reality that was mine.

(Leaning forward, speaking intently but half-humorously:) I have memories of being Ruburt—but the Ruburt I was is not the Ruburt that Ruburt is in his reality. He surprises me, and his reactions alter my past. In his terms I am a future self, with far greater knowledge, yet he uses that knowledge to alter his present reality; and when I was Ruburt I did not have that knowledge. You can say then that I am altering my own past, but Ruburt's present experience also changes my present experience—and so there is an unending interchange.[5]

The same kind of interrelationship occurs with each individual now alive, in your terms, whether or not conscious awareness is involved. Ruburt is exploring time as he probes the reality of his own psyche, then.

You must begin any study from your own viewpoint, from your own ledge, but your personal living experience is always the main source of information. Within you as you know yourself are all of the hints you need, if you are but willing to follow them; and these will not destroy the fabric of physical reality, but instead show you more clearly the structure of its miraculous patterns.

Give us a moment . . . End of dictation.

(11:01. But hardly of the session. Once again, following his recent custom, Seth delivered several additional pages of material on topics not connected to "Unknown" Reality. End at 11:30 P.M.)

NOTES: Session 728

1. In the 13th session for January 6, 1964, Seth told us: "I will at a later date try to discuss the question of time. Any of these discussions are of necessity of a simple and uncomplicated nature. If I speak in analogies

and images, it is because I must relate with the world that is familiar to you." And, of course, Seth has been taking time to talk about time ever since. In Volume 1 of *"Unknown" Reality* see, for instance, his opening delivery for Session 688: "These CU's *(or units of consciousness)* therefore can operate even within time, as you understand it, in ways that are most difficult to explain. Time not only goes backward and forward, but inward and outward."

2. Seth, in the 683rd session for Volume 1: "Reincarnation simply represents probabilities in a time context (underlined)—portions of the self that are materialized in historical contexts."

In the 82nd session for August 27, 1964: "When man realizes that he himself creates his personal and universal environment in concrete terms, then he can begin to create a private and universal environment much superior to the one that is the result of haphazard and unenlightened constructions.

"This is our main message to the world, and this is the next line in man's conceptual development, which will make itself felt in all fields, and in psychiatry perhaps as much as any.

"When man realizes that he creates his own image now, he will not find it so startling to believe that he creates other images in other times. Only after such a basis will the idea of reincarnation achieve its natural validity, and only when it is understood that the subconscious, certain layers of it, is a link between the present personality and past ones, will the theory of reincarnation be accepted as fact. I have been prepared to give you this present information, but a suitable opportunity did not seem to present itself. . . ."

3. I like Seth's passage after 10:31 in the 727th session: ". . . one part of the [human] body knows what is happening to every other part, and the body as a whole knows its precise position on the surface of the planet. It is biologically aware of all the other life-forms around it to the most minute denominator."

4. In the 683rd session for Volume 1, see the flower, bulb, and time analogies given after 10:37.

5. Point 5 at the start of this session contains my note that later I added to Appendix 18 a few of the comments Seth made in last night's ESP class, concerning his connections with Jane. Seth obviously elaborated on that material here, but instead of quoting it in Appendix 18 also, I thought of letting the reader first come across it in this session; and so, to whatever tiny extent, this additional information now alters each reader's present reality by changing his or her conception of that Jane-Ruburt-Seth relationship.

Session 729
January 13, 1975
9:16 P.M. Monday

(I can add later that this is the only session in the two volumes of "Unknown" Reality to be witnessed by someone other than myself. Our visitor was a young man I'll call William Petrosky. He's a member of Jane's ESP class, lives in New York City, and was in Elmira a day early to conduct some personal business.

(For pretty obvious reasons as far as we're concerned, Jane and I prefer that Seth hold his book sessions in private, although Seth himself is more flexible here than we are. But as Jane has said, things are "calmer" psychically when we're by ourselves: In trance or out, she can concentrate upon the work at hand, free of the presence of a third individual—one who is bound to radiate his or her own psychic characteristics. Nor does it particularly matter if the witness remains silent; Jane still picks up elements of that "extra" personality, and reacts to them.

(Earlier this evening, Will had commented that Seth seldom addressed him by name in class sessions.)

Good evening—

("Good evening, Seth," I said.)
—and good evening.
(Will: "Good evening, Seth."
(Leaning forward, amused:) I will call you William, and you cannot say that I have not used your name.
(Will, smiling: "Okay."
(Pause.) Dictation. Now: As soon as you label yourself you are setting limitations, putting up boundaries and defining the reality of your psyche—usually according to quite limited beliefs.

You think that the self must begin or end someplace. There must be a fence around it, a yard of identity in which you can feel safe. I have said many times that there are no limitations to the self. You seem to be afraid that the self will bleed out and lose "itself" in a maze in which all identity is lost. Yet you recognize that your self is a far greater dimension than you usually suppose, so you speak in terms of reincarnation. This allows you to imagine greater realms of identity while still holding your concepts of selfhood intact. You think of being one self after another, each identity being neatly separated from the others by a passage of years, an obvious death and an obvious birth.

The idea of counterparts[1] somewhat shatters that old concept, yet you still want definitions for the self so that you know where you "stand." You are so taken with the idea of labels that many follow astrology blindly. You are born at a certain time, at a certain place, under certain conditions—but consciousness always forms the conditions. If it is to some extent affected by those conditions, then, it is because the effects follow in the same way that a painter is affected by the landscape that he has himself created. So you decide to be born, say, in a certain month when the planets are thus-and-so. Ahead of time, you choose the seasons of your birth.

In the most simple of terms, you are deciding upon the environment. A violet springs to life in the backyard, but the violet must stay there. Its whole growth is dependent upon the weather conditions in that particular area, even though those conditions themselves result from overall planetary activity. You walk out of the place and time of your birth, however, as the flower cannot.

(9:29.) Now: In greater terms, probabilities operate to an extent you may not suspect. For one thing, any focus point of physical life is caused by a merging of probabilities. Our session is being witnessed by a student, a most intelligent young man *(humorously)*. He also helps Ruburt with correspondence. Earlier tonight he wrote to a woman who has the same birthdate as Ruburt. In our last session I compared a year to a ledge on a mountain. I said that the

seasons came and went, and that many crops of spring flowers grew
there over a period of time. So each year, in those terms, is like a
ledge.

Say, again, that the year is 1940. All of those born on a
particular date in 1940 will not necessarily be born "at the same
time" at all. What you think of as 1940 is but one season on that
ledge, the season that you recognize. Flowers from the spring of one
year "do not see" or mix with the flowers of the following spring, or
with those of the spring before. In the same way, those born in 1940
"at one season" do not, in a greater context, mix with those born in
the same year either.

The word "season" here may be misleading. Give us a
moment . . . Each year is like one ledge, however, bringing forth
countless variations of the characteristic "flora" growing there. Each
of those separate years, say, each of those 1940's, or 1920's, or
1950's, carries on its own line of development. Time expands
inwardly and outwardly in those terms—it does not just go forward.

Again: Your reality is like a shining platform, a surface
resting upon probabilities. You follow these so unconsciously and
beautifully, you swim through them so easily, that it does not occur
to you to question your origin, or the medium in which your
experience has its existence. All of those sharing any given birthdate,
however, sharing even place as well as time, do not have the same
"destiny"; but more, they do not share the same conditions necessarily. They are each affected by their own probability system at
birth, and those conditions drastically alter the nature of their
development.

The very practice of pinpointing the time of physical birth
at conception itself errs. There is no point at which you can say in
basic terms (underlined twice) that an individual is alive,[2] though
you do find it more practical to accept certain points of life and
death. It is true that you emerge into space and time at a certain point
in your perception. Your consciousness has been itself long before,
however.

In an even larger context, difficult I know for you to
follow, the son is the father of his father in quite as valid a way as he is
the son, and vice versa.

Once you free your consciousness from limited concepts
of time and self, then you can begin to explore the unknown reality
that is the unrecognized self.

(Louder:) Now you may take a break—and (again humorously) I will return, William.

(9:47 to 10:09.)

Now: Dictation: When you think in conventional terms about astrology, it is as if you are looking at the cover of a book, not realizing that there are many pages within it.

Consciousness, being active within all cellular structures, triggers itself ahead of time [in each case], so to speak, to react to certain conditions and not to others. Many are born the same day of any given year, and generally within the same time period—but individually the inner triggering may be far different, so that while the overall conditions at birth may appear more or less the same, the inner reactions to them will vary widely. Period.

Some persons will be much more affected by, and sensitive to, other probabilities—which, for instance, do not show at all in conventional astrological "charts."

Those charts emphasize one line of probabilities at the expense of all others. Interpretations based upon the charts then will make more sense to those who have chosen the same probable birth circumstances—but they will be of no value to those who were born at the same time, in your terms, but who follow a different order of probabilities.[3]

(10:17.) Now give us a moment ... As the cells operate with the knowledge of probable actions and still maintain the physical body in your chosen system, so the psyche, operating in the same way, "seeds" itself in many different probabilities. In this case specifically, I am speaking of other physical probabilities—alternates, in other words, of the world as you know it. Those alive with you, your contemporaries, do not all belong to the same probable system. You are at a meeting ground in that respect, where individuals from many probable realities mix and merge, agreeing momentarily to accept certain portions of the same space-time environment.

Because you focus upon the similarities in experience, and play down the variances, then the oftentimes greater dissimilarities[4] in so-called experience escape you completely. You take it for granted that memory is faulty if you do not agree with another person on the events that happened at a certain place and time—say those in a recently experienced historical past. You take it for granted that interpretations of events change, but that certain definite events occurred that are beyond alteration. Instead, the events themselves are not nearly that concrete. You accept one probable event. Someone else may experience instead a version of that event, which then becomes that individual's felt reality.

These events may be quite different indeed, and the separate interpretations make quite valid explanations of separate variations. In your terms, one event can happen in many different ways.

All of this is fine theory, esoteric but hardly practical—unless you begin to question the nature of your own thoughts, and begin to explore the reality of those events that you <u>seem</u> to encounter.[5]

(10:25.) Give us a moment... (Pause.) Back to our flowers. Any wildflower on our mountain ledge *(see the 728th session)* will view the valley below from its own perspective, and see stretched about it the environment with which it is familiar. Generally speaking, the others flowers born in the same spring will die at about the same time. The next year the new flowers will see a slightly different landscape, yet the overall patterns will be the same. Violets will grow where there were violets before. The houses in the valley will be in the same "place." If <u>you</u> looked at that same landscape one summer and then the next, you might say: "Ah, the violets always grow there, and it is good to see the lilies of the valley in the shadow of the same rock." You might realize that the flowers you pick are <u>not</u> the same flowers that you picked last year at the same spot, but the very nature of <u>your</u> focus would cause you to concentrate upon those differences only when you were forced to. Otherwise you would think: "Violets are violets, and they are always here each spring."

The vast unexplainable difference that exists as far as the <u>flowers</u> are concerned is something else again—for on that scale the flowers that you pick are utterly themselves in their own world, from which to a certain extent you have taken them.

Unimaginable differences would be present if those posies could see the same environment of the year before, and all of the minute variations that you ignore would be gigantic; different enough indeed so that at their level the flowers might think that a different kind of reality was involved. So there are variations, and highly significant probabilities, operating even between those born generally in the same month of the same year—not only in terms of exterior conditions, but of inward ones.

Consciousness does not simply choose to be born at a certain place in space and time, but it also endows its physical organism ahead of time with certain inner triggers so that it will <u>respond to</u> those conditions in highly individualistic ways.

I am not even hinting at predestination or predetermination. Let us try another simple analogy. A seed "knows" that it will come to life in the middle of a pot in someone's living room. Say it is a tomato seed, and our house owner decides to start a plant from scratch. <u>All</u> cellular life is precognitive, in your terms. The seed then knows that the sun comes, say, from the west in this particular room. It begins to respond in that manner before the shoot emerges.

The shoot does not simply react to the direction from which the sun shines, but senses this far before, and the seed sensitizes itself "ahead of time" to those conditions. It could grow to the east just as well. The trigger is not the sun's direction on its own, but the plant's innate knowledge of that direction. The plant is not predestined to grow toward the west, for example.

(Very intently:) In the same manner, the self knows ahead of time the best conditions for its own development, in light of the time and the place of its chosen birth. It has, however, literally endless probabilities to choose from, to fulfill its abilities while maintaining a workable selfhood.[6] Consciousness chooses the best overall conditions available for its own purposes of growth. It then preconditions its own organism to respond or not to respond to the time and place of birth, to exaggerate or minimize, to negate or accept.

The emergence of consciousness into those physical conditions automatically alters them—a fact not recognized by astrologers. Each child born alters the entire universe,[7] and changes the world of its time and birth by bringing into it action not there earlier, in your terms, and by impressing the universe with the stamp—the indelible stamp—of its reality. Each child chooses its own probable version of any given birthdate. Such dates are obviously not just points in time, pinpointed in space. In the first place, since all time is simultaneous, you are always dying and being born, and your later experience affects the time of your birth.

I admit that a birthday operates as a handy reference. But if you realized that your consciousness did exist before that time, your memory will open up, and your accepted birthdate will appear far less important. "Coming out of the womb" is an event, and much better to use than "birth." In greater terms—far greater terms than you imagine—you are aware of probable "births," and your other parentages [that are] quite as legitimate as the personal history you now accept.

The self is not limited. The true meaning of that statement may sometime dawn. The idea of one personhood still closes your eyes to the greater multipersonhood that is your true reality. Often your dreams give you a hint of this kind of existence.

You may take a break.

(10:59 to 11:18.)

Dictation: You view the heavens and the universe, the planets and the stars, from your own focus—a highly limited one in certain terms.

In the first place you are looking at one <u>version</u> of the universe, as it seems to exist at the moment of your perception. The entire nature of a personality cannot be considered in its totality in that small context.

The personality itself is not only independent of space and time, but uses the illusions that result for its own purposes. All things are related, but they do not act in a certain way <u>because</u> the planets were such-and-such at your birth. There <u>is</u> a relationship, but it is not causal.

It is quite as true to say that the planets behave in a certain way because you are what you are, as it is to turn the statement around, as is generally done. The very positions of the planets and the stars are effects of the senses—perceptions that would have no meaning were it not for your own kind of consciousness. Those perceptions, then, cannot <u>cause</u> you to behave in any given way <u>because</u> of conditions that have no meaning outside of your own consciousness.

(*Pause.*) Now: The universe exists, but it takes the shape and form that you recognize only in your own perceptions. The motion of the planets, indeed their very perceived reality, exists in far different terms.

Give us a moment . . . The universe is seeded with various kinds of consciousnesses. Some of these appear to you as planets or stars,[8] as they "intrude" into your field of actuality. As such they appear to behave in a certain fashion, to take a certain form, to have certain effects. You and the stars are simultaneous events, each conscious and aware but in different "scales" of actuality—as your scale of consciousness is different from that of the violets.

With physical perception the picture all fits, of course. You realize that someone—some interested observer—viewing the earth from another planet in another galaxy, would be seeing what you think of as earth's past. But as I pointed out, "he" might also be seeing earth's future,[9] according to "his" viewpoint. This would in no way alter your reality. The positions of the stars and planets, however, and your time scheme, cannot be depended upon to give an indication of "causal" effects. The personality simply exists in greater terms.

Give us a moment . . . Using conventional astrology, you will find certain correlations, because of particular events occurring, that are indeed interrelated. Yet many individuals will not discover semblances of themselves in the charts of astrology simply because their chosen probabilities are, qualitatively speaking, so different from the "norm."

When astrology works, it works because the astrologer is

using his or her creative and psychic abilities, and then projecting that knowledge into a pattern that is of itself too small to contain it. The chart then simply becomes an aid.

I understand that some of this will be difficult to follow. The only other recourse, however, is to repeat myths and tales that you have outgrown. <u>The stars and planets simply are in more than one place at one time.</u> I admit that your perception of them makes them appear to be relatively stable, and you are biologically tuned in to that perception. Your experience of time and motion, as you know, is relative, and in comparison with your own relatively brief lives the planets seem to endure for almost endless periods. This is your viewpoint as you look out from your ledge.

(11:40.) Give us a moment... Other minute creatures might well mark portions of their lives with your coming and going, and imagine that your position at their birth regulated their activity. Imagine them making up charts correlating their lives with your own. Are you in the habit of pacing the floor? In another scale of time, how many ages might it seem to take for your shadow to cross from one side of the room to another? The analogy is not as far-fetched as it may seem, for certainly your shadow will affect the temperature of the room minutely, and alter other conditions there in ways you would never comprehend, often causing gigantic variations to a consciousness on another scale.

An imaginary ant, a philosophical one, might sit and in its own way contemplate how often you walked the floor in a period that might seem like a year to it. It might try to calculate your next passage ahead of time, so that—prudent ant!—it could run "out of the way" in time to avoid your footsteps.

Your rumbling tread might shake its tiny home beneath certain floorboards, or in the crevices between. I admit that I am stretching our ant tale here, but imagine further that our little fellow becomes familiar with everyone in, say, an apartment house, learning to recognize all of the footsteps that go up and down the stairs. Our philosopher keeps in touch with the other ants, until with time and work and patience, a chart is made and calculations drawn. An ant born at three o'clock in the afternoon, when Miss X comes home with her boyfriend, is apt to have a hard time of it—for the couple runs about exuberantly, shaking all of the establishment, and tumbling the dust in the inner crevices.

I am not comparing astrologers with ants. I am, however, trying to show you that you are not ruled by the stars—and that when you <u>behave</u> as if you are, then you are showing as little comprehension of your true position as our ant did. You are small in relationship to the stars, also, but when you seek to place your fate in their hands, figuratively speaking, then it does seem as if you have little control over your own destiny.

(*Forcefully:*) You are consciousnesses at particular points of experience, and in other kinds of reality you twinkle like stars.

Give us a moment . . .

Now: We will shortly end our session. I am glad that you came.

(*Will: "So am I."*)

Now, I am not going to tell you anything, and that always infuriates you and makes you happy at the same time. Instead, I give you methods that you can use to make your own reality by following your will (*with humorous emphasis*) as far as you want to; and because of this evening's session and the energy involved, you have the opportunity for some splendid dream activity. You will have it whether or not you remember it, but I hope you can remember it. Do not hassle it.

(*Will, laughing: "Okay."*)

Now that is the end of the session.

(*"Good night, Seth," I said at 11:57 P.M. And added a couple of days later, when I typed the session from my notes: After the session Will Petrosky spent the night with friends here in Elmira. When we saw him in class the next evening, he had no special dream activity to report.*)

NOTES: Session 729

1. See the 721st session at 11:11.

2. See Note 1 for the 727th session; it contains references to two sessions on the fetus, as Jane excerpted them for *The Seth Material.* Now see the 557th session for Chapter 13 of *Seth Speaks;* Seth presented additional information on the various ways reincarnating personalities associate themselves with the fetus. And after 11:24 in the 688th session, for Volume 1 of *"Unknown" Reality,* he talked about the present and future physical perceptions of the infant.

3. Jane and I appear to be two of those individuals "who follow a different order of probabilities" as far as astrology is concerned. Beyond some general reading we've done on the subject—both pro and con—we know little about it. However, horoscopes that readers have cast for us, after we've given the requested information about our births, seldom show much correlation with the Jane and Rob we think we know—nor will one person's charts for us agree with those prepared by others. We've ended up feeling that astrology, as it's presently practiced, is too limited in conception.

Seth has briefly referred to astrology a few times over the years. As an example, Appendix 21 contains the remarks he made in ESP class last

November 26, 1974, concerning the "hidden variables" that can be associated with a recognized birthdate. For the moment, then, Jane and I think that Seth's material on astrology in this 729th session (and, it soon developed, in the 730th) can serve as his answer to those who have asked for his opinion about it.

    4. See Note 5 for Session 721.

    5. I think that in his material from 10:17 to 10:25 here, Seth very neatly summarizes much of his thinking about how each of us constantly moves through a multitude of probable realities, meeting certain others in any one space-time environment, perceiving individual *versions* of any given event . . . Very useful information. Jane and I try to keep it in mind.

    6. See the 565th session as it's continued in Chapter 16 of *Seth Speaks.* Seth talked about the myriad probable actions available to any self. After 10:19: "To the extent that you are open and receptive, you can benefit greatly by the various experiences of your probable selves . . . often what seems to you to be an inspiration is a thought experienced but not actualized on the part of another self . . . Ideas that you have entertained and not used may be picked up in this same manner by other probable you's. Each of these probable selves [considers itself] the real you, of course, and to any one of them you would be the probable self; but through the inner senses each of you are aware of your part in this gestalt."

    7. For some analogous Seth material—on how the "slightest perception alters every atom within your body"—see Note 24 for Appendix 18.

    8. See Note 3 for the 713th session.

    9. See Session 712 at 9:40. The whole of Seth's first delivery for that session can supplement his data in this one. Also refer to his concluding paragraphs (after 10:52) for the 727th session.

Session 730
January 15, 1975
9:17 P.M. Wednesday

(As we lay in bed after last Monday's session, Jane told me: "I've got it—from Seth, I think: A really complete *astrological chart would have to include not only the time of your birth, but that of your death." Which would pose a few obstacles, I thought as I fell asleep. . . .*

(This evening, Jane had many thoughts and images before the session got under way. "It's about astrology. Actually, I mean it's about the birth of consciousness.")

Good evening.

("Good evening, Seth.")

Dictation: Usually you think in terms of a hypothetical whole self or consciousness, emerging at birth and disappearing at death. There are, however, learned arguments in which professors debate such questions. Some astrologers use the time of conception in their calculations, while others prefer the date of birth. Various religions have decided that the "soul" enters the fetus at its conception, while others argue that consciousness cannot be considered a human soul until some time later, just prior to birth.

The same kind of questions occur at the other end of the scale: When does death actually come? In most of these debates, this hypothetical self or consciousness is taken as the measure.

Give us a moment . . . In the first place, again, the self or soul in this case is not a thing of measurement—nor is it necessarily some thing that suddenly arrives and then disappears.

The physical self as you know it is a focus of consciousness that forms a personality in response to that focus. It is very difficult to make analogies here, but I am foolhardy enough to try it. *(Pause.)* It seems to you that any naturally aborted fetus has no physical life at all, that such life has been denied to it for some reason. Instead, the fetus experiences another level: physical life at a different scale, that in your terms would apply to the distant past.

In, I repeat, conventional ideas of evolution,[1] this would be a period in which your kind of consciousness experimented with a water environment, with fins instead of lungs. In certain terms this gives the consciousness a look at particular portions of the species' "past." It also provides that consciousness with firsthand knowledge psychically and directly. Again—most difficult to explain (exclamation point)! Particularly without offending your ideas of selfhood—yet each of you "alive" died in just such a manner.

While in conventional terms you think of long centuries' duration, in which finned creatures rose from the seas, some "becoming" reptiles and finally mammals, many did not make that journey but "fell" along the way. So in those terms, and following that analogy, the psyche makes the same kind of adjustments and life-changes. You have each existed many times, then, as fetuses "who did not make it." Not necessarily because you did not want to be born, but because those experiences were in themselves legitimate,[2] and in your present state are written in the "memory" of your physical being.

(Intently at 9:36:) Now this does not mean that your personality as you know it was often trapped within a womb, destined to die there, or that a hypothetical whole self would not be born. It means that the archaeology of your psyche as it is physically focused carries those experiences. The self is not . . . *(pause, eyes closed)* . . . give us a moment; I am searching for a good analogy . . . the self is not like a clay figure coming from a potter's oven, so that you can say: "Ah, here is a self, and nothing can be added to it." You have always existed as a probable self, though you were not focused in the knowledge of your own experience.

(In parentheses: You may have been focused quite well in other realities, but I am speaking of your earthly existence as you understand it.)

At any point now you can literally become more yourself. In that regard, you are born by degrees. In certain terms you have discarded portions of yourself, so you died by degrees—but the two, the living and the dying, occur at once.

To a certain extent what you are was latent in the fetus, but there is no one point when "the full awareness of the soul enters into the flesh." The process is gradual. In physical terms it begins before your own parents are born.

Give us a moment. *(Long pause.)* The chart of events at the time of your "birth" is like one small snapshot of someone's backyard in the afternoon. Here in this analogy, the entire earthly personality could be compared to the world. Now as long as you make your deductions according to that one picture, there will be correlations that apply—but only to that small specific area.

In your terms, the person at birth is affected by multi-dimensional conditions, and the collective position of the planets is but one very minute indication of the other realities involved. Ruburt is correct: Even in conventional terms a true horoscope would have to involve the time of death in your temporal reality, as well [as that of birth]. Your focus of attention forms boundaries that predispose you to believe in a point at which your consciousness emerges, as you understand it, and a point when it is no longer effective, or dies. Your beliefs in such concepts limit your perception, for by altering the focus of your attention you can to some extent become aware of perception before and after the recognized points of birth and death.

You grant soulhood only to your own species, as if souls had sizes that fit your own natures only. You preserve these ideas by thinking of animals as beneath you. Then, however, you must wonder when the soul enters the flesh, or when the alien fetus becomes one of your own, and therefore blessed by the gods and granted the right to life.

But all things have consciousness, and in those terms possess a soul-nature. There are no gradations as to soul. Soul is the life within everything that is. Of course the fetus "has a soul"—but in the same way, if you think in those terms, then each cell within the fetus must be granted a soul *(leaning forward with humorous emphasis, voice deeper)*. The course of a cell is not predetermined. Cells are usually very cooperative, particularly as they form the structures of the body.[3]

(10:02.) Give us a moment . . . But the body is a context that they have chosen to experience. In fulfilling themselves the cells aid your own existence, but in a framework they have chosen. They

can reject certain elements within their existences, however, change their courses or even form new alliances. They have great freedom within what you think of as the framework of your reality. If their paths cannot be charted, and can indeed constantly surprise you, then why do you think that your course can be mapped out ahead of time by reading the positions of the stars at your birth?

The cells are not inferior as far as you are concerned, even though they form part of the structure of your physical being. They are not even less conscious. *(Emphatically:)* They are conscious in a different fashion. There is no need to "romanticize" them, or to think of them as little people, but each of them possesses a highly focused consciousness, and a consciousness of self. You like to think—again—that only your own species possesses an awareness of its own selfhood. There are different kinds of selfhood, and an infinite variety of ways to experience self-awareness.

(With much animation:) As an example, it appears to you that animals do not reflect upon their own reality. Certainly it seems that a cell has no "objective" knowledge of its own being, colon: as if it is without knowing what it is, or without appreciation of its own isness. You are quite wrong in such deductions. Nor are there necessarily gradations in which one kind of consciousness progresses in rigid terms from a lower to a higher state. Any cell has practical use of precognitive abilities,[4] for example, that quite escape you, yet many of you assign such abilities to "higher" souls. Each kind of life has its own qualities that cannot be compared with those of others, and that often cannot be communicated.

Now: All of this may seem to have little to do with the nature of reincarnation, as you think of it, or with counterparts as I have explained them. Yet it is vital that you throw aside old concepts of the self and of the soul before you can begin to understand the freedom of your own selfhood.

Are you tired?

(10:18. "No." Actually I was, but Jane was doing so well as Seth that I hated to interrupt her delivery of the material.)

Stop me when you want to.

This evening Ruburt read some [just-published] material about dolphins and whales. It contained strong hints that those creatures are geniuses, possessing the ability of abstract thought to a high degree.[5] Such is indeed the case

Now dolphins deal with an entirely different dimension of reality. There is as yet no method of communication that can allow you to perceive their concepts of selfhood, or their [collective] vision of existence. They are sensitive, self-aware individuals. They are altruistic. They understand the nature of relativity,[6] and they have different ways of passing on information to their young. They are not higher or lower than your own species. They simply represent a different kind of selfhood.

Now there is some relationship, at least in terms of our discussion, between the reality of the dolphins and the reality of the fetus. In your terms the fetus lives in primeval conditions, reminiscent of periods in the species' past. It relates in its own way to its environment. Now for some consciousnesses this is sufficient. In your terms, again, for each of you, it was sufficient.

Give us a moment, and rest your fingers.

(Pause from 10:25 to 10:27.)

The soul is not a unit that is definable. It is instead an undefinable quality. It cannot be broken down or built up, destroyed or expanded, yet it can change affiliation and organization, and its characteristics, while ever remaining itself.

The soul within the fetus cannot be destroyed by any kind of abortion, for instance. Its progress cannot be charted, for it will always escape such calculations. Its history is in the future, which always creates the past.

Take your break.

(10:31. Jane was out of her very excellent trance at once. "That was one of those times when the material was coming through so great that I could have continued until morning. That feeling of freedom is fantastic," she said, then tried an analogy: "I'm as free as a great runner who breaks a world record when her chest hits the tape. . . ."

(Not only that: Jane now had several other channels of data available from Seth. "God, I get impatient!" she exclaimed. "But in physical reality I can get only one of them at a time, and you can write just one sentence at a time.[7] Oh, forget it, Seth," she added, half laughing, for that "energy personality essence" was ready with comments on what she'd just told me. Jane got up and walked around the living room, where we were holding the session. When she went into the kitchen she picked up more from Seth on astrology.

(As break neared its end, Jane said that Seth was going to give the material available through one of the other channels open from him tonight. This decision was strictly her own, of course, and was motivated by a very successful out-of-body experience she'd had last night, following ESP class. Jane was especially happy that today she had found interesting correlations with part of her adventure through a friend [Mary] who is also a class member.

(Returning at 10:54, then, Seth not only came through with the material Jane wanted,[8] but devoted considerable time to some other information for her. He ended the session at 11:45 P.M.)

NOTES: Session 730

1. Appendix 12 contains much material on conventional theories of evolution, as well as on Seth's and my own often countering views.

2. While Seth was giving his material on the fetus, I found myself recalling some ideas I've mentioned to Jane at various times during the last couple of years, and have written about briefly:

I think it very likely that aborted fetuses and those infants who die early in "life"—say within a few months after birth, especially—never intended to stay long within camouflage (physical) reality to begin with; the consciousnesses within those small human structures came just to momentarily sample our world of matter, whether from inside the womb or out of it. Considering their viewpoints, it's not tragic that they "die" unborn, or at such young ages, although in ordinary terms the parents involved will almost certainly mourn deeply. (Perhaps these notions will be of some limited comfort to those who have written us with related questions.)

But for such consciousnesses the bulk of their activities will be elsewhere, possibly in other probable realities, possibly in nonphysical realities that we can hardly imagine from our own vantage points. Those who die unborn, or young, choose to touch upon physical reality to fulfill certain needs; they glimpse it as one might a view through the window of a passing automobile. I really believe that those "certain needs" can have vast implications, by the way, but this isn't the place to attempt a discussion of such aspects of reality.

Of course, these ideas would apply to any form of life as we ordinarily think of that quality. They would be a commonplace in the animal world, for instance; witness the quick deaths of certain newborn kittens in a litter (as Jane and I have); or consider the puppy in an animal shelter, or pound, certain to be put to death in a few days if no one gives it a home. The young dog won't live long, yet I think that in its own way it must understand that great "risk"; for specific reasons its consciousness decided upon its brief look into temporal reality. (This kind of thinking usually reminds me of a certain statement Seth made half a dozen years ago; see Note 7 for Session 727: "Creatures without the compartment of the ego can easily follow their own identity beyond any change of form.")

Seth's discussion in this evening's (730th) session also reminded me of an article I'd clipped from a metropolitan newspaper in 1974. The gist of the piece is that each year in this country an estimated several thousand seriously defective infants are quietly left to die, without treatment, after most careful consideration by the parents and doctors involved.

On a more personal level, Jane herself naturally aborted a three-month-old fetus, less than a year after our marriage in 1954 (and nine years before she initiated these sessions). Seth has said very little about this event, nor have we asked him to. He did remark some time ago in a private session that the miscarriage spontaneously came about because the personality inhabiting the fetus "changed its mind," and withdrew from the physical world. At some indefinite date we do plan to invite Seth to discuss the whole situation in detail.

3. All 200 billion (approximately) of them. . . .

4. "The cells precognate." See Note 3 for the 727th session.

5. The superior intellectual and altruistic characteristics of dolphins and other cetaceans are well known, if barely understood in detail. Seth commented on dolphins some 10 months ago in his final delivery for the 688th session in Volume 1 of *"Unknown" Reality*; he cited them as being not only similar to certain species that had lived on our own planet in the far past, but as representing bleed-throughs from probable realities in which water-dwelling mammals predominate.

Note 9 for the 688th session contains a description of Jane's work on an early unfinished novel, *To Hear A Dolphin*, which she began a couple of months before Seth first came through in late 1963.

6. I'd say that in a context like the one he uses here, Seth automatically refers to Albert Einstein's special and general theories of relativity. Within the overriding constancy of the speed of light, all phenomena in our camouflage reality—motion, velocity, mass, matter, time, space, gravitation, and so forth—are seen as relative to each other. Space and time, for instance, are not separate or uniform entities, but closely related intuitive "constructs" of consciousness; mass is a form of energy; motion is not absolute, but relative to the motion of something else; two observers, each moving at a different velocity relative to a common sequence of events, will perceive those events in different courses of time.

According to Seth, then, in its own way the dolphin (and the whale, of course) grasps such phenomena—and without the aid of the very sophisticated written calculations and the physical instruments we humans use.

7. Jane first experienced the multiple-channel effect with Seth not long after she began delivering *Personal Reality*; see Session 616 for Chapter 2.

8. I can add later that in Chapter 17 of *Psychic Politics* Jane presented both her own notes on her out-of-body experience, and the material Seth gave on it the next evening in the 730th session.

As noted during the last session break, Jane had tuned in to additional Seth material on astrology. I now add, with regret, that that information was never recorded.

Session 731
January 20, 1975
9:38 P.M. Monday

Good evening.

("Good evening, Seth.")

Dictation. *(Slowly and quietly:)* Your present idea of identity is maintained only because you grant as valid such small aspects of your own reality.

In other words, your accepted concepts of selfhood would disappear if you ever allowed any significant subjective experience to intrude. "The Absent Self"—the absent or unknown self—is the portion of your own existence that you do not ordinarily perceive or accept, though there is within you a longing for it.

Much of *"Unknown" Reality* is involved with the breaking up of theories that <u>have</u> been long accepted, but that prevent you from perceiving the powerful nature of those absent portions of the self. As you focus upon certain details from a larger field of physical reality, so then you focus upon only the small portion of yourself that you consider "real."

You carry within you, however, the deep knowledge of experience that in your terms would be prior, yet in your cells and your own deeper mind such information is current.

Give us a moment . . . Selfhood overspills with great luxurious outcroppings, yet you jealously guard against such creativity. To a certain extent you do carry the knowledge of your forefathers within your [cells'] chromosomes,[1] which present a pattern that is not rigid but flexible—one that in codified fashion endows you with the subjective living experience of those who, in your terms, have gone before. As Ruburt recently suspected, some very old cultures have been aware of this.[2] Period. While being independent individuals their members also identified with their ancestors to some extent, accepting them as portions of their selfhoods. This does not mean that the individual self was less, but was more aware of its own reality. A completely different kind of focus was presented, in which the ancestors were understood to contribute to the "new" experience of the living; one in which the physically focused consciousness clearly saw itself as perceiving the world for itself, but also for all of those who had gone before—(gradually louder for emphasis:) while realizing that in those terms he or she would contribute as well as the generations past.

The animals were also accepted in this natural philosophy of selfhood as the individual plainly saw the living quality of consciousness. The characteristics of the animals were understood to continue "life," adding their qualities to the experience of the self in a new way.[3] You had better put "life" in quotes in that last sentence.

(Pause.) The human body would be used in earth's great husbandry as, from it, dying and decaying, new forms would arise. This was a give-and-take in which, for instance, a jungle neighborhood was truly home, and all was a portion of the self psychically, spiritually, and physically.[4]

(Pause at 9:57.) Let those who will, laugh at tales of spirits turning into the trees[5]—a simplistic theory, certainly, yet a symbolic statement in such societies: The dead were buried at home in the same close territory, to form in later times the very composition of the ground upon which religions grew. Again, your limited concepts of selfhood make what I am saying difficult for you to perceive.

(With emphasis:) I am not saying, for example, that the living conciousness of each individual returned to the earth literally, but that the physical material permeated and stamped with that consciousness did, and does. Again, even the cells retain knowledge of all of their affiliations. In physical terms the consciousness that you understand is based upon this.

Give us a moment . . . Selfhood is poorer when it does not at least intuitively understand this heritage.

Give us a moment . . . Those intimate realizations, however, had to be counterbalanced in line with certain purposes set by your species, and even for that matter momentarily set aside so that other abilities and characteristics could emerge. The species' sense of curiosity would not allow it to stay in any home territory for long,[6] and so the sense of intimacy was purposely broken. It would become highly important again, however, when the planet was populated extensively, as it is now—only the original feeling of home area has to be extended over the face of the earth. The "absent" portions of the self are ready to emerge. The other, to you probable, lines of consciousness can now come into play.

These different lines of focus will each show you other aspects of your own reality, as individuals and as a species.

Take your break.

(10:13 to 10:29.)

I said once that no knowledge exists outside of consciousness.[7]

In those terms, neutral data are not transferred through the chromosomes. Consciousness passes on information through "living" vehicles. Whether physically materialized or not, knowledge is possessed by consciousness. It is always "individualized" (pause), though not necessarily in your terms.[8]

Give us a moment . . . The information carried by the chromosomes is not general, but highly specific. It is codified data (itself alive) that contains within it the essence of ancestral knowledge—change that to ancestral experience—of specific ancestral experience. Biologically you do indeed carry within you, then, the memories of your particular ancestors. These form a partial basis for your subjective and physical existence, and provide the needed support for it.

Since one portion of your heritage is physical, in those terms, those memories can be translated again, back into emotional and psychological events, though usually they are not in your societies.

To that extent the so-called past experience of your ancestors and of your species is concurrent with your own, biologically speaking. That is but one line, however, covered by the chromosomes. You have "another line" of existence that also serves as a support for the one that you presently recognize. It includes other interweaving physical relationships that bind you with all others upon your planet at the same adjacent level of time. That is, to some extent or another you are related to all of those alive upon the

planet. You are time contemporaries. You will have a far closer relationship with some than with others. Some will be your counterparts.

(10:45.) Give us a moment . . . These may or may not be
closer to you than family relationships, but psychically speaking they
will share a certain kind of history with you. You will also be
connected through the physical framework of the earth in the large
give-and-take of its space-time scheme.

A third line supporting your selfhood as you think of it is
the reincarnational one.[9] This is somewhat like the ancestral line
(long pause), and there are also reflections in the genes and chromosomes undetected by your scientists. The ancestral and reincarnational lines merge to some extent to form what you think of as your
genetic patterns ahead of time, so to speak. Before this life you chose
what you wished from those two main areas.

Reincarnational experience is also transmitted, then, and
can be retranslated from a biological code-imprint into emotional
awareness. Again, however, as you are not your parents or your
ancestors, you are not your "reincarnational selves."

Here also ideas of time hamper you, for I must explain all
of this in temporal terms. Since time is simultaneous, at other levels
your ancestors knew of your birth though they died centuries ago in
recognized continuity. The same applies to reincarnational existences that you think of as occurring in the past.

You cannot say that your ancestors, like some strange
plants, were growing toward what you are, or that you are the sum of
their experiences. They were, they are, themselves. You cannot say
that you are the sum of your past reincarnational lives either, and for
the same reasons. You cut off the knowledge of yourself, and so
divisions seem to occur. You are somewhat like a plant that recognizes only one of its leaves at a time. A leaf feels its deeper reality as a
part of the plant, and adds to its own sense of continuity, and even to
its own sense of individuality. But you often pretend that you are
some odd dangling leaf, with no roots, growing without a plant to
support you.

(Jane, as Seth, pointed to the angelwing begonia that sat on the
narrow coffee table separating us.)

All of the leaves now growing on this plant could be
thought of as counterparts of each other, each alive and individual in
one time, each contributing yet facing in different directions. As one
leaf falls another takes its place, until next year the whole plant, still
living, will have a completely new set of leaves—future reincarnational selves of this batch.

You are not plants, but the analogy is a simple one. And if you will forgive me—overall it holds water *(amused)*.

Take your break.

(11:06 to 11:25.)

There is a constant interaction in the plant, between its parts, that you do not perceive. The leaves now present are biologically valid, interrelating in your terms. Yet in <u>time</u> terms each leaf is also aware of the past history of the plant, and biologically they spring up from that "past."

Each leaf seeks to express its leafhood as fully as possible. Leaves take in sun, which helps the plant itself grow *(through photosynthesis)*. The development of the leaves, then, is very important to the plant's own existence. The cells of the plant are kept in contact with the environment through the leaves' experiences, and future probabilities are always taken into consideration. The smallest calculations involving light and dark are known. The life of the plant and its leaves cannot be separated.

(Long pause.) The plant has its own "idea" of itself, in which each of its leaves has its part. Yet each leaf has the latent capacities of the whole plant. Root one, for instance, and a new plant will grow.

Selves *(spelled)* have far greater freedom than leaves, but they can also root themselves if they choose—and they do. Reincarnational selves are like leaves that have left the plant, choosing a new medium of existence. In this analogy, the dropped leaves of the physical plant have fulfilled their own purposes to themselves as leaves, and to the plant. These selves, however, dropping from one branch of time, root themselves in another time and become new plants from which others will sprout.

("Do you mean 'new selves' instead of 'new plants'?")

Correct.

The larger self, then, seeds itself in time. In this process no identity is lost and no identity is the same, yet all are interrelated. So you can theoretically expand your consciousness to include the knowledge of your past lives, though those lives were yours and not yours. They have a common root, as next year's leaves have a common root with the leaves now of this plant *(pointing again to the begonia)*.

Such knowledge, however, would automatically affect those past lives. Ideas of cause and effect can hold you back here, because it seems to you that the leaves of next year come as an effect caused by this year's leaves.[10] To the plant and its innate creative pattern, however, all of its manifestations are one—an expression of itself, each portion different. The knowledge of its "future" leaves, as potential pattern, exists now. The same applies to the psyche. In that greater realm of reality there is creative interplay, and interrelationships between all aspects of selfhood.

　　　　End of dictation and of session. My heartiest regards and a fond good evening.

　　　　("Thank you, Seth, and good night." 11:49 P.M.)

NOTES:　Session 731

　　　　1. As defined in Note 9 for Session 682, in Volume 1 of *"Unknown" Reality:* "Chromosomes are microscopic bodies into which the protoplasmic substance of a cell nucleus separates during cell division. They carry the genes, the factors or units—'blueprints'—that determine hereditary characteristics."

　　　　In Volume 2, see Note 14 for Appendix 12.

　　　　2. After the session Jane told me she'd had the thought during an idle moment early last week, but had forgotten to mention it. She wasn't able to elaborate upon her original idea now.

　　　　3. Seth packed a lot of information into the short 689th session for Volume 1. He discussed the innumerable experiments of consciousness with animal-man and man-animal forms; the great communication between man and animal in ancient times, and the deep rapport of both with their natural heritage; psychic and biological blueprints and cellular precognition; the growth of man's ego consciousness; the beginnings of our god concepts and mythology; and more.

　　　　4. In Volume 1, see the 687th session at 10:45, when Seth said: "Biologically the man knows he has come from the earth. Some of his cells have been the cells of animals, and the animal knows he will look out through a man's eyes." Then see Note 3 for that session—especially Jane's poem, *Illumination.*

　　　　5. For some related tree material, see Note 7 for Session 727.

　　　　6. In Volume 1: See the material from 10:49 to 11:22 for the 684th session. In Volume 2: See the 716th session, for instance.

　　　　7. Seth evidently referred to the material he gave on the conscious attributes of information for Chapter 3 of *Personal Reality*. Note 1 for Session 697, in Volume 1, contains quotations from those comments, as well as a few other references.

　　　　Actually, Seth has been describing in various ways the indissoluble relationship between consciousness and information (or consciousness and anything else), ever since Jane began holding the sessions over a decade ago. I tried a little experiment. From the more than 64 three-ring binders, or volumes, as we call them, that hold the typed transcripts of our sessions, I picked out the second binder. Within it were sessions 16 to 23 inclusive, covering the period from January 15 to February 5, 1964. Five of the eight sessions contained material applicable to this note. Seth, in the 18th session, for example:

"As you have probably supposed by now, there is consciousness in everything. Visible or invisible to you, each fragment of the universe has a consciousness of its own. Pain and pleasure, the strongest aspects of all consciousnesses, are experienced by every fragment, according to its degree. Differentiation is of course various, and it is in the degree of differentiation that consciousnesses are different."

8. Someday, I'd like Seth to enlarge upon the tantalizing implications contained within this statement.

9. When Seth mentions reincarnation now, I usually think of a certain delivery of his in Volume 1. After 10:45 in the 683rd session, see the paragraph of material beginning with this phrase: "Reincarnation simply represents probabilities in a time context. . . ." Also see Note 3 for that session.

10. Besides quoting from the 18th session in Note 7, above, I presented excepts on tree consciousness from the same session in Note 7 for Session 727. Let me briefly continue that early Seth material here: "In drawing up his list of so-called natural laws, I have said *(in the 16th session)* that man decided that what appeared to be cause and effect to him was, therefore, a natural law of the universe. Not only do these so-called laws, which are not laws, vary according to where you are in the universe, they also vary according to what you are in the universe. Therefore, your tree recognizes a human being, though it does not see the human being in your terms. To a tree the laws are simply different. And if a tree wrote its laws of the universe, then you would know how different they are."

And from the 521st session (after 10:17) for Chapter 4 of *Seth Speaks*: "The word 'result,' you see, automatically infers cause and effect— the cause happening before the effect—and this is simply one small example of the strength of such distortions, and of the inherent difficulties involved with verbal thought, for it always implies a single-line delineation."

Session 732
January 22, 1975
9:10 P.M. Wednesday

(Neither Jane or I could remember what Monday evening's session is all about—even though I'd read part of it from my "shorthand" notes to the members of ESP class last night. I still have to type the session.)

Dictation.

("Good evening, Seth.")

Good evening. Now: I have spoken about counterparts in Ruburt's class.[1] Many of the students became deadly serious as they tried to understand the concept.

Some wanted me to identity their counterparts for them. One student *(Fred),* a contractor, said little. Instead, during the last week he let his own creative imagination go wherever it might while he held the general idea in his mind. He played with the concept, then. In a way his experiences were like those of a child—open, curious, filled with enthusiasm. As a result he himself discovered a few of his counterparts.[2]

Most people, however, are so utterly serious that they

suspect their own creativity. They expect that its products will be unreal or not valid in the physical world. Yet there is a great correlation between what you think of as creativity, altered states of consciousness, play, and "spiritual" development.

When you create a poem or a song or a painting you are in a state of play, of enjoyment, of freedom. You intend to make something different, to produce a new version of reality. You create out of love, for the sake of the experience. At one time or another almost everyone has that kind of experience, but children have it often. They compose songs and music and paintings in their heads. They alter the focus of their consciousnesses frequently. They do not stop to ask whether or not the play is real or pertinent. Physically, play develops their body mechanisms. It also flexes the great capabilities of their minds.

(Pause.) When you think, colon: "Life is earnest," and decide to put away childish things, then often you lose sight of your own creativity and become so deadly serious that you cannot play, even mentally. Spiritual development becomes a goal that must be attained. The goal is to be achieved through hard work, and as long as you believe this you do not understand what the spirit is.

I keep returning to natural analogies—but plants do not work at developing their potential. They are not beautiful because they believe it is their responsibility to please your eye. They are beautiful because they love themselves and beauty. When you are so serious, you almost always distort the nature of your own spirit as far as your understanding of it is concerned. You cannot let your guard down long enough to discover what it is. You keep looking for new rules or regulations, or methods of discipline.

Give us a moment . . . You keep searching for a new "ascended master," or guru, to keep you in line and point out THE WAY—in capitals.

In their own ways children are quite aware of their counterparts, and of other portions of their individual realities. They relate to their counterparts in dreams. They sometimes see them as "invisible" companions. You dream of your own counterparts frequently, but you are so afraid of maintaining what you think of as the rational adult self that you ignore such communications.

People have written here asking about soul mates.[3] In certain circles this is the latest vogue. The idea is an old one; it is based upon the reality of counterparts, and presents another version of the theory. But, again, it is treated with an almost pompous seriousness. (Pause.) Many of those who use the term do it to hide rather than to release their own joyful abilities. They spend time searching for their soul mates—but the search involves them in a pilgrimage for a kind of impossible communication with another, in which all division is lost, with the two then trying to join in a cementing oneness, suffocating all sense of play or creativity. You are not one part, or one half, of another soul,[4] searching through the annals of time for your partner, undone until you are completed by your soul mate.

(A one-minute pause, eyes closed, at 9:42.) When you become too intent to maintain your reality you lose it, for you deny the creativity upon which it rests.

(Long pause.) I am not denying the importance of true reason. Certainly I am not telling you to ignore the intellect. But you do often ignore the playfulness of the intellect, and force it to become something less than it is.

Take your break.

(9:45 to 9:55.)

Many of you have daydreams in which you actually see yourselves as your counterparts, and portions of their lives sometimes come through to you as you go about your chores.

You pay little heed, however. You think that this is just your "imagination." The unknown reality is alive in your own psyche. There are hints of it in all of your experience. You would not be alive, in your terms, if first you did not imagine yourself as you are. Play is, in fact, one of the most practical methods of survival, both individually and for the species. Within its framework lie the secrets of creativity, and within the secrets of creativity lie the secrets of being.

The life that you consider real represents one narrow stratum of even your physical experience. I am not speaking here of other realities that could add to that dimension. (Pause.) Play brings you a needed rest from your distorted concepts of selfhood, and many of the world's finest inventions have come when the inventor was not concentrating upon work, but indulging in pastimes or play.

(Pause.) You are involved with some of your counterparts more or less directly, while others live in different lands, and are sometimes separated also in terms of age differences or culture—qualities with which you would find it difficult to relate.[5] Intuitively, you know who the counterparts are in your daily experience. This does not mean that if you become consciously aware of such affiliations you must then feel it your responsibility to form a kind of culture of counterparts, or to try and affect other people's lives by reminding them of your relationship. You are each individual. Some of the people you dislike most heartily may be counterparts.[6] Each of you may be exploring different aspects of the same overall challenge.

There is nothing esoteric about families. They represent the kind of relationships that you take for granted. The same applies to counterparts, except that you are not ordinarily familiar with the term or concept.

Certain members of a family often act out particular roles, however, for the family as a whole. One might be the upstart, another the perfect achiever. Psychologists now often try to deal with the family as a whole, by allowing the different members to see how they may be exaggerating certain tendencies at the expense of others.

The upstart, for instance, may be displaying all of the bold aspects inhibited by other family members. Through this person the others may vicariously share the excitement or suspense of those experiences that are otherwise blocked. On the other hand the achiever may be completely hiding such impulses, while expressing faithfully the desires of other family members for "excellence" and discipline. Now the same can apply to counterparts, and those in your experience can show to you, in exaggerated form, comma, abilities of your own upon which you have not chosen to concentrate. You can learn much from your counterparts, therefore, and they from you. Those counterparts that you meet will be working, playing, and being more or less within your own culture. This does not mean that you are bits and pieces of some hypothetical whole self.

(Pause at 10:20.) Pretend that the psyche is a plant sending out seeds of itself in many directions, each seed growing into a new plant in different conditions. Growing to planthood, those seeds send out further new variations. A handful of seeds from any tree might fall in the same backyard. Others might be blown for miles before they land.

You usually live with your physical family, though this does not always apply; sometimes your ancestors come from various countries, so there is a physical lineage that you understand. There are often homecomings, where distant relatives return to the homestead. Now psychically the same applies in terms of counterparts. If you belong to any particular groups, often your closest counterparts will also be there. You will be a counterpart from their viewpoint, by the way. Many political, civic, educational or religious groups are composed of counterparts.

("And conventional families?" I asked Seth. I thought many readers would come up with that question at the same time I did.)

We will get to that. I purposely did not add that.

These counterparts form psychic families. They are family representations on another level. First of all, such groups have a built-in focus—political, civic, religious, <u>sexual</u>, or whatever. *(Pause.)* Certain members of the group express the repressed tendencies of others. Yet each is supported through a common sense of belonging, so that the group sometimes seems to have its own overall identity, in which each member plays a part. Any reader can easily discover this by examining the groups to which he or she belongs.

(10:30.) Now there are races, physically speaking. There are also psychic counterparts of races—families of consciousness, so to speak—all related, yet having different overall characteristics or specialties.

Most of the people who come to Ruburt's classes are Sumari,[7] for example. There are eight other such psychic families—nine in all. Some of Ruburt's students are counterparts of each other. Many of the people who come here come home in the ways that [members of a physical] family attend a reunion.

You may change the names if you prefer.

Peter Smith is a counterpart of Joseph's.[8] Sue *(Watkins)* and Zelda are counterparts of Ruburt's—or Ruburt is a counterpart of Sue and Zelda.

Alan Koch and Ruburt are counterparts. Carl Jones[9] and Bill Herriman and Bill Granger are counterparts. Norma Pryor is a counterpart of Joseph's, and vice versa. The young man from Pennsylvania who comes every other week is a counterpart of Ruburt's. But [all of] this applies to any group.

Give us a moment . . . The Sumari are naturally playful—inventors, and <u>relatively</u> unfettered. They are impatient, however.[10] They will be found in the arts and in the less conventional sciences.

The unknown reality. You have inner affiliations. What are they? I will outline the inner psychic species, and it is up to you to discover to which one you belong.

(Loudly and humorously:) Take your break, or end the session as you prefer.

("The break's okay.")

(10:45. With one exception—that of Sue Watkins—all the names given by Seth, involving counterpart relationships, have been changed. Most of the people are members of Jane's class; some have met certain of their counterparts, but not others; Jane, Sue, and I are the only ones who know everyone Seth named. During break Jane came through with additional psychic affiliations among her students, but it isn't necessary to discuss them here. She couldn't say whether Seth would indicate any more counterparts after break.

(I told her I'd been rather surprised when Seth had so baldly stated that there were only nine families of [human] consciousness upon our planet. The

*number seemed too small, too arbitrary. I also remarked upon my under-
standing that usually neither she nor Seth liked to categorize new information so
definitely. Jane, while agreeing, couldn't elaborate upon this very much, beyond
saying that she felt each family could have subdivisions, and/or combine with
others, so that mathematically at least there existed the possibility of "a lot" of
them. I liked that idea much better. Strangely, neither of us had ever asked Seth
to name any of the other families of consciousness, following Jane's Sumari
breakthrough some three years ago—but at the end of this session see the
material about the family of consciousness Sue Watkins had tuned in to back
then.*

(Resume at 11:02.)

Now: I am using this group of Ruburt's class as an
example, but the same applies, again, to any group.

The Sumari are rambunctious, in certain terms anti-
authority, full of energy. They are usually individualists, against
systems of any kind. They are not "born reformers," however. They
do not insist that everyone believe in their ideas, but they are
stubborn in that they insist upon the right to believe in their own
ideas, and will avoid all coercion.

In class, Emma *(Hariston)* and Jack *(Pierce)* are counterparts. *(To me:)* You and Jack are counterparts, but you and Emma are
not.

(Pause.) Earl *(Williams)* and Sam *(Garret)* are counterparts.
To my readers these names mean nothing. Yet in each case the relationships noted indicate inner realizations and connections. The
same realities appear in each of your lives. Will Petrosky and Ben
(Fein) are counterparts. Will *(who, incidentally, witnessed the 729th
session)* is a very intellectual young man—proud of it, though he goes
to great effort to show he is one of the boys. On the other hand, Ben
Fein trusts his intuitions fully, and relies upon them, yet to some
extent fears his own great energy. In many respects he is a child, and
utterly spontaneous.

Will dreams of being spontaneous. Yet even in this open
[class] group, Ben's spontaneity becomes embarrassing to adults free
enough to play with the idea of spontaneity while not trusting it
completely. Ben is afraid of the intellect. He is frightened that it will
"pull him down."

Now any group will show the same kind of interrelationships.* You can see them for yourselves. There is great diversity
within the family of consciousness called Sumari, as there is within

*See Appendix 25.

any physical race, and there is also great variety within other psychic families.

(11:14.) You choose to be born in a particular physical family, however, with your brothers and sisters, or as an only child. So, generally speaking, your counterparts are born in the same psychic family as your contemporaries. These families can be called Gramada—

("Wait," I asked, "do you want to spell those?" Jane, as Seth, nodded. Then rapidly, almost with a lilt, as though singing, she spelled out eight names. I added Sumari to the list. Where necessary I've also indicated syllabification and accentuation, following Seth's own delivery.)

1. Gra-ma´-da
2. Su-ma´-fi
3. Tu´-mold
4. Vold
5. Mil´- *(pause)* u-met
6. Zu´-li
7. Bor-le´-dim, closest to Sumari.

(As Jane spelled out "Borledim," I thought she might go into song.)

8. Il´-da
9. And Su-mar´-i

Now these categories do not come first. Your individuality comes first. You have certain characteristics of your own. These place you in a certain position. As you are not a rock or a mineral, but a person, so your individuality places you in a particular family or species of consciousness. This represents your overall viewpoint of reality.

You like to be an initiator or a follower or a nourisher. You like to create variations on old systems, or you like to create new ones. You like to deal primarily with healing, or with information, or with physical data. You like to deal with sight, or sound, with dreams, or with translating inner data into the working psychic material of your society. So you choose a certain focus, as you choose ahead of time your physical family.[11]

(Pause.) End of session. My heartiest regards, and a fond good evening.

("Thank you, Seth, and the same to you."

(11:27 P.M. "I get so screwed up at times," Jane said, as soon as she was out of an excellent trance following the rather abrupt end of the session. "Here I think the stuff is great, but then I worry about how the reader's going to relate to it . . . . I knew I was spelling out those names."

(I wondered if the attributes or vocations Seth had recited could be directly related to the families of consciousness he'd given just previously, and

Jane said this was the case. Neither of us could tell what went with what, though; perhaps we'll get information that will help us make some connections; perhaps I can present a list of such correlations in a note.

(Then Jane remembered that our friend Sue Watkins had had something to do with Seth naming a second family of consciousness shortly after Jane had brought the Sumari concept through several years ago [see Note 10]. But the thing was, Jane mused now, that she didn't think "Sue's family" was on the list Seth had just given: "It was something like Gramada, but that wasn't it. . . ." I made a note to check with Sue, whom we don't see in every class anymore, since at this time she's living outside of Elmira; I also want to see what I can find in the sessions, so that we can ask Seth to clear up any discrepancy.

(While we were having a snack Jane "picked up," presumably from Seth, that the psychic families were "like your overall mood, the predominant one you carry through your lifetime. . . ." Then she had an interesting comment as we made ready for bed; it pertained to the question I'd asked Seth about counterparts in families: "I think that maybe the family unit is designed more to take care of the reincarnational framework, instead of dealing so much with counterparts." I wondered how all of this fit in with probabilities, but by then we were getting too sleepy to figure anything out.

(Finally, and perhaps prematurely: Left untapped so far in all of this is any material from Seth on whether the counterpart and family-of-consciousness mechanisms apply to other species. If they do, I remarked to Jane as I typed this session the next day, then Seth must have a great amount of extremely interesting information on those concepts in relation to animals, say, or birds, insects, and marine life—not to mention bacteria and viruses; perhaps, also, submicroscopic entities down to the molecular and atomic levels, or even "below," are involved. I added that I hoped we'd soon begin to get the material we wanted on all of those categories, and others, and that Seth's flow of information on such topics would continue as the years passed. I planned to remind him often of our desires here.)

NOTES: Session 732

1. It will be remembered that Seth first mentioned his concept of counterparts in the ESP class session for Tuesday evening, November 18, 1974, rather than in dictation for *"Unknown" Reality*; see the opening notes for Session 721. In those notes I also referred to the experiences of my Roman and Jamaican counterparts—episodes that, I wrote, "played some considerable part in establishing a foundation, or impetus for such a development" (as the counterpart one). Then see all of Seth's material on counterparts in the 721st session itself.

2. Fred received his information in the form of several most

delightful, externalized visions. He saw two of his contemporary counterparts in them. Both were female. One was a peasant in Turkey; she was "either 62 or 63 years old." The other was a very tall, handsome and intelligent black in her late 20's, who was a "socialite" living in California.

3. Our dictionary defines a soul mate as one of the opposite sex with whom an individual "has a deeply personal relationship"—a mundane enough description. Jane and I had thought the term, along with its implications, rather out of style until the publication of *The Seth Material* in 1970. Then we began to get letters from readers who either asked for Seth's help in finding soul mates, or for his verification that such counterparts had, indeed, already been located.

4. See Seth's very acute discussions of the soul (or entity) in sessions 526–28 for Chapter 6 of *Seth Speaks.* He came through with many excellent points. I've always been intrigued by the remark he made just before 10:43 in the 526th session: "You are one manifestation of your own soul." Then in Chapter 9 of *Personal Reality,* see the 637th session at 10:20: "A group of cells forms an organ. A group of selves forms a soul. I am not telling you that you do not have a soul to call your own. You are a part of your soul. It belongs to you, and you to it."

That material bothered Jane, as I wrote at the end of the session, since "she wasn't taken with the idea of a group soul, say, or of sharing a soul." For Seth's resolution of this little dilemma, see Session 638 in the same chapter.

To me, beside whatever relationship it might have with counterpart reality, the soul-mate belief embodies strongly distorted versions of the ideas contained in the two Seth passages quoted above.

5. Seth has already referred to counterpart relationships at the extremes of distance, and, to a lesser extent, in terms of age and cultural differences. Jane and I can represent the direct involvement of counterparts; see the 726th session after 11:40. Then see Seth's material in Appendix 21 on the counterpart association that Florence, a student in ESP class, has with a young man in China. I'm almost 10 years older than Jane; Florence is probably 25 years older than her Chinese counterpart.

6. Seth's line about the dislike that can exist among counterparts is hilarous, nor am I being facetious in so commenting. To use the members of ESP class as a general example, Jane and I have often noted the variety of feelings, ranging from the most positive to the most negative, that her students exhibit toward one another. The interesting thing about Seth's statement is that with counterpart theory in mind one can gain a fresh appreciation of how underlying emotions and motives flow among certain individuals, sometimes surfacing in feelings of dislike, for instance, to whatever degree. And, of course, my thinking here is in line with material Seth himself soon gives in this session.

7. In Volume 1 of *"Unknown" Reality,* see the Sumari material and references in Appendix 9, and notes 2 and 3. In Volume 2, Seth discussed the Sumari language at 11:18 in the 723rd session; also see notes 9 and 11.

8. I began these notes several weeks after the 732nd session was held, so that I had some camouflage time to sort out events, and to let others happen.

Originally, however, I felt a surge of uneasiness as soon as Seth mentioned that my friend, artist Peter Smith, is a counterpart of mine. When I checked the 724th session, I affirmed the reason for that reaction: Seth had stated therein that Peter and I were *not* counterparts, although "closely enough allied so that in certain terms you 'share' some of the same psychic memories. . . ." Why the contradiction, I wondered, even if Seth had qualified it? Neither Jane nor I believed I'd mistakenly recorded Seth in either the 724th or the 732nd session; we planned to ask him soon for clarification.

Sue Watkins, who had introduced Peter to Jane and me in 1973, was involved in the question through her friendship with all of us. It was Sue who verified that several months ago Peter had described to her what he now felt to be the same psychic event I'd tuned in to just a few weeks ago (on December 3, 1974)—only Peter's experience had taken place in 1967! I called my version of it my "fourth Roman," and presented an account of it in Appendix 22; through internal pictures I saw, in Jerusalem in the first century A.D., the violent death of my traitorous Roman-soldier counterpart.

Before I got around to asking Seth about whether or not Peter Smith and I were counterparts, Sue had enough time to do some thinking of her own about the subject. As she's done before (in Volume 1, see the opening notes for Session 692, with Note 2), Sue produced some excellent writing on matters psychic—this time on possible variations within the counterpart relationship. Here are abbreviated excerpts covering a few of the ideas she wrote down at my request:

"The thought occurred to me that perhaps Seth's remarks (in sessions 724 and 732) were more pertinent to the situation than we imagined. What if at one time Peter and Rob had *been* counterparts, and, having served a purpose, somehow 'became' no longer counterparts? Once you 'killed your enemy,' (and therefore yourself)—like the Roman soldier in Jerusalem—and realized it, did something change the counterpart connection? Do counterparts slide in and out of interconnections, according to needs, beliefs, and the experience of the present personalities involved?

"As Seth has noted before—and as we *feel*, I think—there are distinct connections between Peter and me and Rob and Jane, in terms of age differences, creative abilities, belief patterns, et cetera. Not that I think the four of us are involved in a counterpart association now—just that perhaps we have been, or that our friendship is a recalling of that kind of connection. Or that we recognize certain *possibilities* in each other and react (rather humorously, I think) to those.

"An idea came to me a few days ago, when I was thinking about my fascination with the time of Henry VIII (in 16th-century England). I wondered, 'Whatever happened to Henry?' Suddenly I had the thought that maybe in linear terms Henry is now 'many' people—that he has a *number* of offshoots or counterpart personalities alive at once. So, theoretically, you could get all the Henry people together now, have them alter their consciousnesses to a certain degree, and compile from them an amazing multilevel, multifaceted portrait of Henry VIII—assuming, of course, that one would be willing to accept such subjective experiences as valid. What a wonderful, weird view of 'history'—and probably a truer one than we're used to. . . ."

And in his own way Seth confirmed one of Sue's projections. From a deleted session that I prefer not to date here because of other, personal reasons: "I may have slipped up, but I do not think so: I do not believe I gave the information about you and Peter in book dictation (for *'Unknown' Reality*), in order to keep the material simple enough for the reader—although you chose to include that (724th) session in the book anyhow. But you and Peter are and are not counterparts. You do share psychic memories, and hold in common the memories of other selves who did live in the time of your *(fourth)* Roman-soldier incident.

"Those memories exist as patterns. In this life, each of you come together and part, come together and part again, forming a counterpart relationship when it suits your purposes, as streams of consciousness mix and merge, and then separate.

"These counterparts are psychic relationships, formations that in the deepest terms flow into historic time and out of it. Some, in your terms, last a lifetime. Others represent psychic encounters that happen between two individuals at several points, say, but are not continuous. They may be no less intense, however."

9. Carl Jones is mentioned in the 561st session for Chapter 14 of *Seth Speaks*.

10. Jane initiated the Sumari development on her own, in the ESP class for November 23, 1971. The next night Seth began discussing that psychic event in the 598th session. During one delivery he remarked somewhat humorously that the Sumari "want someone else to take care of what they have created . . .", that "they don't hang around to cut the grass. . . ." Jane quoted short passages from the session in Chapter 7 of *Adventures in Consciousness*.

In *Seth Speaks*, see chapters 11–13. Seth delivered much material about reincarnation, including "the time of choosing" between lives, recreating and changing events in past lives, and past and present reincarnational family relationships; probabilities; dreams; the fetus, and so forth.

Session 733
January 27, 1975
9:25 P.M. Monday

Good evening *(quietly.*

("Good evening, Seth.")

Dictation: When you are in an airplane looking down upon the planet, then you see the mountain ranges and the valleys, the rivers, plateaus, cities, fields and villages. To some extent you realize that the world has physical contents, existing at one time yet varying in their characteristics. In those terms, the world is composed of its physical ingredients. That "package" is the only part of the picture that you see, however.

Psychically, your world is composed of the contents of its consciousness. You have maps of continents and oceans, and in the entire view each portion is like a piece of a jigsaw puzzle, all fitting together perfectly, smoothly flowing into the natural structure of the world. So at any given time there is a world consciousness, a perfect jigsaw of awareness in which each identity, however large or small, has its part.

There are earthquakes that erupt physically, and tracings are made of them. There are also inner earthquakes of consciousness from which the physical ones emerge—storms of mind or being, eruptions in which one segment of the world consciousness, repressed in one area, explodes in another.

If you could orbit your planet in a different kind of craft, you could view the psychic contents of the world, seeing the world consciousness shining far more brilliantly than any lighted city. You could spot the point of intense activity, see the birth of new myths and the death of old ones as certainly as you might be able to see a mountain slide or a tidal wave. The physical portions of earth are all related. So does consciousness form its own kind of inner structures from which, again, the physical ones emerge. You are indeed counterparts, then, each of the other. Yet as there is great variety to physical form, so counterparts follow a still more expansive inner freedom that finds an even greater diversity of characteristics.

As I have certainly hinted, the body is a miraculous organism, and you have barely learned the most simple of its structures.[1] You do not understand the properties of soul or body, yet the body was given to you so that you could learn from it. The properties of the earth are meant to lead you into the nature of the soul. You create physical reality, yet without knowing how you do so, so that the wondrous structure of the earth itself is meant to lead you to question your own source. Nature as you understand it is meant to be your teacher. You are not its master.

(Louder:) The creator is not the master of his creations. He is simply their creator, and he creates because he does not attempt to control. Period.

(9:45.) When you try to control power or people, you always copy. To some extent the world copies itself, in that there are patterns.[2] But those patterns are always changed to one extent or another, so that no object is ever a copy of another—though it may appear to be the same.

(All emphatically and joyously:) In your terms, the world is intensely different from one moment to another, with each smallest portion of consciousness choosing its reality from a field of infinite probabilities.[3] Immense calculations, far beyond your conscious decisions as you think of them, are possible only because of the unutterable freedom that resides within minute worlds inside your skull—patterns of interrelationships, counterparts so cunningly woven that each is unique, freewheeling, and involved in an infinite cooperative venture so powerful that the atoms stay in certain forms, and the same stars shine in the sky.

The familiar and strange are intimately connected in your most obvious, your simplest utterance. You are surrounded by miracles. Why, then, does the world so often seem dour and cruel? Why do your fellow beings sometimes seem like unfeeling monsters—*(loudly:)* Frankensteins not of body but of mind, spiritual idiots, ignorant of any heritage of love or truth or even graceful beasthood? Why does it seem to many of you that the race, the species, is doomed? *(Whispering:)* Why do some of you feel, in your quiet moments, such a sentence just?[4]

You make your own reality.

That goes by itself in a separate paragraph.

(Loudly:) Generally speaking (underlined), most of you live in your own world, with others of your kind. Those of you who do not believe in war have not experienced it. It may have surrounded you, but you did not experience it. Those of you who do not believe in greed have not suffered its "consequences." If you still see it, it is because it is a part of your reality. If you are honestly not greedy, yet you see greed, then perhaps you are serving as an example to others—but you form your own reality.

(10:01.) There are more worlds than you suppose, and in your own private experience each of you contributes to the world that you know. You and your counterparts together form it. Your physical body alone is equipped to perceive far more than you presently allow it to. Physically you are a part of every other person upon the earth, and you have a connection with each leaf and frog and nail.

You choose the city or state or country in which you live. No one forces you to stay there unless you are looking for an excuse to remain. So you choose your psychic land as well. You can travel from one psychic land to another as you can journey into other parts of the physical world. Some great travelers never left the country of their birth.

(Again loudly:) Michelangelo[5] roamed the centuries, picking up visions and ideas as others might buy postcards, journeying from one country to a foreign land. His genius shows you what you are, and yet it is but a hint of the potential with which your species is endowed.

In the light of such ideals, surely you seem wanting—yet your reality is one in which the greatest freedoms have been allowed.

This means that you have given yourselves full range so that all probabilities could be explored, and none left out that were physically feasible.

(Again louder:) This species gave itself no "preordained" taboos.

The infinite ranges possible to human capabilities would be explored—and those who chose that route said, quote: "We will trust that our creativity will find its own way, and if there are nightmares we will waken from them. We will even learn from them. We will dare to push aside the dimensions of being into those realms in which only the gods have gone before—and through our utter vulnerability to experience, discover the divinity that gives our humanity its meaning. And (whispering) through the compassion that we have learned, will we be able to understand the divine errors[6] that gave us the gift of our birth. Souls and molecules each are learning, each are forming realities, each are a part of a divinity in which each counterpart has a part to play."

Break.

(10:18. Jane's trance had been deep, her delivery often fast and impassioned. She'd felt a great energy sweeping through her, she told me. In volume, her voice had ranged up and down the scale—a most unusual demonstration as far as these sessions for "Unknown" Reality are concerned; usually she has Seth come through in a rather businesslike, routine manner, with any milder voice or speed effects taking place within that framework.

(Jane was quite relaxed. "Now I don't know what to do—I could go to bed or continue the session for hours. . . ." She'd spent most of her day writing lyrics for rock music—for reasons not necessary to go into here—and now that activity reminded her of a poem she'd written in May 1963, well over six months before she began speaking for Seth. She recited the first verse:

Magic is my middle name,
I was so brave and tall.
No one knew who I was then,
Myself least of all.

(Jane hasn't written for music before, and found that creative activity very refreshing.

(Instead of ending the session she took time out for a peanut-butter sandwich and a glass of milk. Then at 11:15: "I'm just waiting . . ." Then: "Now I'm getting different things but they aren't clear, so I'll just wait . . ." Then at 11:20: "I'm getting one of those frustrating things that's too big—too massive, really,—to be verbalized. There's a sense of strain. I'm trying to go beyond myself . . . Now I'm almost getting it . . ." Jane, half smiling, bemused, *shook her head. "Well, I'll see, Rob. I'll just see. . . ." She lit a cigarette and took off her glasses. Quietly at 11:50:)*

I dwell, in a way, in a realm that is more <u>direct</u> than yours. That is one image. I allow myself greater acknowledgment of my being. I speak with the wisdom, for example, that your cells would utter if they had speech.

I am more aware of my reality than you are of yours, but the terms of being are the same in every place and every time. They bring forth the greater comprehension of each self, <u>of</u> itself. (*Long pause.*) Ruburt experiences now what he calls a massive quality, a physical and psychic expansion of consciousness in which the dear familiar world seems small—yet twice precious. So does it appear to my consciousness.[7]

The petty wars, even those still to be fought, are but dim memories, once vital but lost as nightmares in greater awakenings. So even in this moment Ruburt faintly feels a nostalgic memory for lives come and gone, as you might for fond dreams barely recalled.

They represent a present unique beyond telling, alive in <u>each</u> consciousness, more important than you recognize. There are no real rules to be followed that will bring you into such an encounter with the present moment of reality—only a <u>trust</u> in the nature of your being. And that trust <u>is</u> within you whether or not you recognize it, for it gives you your present experience; and no matter how your mind questions, it rides securely in the great creativity of the soul.

That soul constantly creates the body, and each individual on the face of the earth at any given time places his or her trust in that reality. That feeling of certainty is the same that any plant knows. Any idea, creative insight, or dream, rides upon the same sure thrust.

End of dictation. End of session, and a fond good evening.

(*"Thank you, Seth, and the same to you."*)

(*12:05 A.M. Jane said her "massive" feeling was gone now. She added that she didn't think she'd held anything back; but at the same time, she had sensed information we weren't ready for yet—or that, to put it another way, lay in our future.*)

NOTES: Session 733

1. Seth, way back in the 23rd session for February 5, 1964: "Nor do I know all the answers. It is, however, a fact that even man, in his blundering manner, will discover that he himself creates his own physical

universe, and that the mechanisms of the physical body have more functions and varieties than he knows."

2. At about the time Seth was producing his material on patterns for *"Unknown" Reality*, Jane was dealing with the same concept from her own much more personal viewpoint. See Chapter 18 of *Politics:* "It's the entire human element that is so perplexing, vast, humorous, and tragic all at once. To some extent, my humor helps me avoid pitfalls, and lets me help others to see their lives in better perspective.

"Then I understood something else: The phone calls, visits, and letters were falling into patterns, just as the subjective events of my life had been doing. They came in clusters, dealing with certain particular questions and subject matter. Each call gave me the opportunity to see how various people organized exterior reality according to inner politics. Amazing that I hadn't seen the connections earlier."

3. See Seth's material on his units of consciousness, or CU's, in sessions 682–83 for Volume 1 of *"Unknown" Reality*. In the 682nd session after 9:47, for example, he discussed relationships between CU's and probable realities.

4. I felt distinctly uncomfortable here as I took down Seth's vehement words. For whatever reasons, he sounded too much like I had at the supper table tonight, right after I'd scanned the headlines of the front page of our daily newspaper.

5. See Jane's comments about Michelangelo (Buonarroti) at the end of the 721st session.

6. Much of Seth's material in this session (and in this paragraph), along with his obviously intense feelings about what he was saying, reminded me of a group of sessions he gave well over a decade ago on the three creative dilemmas of All That Is. In them he discussed at length the "agonized search" for expression of the powers of creativity and existence, and how the beginning of that search "may have represented the birth throes of All That Is as we know it."

Those sessions, 426–28, were held in August 1964, and Jane presented excerpts from them in Chapter 18 of *The Seth Material.*

7. For material concerning some of Jane's experiences with massiveness, see the opening pages of Appendix 19, as well as its Note 2. Not only is Seth Two involved; Volume 1, of *"Unknown" Reality*, as well as *Personal Reality*, are referred to.

Seth's almost casual remark here: "So does it appear to my consciousness," embodies a new thought for us in connection with Jane's adventures with massiveness; it's the kind of clue about the Seth phenomenon that we're always interested in getting. I also think the statement represents one way in which Jane, while speaking for Seth, interprets his reality for us in terms we can understand.

Session 734
January 29, 1975
9:10 P.M. Wednesday

(See Appendix 26 for some of the family-of-consciousness material that Jane delivered for Seth in ESP class yesterday evening.

("I'm at the point now where I know what Seth's going to talk about," Jane said a few minutes before the session began. "I feel funny waiting, though—edgy, or restless. Maybe it's the wind. Seth's there, but he doesn't quite make it through. . . ."

(The weather had been fluctuating dramatically all day. It turned extremely windy tonight—so much so that I thought about tornadoes, although we'd heard no radio warnings about them. This afternoon the temperature had registered better than 50°; it still read considerably above freezing, even if the chill factor generated by the wind made the night seem much colder. Finally:)

Good evening.

("Good evening, Seth.")

Dictation: There is a connection between counterparts and the families of consciousness.

As you and your brothers or sisters might belong to the

573

same physical family, so generally are you and your counterparts part of the same psychic group of consciousness.[1] Remember, however, that these psychic groups are like natural formations into which consciousness seems to flow. Your own interests, desires, and abilities are not predetermined by your membership in a given psychic family. Underline that entire sentence.

For example, you are not creatively playful because you are Sumari. Instead, you join the Sumari grouping because you are creatively playful. The groups of consciousness, then, are not to be equated with, say, astrological houses.

Taking the Sumari as an example, there can be overly intent, ponderous, or simply dour Sumari who have not learned to use their creativity graciously, or with joy. Yet that joyful use of ability will be their intent. At particular periods of history, in your terms, different families may predominate.

(Long pause. The wind burst against our apartment house in great forceful thrusts that were most unusual for this section of the country. The house actually shook at times. I found myself thinking that occasionally the trite phrase, "the howling wind," was a very apt one.)

The psychic groups, however, overlap physical and national ones. The Sumari are extremely independent, for instance, and as a rule you will not find them born into countries with dictatorships. When they do so appear, their work may set a spark that brings about changes, but they seldom take joint political action. Their creativity is very threatening to such a society.

However, the Sumari are practical in that they bring creative visions into physical reality, and try to live their lives accordingly. They are initiators, yet they make little attempt to preserve organizations, even ones they feel to be fairly beneficial. They are not lawbreakers by design or intent. They are not reformers in the strictest sense, yet their playful work does often end up reforming a society or culture. They are given to art, but in its broadest sense also, trying to make an "art" of living, for example. They have been a part of most civilizations, though they appeared in the Middle Ages *(A.D. 476–c. A.D. 1450)* least of all. They often come to full strength before great social changes. Others might build social structures from their work, for example, but the Sumari themselves, while pleased, will usually not be able to feel any intuitive sense of belonging with any structured group.[2]

(9:38. The wind continued to beat strongly at the house. Jane paused in trance for some moments, her eyes closed as if to repel the noise.)

There is no correlation between the families of consciousness and bodily characteristics, however. Many of the Sumari choose to be born in the springtime,[3] but all those born in the spring are not

Sumari, and no general rule applies there. They also have a liking for
certain races, but again no specific rules apply. Many of the Irish, the
Jews, the Spanish, and some lesser numbers of the French, for
instance, are Sumari—though they appear in all races.

Generally speaking, America has not been a Sumari nation, nor have the Scandinavian countries or England. Psychically
speaking, the Sumari often very nicely arrange existences in which
they are a minority—in a democracy, say, so that they can work at
their art within a fairly stable political situation. They are not
interested in government, yet they do rely upon it to that extent.
They are apt to be self-reliant within that framework. Their recognized artistic abilities may predominate or be fairly minimal.

Sumari is a state of mind, a slant of being. They are not
fighters, nor will they generally advocate a violent overthrow of
government or mores. They believe in the creativity of change,
naturally occurring.

Nevertheless, they are often part of the cultural underground simply because they are seldom conformers. A Sumari is
very uncomfortable as a member of any large commercial venture,
particularly if the work involves habitual or boring routine. They are
not happy on assembly lines. They like to play with details—or to use
them for creative purposes. They often go from one job or profession to another for that reason.

(9:55.) If you begin to look into the nature of yourself, and
feel intuitively that you are a Sumari, then you should look for a
position in which you can use your inventiveness. Sumari enjoy
theoretical mathematics, for example, yet make miserable book-
keepers.

In the arts, Picasso was a Sumari.

(9:57.) Give us a moment . . . Many entertainers are Sumari. You will seldom find them in politics. They are not usually
historians.

(Long pause.) There are few with any position within
organized religions. Because of their feelings of self-reliance, however, you can find them as farmers, working intuitively with the land.
They are equally divided between the sexes. In your society, however, Sumari qualities in the male have until lately been frowned
upon to some degree.

Take your break.

(10:01 P.M. Her trance hadn't been particularly deep, Jane said,
yet now she proceeded to underestimate by almost half the 51 minutes she'd been
"under." She still felt unsettled; she still wasn't sure that her odd state resulted
from the tumultuous weather.

(I wrote down two questions for Seth, and read them to her:

(1. Granting Seth's concept of time: Does the reincarnating personality usually choose to experience its simultaneous lives through various families of consciousness, or is it more likely to remain "loyal" to one such family in all of them? At the start of tonight's session Seth had remarked that generally speaking counterparts are part of the same psychic family, but I wanted to know if reincarnating personalities are also.

(2. And based upon my comments at the end of Session 732: How do animals, and other life or "nonlife" forms, fit into the counterpart and family-of-consciousness ideas?

(After listening to me discuss the second question for a couple of minutes, Jane said she had an answer to it, or at least a partial one. Her material was presumably from Seth, although she would give it. Just as she began speaking she was interrupted by a heavy knocking—first at the door to the public hall that separates the two apartments we occupy on the second floor, then at each of the apartment doors themselves. A feminine voice cried out for Jane. We waited. The persistent racket, penetrating the wind noise, meant just what we thought it would: an end to the evening's session. When I opened the door I faced a comely but very agitated woman whom I'll call Barbara. She was probably in her early 40's. An expensive suitcase sat beside her.

("Aren't you expecting me? Seth told me you would be. . . ."

(Neither Jane nor I had expected our unexpected out-of-state visitor, of course. I can note later that Jane dealt more extensively with the whole episode in Chapter 18 of Politics—[and also that it's interesting to compare our individual accounts of the same event, even though mine is much shorter]. Just let me state here that we found ourselves confronting a well-educated individual who was deeply afraid of her own energy. Because of that fear she had developed certain problems that were severe enough to keep her from working at her profession in the law.

(Barbara insisted that she wanted help, but as in other cases that Jane and I have encountered, her focus upon her distress was so intense that we couldn't breach it; certainly not in the little time available. Neither could Seth, who eventually came through—a course of action Jane hardly ever allows to happen in that kind of circumstance. Barbara just couldn't grasp that she was creating her own reality.

(After two frustrating hours I took her to a motel. The wind had abated considerably, but the night was much colder. When I returned I was able to tell Jane that Barbara had made a decision: Tomorrow she was going to journey by airplane halfway across the country—to see another psychic who would surely be able to help her.

(And Jane had something to tell me: She had been able to account for her strange restlessness this evening as soon as Barbara appeared, for she realized she'd been "picking up" that the session would be interrupted. "Of course," we said now, using that very valuable attribute called hindsight. But

each time Jane gets this kind of confirmation of her abilities, it seems that both of us are surprised anew.

> *(Now see Note 4 for material concerning the two questions I'd noted at 10:01.)*

NOTES: Session 734

1. See the 732nd session at 11:14.

2. Jane and I are Sumari (see notes 7 and 10 for Session 732). I can write that many of the characteristics Seth mentioned this evening apply to us, as we've learned over the years—especially those concerning our love of art, our being initiators, and our desires to be free of social structures. At the same time we readily agree that organizations are indispensible within the world's very complicated cultures. We do have strong interests in national and world politics. Yet if our work is to ever result in social changes of any kind, those changes will have to be carried through by others, for primarily Jane and I work alone.

In a way, however, Seth may do Jane and me something of an injustice when he remarks, for instance, that the Sumari "don't hang around to cut the grass. . . ." (Again, see Note 10 for Session 732.) Jane and I may be involved with the arts, and impatient at times, but we're also extremely tenacious when we decide to do something we consider worthwhile. I doubt that the Seth material would exist in its present recorded form if we weren't that way.

3. In view of Seth's statement that "Many of the Sumari choose to be born in the springtime," I decided to poll the members of Jane's class for their months of birth. At various times, and usually in connection with other subjects, Seth has referred to many of them as being Sumari. Actually, I took my little survey on February 4, the evening following next Monday's session, but give the rather ambiguous results here because of the predominately Sumari material in this (734th) session. Here's the month-birth breakdown of the 37 people present for that particular class (including Jane and me):

January	2	July	3
February	4	August	4
March	7	September	2
April	4	October	1
May	3	November	1
June	4	December	2

Total—37

These figures can hardly be definitive in any sense, however; they're meant only to point out some interesting directions for study, involving groups and the various families of consciousness to which their members may belong. I'll simply note, then, that 24 of the 37 students in Jane's class were born in the first half of the year. From that point on, the figures can be assembled and interpreted in different ways. Obviously they'd change within limits from class to class, depending not only on which members were in attendance, but on which ones are Sumari. Seth hasn't pointed out every Sumari in class; some have strong feelings about belonging to that family of consciousness, but others don't.

How one chooses to define "spring" also enters in, of course. Astronomically, spring in the Northern Hemisphere covers the period from about March 21 to June 21 or 22, although many just think of it as embracing March, April, and May. (Jane was born on May 8, I was born on June 20. She's half English, one-quarter Irish, one-quarter French and Canadian Indian. My English ancestry is leavened with a bit of Irish and German.)

We may not be able to pin Seth—as that energy personality essence calls himself—down to one physical race, but he *is* a Sumari: "And a very high lieutenant indeed, I will have you know," he told us with much humor in his first session on the Sumari family of consciousness, the 598th for November 24, 1971. A month later he offered more insights on his own reality—the kind of information we're always interested in acquiring (as I wrote in Note 7 for the 733rd session). From Session 601 for December 22 of that year, then:

"As my name basically makes little difference, so does the name Sumari make little difference. But the names signify an independent, unique kind of consciousness that makes use of certain boundaries.

"Your [Sumari] consciousness is that kind of consciousness, and so is mine, except that my boundaries are far less limited than your own, and I recognize them not as boundaries but as directions in which recognition of myself must grow. The same applies to the Sumari as such. In other words, this is not an undifferentiated consciousness that addresses you now, but one that understands the nature of its own identity.

"It is a personal consciousness. The difference in degree, however, between my recognition of my identity and your recognition of your own reality is vast. Do you follow me?"

"Yes," I said. (I underlined Seth's phrase above because I think that in it he expressed an important, creative aspect of his reality.)

"The point is that I am not impersonal any more than you are, in those terms, and in those same terms the Sumari are also individual and to that extent personal. You are a part of the Sumari. You have certain characteristics, in simple terms, as a family might have certain characteristics, or the members of a nation."

4. Strange, how things can develop or not in our camouflage reality. I'll explain what I mean by referring to my two questions for Seth in reverse order. At the end of the 732nd session I expressed the hope that "... we'd soon begin to get the material we wanted..." from him on whether the counterpart and family-of-consciousness mechanisms applied

to other species and forms than our own; hence my second question this evening. With Seth's evident help, Jane herself began at least a partial answer—one that was cut off by our visitor, Barbara, pounding upon our door. Jane's focus and concentration on the subject were broken, and we didn't return to it at the time. Not only that: I must note that even several years later we've still acquired no Seth material at all on such possible counterpart and family-of-consciousness roles. I also let go (although not consciously and deliberately) my plans to keep after Seth for that kind of information.

If we'd encouraged him to begin answering question No. 2, then, Jane and I assume that as time passed much of his succeeding work would have been changed and enlarged in scope to some observable degree. Seth could have based future sessions upon the additional conscious knowledge already given us; we'd have possessed the larger frame of reference necessary to accommodate even more new material.

Although in this note I've stressed the "what-might-have-been" aspects of that second question, the same thinking can apply to the first one also, in which I wanted to know how many families of consciousness might be chosen by the reincarnating personality during its "cycle" of simultaneous lives. Yet my feelings of regret here aren't as great as they are for having missed out on something good with question No. 2.

Session 735
February 3, 1975
9:12 P.M. Monday

*(Last Thursday I finished the final pen-and-ink drawing of the 40
I'd planned for Jane's book of poetry,* Dialogues of the Soul and Mortal
Self in Time.[1] *I spent Friday checking the batch, then on Saturday morning I
mailed them to Tam Mossman, Jane's editor at Prentice-Hall. That afternoon
we talked with a real-estate agent, Debbie [not her real name], whom we've
known for some time. Sunday we rested. And today we began house hunting.[2]*

*(From the outside only, Jane and I inspected several homes in
Elmira. The first one we looked at—a bungalow on a Foster Avenue—intrigued
us considerably. Our interest was hardly coincidental, though. Debbie had
pointed out a photograph of it in a local real estate catalog, and we were quite
aware that it bore a good resemblance to the house we'd considered buying in
Sayre, Pennsylvania, in the spring of 1974.[3] Besides being bungalows, both
houses were of about the same age, and even of similar colors.*

*(Jane and I were also interested in the fact that we'd seldom been on
Foster Avenue, even though it lay within comfortable walking distance of the
apartment house we lived in on Water Street; nor could either of us recall having*

noticed the "Foster Avenue place" before. We speculated that we'd "homed in on it" now, as if for the first time, because our combined focus was opening up in the direction of homes.

(That concentration upon places to live reminded us of families, of course—"regular" families as well as Seth's families of consciousness. While I drove us back to our apartment house for supper we discussed the incredibly complicated roles and events surrounding those different kinds of organizations—whereupon Jane came up with a most apt phrase: "The genealogy of events. . . ." She laughed, then added: "As families of people have their genealogies, so do families of events."[4]

(As we waited for the session to begin Jane abruptly received a block of impressions from Seth. They concerned the opposing uses of personal power by two individuals whom we'd encountered within the last week: the woman lawyer who had interrupted the session last Wednesday evening, and who is so afraid of her power; and the young classical guitarist who had visited us last night, and who revels in the positive use of his power. The impressions are for use in either "Unknown" Reality, *Jane said, or in* Psychic Politics.[5] *She grinned: "Thanks, Seth." Then she launched into the session before I could finish these notes. I came back to them at first break.)*

Good evening.

("Good evening, Seth.")

Dictation. Give us a moment . . .

The Sumari characteristics do not exist in isolation, of course. To one extent or another, each family of consciousness carries within it the characteristics inherent in all of the families. There is, therefore, great diversity.

The Sumari abilities are highly creative ones, however. To a large extent they have been inhibited in your society. I have been speaking of them here so that each individual can learn to recognize his or her own degree of Sumariness. The playful, creative elements of personality can then be released. These qualities are particularly important as they add to, temper, or enhance the primary characteristics of the other families of consciousness.

(Pause.) If you are a "reformer," a "reformer by nature," then the Sumari characteristics, brought to the surface, could help you temper your seriousness with play and humor, and actually assist you in achieving your reforms far easier than otherwise. Each personality carries traces of other characteristics besides those of the family of consciousness to which he or she might belong. The creative aspects of the Sumari can be particularly useful if those aspects are encouraged in any personality, simply because their inventive nature throws light on all elements of experience.

The psyche as you know it, then, is composed of a mixture of these families of consciousness. One is not superior to the others. They are just different, and they represent various ways of looking at physical life. *(Pause.)* A book would be needed to explain the dimensions of the psyche in relation to the different families of consciousness. Here, in this manuscript, I merely want to make the reader aware of the existence of these psychic groupings. I am alert to the fact that I am using many terms, and that it may seem difficult to understand the differences between probable and reincarnational selves, counterparts and families of consciousness. At times contradictions may seem to exist. You may wonder how you are you in the midst of such multitudinous psychic "variations."

An apple can be red, round, weigh so much, be good to eat, sit in a basket, but be natural on a tree. It can be tart or sweet. You can find one on the ground, or on a table or in a pie. None of these things are contradictory to the nature of an apple. You do not ask: "How can an apple have color and be round at the same time?"

(Long pause.) You can look at an apple and hold it in your hands, so it is obvious that its shape does not contradict its color. You see that an apple can be red or green or both. If I said: "Apples sit quietly on a table," you would have to agree that such is sometimes the case. If I said: "Apples roll down grassy inclines," you would also have to agree. If I said: "Apples fall down through space," you would again be forced to concede the point. It would be clear to you that none of these statements contradicted each other, for in different circumstances apples behave differently.

(9:40.) So far, you do not hold your consciousness in your hand, however. When I speak of the behavior of your psyche, then, you may wonder: "How can my psyche exist in more than one time at once?" It can do this just as an apple can be found on a table or on the ground or on the tree.

(Then:) Change that last sentence to read: "just as apples. . ." *(My emphasis.*

(Occasionally Seth will make this kind of correction in his material.)

The inside dimensions of consciousness cannot be so easily described, however. If you ask: "How can I have reincarnational and probable selves at once?", you are asking a question comparable to the one mentioned earlier, colon: "How can an apple have color and be round at the same time?"

(9:45.) Give us a moment . . . A young man was here last evening. He possesses great mastery of the guitar. As he played, it was obvious that any given composition "grew" from the first note,

and had always been latent within it. An infinite number of other "alternate" compositions were also latent within the same note, however, but were not played last night. They were quite as legitimate as the compositions that <u>were</u> played. They were, in fact, inaudibly a part of each heard melody, and those unheard variations added silent structure and pacing to the physically actualized music.

Following this analogy, in the same way each psyche contains within it infinite notes, and each note is capable of its own endless creative variations. You follow one melody of yourself, and for some reason you seem to think that the true, full orchestra of yourself will somehow drown you out *(intently)*.

When I speak in terms of counterparts, then, or of reincarnational selves and probable selves, I am saying that in the true symphony of your being you <u>are</u> violins, oboes, cymbals, harps—in other words, you are a living instrument through which you play yourself. You are not an instrument upon which you are played. You are the composer and the symphony. You play ballads, classical pieces, lyrics, operas. One creative performance does not contradict the others.

Take your break.

(9:58 to 10:16.)

Life as you think of it is far from being inflexible.

Returning to our comments about the alternate compositions, you can at any time bring into your own life-composition elements from any "alternate" ones. Period.

Some people structure their lives around their children, others around a career, or pleasure, or even pain. Again, these are simply certain focuses that you choose, that direct your experience. You can add other focuses while still retaining your own identity—indeed, enriching it.

Sometimes you act as though one ability contradicts another. You think: "I cannot be a good parent and a sexual partner to my mate at the same time." To those who feel this way a definite contradiction seems implied. A woman might feel that the qualities of a mother almost stand in opposition to those of an exuberant sex mate. A man might imagine that fatherhood meant providing an excellent home and income. He might think that "aggressiveness,"[6] competition, and emotional aloofness were required to perform that role. These would be considered in opposition to the qualities of love, understanding, and emotional support "required" of a husband. In actuality, of course, no such contradictions apply. In the same way, however, you often seem to feel that your identity is dependent upon a certain highly specific role, until other qualities quite your own seem threatening. They almost seem to be unself-like.[7]

To some degree you feel the same way when you en-counter the concept of probable selves, or of counterparts. It is as though you had an unlimited bank of abilities and characteristics from which to draw, and yet were afraid of doing so—fearing that any addition could make you less instead of more. If all of this goes on personally, as you choose one melody and call it yourself, then perhaps you can begin to see the mass creative aspects in terms of civilizations that seem to rise and fall.

So you look back through the historical past. All of the counterparts alive as contemporaries then form, together, a musical composition in what you think of as a present; and once that multi-dimensional song is struck then its past ripples out behind it, so to speak, and its future sings "ahead." But the song is being created from its beginning and its end simultaneously. In this case, how-ever, it is as if each note has its own consciousness and is free to change its portion of the melody. Yet all are in the same overall composition, in "time," so that time itself serves as the scale (gesturing) in which the [musical] number is written—chosen as a matter of organization, focus, and framework.

Now in music the pauses are as important as the sounds. In fact, they serve to highlight the sounds, to frame them. The sounds are significant because of their placement within the pauses or silences. So the portions of your psyche that you recognize as yourself are significant and intimate and real, because of the inner pauses or silences that are not actualized, but are a part of your greater being.

Now imagine a composition in which the pauses and the silences that you do not hear are sounded—and the notes that you hear are instead the unheard inner structure.

In the last few sentences there is an intuitive "definition" of probable and reincarnational selves, and counterparts, in rela-tionship to the self that you know. In your case, however, you can change your own pacing, add variations, or even begin an entirely new composition if you choose to. Now many people have done this in very simple, mundane ways by suddenly deciding to use abilities they had earlier ignored. A man of letters, for instance, at the age of 40 suddenly remembers his old love of carpentry, reads do-it-yourself manuals, and begins his own home repairs. After disdain-ing such activities as beneath him for years, he suddenly discovers an intimate relationship with earth and its goods, and this appreciation adds to words that before may have been as dry as ash.

(10:48.) In that case, you see, there would be in another reality a carpenter or his equivalent with a latent love of words, unexpressed—and that individual would then begin to develop; reading books on how to write, perhaps, and taking up a hobby that would allow him to express in words his love of the land and its goods. *(With emphasis:)* The creativity of the psyche means that no one world or experience could ever contain it. Therefore does it create the dimensions in which it then has its experiences.

Each portion, by whatever name, contains within it the latent potentials of the whole. If the unknown reality exists, it is because you play one melody over and over and so identify yourself, while closing out, consciously at least, all of the other possible variations that you could add to that tune.

Give us a moment . . . Do you want to rest your hand?

("No.")

There are many kinds of music. I could say: "Music is triumphant," or "Music is tragic." You would understand that I am not contradicting myself. You would not say, or *(humorously)* at least I hope you would not say: "Why would anyone write a composition like Tchaikovsky's *Pathétique*?"[8] Why would a composer choose a somber mood? The music itself would have its own sweep and power, and would indeed be <u>beautiful</u> beyond all concepts of good and evil.

(All very intent, leaning forward, eyes wide and dark:) In some manner, even a tragic composition of merit transcends tragedy itself. The composer was <u>exultant</u> in the midst of the deepest emotions of tragedy, or even of defeat. In such cases the tragedy itself is chosen as an emotional framework upon which the psyche plays. The framework is not thrust upon it, but indeed <u>chosen</u> precisely because of its own characteristics—even those of despondency, perhaps.

Tasting those qualities to the utmost, from that framework the psyche probes the fires of vitality and being as <u>experienced</u> from that specific viewpoint, and the despondency <u>can</u> be more alive than an unprobed, barely experienced joy. In the same manner, certain individuals can and do choose life experiences that involve great tragedies. Yet those tragic lives are used as a focus point that actually brings into experience, through comparison, the great <u>vitality</u> and <u>thrust</u> of being.

(Still in the same intense manner:) This does not mean that a tragic life is more vital than a happy, simple one. It just means that each individual is involved in an <u>art of living</u>. There are different themes, instruments, melodies—but existence, like great art, cannot be confined to simple definitions.

From the outside, for instance, it might seem as if a young person dies because in one way or another he or she is dissatisfied with life itself. Certainly it is usually taken for granted that suicides are afraid of life. However, suicides and would-be suicides often have such a great literal lust for life that they constantly put it into jeopardy, so that they can experience what it is in heightened form. The same applies to many who follow dangerous professions. It is fashionable to suppose that these people have a death wish. Instead, many of them have an intensified life wish, so to speak. Certainly it seems destructive to others. To those people, however, the additional excitement is worth the risk. The risk, in fact, gives them an intensified version of life.[9]

This is obviously not the case with all suicides[10] or would-be suicides, or all risk-takers. But those elements are there. A person who dies at 17 may have experienced much greater dimensions of living, in your terms, than someone who lives to be 82. Such people are not as unaware of those choices as it seems.

You may take a break or get Ruburt his cigarettes, as you prefer.

("We'll take the break, then."
(11:15 to 11:31.)

This does not mean that you cannot alter your experience at any given point.

Take a hypothetical young woman named Mary, who is partial to the kinds of experiences just mentioned. Temperamentally, she seeks out crisis situations. She may initiate suicide attempts. On the other hand she may entertain no such ideas, but be murdered at the age of 17.

(Forcefully:) We are certainly not condoning the murderer—but no slayer kills someone who does not want to die, either.

He picks, or she picks, victims as intuitively as the victim seeks out the slayer. On the other hand, Mary's experiences in life may make her change her mind, so to speak, so that at 17 she encounters a severe illness instead, from which she victoriously recovers. Or she might narrowly miss being murdered when a bullet from the killer's gun hits the person next to her. On an entirely different level and in a different way, she might have no such experiences but be a writer of murder mysteries, or a nurse in surgery. The particular variations that one person might play are endless. You cannot consciously begin to alter the framework of your life, however, unless you realize first of all that you form it. The melody is your own. It is not inevitable, nor is it the only tune that you can play.

To some extent you can actualize portions of your own

unknown reality, and draw them into the experienced area of your life. There is an obvious relationship between one note and another in a musical composition. Now in terms of physical families and in larger terms of countries, there is a relationship between realities, which constantly change as the notes do. To some extent your reality is picked up by your contemporaries. They accept it or not according to the particular theme or focus of their lives.

(11:45.) Give us a moment . . .

(From its position on a bookcase some 10 feet away, the telephone began to ring—to faintly buzz, actually, since we'd turned down its bell before the session. Still, I was afraid the repetitious noise might bother Jane as she sat quietly in trance. Her eyes were closed.)

In those terms, you are not a part of any reality that is not your own. If you share it with others, it is because others are concerned with variations of the same theme. This applies in terms of world goals "at any given time."

(Still buzzing . . .) Give us a moment . . . For example: In certain terms, you are working with the challenge of how best to use the world's resources. Some countries will overproduce. Others will underproduce. Contradictions seem to occur. Some people will be overfed while others starve; some sated with material conveniences, others relatively ignorant of them. These are variations of the same theme, you see. In overall terms contemporaries are working on the same group of challenges, though either oversupply or great lack might show itself at any particular place. Perhaps, however, the challenges could not be clearly delineated without those extravagances of degree.

(The phone stopped ringing—at last.) As contemporaries, counterparts choose a particular time framework. The time format alone makes certain focuses clear, that in your terms could not be made in another context. What you learn in your present about industry— "progress"—and the equitable sharing of the earth's products, could only be learned in a context in which industrialism was <u>experienced</u> as going too far, where technology was seen and known as a growing jeopardy.

(Again forcefully:) In terms that I admit are difficult to describe, the creative solutions will change the course of history <u>in the past,</u> so that variations are taken, and technology does not progress <u>in the same way</u> that it "has" in your experience.

I have said before that personally you can change your past from the present.[11] The same applies to civilizations.

I will end the session. My heartiest good wishes and a fond good evening.

(12:01 A.M. The ending was quick. Jane's trances and deliveries

had been excellent—strong and vital. "Seth's going into historical probabilities in the next session," she said. "I could go into that stuff right now, I feel so good. I could do it for another hour without any hassle. There's a lot there on national counterparts, too."[12] Then while I wrote this note she proceeded to tell me more about what Seth had in mind.

(I knew that if I encouraged her she'd go back into the session. I was tempted, but it was after midnight; we had ESP class coming up in 19 hours, with much to do in the meantime. And my writing hand was getting tired.

("Tonight I did have the feeling—for the first time—that 'Unknown' Reality was heading toward an end," Jane said, "that Seth will soon be getting ready to tie it up, and incorporate the ending with the beginning . . . Not right away; but it's the first time I've felt that."

(Actually, she now had many channels open from Seth. It seemed that every topic we mentioned engendered another one. Seth even had "a bunch of stuff" available on Jane, myself, and music. This included data on my starting to take violin lessons when I was eight years old—an event I hadn't thought of for what seemed to be decades [it took place in 1927], but which I was able to instantly recall as soon as Jane mentioned it.)

NOTES: Session 735

1. I was about a month behind schedule in finishing the illustrations for *Dialogues*; see Note 1 for the 705th session. The delay doesn't matter in this case, though. Jane's publisher still has plenty of "lead time" for the production of the book, since it won't be marketed until the fall of 1975.

2. Every so often I've referred to the inconveniences of apartment living for us, especially those involving that ever-present, ever-growing traffic noise. During break for the 726th session, which was held on December 16, 1974, I wrote that we planned to start looking for a house of our own as soon as I finished the illustrations for *Dialogues*. Our need for a certain kind of privacy and quiet has become very strong. At the same time, we want to avoid the sense of isolation that might result if we move into the country. I'd probably like that, but realized some time ago that such a situation would bother Jane considerably.

The 726th session was held on a Monday night, and was the last one for *"Unknown" Reality* for the year. During a private session on the Wednesday night following, Seth had a few things to say relative to our upcoming house adventures:

"Give us a moment . . . Do not buy a house with a dirt cellar. Do not buy a house heated by oil. The fumes are not good. A house facing the east is good in your section of the country. Use your psychic abilities to ascertain the house's atmosphere, by all means—and no matter how fine it seems, do not buy it if you do not feel comfortable inside. It should have a fireplace because of the reminders of the hearth. It should not be sided with aluminum or other metal. In your area it should not face the south. This also has to do with the ways you use energy, so these are not general precepts for others to follow. Check with your pendulums.

"Even in the country, houses can have a closed quality if the mountains or trees press too tightly. The land that you own is important, but the visible land that you do <u>not</u> own is also, and you should be in sight of a mountain or some open area, while still having a private 'secret' area also."

It will be interesting to see how many of the points Seth mentioned above tally with the place Jane and I finally acquire.

For those who may be puzzled by Seth's reference to "pendulums," I'll quote a paragraph of my own for the 619th session at 10:01, in Chapter 4 of *Personal Reality:*

"The pendulum is a very old method. I use it, with excellent results, to obtain ideomotor—"subsconscious"—responses about knowledge that lies just outside my usual consciousness. I hold a small heavy object suspended by a thread so that it's free to move. By mentally asking questions, I obtain 'yes' or 'no' answers according to whether the pendulum swings back and forth, or from side to side."

3. In Volume 1 of *"Unknown" Reality*, see sessions 693–94, with their notes.

4. I can note later that during the next few weeks we were to recall that creative insight more than once.

5. In very gentle ways, Jane did eventually use some of Seth's impressions relative to both people—but cast in her own vernacular—for Chapter 18 of *Politics.* In that chapter she also began presenting, again from her viewpoint, material on our house-hunting activities; she plans to continue doing so in subsequent chapters.

6. For some of Seth's material in *Personal Reality* on true aggression, see Session 634 for Chapter 8, and Session 642 for Chapter 11.

7. In Volume 1, see Appendix 2 for Seth's discussion of the conflicts I felt between my artistic, writing, and sportsman selves. I spent a number of years working to resolve those feelings. From the private session for January 30, 1974, which I quoted in Appendix 2: "Your father's creativity . . . had its side of secrecy, privacy and aloneness . . . you identified creatively with his private nature. The writing self became latent as the sportsman did, yet the writing self and the artist were closely bound. You felt conflicts at time. It never occurred to you that the two aspects could release one another—one illuminating the other—and both be fulfilled. Instead you saw them as basically conflicting. You believed the painting self had to be protected . . . as you felt that your father had to protect <u>his</u> creative self in the household. . . ."

And in a note for that session I wrote: "Years ago, when Jane and I began living in Sayre, Pennsylvania, not long after our marriage in 1954, I began telling myself that before I reached the age of 40 I'd know whether I wanted to concentrate upon writing or painting—but that if I'd failed to do so before that date, I would then decide upon one or the other of those creative arts. I turned 40 in 1959–and chose painting."

8. It's no coincidence that Seth used the *Pathétique* here in his material. The symphony is, probably, Jane's and my favorite musical composition. We "discovered" the *Pathétique* during our courtship 21 years ago, and many times during the following months we listened to the two scratchy old records that carried the piece. But even then we were impressed—awed—by its creative power, over and above the obvious emotional connotations we put upon it.

9. Much of Seth's material in Chapter 18 of *Personal Reality* applies here; see especially Session 665. Then see (in the same book) Session 667 for Chapter 19.

10. For some Seth material on suicide, see the first delivery for the 546th session, in Chapter 11 of *Seth Speaks*. In the 642nd session for Chapter 11 of *Personal Reality*, Seth mentioned that suicide can be "the result of passivity and distorted aggression, and of natural pathways of communication not used or understood."

11. See the 657th session for Chapter 15 of *Personal Reality*; Seth talked about how to "repattern your past from the present."

12. A note added later: I'm sorry to write that Seth didn't discuss historical probabilities in the 736th session, or national counterparts either. I forgot to remind Jane of those topics before that session, just as I forgot to ask Seth about them while he was speaking. Several more sessions were held before I discovered the lapse, which occurred partly because I hadn't typed the 735th session yet, and neglected to refer to my handwritten notes, and partly because in the meantime Seth had returned to his material on the families of consciousness. My error was unfortunate, since I feel that his information would have been most original, enhancing future sessions.

My comments here are certainly reminiscent of those in Note 4 for the last session: I explained how Jane and I missed out on what I think would have been excellent material simply because she was interrupted by a visitor just as she began to deliver it. Then see Note 2 for Appendix 22, which contains some of the reasons why we often find it difficult to return to a certain session to flesh out a certain subject.

(I should add that those reasons do not involve any particular unwillingness on Seth's part to do this, nor is it that those data we want may have evaporated beyond his recall.)

Session 736
February 5, 1975
9:24 P.M. Wednesday

(One of the first houses Jane and I looked at yesterday occupied a hillside corner lot in West Elmira, on a street we'd never been on before. Our friend in real estate, Debbie, had directed us to it from a photograph in the same catalog she'd used to point out the Foster Avenue place, which we had inspected Monday. In fact, both houses are pictured, one above the other, on the same page of the catalog. See the opening notes for the last session.

(The house that was for sale—and which we came to call the "hill house"—was empty and locked. There were other homes about, but each one had a feeling of privacy amid its thick insulation of trees. We rather casually surveyed the place in question from our car. At the time it didn't "turn us on." It bore no similarity to those in Sayre, or on Foster Avenue in Elmira. It was a ranch-style, cedar-sided dwelling that had just been painted a dark green—a conventional one-story affair with white shutters, a fireplace, a picture window, an attached double garage in back, and many trees and shrubs. Part of the front lawn was rather steeply banked, part of the curving flagstone walk was stepped as it rose up to the porch. The house faced the south; before it in the valley lay

591

Elmira itself, almost hidden by trees; beyond the city the hills rose in tiers. Streets—without sidewalks—passed the hill house on but two sides, at the southwest corner, and each one dead-ended less than a block away. In back of the house to the north and east, woods rolled up the gentle curve of the hill and over its top.

(The above notes and my speculations to follow, all added later, look ahead to sessions 738–39 for February 19 and 24 respectively. I'm inserting the material here to continue the record of our house hunting in an orderly way, and to show how even an important perception [in this case of a house] can at first make hardly any conscious impression upon the perceiver—although here two perceivers, Jane and I, were involved.

(But, I think, in those terms there can be an appreciable lag before an original perception-event takes on any special significance for the concerned person or persons. During that lapse, that first impression is being modified and enhanced within the psyche by subsequent events and understandings; it starts to build up in importance; then, when all of the intuitive-creative "work" has been done, the original perception emerges—or bursts—into consciousness. It's mature now, it makes sense: "Why didn't I see that before?" Something new is known. Those synthesized data are available for fresh conscious decisions.

(Now Jane's and my psyches were involved in this other-than-conscious activity concerning the hill house for 16 days from the time we first saw it. During that period we held the 737th session [on February 17], but since we weren't consciously concerned with that particular place then, we neither talked about it nor asked Seth to comment; instead, on his own during the session, Seth discussed the house on Foster Avenue as representing a probability, and a pretty likely one, that we could choose to explore. Seth didn't suggest that we buy that particular place, and had he done so I'm fairly sure we'd have rejected the idea. Jane and I were free to make our own joint decision—and all the while, both of us were unconsciously processing the hill-house situation.

(Because we'd been looking at houses today, Jane was excited: "How am I going to get my mind on the session?" Just before Seth came through, she reread his list of the families of consciousness that he'd given for the 732nd session. She did so, I quickly learned, for both practical and intuitive reasons.)

Good evening.

("Good evening, Seth.")

Dictation. House information later if you want it. There is a tie-in here with Sumari characteristics.

("Okay.")

Dictation: Generally, the Sumari have the capacity to reach out emotionally to others and empathize. To some extent this feeling for humanity often serves as an impetus for creative work. Many of them also have a mystical sense of connection with nature. At the same time they can be relative isolationists, wanting to work in solitude.[1]

Various kinds of seemingly contradictory characteristics may appear, then. One Sumari may have many deeply rewarding personal relationships. Another might find friends a distraction. One Sumari might enjoy performing in front of an audience, while another might not even be able to bear the thought. Since each person is unique, the various Sumari characteristics will then appear quite differently. Some live in cities, basking in the emotional nearness of others, content with a few flowerpots for a reminder of nature's beauty. Another might have a farm. In most cases, however, the slant of consciousness is primarily creative. Period.

I am not, again, going into detail about the other families, but I will briefly discuss them because counterparts will generally belong to the same family.

The first family that I mentioned (Gramada[2]), for example, specializes in organization. Sometimes its members follow immediately after a revolutionary social change. Their organizational tendencies are expressed in any area of life, however. They are behind art schools, for instance, though they may not be artists themselves. They may set up colleges, although they may or may not be scholars.

The founders of giant businesses often belong to this family, as do some politicians and statesmen. They are active, vital, and creatively aggressive. They know how to put other people's ideas together. They often unite conflicting schools of thought into a more or less unifying structure. They are, then, often the founders of social systems. In most cases, for instance, your hospitals, schools, and religions, as organizations, are initiated by and frequently maintained by this group.

(9:38.) These people (the Gramada) have excellent abilities in putting together solitary concepts that might otherwise go by the wayside. They are organizers of energy, directed toward effective social structures. They usually set up fairly stable, fairly reasonable governments, schools, fraternities, although they do not initiate the ideas behind those structures.

The next group (Sumafi) deals primarily with teaching. Again, the relationship with others is good, generally speaking. They may be gifted in any field, but their primary interest will be in passing on their knowledge or that of others. They are usually traditionalists, therefore, although they may be brilliant. In a way they are equally related to the family just mentioned (Gramada), and to the Sumari, for they stand between the organized system and the creative artist. They transmit "originality" without altering it, however, through the social structures.

I say that they (the Sumafi) do not alter the originality. Of course any interpretation of an event alters it, but generally they

teach the disciplines while not creatively changing the content. As
historians, for example, they pass down the dates of battles, and
those dates are considered almost as immaculate facts, so that in the
context of their training they see no point in questioning the validity
of such information.

In the Middle Ages they faithfully copied manuscripts.
They are custodians in a way. Again, there are infinite variations.
Many music or art teachers belong in that category, where the arts
are taught with a love of excellence, a stress upon technique—into
which the artist, who is often a Sumari (although not always, by any
means) can put his or her creativity. Period.

Do you have that?

("Yes." But the pace had been fast.)

Give us a moment . . . The next family *(Tumold),* in the
order given, is primarily devoted to healing. This does not mean that
these people may not be creative, or organizers, or teachers, but the
primary slant of their consciousness will be directed to healing. You
might find them as doctors and nurses, while not usually as hospital
administrators. However, they may be psychics, social workers,
psychologists, artists, or in the religions. They may work in flower
shops. They may work on assembly lines, for that matter, but if so
they will be healers by intent or temperament.

I mention various professions or occupations to give clear
examples, but a garageman may belong to this *(Tumold)* group, or to
any group. In this case the garageman would have a healing effect on
the customers, and he would be fixing more than cars.

(A one-minute pause at 9:59.) Give us a moment . . . The
healers might also appear as politicians, however, psychically healing the wounds of the nation. An artist of any kind, whose work is
<u>primarily</u> meant to help, also belongs in this category. You will find
some heads of state, and—particularly in the past—some members
of royal families who also belong to this group.

(10:02.) Give us a moment . . . Those in the next group
(Vold), are primarily reformers. They have excellent precognitive
abilities, which of course means that at least unconsciously they
understand the motion of probabilities. They can work in any field.
In your terms <u>it is as if</u> *(louder)* they perceive the future motion or
direction of an idea, a concept, or a structure. They then work with
all of their minds to bring that probability into physical reality.

In conventional terms they may appear to be great activists and revolutionaries, or they may seem to be impractical
dreamers. They will be possessed by an idea of change and alteration, and <u>will feel,</u> at least, driven or compelled to make that idea a

reality. They perform a very creative service as a rule, for social and political organizations can often become stagnant, and no longer serve the purposes of the large masses of people involved. Members of this *(Vold)* family may also initiate religious revolutions, of course. As a rule, however, they have one purpose in mind: to change the status quo in whatever the area of primary interest.

It is already easy to see how the purposes of these various families can intermesh, complement each other, and also conflict. Yet all in all, almost, they operate as systems of creative checks and balances.

(With a smile, eyes wide:) Take your break and check your balance.

(10:12. Jane's delivery had been somewhat faster than usual. While we talked now she interrupted herself to say that she"got in a flash" the main activities, the predominant slants of consciousness, of the next three families on Seth's list: the Milumet, the Zuli, and the Borledim. Yet when she tried to describe their attributes for me she had difficulty in doing so; the information was peculiarly evanescent, she said.

(She did remember that Milumet represented many mystics, then added rather humorously that she didn't think the name fit the activity—she thought Zuli a much better mystical appellation. All of this, of course, while Jane herself is a Sumari *mystic.[3] But some mystical differences began to emerge when Seth resumed dictation at 10:40.)*

Now: Dictation: The next family *(Milumet)* is composed of mystics.

Almost all of their energy is directed in an inward fashion, with no regard as to whether or not inner experience is translated in usual terms. These persons, for instance, may be utterly unknown, and usually are, for as a rule they care not a bit about explaining their interior activities to others—nor, for that matter, even to themselves. They are true innocents, and spiritual. They may be underdeveloped intellectually, by recognized standards, but this is simply because they do not direct their intellect to physical focus.

Those belonging to this *(Milumet)* family will not be in positions of any authority, generally speaking, for they will not concentrate that long on specific physical data. However, they may be found in your country precisely where you might not expect them to be: on some assembly lines that require simple repetitive action—in factories that do not require speed, however. They usually choose less industrialized countries, then, with a slower pace of life. They have simple, direct, childish mannerisms, and may appear to be stupid. They do not bother with the conventions.

(Long pause.) Strangely enough, though, they may be

excellent parents, particularly in less complicated societies than your own. Period. In your terms, they are primitives wherever they appear. Yet they are deeply involved in nature, and in that respect they are more highly attuned psychically than most other people are.

Give us a moment . . . Their private experiences are often of a most venturesome kind, and at that level they help nourish the psyche of mankind.

The next group *(Zuli)* is involved mainly with the fulfillment of bodily activity. These are the athletes. In whatever field, they devote themselves to perfecting the capacities of the body, which in others usually lie latent.

To some extent they serve as physical models. The vitality of creaturehood is demonstrated through the beauty, speed, elegance, and performance of the body itself. To some extent these people are perfectionists, and in their activities there are always hints of "super" achievement, as if even physically the species tries to go beyond itself. The members of this family actually serve to point out the unrealized capacity of the flesh—even as, for example, great Sumari artists might give clues as to the artistic abilities inherent, but not used, in the species as a whole. The members of this group deal, then, in performance. They are physical doers. They are also lovers of beauty as it is corporally expressed.

(Long pause at 11:01.) Members of this *(Zuli)* family can often serve as models for the artist or the writer, but generally speaking they themselves transmit their energy through physical "arts" and performance. In your terms only, and historically speaking, they often appeared at the beginnings of civilizations, where direct physical bodily manipulation within the environment was of supreme importance. Then (underlined), normal physical reactions were simply faster than they are now *(intently),* even while normal body relaxation was deeper and more complete.

End of dictation. Take a break or end the session as you (underlined) prefer *(amused.*

("We'll take the break.

(11:05. Jane said the sounds of traffic rising up from the corner just southwest of our second-floor apartment had bothered her after last break, and that in part this accounted for the shorter delivery. I'd been able to tell when her discomfiture started, I thought, for her once-rapid delivery slowed, then began to fluctuate.

(Seth returned at 11:19. For a couple of pages of notes he discussed the house we'd looked at on Foster Avenue two days ago. This material came through even though we had our first viewing of the "hill house" yesterday; see the notes [added later] at the beginning of tonight's session. Seth's information

on the Foster Avenue place, and our present and potential relationships with it, was very illuminating. He helped explain the psychic attractions Jane and I feel for the house, without implying a commitment toward it [through purchase, for instance] in any way. Some of those present and potential relationships, incidentally, actually stem from our childhood days.

(Here's one point brought out in that deleted material: Since Seth had told Jane and me long ago that the three of us belong to the Sumari family of consciousness,[4] we were more than curious now when he declared that the woman who presently owns the house on Foster Avenue is also a Sumari: "[She] added Sumari characteristics of expansiveness." But to go a step further: According to Seth the house's previous owner for many years, a male now deceased, had also been Sumari. It's quite intriguing to watch such psychic and physical connections unfold.

(End at 11:30 P.M.)

NOTES: Session 736

1. Naturally, Seth's material here began to sound very reminiscent of Jane's and my own Sumari characteristics—especially those concerning the "mystical sense of connection with nature" that each of us feels, and our individual desires "to work in solitude."

2. Now Seth began a rundown of the roles played by each of the families of consciousness as he'd listed them in the 732nd session. Note that he didn't name any of them tonight, merely calling each one the "next family," and so forth. Since Jane had already refreshed her memory of those psychic groupings before the session, and, presumably, would deliver Seth's material on them in the proper order, I matched up their names with the successive blocks of data given in the session. Perhaps I should have double-checked by asking Seth to rename the families, in order, but I didn't think it necessary.

3. See Appendix 1 for Volume 1 of *"Unknown" Reality*.

4. See notes 2 and 3 for Session 734.

Session 737
February 17, 1975
9:26 P.M. Monday

(We skipped last week's two regularly scheduled sessions so that Jane could rest, and so we'd have more time to spend house hunting. House notes and material are presented after first break. Jane did hold ESP class on Tuesday night, February 11, though.

(Now these notes hark back to the end of the 732nd session, when I wrote a paragraph concerning Sue Watkins, our longtime friend who attends class as often as she can these days from the small town where she now lives, some 35 miles north of Elmira. Jane listed Seth's families of consciousness last month in Session 732, but wound up the evening's work thinking that several years ago, soon after she'd initiated the Sumari breakthrough, Sue had psychically tuned in on the name of a second family of consciousness—one that Seth didn't give in the 732nd session. Jane thought the family name was similar to the "Gramada" that Seth had described; at session's end I wrote that I intended to check our records for the missing name, and to ask Seth about it—but I neglected to do either of those things. One of the reasons for my failure to settle the matter right away was the lack of any immediate pressure to do so, for we

598

hadn't seen Sue since before the 729th session was held; that's over five weeks ago now; newspaper work has often kept her too busy to make the trip to Elmira.

(Sue did attend class last Tuesday evening, however, arriving just in time before it began to read the transcript for the 732nd session. Then during class she handed me a note that I'll paraphrase a bit here: "In a session on Sumari I witnessed in 1971 or early 1972—I picked up a family-of-consciousness name, and Seth said it was 'Grunaargh.' It wasn't on the list given last month."

(Class was a very busy one, with over 40 people present. When Seth came through Sue had time for but one question: Was Grunaargh connected to any of the families of consciousness Seth had named in the 732nd session? "It is indeed," Seth answered. "It is related to one already given."

(Sue's note intrigued me anew: After class I promised her that not only would I search our files about Grunaargh, but that with Seth's help Jane and I would eventually get more information on that family, and present it somewhere in the notes for "Unknown" Reality. The point I want to make here is that others beside Jane can intuitively divine material on the families of consciousness. Actually, for whatever reasons, Sue had glimpsed a family other than Sumari before Jane had. Going through back sessions late this evening, I found what I wanted: Sue had picked up on the Grunaargh[1] during the 598th session, which she'd recorded for me the evening after Jane had made the whole Sumari breakthrough in class, on November 23, 1971.

(Before tonight's session Jane told me that she felt the Grunaargh represented a variation of Seth's Gramada family of consciousness. "But the important things are the family characteristics," she said, "by whatever name. The similarities in the two names are legitimate, I think. There are also family combinations, and these will have their own names." Then she reminded me that several times during the past week she'd felt that Borledim, the next family of consciousness on Seth's list, is strongly concerned with parenthood and related roles.)

Good evening.

("Good evening, Seth.")

Now: Dictation *(quietly)*.

The next family *(Borledim)* deals primarily with parenthood. These people are natural "earth parents." That is, they have the capacity to produce children who from a certain standpoint possess certain excellent characteristics. The children have brilliant minds, healthy bodies, and strong clear emotions.

While many people are working in specific areas, developing the intellect, for example, or the emotions or the body, these parents and their children produce offspring in which a fine balance is maintained. No one aspect of mind or body is developed at the expense of another aspect.

The personalities possess a keen resiliency of both body and mind, and serve as a strong earth stock. It goes without saying that members of one family often marry into other families. Of course the same thing happens here. When this occurs new stability is inserted, for this particular family acts as a source-stock, providing physical and mental strength. Period. Physically speaking, these people often have many children, and usually the offspring do well in whatever area of life is chosen. *(Pause.)* Biologically speaking, they possess certain qualities that nullify "negative" codes in the genes.[2] They are usually very healthy people, and marriage into this group can automatically end generations of so-called inherited weaknesses.[3]

These people *(the Borledim)* believe, then, in the natural goodness of sex, the body, and the family unit—however those attributes are understood in the physical society to which they belong. As a rule they possess an enchanting spontaneity, however, and all of their creative abilities go into the family group and the production of children. These are not rigid parents, though, blindly following conventions, but people who see family life as a fine living creative art, and children as masterpieces in flesh and blood. Far from devouring their offspring by an excess of overprotective care, they joyfully send their children out into the world, knowing that in their terms the masterpieces must complete themselves, and that they have helped with the underpainting.

[The Borledim] are the stock that so far has always seen to it that your species continues despite catastrophes, and they are more or less equally distributed about the planet and in all nationalities. They are most like the Sumari. They have the same love of the arts, the same general attitudes. They will usually seek fairly stable political situations in which to bear their children, as the Sumari will to produce their art. They demand a certain amount of freedom for their children, however, and while they are not political activists, like the Sumari their ideas often spring to prominence before large social changes, and help initiate them. The one big difference is that the Sumari deal primarily with creativity and the arts, and often subordinate family life *(as Jane and I have done)*, while this family thinks of offspring in the terms of living art; everything else is subordinated to that "ideal."

The Sumari often provide a cultural, spiritual, or artistic heritage for the species. This *(Borledim)* family provides a well-balanced earth stock—a heritage in terms of individuals. These people are kind, humorous, playful, filled with a lively compassion, but too wise for the "perverted" kind of compassion that breeds on other individuals' weaknesses.

An artist expects his paintings to be good—or, if you will

forgive a jingle: at least he should. These people expect their children to be well-balanced, healthy, spiritually keen, and so they are. You will find members of the Borledim family in almost any occupation, but the main consideration will be on the physical family unit.

These parents do not sacrifice themselves for the sake of their children. They understand too well the burden that is placed upon such offspring. Instead, the parents retain their own clear sense of identity and their individual characteristics, serving as clear examples to the children of loving, independent adults.

The next family *(Ilda)* is composed of the "exchangers." They deal primarily in the great play of exchange and interchange of ideas, products, social and political concepts. They are travelers, carrying with them the ideas of one country to another, mixing cultures, religions, attitudes, political structures. They are explorers, merchants, soldiers, missionaries, sailors. They are often members of crusades.

(10:01.) Throughout the ages they have served as the spreaders of ideas, the assimilators. They *(the Ilda)* turn up everywhere. They were pirates and slaves as well, historically speaking. They are often primarily involved in social changes. In your time they may be diplomats, as they were also in the past. Their characteristics are usually those of the adventuresome. Very seldom do they live in one place for long, although they may if their occupation deals with products from another land. Individually they may seem highly diverse in nature, one from the other, but you will not find them as a rule in universities as teachers. You might find them as archaeologists in the field, however.

A good many salesmen belong in this *(Ilda)* category. In your terms they may be cosmopolitan, and often wealthy, so that frequent travel is possible. On the other hand, however, in certain frameworks, a humble merchant in a small country who travels through nearby provinces might also belong to this family. These are a lively, talkative, imaginative, usually likeable group of people. They are interested in the outsides of things, social mores, the marketplace, current popular religious or political ideas. They spread these from place to place. They are the seed-carriers, both literally and figuratively.

They can be "con men," selling products supposed to have miraculous values, blinding the local populace with their city airs. Yet even then they will be bringing with them the aura of other ideas, often inserting into closed areas concepts with which others are already familiar.

The members of that family of consciousness provide

frequent new options. They may be scientists, or the strictest kind of conventional missionaries abroad in alien lands. In your present time they are sometimes Indians (from India, that is), or Africans or Arabs, journeying to your civilizations. They add to the great flow of communication. They may be emotional rather than intellectual, as you understand those terms *(pause),* but they are restless, usually on the move. They can be actors, also.

In the past some *(Ilda)* have been great courtesans, and even though they were not able to travel physically, they were at the heart of communicaiton—that is, a part of court life, or involved with diplomats who did travel.

(Pause at 10:24.) Many of the courtesans who ruled the salons of Europe belonged in the *(Ilda)* category, then. The Crusades[4] involved great movement of this family, in which trade and commerce, and the exchange of political ideas, were far more important than the religious aspects. Some members of this family served as initiators of new orders in the *(Catholic)* church in the past— the worldly Jesuits, for example, and some of the more sophisticated popes[5] *(amused),* who had a fine eye out for commerce and wealth. These people may be appreciators of fine art, but usually for its commercial value.

Now you can often find them in the departments of government, in those areas where travel is involved, or in finance. They frequently enjoy intrigue. All in all, they mix mores.

Take your break.

(10:30. "I've got the feeling he likes that last family," Jane said as soon as she was out of trance, then added, laughing: "I've got the feeling he likes them as well as Sumari. I was picking up all kinds of things about them." Yet her delivery had been even in pace and emphasis. Now see Note 6 for more family-of-consciousness material.

(So far, Jane and I haven't been able to find a home that we intuitively feel is the right one, although the place on Foster Avenue has intrigued us considerably since we first saw it on February 3. [Since then we've looked at many other houses.] Last Thursday afternoon [February 13], Jane was busy with her creative writing class so I went house hunting alone. Without feeling any great curiosity I checked out one place we'd seen before: the hill house. Once again I thought it wouldn't do for us. Jane agreed when I asked her about it at the supper table.[7]

(The next day, Friday, Jane had an auditory "psychic" experience of sorts about the Foster Avenue situation; Saturday morning we made a formal offer to buy the house in question. For our own reasons we offered a low price, and it was promptly refused. The rejection didn't completely close out our interest here—or Seth's either—but it did help us put the whole matter in better

perspective. Note 8 covers Jane's inner experience and the details surrounding our house offer. [At 12:06 this evening Seth also refers to Jane's auditory intuition.]

(Then in Sayre, Pennsylvania, this afternoon [Monday the 17th], we found ourselves participating in house-related developments that took us back in time more than nine months.[9] Jane and I don't believe in coincidences. We'd considered the Sayre episodes finished last year; yet today the echoes of those earlier events were so prominent that I came to think of them as actual projections from the past into the present, and so into the future, in a most practical manner. Today Jane and I very clearly felt those connections—or probabilities, if one chooses—developing. Seth remarks upon some of them after break, but the best we can offer are a few hints; otherwise all of these house notes would be much longer.

(Jane had declared before the session began tonight that she thought Seth would go into our house affairs in connection with probable realities, but that such material wouldn't go with his book dictation on the families of consciousness. I facetiously replied that if the information didn't fit into "Unknown" Reality we'd "force it to." I was only half putting her on. Anything on our house hunting, I thought, would be welcome here because it would help unite these late sessions for "Unknown" Reality with some of its much earlier ones [in Volume 1, as it turned out]. It almost seemed as though we'd planned things this way.

(Resume at 11:01.)

Now: Give us a moment.

You may or may not use this in the book as <u>you</u> prefer— that is, dictation can continue smoothly without this passage, or it can be inserted at this place.

There are all kinds of Sumari, as there is great diversity within each family of consciousness.

Your house hunting serves, however, as an excellent example of the ways in which Sumari are attracted to other Sumari, even in connection with probabilities in your system. The same relationships could be seen with other family interconnections. You have already noticed a similarity in the two houses thus far that have attracted your attention.

The first *(in Sayre)*, mentioned far earlier in *"Unknown" Reality*, you thought was definitely sold, and today you discovered that the sale was not that final.[10] As you discussed these issues a rather important main point escaped your minds: The man who owned the first house *(Mr. Markle)* was a dealer in antiques and precious stones, utterly devoted to his work and engrossed in it, considering it his art. The house has a garden on one side, with high trees, and a yard on the other, and was relatively shielded. The man's family took second place to some extent. The kitchen and dining areas were small. He had his office downstairs and he often worked at home. His art came first.[11]

The second house *(on Foster Avenue in Elmira)* was owned for years by the people who gave it its character. The large living room was so spacious just so that it could hold a grand piano. The man who owned the house thought of pianos as his art *(he was in the business of selling them)*, and the living room was simply meant to set a piano off.

Again, you have a small kitchen, a garden and some sheltered privacy. Both homes appealed to you, however, because the people who lived in them organized their houses about their work. This is what you picked up and reacted to. You did not react to the attitudes of others in those families who "had to put up with those conditions," because to you they are natural.

Neither house expresses your own particular individualistic ways of life, of course, but each one comes close enough to intrigue you, and either one could be made to suit your purposes quite easily. You were attracted also because the people who put their greatest imprint upon those houses so shared some of your tendencies. In the second house your ideas of privacy were shown to you, carried to an extreme, where the windows would not even open. In the first house the stairs to the second floor were purposely steep, and never altered, because no one was invited to view the private family bedrooms. The stairs were meant to be formidable.

Now let us look at your real-estate agents.

As mentioned much earlier, the real-estate couple who showed you the first house, in Sayre *(see Note 11)*, have definite artistic leanings. The woman particularly likes the house, and thought you would. She identified with your ideas of art and work, and saw a probable variation of herself happily ensconced in such surroundings.

Your second real-estate lady *(Debbie)*, leading you unerringly to the Foster Avenue house, did so for the same reasons. She paints as a hobby.[12] You did not consciously pick out real-estate people who had artistic connections, but you were led to them and they to you. You recognized each other's characteristics.

(11:25.) Now: When you make any important decision you automatically rouse all portions of your psyche. You set probabilities into motion. The kind of decision to some extent organizes the patterns. This should be obvious. But when you decide to move you are putting yourself in league with others who also make the same decision. Someone who moves will leave a house or an

apartment vacant for someone else to move into. Unconsciously, then, the movers are in league with each other. There are sympathetic probabilities set up.

The [other] couple also interested in the Foster Avenue house are musicians—attracted to it for the same reasons that you were. You would find their house in Sayre interesting. They are primarily teachers of music, however. Their purposes do not necessarily involve the same kind of privacy that you want, although they think it attractive.[13]

You find typical ranch-style homes, generally now, uncomfortable because—and this should be obvious—they are given over mainly to family living of a particular kind, colon: a kind that obviously separates work from living areas. Work is definitely done outside of the house.

Since you both work at home, those houses do not fit you, generally speaking.[14] Work is not incorporated into daily family life, but certainly exists apart from it—something you find, each of you, relatively inconceivable. You can see farms better, though you are not farmers, simply because there also work and home life are one.

Both houses, therefore, still exist in your practical present as probable acquisitions, because you have not dismissed them. Years ago *(in 1964)*, you were interested in another house *(also in Elmira)*; again, it had been owned by an artist. A coincidence? Hardly.

I suggested that you take it *(but see my note in the material at next break)*. It would have been good for you both, but you were afraid of it, and your feelings had much to do with the contract being turned down *(by the Veteran's Administration)*. That house represented what each of you thought of as unbridled, undisciplined creativity. It was dirty and cluttered. The artist had children who ran about without any control. There was much playfulness there, however, that could have tempered some of your great mutual seriousness at the time. You did not choose to accept such a probability then, any more than you could have accepted my advice all the way. The authorities turned the contract down—but the authorities stood for the inner disciplinarians, and you did not want to share your road with the world; nor did you want, later, to share your driveway *(for the Sayre house)* with your neighbor.

End of session, or take a break as you prefer.

("We'll take the break."

(11:43. I told Jane that, once heard, much of Seth's material had the quality of being so obvious that we in turn seemed to be quite opaque not to have reached the same conclusions ourselves. After considering the alternatives

Seth suggested immediately following last break, I decided to leave his delivery in place in the session as a guide for the reader; parallels can be drawn with many other situations, I think, having nothing to do with art or houses.

(Considering parallels, here's another of the many "connections" that Jane and I have become aware of since we began our housing odyssey last year [already we've compiled a list of 30 similar relationships]: Three out of the four dwellings that in one way or another we've been seriously involved with possess driveways shared by next-door neighbors—Mr. Markle's in Sayre; the apartment house we live in now; *and the house in Elmira that we considered buying in 1964. Only the Foster Avenue place is exempt here. I see such connections as symbols running through our personal experiences.*

(A clarification: Seth didn't actually suggest that Jane and I buy the "1964 house." His statements just before break that he did so are distortions on Jane's part, I would say, while speaking for him tonight; even in trance, her memory could have been in error—or she could have been touching upon another probable reality. What Seth did talk about, and quite legitimately, were the benefits we'd enjoy if we did acquire that place. He discussed the whole affair in the 65th session for Sunday, June 28, 1964, using passages like: "I am certainly not going to make any decisions for you. The house you looked at today should prove an excellent buy . . ." and, "If you purchase the house . . ." and, "You will have to make your own decisions."[15]

(Resume at 11:55, with a few deletions as indicated.)

Now: You chose your present neighborhood particularly because when you moved here *(from Sayre in 1960)* it was highly professional. Work and home were united. The dentist next door lives and works in the same house. So did the other dentist around the corner, and the chiropractor beside him. There was a uniting factor that you recognized, where office and home were in the same location.

For that reason, <u>certain</u> so-called city locations could serve you well. That is, Elmira is no metropolis, but there are areas where old homes with grounds exist amid other old homes now given over to offices of one kind or another.

The suburbs obviously will not suit you unless you find a house apart from others while in the same general area. You like both the [Sayre and Foster Avenue] houses thus far because their grounds set them apart from the neighbors and give clearly defined boundaries—very important to both of you.

Give us a moment . . . Because there are such inner connections as mentioned *(at 11:25)*, your intents are going outward, to be picked up by others. *(With emphasis:)* It would take a book to probe into the probabilities alone being roused at this time, for example, by all of those interested in either of those two houses.

The present owner, even, of the Foster house thinks of it as "work," since she herself is a . . . working [real-estate] person. Ruburt finds the rugs there out of place, however, because they do not fit in with his ideas of work areas. The owner, however, is quite proud of them. Her work in that respect is to decorate, and the rugs represent her idea of what belongs in the house.

The hints I have given you should be of help . . .

(12:06.) The [inner] voice said: "Wait a few days," because Ruburt unconsciously knew that the . . . owner . . . already had a higher offer that might very well fall through—in which case she would later be more amiable to negotiation.[16]

End of session, unless you had something else you wanted to ask.

("Do you want to say something more about that auditory experience of Jane's?")

I cannot answer that quickly, of course. Briefly, however, Ruburt's own information is correct, and 't did come from "the library." I can elaborate when you want.

Another point, however: Both houses also have built-in bookcases—physical versions, in other words, of Ruburt's library. If you want the entire explanation now you can have it. Otherwise—

("On second thought I'm afraid we'll have to wait. . . ." I'd just realized how tired I was.)

All right. *(Louder:)* My heartiest regards, you house hunters, you.

("Good night, Seth. Thank you very much."
(12:13 A.M.)

NOTES: Session 737

1. A note added a couple of weeks later: Session 738 and Appendix 27 (for Session 739) contain additional material showing the special meaning that Grunaargh has for Sue Watkins.

2. See Note 1 for Session 731.

3. It would seem that a computerized study could be rather easily organized to investigate statements of Seth's like this one. However, results might depend on whether Seth-Jane could identify enough members of the Borledim who had married partners from other families of consciousness.

4. The Crusades took place mainly during the 12th and 13th centuries, and consisted of a number of military expeditions organized by Christians to recover the Holy Land from the Moslems.

5. See item No. 3 in the opening notes for the 728th session.

6. I listed the families of consciousness (along with simple clues to their pronunciations) when Seth first gave them at 11:14 in the 732nd session. Here I'll not only remind the reader of the sessions in which Seth described the characteristics of each family, but will try to summarize in a few words the overall function of each one.

1. Gramada . . . (736)	To found social systems
2. Sumafi . . . . . (736)	To transmit "originality" through teaching
3. Tumold . . . . (736)	To heal, regardless of individual occupations
4. Vold . . . . (736)	To reform the status quo
5. Milumet . . . . (736)	To mystically nourish mankind's psyche
6. Zuli . . . . (736)	To serve as physical, athletic models
7. Borledim . . . (737)	To provide an earth stock for the species through parenthood
8. Ilda . . . . (737)	To spread and exchange ideas
9. Sumari . . . . . (723, 732, 734–36)	To provide the cultural, spiritual, and artistic heritage for the species

See the opening notes for this session, plus Note 1, for material and references concerning the Grunaargh family of consciousness, which is related to the Gramada.

Except for the Sumari, which Jane and I choose to be allied with, there's much we don't know about the families of consciousness; the material is all so new. Yet my observation can even apply to aspects of our relationship with the Sumari. For instance, were any of our now-deceased parents Sumari? And regardless of whatever family each of those four people had belonged to, how had their individual family predilections affected their Sumari children? Seth's data in these recent sessions give us clues, but we need time to put it all together.

In more general terms, how do the members of each family operate through the mechanics of reincarnation? Or of probabilities or counterparts? It's also important to keep in mind what Seth told us in his first delivery for the 735th session: "Each personality carries traces of other characteristics besides those of the family of consciousness to which he or she might belong . . . A book would be needed to explain the dimensions of the psyche in relationship to the various families of consciousness."

And Jane herself has been thinking about the whole subject of psychic interrelationships since holding the 732nd session almost a month ago. She wrote recently: "We regard Seth's material on counterparts and families of consciousness as excellent *explanations*—as thematic *frameworks* that help us perceive and organize facets of our greater reality that are ignored by conventional academic disciplines. Seth's explanations *stand for* aspects of reality that usually escape us.

"Now it seems so obvious that there must be such alliances as Seth's families of consciousness, and that each of us alive at any given time takes part in one or more of such psychic groupings—just as we form, say, nationalistic affiliations on ordinary levels.

"But the names and designations aren't meant to be taken *too* literally; these aren't to be interpreted as esoteric clubs or brotherhoods, but as natural psychic 'conglomerations' to which we all belong."

7. Added later: See the notes on the hill house at the beginning of the 736th session. In them I wrote about the delay involved before Jane's and my perceptions of that particular dwelling blossomed within our conscious minds in any meaningful way; the results of that joint metamorphosis are described in sessions 738–39. In the meantime, then, Seth's material in this (737th) session deals only with the house on Foster Avenue, in Elmira, and—as discussed shortly—with Mr. Markle's house in Sayre, Pennsylvania, since those two places were the ones we were consciously interested in at the moment. Seth made no predictions, about the hill house or any other, nor did we ask him to.

8. As she lay down for a nap last Friday afternoon, Jane asked her inner self to let her know what to do—specifically—about buying the house on Foster Avenue. She fell asleep, then drifted off into a relatively bland dream. Suddenly a male voice burst loudly through that dream fabric in a very intrusive way, saying only: "Wait a few days."

Jane woke up. "That wasn't Seth's voice, but I recognized it as giving me the answer I wanted," she told me later. "I had no doubt. It was even clearer because the dream, which I can hardly remember, was so vague. But even after I got the answer I was too worked up to follow it. I wanted to do something, take some action." The result was that on Saturday we made our low offer for the Foster Avenue place, as described in the notes at first break. We did so mainly to relieve the psychic charges we'd built up concerning it, thinking that if we were so inclined later we could make a higher bid.

Our tactics were successful in freeing us, and I suspected that we were through with Foster Avenue. Since we'd achieved our goal here, we made no immediate plans to try to find out whether others would offer more for the house.

We speculated over the weekend that three layers or portions of Jane's self had been involved in her auditory experience:

1. Her dreaming self, which had provided a comfortable fabric or framework.

2. Her intrusive or "library" self—not Seth. (The library connotations are briefly referred to below. Seth also touches upon them at session's end.)

3. Her conscious self, the recipient of the information, in usual terms, and the portion of her psyche that put it all together.

As Jane wrote at about this time in her manuscript for *Psychic Politics*: "So in house hunting I can almost feel the *shape* of my ideas and beliefs looking for their proper house." My opening notes for sessions 714–15 each include material on Jane's psychic library, and Seth himself discussed it in the latter session. *Politics*, of course, contains extensive material on the same subject (as well as on our house-hunting adventures).

It might be added later here that on succeeding days Jane had several more auditory-type experiences, all involving topics other than houses or *"Unknown" Reality*. In none of those episodes was she aware of Seth's voice, *per se*, but even so we see relationships between them and the time she *did* hear his voice; see my description of that event at the beginning of the 710th session.

9. In Volume 1 of *"Unknown" Reality*, see sessions 693–94 for April 29 and May 1, 1974.

10. This afternoon Jane and I had spontaneously decided to lay our work aside and go for a drive. We needed the brief change. Neither of us had any conscious intentions of making the trip to Sayre, which lies just across the New York State border in Pennsylvania, some 18 miles east and south of Elmira. We found ourselves doing so, however; we also found ourselves driving past the house we'd considered buying there last year. I received a distinct shock of surprise when I saw the familiar "For Sale" sign still tacked to the front of the house. So did Jane—although she's never been drawn to it in the way that I am. We'd been informed months ago that the place had been sold. This new joint perception of ours set a whole group of events into motion—all of which were connected to those described in sessions 693–94 (see Note 9).

11. The Johnsons, the husband-and-wife real-estate team who had taken us through Mr. Markle's house in April 1974, gave us the objective information in this paragraph. I could verify those facts myself, and add a bit to them, for even 43 years later I remembered Mr. Markle and his family well. Prior to 1931, the Buttses and the Markles lived only a block apart; in Volume 1, see Note 2 for the 693rd session.

Seth's material on Mr. Markle's feeling for his art, however, is his (Seth's) own. I couldn't help here; as a boy of less than 12, I hadn't been that consciously aware of subjective states other than my own. Although I remember my parents talking about Mr. Markle, I have little idea of how much they may have understood—or *mis*understood—his basic life-style.

12. Seth didn't mention that for several years Debbie also taught art in Elmira's public grade schools.

13. Here Seth touches upon several ramifications involving our house affairs that I've been saving to present all at once, if briefly. This note, then, will enlarge upon the fertile field of connections, or probabilities, that is enveloping Jane and me, the houses in Sayre and Elmira, the real-estate agents we've been dealing with (the Johnsons and Debbie—who are not acquainted), and some other people.

When Debbie took Jane and me through the Foster Avenue house on February 5, she told us that another couple—*who live in Sayre*, and whom I'll call the Steins—had also inspected the property and planned to make an offer for it, while trying at the same time to sell their present home. Without thinking too much about it, we mentally filed this bit of news along with the connections that had developed out of our house-hunting episodes last year; even now, we still didn't realize just how the complicated relationships between those events of April 1974, and now, were to continue growing. For instance: When Jane and I "rediscovered" Mr. Markle's house in Sayre today (February 17), and saw to our considerable surprise that it might still be for sale, we at once visited the Johnsons, who had shown us through it last year. We were then in for another surprise—for the Johnsons are the agents in charge of selling the Steins' residence in Sayre.

I want to emphasize here that the Steins, who are teachers of music, have been attracted to a home in Elmira that was owned for many years by a man who, as a merchant, had strong connections with music in general and pianos in particular. Mr. Stein, incidentally, teaches in Elmira—hence the decision by him and his wife to move here and so eliminate his workday traveling between Sayre and Elmira.

Seth commented that Jane and I would be interested in the Steins' home in Sayre. Not so. We looked at it today in passing after the Johnsons told us it was for sale; the truth is, we saw nothing about it that turned us on.

(I should add that the reasons Jane and I made our low bid for the Foster Avenue house were entirely unrelated to whatever offers the Steins, or anyone else, had made or might make for the place. See the notes for first break, and Note 8.)

14. A couple of weeks later I felt considerable humor upon rereading Seth's statement here: See the notes about the hill house, inserted at the beginning of the 736th session.

15. A note added later: Another house connection is that the place Jane and I were drawn to in 1964 perches on a hillside just west of Elmira proper, as does the hill house. The two are separated in our experience of time by 11 years, but their physical existence is simultaneous: They lie within walking distance of each other—less than half a mile apart—on the north side of the same highway.

16. But on conscious levels Jane was too impatient to follow her own inner counsel. See the notes at first break, and Note 8.

17. Surely Seth's information about Jane's auditory experience would have been very interesting—but I must note much later that we never received it.

Session 738
February 19, 1975
9:27 P.M. Wednesday

(*Today Jane and I spent several discouraging hours driving through and around Elmira, inspecting homes that were for sale. Nothing seemed suitable. Then, as we were passing through the outskirts of West Elmira late in the afternoon, I spontaneously turned onto an avenue that we'd first traveled on February 4.*

(*Jane was momentarily surprised. "Hey—where are we going?"*

(*"Let's take another look at that house up here on the hill," I said, and our car began the long steady climb toward a certain dead-end road . . . So we looked at the hill house again—if from the outside only—but this time we really looked at it. Our inner cogitations about it were beginning to flower. Mine came into consciousness before Jane's did, but she soon caught up with me. [See the notes prefacing the 736th session.]*

(*Seth had used more than half of Monday's session to discuss our house hunting in connection with Sayre and Foster Avenue. Some of his related material there had been fairly personal, but we'd left it in place because of its general application. When Seth added the hill house to his list tonight, however,*

*his connecting information about Jane and me was so intimate that we decided
to delete parts of it. But I've reassembled the remainder in the proper order, and
it's more than enough to show how closely such "objective" things as houses can
be bound up with beliefs and emotions.*

*(After supper tonight I asked Jane if Seth would comment on the
Grunaargh family of consciousness. This is the one Sue Watkins had "picked up
on" several years ago; see the notes preceding the last session. I've come to think
of those data involving Sue and "her" family as cropping up every so often like
counterpoint to other themes in this 6th section.)*

Good evening.

("Good evening, Seth.")

Now first the house.

("Okay.")

Because that house is on a hill it has certain advantages.
Looking down at the town gives the kind of perspective that each of
you enjoys—as here *(in the apartment house)* you look down from the
second story.

The aspects of nature there are important, however, and
will be most refreshing. The air itself is clearer and cleaner.

Give us a moment . . . You both seem informal, yet your
informality exists within its own rather formal structure. The places
so far have had a certain formality, within which, in contrast, you are
informal. The formality of the position of the house upon its hill
provides a structure of its own. The same house on low land would
not suffice, you see. It is the entire picture that is important. You do
not understand your own mixtures of order and spontaneity, formality and informality.

Houses themselves have a quality, a life, that is picked up
by potential buyers. Certain houses repel you and Ruburt. They will
positively attract others, however, so the qualities in the houses that
appeal to you two are precisely the ones that have turned off others,
and prevented their sale.

It is highly important that you move. You both do need
privacy for your work and because of your natures, but this does not
mean that you should try to find a place with no [distractions] within
miles. It <u>does</u> mean that you settle for a reasonable amount of
privacy, in that you do not carry the idea to extremes.

There are alliances and understandings in neighborhoods—signs for others to read. The front entrance of the Foster
Avenue house was not even used. The hill house is set up high.
Anyone who walks up the steps from the street knows [he or she is]
making a trip. Your daily environment is very important to your
work, and to Ruburt. You require certain things of your art, and

therefore you want the same things in your surroundings. Once you had it where you live now, for all of your criticism. Now it is gone, and you are different.

(And inevitably so, I thought.)

At this time of your lives it is important that you act. I am telling you that of the [Elmira] houses in your mind it really makes little difference which one you choose. Neither is perfect. You would find yourselves quite hampered in [any] idealistically perfect environment. You need some give-and-take. Either place could well be made to suit your specific needs, and each reflects strong elements of your personalities.

(10:15.) Give us a moment . . . I am trying to give you the best information I can. The hill house has its own kind of inner light. This is not possessed by the Sayre house, and I recommend against that house regardless of price. It has a built-in darkness that no amount of applied light would disperse. Nor will either of you ever—particularly you, Joseph—be satisfied with sharing a driveway.[1] The hill house, because of its location, adds a spaciousness that is inside the Foster Avenue house; but either way, you have an open feeling in terms of expansion.

(10:28 to 10:32.)

Now: Once I gave you a recommendation, and you did not really take it.[2] I can foresee probabilities, but you make your own reality, and I will not take the responsibility. Taking that for granted, and knowing your characteristics, I have more to say. You may not like it.

The Foster house represents many things, and though it is not on a hill it stands for your feelings of secrecy and privacy. The windows do not open. It is dark, yet it is large, and in its way elegant. The hill house has some privacy. It does not have secrecy, and while you have a view you cannot hide in it. It is too contemporary.

The Foster Avenue house has a certain decadence. Do you follow me.?

("Yes.")

The hill house does not. It represents a kind of challenge you have thus far not accepted. As given, however, it still possesses qualities that do go in with your natures.

Give us time . . . The hill house represents the future, and the contemporary qualities of it. I suggest—and only suggest—that that be your choice, because it is the most daring of the ventures for you, and because the hill will give you a view in many more ways than one.

Give us time . . . When you live in a house that belongs conspicuously to another age, you are to some extent avoiding the contemporary nature of life. Ruburt may find himself furnishing the place more formally than another one, yet the open quality of the air is the kind that you do not hide in.

("You're talking about the hill house.")

I am indeed. If some rooms are small you can enlarge them. Take a break.

(10:45. "I feel sad," Jane said as soon as she was out of a very good trance. "I feel funny—like some part of me wants to burrow into that house on Foster Avenue. Walk around that yard all alone at night. . . ."

("I think Seth gave good advice," I said.

("I'm shocked," she countered. "For a while I loved the idea of that place. But he's so fucking smart—Seth—"

("You got what you wanted: answers."

("I know. I said before the session that if we got house material I really wanted good answers, that I'd stay out of it as much as possible. . . ." Jane went into the kitchen, looking for matches. All in all, I thought she was "recovering" quite easily from Seth's data, and that she was helped here because we'd revisited the hill house today. Every so often someone wants to know about the extent to which we follow Seth's advice or information, and I suppose a good answer is that we may decide to go along with it if it suits our conscious purposes to do so. Sometimes we don't agree with what Seth tells us even when we know *it's good counsel. [However, Jane and I freely admit that on occasion we've made the wrong choice in deciding to ignore what Seth had to say; in retrospect we've seen that he gave out very valid material.]*

("Oh, hell, I'm getting more," Jane laughed, coming back into the living room. She sat down. "I'll have to say that when I ask for straight stuff, I get it." She still looked at bit teary, but at the same time I was sure now that we'd steered away from any probable reality involving Foster Avenue—and perhaps Sayre too, I thought, considering Seth's material at 10:15 tonight.[3]

(Once again, some very personal portions of Seth's delivery are excerpted. Resume at 11:02.)

Now: The hill environment is as important to your painting as the ready-made workroom in the Foster Avenue house. The very air is inspiring, so that you will paint more there even if your work area is not immediately as good. The sunny nature [of that house], regardless of what Ruburt thinks now, will help him creatively and physically—but the hill house represents a decision to face the world while maintaining certain necessary and quite reasonable conditions. It provides privacy yet openness. The hillside is not yours, <u>yet it is your view</u>, and it has strong evocative connections with your creative lives. A definite change in living patterns and of psychic attitude will result, that would not happen in the house on Foster Avenue.

This also means that greater adaptability is required, but it will be to the good. The whole difference here is the quality of nature as it surrounds both places. The one invites you to roam, the other to stay inside. Both houses have Sumari characteristics, but in different combinations. You both need the sun.

(Then at 11:21, here presented verbatim:) Now a note: I do not want to get into family variations, but Sue Watkins picked up a variation of the Gramada family of consciousness *(the Grunaargh)*— quite legitimate, and at the time very good on her part.[4] People love to make divisions. There are then what you can call subfamilies, combinations, highly creative. All divisions are simply for the purpose of organizations of consciousness. The families mix and interrelate, so that you could indeed subdivide them, but for my purpose there is little point to this.

As the physical races mix, so do the psychic ones. Every once in a while, in your terms, a new family forms out of such subgroups. So the families are meant to be understood as general categories into which earth-tuned consciousnesses fall more or less naturally.

Reading this section of *"Unknown" Reality*, each person should be able to feel an identification with a family. Yet he or she might also find within strong characteristics of another one, in which case the individual is in the same position as someone who is, say, part Irish and part French in physical terms.

Now it is fairly unusual to be half Italian and half Chinese, though it is possible; so some of the psychic families join more easily with certain others, and some who are very sympathetic to each other find it quite difficult to blend. The "natural earth parents" [the Borledim] and the Sumari, for instance, are very close, and yet have great difficulty in merging, because one considers the family itself as art, and the other subordinates the family for a different kind of art. Often they do not even recognize each other as having many of the same characteristics.

(11:41. That was that on the families of consciousness for the evening. Jane proceeded to deliver for Seth a few more paragraphs of house material, here deleted, followed by this exchange:)

That is the end of the session, unless you have questions.

("No, I think you've already answered them all for now.")

I think I have.

("And very well, too."
(With a smile:) I think I did a pretty good job.
(End at 11:45 P.M.)

NOTES: Session 738

1. See the notes on the shared-driveway situation as presented at the 11:43 break for the last session.

2. Once again, see the notes at the 11:43 break for the 737th session—this time about the "1964 house."

3. The day after this (738th) session was held I wrote to the real-estate agents in Sayre, the Johnsons, informing them that Jane and I were withdrawing any interest we had in the Markle house. We sent the notice not only because of Seth's material in the session, but because we felt that on our own we'd intuitively resolved a certain probable course of action—just as we'd done concerning the house on Foster Avenue in Elmira. (See Note 8 for Session 737.)

With some surprise, then, considering the 53 years that Mr. Markle's house has been a portion of my psyche, to whatever degree, I found myself turning away from intensifying that involvement. My realization that Jane wasn't drawn to the place that much had something to do with my decision, although she was willing to make the purchase—but still, I deliberately passed up the opportunity to spend the later years of my life in the main environment I'd known between the ages of 3 and 12. I felt regret and a strong attraction, but in some way realized that Sayre wasn't the course to follow. Jane agreed, and we made conscious decisions to go elsewhere.

4. See the opening notes for the last session.

Session 739
February 24, 1975
9:25 P.M. Monday

(On Friday, February 21, Jane and I not only saw the hill house from the inside for the first time—but decided to buy it. We made up our minds quite effortlessly while being taken through it by a real-estate agent. Of course we knew what Seth had suggested during last Wednesday's session, and his advice was valuable; at the same time we'd been strongly inclined to make the purchase after looking at the house anew that Wednesday afternoon. At the Realtor's office two days later, then, we signed the initial papers leading to the final purchase, which will be consummated in a couple of weeks or so.

(As I wrote at the start of the 736th session, we first encountered the hill house on February 4, on just our second day of searching. A period of gestation lasting well over two weeks had to follow, though, before we understood what we'd seen; during that time we investigated perhaps 35 other places.[1]

(These notes give me a chance to hint at another in the series of "house connections" that Jane and I have become so much aware of this month—for there is a close professional relationship between the owner of the Foster Avenue house and the real-estate agency through which we're buying the house on the hill. Jane and I had heard of this association in a remote way, but it *had no meaning for us until we committed ourselves to the hill house; the agency concerned is but one of many we'd contacted; yet also involved is our friend Debbie, who works for another real-estate firm, and who had first called our attention to the hill house. There are more intertwinings here [including some art elements] than it's necessary to describe; but studying just this one complex house connection, then seeing how it combines with some of the others we've become conscious of, leaves Jane and me more than a little bemused by this interlocking reality we're creating.[2]*

(In tonight's relatively brief session Seth discussed our house adventures in quite a personal way, yet also passed along some related concepts of a more general nature. I've deleted certain portions of his material about us while leaving other parts for presentation here, since they do extend his recent work for "Unknown" *Reality.)*

Now: Good evening.

("Good evening, Seth.")

This is not dictation. Once you made up your minds to, you found your house—with characteristic swiftness, let me add, and you avoided several pitfalls.

Ruburt was correct: The picture of you, taken on the hill in the front yard *(by a friend)*, portrays you as far as your stance toward the hill house and land is concerned. Ruburt was never athletically inclined, but always loved nature. The house and the grounds will allow you to pick up on old feelings that he had discarded, renewing to some extent a "fresh air" image that he once found natural.

The hill house neighborhood is composed of a rather beneficial balance: No particular family of consciousness predominates. Instead, a love of woods and trees transcends such classifications. The area has brought together diverse kinds of people, united by love of nature, some airy spaces, and some privacy... The people are also achievers of one kind or another, and while [your goals may be different] you appreciate the fact that they are trying to do something with their lives. Many are aware of their limitations. Many dabble in the arts.

Some are patrons of the arts. They possess a great curiosity about artists, writers, or others who have chosen a different route, and achieved in that fashion. They needed you there. This does not mean that some of your characteristics may not seem as strange to them as some of theirs may seem to you.

(Pause at (9:45.) Quite simply, few of them have known people who have devoted themselves to their art. They have only met them at receptions *(with amusement).* They have an almost childlike wonder and curiosity about such matters, and will actually give you as much privacy as you want.

Your psychic work will also help them question the values

of their lives. In any case, barriers will drop on both sides. Many of the children are grown, and the adults have more time to think and ponder. They also need to see other life-styles. The mixture of families of consciousness allows you also to take a close look at the ways in which these tendencies merge to form communities. You are not moving into a closed psychic area, then, where everyone sees the world as you do, even generally speaking. Nor should you.

For you, Joseph *(as Seth calls me),* the place is reminiscent. You are also presented, whether you know it or not, with certain artistic challenges that the landscape itself will provide, and that you have chosen.

I mentioned that the air was cleaner on the hill. You will also have another kind of freedom: Your psychic and other creative work will be easier simply because you will not have others so close to contend with in terms of thought patterns.[3]

(And now verbatim:) The fireplace in the hill house is advantageous, as the one in the house on Foster Avenue would have been, simply in that the open hearth represents an inner source of strength and stability. The open flame, the source of cave heat, is evocative, and represents a closeness with the origins of light and life.

Now: An open fire elicits certain responses from the cells[4] that, for instance, a furnace does not. The effect of the light plus the warmth on the skin is extremely healing. People sit by a fireplace in wintertime because it is unconsciously recognized that recuperative and therapeutic results occur. Simply put, the cells respond to firelight in somewhat the same manner that flowers do to sunlight. The stimulation is much more than skin deep, however, and an open fire is cleansing. It even helps clear the blood.

Cavemen recognized this. I am not suggesting that you use your fireplace instead of the furnace. I am saying that in wintertime there are definite health-value effects to be felt when you sit in front of an open fire. Two evenings a week would be quite effective.

The proximity of so many trees also has considerable health value, and to those doing psychic or other creative work the effects are particularly conducive to a peaceful state of mind. Trees are great users and yet conservators of energy, and they automatically provide much vitality to areas in which they are plentiful. This is physically obvious in scientific terms. Besides that, however, the consciousnesses of trees are remarkably kind and enduring.[5]

Now you think of dogs as friends of man, and you personify dogs in human terms. You think of them sometimes as guardians. In those terms, now, trees are also guardians. They are attached to the people they know. You cannot put a leash on them and walk them around the block, yet trees form a protective barrier about, say, a home or a neighborhood. They are actively <u>concerned</u>. They have personalities—certainly to the same extent that dogs do, yet of an entirely different nature. They respond to you. The trees in that *(hill house)* neighborhood then are particularly friendly, strong, and protective, and they will help renew your energies.

The air there is dryer in a certain way. Now ocean air is wet but it is healthy. River air is wet, but it may be healthy <u>or</u> unhealthy, according to the nature of the river, the land, and the attitude of the people. After the flood [in your area], the river air is felt to be a threat, and to many it is therefore unhealthy. At some time I will give you information discussing the reasons why some people, after being flooded in one location, then move to another equally threatening environment.

The hill property represents a certain kind of security, then—financial, spiritual, and artistic—but an open security, in which there is relative privacy without an overemphasis upon secrecy, which is something different.

Take your break.

(10:17 P.M. Jane's delivery had been very steady. She told me now, however, that she was entering a relaxed state. Her very pleasant situation continued to deepen, so we decided to let the rest of the session go.

(The flood referred to by Seth took place on June 23, 1972. It was caused by the massive tropical storm, Agnes, and devastated many areas in New York, among other eastern states. Low-lying portions of Elmira were much damaged. Jane and I were involved in it, and Seth discussed our experiences in Personal Reality; *see Chapter 1, for instance.*

(Now this is the right time to refer the reader to Appendix 27, which contains Sue Watkins's account of her past-life involvement with the Grunaargh family of consciousness.)

NOTES: Session 739

1. I want to note here that at the same time Jane and I decided to buy the hill house, we learned that the house next door, to the west, would soon be for sale; because of a job transfer its owner would be moving with his family to California this summer. No "For Sale" sign had yet been set up in the front yard. Although Jane and I liked the place well enough, we had no doubt that the hill house was the one for us.

Our own plans to relocate, however, plus those of the family next door (whom we'll never get to know), reminded me of the material Seth gave at 11:25 for the 737th session, to the effect that any important decision we make organizes the patterns of probability set into motion: "This should be obvious . . . Unconsciously, then, the movers are in league with each other. There are sympathetic probabilities set up."

So, I said to Jane, not only are we stirring things up by moving out of the apartment house, but we're entering a situation where *we* will be staying put while others move away. Obvious, but intriguing: We'll be joining the present residents of the hill neighborhood in forming a newer psychic and psychological entity than the one that existed before we arrived. Yet the full picture of our moving should include not only the myriad probabilities growing out of our own actions, but all of the probable developments involving that house next door: Whatever happenings take place there—which we'll help create—are bound to have their effects upon us.

If one wanted to outline an event such as our moving from an arbitrary beginning to an arbitrary end, I added, it could be from the time we first looked at Mr. Markle's house in Sayre, in April 1974, to sometime in the summer of 1975, when we think the situation next door will be resolved with the arrival of "new" people. It'll be interesting to see what—if any— house connections develop.

2. Here's another house connection—one that developed last Thursday, the day after the 738th session was held.

In the 737th session, after 11:55, Seth mentioned the "other dentist" who lived and worked around the corner from the apartment house Jane and I moved into in 1960, upon our arrival in Elmira. We soon became acquainted with him and his family on a very casual basis, since the back of his property abuts the west yard of the apartment house. Several years ago our medical friend moved to a more residential area in Elmira— just where we didn't know—but kept his offices in his original home. Then on Thursday we learned that he'd bought the place across the street from the hill house. The family still lives there.

(We've also discovered that several other professional people who live near the hill house maintain offices in the old near-downtown neighborhood surrounding the apartment house.)

3. I found Seth's statement about contending with the thought patterns of others a particularly apropos one, since Jane and I have lived in apartment houses for many years (and are only now preparing to give up that kind of life.) A question: How does that steady psychic exchange affect all of those who work and/or live in high-rise complexes, for instance?

4. Seth's material here reminded me of a remark he made in the 504th session, which is presented in the Appendix of *The Seth Material;* he was discussing the perceptions of the fetus as mediated by electromagnetic energy (EE) units: "Cells are not just responsive to light because this is the order of things, but because an emotional desire to perceive light is present."

5. See Seth's discussion of tree consciousness in Session 727; Note 7 for that session contains excerpts from his tree data in the 18th

session (for January 22, 1964) and in the 453rd session (for December 4, 1968). Here's some more related material from the 18th session:

"As your body senses temperature changes, so it also senses the psychic charge not only of other human beings but also, believe it or not, of animals, and to a lesser extent . . . of plants and vegetative matter. Your tree builds up a composite of sensations of this sort, sensing not the physical dimensions of a material object, whatever it is, but the vital psychic formation within and about it.

"The table beside Ruburt senses him even as Ruburt senses the table . . . The abilities of the tree are latent in man as, dear Joseph, are the abilities of man latent in the tree."

Session 740
February 26, 1975
9:35 P.M. Wednesday

(In ESP class last night Jane told all of her loyal students, some of whom have been with her almost from the time she began holding such meetings in the summer of 1967, that class was suspended until we'd moved into the hill house and settled down a bit—however long that might take.

(Jane and I were inside "our" hill house for only the second time this afternoon. Again we were accompanied by a real-estate agent; because of insurance regulations we're not allowed to have a key to the place yet, although we've been told that this dilemma will be resolved very soon. In the meantime I've begun what seems to be an awesome task: packing many of our possessions into an endless series of cartons that had once held things like wine, mayonnaise, cereal, pipe fittings, and so forth.

(Just before the session Jane began to edge into an altered state of consciousness other than the one she uses for her "Seth trance," as she put it. For a few moments she sat quietly with her eyes closed. She felt "the idea, mentally, of something shaped like a television screen" off to her right. By now I was writing down what I could. "And now it's coming closer. I don't know what it

624

is, or what it has to do with the session, if anything." She paused, then resumed in the past tense: "It came up fairly close to me. I walked through it and down a long chute. There were coils in there. They did things with me—healing things— then dropped me back in my chair.

("I had the feeling that Seth was in this chute or tunnel, in miniature, and that he looked like he does in your portrait of him, only in full length."[1]

(Back to the present: "Oh—he comes forward, then retreats, oscillating real fast. But in some way the Seth thing in this is in the background. Now he's turning around, this miniature Seth. He's walking away, out of the chute and into this great big Seth who's like a statue.

("Then in the eyes of this Seth there are two little Seths looking out. Both of these images are like your portrait. Now they climb out of the eyes; with their bodies they make a garland around the big Seth's head; they sit on it back-to-back like a pair of bookends." Pause, eyes closed. "Wow—a whole bunch of these little Seths climb up on top of the giant head—but in perfect poses. They're very stylized, but all real. And Seth will explain it," Jane abruptly said, evidently quite surprised. "The little images face in all directions around the head of the big Seth. I know it's not right, not a good analogy, but they're like gargoyles on a steeple . . .

("It's all very distant now. I never saw the entire giant-sized figure of Seth. The head and the arms were clearest. The whole thing was an immeasurable distance from me."

(After another pause: "Okay, I think we can have a session now. But until Seth said so, I didn't know he'd explain any of this.")

Now: Give us a moment.

("Good evening, Seth.")

Dictation *(quietly)*: Ruburt saw the images in a particular fashion so that he could understand certain information about the nature of the psyche.

The giant image of myself, never clearly glimpsed by Ruburt, represents my own greater reality. In a particular fashion, that identity cannot be fully expressed within the confines of any one form, any more than yours can. Period. Ruburt saw many miniature versions of me. In his inner vision these appeared as identical, simply so that he would identify them as portions of myself. They are actually quite different, one from the others.

Each one is involved in its own context of reality, each one pursuing its own directions for its own purposes. One of those "Seths" was born in your space and time. That Seth then seeded himself, so to speak, in the space-time environment you recognize— appearing through the centuries, sending out offshoots of "himself," exploring earthly experience and developing as well as he could those potentials of his own greater identity that could best be brought to fruition within a creature context.[2]

That one Seth was endowed with his own inner blueprint. The blueprint gave him an idea of his potentials, and how they could be best fulfilled in earthly terms.[3]

Give us a moment... The self, as I have said [many times] before, is not limited. It can therefore split off from itself without being less. This Seth might be "born" two or three times in one century—or more—and then in your terms not appear for five or ten centuries. Each Seth would be completely independent, however, and each appearance would signify the creation of a new personality—not simply a new version of an old one.

Each would be inherently aware of its own potentials and "background," but each would tune in to a particular point of that so-called background.

What I am saying here applies to the greater identity of each reader. Give us a moment... Because you are usually so worried about preserving what you think of as your identity, we use terms like reincarnational selves or counterparts. If you truly understood the nature of your individuality, however, you would clearly see that there is no contradiction if I say that you are uniquely yourself, that your individuality has an indestructible validity that is never assailed, and when I also say that you are at the same time connected with other identities, each as sacredly inviolate as your own.

(9:53.) You are used to thinking of exterior organizational patterns. You might live in a city and a state and a country at one time, yet you do not think that your presence in one of these categories contradicts either of the other two. So you live amid psychic organizations, each having its own characteristics. You may consider yourself Indian though you live in America, or American though you live in Africa, or Chinese though you live in France, and you are quite able to retain your sense of individuality.

So the psychic families, or the families of consciousness, can be thought of as natives of inner countries of the mind, sharing heritages, purposes, and intents that may have little to do with the physical countries in which you live your surface lives. People are born in any month of the year in every country. All those in Norway are not born in January or August. In the same way, all the members of any given psychic family are spread across the earth, following inner patterns that may or may not relate to other issues as they are currently understood.

Certain families have a liking for certain months of birth,[4] but no specific rules apply. There is indeed an inner kind of order that unites all of these issues; yet that inner order is <u>not</u> the result of laws, but of spontaneous creation, which flows into its own kinds of patterns. You see the patterns at any given time and try to make laws of them.

I am trying to stretch your imaginations, and to help you throw aside rigid concepts that literally blind you to the dimensions of your own reality. Again—you are biologically equipped to perceive far more of that reality than you do.[5]

Give us a moment . . . *(A one-minute pause.)* You are not a miniature self, an adjunct to some superbeing, never to share fully in its reality. *(Long pause.)* In those terms you <u>are</u> that superself—looking out of only one eye, or using just one finger.

Much of this is very difficult to verbalize. *(Long pause.)* You are not subordinate to some giant consciousness. While you think in such terms, however, I must speak of reincarnational selves and counterparts, because you are afraid that if you climb out of what you think your identity is, then you will lose it.

Take your break.

(10:11. I think that in his delivery since 9:53 especially, Seth did a good job of making some important points in a very brief way.

(Jane's rather intent delivery had slowed noticeably during the last 10 minutes. "Boy," she said, "I was getting stuff toward the end that neither of us—Seth or me—could verbalize. There wasn't anything in my thought patterns that he could make words out of to express what he wanted to say. I vaguely felt it, but it was pretty alien to my psychological experience." At the moment, at least, I couldn't recall hearing her voice such ideas just that way before in the sessions.[6]

(Then: "Wait—I'm starting to get something on it," Jane suddenly said. "He's found something in my thought patterns he can use . . ." She sat with her head down. "I'm getting a whole lot of stuff now. I'm embarrassed to say it," she laughed, "but I've got the feeling that if I rubbed right here between my eyes—you know, the third eye thing—I could get a lot more information. . . ."[7]

(Jane didn't rub between her eyes—and without leaving her chair she went back into the session within a very few minutes. Her eyes were closed. Her delivery was so subdued at first that I wondered if she was using her Seth voice. Resume at 10:15.)

Now: We will see if we can express some concepts about the self in a new way. In his own *Psychic Politics* Ruburt has presented from his *(psychic)* library some information concerning official and unofficial numbers.[8]

(Pause, hand to closed eyes.) Between each official number in

a given series he envisions literally infinite space. The infinitesimal becomes infinite.

Now *(eyes open):* In the same way the most infinitesimal self is infinite, and the most finite self, carried to the extremes of itself, is infinite. Each of you is part of an infinite self. That infinite self appears as a series of finite selves in your reality.

Beneath that perceived reality, however, each finite self, carried to its degree, is itself infinite. Now here is one for the books *(with amusement):* but there are different kinds of infinities. There are different varieties of psychological infinities that do not meet—that is, that go off in their own infinite directions.

(Now for a few moments Jane rubbed in a circular motion between her closed eyes.)

As long as you believe that as individuals you belong in any given series, you appear to yourselves as finite.

You think in terms of linear time, and the best you can do to imagine your deeper reality is to consider reincarnation in time. It is a matter of focus. You usually identify with the outside of yourself, and with the outside of the world. You do not, for example, usually identify with the inside of your body, with its organs, much less its cells or atoms—yet in that direction lies a certain kind of infinity *(intently).*

If you would identify with your own psychological reality, following the inward structure of thoughts and feelings, you would discover an inward psychological infinity. These "infinities" would reach of course into both an infinite past and future. Yet true infinity reaches far beyond past or future, and into all probabilities—not simply straightforward into time, or backward.

(10:29.) There is literally an infinity in each moment[9] you recognize, as numerically there is an "infinity" behind or within any prime number[10] *(3, 97, 863, et cetera)* that you recognize.

There are infinite versions of yourself, but no one negates the others, and each is connected with the others, and aids and supports them. There are other quite legitimate numerical systems that you do not follow. There are other kinds of psychological organizations also. In those terms Ruburt has learned, or rather Ruburt is learning, to alternate a series–to bring information from one [neurological series] to another, so to speak.

However, none of this is apart from normal living. Whether or not they want to mention it here in *"Unknown" Reality,* both Ruburt and Joseph have learned to correlate data so that some of the implications involved in a simple move from one house to another become apparent. They are not mathematicians. They will not statistically analyse the results. Yet I tell you that the moves that you make in daily life have indeed infinite effects—and I am not using the word loosely.

Now take your break.

(10:36. "Wow," Jane exclaimed as she emerged from her short but excellent delivery. "Before the session I didn't feel a thing. I was just sort of happily dopey—no ideas at all. But I really clicked in before this break. Seth finally found something he could use to make analogies. I wasn't aware of traffic noise or anything else . . . The whole thing surprises me: Look what I'd have missed if I'd decided not to have a session. And I didn't know Seth was going to explain those visions until I got that flash from him just before he came through. I have the feeling that inside that experience I traveled a great distance. . . ."

(Concerning Seth's remark about "a simple move from one house to another" for Jane and me: This includes all of the other people involved, too. In the previous five sessions I've inserted just enough "house connections" to indicate what's been materializing for us in this area, without digressing to write a much longer history. Our list of such interrelationships contains over 40 items so far, and continues to grow. However, many of these are made up of several related events, figures, et cetera, and so could be legitimately divided further if we chose to do so.[11]

(Jane and I do not ascribe the elements making up our house adventures to that old catchall, "coincidence," of course; at the same time we have no plans to statistically attempt anything with them either. So many variables are present that a separate analysis would be required for each individual involved—with "boundaries," say, set as to the number of items to be considered in each case. Then what about temporal boundaries? Truly, for myself the whole house thing had its origins in my early childhood, over half a century ago. But Jane, being younger, would designate quite different limitations in time. . . .

(A query: With the individual analyses done, would it be possible to incorporate them all into one masterwork? Such a project would be a formidable one, I think, and would take at least a book in itself.

("I'm just waiting," Jane said finally, after we'd each had a little something to eat. "I feel unsettled. I think there's another bunch of material there. Seth's going to get it if I can do it—if he can find some more thought patterns he can use." A long pause. "Now, I'll try. . . ."

(Very quietly at 11:06:)

Imagine a string of different-colored Christmas tree lights, all glowing on a given tree. In this series of lights, any one light can go out while the others continue to shine. You are familiar with that arrangement.

However, in our imaginary assortment there are many such strings, and when a light goes out on one string "it" almost automatically appears on another string. Now generally speaking the lights are all lit at once on any given string, except for those that now and then go out.

Pretend that you are very tiny, and moving slowly about the tree so that you see only one light at a time. It appears that one light exists before the other, then, and each one is so brilliant to your focus that it blots out the lights before and after it. You may have a dim memory of the light you "saw" before, however, and so you think: "Aha, the bulb I see is my life, but I'm sure that long ago I had a different life—and perhaps another one lies ahead of me." But unless you step far back from the tree you will not realize that the entire string of lights exists at once. Nor will you understand that when one light goes out in a strand it appears somewhere else on the tree in another strand.

If you were still tinier, then any given bulb itself might seem to emit not a steady light at all, but a series of waves, and you might identify your life with any given wave, so that great distance might be perceived between one wave and the next.[12]

(Pause at 11:20.) Experiencing that kind of series could lead to entirely different kinds of perception, in which infinities *(pause)* existed *(pause)* within a scale of its own. (In parentheses: The series would have its own kind of infinit<u>ies</u>.)

("A singular 'its' but a plural 'infinities'?" I asked. Jane, as Seth, nodded in agreement.)

A tree could be wired with lights, with each one having its own particular series [of waves]. The people who put up the tree might experience one Christmas Eve, while other consciousnesses, tuned in to the different series, could experience endless generations[13]—and <u>their</u> perceptions would be quite as legitimate as those of the light-watchers who had erected the tree.

This is not necessarily the best analogy, but I wanted to make the point that various scales of awareness contain their own infinities, no matter how finite they may appear to be.

The soul, so-called, is not related to size or duration in space and time, except insofar as it is wedded to experience within those contexts.

Give us a moment . . . That will be the end of dictation. Take a break or end the session as you prefer.

("We'll take the break and see what happens.")

(11:29 P.M. "That's as far as we can carry it tonight," Jane said, meaning book material. She wasn't so sure about ending the session itself. We sat waiting. Five minutes later she said: "Well, I guess that's it," and the session was over.)

NOTES: Session 740

1. See the picture section in Prentice-Hall's editions of *The Seth Material* for a cropped, black-and-white reproduction of my oil portrait of Seth, "in the form in which he chose to appear to Rob," as Jane wrote in Chapter 8 of that book. Seth first announced his presence by name in the 4th session for December 8, 1963; I painted him in 1966.

2. Quite a few of the diagrams I drew for Jane's *Adventures in Consciousness* (which is to be published by Prentice-Hall in the spring of 1975) illuminate Seth's material in this paragraph. See the opening notes for Session 718 of *"Unknown" Reality.*

3. Seth discussed his "blueprints for reality" a number of times in Volume 1 of *"Unknown" Reality.* See the 696th session, for instance: "Each probability system has its own set of 'blueprints,' clearly defining its freedoms and boundaries . . . These are not 'inner images of perfection,' and to some extent the blueprints themselves change . . . As an individual you carry within you such a blueprint, then; it contains all the information you require to bring about the most favorable version of yourself in the probable system you know . . . In the same fashion the species *en masse* holds within its vast inner mind such working plans or blueprints."

4. In Note 3 for Session 734, see my exploration of the months of birth for some of the members of ESP class—many of whom are Sumari.

5. In the 685th session for Volume 1, Seth stated that the consciousnesses of our cells are eternal, and that biologically we're equipped to explore many more probable realities than we know. In the 686th session he discussed our cells' comprehension of the past, present, *and* future, as well as our cellular responses to a variety of neurological pulses besides that certain range we're egotistically focused upon. See his first delivery for that session.

6. But in appendixes 4 and 5 for Volume 1, see Jane's own material on other-than-usual neurological pulses, or speeds. Seth examined our neurological pulses—and habits—at 12:19 in Session 686.

7. In all of the sessions, Jane has mentioned the third (or "back") eye of occult lore only once before—in Session 612 for September 6, 1972—and she'd been somewhat embarrassed then, too. See the opening excerpts from the 612th session in Appendix 19, with Note 5. In that note I speculated about "what intuitive knowledge she might possess that led her to talk about" the third eye at that time. We had the same questions all over again, without intending to investigate them any more now than we did then.

8. We think it quite likely that Seth's material in this delivery, and some of Jane's in *Politics,* grew out of reading we did earlier this month on "new" forms of mathematics—which embody some ideas that are actually many centuries old. Involved, however, are very interesting "nonstandard" methods of regarding time, quantum theory, the infinite and the infinitesimal in numbers, model theory, and other mathematical tools.

At least as she understands these concepts, Jane—and Seth—
"took off" from them in individual, creative ways. For Chapter 19 of *Politics*
(which is to be published in 1976) Jane transcribed from her library, in part:
"If you imagine the official numbers 1 to 10 in a row, then there would be
an infinite number of unofficial 1's hidden in the 1 you saw, and an infinite
number of spaces between the official 1 and 2. The position of the 1 on the
paper would represent our sense-data world, while the invisible 1's behind
the official 1 would represent the official 1's hidden values and infinite
probabilities."

And: "It's significant that we apply numbers to time, but as
there are unrecognized spaces between numbers, there are unrecognized
spaces (psychologically invisible) between or within moments, and some of
the events of our bodies are 'too small' for us to follow, focused as we are in
our prime series. These body events actually are 'infinitesimal but infinite,'
following their own patterns that merge with ours."

There are, of course, close relationships concerning this delivery of Seth's for the 740th session, the material in this note, and the
musical analogies Seth presented in the 735th session, when he discoursed
upon the inaudible variations inherent in the compositions played by the
young classical guitarist who'd visited us over the weekend of February 2.
(I've been saving this reference for this particular note.) At 9:45, for
instance, in that 735th session: "An infinite number of other 'alternate'
compositions were also latent within the [first] note, however . . . They were
quite as legitimate as the compositions that were played . . . and . . . added
silent structure and pacing to the physically actualized music."

For the same session Seth also offered evocative analogies
involving heard and unheard musical compositions on the one hand, and
counterpart, probable, and reincarnational selves on the other.

9. For some quotations (and references) from Volume 1 on the
moment point, see Note 11 for Appendix 12.

10. In mathematical terms: A prime number is a whole num-
ber (not a fraction, for instance) that cannot be exactly divided by any other
whole number except itself and 1.

11. This house connection is a good example of the kind that's
not only made up of a number of related elements, but extends over a
longer period of time. Because of those combined attributes, I'm adding
this note to the (740th) session in October 1975, six months after Seth
finished dictating Volume 2 of *"Unknown" Reality*. All names have been
changed.

In Note 1 for Session 739 I wrote that when Jane and I decided
to buy the hill house (on February 21, 1975) we learned that the place next
to it on the west would soon be for sale. I also commented that it would "be
interesting to see what—if any—house connections develop."

Not long after we moved into the hill house (in March) our new
acquaintance and next-door neighbor to the east, Frank Corio, told us he
knows Louise Akins; she was one of the first students to attend Jane's ESP

class, in September 1967. An interesting tidbit, we thought, considering that Elmira is a city of close to 50,000 people, and in turn is surrounded by a similar number residing in smaller communities. I added Frank's information to our list of house connections, then forgot about it.

Frank is also in real estate, although he has no professional associations with the Johnsons, Debbie, or the agency through which we bought the hill house. The house west of us became vacant this year in early summer. In the fall Frank Corio was given the job of selling the place, and soon did so—to a family, the Millers, who were moving to Elmira from a distant state. Next, Jane and I found out from Mrs. Miller that she too knows Louise Akins.

The odds against such a "coincidence" developing would be astronomical—except that the Millers had lived in a neighborhood close to the hill house several years ago (when the acquaintanceship with Louise Akins had been made), had moved out of state, then returned to buy the house next-door to us. The house connection is still unique, however, considering that in the hill house Jane and I found ourselves bracketed east and west by people who knew one of her early students—who had in turn mentioned Jane to *them*. Interesting, that Frank Corio had been instrumental in bringing the Millers back to their favorite neighborhood, when in a city the size of Elmira there are at any time a number of homes for sale in "desirable" neighborhoods, including "ours."

Jane and I certainly don't think the fact that Frank and Mrs. Miller know Louise Akins was the reason the Millers moved next-door to us, yet it *is* one factor to be considered among a myriad of others—money, availability, and so forth. Why did Jane and I move into a neighborhood in which such a house connection could develop to begin with? Why was Frank Corio assigned the task of selling the house next door to us? Why did the Millers encounter him at just that particular time, and why was he, of all the real-estate agents in Elmira, the one who succeeded in selling them the house they bought?

Such connections and questions, whatever their strength and the conscious or unconscious motivations behind them, make a fascinating area for study. Once again, we were reminded of Seth's material at 11:25 for the 737th session, when he told us that "movers are in league with each other."

In concluding this note, I should add that our neighbor, Frank Corio, was involved in other house connections with Jane and me—some of them quite as intriguing as the one just described.

12. Seth's ideas in this paragraph and the one just preceding it are consistent with his material in a number of sessions for Volume 1. In sessions 681 and 684, for instance, he discussed the on-off fluctuations of our physical universe and everything within it, moment points, probabilities, Jane's sensations of massiveness, the basic unpredictable motion of any wave or atom, and much more. In sessions 682–83, he stressed the nature of his CU's, or units of consciousness. Then in Volume 2, Seth

likened his own identity to that of a wave formation; see the excerpts from the 775th session in Appendix 18, with Note 35.

I also think his use of "great distance" this evening (just before 11:20) is somehow related to the feeling of "immeasurable distance" that Jane experienced in her vision as she sat for the session.

13. In retrospect we can see how the mystical Jane has always tried to intuitively penetrate the nature of reality through her art; I've illustrated that learning process by presenting selections from her early poetry at apropos times throughout the two volumes of *"Unknown" Reality*. I also gave some background information on Jane's nature (with a poem) in Appendix 1 for Volume 1.

One of those steps in Jane's self-directed search for understanding is referred to in Note 5 for Session 681 (in Volume 1), which contains three lines from her poem, *More Than Men*. She wrote it in 1954, when she was 25 years old. That was the year we married. The Seth material's inception lay nine years ahead of us; neither of us knew what mediumship was. Yet, as Jane said recently: "It was there in the poetry all the time, only I didn't understand." Now I want to offer that poem in full.

More Than Men

More than men
Have walked these shores in twilight.
More gods than ours have risen altars fair.
The earth is filled
With songs not of our singing,
There are worlds about us in which we have no share.

Between each ticking of the clock
Long centuries pass
In universes hidden from our own.
And our time's eons are far less than breath
Or the flight of a leaf by the wind blown.

Session 741
April 14, 1975
9:21 P.M. Monday

("All I know," Jane said tonight at 8:50, "is that I want to get back to the sessions again. I don't care whether we get stuff on "Unknown" Reality, or personal material, or what. Just so we get going—I'm always nervous about starting things up again after a layoff. . . ."[1]

(She made her remarks after I'd read her Seth's last session [the 740th for February 2] from my notes earlier this evening; I still don't have it typed. Incredibly, that session is already six weeks old. We've been involved in so many activities since then that it's difficult to decide which of them to refer to in these notes, and to what extent. Except for the few listed below, then, it may be sufficient to just state that we've been in our hill house for a month, and that after much hard physical labor[2] we've settled down enough to resume our natural rhythms of painting, sessions, books, and play. I have a room I'm converting into a studio, and one in which to work on this manuscript. And for the first time since we married 20 years ago [in 1954], Jane has a room to herself for her own writing—if she chooses to use it. So far she's preferred to work before the picture window in the living room.

(*Our house connections continue to accumulate, often in unexpected ways. From her own viewpoint Jane has already produced for* Psychic Politics *some very perceptive material on our move to the hill house: "So we made our own special place in more ordinary terms, by symbolizing that particular house and corner, marking it ours, stamping it with the imprint of living symbols which we transposed upon it. Henceforth it had a magic quality."*[3]

(*Jane hasn't restarted ESP class yet. We'e not sure when we'll be able to manage that. Class may have to wait until Seth finishes his work on* "Unknown" Reality.

(*We've largely finished correcting proofs on both the text and the drawing captions for Jane's* Adventures in Consciousness, *which will be published in June. We've also seen a first color proof of the jacket design for her* Dialogues, *scheduled for publication next fall.*[4]

(*As if to celebrate our way of life and work in the house on the hill, we were visited last Saturday by Tam Mossman, Jane's editor at Prentice-Hall, and a publishing colleague of his. One result of our meeting [as I wrote at the beginning of the Introductory Notes for Volume 1], was the decision to publish this long manuscript for* "Unknown" Reality *in two volumes.*[5]

(*In ordinary terms, I think that during our first month in the hill house we've been busy forming a fresh psychic atmosphere within which we can feel comfortable—and that anyone in a similar situation intuitively does the same thing. Perhaps not until a start is made in this way can any of us initiate certain functions in the "new" place. Actually, then, we seek to wed the old environment with the new, using the psyche as a bridge between the two worlds. Now when Jane and I drive past the old house we lived in on Water Street, close by downtown Elmira, we engender within ourselves mixed feelings of strangeness and familiarity. We see the intimately known windows of the two apartments we shared still vacant, the blinds hanging at careless angles. Friends have told us both places are being redecorated to a modest degree. "I'm glad they're being changed," Jane said the other day, in a strangely possessive response. "That means the world we had there can't ever be entered by anyone else."*

(*In that big, intriguing house her whole psychic world—and mine— had begun to open up late in 1963; various aspects of that becoming are detailed in her different books. Yet when Jane left the Water Street apartments that day in March, she never looked back: When she's through with something, she's through with it. She's remarkably free in that way. I'm the one who's apt to become attached to old things, old places, to look back with a bit of nostalgia. Now as we waited for tonight's session to begin, our 14-year-old cat, Willy, dozed on the couch beside me. At the same time our black cat, Rooney, who'd died in his fifth year, lay in his grave in the backyard of the house on Water Street.*[6]

(*Jane lit a cigarette and sipped at a beer. Then she took off her glasses. By the time she laid them on the coffee table between us she was in trance. Speaking as Seth, she began to very comfortably and easily deliver the next session for* "Unknown" *Reality.)*

Good evening.

("Good evening, Seth.")

Dictation *(quietly and humorously)*: The unknown reality appears [to be] invisible only because you do not accept it in your prime series of events. *(See the last session.)*

It is as if you had trained yourselves to respond to red lights and to ignore green ones, for example—or as if you read only every third or fourth line on a page of a book.

You attend to matters that seem to have practical value. Whether or not you understand what space is, you move through it easily. You do not calculate how many steps it takes you to cross a room, for instance. You do not need to understand the properties of space in scientific terms, in order to use it very well. You can see yourselves operate in space, however; to that extent it is a known quality, apparent to the senses. Your practical locomotion is involved with it so you recognize it. Its mysterious or less-known properties scarcely concern you.

Now, you move through probabilities in much the same way that you navigate in space. As you do not consciously bother with all of the calculations necessary in the process of walking down the street, so you also ignore the mechanisms that involve motion through probable realities. You manipulate through probabilities so smoothly, in fact, and with such finesse, that you seldom catch yourself in the act of changing your course from one probability to another.

(9:34.) Take a very simple action: You stand at a corner, wondering which direction to take. There are four streets involved. You briefly consider streets One and Two, but rather quickly decide against them. You stand for a moment longer, gazing down Street Three, taking in the visual area. You are somewhat attracted, and imagine yourself taking that course. Your imagination places you there momentarily. Inner data is immediately aroused through conscious and unconscious association. Perhaps you are aware of a few memories that dimly come to mind. One house might remind you of one a relative lived in years ago. A tree might be reminiscent of one that grew by your family home. But in that instant, inner computations occur as you consider making a fairly simple decision, and the immediate area is checked against all portions of your knowledge.[7]

You then look at Street Four. The same process happens

again. This area also takes your attention. At the same time you almost equally hold in your mind the image of Street Three, for you can see them both at once from this intersection.

Let us say that you are almost equally attracted to both courses. You teeter between probabilities, having the full power to choose one street or the other as physical experience. If you had to stand there and write down all the thoughts and associations connected with each course of action before you made your decision, you might never cross the intersection to begin with. You might be hit by an automobile as you stood there, lost in your musings.

In the same way, it would take you some time to even walk from a table to a chair if you had to be consciously aware of all of the nerves and muscles that must first be activated. But while you stand almost equally attracted by streets Three and Four, then you send out mental and psychic energy in those directions.

Past associations merge with present reality and form a pattern. Mentally, a part of you actually starts out upon each street— a projected mental image. Period. As you stand there, then, in this case two such projected images go out onto streets Three and Four. To some extent these images experience "what will happen" if you yourself take one direction or the other. That information is returned to you instantaneously, and you make your decision accordingly. Say you choose Street Four. Physically you begin to walk in that direction. Street Four becomes your physical reality. You accept that experience in your prime sequence of events. You have, however, already sent out an energized mental image of yourself into Street Three, and you cannot withdraw that energy.

(9:53.) The portion of you that was attracted to that route continues to travel it. At the point of decision this alternate self made a different conclusion: that it experience Street Three as physical reality. The self as you think of it is literally reborn in each instant, following an infinite number of events from the one official series of events that you recognize at any given "time."

There is something highly important here concerning your technological civilization: As your world becomes more complicated, in those terms, you increase the number of probable actions practically available. The number of decisions multiplies. You can physically move from one place on the planet to another with relative ease. Centuries ago, ordinary people did not have the opportunity to travel from one country to another with such rapidity. As space becomes "smaller," your probabilities grow in complexity. Your consciousness handles far more space data now. (In parentheses: I am speaking in your terms of time.) Watching television, you are aware of events that occur on the other side of the earth, so your consciousness necessarily becomes less parochial.[8] As this has happened the whole underline{matter} (smiling) of probabilities has begun to assume a more practical cast. Civilizations are locked one into the other. Politicians try to predict what other governments will do. Ordinary people try to predict what their government might do.

More and more, you are beginning to deal with probabilities as you try to ascertain which of a number of probable events might physically occur. When the question of probabilities is a practical one, then scientists will give it more consideration.

The entire subject is very important, however. As far as a true psychology is concerned, individuals who are made aware of the existence of probable realities will no longer feel trapped by events. Your consciousness is at a point where it is beginning to understand the significance of "predictive action"—and predictive action always involves probabilities.

In certain terms (underlined), you are the recognized "result" of all of the decisions you have made up to this point in your life. That is the official [9] you. You are in no way diminished because other quite-as-official selves are "offshoots" of your own experience, making the choices you did not make, and choosing, then, alternate versions of reality.

You follow the prime series of events that you recognize as your own, yet all of you are connected. (Long pause, eyes closed.) These are not just esoteric statements, but valid clues about the nature of your own behavior, meant to give you a sense of your own freedom, and to emphasize the importance of your choice.

Take your break.

(10:23. Jane was very quickly out of a fine trance that had lasted for just over an hour. Willy had slept beside me all of the time, twisting himself into a variety of positions. "I feel relaxed, relieved, and exhausted, now that we've started things up again," Jane said, yawning. "I almost think I could go to bed right now, but I know I won't. There: I just picked up the next two or three sentences for after break," she said as she got up and moved about, "but they can wait."

(Resume at 10:53.)

Now: Dictation again (loudly).

Whenever you try to predict behavior or events, then, you are dealing with probabilities.

However, it seems to you that all action in the past is fixed and done, while behavior in the future alone is open to change—so the word "prediction" assumes future action. Basically, the past is as open to change as the future is. When you are dealing with historic events you believe that no prediction is involved. Personally and as a species, you are convinced that there is a one-line series of finished events behind you.

In *The Nature of Personal Reality* I stated that the point of action occurs in the present.[10] In *Adventures in Consciousness* Ruburt said, quite properly, that time experience actually splashed out from the present to form an apparent past and future.[11]

When you seemingly look backward into time, and construct a history, you do so by projecting your own prime series of events into the past as it is understood. Obviously you read the past from the present, but you also <u>create</u> it from the present as well. You accept certain data—your present recognized series of events—then use that series as a measuring stick, so to speak: It automatically rejects what does not fit. At certain levels of experience this makes little difference. All data agree. No rough spots show.

(11:05.) Give us a moment . . . *(Pause.)* You build smooth structures of beliefs, then look at reality using the beliefs like glasses—tinted ones. Period. Opposing information will literally be invisible to you.[12] It will be ignored or cast aside.

It has been fashionable to think in terms of straight-line evolution, for example. As mentioned earlier in this book,[13] the accepted theory of evolution is highly simplistic. Your species did not come from one particular source. You have many cousins, so to speak. Some traces of that lineage remain in your time. However, when you look "backward" at the planet you actually try to predict past behavior from the standpoint of the present.

You do this personally in your intimate lives to some degree also, as you view your earlier days. You blot out events that do not fit your present concept of yourself. They literally become nonexistent as far as you are concerned. In such fashion you block out aspects of your own reality—and consciously, at least, cut down on your choices.

Give us a moment . . . The species as you know it has within it, intrinsically, many abilities and characteristics that go unrecognized because you do not accept them as a part of your biological or spiritual heritage. Therefore they become latent and invisible, practically speaking. The same applies individually, when you deny yourselves the rich mixture of consciousness and experience that is available through a recognition of the manipulation of probable realities.

You alter your experience in each instant, quite drastically. Each individual possesses far vaster opportunities for choice than are realized. You are denied tomorrow's wisdom only because you believe time is a closed system.[14] It is true that you are subject to birth and death, yet within that framework far greater dimensions of experience are possible than are usually experienced.

You are all counterparts of each other who are alive at any given earth time. By really understanding this you could come to terms with the ideas of brotherhood that religions have taught for so long.

End of session.

("Thank you, Seth," I said, after the sudden ending.

(Still in full trance, her eyes very dark, Jane stared at me. Then I watched the Seth personality begin to recede, to fade. Jane blinked a few times, and Seth was gone. 11:26 P.M.)

NOTES: Session 741

1. Checking, I soon discovered that Jane had said much the same thing as we sat for the 708th session, following a three-month break in book sessions. See the opening notes.

2. A number of our friends—some of them members of ESP class—helped us move on Saturday, March 15. They even furnished the trucks. Their strenuous efforts will be endlessly appreciated: Anyone who has ever carried heavy furniture, or innumerable boxes of goods, up and down steep and turning flights of stairs will understand the gratitude Jane and I feel.

3. This passage is from Chapter 20 of *Politics.* Then see Chapter 21 for more of Jane's material on our moving.

4. Material (and further references) concerning production details for *Adventures* and *Dialogues* can be found in the opening notes for sessions 718 and 735. Also see Note 1 for the latter session.

5. Five months ago, in the 721st session, I noted Jane's speculations "that *'Unknown' Reality* might prove to be so long that it could go into *two volumes*–a probable development I hardly took seriously."

6. For material on the death—and life—of Rooney, see these sources: in *Personal Reality,* sessions 638–39 in chapters 9 and 10, respectively; in *Dialogues,* Part 3.

7. Seth gave two blocks of material in *Seth Speaks* that are analogous to what he tells us here. In Chapter 7, see the 530th session at 9:30, when he discoursed upon our frequent projection of "replica images" or "pseudophysical forms" to vividly desired locations. In the 565th session at 9:30, for Chapter 16, he used the example of one's possible responses to a telephone call to show how all "probable actions are equally valid," no matter which one of them is physically actualized.

8. In Chapter 10 for *Personal Reality,* see the 675th session from 11:51. In Volume 1 of *"Unknown" Reality,* see the 686th session from 10:37.

9. See Note 2 for Session 695, in Volume 1.

10. Among the sessions for *Personal Reality* in which Seth stressed that "the present is the point of power," see the 657th in Chapter 15.

11. See Chapter 10 of *Adventures*.

12. For one of the ways in which Seth explicates the idea that we're blind to information—or beliefs—that we don't agree with, see the 617th session for Chapter 3 of *Personal Reality*.

13. See Session 705 and Appendix 12.

14. In Volume 1, see Note 4 for Session 680, and Note 2 for Session 688.

Session 742
April 16, 1975
9:29 P.M. Wednesday

Good evening.

("Good evening, Seth.")

Dictation. The whole idea of probable realities seems strange or esoteric only because you are not used to following your own thought processes.

You shut them off any time they do not conform to current beliefs about the nature of the self, or about reality in general. The deepest meanings of probabilities lie, however, precisely in their psychological import.

(Pause.) You have become so hypnotized by a one-level kind of thought that anything else seems impractical. You concentrate upon those decisions that you make, and disregard the processes involved. This has been carried to an extreme, you see: Often you are so disconnected from those inner workings that your own decisions then appear to come from someplace else. You may be convinced that events happen <u>to</u> you, and are beyond your control,

simply because you are so out of touch with yourself that you never catch the moments of your own decisions.

Then you feel as if you are the pawns of fate, and the idea of probable actions seems like the sheerest nonsense. Each event seems inevitable. If this attitude is carried to excessive lengths, then it even appears that you have no hand at all in the making of your own reality. You will always feel yourself a victim.

The unknown reality is your psychic, spiritual, and psychological one, and from it your physical experience springs.[1]

That inner, all-pervasive existence becomes known to the extent that you grow more responsive to your own inner environment. This does not mean that you become entirely self-centered, blind to the rest of the world. It does not mean that you must meditate for hours, or study your own thought processes with such vigor that you ignore other activities. It simply means that you are <u>aware</u> of your own life as clearly as possible—in touch with your thought processes, aware of them but without overdue concern or overanalysis. They are as much a part of your inner environment as trees are of your exterior world. There are different species of selves in the same fashion. There are different species of worlds.

New paragraph *(as Seth often declares)*. When you identify with only one particular level of your thought processes, however, the others—when you sense them—appear alien. You begin to feel threatened, determined to uphold your old ideas of selfhood. Plants grow many leaves. One leaf does not threaten the existence of others, and the plant is not jealous of its own foliage. So there is no need to protect your own individuality because it may send out other shoots into probable realities. This is simply the self growing in different directions, spreading its seeds.

(Pause at 9:52, eyes closed.) Joseph and Ruburt have moved into a "new"[2] house. In so doing they have traveled through probabilities, as each of my readers has under similar circumstances. *(Long pause.)* They identify with the selves who moved into the new "hill house." In a sense they are different people now than they were when *"Unknown" Reality* was begun *(some 14 months ago)*. However, many of my readers are also different people now than they were when they began to read this work.

Let us go back approximately two months in your time. Ruburt and Joseph were looking for a house. They had already seen one on the inside, as mentioned earlier in *"Unknown" Reality*.[3] This manuscript, for that matter, was begun precisely at the point in time that Ruburt's and Joseph's latest adventure with probabilities began. Two months ago, however, they were attracted to "the Foster

Avenue house," as they called it (change the name if you want to). They drove past it often, and went inside. Ruburt imagined his classes being held there. Imaginatively both Ruburt and Joseph saw themselves living there, and a certain amount of psychic energy was projected into that house.

In a probable reality, a Ruburt and a Joseph now live there. In the world that you recognize as official, however, they moved into the hill house. To some extent both of them are aware of the inner processes involved in the final decision. I do not mean that they are simply familiar with the exterior thought processes involved, such as: "The hill house is better constructed," or "It has a fine view." I am speaking of deeper mechanisms of consideration *(pause)*, in which correlations are made between interior and exterior realities. *(Pause.)* It is obvious that when you move from one place to another you make an alteration in space—but you alter time as well, and you set into motion a certain psychological impetus that reaches out to affect everyone you know. *(Long pause.)* When a house is vacant all of the people in the neighborhood send out their own messages. To a certain extent any given inhabited area forms its own "entity." This applies to the smallest neighborhood[4] and to the greatest nation. Such messages are often encountered in the dream state. Empty houses are psychic vacancies that yearn to be filled. When you move, you move into other portions of your own selfhood.[5]

Take your break.

(10:11. "I've been doing this book for so long by now," Jane commented, "that I don't know if it's a great big sprawling thing without any order, or what. I've lost all track of whatever sense of continuity it's got," she amended. "When I come out of trance I don't know what the thing's all about. . . ." Out of habit, Jane—and consequently Seth—still talked about "Unknown" Reality *as being one entity, even though just five days ago we'd learned from her editor that it would be published in two volumes.*

(The tenor of Seth's material tonight led me to think that he was close to finishing "Unknown" Reality, *but since Jane evidently didn't feel that way I said nothing about it. Resume at 10:29.)*

In fact, you move into new areas of the self all of the time. The species is now entering such a phase, a period in which it will come more into its own. Mankind will be entering its own new house, then—but the physical changes will be the results of interior ones, and alterations in main lines of probabilities.

Christian theology sees the end of the world in certain terms, with a grand God coming to reward the good and to punish the wicked.[6] That system of belief allows for no other probability. Some see the end of the world coming as a greater disaster, or envision man finally ruining his planet. Others see periods of peace and advance—and each probability will happen "somewhere." However, many of my readers, or their offspring, will be involved in a new dimension of selfhood in which consciousness is fully explored and the potentials of the soul uncovered, at least to some extent.

Human capabilities will be seen as what they are, and a great new period of development will occur, in which all concepts of selfhood and reality will be literally seen as "primitive superstition." The species will actually move into a new kind of selfhood.

Theories of probabilities will be seen as practical, workable, psychological facts, giving leeway and freedom to the individual, who will no longer feel at the mercy of external events—but will realize instead that he (or she) is their initiator.

Now, you squeeze the great fruit of your selfhood into a tiny uneasy pulp, unaware of the sweetness of its juices or the variety of its seasons. You look at the outsides of yourselves as if a peach were aware only of its skin. In the reality I foresee, however, people will become familiar with far greater aspects of themselves, and bring these into actualization. They will be in touch with their own decisions as they make them.

If they become ill, they will do so knowing they choose the condition in order to emphasize certain areas of development, or to minimize others. They will be aware of their options, comma, consciously. The great strength and resiliency of the body will be much better understood; not because medical science makes spectacular discoveries—though it will—but because the mind's alliance with the body will be seen more clearly.

In this probability of which I speak, the species will begin to encounter the great challenge inherent in fulfilling the vast untouched *(forcefully)*—underlined—potential of the human body and mind. *(Long pause.)* In that probable reality, to which each of you can belong to some extent, each person will recognize his or her inherent power of action and decision, and feel an individual sense of belonging with the physical world that springs up in response to individual desire and belief.[7]

(10:59.) Give us a moment . . . *(Jane, in trance, lit a cigarette.)* Your ideas of Atlantis are partially composed of future memories. They are psychic yearnings toward the ideal civilization—patterns within the psyche, even as each fetus has within it the picture of its own most ideal fulfillment toward which it grows.

Atlantis is a land that you want to inhabit, appearing in your literature, your dreams, and your fantasies,[8] serving as an impetus for development. It is real and valid. In your terms it is not "yet" physical fact, but in some ways it is more real than any physical fact, for it is a psychic blueprint.[9]

It carries also, however, the imprint of your fears, for the tales say that Atlantis was destroyed. You place it in your past while it exists in your future. Not the destruction alone, but the entire pattern seen through the framework of your beliefs. Beside this, however, many civilizations have come and gone in somewhat the same manner, and the "myth" [of Atlantis] is based somewhat then on physical fact in your terms.[10]

The species then moves into its own new houses. Atlantis is the story of a future probability projected backward into an apparent past.

Give us a moment . . . Your planet as you know it is a certain kind of focus point for consciousness. At your level you think it is divided into areas of land and water—continents and oceans, islands and peninsulas, cities and woods—because that is all you perceive. Your consciousness is tuned in to frequencies of perception that give you that impression. A cat's world, or an insect's or a plant's, are each far different, yet equally valid.

As simply as I can explain it, your planet is also "divided" into time and probability areas. Period. So many civilizations exist at once, then, and there are certain bleed-throughs. In your terms some civilizations are real and perceivable, and some are not.

(*Loudly:*) End of session. It is a good place to end, and to start the next one.

(*"All right."*)

I bid you a fond good evening.

(*"Thank you, Seth—"*)

(*Loudly and with amusement:*) I have plenty of comments about your personal situations, but I wanted to get back into the book first.

(*"Oh. Very good. Thank you, and good night."*)

(*End at 11:10 P.M. Jane's trance had been excellent. "You don't have to put this in," she said, "but I feel like I do every once in a while—I really let it out—I feel relieved and ready to collapse.*

(*"I don't know why, but I sometimes think that it's a tremendous strain to do this—have these sessions, and so forth—but I'm determined to explore this reality as much as I can, to get all I can out of it. Then sometimes I think there's nothing to it. Everyone has their hassles, so why should I have any more—or less? I really think I have less trouble than a lot of people."*

(*I read to Jane the few paragraphs of material Seth had given on Atlantis. Both of us thought it quite sensible, although it brought up questions I'll get to shortly. I'll have to admit that we cringe a bit when Seth talks about cultish concepts like Atlantis. We always think that such beliefs, while serving a variety of quite legitimate creative and psychic purposes, are very likely to be more mythic than physically factual. The word "physically" is important here. From these remarks it's easy to see that we feel much more comfortable with the ideas about Atlantis that Seth advanced in this session. "He's got more on it, too," Jane said now, but she didn't go back into trance.*

(The questions I referred to concern the fact that once in The Seth Material *and nine times in* Seth Speaks, *by my count, Seth spoke of Atlantis as being in our historical past. He did so this evening also, of course, when he remarked at 10:59 that our "ideas of Atlantis are <u>partially</u> composed of <u>future</u> memories"—thus leaving room for past manifestations. Seth's theory of simultaneous time, which can encompass the notion of future probabilities projected backward into an apparent past, for instance, leaves great leeway for the interpretation of events or questions, however, and makes the idea of contradiction posed by an Atlantis in the past and one in the future too simple as an explanation. At any given "time," depending on whatever information he's given previously, Jane could just as easily quote Seth as placing Atlantis in our historic past, or in a probable past, present, or future—or all four "places" at once, for that matter. Any or all of these views would simply be repatterning other dimensions of time from our "present point of power."*

(Questions of reincarnation enter in also. Seth has connected himself with Atlantis only once, but he did so very definitely; from the 588th session for Chapter 22 of Seth Speaks: *"I was . . . born in Atlantis." Jane and I felt those same uneasy twinges then, too, but chose not to explore them at that time.*

(After this evening's session, however, we decided we'd like to know why in Seth's view Atlantis had moved from its long, if uneasy residence in our "historical past" forward into a future probable reality. We resolved to ask him to explain—but strangely enough, I note later, a month passed before we got around to a session on the subject. By then, Seth had been through with "Unknown" Reality for three weeks. Now I refer the reader to Note 11 for quotations from the session, the 747th, in question.)

NOTES: Session 742

1. This is a good place to insert these excerpts from the session Seth gave for ESP class on February 16, 1971, three years before starting *"Unknown" Reality.* While it leads to a number of questions, his material still sums up certain important meanings that lie behind or within the overall concept of probable realities.

"Now I am going to say good evening shortly, but remember—you call this your universe and your reality, and it is indeed, for you form it. Within you also is the knowledge of other great experiments that are being tried, just as other probable systems are aware of the experiments you are involved with. I am speaking in your terms only, which means that to some extent I am hedging—but other civilizations have gone your route. Some have failed, but the inhabitants of some earths have succeeded very well.

"As you think of it, your future is not set. You can follow any road you choose, but—until you realize that as individuals you each form your own personal life, and have a part in the mass creation of reality—there is much learning ahead for you. This is a lesson you are meant to fully understand within physical reality.

"You are meant to judge physical reality. You are meant to realize that it is a materialization of your thoughts and feelings and images, that the inner self forms that world. In your terms, you cannot be allowed to go into other dimensions until you have learned the great power of your thoughts and subjective feelings. So even when you think you destroy, you destroy nothing. And when you think you kill, you kill nothing. When you imagine that you can annihilate a reality, you can only assault it as you know it. The reality itself will continue to exist.

"Because you cannot follow a thought, you wonder where it has gone; has it fallen off some invisible cliff in your mind? But because you can no longer hold that thought in consciousness does not mean it no longer exists, that it does not have a reality of its own, for it does indeed. And if a world escapes you—if you cannot follow it and think it has been destroyed—then the same thing applies to the world as to the thought. It continues to live.

"Now, what I have said should inspire questions within you. . . ."

Much in these passages fits in with material I've presented in Appendix 12, on the reasons behind the pain and suffering in the world. Early in that appendix, then, see the quotations from the 580th session for Chapter 20 of *Seth Speaks,* and from the 634th session for Chapter 8 of *Personal Reality.*

2. Our "new" hill house is really 21 years old. It seems new to Jane and me, though—and to Seth too, we notice. Calling it new is a pretty convenient way for us to distinguish it from the much older apartment house we vacated last month. Actually, however, we're using the word "new" to indicate our present physical and psychological states. In that sense, if the house we've just moved into was physically older than the one we left behind, I suppose we'd still call it new.

3. See the notes at the start of the 735th session for February 3, 1975.

4. See Note 1 for Session 739, and Note 11 for Session 740.

5. I borrowed liberally from these very perceptive lines of Seth's in order to conclude the Epilogue for Volume 1 of *"Unknown" Reality.*

6. According to some Christian sects, all of this is to transpire at the Parousia, or the anticipated Second Coming of Jesus Christ, during the Last Judgment. In the Bible, see Daniel 7:13, Matthew 24, and so forth.

7. Naturally, Seth's discussion since break reflects much of his

material throughout *Personal Reality.* Then in Volume 1, see his comments just before 11:26 for Session 687: "I am saying that the individual self must become consciously aware of far more reality . . . Your species is in a time of change. There are potentials within the body's mechanisms, in your terms, not as yet used. Developed, they can immeasurably enrich the [species] . . . If some changes are not made, the [species] as such will not endure."

    8. See Appendix 14.

    9. See Note 3 for Session 740.

    10. In Volume 1, quotations from Seth's material just given on Atlantis are presented in Note 3 for Session 702.

    11. I found it quite difficult to extract from the 747th session the material I wanted for this note on Atlantis, so interwound is it with closely related information on early man and animal kingdoms, the expanding-universe theory, archaeology, Jane's other work, All That Is, and so forth. (Some of those topics have been discussed in earlier sessions or notes, but no such references are given here, nor is any new backup material offered.)

    Jane and I regard Seth's latest delivery on Atlantis as still being only a partial explanation of the whole question of myth and fantasy versus "physical fact," no matter what time schemes may be involved. We intend to explore it all as much as we can in "future" work.

    From Session 747, for May 14, 1975:

    "Atlantis. First of all, take it for granted—as you do—that your ideas about the age of the earth are erroneous. There were intelligent human beings far earlier than is supposed; and because you assume a one-line kind of progression from an apelike creature to man, you ignore any evidence that shows to the contrary. There were highly developed human beings with elaborate civilizations, existing simultaneously with what you might call animal kingdoms—that is, more or less organized primeval animal tribes, possessing their own kinds of 'primitive' cultures.

    "Those animal kingdoms, some of them, utilized tools. Their senses were extremely acute, and their 'cultures' dealt with a kind of transmission of knowledge that made a highly complicated vocabulary unnecessary.

    "Those species did not vie for domination of the earth, but simply shared the same general environment with the more sophisticated groupings beyond their own perimeters. There were many highly technical human cultures, but in your terms not on a global scale. The legend of Atlantis is actually based upon several such civilizations. No particular civilization is the basis, however. Apart from that, the legend as picked up, so to speak, by Plato *(see Appendix 14)* was a precognition of the future probability, an image of an inner civilization of the mind actually projected outward into the future, where it would be used as a blueprint, dash—the lost grandeur, as, in other terms, Eden became the lost garden of paradise.

    "Ruburt has implied in [his novel] *The Education of Oversoul Seven* that some archaeological discoveries about the past (underlined) are not discovered in your present because they do not exist yet. Now such concepts are difficult to explain in my kind of prose, and in your language. But in certain terms, the ruins of Atlantis have not been found because they have not been placed in your past yet, from the future.

"Now the future is probable. However, in your terms there are ruins of the civilizations that served as the 'concrete' basis for the one Atlantean legend. Those civilizations were scattered. The so-called ruins would not be found in any one place as expected, therefore. There are some beneath the Aegean Sea, and some beneath an offshoot of the Atlantic, and some beneath the Arctic, for the world had a different shape.

"In far greater terms *(louder, humorously),* at the risk of repeating myself, time is simultaneous, so those civilizations exist along with your own. Your methods of dating the age of the earth are very misleading.

"In your terms, from your present you 'plant' images, tales, legends, 'at any given time,' that seem to come from the past, but are actually like ghost images from the future, for you to follow or disregard as you choose.

"Atlantis and the Garden of Eden are the same in that regard.

"When you think that perhaps your species came from another planetary system, in time terms, then of course you are still dealing with old concepts. In your usual terms of thinking, the earth does not exist at all *(emphatically)*—not if you are considering it as a chunk of matter occupying a certain position in a physical cosmos. It is really futile to question whether the universe came from a big boom *(again emphatically, humorously)*, or is constantly expanding (though in those terms I have said it continually expands, as an idea or a dream does). I am not saying the universe does not exist—only that it does not exist in the way that it seems to you.

"By itself *(with a smile, almost an outright laugh)*: The truth of the matter is far more spectacular.

"All That Is creates its reality as it goes along. Each world has its own impetus, yet all are ultimately connected. The true dimensions of a divine creativity would be unendurable for any one consciousness of whatever import, and so that splendor is infinitely dimensionalized *(most intensely throughout),* worlds spiraling outward with each 'moment' of a cosmic breath; with the separation of worlds a necessity; and with individual and mass comprehension always growing at such a rate that All That Is multiplies itself at microseconds, building both pasts and futures and other time scales you do not recognize. Each is a reality in itself, with its own potentials, and with no individual consciousness, however minute, ever lost.

"In that kind of framework, how can I explain an Atlantis? It exists both in your past and future, a probable world that some of you will choose from a model placed in the past of your future—partially based upon fact, in your terms, but with its greatest validity lying in its possibilities."

Session 743
April 21, 1975
9:46 P.M. Monday

(I read the last part of Wednesday's session to Jane from my notes. "I've got the nostalgic, uneasy feeling that he's going to wind up the book soon," she said, "especially after listening to that material just before the Atlantis stuff. I didn't feel that way when I had the session, but I do now. I've said it before, I know, but this book started when we were thinking of moving. and now we're settled in a new place, so that makes a good time to end it."

(Jane paused. She still habitually referred to "Unknown" Reality as a one-volume work—even as Seth himself did in the session this evening— despite the decision made 10 days ago to publish it in two volumes. "I feel sort of sorry," she continued, "because here the sessions will stop again just after we got back into them. You'll need time to finish the notes and do all that typing. . . ."[1])

Good evening.

("Good evening, Seth.")

Dictation: No book entitled *The "Unknown" Reality* can hope to make that reality entirely known.

It remains nebulous because it is consciously unrealized.

The best I can do is to point out areas that have been relatively invisible, to help you explore, actually, different facets of your own consciousness.[2] To some extent this book has been written to help you exercise your own intuitive and mental capacities from a different viewpoint.

In a way, it is meant to familiarize you with elements of your own reality of which you may have been unaware, and to introduce you to certain subjective states of mind that are automatically aroused because of the manner in which the book was produced. Period.

Besides this, however, it contains what you may call <u>cues</u> that automatically open up greater levels of your own awareness, and hence bring into your conscious life some recognition of the unknown reality in which you also have your being. The subject matter itself entices your imagination. That intuitive faculty will then illuminate the intellect so that it learns to question in a broader, more exciting and <u>productive</u> manner than perhaps it did before.

I am well aware that the book raises many more questions than it presents answers for, and this has been my intent. The unknown reality will become known to the extent that you form new questions, and forget the old frameworks in which answers and myths were automatically given in response. If this book "works," then many old questions will be seen as relatively meaningless, formed not after any intimate encounter with basic issues, but in response to old dogmas.

The "proper" questions about the unknown reality will automatically bring more of it into your experience.

Give us a moment . . . Many of the questions you think were <u>not</u> answered in this book, however, <u>have</u> been answered—but from a different angle, colon: the answers presented in such a way that they will entice you to further creative thought.

<u>You</u> are the unknown reality, to the extent that you do not recognize, realize, or experience the many facets of your own being. As always, I say that the answers lie within yourself, not in the exterior world.

(10:09.) Clues may indeed be found there, however, because the exterior conditions mirror so perfectly your inner, individual and mass experience.

Give us a moment . . . This book itself, because of the method of its production, is an excellent example of the unknown reality becoming, if not "known," then recognized. Do not look for neat answers or tidy solutions, for when you do your explanations and theories will always be too small. There is always an unknown reality to some extent, for the miracle of your being works outside of the kind of explanations that you so often seem to require.

Your ready answers end up limiting your own experience, because you try to fit your subjective behavior into the cramped boot of preconceived ideas. Your experience creates new questions in the same way that a painter creates new paintings.

(Long pause.) The unknown reality, dash—Many of you, I know, would like to find in this book answers pertaining to Atlantis, the Bermuda Triangle, UFO's[3], and many other such questions. Those matters certainly seem pertinent in the framework of your experience and beliefs. You already have a great variety of explanations offered: Writers in many fields have produced books about such topics. By far the greater questions, however, are those pertaining to the unknown reality of the psyche, and those that relate to the kind of being who perceives in one way or another an Atlantis, a Bermuda Triangle, a UFO—for in greater terms, until you ask deeper questions about yourselves, these other experiences will remain mysterious. You cannot understand perceived events unless you understand who perceives them. You must learn more about the slant of your own consciousness before you are in a position to ask truly pertinent questions about the reality that you perceive.

(10:23. As Seth, Jane paused during an intent delivery.)

Are your fingers tired?

("No," I said. At the same time, I was thinking as I wrote that Seth's sentence, above: "You cannot understand perceived events unless you understand who perceives them," embodied one of his best ideas in "Unknown" Reality.)

Give us a moment, then.

(Still in trance, Jane took a sip of wine and lit a cigarette.)

There are many who will give you answers to such questions. The answers will be couched in a framework of beliefs that you have held individually and collectively for some time. In this book I am purposely trying to lead you into a larger, more expansive way of looking at yourself and the world in which you live.

When I consider those (Atlantis, UFO's, and so forth) and other such matters, it will be from a much different perspective. By then you—my readers—will be familiar enough with the unknown reality to understand answers given in a different context. Period.

This book had no chapters [in order] to further disrupt your accepted notions of what a book should be. There are different kinds of organizations present, however, and in any given section of the book, several levels of consciousness are appealed to at once. (Intently:) The threads of the work are interwoven so that various portions of your consciousness are sent out, so to speak, on separate journeys of thought and imagination. Yet these side trips are also related. They intertwine, not only through the psychic organization that I have given to *"Unknown" Reality*, but because of the great uniting nature within the consciousness of each reader.

Again, Ruburt and Joseph have moved to a new place. Each reader has also journeyed to a new position within the psyche, however. This book is a bridge between realities. Reading it, each person sets out upon a psychic pilgrimage through the unknown realities of his or her own consciousness and experience. No one can predict the destination.

(Pause.) I am a part of your unknown reality, and you are a part of mine. To some extent in these pages our realities meet. To the extent that you do not know yourself, you do not know your world. To the extent that you do not know yourself, you do not know your husband, or wife, or mother and father. To the extent that you do not know yourself, you do not know what God is. To the extent that you do not know yourself, you do not know what nature is. The unknown reality exists to the extent that you do not travel joyfully through the intimate lands of the psyche, to the extent that you do not directly experience your life as original *(forcefully)*, but accept labels put on it by others. The unknown reality exists as a challenge, an exciting endeavor, as each individual becomes consciously aware of intimate subjective feeling. Do not overlay the personal daily aspects of your life with preconceived ideas about who you are, what you are, where you are, why you are. Become aware of the original nature of any given moment as it exists for you.

(Pause.) Forget what you have been told about time and space. Refuse to accept ideas that limit the dimensions of your own natural being. Again, the unknown reality is what you are.

(And louder:) End of dictation. <u>End of book</u>. Take a break.

(10:50. Jane was soon out of trance—but she had a very, very long face.

("That was an excellent dissertation," I said.

("I'd rather be starting a book than ending one, I guess." She sat quietly. I thought she wanted to cry, but wouldn't let herself do so.

("I do have a couple of questions," I continued. "We can talk about them before break ends. I'd like to add them to the book material tonight—along with Seth's answers, that is."

(For the moment, though, we ate cookies and indulged in small talk. I could see that Jane was not only sad that the long project was finished for her, but uneasy, too; she was suddenly set loose, released from a framework that had come to be very familiar over the last 14½ months. Not that her new freedom

hadn't been expected. But she's so creative that as soon as she is through with one undertaking she's ready to launch into another; and this applies even though she's been working on Psychic Politics *outside of the Seth framework. That's her focus in life [and mine, too]: the full commu...ent to artistic production. I'd often heard her comment about being in a kind of limbo between works. Her abilities demand use and release.*

(As Jane moved about, I wrote out my two questions for Seth— while thinking of a third:

("1. What do you think about this work being published in two volumes?

("2. In our terms of time: What were some of your other activities, in other realities, while you were giving 'Unknown' Reality through Jane for well over a year?

("3. I suppose it's quite evident why you finished 'Unknown' Reality right after we moved into our 'new' house, but will you reassure Jane by commenting on this, and on future works?"

(When Jane sat down again I read the questions to her. Our cat, Willy, jumped up into her lap. "I'm still appalled," she said dejectedly. "Here my part in the thing is done, but you've got to live with it for a long time yet while you do the notes and typing. I wish there was some way each book could be turned into print instantly, so that we could go on to the next one . . . I can't help it—every time Seth finishes a book I feel like crying."

("And why not? It's a perfectly natural reaction," I said. But an interesting point came out as we talked: Jane doesn't experience that strong nostalgia when she finishes one of her "own" books.

("Well, I'm just waiting now," she said finally. "I can feel session material there, but I don't know what it'll be about. I'm just waiting until I get over the shock. . . ."

(Resume at 11:27.)

Now: I will answer your questions on Wednesday. But I have a few remarks.

(Which was Seth's way of leading us into other than book material. For a little while he discussed Jane's Politics, *our relationship with others through the mail and by telephone, and a different kind of "inner listening" that we'd become involved in. Then he wound up the evening's work with a remark that I took to be a reference to my third question:)*

I bid you then a fond good evening for now, from my unknown reality to yours. You can have all the books that you want, when you want them, and at your own pacing.

("Thank you, Seth. Good night."

(11:44 P.M. And so, even though Seth had declared the end of "Unknown" Reality *this evening, it will still include at least part of the next session.)*

NOTES: Session 743

     1. A note added four months later: Jane needn't have worried. The sessions didn't come to a halt after all. With the arrival of warmer weather we did take an occasional break from psychic work, but for the most part the sessions were held regularly even though Seth was through with *"Unknown" Reality*. Some of them were private, but Seth also covered a number of interesting topics of a more general nature—material we'd like to see published eventually. (His comments in the 750th session as to why *"Unknown" Reality* was written, are quoted in the Introductory Notes for Volume 1.)

     We finally rested from the sessions for most of July, although Jane continued working on her *Psychic Politics,* among other projects. Then, in the 752nd session for July 28, 1975, Seth plunged into his next book: *The Nature of the Psyche: Its Human Expression.* He's well into it at this writing, and as Jane and I have planned things, the notes for it will be very short. It should be published a few months after this present volume is issued.

     2. I ended up by using Seth's opening passages here, plus a couple of later ones from this session, in the notes introducing Volume 1.

     3. See Appendix 20 for Volume 2.

Session 744
April 23, 1975
9:33 P.M. Wednesday

(Yesterday Jane received from her publisher the galley proofs for her book of poetry, Dialogues of the Soul and Mortal Self in Time.[1] *The story of that work's creation is interwound throughout* Personal Reality.

(I read to Jane again the three questions I'd noted down for Seth during break in Monday's session. As I suspected he might do, Seth began this evening's session by dealing with the second one. Not all of his material tonight is given over to questions, however; much of the rest of it, covering matters other than those relating to "Unknown" Reality, is deleted.)

Good evening.

("Good evening, Seth.")

Now: In a way, it is quite difficult to tell you what I have been doing with my time *(humorously emphatic)* while I have been involved in the production of *"Unknown" Reality*—and therefore, to some extent at least, inclined toward your time.[2]

In a manner of speaking your experienced, practical reality is made up of events that seem entire to you, or relatively complete, while from my dimension it is apparent that your recognized events are simply portions of larger ones. I move naturally, then, in a realm of greater dimensionalized events.

In your terms I see not only greater chunks of time than you do, but I can to some considerable extent view the probable actualizations of events and times.

Now: An artist does the same thing in different terms, when he or she imagines the probable versions that a painting, or a book or a sculpture, for example, might take. *(Pause.)* The artist does not usually understand, however, that those probable art productions do literally exist; he perceives only the final, physically chosen work. Speaking simply, some of us are able to hold intact the nature of our own identities while following patterns of probable realities in which we also play a part.

In your reality, the *"Unknown" Reality* we have just finished is the only version of that manuscript. Instead it is, of course, the only version you <u>recognize</u>. When we are working on such a project here (in your reality), we are working on probable books also, and those are as real as your official one. In ways too difficult to explain now, your probabilities are connected by certain themes, intents, purposes. Some of these appear as subsidiary interests in your own lives, for example. Others may well be recognized by you as prime concerns, and still others may be so latent that you are unaware of them. So we have been working on a probable *"Unknown" Reality*—in fact, on many probable *"Unknown" Reality*s. Not mere versions, but variations.

In one reality, of course, the work was finished at the Foster Avenue house *(in Elmira, New York).* In another it was finished in Sayre *(Pennsylvania).*

Now that is what I have been doing as far as <u>your</u> reality is concerned—that is, in my relationship with you. It is a multidimensional version of what Ruburt does in simple terms when he writes a book of his own.

I've also helped in the construction, so to speak, of Ruburt's [psychic] library,[4] and I hope that he will be able to meet me there, in surroundings in which he feels confident and at home, and yet on neutral ground. *(Smiling:)* He does not want my <u>apparition</u>, you might say, to intrude upon a physical living room, particularly, <u>yet he wants to meet me</u> *(much louder, leaning forward)* <u>in an out-of-the-way place.</u>[5]

Now that is a sensible arrangement. He is the one who has to deal primarily with the practical aspects of our relationship, and in the business of translating my reality into your world.

(Long pause at 9:56.) I quite approve, for in greater terms I do not belong in your living room in that particular fashion. My reality is far more apparent than any apparition's. Ruburt does well because he explores so cleverly, and keeps his strands of reality in good order.[6]

(Long pause at 10:01.) Others have indeed sensed me—Sue [Watkins][7] for example—but the relationship there is far different, and it is important for Ruburt that he have clear-cut areas, which I respect.

Any such appearances, by the way, would also add to much superstitious nonsense. On the other hand, there is much for Ruburt to learn about my reality. Until he understood the inward order of events[8] he would not be able to meet me there—so the library can serve us both in that regard.

(Pause at 10:05. Now Seth took off into some areas involving Jane that were more personal; at the same time he gave material on the third and then the first of the questions I'd listed during break for the last session. I thought I'd include a few quotations from him on both issues, while eliminating portions of the session that deal with other matters entirely. I think the information on Jane is quite relevant to both her work and her life in general.)

Give us a moment . . . I am not here going into Ruburt to any great degree, but I do have some information. Obviously he is in the middle of a learning adventure, trying to do far more with his ordinary consciousness than most people, and trying to solve his problems and encounter his challenges without relying upon old structures of belief . . . He has done this even though he has been working in relatively untried areas, where there <u>seem</u> to be few certainties.[9]

The Nature of Personal Reality [our last book] is there for others to follow. Others, however, did not have a hand in producing it. They will try out the ideas, many of them, to the best of their ability, and learn and gain much—all the time *(much more forcefully:)* <u>hanging on safely to the banners of conventional beliefs.</u> Ruburt has allowed himself no such comforts. He should remember that many people have far greater hassles . . . with health, personal relationships, finances and vocations, and without any satisfying accomplishments to offset their misfortunes.

(Long pause at 10:23, eyes closed.) I make recommendations now and then, and now and then you see fit to follow them . . .[10] Considering Ruburt's challenges, he has done extremely well as he cleared away the debris that literally surrounds the lives of most people . . . In a way his progress has been dependent upon the state of his learning, so that he has been trying to stretch the abilities of

normal consciousness by drawing in other "strands."[11] Yet because he was the one so involved, he had to test each strand; and in the meantime he still had his "old" consciousness, with its habits, to contend with.

The [Seth] material is endless. I organize it for your benefit. If you want to divide it into two volumes, that is fine. You will find several points where this can be done,[12] and I will answer any questions that you have.

In a way, Ruburt's book *(Psychic Politics)* will continue our material from another viewpoint while you are preparing our "Unknown" Reality.

God bless your fingers—

("They're okay.")

—and a hearty good evening.

("Thank you, Seth. The same to you. Good night."

(11:01 P.M. And so Volume 2 of "Unknown" Reality *is finished. Now I want to briefly summarize for the reader two subjects—"house connections" and ESP class—that have been mentioned often in the sessions for Section 6. See notes 13 and 14.)*

NOTES: Session 744

1. A note added later in the year: *Dialogues* was published by Prentice-Hall in September 1975.

2. See the material on Seth's concept of simultaneous time as given in the concluding notes for Session 724. Included are some very intriguing excerpts from the 14th session, which was held over 11 years ago. Seth: "While I am not affected by time on your plane, I am affected by something resembling time on my plane . . . It is therefore still a reality of some kind to me." In this case, I added the underline myself for emphasis.

To Seth's remarks in that early session I'd now like to add what he said a decade later in our time. From the 514th session for Chapter 2 of *Seth Speaks:* "Consciousness is not dependent upon form, as I have said, and yet it always seeks to create form. We do not exist in any time framework as you know it. Minutes, hours, or years have lost both their meaning and their fascination. We are quite aware of the time situations within other systems, however, and we must take them into account in our communications. Otherwise what we say would not be understood."

3. Following Seth's material in these paragraphs, then, there are of course a number of other Janes and Robs busily living out their lives in a cluster of associated probable realities—and all of those Janes and Robs are just as *real* to Seth as *we* are. I've had the thought before. It's a somewhat chastening one, I said to Jane, joking, since it means that from Seth's viewpoint we could be just two more individuals.

All sorts of interesting questions arise. Perhaps Seth likes some of those other versions of ourselves more than he does *us*. (didn't ask him if I was right, though.) It might even be that his favorite Jane inhabits one probable reality, his favorite Rob another. How does Seth tell all of us apart? What age differences are there among us? In which reality did we produce the "best" version of *"Unknown" Reality*? The worst? Moreover— what do all of those other Janes and Robs think of *their* Seths? And so on. . . .

4. Jane describes in Chapter 1 of *Politics* the onset of her ability to perceive her psychic library. For library material in Volume 2 of *"Unknown" Reality*, see the notes at the start of Session 714, and Seth's dictation for Session 715.

5. Jane has yet to see Seth's apparition, however, or to meet him in her library or any other "out-of-the-way place." In Note 2 for Appendix 11, in Volume 1, I refer to the time she set out to "find" Seth.

6. Seth spoke of "strands of reality" here, we think, because today Jane had been going over her material on the stages of consciousness and strands of consciousness for chapters 24 and 25, respectively, of *Politics*.

7. In Session 594 for the Appendix of *Seth Speaks*, see Sue's material on how she sensed Jane's and Seth's "speeds"—as well as her own.

8. Appendix 18 for Volume 2 of *"Unknown" Reality* contains much material "on the complex relationships involving Jane-Ruburt-Seth [and also Rob-Joseph]." Jane devoted Chapter 15 of *Adventures* to a discussion of the inner order of events and "unofficial" perceptions.

9. Material on the psychic and physical challenges that Jane chose to deal with in this life can be found in sessions 708 and 713 (among others). In the former, see Seth's delivery after 11:40, as well as the notes at the end of the session; in the latter, see the opening notes, and Seth's discussion after 11:26.

10. See the notes at 10:45 for Session 738, concerning "the extent to which we follow Seth's advice or information. . . ."

11. See the opening notes for the 725th session, as well as the session itself, for material on strands of consciousness.

12. I used Seth's lines in this paragraph early in the Introductory Notes for Volume 1.

13. During the 10:36 break for Session 740, which was held a couple of months ago, I wrote that the list of house connections associated with our move to the hill house had grown to over 40 items, "and continues to grow." Jane and I have now accumulated more than 60 such inter-relationships, and they range all the way from color and architectural similarities among the various houses we've either lived in, or felt strong emotional and psychic attachments for, to human connections like the following one. It's neither the most inconsequential item on our list, or the most spectacular—but recently we learned through a close relative of the Steffans (I'll call them), the couple from whom we bought the hill house, that at a small social gathering over two years ago Jane had spontaneously given something of a psychic "reading" for Mrs. Steffans. Moreover, *this event had taken place in the apartment house we lived in on Water Street*; not in our

own quarters there, however, but in the apartment of another tenant whom we've known for a number of years.

Jane hadn't met Mrs. Steffans before, and never saw her again. (I wasn't involved in the little scenario.) The Steffanses moved out of Elmira some months before we purchased the hill house through a real-estate agency.

Stranger still, that reading marked one of the few times—and certainly the last, to the best of our mutual recollection—that Jane has "tuned in to" an individual under such circumstances. "I just did it because I liked her after we got talking," Jane said, once the Steffanses' relative had reminded her of the affair. "But I don't think I precognitively picked up that we were going to buy their house two years later, or anything like that. We didn't know this place [the hill house] even existed then. Hell, we didn't even know the *street* existed."

Let me note at the end of this account that the mutual friend who introduced Jane and Mrs. Steffans has participated in some of our other house connections also—a function similar to the one enacted by our new acquaintance, Frank Corio, whom I referred to in Note 11 for Session 740. Jane and I saw this kind of situation develop with several other individuals also, once we began our active house hunting in Sayre, Pennsylvania, in April 1974.

It seems, then, that at least on unconscious levels (and for their own reasons also, of course), certain individuals chose to act as catalysts or expediters, helping us to achieve our particular goals. Such role-playing could be studied as an attribute of certain families of consciousness.

14. This final note is added well over a year after Jane finished delivering *"Unknown" Reality*. As I wrote at the start of the 740th session, Jane suspended ESP class on February 26, 1975, to give us time to not only prepare for our move to the hill house (in March), but to settle down afterward.

As might be expected, the class hiatus soon began to have a ripple effect: The longer we delayed making up our minds as to whether we'd have the time to resume class, the more Jane's students began to scatter. The younger people, especially those who weren't natives of the area to begin with, began to fan out across the nation, and even into foreign lands, continuously searching for more of that indefinable essence or quality many of them called "truth." They took Seth's ideas with them, however, and with considerable interest Jane and I thought of them as not only looking for truths but meeting counterparts. Why not, indeed? According to Seth's views, such encounters with other portions of their whole selves would be inevitable.

We also applied the counterpart ideas to ourselves. Seth named a number of counterparts among class members in the 732nd session—including, for example, a total of nine involving Jane and me (counting the psychic relationships between us)—and I wrote about those connections in Appendix 25 for that session.

As class gradually receded into the past, through our own default, as it were, Jane and I kept in touch with some of our local counterparts from class, while we saw less and less of certain others. Each choice seemed to be a matter of mutual, unspoken agreement among all concerned, and we kept in mind that each individual had the complete freedom to do as he or she wished about maintaining contact with us—just as we had in our relationships with them.

Of my three class counterparts other than Jane, then, it developed that Norma Pryor and Jack Pierce soon embarked upon their own paths, which hardly ever cross mine even though we don't live that far apart. Peter Smith and I still see each other often. On Jane's part, one of her counterparts, Zelda, has traveled far away, although maintaining a tenuous, infrequent contact by mail. Jane has met Alan Koch but twice physically, yet feels allied with him. Sue Watkins remains close (to both of us, by the way), even though she now lives in a small community that's well over an hour's travel north of Elmira. And Jane has seen her fourth counterpart, "the young man from Pennsylvania . . . " but once since class stopped meeting.

The longer we went without class, the more Jane and I saw how much its demise paralleled the ending of *"Unknown" Reality*. Both events were inevitable, we came to understand; both had had their time; our regrets about the finishing of both are real, while simultaneously we heartily agree that the nature of life in this physical—or "camouflage"—reality is one of unending change and renewal. Even though we may never again see many of those counterparts we'd known, we realize that all of us are indissolubly joined. Nor is the fact that a number of us are physically separated (or invisible to each of the others) of great importance, for as Seth told us recently in a private session:

"In a strange fashion, of course, the word 'invisibility' has meaning only in your kind of world. There is no such thing as true psychological invisibility . . . The physical world is dependent upon the relationship of everything from electrons to molecules to mountains to oceans, and in the scheme of reality these are all interwoven with exquisite order, spontaneity, and a logic beyond any with which you are familiar.

"The counterpart idea is merely a small attempt to hint at that interrelationship—an interrelationship that of course includes all species and forms of life."

APPENDIX 12
(For Session 705)

(Originally I planned this appendix on evolution to contain just three widely separated excerpts from Seth's material: an early unpublished session, a few passages in Seth Speaks, *and one in Volume 1 of* "Unknown" Reality. *The appendix, however kept growing as I worked on it; I found myself adding quotations from other sessions, along with comments derived from my own reading and from conversations Jane and I had on the subject.*

(I learned that "evolution" can mean many things. Like variations on a theme, it can be progressive or relatively sudden, convergent or divergent. I also learned that once I began to study it, a great amount of material presented itself, seemingly without effort on my part; the information ranged all the way from paleontological studies to current biological research on recombinant DNA, and I found it in newspapers, scientific journals and popular magazines, in books and even on television. [I'm sure others have had similar experiences: Once a subject is focused upon, data relative to it seem to leap out from the background welter of daily events and "facts" surrounding one's life.] Almost automatically, many of the notes for this appendix came to deal with the scientific thinking about evolution, and I realized that I wanted them to show the differences [as well as any similarities that might emerge] between Seth's concepts and those "official" views prevailing in our physical reality.

(Our beliefs and intents cause us to pick "from an unpredictable group of actions," or probabilities, those that we want to happen, as Seth tells us in the 681st session in Volume 1; therefore, from my physically oriented probability the considerable work I've put into this paper is an examination of evolution in connection with a number of Seth's concepts. Religious questions connected with evolution aren't stressed as much as some might like, although they aren't ignored either—but to go very far into religious history would lead away from the focus I've chosen.

(I found some of the excerpts, notes, and comments very difficult to assemble and interpret, and others easy to do. The Seth material is incomplete, of course; new information "intrudes" constantly, and in so doing often takes off from a given subject in fresh directions. Some of this process has to do with Jane's own character: She likes new things, new ideas. Yet in her own way she—and Seth as well—eventually returns to earlier material. Interpretation of old and new together calls for a system of constant correlations, then, and I use that approach as often as I can.

(Even so, as I worked on this appendix I wondered again and again why I was investing so much time in it. The answers proved to be simple once I understood them: I ended up shocked to discover how little real evidence there is

to back up the idea of evolution, and fascinated by the limits of scientific thinking. I was quite surprised at my reactions. Somehow Jane and I always understood, to make an analogy, that Seth's kind of "simultaneous" reincarnation [or anyone else's kind, for that matter] wasn't acceptable in our Western societies at this time in history; we could trace out many reasons why this is so. But some time passed before I realized that our ruling intellectual establishments were advancing notions about evolution that were not proven in scientific terms— then teaching these "facts" to succeeding generations. Finally, the humor of the whole situation got through to me: As some have very clearly noted, in the biological and earth sciences especially, circular reasoning often predominates: The theory of evolution is used to prove the theory of evolution.

(The first quotes I've put together, then, are from the 44th session for April 15, 1964. In that session Seth gave us his interpretations of some of the basic laws or attributes of the inner universe, but it will be quickly seen that he was really discussing space and time,² as those qualities are perceived in his reality and in ours. In our world, of course, space and time form the environment in which conventional ideas of evolution exist. For that matter, all of the material in this appendix shows the interrelationship between our ideas of serial time and Seth's simultaneous time. Connected here also is the philosophical concept known as "naive realism," which will be discussed briefly later.

(This presentation from the 44th session shows clearly just how much of his philosophy Seth had given Jane and me by then. He spoke very forcefully:)

I have said that the mind cannot be detected by your instruments at present. The <u>mind</u> does <u>not</u> take up space, and yet the mind is the value that gives power to the brain. The mind expands continuously, both in individual terms and in terms of the species as a whole, and yet *(with amusement)* the mind takes up neither more nor less space, whether it be the mind of a flea or a man.

I have also said that basically the universe has <u>no more</u> to do with space <u>in your terms</u> than does the dream world.

Your idea of space is some completely erroneous conception of an emptiness to be filled. Things—planets, stars, nebulae— come into being in this physical [camouflage] universe of yours, according to your latest theories, and this universe expands— pushed so that its sides bulge, so to speak, the outer galaxies literally bursting into nowhere. True inner space is to the contrary vital energy, itself alive, possessing abilities of transformation, forming all existences, even the camouflage reality with which you are familiar, and which you attempt to probe so ineffectively.

This basic universe of which I speak expands constantly in terms of intensity and quality and value, in a way that has nothing to

do with your idea of space. The basic universe beneath all camouflage does not have an existence in space at all, as you envision it.
Space is a camouflage . . . This tinge of time is an attribute of the
physical camouflage form only, and even then the relationship
between time and ideas, and time and dreams, is a nebulous
one . . . although in some instances parts of the inner universe may
be glimpsed from the camouflage perspective of time; only, however, a small portion.

If the dream world, the mind, and the inner universe do
exist, but not in space, and if they do not exist basically in time,
though they may be glimpsed through time, then your question will
be: In what medium or in what manner do they exist; and without
time, how can they be said to exist in duration? I am telling you that
the basic universe exists behind all camouflage universes in the same
manner, and taking up no space, that the mind exists behind the
brain. The brain is a camouflage pattern. It takes up space. It exists
in time, but the mind takes up no space and does not have its basic
existence in time. Your camouflage universe, on the other hand,
takes up space and exists in time.

Nevertheless the dream world, the mind, and the basic
inner universe do exist . . . in what we will call the value climate of
psychological reality. This is the medium. This takes the place of
what you call space. It is a quality which makes all existences and
consciousness possible. It is one of the most powerful principles
behind or within the vitality that itself composes from itself all other
phenomena.[3]

One of the main attributes of this value climate is spontaneity, which shows itself in the existence of the only sort of time
that has any real meaning—that of the spacious present.

The spacious present does not contradict the existence of
a future as you conceive it. Now this may appear contradictory, but
later I hope that you will understand this more clearly. The spacious
present, while existing spontaneously, while happening simultaneously, still contains within it qualities of duration.

Growth in your camouflage universe often involves the
taking up of more space. Actually, in our inner universe . . . growth
exists in terms of the value or quality expansion of which I have
spoken, and does not—I repeat—does not imply any sort of space
expansion. Nor does it imply, as growth does in your camouflage
universe, a sort of projection into time.

I am giving it [this material] to you in as simple terms as
possible. If growth is one of the most necessary laws of your

camouflage universe, value fulfillment corresponds to it in the inner-reality universe.[4]

Now, the so-called laws of your camouflage physical universe do not apply to the inner universe. They do not even apply to other camouflage planes. However, the laws of the inner universe apply to all camouflage realities. Some of these basic laws have counterparts known and accepted in various camouflage realities. There are diverse manifestations of them, and names given to them.

These fundamental laws are followed on many levels in your own universe. So far I have given you but one, which is value fulfillment. In your physical universe this rule is followed as physical growth. The entity follows it through the cycle of [simultaneous] reincarnations. The species of mankind, and all other species in your universe on your particular horizontal plane, follow this law [value fulfillment] under the auspices of evolution *(my emphasis)*.[5] In other camouflage realities, this law is carried through in different manners, but it is never ignored.

The second law of the inner universe is energy transformation.[6] This occurs constantly. Energy transformation and value fulfillment, both existing within the spacious present [or at once], add up to a durability that is at the same time spontaneous . . . and simultaneous.

You may see what we are getting at here. Our third law is spontaneity, and despite all appearances of beginning and end, of death and decay, all consciousnesses exist in the spacious present, in a spontaneous manner, in simultaneous harmony; and yet within the spacious present there is also durability.

Durability is our fourth law. Durability within the framework of the spacious present would not exist were it not for the laws of value fulfillment and energy transformation. These make duration within the spacious present not only possible but necessary. . . .

(The "value climate of psychological reality," first mentioned in the [44th] session just quoted, is also dealt with through analogy in the 45th session. Portions of that material are given as Appendix 8 in Volume 1; in that session also Seth stated that "value expansion becomes reincarnation, and evolution and growth." [Seth's own kind of simultaneous time, of course, easily accommodates all three concepts, although this appendix isn't concerned with reincarnation.]

(Seth material on evolution is presented twice in the 582nd session for Chapter 20 of Seth Speaks—*not only in the session proper, but from an ESP class delivery given a few days later, on April 27, 1971. In class, Seth discussed Charles Darwin and his theory of evolution,[7] and that material, some*

of which wasn't published in the 582nd session, is the source for my second group of excerpts:)

He [Darwin] spent his last years proving it, and yet it has no real validity. It has a validity within very limited perspectives only; for consciousness does, indeed, evolve form. Form does not evolve consciousness. It is according to when you come into the picture, and what you choose to observe . . . Consciousness did not come from atoms and molecules scattered by chance through the universe . . .

Now, if you had all been really paying attention to what I have been saying for some time about the simultaneous nature of time and existence, then you would have known that the theory of evolution is as beautiful a tale as the theory of Biblical creation. Both are quite handy, and both are methods of telling stories, and both might seem to agree within their own systems, and yet, in larger respects they cannot be realities . . .

Within you, concepts and actions are one. You recognize this, but your mental lives are often built around concepts that, until recently, have been considered very modern and very "in," such as the idea of evolution . . . In actuality, life bursts apart in all directions as consciousness does. There is no one steady stream of progress.

(To a student:) Now last week, when Ruburt [Jane] was speaking about the natives who are such expert dreamers, you asked: "But why are they not more progressive?" Yet I know you realize that your own progress as a civilization will, in your terms, come to a halt unless you advance in other directions. This is what your civilization is learning: that you cannot rape your planet, that life did not begin as some isolated [substance] that in the great probabilities of existence met another [similar substance], and another, and then another, until a chain of molecules could be made and selves formed. Using an analogy, neither does consciousness exist as simple organisms separated by vast distances, but as a complicated gestalt.

(From the beginning, then, Seth has referred to evolution in his material. He attaches his own meanings to it, however, and as I show in this appendix, does not imply that all life as we know it on this planet evolved from a single primeval source. [See notes 5 and 7.]

(I think it more than a coincidence that in these excerpts from Seth Speaks, *Seth mentions Darwin's theory of evolution and the Biblical story of creation in the same sentence, for those systems of belief represent the two poles of the controversy over origins in our modern Western societies: the strictly Darwinistic, mechanistic view of evolution, in which the weakest of any species are ruthlessly eliminated through natural, predatory selection; and the views of*

the creationists, who hold that God made the earth and all of its creatures just as described in the Bible.

(Many creationists believe that the Bible is literally true. [An undetermined number of scientists hold creationist views, by the way, but I have no statistics to offer on how many do.] The Bible certainly advocates at least a relative immutability of species, rather than a common ancestry in which a single cell evolved into a variety of ever more complex and divergent forms. In between these opposites there range all shades of meaning and interpretation on evolution. Theistic evolutionists and progressive creationists, for example, try to bring the two extremes closer together through postulating various methods by which God created the world and then, while remaining hidden, either helped it to evolve to its present state in the Darwinistic tradition, or, through a series of creative acts, brought forth each succeeding "higher" form of life.

(Ironically, Charles Darwin's natural selection, "the survival of the fittest," [a phrase that Darwin himself did not originate, by the way], allows for all sorts of pain and suffering in the process—the same unhappy facts of life, in Darwin's view, that finally turned him into an agnostic, away from a God who could allow such things to exist! As I interpret what I've read, Darwin didn't deny the existence of a god of some kind, but he wanted one that would abolish what he saw as the "upward" struggle for existence. According to the geological/fossil record, this conflict had resulted in the deaths of entire species. Darwin came to believe that he asked the impossible of God. Instead, he assigned the pain and suffering in the world to the impersonal workings of natural selection and chance variation [or genetic mutation]. For Darwin and his followers—even those of today, then—nature's effects gave the appearance of design or plan in the universe without necessitating a belief in a designer or a god; although, as I wrote in Note 7, from the scientific standpoint this belief leaves untouched the question of design in nonliving matter, which is vastly more abundant in the "objective" universe than is living matter, and had to precede that living matter.

(As counterpoint to Darwin's ideas, here briefly are some of Seth's comments on the human condition, and that of the animals. The material is from two sessions. The first one is the 580th [for April 12, 1971] from, once again, Chapter 20 of Seth Speaks. *Seth talked about the innate creative ability of human beings—even in creating war. Then he continued:)*

Illness and suffering are not thrust upon you by God, or by All That Is, or by an outside agency. They are a by-product of the learning process, created by you, in themselves quite neutral . . . Illness and suffering are the results of the misdirection of creative energy. They are a part of the creative force, however. They do not come from a different source than, say, health and vitality. Suffering is not good for the soul, unless it teaches you how to stop suffering. That is its purpose . . .

I have mentioned before that everyone within your system is learning to handle this creative energy; and since you are still in the process of doing so, you will often misdirect it. The resulting snarl in activities automatically brings you back to inner questions.

(The second session quoted is the 634th [for January 22, 1973] in Chapter 8 of Personal Reality. *Seth discussed the repression of natural aggression, and mentioned the sense of guilt that arose in early man with the birth of compassion. Then:)*

Animals have a sense of justice that you do not understand, and built into that innocent sense of integrity there is a biological compassion, understood at the deepest cellular levels . . .

A cat playfully killing a mouse and eating it is not evil. It suffers no guilt. On biological levels both animals understand. The consciousness of the mouse, under the innate knowledge of impending pain, leaves its body. The cat uses the warm flesh. The mouse itself has been hunter as well as prey, and both understand the terms in ways that are very difficult to explain.

At certain levels both cat and mouse understand the nature of the life-energy they share, and are not—in those terms—jealous for their own individuality . . . Man, pursuing his own way, chose to step outside of that framework—on a conscious level . . .

(This kind of material from Seth is deceptively simple, but upon reflection it can be seen to offer much. Jane and I think its implications are often missed by many who write us with questions about the pain and suffering in the world. Undoubtedly Seth has much more to say on the subject, and we hope to eventually obtain that information. Certainly individual and mass beliefs will be involved [along with the natural and unnatural guilt Seth discussed in the sessions making up Chapter 8 of Personal Reality]. *I'd say that just understanding the complicated relationships between mass beliefs and illness alone, for example, will require much material from Seth and much time invested upon our parts.*

(For the most part Seth's ideas are far away from thoughts of replicating genes or the second law of thermodynamics. Through Jane, he grapples with the mysteries of existence in emotional terms, rather than through the impersonal, "scientific," and really unproven concepts that life originated by accident [more than 3.4 billion years ago,[8] to give a late estimate], and perpetuates itself through chance mutations. Darwin's objective thinking, then, cut him off from such comprehensions as Seth advocates. The same was true for many scientists and theistic thinkers in succeeding generations, and in my opinion this holds today. I suggest that the entire 634th session in Personal Reality *be read with this appendix, for in it Seth explored some connections between animal and man—including the* evolution *[my emphasis] by man of "certain animal capacities to their utmost." At practically the same time, in the*

637th session for the following chapter [9], he could tell us: "Note: I did not say that man *emerged from the animals."*

(Over a year later Jane supplemented such remarks by Seth with some trance material of her "own"; see Appendix 6 in Volume 1 of "Unknown" Reality. According to her, if man didn't emerge from the animals, there were certainly close relationships involved—a dance of probabilities between the two, as it were. As I noted at the beginning of this appendix, the Seth material is still incomplete, and new information requires constant correlation with what has come before. Jane's own material—including whatever she comes up with in the future—ought to be integrated with Seth's, also, and eventually we hope to find time to do this. Although she left Appendix 6 unfinished, it contains many ideas worth more study: "Some of the experiments with man-animals didn't work out along our historic lines, but the ghost memories of those probabilities still linger in our biological structure . . . The growth of ego consciousness by itself set up both challenges and limitations . . . For many centuries there was no clear-cut differentiation between various aspects of man and animal . . . there were parallel developments in the emergence of physical man . . . there were innumerable species of man-in-the-making, in your terms. . . ." [I can add that just as Jane supplemented Seth's material on early man, he in turn has added to hers in a kind of freewheeling exchange; his information is presented later in this appendix.]

(The third excerpt I'd originally planned to use is from the 690th session in Volume 1, and shows that even when Seth talks of evolution in our terms of ordinary time, he means something quite different from that conventional definition of linear change: Precognition is one of the attributes of the growth through value fulfillment that he described in the [already quoted] 44th session. I also want to use this material to lead into short discussions of "naive realism," and evolution at the level of molecular biology. Seth:)

I have said that evolution does not exist as you think of it, in any kind of one-line ape-to-man sequence. No other species developed in that manner, either. Instead there are parallel developments. Your time perception shows you but one slice of the whole cake, for instance.

In thinking in terms of consecutive time, however, evolution does not march from the past into the future. Instead, precognitively the species is aware of those changes it wants to make, and from the "future" it alters the "present" state of the chromosomes and genes *(see Note 14)* to bring about in the probable future the specific changes it desires. Both above and below your usual conscious focus, then, time is experienced in an entirely different fashion, and is constantly manipulated, as physically you manipulate matter.[9]

(Seth's ideas aside for the moment, biologists faithful to Darwin's theories don't want to hear anything about the precognitive abilities of a species, nor do they see any evidence of it in their work. In evolutionary theory, such attributes violate not only the operation of chance mutation and the struggle for existence, but our ideas of consecutive time [which is associated with "naive realism"—the belief that things are really as we perceive them to be]. Not that scientifically the concept of a far more flexible time—even a backward flow of time—is all that new. In atomic physics, for example, no special meaning or place is given to any particular moment, and fundamentally the past and future all but merge in the interactions of elementary particles—thus at least approaching Seth's simultaneous time.[10] At that level there's change, or value fulfillment, but no evolution. To Jane's and my way of thinking, if there's value fulfillment there's consciousness, expressed through CU's, or units of consciousness.

(But to some degree many scientists outside physics regard such esoteric particle relationships as being of theoretical interest mainly within that discipline; the concepts aren't seen as posing any threat to biology, zoology, or geology, for instance, nor do they tinker with naive realism. The biological sciences can cling to mechanistic theories of evolution by employing the conservative physics of cause and effect to support their conclusions while being aware, perhaps, of the tenets of particle physics. Such "causal analysis" then proves itself over and over again—a situation, I wryly note, that's akin to the criticism I've read wherein the theory of evolution is used to prove the theory of evolution. [I mentioned such circular reasoning near the beginning of this appendix.]

(I find it very interesting, then, to consider that the theory of evolution is a creature of our coarser world of "physical" construction. Our ordinary, chosen sensual perceptions move us forward, within "the time system that the species adopted," as Seth commented in Chapter 8 of Personal Reality. *And Seth's explanation of the moment point[11] encompasses the seeming paradox through which consecutive time can be allowed expression within simultaneous time.*

(Naive realism, the philosophical concept that's been mentioned a few times in this appendix, enters in here. It could, however, be considered at just about any time, since its proponents believe that it's unconsciously involved in practically all of our daily activities. Simply put, naive realism teaches that our visual and bodily senses reveal to us an external world as it really is—that we "see" actual physical objects, for instance. Disbelievers say that neurological evidence contradicts this theory; that from the neurological standpoint the events in our lives and within our bodies depend upon interpretation by the brain; that we can know nothing directly, but only experience transmitted through—and so "colored" by—the central nervous system. The perceptual time lag, caused by

the limited speed of light, is also involved in objections to naive realism. I merely want to remind the reader that in ordinary terms naive realism, or some mind-brain idea very much like it, is habitually used whether we're considering evolution within a time-oriented camouflage universe, painting a picture, or running a household. And after many centuries, the debate over the relationship between mind and brain continues, if first the existence of the mind is even agreed upon!

(Is there really *"something out there?" That was one of the questions I asked Jane not long after she began giving these sessions late in 1963. I'd say that we still have but a partial answer [the same situation that applies to a lot of our other questions, too], although Seth came through with what I think of as a key passage in the 23rd session for February 5, 1964:)*

Because I say that you actually create the typical camouflage patterns of your own physical universe yourselves, by use of the inner vitality of the universe in the same manner that you form a pattern with your breath on a glass pane, I do not necessarily mean that you are the creators of the universe. I am merely saying that you are the creators of the physical world as you know it—and herein, my beloved friends, lies a vast tale.

(And a decade later we're still unraveling that tale, with Seth's help. I'll digress here for a moment to note that we expect to be so occupied for the rest of our lives: The intellectual and emotional challenges posed by the Seth material are practically unlimited.

(Yet, as far as he went in Chapter 5 of Personal Reality, *Seth was pretty definite in his ideas about physical reality. It seems to me that he combines certain aspects of naive realism with some of the objections to it; see the 625th session for November 1, 1972:)*

Because you are flesh and blood creatures, the interior aspects of perception must have their physical counterparts. But material awareness and bodily response to it would be impossible were it not for these internal webworks . . . I am saying that all exterior events, including your own bodies with their insides, all objects, all physical materializations, are the outside structures of inside ones that are composed of interior sound and invisible light, interwoven in electromagnetic patterns.

Beneath temporal perception, then, each object and event exists in these terms, in patterns that interact with each other. On a physical level you seem to be separated from everything that is not yourself. This is not true, but in your day-to-day existence it seems to be, and it is an assumption that you usually take for granted . . .[12]

Again, we run into difficulties in explanation simply because there are few verbal equivalents for what I am trying to say.[13]

(Within that temporal framework, investigators have recently dis-covered great biochemical differences among human beings at the molecular level: The genetic structures of numerous proteins [see Note 5] have been shown to be much more varied than was suspected. Even more pronounced are the differences among proteins between species. Each of us is seen to be truly unique—but at the same time those studying biological evolution express concern about whether their discoveries will challenge Darwinistic beliefs. Instead, I think that what has been learned so far offers only possible variations within the idea of evolution, for the talk is still about the origin of life out of nonlife, followed by the climb up the scale of living complexity; most evolutionists think that natural selection, or the survival of the fittest, still applies.

(Any role that consciousness might play in such biochemical processes isn't considered, of course, nor is there any sort of mystical comprehension of what we're up to as creatures. No matter how beautifully man works out a hypothesis or theory, he still does so without any thought of consciousness coming first. Through the habitual (and perhaps unwitting) use of naive realism, he projects his own basic creativity outside of himself, or any of his parts. He also projects upon cellular components like genes and DNA[14] learned concepts of "protection" and "selfishness": DNA is said to care only about its own survival and "knowledge," and not whether its host is man, plant, or animal. Only man would think to burden such pervasive parts of his own being, and those of other entities, with such negative concepts! Jane and I don't believe the allegations— in its own terms, how could the very stuff controlling inheritance not care about the nature of what it created? I'm only half joking (is there a gene for humor?) when I protest that DNA, for example, doesn't deserve to be regarded in such a fashion, no matter how much we push it around through recombinant techniques.[15]

(I'm projecting my own ideas here, but I think that in all of its complexity DNA has motives for its physical existence [as mediated through Seth's CU's, or units of consciousness] that considerably enlarge upon its assigned function as the "master molecule" of life as we know it. Deoxyribonu-cleic acid may exist within its host, whether man, plant, or animal—or bacteria or virus—in cooperative altruistic ventures with its carrier that are quite beside purely survival ones. Some of those goals, such as the exploration of concepts like the moment point [see Note 11], or probabilities [and reincarnation[16]], really defy our ordinary conscious perception. In terms we can more easily grasp, social relationships within and between species may be explored, starting at that biochemical level and working "upward." Basically, then, an overall genetics of cooperation becomes a truer long-run concept than the postulated deadly struggle for survival of the fittest, whether between man and molecules, say, or among members of the same species. Once again we have consciousness seeking to know itself in as many ways as possible, while being aware all of the

time, in those terms, of the forthcoming "death" of its medium of expression, DNA, and of DNA's host, or "physical machine."

(I continue my projections by writing that to a molecule of DNA the conventional notion of evolution—could such an entity grasp that idea, or even want to—might be hilarious indeed, given its own enhanced time scheme.[17] *Actually it would be more to the point if, perhaps with the aid of hypnosis and/or visualization, we tried from our giant-sized viewpoints to touch such minute consciousnesses with our own,*[18] *and so extend our knowledge in unexpected ways. Some probable realities might be reached—potential conscious achievements that I think are already within the reach of certain gifted individuals, Jane among them.*[19] *Jane and I would rather say that the variability among humans [or the members of any other species] at the molecular level is a reflection of Seth's statement that we each create our own reality, with all that that implies.*

(I want to add here that our real challenge in knowing our own species, and others, may lie in our cultivating the ability to understand the interacting consciousnesses involved, rather than to search only for physical relationships supposedly created through evolutionary processes. The challenge is profound. The consciousnesses of numerous other species may be so different from ours that we only approximately grasp the meanings inherent in some of them, and miss the essences of others entirely. To give just two examples, at this time we are surely opaque to the seemingly endless search for value fulfillment that consciousness displays through the "lowly" lungfish and the "unattractive" cockroach. Yet those entities are quite immune to our notions of evolution, and they explore time contexts in ways far beyond our current human comprehension: As far as science knows, both have existed with very little change for over 300 million years.

(It should be clear, then, that in our camouflage reality the ordinary concept of evolution becomes very complex if one chooses to make it so. The process can be discussed from many viewpoints; Jane and I think that such inquiries could easily "evolve" [to make a pun] into a book, either to bolster Seth's ideas on the subject, for instance, or to refute them. I now have on file materials that support or reject any stance on evolution that one cares to take. But it never fails, as "they" say: The members of each "pressure group," whatever its orientation, want to see things their way—very human performances, I'm afraid. Once it's created, each school of thought takes upon itself, and often with great intellectual and emotional arrogance, the right to advance its own belief systems in the world at the expense of its rivals.

(But, I asked Jane recently, why do our sciences and religions take it all so seriously? I wasn't really too earnest. If we truly owe our physical existence to the chance conglomeration of certain atoms and molecules in the thickening scum of a primordial pond or ocean [to discuss only mankind here], then certainly we'll never come this way again in the universe; and moreover, our

*emotional and intellectual attributes must rest upon the same dubious begin-
ning. Aside from the lack of evidence to back up such "scientific" speculations,
what thinking or feeling values, I wonder, can make such a belief system so
attractive? Surely very limited ones in linear terms, fated to never get beyond
those incessant questions about what came before the beginning. To paraphrase
some other material Jane wrote not long ago: "But the earth and all upon it are
given. To imagine that such an entire environment is an accident is intellectually
outrageous and emotionally sterile."*

*(And this is the ideal place to insert the poem she wrote not long
afterward:*

Science Convinces Me of Magic

*Science convinces me of magic
More each day.
To think that you and I,
The tiniest blade of grass
And highest mountain,
The smallest ant
And the Empire State Building
(and all the shops, streets,
and people in modern-day Manhattan)
All exist because
Some elemental dice
Just happened to
Fall together right!
Dice thrown by no hand
Or intent,
Because neither were
Invented yet.*

*(Jane and I certainly do not hold creationist views [see Note 1]. As I
wrote near the beginning of this appendix, to go very far into religious history
would lead away from the subject matter I planned to cover; but to us science is
as far away from Seth's philosophy in one direction as religion is in the opposite
direction. The species' religious drives have been around a lot longer than its
scientific ones, however, so I found myself looking for broad correlations between
the two, in that under each value system the individual carries a very conscious
sense of personal vulnerability. Before Darwinism, to use that concept as an
example, man at least felt that God had put him on earth for certain purposes, no
matter how much man distorted those purposes through ignorance and war.
According to Judaism and Christianity, among many religions, man could seek
forgiveness and salvation; he had a soul. After Darwin, he learned that even his*

physical presence on earth was an accident of nature. He was taught—he taught himself—that ideas of souls and gods were ridiculous. Either way, this very fallible creature found himself vulnerable to forces that consciously he couldn't understand—even though, in Seth's view, down through the millenia man had chosen all of his religious and antireligious experiences.

(As far as I can discover, science pays very little attention to any philosophical questions about why we're here, even while most definitely telling us what's true or not true. And while postulating that life is basically meaningless or goal-less [DNA doesn't care what its host looks like, for instance], science fights awfully hard to convince everyone that it's right—thus attaching the most rigid kind of meaning or direction to its professional views! [If I were very cynical, I'd add here that to Jane and me it often seems that science wants only what science believes.] At the same time, in mathematical and biological detail much too complicated to go into here, the author of many a scientific work in favor of evolution has ended up by undermining, unwittingly, I'm sure, the very themes he so devoutly believes in. I've hinted at some of those paradoxes in certain notes [mainly 5 through 8] for this appendix.

(In the current literature I read that a typical famous scientist—one of many leaders expressing such views these days—is very pessimistic about the state of the human species, given its many dilemmas. I also note that he seems to be most unhappy while stressing his agnosticism,[20] which is the kind of belief system that perpetuates standard evolutionary doctrines. Building upon those limited assumptions, the individual in question tells us how ironic it is that the "new" portions of the human brain, those that have evolved within the last two million years, are responsible for the moral and technological problems our species now faces. The brain's great creative neocortex is held especially accountable for problems that may lead to humanity's self-destruction. None of these challenges, as Jane and I habitually call them, are seen as distorted expressions of the kind of creativity Seth has described many times.[21]

(Within such a gloomy framework, then, I think it legitimate to ask how the species can consciously stress its accidental presence in the cosmos, yet demand that its members be the most "moral" of creatures. If science insists that there was, and is, no design or planner behind man's emergence, then how can man be expected to act as if there was, or is? Seth hasn't said so yet, but I think such contradictions play an important negative role in present world conditions. The attitude that life is a godless thing is so pervasive—and not only in Western cultures—that in Seth's terms it can be called an invisible mass core belief.

(I'm happy to note that Seth's ideas oppose much of the "modern" thinking that we're fated to bring about our own end as a species, whether by nuclear warfare or in some other equally devastating way. From his own viewpoint, Seth recently discussed such fears in a session given for Jane's ESP class:)

. . . in certain terms the theory of evolution, as it is

conventionally held, has caused unfortunate beliefs. For how can you look at yourselves with self-respect, with dignity or with joy, if you believe that you are the end product of forces in which the fittest survive? Being the fittest implies those given most to what would appear to be murderous intent—for you must survive at the expense of your fellows, be you leaf, frog, plant, or animal.

You do not survive through cooperation, according to that theory, and nature is not given a kind or creative intent, but a murderous one. And if you see yourselves as the end result of such a species, then how can you expect goodness or merit or creativity from yourselves, or from others? How can you believe that you live in a safe universe when each species exists because it survives through claw, if it must hunt and kill out of murderous intent, as implied in the theories of evolution and of reality itself?

So when you think of your beliefs and who you are, you must also think of your species, and how you are told your species came to be. For your private beliefs are also based upon those theories, and the beliefs, culturally, of your times.

It is seldom that you really question your biological origins, what they mean, and how you interpret them. Are you physically composed of murderous cells, then, each spontaneously out to get the others? If so, your physical being is more miraculous a product than even I have ever told you! If your cells did not cooperate so well, you would not be listening to this voice, and it would make no sound. As you listen to me, the cooperative, creative adventure within your bodies continues, and in terms of continuity reaches back prehistorically and into the future. Because consciousness creates form with joy, there is no murder that you have not projected out of misunderstanding and ignorance of the nature of that consciousness.

Roots do not struggle to exist. One species does not fight against the others to live. Instead creativity emerges, and cooperatively the environment of the world is known and planned by all the species. What appears to be struggle and death to you at those levels is not, now, for the experience of consciousness itself is different there, as is the experience of your own cellular composition.

(Then soon afterward, Seth had this to say in a private session:) Your body knows how to walk. The knowledge is built in and acted upon. The body knows how to heal itself, how to use its nourishment, how to replace its tissues—yet in your terms the body itself has no access to the kind of information the mind possesses. Being so ignorant, how does it perform so well?

If it were scientifically inclined, the body would know that such spontaneous performance was impossible, for science cannot explain the reality of life itself in its present form, much less its origins. Consciousness within the body knows that its existence is within the body's context, and apart from it at the same time.

(I repeat that when Seth discusses evolution his meaning differs considerably from the scientific one—which, with various modifications, is even accepted by a number of religious thinkers. As I show at the end of this appendix, Seth allows for a much greater range of simultaneous origins; in our reality these imply growth and development out of that "basic" group of species for the most part, with multidimensional purposes operating inside an enhanced time scheme that includes probabilities, reincarnation, counterparts,[22] *precognition, and other concepts, meanings, and beliefs. All of these qualities are manifestations of All That Is, or consciousness, or energy, or whatever. Probabilities aside, when Seth talks about cells [or their components] recombining as parts of plant or animal forms, as he does in the 705th session, Jane and I don't take that to mean the evolution, or alteration, of one species into another—but that a unity of consciousness pervades all elements in our environment, whether "alive" or "dead." With the concept of probabilities in mind, however, much of the "thrust for development and change" that Seth also mentions as existing inside all organisms, could just as well take place in those other realities. Early in this appendix, I described how Seth continually built upon material that he'd given before, and that processes of correlation between old and new resulted. At this time, my ideas here represent a correlation between Seth's material on evolution in the 705th session [which led to this appendix], and his later statements on origins, referred to above. We hope to learn much more about the whole business of evolution. And behind all, Seth insists upon the condition that each of us chose to experience this camouflage reality within this historical context.*

(My thought is that because of that choosing, common denominators must lie beneath the clashing beliefs about evolution, and that a good place to start looking for such unifying factors is within the theory, or the framework or idea, of simultaneous time—however one wants to try to express such a quality within serial terms. The search would be a complicated one. At the same time, I admit that ideas like this always remind me of Seth's comments in the class session for June 23, 1970, as excerpted in the Appendix for Seth Speaks:*)*

In this reality, [each of] you very nicely emphasize all the similarities which bind you together; you make a pattern of them, and you very nicely ignore all the dissimilarities . . . If you were able to focus your attention on the dissimilarities, merely those that you can perceive but do not, then you would be amazed that mankind can form any idea of an organized reality.

(However, collectively we do share an agreed-upon reality, even if one subject to many stresses. The next two excerpts to be presented from Seth

came through in a couple of sessions delivered some time after he'd finished "Unknown" Reality. I've put them together for easy reading. Their inspiration was my work here and the discussions on evolution that Jane and I led in ESP class. As noted with the quotations given in Note 13, eventually this material will be published in its entirety as part of a Seth book; perhaps then it can be used as a guide for the sort of investigation just mentioned. In the meantime, the thoughts below can at least help orient some fresh thinking about the beginning of our planet, of all the species upon it, and indeed of the universe itself. Seth began:)

There are verbal difficulties having to do with the definition of life. Because of the psychological strength of preconceived notions, I have to work around many of your concepts. Your own kind of conscious mind is splendid and unique. It causes you, however, to interpret all other kinds of life according to your own specifications and experiences.

There is no such thing, in your terms, as nonliving matter. There is simply a point that you recognize as having the characteristics that you have arbitrarily ascribed to life, or living conditions. For there is no particular point at which life was inserted into nonliving matter.

If we must speak in terms of continuity, which I regret, then in those terms you could say that life in the physical universe, on your planet, "began" spontaneously in a given number of species at the same time. Words do nearly forsake me, the semantic differences are so vast. In those terms there was a point where consciousness, through intent, impressed itself into matter. That "breakthrough" cannot be logically explained, but only compared to, say, an illumination—that is, a light occurring everywhere at once, that became a medium for life as you define it. It had nothing to do with the propensity of certain kinds of cells to reproduce—[all cells are] imbued with the "drive" for value fulfillment—but with an overall illumination that set the conditions in which life was possible as you think of it; and at that imaginary, hypothetical point, all species became latent. The inner pulsations of the invisible universe reached certain intensities that "impregnated" the entire physical system simultaneously. That illumination was everywhere then at every point aware of itself, and of the conditions formed by its presence.

At the same time, EE units *(see Note 3)* became manifest. I have said, for example, that the universe expands as an idea does, and so the visible universe sprang into being in the same manner. The same energy that gave birth to the universe is, in those terms, still being created. The EE units contain within themselves the latent knowledge of all of the various species that can emerge under those conditions. It is according to your relative position. You can say that it took untold centuries for the EE units to "initially" combine, forming classifications of matter and various species, or you can say that this process happened at once. In your terms, each species is aware of the condition of each other species, and of the entire environment. <u>In those terms</u> the environment forms the species and the species form the environment. There were fully developed men—that is, of full intellect, emotion, and will—<u>living at the same time</u>, in your terms, as those creatures supposed to be man's evolutionary ancestors.

[However, as] you begin to question the nature of time itself, then the "when" of the universe is beside the point. The motion and energy of the universe still comes from within. I certainly realize that this is hardly a scientific statement—yet the moment that All That Is conceived of a physical system it was invisibly created, endowed with creativity, and bound to emerge [into physical reality].

There <u>is</u> a design and a designer, but they are so combined, the one within the other, the one within and the one without, that it is impossible to separate them. The creator is within its creations, and the creations themselves are gifted with creativity. The world comes to know itself, to discover itself, for the planner left room for divine surprise, and the plan was nowhere foreordained. Nor is there anywhere within it anything that corresponds to your "survival of the fittest" theories.

(Seth's statement just given, that fully developed men coexisted with their supposed ancestors, led to our request that he follow through with more information on the subject. He's done so to some extent, and here we're presenting material from one of those later sessions to show his thinking. He continues to confound accepted evolutionary theory. As usual, however, Seth's new data obviously imply new questions that we haven't gone into yet. But at least, I told Jane, he's said certain things that we can ask questions about, whether from the viewpoint of evolution, time, language, civilization, or whatever. The excerpts to follow, incidentally, are those I referred to earlier in this appendix, when I wrote that just as Jane had supplemented Seth's material on early man with some of her own [as given in Appendix 6 in Volume 1], he in turn added to hers:)

In your terms of history, man appeared in several different ages—not from an animal ancestor in the way generally supposed. There <u>were</u> men-animals, but they were not your stock. They did not "lead" to anything. They were species in their own right.[23]

There were animal-men. The terms are for your convenience. In some species the animal-like tendencies predominated, in others the manlike tendencies did so: Some were more like men, some more like animals. The Russian steppes had a particular giant-sized species. Some also I believe in Spain—that area.

There is considerable confusion, for that matter, as to the geological ages as they are understood.[24] Such species existed in many of these ages. Man, as you think of him, shared the earth with the other creatures just mentioned. In those terms so-called modern man, with your skull structure and so forth, existed alongside of the creatures now supposed to be his ancestors.

There was some rivalry among these groups, as well as some cooperation. Several species, say, of modern man died out. There was some mating among these groups—that is, among the groups in existence at any given time.

The brain capacities of your particular species have always been the same . . . Many of the man-animal groups had their own communities. To you they may seem to have been limited, yet they combined animal and human characteristics beautifully, and they used tools quite well. In a manner of speaking they had the earth to themselves for many centuries, in that modern man did not compete with them.

Both the man-animals and the animal-men were born with stronger instincts. They did not need long periods of protection as infants, but in an animal fashion were physically more agile at younger ages than, say, the human infant.

The earth has gone through entire cycles unsuspected by your scientists. <u>Modern</u> man, then, existed with other manlike species, and appeared in many different places on the earth, <u>and at different ages</u>.

There were then also animal-man and man-animal civilizations of their kinds, and there were complete civilizations of modern man, existing [long] before the ages now given for, say, the birth of writing *(in 3100 B.C.*

(My position after writing this appendix is that in scientific and religious terms we know little about our world [and universe], its origins, and its amazing variety of forms, both "living" and "nonliving." Our own limitations may have something to do with our attitudes here, yet Jane and I have become very careful about believing science or religion when either one tells us it can explain our world, for each of those disciplines ignores too much. No matter what the source of this camouflage reality may be, our conscious lack of knowledge and understanding as we manipulate within it, through naive realism or any other system of belief or perception, ought to make us humble

indeed; all arrogance should be transcended as we become more and more aware of the limitless beauty, complexity, and mystery that surrounds us, and of which we are part. Jane and I just don't think it all came about through chance! The mind can ask too many questions to be satisfied with mechanistic explanations, and nurturing that characteristic of dissatisfaction alone may be one of the most valuable contributions the Seth material can make.

(To us, even "ordinary" linear knowledge as it accumulates through the next century or two, not to mention over longer spans of time, is certain to severely modify or make obsolete many concepts about origins and evolution that today are dispensed by those in authority—and which most people accept unthinkingly.

(For some years now, organized religion as a whole has been suffering from a loss of faith and members, stripped of its mysteries by science, which, with the best of intentions, offers in religion's place a secular humanism—the belief that one doesn't need blind faith in a god in order to be morally concerned for the common welfare; paradoxically, however, this concern is most of the time expressed in religious terms, or with religious feeling. Yet science too has experienced many failures in theory and technology, and knows a new humility; at least partly because of these failures, anti-intellectualism has grown noticeably in recent years.

(Now we read late surveys that show an increase in religious faith, and statements to the effect that science does not claim to reveal absolute truth, that any scientific theory is valid only until a variance is shown. Jane and I certainly aren't turned on to realize that a major religion, for instance, teaches the "facts" of man's basically corrupt and sinful nature; surely a religion in the best sense can offer beliefs superior to those! At the same time, we take note of the latest efforts of biological researchers to explain how, millions of years ago, a primitive DNA molecule could begin to manufacture the protein upon which life "rides," and thus get around the contradiction posed in Note 8: What made the protein that sustains the processes of life, before that life was present to make the protein? The scientists involved hope the new hypothesis will survive further tests and become "fact," thus giving clues to the riddles of origins and evolution. But to briefly paraphrase material Jane came through with not long ago [and which, again, will eventually be published]: "How does one deal with new facts that undermine old facts, in whatever field of endeavor? Do you say that reality has changed? Upon examination, facts give."

(And as I work on this appendix, Seth has already remarked in the 709th session, just before break at 10:35:)

You are well acquainted with the exterior method, that involves studying the objective universe and collecting facts upon which certain deductions are made. In this book [Volume 2], therefore, we will be stressing interior ways of attaining, not necessarily facts, but knowledge and wisdom. Now facts may or may not give you wisdom. They can, if they are slavishly followed, lead you away from true knowledge. Wisdom shows you the insides of facts, so to speak, and the realities from which facts emerge.

(The search, then, is on for new unities and meanings; a convergence, one might say, of the realities of science, nature, religion—and, of course, mysticism. By mysticism I mean simply the intuitional penetration of our camouflage reality to achieve deeper understandings relative to our physical and mental environments—and such comprehensions are what Jane seeks to accomplish through her expression of the Seth material.[25] In that sense, it isn't necessary here to discuss attaining "ultimate" knowledge—it will be enough to note that as one person Jane can use her abilities to help unify a number of viewpoints. She can also bring to consciousness the idea that no matter what our individual orientations may be, collectively we do have overall purposes in the world we've created. This realization alone can be a transforming one; as I show in the Introductory Notes for Volume I of "Unknown" Reality, it can be a most useful one in practical, everyday life as well. Within that sort of framework, the evolution referred to by Seth—in whatever way it may concern the development of ideas, planets, creatures, or anything else—makes sense.)

NOTES: Appendix 12

1. Over the years, my outside reading on evolution has covered many often conflicting viewpoints. Whether their beliefs are rooted in the tenets of conventional biology (Darwinism), for instance, or allied with those of the creationists (who hold that God made the earth and all of its creatures, just as described in the Book of Genesis), the advocates of rival theories have impressed me as having at least one thing in common: No matter how violently they may disagree, their arguments lack all sense of *humor.* This is serious stuff, world! Whatever happened to the spontaneity and joy in life? For surely, I found myself thinking as I read all of those antagonistic ideas, spontaneity and joy were the very ingredients that Seth would place uppermost in any theory or scheme of life's "beginnings," regardless of its philosophical stance.

2. As I wrote in the Introductory Notes for Volume 1 of *"Unknown" Reality*, "I think it important to periodically remind the reader of certain of Seth's basic ideas throughout both volumes. . . ." His simultaneous time, or spacious present, is certainly such a concept. Yet in the next paragraph I added that in my opinion, "Seth's concept of simultaneous time will always elude us to some extent as long as we're physical creatures. . . ." To me the challenge of confronting that idea is well worthwhile, however, for to grasp it even partially is bound to enlarge one's view of reality.

A close analogy to this material can be found in remarks Seth made in the 682nd session for that first volume: "<u>The idea of one universe alone is basically nonsensical.</u> Your reality must be seen in its relationship to others. Otherwise you are always caught in questions like 'How did the universe begin?' or 'When will it end?' All systems are constantly being created."

Then see the 688th session for Seth's discussion of closed systems and the backward and forward, inward and outward motions of time.

In light of the excerpts to come in this appendix from the 44th session, it should be noted that when Seth used the term "camouflage," he referred not only to our physical world as one of the forms (or camouflages) taken by basic reality, but to another kind of time as well—the medium of successive moments the outer ego is used to, and in which our ordinary world exists.

Seth's first mention of "camouflage" is described in Volume 1; see Note 3 for Appendix 11.

3. In this 1964 session, Seth was several years away from any attempt to elaborate upon the vitality that "composes from itself all other phenomena." In October 1969 he began his material on EE (electromagnetic energy) units. These, he declared, exist just below the range of physical matter, and accrete in response to emotional intensity; eventually, they form physical objects. See sessions 504–6 in the Appendix of *The Seth Material,* and the 581st session (held in April 1971) in Chapter 20 of *Seth Speaks.*

In Volume 1, Seth carried this material a step further through his description of his CU's, or "units" of consciousness. "I do not want you to think of these units as particles," he said in the 682nd session (given in February 1974). "There is a basic unit of consciousness that, expressed, will not be broken down. . . ." Also see sessions 683–84.

4. This paragraph and the preceding one were used as a footnote for the 637th session in Chapter 9 of *Personal Reality.* That session, held 18 months ago, contains material appropriate to this appendix: As an analogy, Seth compares the "evolution" of souls in terms of value fulfillment to cellular growth in our physical reality.

5. According to my interpretation of this sentence, Seth stops short of telling us that in our reality all species—man, animals, and plant life (and viruses and bacteria too, for that matter)—developed from a single primordial living source. Evolutionary theory maintains that such a source spontaneously came into being, riding upon various protein molecules (or certain other kinds of molecules) that had themselves chemically—and miraculously—evolved out of nonliving matter, then demonstrated the ability to duplicate themselves. (When Seth came through with this 44th session, neither Jane nor I had enough background information about theories of evolution to ask him to be more specific. Proteins, for instance, are very complex chains of amino acids, and consist of nitrogen, oxygen, hydrogen, carbon, and/or certain other elements. They exist in great

variety in all animal and vegetable matter; in the body each protein supports a very definite function.) But the view that all life had a common origin, that by pure chance it originated on the earth—*just once*—without the aid of God, or any sort of designer, is today accepted by most scientists in biology and related disciplines. Such thinking stems from the work done in the 19th century by the English naturalists Charles Darwin and Alfred Wallace.

However, Jane and I believe that at most the "facts of evolution" make up a working hypothesis—or unproven proposition—only, for many of evolution's tenets, especially those involving energy/entropy (see Note 6), are open to serious challenge. There's plenty of evidence around for changes occurring *within* species, but the "upward" transmutation of one species into another has not been scientifically proven from the index fossil record, nor has it been experimentally verified. The arguments about evolution can get very technical, so in my notes I'm referring to those aspects of the subject in the barest terms possible.

In Volume 1, see Appendix 6 for Session 687, and Session 689 with its notes.

6. Ever since Seth came through with the material in this (44th) session 10 years ago, I've been interested in comparing his second law of the inner universe with the second law of thermodynamics of our "camouflage" physical sciences. Both deal with energy, yet to me they're opposites. At the same time I see them as linked through our distorted perception of that inner reality, thus pointing up Seth's statement just given, that "the so-called laws of your camouflage universe do not apply to the inner universe." (When this session was held Jane knew nothing of the three laws of thermodynamics, or how they define energy/heat relationships in our universe. Nor is she concerned with them now, *per se*; they're simply outside of her interests.)

Seth has always maintained that there are no closed systems, that energy is constantly exchanged between them, regardless of whether such transfers can be detected. (In Volume 1, see Session 688, plus Note 2 for the same session.) The second law of thermodynamics, on the other hand, tell us that our universe *is* a closed system—and that it's fated to eventually run down because the amount of energy available for useful work is always decreasing, even though the supply of that energy is constant. A measure of this unavailable energy is called entropy.

I think it obvious that by "energy transformation" Seth doesn't mean that the energy (or consciousness, to my way of thinking) in our system is inevitably decreasing. I can best express it intuitively: In physics, that well-known second law of thermodynamics may usually be so reliable for us, distorted as it is, just *because* of our limited physical interpretation as mediated by the central nervous system.

At the same time, it's worth noting that the second law of thermodynamics is still questioned by some theoreticians—the idea being that it's impossible to prove a scientific "truth" in each of an unlimited number of instances.

7. Charles Darwin (1809–1881) published *On the Origin of Species* in 1859. In his book Darwin presented his ideas of natural selection—that all species evolve from earlier versions by inheriting slight (genetic) variations through the generations. (See Note 5.) Thus, in a process called gradualism, there has been over many millions of years the slow development of flora and fauna from the simple to the complex, with those structures surviving that are best suited to their environments—the "survival of the fittest," in popular terms.

Any biologist who is a true Darwinist would find these statements of Seth's to be anathema: "Psychic and religious ideas, then, despite many drawbacks . . . are far more important in terms of 'evolution' than is recognized." And: "I am telling you that so-called evolution and religion are closely connected." (From the 690th session, in Volume 1.) Such a scientist would have the same reaction to Seth's statement that "Consciousness always creates form, and not the other way around." (From the 513th session, in Chapter 2 of *Seth Speaks.*)

It's often been claimed that Darwin's natural selection, while ruling out any question of design or a planner—God, say—behind living matter, leaves unexplained the same question relative to the structure of *non*living matter, which in those terms obviously preceded life. I'd rather approach that argument through another statement Seth made in Chapter 20 of *Seth Speaks* (in the 582nd session): "You are biologically connected, chemically connected with the Earth that you know. . . ." How is it that as living creatures we're made up of ingredients—atoms of iron, molecules of water, for instance—from a supposedly dead world? In the scientific view we're utterly dependent upon that contradictory situation. No one denies the amazing structure or design of our physical universe, from the scale of subatomic particles on "up" (regardless of what cosmological theory is used to explain the universe's beginning). The study of design as one of the links between "living" and "nonliving" systems would certainly be a difficult challenge—but a most rewarding one, I think—for science. I have little idea of how the work would be carried out. Evidently it would lead from biology through microbiology to physics with, ultimately, a search that at least approached Seth's electromagnetic energy (EE) units and units of consciousness (CU's). Yet according to Seth, both classes of "particles" are in actuality nonphysical; as best words can note, they have their realities on scales so minute that we cannot hope to detect them through our present technology. . . .

Yet here we run into irony and paradox: Any scientist who considered the existence of Seth's EE units and CU's would be called a heretic by his more conventional colleagues, for he would be acknowledging the possibility that *all* matter, being made up of such conscious entities, was living. From that viewpoint, at least, there would be no link through design to be discovered.

In connection with material in this note, I think it quite interesting and revealing that several millennia before Darwin, man *himself* began playing the role of a designer within the framework of nature, through his selective breeding of animals and his hybridization of plants. These activities certainly represent evolution through conscious intent, guided by the same creature who insists that no sort of consciousness could have been responsible for the origin or development of "life," let alone the "dead" matter of his planet. Not only that: We read that even now in his laboratories man is trying hard to *create* some of that life itself. This is always done, of course, with the idea that the right combination of simple ingredients (water, methane, ammonia, et al.) in the test tube, stimulated by the right kind of energy under just the right conditions, will automatically produce life. It's confidently predicted that eventually at least one such experiment will succeed. I have yet to see in those accounts anything about the role consciousness will play in this truly miraculous conversion of dead matter into that of the living. Perhaps those involved in the experiments fear that the idea of consciousness will impugn the scientific "purity" of their work.

Finally, in this appendix I haven't used the term "Neo-Darwinism" in order to avoid confusion with the familiar Darwinism that most people—including scientists—still employ. Neo-Darwinism is simply the original idea of natural selection in plants and animals updated to take present-day genetics into account.

8. Very briefly, for those who are interested: It's often been shown mathematically that contrary to Darwinistic belief, enormous time spans (in the millions of years, say) will not aid in the chance formation of even the chemical precursors to life—the protein or nucleic acid molecules—but will instead make their creation even less likely. For with time, the even distribution or equilibrium of matter increases, moving it away from the ordered sequences necessary to support life. Scientifically, in the closed system of our universe, the second law of thermodynamics and entropy eventually conquer all. (See Note 6.)

Nor can solar energy be thought of as the agent that directly turned nonliving matter into its living counterpart; in those terms, life required its intermediate molecules, which sunlight is not able to construct. Life needs protein in order to "be," and to sustain it through metabolism—*then* it can use solar energy! Darwin's theory that life arose by chance poses a basic contradiction: What made the protein that sustains the processes of life, before that life was present to make the protein?

Many times in laboratory studies, substances called proteinoids (often misleadingly defined in dictionaries as "primitive proteins") have been observed forming from amino acids, which are subunits of proteins. Some researchers think of proteinoids as the forerunners of the protein that life needs to ride upon, but for quite complex scientific reasons, proteinoids are far from being true biological proteins and do not lead to life. Jane and I strongly object to being told that dead matter turns itself into living matter. Just how does this transformation come about?

Evolutionary thinking is challenged not only by questions of protein synthesis, and energy/entropy (see Note 5), however. Equally insistent are the puzzles posed by the missing intermediate forms in the fossil record: Where *are* all the remnants of those creatures that linked birds, reptiles, cats, monkeys, and human beings? The hypothetical evolutionary tree of life demands that such in-between forms existed; it seems that by now paleontologists should have unearthed enough signs of them to make at least a modest case for their belief systems; the lack of scientific evidence is embarrassing. Since my mind works that way, I could make minutely detailed drawings of a graduated series of such entities (gradualism being a basic premise in Charles Darwin's theory), but would the creatures shown have been viable? Could they actually have existed for the necessary millennia while evolving into the species whose fossil remains *have* been discovered, or that live today? As indicated in Note 5, evolutionists are serving goodly portions of speculation along with inadequate theory—or, really, hypothesis.

9. Seth prepared the way for these statements by declaring in the 684th session, in Volume 1: "It is truer to say that heredity operates from the future backward into the past, than it is to say that it operates from the past into the present. Neither statement would be precisely correct in any case, because your present is a poised balance affected as much by the probable future as the probable past."

10. See Note 2 for this appendix. Then, in Volume 1 see the material on time reversal and symmetry in Note 6 for Session 702.

11. Both of these references originate in the first volume of this work. Seth, in Session 681: "In your terms—the phrase is necessary—the moment point, the present, is the point of interaction between all existences and reality. All probabilities flow through it, though one of your moment points may be experienced as centuries, or as a breath, in other probable realities of which you are a part." Also see notes 1 and 5 for the same session.

And Seth, in Session 683: "All kinds of time—backward and forward—emerge from the basic unpredictable nature of consciousness, and are due to 'series' of significances."

12. I'm not sure how something like naive realism fits in with out-of-body travel (or "projection"), however. I've read nothing about the two together, nor have I yet asked Seth for what will surely be some very interesting material on such a possible relationship. Paradoxically, our perceptions while out-of-body can be more tenuously connected to temporal reality than usual, yet more acute at the same time. I was aware of the accustomed physical world during a projection that's described in *Seth Speaks* (see the 583rd session in Chapter 20), and in some other dream-connected out-of-body situations. However, our use of naive realism must often govern what we allow ourselves to experience while consciousness is separated from the body. I also think that some out-of-body travels, apparently to "alien" nonphysical realities, may actually be based instead upon interior bodily states or events. But there are times when the projecting consciousness, free of frameworks like naive realism, at least approaches truly different realities, or probabilities. Jane has had some

success here; in Chapter 6 of *Adventures,* see her projection experience involving "Dr. Sam's house."

13. A note added much later: Sometimes things develop in unexpected ways: One might say that several years later Seth continued the material just presented. By the time he did so he'd been through with *"Unknown" Reality* for quite a while, but I was still working on the notes and appendixes for Volume 2. As I wrote Appendix 12 in particular I discussed with Jane the passages on naive realism; soon afterward Seth began to refer to the subject during scheduled sessions, and one of them contained the excellent information below. (Only one part of that session is quoted, but eventually it will be published in its entirety as part of a Seth book.) Very evocative, to consider how consciousness *chooses* to manifest itself physically, in direct contradiction to the mechanistic beliefs held so tightly—and with so little humor—by those adhering to Charles Darwin's theory of evolution. From Session 803:)

"You perceive your body as solid. Again, the very senses that make such a deduction are the result of the behavior of atoms and molecules literally coming together to form the organs, filling a <u>pattern</u> of flesh. All other objects that you perceive are formed <u>in their own way</u> in the same fashion.

"The physical world that you recognize is made up of invisible patterns. These patterns are 'plastic,' in that while they exist, their final form is a matter of probabilities directed by consciousness. Your senses perceive these patterns in their own way. The patterns themselves can be 'activated' in innumerable fashions. *(Humorously:)* There is <u>something out there</u> to observe.

"Your sense apparatus determines what form that something will take, however. The mass world rises up before your eyes, but your eyes are part of that mass world. You cannot <u>see</u> your thoughts, so you do not realize that they have shape and form, even as, say, clouds do. There are currents of thought as there are currents of air, and the mental patterns of man's feelings and thoughts rise up like flames from a fire, or steam from hot water, to fall like ashes or like rain.

". . . these patterns of probabilities themselves are not inactive. They are possessed by the desire to be-actualized (with a hyphen). Behind all realities there are mental states. These always seek form, though again there are other forms than those <u>you</u> recognize."

14. Deoxyribonucleic acid, or DNA, is often referred to as the "master molecule," or the "basic building block" of life. DNA is an essential component of the protoplasmic substance of which genes and chromosomes are formed in the cell nucleus, and governs the heredity of all living things.

15. In microbiology, the first stages of the exciting and controversial "genetic engineering" are at hand. This long-sought goal of science involves the very sophisticated recombination of DNA from such different life forms as plants and mammals, say, into new forms not seen on

earth before. Such work has been called vital for the understanding of many things—the genetics of all species, the control of at least some diseases, great improvements in the quality of food plants, and so forth. It's also been called outright interference with the evolutionary constraints that prevent the interbreeding of species. Although risks may be present in DNA research, such as the unforeseen creation of new diseases, it seems that within strict safeguards recombinant techniques are here to stay.

Once again, however, it's obvious that as a whole, science is far removed from Seth's idea that each of us—whether that "us" is a human being or a molecule of DNA—creates our own reality. And what if we *can* learn to assemble sections of DNA from various life forms into new forms? To at least some extent such basic genetic substances *would* cooperate in the efforts at recombination: for no matter what kind of life developed, it would represent a gestalt of myriad consciousnesses, embarking upon unique explorations.

In Note 7 (also see Note 5), I wrote that for centuries now—most of them obviously preceding Darwin—man himself has been playing the role of a designer through his creation of certain breeds of animals and hybrid plants. But we see now that man is no longer content to bring about changes *within* species, as in cattle, for instance: With vast excitement he faces the challenge of "engineering" new kinds of life. Those urges are creative even when, as a designer, he goes against his own Darwinian concepts that there is no conscious plan involved in the design of his world.

16. In this appendix I've consistently thought of probabilities and reincarnation as being nearly synonymous, while hardly mentioning the latter to avoid making the material unnecessarily complicated. As Seth himself told us in the 683rd session for Volume 1 of this work: "Rein- carnation simply represents probabilities in a time context (underlined)— portions of the self that are materialized in historical contexts."

17. These excerpts from Seth's material in the 690th session, for Volume 1, furnish a close analogy to the sort of "time" available to molecular consciousness: ". . . biological precognition is firmly based in the chromosomes and genes, and reflected in the cells . . . The cells' practically felt 'Now' includes, then, what you think of as past and future, as simple conditions of Nowness. They maintain the body's structure in your poised time only by manipulating themselves in a rich medium of prob- abilities. There is a constant give-and-take of communication between the cell as you know it in present time, and the cell as it 'was' in the past, or 'will be.' "

18. See the information on "the true mental physicist" in Session 701 for Volume 1. Seth discussed how in our future such a scientist will be able to allow "his consciousness to flow into the many open doors *(or inner realities)* that can be found with no instrument, but with the mind." And Seth commented in the same session: "Ruburt has at times been able to throw his consciousness into small physical instruments *(computer com- ponents, for instance),* and to perceive their inner activity at the level of, say, electrons."

19. Jane described one of her adventures with probable realities in Appendix 4 for Volume 1: She tuned in to her own "sidepools of consciousness," her own "probable neurological materializations. . . ." (My personal opinion is that although many may think it difficult reading, Appendix 4 contains some of the most important information in Volume 1.)

20. I remind the reader that an agnostic (as I think Charles Darwin was) is one who believes the mind can know only physical phenomena, and not whether there are final realities, causes, or gods. An atheist believes there is no God.

I should add that the passages on science and scientists in Appendix 12 aren't intended to add up to any general indictment of what are very powerful cultural forces, but to give insights into "where we're at" at this time in linear history. Many scientists *are* agnostic or atheistic. However, Jane and I feel that if science represents the "search for truth," as it so often reminds us, then eventually it will contend with the kind of gifts she demonstrates. Subjective and objective abilities, working together, can create a whole greater than the sum of its parts. A number of scientists, representing various disciplines, have written Jane about the Seth material, and many of them have expressed such views.

The material in Volume 1 on the dream-art scientist, the true mental physicist, and the complete physician (as well as on science in general), applies here. See sessions 700-4.

21. Earlier in this appendix, see Seth as quoted from Chapter 20 of *Seth Speaks* and Chapter 8 of *Personal Reality*.

22. A note added later: I inserted "counterparts" here because in Section 5 of this volume Seth devotes portions of several sessions to his counterpart concept: "Quite literally, you live more than one life at a time" (his emphasis). Among others, see Session 721, here quoted, with its Appendix 21. As the reader studies those particular sessions, he or she will quickly see how counterpart ideas fit in with the subject matter of Appendix 12.

23. I suggest that sessions 562–63, in Chapter 11 of *Seth Speaks,* be reviewed in connection with all of this material. In Volume 1, see Note 4 for Session 689.

24. Without going into detail yet—nor have we asked him to— Seth has insisted more than once that the earth is "much much" older than its currently estimated age of 4.6 billion years.

25. In Volume 1, Jane and mysticism are discussed in the Introductory Notes, Session 679, and Appendix 1 for that session.

APPENDIX 13
(For Session 708)

(Seth's phrase, ". . . you cannot see before or after what you think of as your birth or death. . . ." triggered a set of associations for me, but they proved to have their complications. I thought I remembered a statement he'd made long ago, but now I couldn't locate it within the body of his material. One by one my mental connections fell into place as I searched for it, yet for a time I was quite frustrated while I tried to physically verify my unconscious knowledge of its location.

(First I thought of Seth's assertion in the 92nd session for September 28, 1964, that "trees have their dreams"; [in Volume 1, see the quotations in Note 1 for Session 698]. Then I remembered that he'd come through with extensive material on tree consciousness in a much earlier session. With Jane's help the next day I found that information in the 18th session, which had been held on January 22, 1964. Most of that session is unpublished, although someday we'd like to print it in full. It contains many intriguing ideas—as, for example: "A tree knows a human being also . . . [yet it] does not even build up an image of a man, which is why this is so difficult to explain . . . And the same tree will recognize the same man who passes it by each day."

(Next, the subject matter of the 18th session led me to recall that Seth had also discussed trees several years later. But this time, in spite of my system of indexing each session in at least a fairly adequate fashion, several days passed before I found the passage I wanted. Discovering it involved a patient combing of many sessions and notes. [If the indexes listed everything in detail, they'd end up being almost as long as the sessions themselves.] The search was worth it, though; now I had the key phrase I'd associated with Seth's remark in Session 708. It's underlined below for easy reference.

(Seth, then, in the 453rd session for December 4, 1968:)

To your way of thinking some lives are lived in a twinkling, and others last for centuries, as some huge trees. The perception of consciousness is not limited . . . I have told you, for example, that the consciousness of the tree is not as specifically focused as your own. To all intents and purposes, however, <u>the tree is conscious of 50 years before and 50 years hence.</u>

Its sense of identity spontaneously goes beyond the change of its own form. It has no ego to cut the "I" identification short. Creatures without the compartment of the ego can easily follow their own identities beyond any changes of form. The inner self <u>is</u> aware of this integrity of identity, but the ego focused so securely in physical reality cannot afford this luxury.

APPENDIX 14
(For Session 708)

(The morning after the above session had been held [on September 30, 1974], I asked Jane to write down what she'd told me at about 1:15 A.M. I remembered her description of it at the time, even though I'd been pretty bleary by then, but I wanted her own version for use here. She wrote:)

"As I was getting ready for bed after our last Seth session, I suddenly wondered about Atlantis. Then from Seth, mentally, I thought, I got the information that Atlantis, as it's come down to us in myth and story, was actually a composite of three civilizations. Atlantis is a myth in response to a truth, then, I suppose. Next I got that Plato picked up the Atlantis material himself, psychically—he didn't get it the way he said he did. I never ask Seth about Atlantis; I'm afraid the cultish ideas connected with it turned me off long ago."

(In his dialogues Timaeus *and* Critias, *the Greek philosopher Plato [427?–347? B.C.] described how the fabled island continent of Atlantis sank beneath the ocean west of the Pillars of Hercules—the Strait of Gibraltar— some 12,000 years previously. Looking backward in time, Plato heard the story of Atlantis from his maternal uncle, Critias the Younger, who was told about it by his father, Critias the Elder, who heard about it through the works of the Athenian statesman and lawgiver, Solon, who had lived two centuries earlier [c. 640–559 B.C.]; and Solon got the story of Atlantis from Egyptian priests, who got it from—? Whether Atlantis actually existed in historic terms, its location, the time of its suggested demise, and so forth, are of course points strongly contested by scholars, scientists, and others.*

(Any specific associations that might have brought the Atlantis information to mind were hidden from Jane, though. Neither of us had been reading or talking about it. We were left thinking that the general tone of Seth's material early in the session, especially in his references to such ideas as "historical sequences" and "alternate realities," might have served as a trigger.

(A note added later: Seth himself had some things to say about Atlantis in the 742nd session for Section 6; the session also contains excerpts from the Atlantis material he delivered a month or so after finishing Volume 2 of "Unknown" Reality. Without giving away any "secrets," I can write that on both occasions Seth discussed the subject in conjunction with his postulates about ideals, myths, religion, probabilities, and the simultaneous nature of time.)

APENDIX 15
(For Session 710)

(Today we read a long treatise on the "truths" advocated by "holy men" associated with various Eastern religious philosophies—Hinduism, Buddhism, Taoism, and so forth. Jane's quick and impassioned response through her own writing, as presented below, reflects feelings deeply rooted within her mystical nature, and also illuminates important aspects of the body and direction of the Seth material as a whole. Given those points, she's bound to have differences of belief with other views of reality.

(Yet I think more is involved than choosing among the belief systems offered by Eastern or Western cultures, for instance—that is, in more basic terms each personality would make that kind of choice before physical birth, with the full understanding of the vast influence such a decision would have upon a life's work. Obviously, in those terms of linear time, Jane and I each feel that we chose our present environments.

(Being individualists, then, as I wrote in the Introductory Notes for Volume 1, we don't concentrate upon whatever parallels exist between Seth's concepts on the one hand and those of Eastern religious, philosophical, and mystical doctrines on the other; while we know of such similarities, we're just as aware of how different from them Seth's viewpoint can be, too. I added that even though we have no interest in putting down other approaches to inner reality, still we're firm believers in the "inviolate nature of the individual consciousness, before, during, and after physical existence, in ordinary terms."[1] So, here, we leave it up to the reader to make the intuitive and overt connections between Seth's philosophy and the material Jane wrote today. The interested reader will also be able to compare her composition with certain passages in her long poem, Dialogues of the Soul and Mortal Self in Time, *when that work is published in book form in September 1975.*

(Thus Jane demanded in her composition of this afternoon, October 7, 1974:)

"What is this passion for nonbeing, this denial of sensual life, that drives so many gurus and self-proclaimed prophets? They speak out against desire while propelled by the overwhelming desire to lose themselves. They luxuriate in a kind of cosmic masturbation, titillating their psychic organisms into pitches of mindless excitement; cavorting in orgasms of self-surrender. They bask in a sort of universal steam bath that drives all impurities of individuality or creativity from their souls, leaving them immersed, supposedly forever, in a bliss beyond description; in which, indeed, their own experience disappears.

"Thank God that some god managed to disentangle itself from such psychic oneness, if that's what it's supposed to be. Thank God that some god loved itself enough to diversify, to create itself in a million different forms; to multiply, to explode its being inward and outward. Thank God that some god loved its own individuality enough to endow the least and the most, the greatest and the smallest, with its own unique being.

"The gurus say: 'Give it all up.' One of those we read about today counsels: 'When you want to do one thing, do another instead. Do not do what you want to do, but what you should do.' Never trust the self that you are, the gurus say, but the self that you should be. And that self is supposed to be dead to desire, beyond wanting or caring; yet paradoxically, this nonfeeling leads to bliss. The gurus say that All That Is is within you, yet tell you not to trust yourself. If All That Is didn't want appearances, we wouldn't experience any! Yet appearances, the gurus say, are untruths, changing and therefore false.[2]

"Is my body an appearance, hence an untruth amid the truth which is changeless? Ah dear body, then, how lovely and blessed your untruth, which is sensate and feels desire through the hollowest of bones. How blessed, bodies, leaping alive from the microscopic molecules that combine to walk down the autumn streets; assemble to form the sweet senses' discrimination that perceives, for a time, the precise joy and unity of even one passing afternoon. The body's untruth, then, is holier than all truths, and if the body is an untruth then I hereby proclaim untruth, and truth and all the gurus' truths as lies.

"God knows itself through the flesh. God may know itself through a million or a thousand million other worlds, as so may I— but because this world *is,* and because I am alive in it, it is more than appearance, more than a shackle to be thrown aside. It is a privilege to be here, to look out with this unique focus, with these individual eyes; not to be blinded by cosmic vision, but to see this corner of reality which I form through the miraculous connections of soul and flesh.

"Cherish the gifts of the gods. Don't be so anxious to throw your individuality back into their faces, saying, 'I'm sick to death of myself and of my individuality; it burdens me.' Even one squirrel's consciousness, suddenly thrown into the body of another of its kind, would feel a sense of loss, encounter a strangeness, and know in the sacredness of its being that something was wrong. Wear your individuality proudly. It is the badge of your godhood. You are a god living a life—being, desiring, creating. Through honoring yourself, you honor whatever it is God is, and become a conscious co-creator."

NOTES: Appendix 15

1. In Volume 1 of *"Unknown" Reality*, see the material on Jane, mysticism, and religion in the Introductory Notes, the 679th session, and Appendix 1 for that session. In that first appendix, the notes on Jane as an "independent mystic" (despite her denial that she even thinks of herself as a mystic), are especially appropriate here.

2. From any of Seth's books—let alone Jane's—I could cite a number of comments that question much of the thinking behind different Eastern systems of religious thought. Seth, for example, in the 642nd session in Chapter 11 of *Personal Reality:* "You will not attain spirituality or even a happy life by denying the wisdom and experience of the flesh. You can learn more from watching the animals that you can from a guru or a minister—or from reading my book. But first you must divest yourself of the idea that your creaturehood is suspect. Your humanness did not emerge by refusing your animal heritage, but upon an extension of it."

For ourselves, and even considering Seth's concept of "camouflage" (in Volume 1, see Note 3 for Appendix 11), Jane and I certainly believe that our physical existences and mental experiences are quite "real" in themselves. We could easily take a book to present the reasons for our particular beliefs, examining them in connection with both Eastern and Western religious philosophies. A good general question, we think, and one we'd like to see discussed with our own ideas of the inviolate nature of the individual in mind, has to do with the prevalence of ordinary, daily, conscious-mind thinking and perception throughout much of the world. In historical terms this situation has always existed for the human species; and we think it applies almost equally in Eastern lands, especially among the political leaders and ruling classes within them.

Yet Buddhist belief, for instance, maintains that our perception of the world is not fundamental, but an illusion; our "ignorance" of this basic undifferentiated "suchness" then results in the division of reality into objects and ideas. But why call our generalized awareness an illusion, instead of regarding it as one of the innumerable manifestations that reality takes? No one is free of certain minimum physical needs or of self-oriented thought, I remarked to Jane recently, and each nation strives to expand its technological base no matter what its philosophy may be. Would a widespread use of Eastern religious doctrines be more practical on our earth today, or the kind of self-knowledge Seth advocates? Even given their undeniable accomplishments, why didn't the Eastern countries create ages ago the immortal societies that could have served as models for those of the West to emulate—cultures and/or nations in which all the mundane human vicissitudes (in those terms) had been long understood and abolished: war, crime, poverty, ignorance, and disease?

Certainly the species must be putting its conscious activities to long-term use, however, even with the endless conflicts and questions that grow out of such behavior. During the many centuries of our remembered history, those conflicts in themselves have been—and are—surely serving at least one of consciousness's overall purposes, within our limits of understanding: to know itself more fully in those particular, differentiated ways.

APPENDIX 16
(For Session 711)

(In the opening notes for the 711th session, I referred to Seth's deliveries in ESP class on the previous evening, October 8, 1974. When Jane and I received the transcript of his material at next week's class, we saw that it ran to five single-spaced typewritten pages. Seth talked about many things, but his remarks here, as I've put them together, mainly concerned a subject he'd first discussed with members of class just a week ago [on October 1][1] —the "city" they could start building in their individual and collective dream states:)

There is much I have not told you about your city, for you will have to discover it for yourselves. I am merely encouraging you to focus your joint energies in that direction . . . You will be dealing with symbols, yet you will learn that symbols are reality, for you are symbols of yourselves that live and speak. You do not think of yourselves as symbols [but] there is no symbol that does not have its individual life.

I speak to you of other theoretical realities. I challenge you now to be as creative in another reality as you are in this one. And if it seems to you, because of your beliefs, that you are limited here, then I joyfully challenge each of you to create a city, an environment, and perhaps a world, in which no such limitations occur. What kind of world would you create?

I speak to you from the known and unknown desire that gives you your own birth, and that speaks to you from the tiniest, least-acknowledged thought that flies like a pigeon within your skull . . . And in this moment of your reality, and in the desire of your being, do you even create All That Is. Bow down before no man, no woman, and no belief—but know you are indeed the creators.

For some of you the city will have a theater. For some of you it will not. For those of you who like theater, it will be like none you have ever seen. In it the actors and actresses will take the parts of beliefs—of fleshed beliefs—and the morality play, so to speak, will deal with the nature of beliefs and how they are enacted through the centuries as well as through the hours. That theater then will serve many purposes, even as each of you are exquisite performers, and have chosen the roles and beliefs that you have taken . . .

Now there are books programming out-of-body activity; millions of you are told that when you leave your body you will meet this demon or that demon, or this or that angry god. So, instead, we will form a free city to which those travelers can come, and where those who enter can read books about Buddhism if they prefer, or play at being Catholic. There will also be certain beloved traps set about the city, that will be of an enlightening nature . . . Now listen: You think there is nothing intrinsically impossible about building a platform in [your] space . . . I am suggesting, then, a platform in inner reality. It is as valid—far more valid—as an orbiting city in the sky, in physical terms, and it challenges your creative abilities much more. You need a good challenge—it is fun! Not because you <u>should</u> do it, but because you <u>desire</u> it . . . It is a great creative challenge that you can throw down to yourselves from your future selves.

(*In answer to a question from a student:*) A beloved trap is one that you set for yourself. And so our city will be full of them. When you are tired of playing a Catholic priest, for example, you will fall into your own trap—in which your beliefs [as such a one] are suddenly worked out to their logical perfection, and you see what they mean.

Now when children walk down streets, they count the cracks in the sidewalks. And so our city will have its own kind of tricky walks! There will be sidewalks within, and above and below sidewalks. But it is for each individual to decide which one he or she will follow. When Ruburt (*as Seth calls Jane*) was a young girl he wrote a poem in which he declares:

> You make your own sidewalk,
> And I make my own sidewalk.[2]

And so our city will simply have alternate sidewalks, and they will be beloved traps, set by each self.

I feel no great responsibility for any of your beings. [If I did] then I would be denying you your own power, and therefore seemingly building my own . . . I am here because I enjoy it. I am a teacher, and because I am a teacher I love to teach. A person who loves to teach needs people who love to learn. That is why I am here and why you are here . . . My view of reality is different from your own, and that is fine, and so I can teach. A true teacher allows you to learn from yourself. I enjoy the great vitality and exuberance of your reality, and our city will have joy and exuberance. Now joy sounds quite acceptable, but (*with amusement*) our city will also have fun— which in many spiritual circles is <u>not</u> so acceptable!

(*In that class session Seth had much more to say about the dream city. Because of the individual freedom of creation implied in the city's very existence, and in Jane's early poem in Note 2, I'll close this appendix with another of her verses. This one is from an even earlier poem,* Lorrylo, *written when she was but 15 years old:)*

> *I am the daughter of the wind,*
> *I am the vagabond of time.*
> *I am a spirit, unleashed and free,*
> *Foster child of infinity.*

NOTES: Appendix 16

1. "You can colonize an entire inner level of reality," Seth told that October 1st class. "To do so, you must give your best with dedication and joyful creativity. This will not be an imaginary city. It will have a greater reality than any physical city that you know, and it can, in its own way, shine with brighter lights in inner reality than any nighttime city displays. There, I hope, you will work at developing skills, in terms of the dream-art scientist *(for instance; see Session 700 in Volume 1 of* 'Unknown' Reality*),* and learn other professions than the ones you now know."

2. Seth didn't quote Jane's little poem exactly from 26 years ago, but paraphrased it. It's called *Echo,* and Jane wrote it in 1948, when she was 19 years old. Once again in an early work we see clear signs of the Seth material to come (in 1963). *Echo* begins:

> *I stand upon a block*
> *of stillness.*
> *It is more secure*
> *than any sidewalk.*
> *I bring with me*
> *My own sidewalk . . .*

APPENDIX 17
(For Session 711)

(*I started this appendix 13 months after the 711th session was held. Jane and I have seldom been concerned with trying for strict definitions of qualities like "altered states of consciousness." All of us experience such altered states of consciousness often throughout each day, so the phrase itself should hardly mean anything mysterious—even though others usually look at Jane or me questioningly if either of us uses it in conversation.*

(*Jane, for instance, hasn't had her brain waves formally recorded by an EEG, or electroencephalograph. It's not that she's against that procedure— just that she's much more interested in what she* feels *and* does *than she is in the mechanical records offered by the machine.*

(*There are four recognized [electrical] brain waves, and in speed they range upward from 0 to 26 and more Hertz units, or cycles per second. These rhythms can vary somewhat, and are best thought of as areas of activity. Brain waves overlap. Very simply, delta brain waves are connected with dreamless sleep, theta with creativity and dreams, alpha with a relaxed alertness and changing consciousness; beta—the fastest—with concentration, and with an intense focus upon all of the challenges [and anxieties and stresses, many would say] faced in the ordinary daily world.*

(*Even if beta waves, then, seem to be the "official pulses" of our civilization [to use Seth's phrase from a session that will be quoted in part below], still Jane and I wonder: When aren't we actually in a state of altered consciousness? For no matter which brain rhythm may predominate at any time, that state is certainly an altered one in relation to the other three. But more than this, why not call all actions of the brain "altered" when compared to Seth's concept of the individual personality's whole self, or entity?*[1]

(*We read that in ordinary terms highly creative people [like Jane] usually generate large amounts of theta and low-alpha waves pretty constantly while doing their thing. Measuring and recording brain waves is a complicated task, however; not only is it important which areas or lobes of the brain are monitored—if not all of them—but because of the mechanical limitations of the EEG itself much that goes on in the brain is necessarily missed. In addition, the two hemispheres of the individual brain often show variations in electrical energy states. But most importantly, we think, while the EEG can indicate broad categories of brain activity, it can hardly probe the participant's very individual and subjective content of mind within this camouflage [physical] reality. Nor at this time, given the minimum premise that Jane's speaking for Seth constitutes any indication of "paranormal" activity, do we think that her performance could be identified as such* per se *on the graphs of her brain waves.*

The state of "EEG art" isn't that advanced yet [if it ever will be]. Presumably, however, when speaking for Seth, Jane would show definite changes in all frequency areas in both hemispheres, with the theta and delta ranges altered the most. We also think that her EEG readings would vary once again when she spoke or sang in Sumari, her trance "language."

(Our curiosity about such speculations led me to plan this appendix shortly after the 711th session was held, and I asked Jane if Seth could eventually offer some insights about the brain's electrical reality. He finished dictating Volume 2 of "Unknown" Reality in April 1975, and we finally got around to the session I wanted six and a half months later.

(Seth did give much unexpected material about the brain—and about his own reality, incidentally—but the session turned out to be so long and closely interrelated that I found it very difficult to excerpt; most of the portions I picked out were left hanging, or were too incomplete. Naturally, Seth said what he said from his own viewpoint. I ended up choosing the few quotations gathered together here just to indicate the direction of the information, while hoping that the entire session, with others promised on the subject by Seth, will be published some day.

(From the 760th session for November 10, 1975:)

The beta waves quicken. They seem to be the official pulses of your civilization, giving precedence to official reality, but you have little idea that the psyche is <u>inherently</u> able to seek its conscious experience from all of the known ranges, according to the kind of experience chosen at any given "time."

Beta was not meant to carry the full weight of conscious activity, however, although its accelerating qualities can lead to initiations into "higher" realms of consciousness, where indeed the brain waves quicken. The other patterns *(delta, theta, and alpha)* are highly important to physical and mental stability, being very interwound with cellular consciousness. In cases usually called schizophrenic, the beta acceleration is not supported by the stabilizing attributes of the other known frequencies.

It is possible, then, for a brain to register all of the known patterns at once, though your machines would note only the predominating rhythm.

A kind of inverted beta pattern, difficult to describe, often appears suddenly in the midst of the other ranges, <u>driving through</u> them, accelerating consciousness to a high degree of creativity. The brain waves as they are known are separately registered segments of a greater "whole" kind of consciousness, and your machines are just as segmented, perceiving only those patterns [they were designed to recognize]. Other activity escapes them. They cannot note the rapidity with which you move through all of the known patterns constantly. This behavior can be learned by anyone willing to take the time and effort. Some courage would also help.

I told you that you flashed in and out of the reality that you know.[2] In between one moment and the next of the waking day, there are, in your terms, long delta and theta waves that you cannot recognize. They are not recorded by your machines because quite literally they go in a different, "unofficial" direction. Each official waking brain wave is a peak in your world of a far deeper "wave" of other experience, and represents your points of continuity.

Each beta wave rides atop the other patterns. In normal sleep, the "conscious" wave rides beneath the others, with the face of consciousness turned inward, so to speak. All the recognized characteristics of consciousness are "inverted," probing other realities than the one you know. They are quite effective and lightning fast. In sleep the beta waves are not turned off—the "conscious" part of you, with its beta rhythms, is elsewhere.

In these sessions the full range of brain waves is utilized as you understand them. Here, in a highly creative, disciplined, and yet spontaneous performance, a situation is set up in which knowledge is obtained from the known frequencies, combined so that consciousness can use itself more fully, reaching into many areas closed to one range of consciousness alone. The various diverse, unique characteristics of each level of awareness are given play. In a way this is like an accelerated, chosen, well-organized "conscious" dream venture, in which Ruburt travels through mediums of consciousness until finally he, still being himself, is nevertheless no longer himself (humorously), but me.

He is combining and alternating frequencies so that he literally brings forth a different creature of consciousness—one that in your terms is not alive, yet one whose very reality straddles the life that you know. The most elemental portions of my reality begin at the furthest reaches of your own.

In sleep your ordinary brain waves as you understand them register a chaotic jungle of experience not normally processed. Biologically or psychically, there is little need for such disorientation. The normal waking consciousness, with its characteristic patterns, can indeed follow [into sleep]. A mixture of brain waves would result. Consciousness as you think of it expands tremendously under such conditions. You would follow your own pattern of continuity and understanding, weaving this into the sleep and dream states, forming a "new" pattern that triumphantly combines all, as to some extent this occurs in our sessions.

In an ideal society, each brain wave would be utilized

purposefully. You would go to sleep to solve certain problems . . .
There is an overall general difference, nationally speaking—that is,
people of various nations do differ to some extent in their prevalent
brain frequencies . . . All in all, however, the beta has predominated, and been expected to solve many problems unsuited to its
own characteristics.

Despite your reliance upon one range only, your world of
consciousness draws heavily upon all of the known wave patterns,
and from others of which you are unaware. For now that is the end of
this material, though I will continue it at any time at your request.

NOTES: Appendix 17

     1. See Seth's definition of the entity as given in Chapter 5 of *The
Seth Material.*

     2. In Volume 1 of *"Unknown" Reality*, see Session 684 after
10:07, as well as Note 3.

APPENDIX 18
(For Session 711)

(I'll open this appendix by referring to a pair of short notes I wrote for Volume 1 of "Unknown" Reality. First, Note 6 for Session 686: "We're still acquiring information about the psychic connections between Jane and Seth, of course. Even now, more than 10 years after Jane began speaking for Seth, one might say that each session we hold represents another step in this learning process; we fully expect it to continue as long as the sessions do." Then, Note 3 for the 688th session contains my statement that in an appendix for Session 711, "I assemble from various sessions information on the complex relationships involving Jane-Ruburt-Seth [and also Rob-Joseph]."

(Sometimes, though, I find it quite a challenge to excerpt a number of sessions to illuminate a particular one. I want the passages chosen to make sense on their own, out of context, and to focus clearly on the subject; at the same time, I don't want to include too many or too few of my own notes. But in this appendix, at least, I discovered that it wasn't always possible to achieve both of those goals just as I wanted to—not in connection with each point mentioned. It also became inevitable that at least some elements of Seth's own "separate-but-connected" reality would have to be considered. In addition to those concerns, on occasion I found myself rearranging the quoted discussions a bit—although really to a minor degree—for even greater brevity and clarity. So here's how it all worked out:

(This appendix was inspired by two blocks of material Seth covered in the 711th session: Jane's hearing his voice recently in the sleep state [see her own notes at the start of the 710th session], and the bridge personality she and Seth have created "between dimensions," or between themselves.

(I finally decided that the best way to present the variety of material desired, whether from Seth, Jane, or myself, was in chronological order, letting a composite picture emerge as the work progresses. This system automatically makes room for any references in Volume 1. In actuality the chronology begins long before "Unknown" Reality was started, and continues well beyond the date of its ending, in April 1975. Since the excerpts are still more representative than complete, however, due to the accumulated mass of information available, my own choices enter in: ESP class data are quoted a number of times; included is material summarizing Jane's own theories about the Seth phenomena, as she worked them out in her recently completed Adventures in Consciousness; *but reincarnation, while mentioned often, isn't stressed in terms of particulars— that is, I refer to Seth's statements that he, Jane and I led closely involved lives in Denmark in the 1600's, but those lives aren't studied* per se. *Within our ordinary context of linear time I think of reincarnation, even though in Seth's*

terms it's really a simultaneous phenomenon, as being further away, or more removed, from us physical creatures than the more "immediate" psychic connections and mechanics I want to show as linking Seth, Jane, and myself. And also because of that sense of removal, Seth Two[1] is hardly mentioned at all.

(Perhaps I put this appendix together as I did partly because Jane herself isn't much turned on by reincarnational concepts, although she does like the way Seth insists upon the unlimited attributes of each personality; and within such a "simultaneous" framework there's plenty of room for probable selves, reincarnational selves, and [added later] counterpart selves.[2]

(Seth began talking about his connections with Ruburt-Jane—and, therefore, himself and his own reality—almost from the time these sessions began on December 2, 1963. Such relationships were of great interest to us as we sought to understand the blossoming of Jane's psychic abilities. They still are. Every bit of information helped, although often in the beginning I didn't know enough to follow up answers with more questions. As the sessions multiplied, however, this became more and more difficult to do: There was a steadily widening pool of material to ask questions about!

(I'll begin our chronology by reminding the reader that Note 6 for Session 711 contains a description of how, through the Ouija board, Seth announced himself by that name in the 4th session for December 8. [Note 6 also includes his reasoning about names, as given a decade later.]

(Then, in the 6th session Seth's answer to my question: "Do you have a last name?" couldn't have been more precise: "No." I still think his reply has its own kind of wit, even though it came to us through the board.[3]

(Speaking of names, this is the time to remind all that Seth calls both Jane and me by male names: Ruburt and Joseph. Why does he speak of Jane as a male—and so as "he" and "him?" In Note 6 for Session 679, in Volume 1, I quoted Seth from the 12th session for January 2, 1964:) Sex, regardless of all your fleshy tales, is a psychic phenomenon, merely certain qualities which you call male and female. The qualities are real, however, and permeate other planes as well as your own. They are opposites which are nevertheless complementary, and which merge into one. When I say as I have that the overall entity [or whole self] is neither male nor female, and yet refer to [some] entities by definite male names such as "Ruburt" and "Joseph," I merely mean that in the overall essence, the [given] entity identifies itself more with the so-called male characteristics than with the female.

(Sessions 12 through 15 are briefly quoted in Note 4 for the 680th session, in Volume 1; Seth remarked upon the impossibility of closed systems, his own senses [including something of their limits], his ability to visit other "planes" of reality, and his "incipient" man's form.

(However, from Session 14 [for January 8, 1964], there's other material that can be given here, as well as some that makes an interesting note

at the end of this appendix.[4] *First, from my own note at 11:05: "Jane said that Seth was quite pleased with the new voice, and that she now knows what he's thinking sometimes, even though he doesn't relay it to or through her as part of a message."*

(Then from Seth himself:) In one sense meeting with you costs me little energy, it is true. On the other hand the effort to communicate explanations does involve a very real endeavor on my part. And so you are not the only ones who grow weary in this respect. As I have said, feeling is action, and in my communications to you feeling plays a strong part.

(Nor did Seth agree with Jane's assessment of her reactions to her Seth voice. He was very outspoken—yet his material came through with a much lighter touch than these printed words alone can indicate:) . . . Ruburt's voice sounds rather dreary in this transitional phase, [yet] the one thing that pleases me immensely is the way he can translate at least a few of my humorous remarks and the inflections of my natural speech . . . As a man's voice I fear he will sound rather unmelodious. I do not have the voice of an angel by any means, but neither do I sound like an asexual eunuch, which is all I've been able to make him sound like all night. And incidentally, Ruburt, you were a good brother at one time. The so-called male aspect of your personality has always been strong, but by this I mean powerful. Without the loyalty that you are learning as a woman, your character had many defects—and there, I said I would not get into anything serious.

(Then to me, later yet in the session:) . . . and as a woman [when I knew you], you certainly put your present wife to shame as far as vanity was concerned!

(From the 22nd session for February 4, 1964:) I have never trusted the written word half as much as I trust the spoken word, and on your plane it is difficult to trust either. But I do not feel that I could be myself as easily by means of automatic writing, for example. I do not mind speaking through Ruburt's mouth—somehow the sound of the words is rather pleasant. But seeing myself transformed more or less into plain black and white words on a sheet of paper seems dull and uninteresting. And I have always enjoyed conversation, which is the liveliest of all arts. . .

Because Ruburt deals in words [as a writer], it is easy for me to communicate in this manner. That is, he automatically translates inner data given by me into coherent, valid, and faithful camouflage[5] patterns—into words. My information is not actually given as sound. Its transference is instantaneous on Ruburt's part, and is performed through the workings of the mind, the inner senses,[6] and the brain.

(In Note 3 for the 688th session, in Volume 1, I quoted my own note from the 24th session for February 10, 1964: I described how Jane could sense the whole of whatever concept Seth was discussing—and how, since such a structure was too much for her to handle at once, she could feel Seth "withdrawing it, to release it to her a little at a time in the form of connected words."

(Then Seth himself continued in that 24th session:) Concepts fit together in patterns. In order for there to be communication between us I must disentangle a concept from its pattern, which is somewhat difficult. It is somewhat like having to free a particular word from a strong emotional association. I experience patterns made up of concepts, and you use words in associations.

When I speak through Ruburt I must disentangle the concept. This sometimes leaves me with short ends, because it is natural for me to experience the concepts in their entirety; and yet I must drop very important data by the wayside because you are not capable of handling it, except in consecutive form. I <u>feel</u> concept patterns.[7]

(From the 27th session for February 19, 1964:) There is so much I want to say. When your training is further advanced, <u>much</u> further advanced, we may be able to take certain shortcuts. It is difficult for me to have to string out this material in words, and for you to record it. You see, it is possible in theory for you to experience directly a concept-essence of the material in any given night's session.[8]

As for another advancement made, besides dispensing with the material [Ouija] board, Ruburt has achieved a state in which he can receive inner data from me more readily. But beyond this, he is now able in some small way to contact me . . .

One reason for the success of our communications is the peculiar abilities in you both and the interaction between them, and the use that you allow me to make of them. Ruburt's intellect had to be of high quality. His conscious and unconscious mind had to be acquainted with certain ideas to begin with, in order for the complexity of this material to come through.

In the beginning, for example, there is always a distortion of material by the person who receives it, at least on the topmost subconscious level. So an individual whose personal prejudices are at a minimum is excellent. If, for example, Ruburt's prejudices happen to lie along lines which do not contradict what I know to be true, then all the better, and there is much less resistance.

Information like this <u>is</u> sifted through many layers of subconscious conception, and is subsequently colored. People believing in your organized religions color it in a manner that is highly disadvantageous, and that unfortunately adds to existing superstitions. Ruburt's mind, believe it or not, is much like my own— though, if you'll forgive me, in a very limited fashion. Therefore the distortions are much less distortive, much less harmful, and more easily discovered and cleared... Others less perfectionist than myself are content with more distortion. I am not. Ruburt's *Idea Construction*[9] was rather amazing. The inner senses provided him with much, but nevertheless the ideas contained in it represented an achievement of the conscious mind. I was drawn by this to realize that he was ready for me.

(*To me, later in the session and with much humor:*) You had no problems with parents in the past—and, my dear Yo-Yo, you were an excellent father to me at one time, and if I may say so, at one time I was an excellent father to you. As a son you were helpful, considerate, and kind.

To me this [reincarnational and family material] is all so obvious that I almost hesitate to mention it, but this is because I tend to forget what human existence on your plane actually involves. . .

And now, most devoted friends, a fond good evening. I will always help you to the best of my ability, and as far as I know I will be accessible for your present lifetimes.[10] And my dear Joseph, if you whacked me many times, I got my blows in too. And I made Ruburt one lovely wife—so there, my lovelies.

(*From the 28th session for February 24, 1964:*) As far as Ruburt is concerned, there is no danger [to him in these sessions]. For one thing, I am an extremely sensitive but disciplined, and sensible if somewhat irascible, gentleman, if you will forgive the term. None of the communications from me have been in any way conducive to a development toward mental or emotional instability. (*Smiling:*) I may make bold to remark that I am more stable than you or Ruburt, or your fine psychologist [who just wrote to you].[11]

I also do not take my responsibility lightly, and to a great degree I feel responsible for you, and for any results coming from your communications with me. If anything, the personal advice I have given you both should add to your mental and emotional balance, and result in a stronger relationship with the outside world.

I do depend upon Ruburt's willingness to dissociate.[12] There is no doubt that at times he is unaware of his surroundings during a session. However, this is no more binding upon him than autosuggestion. It is a phenomenon in which he gives consent, and he could, at any time and in a split second, return his conscious attention upon his physical environment.

There is no danger, and I will repeat this: There is no danger of dissociation grabbing ahold of him like some black, vague and furry monster, carrying him away to the netherlands of hysteria, schizophrenia, or insanity... Withdrawal into dissociation as a hiding place from the world could, of course, have dire consequences. Certain personalities could, and have, fallen prey here, but with you, with Ruburt, this is not the case.

Also, Ruburt has experienced and used dissociation, though to a lesser degree, before our communications—that is, in his work—and knows how to handle it.

We have gone into this before, and I have no doubt that we will on endless occasions. And if I succeed in convincing you of my reality as a personality, I will have done extremely well ... Ruburt's subconscious has enough camouflage pattern to enable me to make contact, but not so much as to distort me out of all recognition. I am not his subconscious, though I speak through it. It is the atmosphere through which I can come to you, as the air is the atmosphere through which the bird flies. A certain reassembly of myself is necessary when I enter your plane, and this is done partially by myself, and by the combined subconscious efforts of you, Joseph, and Ruburt. Will this satisfy you for now?

("Sure, Seth," I said, agreeing with the implication that Jane and I would want the same material discussed again—and again. [13] *)*

... and Ruburt did get a rather embarrassing flash from me before the session. I blush to admit the fact, but at one time I did call you Yo-Yo *(see the excerpts for the 27th session.*

("When did you call me that, Seth?")

I called you Yo-Yo when you were my father, and I am not going into any reincarnational material tonight.

(From the 33rd session for March 9, 1964:) I do not bring about the trance state in the manner of which you [Joseph] are speaking. Ruburt switches on another channel, through which my essence can enter more readily. This certainly does involve a looking inward on his part, but it is not self-hypnosis in usual terms—merely a focusing upon an objective inner stimulus ... Any such signs *(as the powerful, deeper Seth voice)* involve camouflage patterns, and do not actually represent direct experience. This is not my voice, for example. It is a representation or approximation of my voice for your edification. Furthermore, in your terms I do not have a voice. But it is a valid representation, and if I say so myself—that's a pun— the voice is much like the one I would use. ....

(From the 49th session for April 29, 1964:) It is much better in the long run to quietly and cautiously advance [in these sessions]. I

am not the Holy Ghost. I do not require or demand the vows of poverty, obedience, and certainly not chastity. I will at all times demand integrity, and perhaps when all is said and done that is my only requirement. *(Then to a friend of a friend of ours—both were present, and among the few to witness a session up to that time:)* Excess enthusiasm can lead to fanaticism, and this at all costs must be avoided.

(From the 54th session for May 18, 1964:) Your Ruburt was, indeed, Seth . . . I have promised to give you more material dealing with the psychic construction of the entity, and its relationship with its various [physical] personalities. In the beginning, I could not tell you in so many words that Ruburt is myself, because you would have leaped to the conclusion that I was Ruburt's subconscious mind, and this is not so.

Ruburt is not myself now, in his present life. He is nevertheless an extension and materialization of the Seth that I was at one time. Nothing remains unchanging, entities and personalities least of all. You cannot stop them in time . . . I am Seth today. I keep my continuity but I change, and offshoots like currents explode into being. Ruburt was myself, Seth, many centuries ago, but he grew, evolved, and expanded in terms of a particular personal set of value fulfillments. He is now a personality that was one of the probable personalities[14] into which Seth could grow. I represent another. I am another.

To make it simpler, we split—this being necessary always so that various possibilities can be brought into action . . . Yet we are bound together, and no invasion [of Ruburt] occurs because in one way of speaking our psychic territory is the same.

(From the 58th session for June 1, 1964:) Ruburt and myself are offshoots of the same entity. The difference in time is but a camouflage distortion. The entity was a particularly strong one, and many of its egos have made the decision to turn into entities . . . And now, my dear patient Joseph, may I tell you that you are also part of that same entity—and this is one of the reasons why I am able to communicate with you both.

(From the 82nd session for August 27, 1964:) When man realizes that he creates his own image now, he will not find it so startling to believe that he creates other images in other times. Only after such a basis [is established] will the idea of reincarnation achieve its natural validity, and only when it is understood that the subconscious, certain layers of it, is a link between the present personality and past ones, will the theory of reincarnation be accepted as fact.

(From the 83rd session for August 31, 1964:) Man sees not even

half of the whole entity which is himself. It is true that on this journey [with the sessions] discipline, some caution and understanding, and much courage, is demanded. This is as it should be. I am helping you in this . . . You are both *(meaning Jane and me)* peculiarly suited for such a pursuit, with a combination of intuitiveness, basic psychic facility, and yet integrated inner identities . . . I also want to add that I am <u>not</u> a control, as mediums speak of controls. I am not, as I believe I have mentioned, a secondary or split personality of Ruburt's. For example, I am not a conglomeration of male tendencies that have collected themselves into a subsidiary personality that struggles for recognition or release. I say that I am an energy personality essence, since that is what I am . . . My name for him is Ruburt,[15] which happens to be a male name simply because it is the closest translation, in your terms, for the name of the whole self or entity of which he is now a self-conscious part.

(*From the 119th session for January 6, 1965:*) Ruburt should learn much of advantage from the book by Jung[16] which he is reading. And I would like to mention here that I am not <u>Jane's</u> animus . . . Nor could I possibly live up to Jane's animus. I use the name "Jane" here rather than "Ruburt" because the animus belongs to Jane and to the present personality. Talk about reflections—because <u>Ruburt</u> has an anima![17]

Scientists have glimpsed the complications of the human body. They have scarcely glimpsed the complicated realities of the mind.

(Jane's account of "a year of testing" Seth's [and her own] psychic abilities is given in chapters 6 through 8 of The Seth Material. *The tests began with the 179th session for August 18, 1965, and finally ended with the 310th session for January 9, 1967, although actually most of them were held during the year following their inception. All that work can't be described here, but we accomplished our main goal: exploring from new angles the relationships involving Jane, Seth, and our physical [camouflage] reality.*

(The tests concerned two main approaches. The first, for our own study, was for Seth to describe objects thoroughly sealed in double envelopes; the envelopes were prepared [unknown to Jane, of course] by myself and by others. The second was for Seth to give long-distance impressions on a regular basis about the reality of an eminent, elderly psychologist at an Eastern university. We met "Dr. Instream," as Jane called him in The Seth Material, *but once, a few weeks after I'd written him in the spring of 1965 about Jane's growing psychic abilities. Seth conducted 83 envelope tests for Jane and me, and within a concentrated period of nine months during that "year of testing," gave impressions for Dr. Instream on 75 occasions; those I mailed to the doctor as they*

came through.[18] *Often both tests were held during each of our twice-weekly sessions.*

(Here's what Seth said after that first, only moderately successful envelope test had taken place in the 179th session:) We are dealing here with something rather unusual *(the tests),* in that we are attempting to permit two personalities to exist side by side, so to speak. Ruburt is not in a deep trance state. I do not supersede his own personality. He <u>allows</u> me, in our sessions, to coexist with himself.

A deeper trance state would allow us to get less distorted information on such a test as this, initially, but our results will improve, and such experiments will be helpful in that the various layers of the two personalities, Ruburt's and my own, will be seen in their operating procedures.

Ruburt will learn very quickly through such practice . . . The distortions that appeared are most helpful, in that they allow Ruburt to differentiate between my own communications and his own thoughts.

(From the 180th session for August 23, 1965:) Tonight's *(second envelope)* test dealt with clairvoyance—I happened to pick up my information that way, although it could just as easily have been obtained through telepathic communication.[19] In the future, tests will be worked out in whatever manner is needed.

I myself operate well clairvoyantly . . . for my own reasons and peculiarities, and usually obtain such information [in that manner]. We will have much to say concerning the ways in which that kind of material is received and interpreted, as this is very important.

(From the 211th session for November 24, 1965:) First of all, as far as the hands are concerned, to be left- or right-handed has to do with inner mechanisms and brain patterns that come first, before the motions of the hands. Characteristically I operated in certain manners that resulted in the primary use of my left hand, when I was focused within physical matter.

Now and then with Ruburt, when I am allowed to manifest myself to a smaller or lesser degree, my own habits therefore show through, for I manipulate his muscles in a different way than he does. But, scientifically, this would not be proof of my existence as an independent personality who has survived physical death. Not that this concerns me, for it does not . . . Or, if you are thinking in terms of secondary personalities,[20] you can prove nothing one way or another. A secondary personality could indeed use gestures that are different [from Ruburt's]. Either way, this would be no proof as to my independent nature. *(With humor:)* I am glad to see that it has been bothering you. You have had a good think session!

    (Seth came through with this material, including his jocular closing remarks, because a good friend of ours had asked many questions as he witnessed the session—one of them being why the right-handed Jane gestured mainly with her left hand while speaking in trance. I hadn't noticed this mannerism.

    (It's of interest to add that as far as she knows Jane was born right-handed, yet does recall her mother saying that she [Jane] was originally left-handed and had been taught to switch handedness. Jane is sure she wasn't compelled to do so in school, say. At the same time, she laughed, in early grades she had much trouble learning to salute the flag with her right hand; she repeatedly used her left hand until she "learned better."

    (Incidentally, it's been many years since she showed any signs of favoring either hand in trance.

    (From the 242nd session for March 16, 1966:) The ego is not the most powerful or the most knowledgeable portion of the self. It is simply a well-specialized part of the personality, fully equipped to operate under certain circumstances[21] . . . When those conditions no longer exist [after "death"], then other layers of the self take over the dominant position, and the personality realigns its psychological components. The ego does not <u>disappear</u>, however; it merely takes a back seat in some respects, as your own subconscious does during physical existence. The ego is under the control of what may loosely be called "the inner self." The survival or nonphysical personality has somewhat the same relationship to the ego as the dreaming personality has to it in physical life.

    When communication takes place between a survival personality and one who exists within the physical system, this involves a reshuffling on the part of the survival personality, where the ego is momentarily given greater reign . . . If this was not done, then in most cases communication would not be possible, just because the survival personality would have such difficulty <u>impressing</u> the personality who was still ego-oriented within the physical system.

    The nonphysical personality does not think in terms of words, but experiences concepts in a much more direct manner. This sort of thing simply could not be understood by the physically focused individual . . . The survival personality's inner self gives this reassembled ego ideas in the same way that, often, the subconscious gives the ego concepts in physical existence. This reassembled ego then attempts to perceive these insights in terms of <u>sense</u> perceptions, which are sent to the physical individual at the other end. Sometimes the communications are made directly, though they must be sifted through the subconscious of the one who is physical. When that person is trained along these lines, however [as Ruburt is], he or she helps in this process, and a <u>psychological framework, like a bridge</u>,[22] is erected that serves to connect the two personalities.

I speak as my whole self to you . . . since my personality structure is more advanced than is usual for communications from other systems. Therefore, I do not need to adopt a past ego [of my own]. Perhaps because this is not necessary, the psychological bridge <u>is</u> required to make my messages comprehensible to Ruburt. This connecting framework does some of the translating for me that a reassembled ego would do. It delivers information to Ruburt in a way that he can understand. Occasionally [in your tests] I do impress him <u>directly</u>, telepathically *(see Note 19)*, with a concept. When he receives data in the form of images the framework is operating. With <u>my</u> direction, this framework uses Ruburt's personal associations to direct his impressions toward the correct point. Then when we are successful I insert the right information.[23]

I am a comunicator. In our case the control personality, so-called, the psychological framework to which I have referred, is entirely passive, and shall remain so.

(In the 263rd session for May 29, 1966, Seth stated that eventually Jane would be able to entirely dispense with the psychological bridge linking the two of them, but she hasn't attained that situation at this writing.

(From the 398th session for March 11, 1968:) Personalities are not static things. Entities are eternal. They are not as nicely nor as neatly packaged out, one to a body, as your psychologists believe. They constantly change. They grow. They make decisions. They use the physical body fully, or they partially depart according to their own inner needs and development.

When psychic gestalts are formed they are not static. They make different alliances until they find their place in a whole identity that serves their purposes, or are strong enough to become indestructable. They are always <u>becoming</u>. They are not closed units.

(To me [Rob]:) Now I hope you will understand me intuitively, for what I have said [tonight] confounds the intellect to some considerable degree. But I speak through Ruburt, and Ruburt is himself and I am myself, yet without your support of Ruburt I could not speak. This in no way minimizes my reality, or Ruburt's.

(The Seth Two phenomenon began to manifest itself through Jane in the 406th session for April 22, 1968. Seth Two exists in relation to Seth in somewhat the same manner that Seth does to Jane, although that analogy shouldn't be carried very far. Even though deep connections endure among the three, then, at the same time, as I wrote early in this study, Seth Two is too far

"away" from Jane [and the subject matter of this appendix] to go into here. See Note 1.

(Now I'll refer the reader to Chapter 20 of Jane's The Seth Material. *She called the chapter "Personal Evaluations—Who or What is Seth?" In it she made a number of excellent points concerning her relationship with Seth and Seth Two; for example: "If physical life evolves [in ordinary terms], why not consciousness itself?" The questions we had at the time can be found throughout the chapter. Indeed, we still have many of them—or, I should note, we're still intrigued by the latest versions of those "old" questions, for like consciousness itself they're endless in their ramifications. But here I want to call attention mainly to the excerpts in Chapter 20 that Jane presented from the 458th session for January 20, 1969. Seth discussed the psychological bridge Jane and he have created between themselves for purposes of communication; yet most of his material came through in response to my question about his availability to us. "We [Rob and I] both know that some sessions seem more 'immediate' than others, and now as Seth continued we saw why," Jane wrote in Chapter 20. Seth, briefly, from the 458th session:)*

I am, however, automatically a part of the message that I bring to you. At times I am "here" more completely than in other sessions. These reasons often have to do with circumstances usually beyond normal control: electromagnetic conditions, psychological circumstances. These could be considered as atmospheric conditions through which I must travel.

As I have told you, projection is involved to some extent, both on my part and Ruburt's. Your *(Rob's)* own presence is also important, whether or not you are present at any given session . . . Now when you watch, say, educational television, you see the teacher, and he speaks. [Actually] you may be watching a film. But the teacher exists whether or not he is speaking at that time, and his message is legitimate . . . It makes no difference whether or not I am myself speaking through Ruburt now, or whether I did this last night in his sleep, and tonight is a film or playback. Again *(with a smile)*: the medium is the message . . .

This does not mean that I use Ruburt as a puppet, and stuff his mouth with tapes as a recorder, that you are always listening to replays, or that emotionally I am not always with you in sessions. It means that in such multidimensional communications more is involved than you suppose.

(Now here's an excerpt from the 458th session that wasn't *given in Chapter 20. It concerns witnesses asking questions of Seth during a session:)*

It is unfortunate that I must use terms of time to explain all of this to you, but as I told you many sessions ago, my time is not your time *(humorously)* . . . Because you ask specific questions at a specific session, it does not necessarily mean that the program has not been prepared, in your terms, earlier. For on many occasions I will see the questions within your mind, or the minds of your witnesses, and [again in your terms] will therefore answer them ahead of time.

Even on such occasions, however, I look in on you closely . . . to see whether or not my message is coming across clearly, and I also learn.

(Later in Chapter 20 of The Seth Material, *Jane quoted Seth from the 463rd session for February 3, 1969. While discussing the impossibility of any medium being an absolutely clear channel for paranormal knowledge, even when "in a trance as deep as the Atlantic Ocean," Seth had some extremely interesting things to say about the nature of perception in general. Presenting a few sentences from that session here serves two purposes: I can remind the reader of important material, and in Note 24 I can offer some unpublished extensions of it from the next session.)*

Information must be sifted through the layers of the medium's personality. Any perception instantly alters the electromagnetic and neurological systems of the perceiver . . . It is a logistic contradiction to imagine, with your physical systems, that any perception can be received without the perceiver's inner situation being altered. I am trying to make it as clear as possible: Information automatically blends with, is intermingled with, and enmeshed with, the entire physically valid structure of the personality.

Any perception is action; it changes that upon which it acts, and <u>in so doing it is itself changed</u>. The slightest perception alters every atom within your body.[24] This, in turn, sends out its ripples, so that as you know, the most minute action is felt everywhere.

(From here on I'll start occasionally presenting excerpts from a few of the sessions Jane has delivered in her ESP class.[25] I've saved some of this material for a considerable time. More often than not I wasn't present when Seth produced his material, and in all cases it was recorded by students; Jane meets with them on Tuesday evening, when I'm usually occupied typing Monday night's private session [or book material, often] from my own notes.

(Class offers an extremely rich learning environment, for Jane as well as her students. Since in this appendix the focus is primarily upon the relationship involving Jane-Ruburt-Seth, however, I can only write here that many other developments of great interest to us [Jane's Sumari songs and poetry, for instance], had their origins within the class framework.

(From the ESP class session for February 16, 1971:) I [come through so forcefully] for several reasons: because that is the way I am, in the guise that I choose to use in my communications, and to

get everyone over the idea that so-called spirits must be sweet-faced, quiet, sober, and dignified. That, for example, is one of my main concerns. I also want each of you to understand that energy is being used—and that the same energy Ruburt uses is available to each of you.

(With much good humor:) For all of those who have in their deepest, most sacred thoughts, imagined that to be quiet was good and to be dignified was pious, then such a performance as mine should certainly make them think!

The voice mechanism, unfortunately, is something that we must work with, and to get my own personality across through the female image and vocal chords, certain adjustments must be made. Beyond this, however, as I have mentioned before in class, it is not out of the inner sense of my invisible heart, but out of the depths of your own psychologies that you make me into a wise old man, and project upon me the authority images that lurk in your own minds. I have always tried to keep you from making this error, and sought to release from within yourselves your own abilities.

(To a particular student:) I remain spontaneous and alive, and do not allow myself to be deadened by your projections upon me. I have a cosmopolitan accent—not sophisticated, but cosmopolitan. You have an accent to me. *(Amused:)* I have spoken many tongues, and in translation this [voice] is what it ends up as, and so we are all stuck with it. Now continue . . .

(From the ESP class session for April 20, 1971:) I am very afraid to tell [all of] you that I have forgotten what I considered to be secrets through the lives I have lived. I certainly know that like any of you I have not always been charitable in the past. I know that I have hated one parent or another. I know, certainly, that once I plundered in the wages of war. I do not come to you as someone who does not know what it is like to be human,[26] and in those personality characteristics that I use when I speak to you, I show you that the emotional life continues . . .

Now my relationship with you [and Ruburt] is indeed a strange one, since you do not relate to me as you do to each other. The—I hope—delightfully human egotistical characteristics that I show help calm your fears and show you that the self as you think of it continues to exist [after physical death]. I have a reservoir of personality banks upon which I can draw, and as a teacher I use the one that is most effective in any given system of reality; this is the one I use here. It is a portion of myself that is the most closely connected with earthly existence, and it is a self that I liked very well, indeed.

I very seldom speak symbolically to you. I speak as literally as possible, but in order that any information may appear within your three-dimensional system, translations of it [through Ruburt] are automatically necessary or you would not perceive it.

(In July 1971 Jane began a book to be called Adventures in Consciousness, *based on the experiences of her students in ESP class. Within a few days Seth mentioned it while dictating Chapter 21 of* Seth Speaks: *See the 587th session. Class was now providing a wealth of material on reincarnation, various states of consciousness, and out-of-body travel. It was also bombarding Jane with questions for which she found no acceptable answers. Her own intuitive experiences were accelerating, and these, she felt, were more and more outgrowing the ordinary concepts of psychology.*

(Jane was particularly bothered by people's attitudes about Seth, for they often considered him as a "spirit guide" in conventional spiritualistic terms. Though almost eight years had passed since Seth had first come through, she'd known for some time that she wanted to explore the whole phenomenon more deeply. Jane believed Seth when he told us he was an "energy personality essence, no longer focused in physical reality"—she just wanted to know more about what he meant by that statement. She was certain, she wrote, that far more than Seth's being a spirit guide was involved, that "in larger terms the abilities of living personality are connected with . . . other facets of creative consciousness."

(Now I'll refer the reader to Note 6 for Session 711, which is the session for which I'm assembling this chronology to begin with. In that note I presented some material on ancient connections with the name, Seth, then quoted Seth on the subject of names from the ESP class session for April 17, 1973. For instance:)

I told Ruburt from our earliest sessions that he could call me Seth. I never said, 'My name is Seth,' . . . for I am nameless. I have had too many identities to cling to one name!

(At the end of Note 6 are a few references to some of Seth's reincarnational names as he gave them while dictating Seth Speaks. *A reference not given there is the 541st session for Chapter 11 of* Seth Speaks. *That session contains information and notes relevant to the concurrent lives that Jane, Seth, and I lived in Denmark in the 1600's. As mentioned at the beginning of this appendix, even though I'm considering the Jane-Ruburt-Seth relationship, I want to avoid becoming too enmeshed within the intertwining connections several personalities would experience in any one set of lives; such particulars would lead too far away from the focus chosen here.*

(Jane and I would rather explore specific reincarnational information in an outright book on the subject, and then only after we'd acquired much more personal [and theoretical] material. We do think that in detail, reincarnation, whether it's seen in ordinary terms or within the "simultaneous" framework espoused by Seth, can be an endless subject.[27]

(From my notes at the close of the 700th session for May 29, 1974,

*in Volume 1: "In our case," Seth said a bit later, "Ruburt almost 'becomes' the
material he receives from me. If certain other beneficial alterations occur, and
further understanding on Ruburt's part, we may be able to meet at other levels of
consciousness—in the dream state, when he is not cooperating in the production
of our book material." For Jane has never met Seth, face to face, you might say,
in a dream. The closest she's come to this situation is in giving a session for him
in the dream state, as she does in waking life.*

(From the ESP class session for July 16, 1974:) In certain terms,
then, you cannot separate yourselves from me [as Ruburt cannot],
nor can I separate myself from you. For we are all portions of an
event that is taking place within the universe, and the universe is
acquainted with all of its parts. When one part of the universe speaks,
then all parts speak. When one portion of the universe dies, all
portions die—but in your terms, to get into the kind of life you know
again, you must exit from space and time so that you can re-enter it.

Now, I can be playful because I am not as serious and
mystical as the rest of you. I am myself, and if you were yourselves,[28]
you would not be so self-consciously profound about your beliefs
and the nature of your reality. *(Humorously, to a certain student:)* You
would trust your mustache!

*(In the opening notes for the 708th session, in this Volume 2, I wrote
that Jane finished* Adventures *in August 1974. She'd started it in July 1971
[as noted a few paragraphs ago], but there was never any straight line of activity
for her on the book from beginning to end. She finished* Seth Speaks. *Then
during a class in November 1971, she first gave voice to her trance language,
Sumari; so besides the other class material she had several more stages of
consciousness—if very dependable ones—to deal with in* Adventures. *At the
same time she worked on her autobiography,* From This Rich Bed *[which still
isn't done]. At times the creative pace grew even more complicated: From March
to July 1972, she put* Adventures *aside completely to write her novel,* The
Education of Oversoul Seven, *when that idea spontaneously came to her.
But overall, Jane discovered that she was frustrated in dealing with class
experiments and records for* Adventures *while she still had so much to learn
about her own connections with Seth. More than ever, she needed larger concepts
of reality to explain her experiences, those of her students, and of some who
wrote.*

(Shortly after Jane finished Seven, *the entire idea for what she calls
"Aspect Psychology" came to her—an "intuitive construct" that she thought was
large enough to contain her experience. At one sitting she wrote 20 or so pages of
material in which she understood her relationship with Seth, Seth Two, the
Sumari, the characters in* Seven, *and other psychic concepts—all as aspects of a
larger self that was independent of space and time. The aspects represented the*

dynamics of personality. As Jane wrote, she realized that the questions she had been struggling with in Adventures *had triggered a new psychology, a new way of approaching the creative portions of human personality.*

(The material itself, of course, came from another *state of consciousness, and this Jane called her "aspects channel." More on aspects came to her spontaneously at intervals during the next two years. Throughout this period she did a great deal of other work: Besides holding class and continuing* Rich Bed, *she produced in their entirety* Dialogues, Personal Reality, *Volume 1 of* "Unknown" Reality, *and started Volume 2. Toward the end of this period the aspects channel began opening up regularly, providing further refinements on her original inspirations. And Jane put it all together; the class experiments she'd started out with in 1971, and all of the later material, became* Adventures in Consciousness: An Introduction to Aspect Psychology. *For Part Two of that book I drew 16 diagrams to illustrate her theories.*

(As she probed the Jane-Ruburt-Seth relationship in Adventures, *Jane found herself developing her own nomenclature, separate from Seth's, for many of the concepts she and Seth had experienced over the years. "But I didn't plan it that way," she said. "That's just the way it all came out." She calls the conscious self the "focus personality," for instance; since it's focused in this physical [camouflage] reality. The focus personality is composed of aspects of the "source self" [or entity]. Each aspect exists independently, in its own dimension of actuality, but the aspects' combined attributes form the basic components of the selves that we know. To Jane, Seth is a "personagram"—an actual personality formed in the psyche at the intersection point of the focus personality with another aspect.*

(Seth, then, would be a message from the source self, except that in this case the messenger is *the message, formed into a richly "worded" psychological structure instead of into dry words on, say, a telegram. Seth in sessions would stand for Jane's Seth Aspect, who does indeed exist in a different kind of reality than ours. But that "invisible" Seth would send out an actual psychological structure that takes over in place of Jane's, as her own structure voluntarily steps aside during sessions. Earlier in this appendix, see the excerpts on the psychological bridge from the 242nd session.*

(From the ESP class session for September 24, 1974:) The excitement [of living] must come from each of you, and not from me. You come here to know yourselves, and that should always be your purpose. I can help you—I can help you—but I am not the person you search for. You are the person you search for. The dimensions of your reality are the important points . . .

In certain terms, and in certain terms only, and speaking now as the psychological bridge personality, then what you perceive in me and these abilities represents a portion of Ruburt that is utterly free in those directions—a portion of the human mind, as you understand it, goes beyond the threshold of itself into other dimensions of actuality; then, as best it can, it translates what it learns, sees, and experiences. It goes out of itself—it launches itself on paths that it does not understand, taking journeys that even Ruburt does not understand; and yet, that one portion of Ruburt's human personality is _that_ free. And so you can see what happens!

(The following excerpt is from an ESP class session that Seth delivered three months after the 711th session [which inspired this appendix] was held on October 9, 1974. As noted much earlier, the chronology for our study of the Jane-Ruburt-Seth relationship "begins long before 'Unknown' Reality was started, and continues well beyond the date of its ending in April 1975." Very soon, then, the quotations to come reach beyond that date: They're usually short, and are from a mixture of class, regular, and private [or "deleted"] sessions. With an exception or two they contain material that ordinarily might not have been published for several years—if ever. But all of them contribute insights into the subject under consideration.

(From the ESP class session for January 7, 1975:) Ruburt can do many things that surprise me—that I did not do in my past, for remember that fresh creativity emerges from the past also, as in Ruburt's novel, *Oversoul Seven.*[29]

My memory does not include a predetermined past in which Ruburt exists. He can do things that did not happen in my memory of that existence, and did not, in fact, occur. Now that is a "mind-blowing" statement, and it applies to each of you. It is important in terms of your own understanding of yourself and the nature of time.

(The following exchange between Seth and a student—Bill, say—took place in the ESP class for February 18, 1975. Seth had been discussing certain psychic aspects of a rather complicated experience involving Jane, myself, and a house. Then he said:) We all learn, as each of us experiences. In certain terms, again, and _only_ in my relationship to Ruburt and Joseph *(as Seth calls Jane and me),* I am a future Ruburt. But only in terms of that relationship—as I may be an uncle to someone here, and an aunt to someone there, an ancestor to someone else, and a descendent of still another person. Or, as _you_ might be.

(Bill: "So, in other words you had this [house] information and you're somehow being reminded of it again through the experience of Ruburt? Because you had it through another life?")

Not in that way at all. That experience of Ruburt's and Joseph's was completely new. I was, in those terms, _not_ the Ruburt that Ruburt _is_. My experiences as Ruburt were different, and

Ruburt's experiences as Seth, in those terms, will be different. Ruburt will be a different Seth than I am.[30]

(Bill: "But you did experience this house event, in order to say it through Ruburt—")

I did not experience it. Ruburt experienced it. I commented on Ruburt's experience . . . In his experience, Ruburt is also free enough so that he can open up certain channels of his mind that then comment upon his activity. Some of those channels lead to my reality. But, I am not some spooky Big Brother experiencing his reality for him!

(The 768th session was held on March 22, 1976, 11 months after Seth had finished dictating "Unknown" Reality. Originally Jane and I deleted the following rather personal material from the session—yet we present it here because in it Seth explores further the connections involving the three of us. My notes at the time show that I was also distinctly surprised by Seth's comments on his emotional behavior at his own "level of activity," but I soon understood my reaction as a sign that we still had things to learn about him, as well as ourselves. In one passage Seth referred to some health difficulties, now resolved, that had bothered me just before our sessions with him began.

(To me:) You have often said that the [Seth] books were Ruburt's. That is true. Yet to a certain degree it is also a simplification.

Ruburt's experience is obviously intertwined with yours. My characteristics as they are displayed through the Seth personality, therefore, come from you as well as Ruburt . . . Triggers were needed also to initiate my emergence into your world through that personality I display. Ruburt's own background and questions were highly vital as such initiating principles. Your questions merged with his. It was the practical impetus of your need at the time, however, that operated as the final emotional trigger—you recall the circumstances.[31]

Ruburt provided himself with a background in which a parent *(Jane's mother)* was steadily, chronically ill,[32] and in which the medical profession with its beliefs was in constant sight. His mother was not medically neglected. His background included far more than sickness and the medical profession, however, but Ruburt knew that the conventional medical framework was not the answer to human ills. As you became more and more incapacitated, the trigger was set to find another solution. Psychic structures interweave, and realities do, one through the other *(as Jane had written a few hours before the session).*

(With a smile:) My personality, as it so richly presents itself,

is *(louder)* to some extent a joint creation of the two of you. This does not mean that I do not have my own reality, for I do, but in my relationship with you and Ruburt, and with your world, I do take certain characteristics that come from each of your realities.

You two do not understand how alike you are. Ruburt is as "detailed" about his own working habits as you both admit you are in yours. He seems to be in awe, relatively speaking, of your simplified "perfectionist" detailed ways, while to a certain extent you seem to be equally awed by his inspired, undetailed ways—a game each of you plays.

In your terms, I am relatively unemotional at my own level of activity. Rather, my emotional behavior does not follow your patterns—that is closer to "the truth." I have long delegated your kind of emotional activity to what you would call unconscious behavior. Our focuses are different, yet the overall coloration of your experiences does come through to me, and through this delightful personality *(Jane indicated herself),* I can to some extent relate to it.

You set upon this adventure, the two of you. It is meaningless to say that the books are Ruburt's. Your ideas of "perfection" and love of detail, or if you prefer, your feeling for the significance of detail that appears exteriorized in your notes, is as present in the inner consistency of the material itself as given by me.

Ruburt keeps track of intuitive details that neither of you are even conscious of, and so there shows an integrity that at least sometimes he is not aware of. You yourselves adopt personalities, though usually you are not aware of doing so. So I adopt a personality that can communicate with your own.[33] In one manner of speaking mine is heroic, larger, and multidimensional. On the other hand, I can operate only mentally in your world. It is Ruburt who must walk down the street.

(From the 775th session for May 10, 1976:) Bits of your consciousnesses,[34] Joseph and Ruburt, go out through these books. I am not speaking symbolically. Those portions will mix with the consciousness of others. Portions of your intent and purpose become theirs. My own psychological reality is not particleized. My identity includes the identities of many others, and they each operate in their own fashion. In those terms I am a wave formation. More specifically, however, and to a lesser degree, each physical person operates partially as a particleized being, and partially in terms of a wave.[35] But identity, being itself inviolate, is on the other hand ever-changing—and there is, in the larger framework of reality, no contradiction.

(Jane stopped holding ESP class on a regular basis early in 1975;

the rhythm of those weekly gatherings was broken when we gave up apartment living to move into our own house in March of that year. In spite of our good intentions class in the old sense was never resumed, as we became more and more involved with producing Seth's and Jane's books, painting, correspondence, and all of the other events that make up our daily lives. The following material came through during a session on March 11, 1977, when a group of former students assembled to hear Seth speak "for old time's sake":)

Now I do not mind being nonscientific, and neither do any of you mind, because if all of your realities were confined to scientific theories you would have no realities at all, and neither would your fine scientists.[36] And in my time, I was also quite a dogmatic scientist. The times were different, however, and then I was even more intolerant in my beliefs than your scientists gen-erally—underlined—are today!

In the terms of my book *("Unknown" Reality)*, I was a dream-art scientist,[37] but I was very dogmatic, and I demanded that others follow <u>my</u> symbols and not their own. And that is why I now so carefully tell you to follow your own ways.

(Finally, I'll close this appendix with a couple of quotations from Seth that I return to again and again. [These in turn lead to a last note.] In Chapter 3 of Seth Speaks, *see the 519th session for March 23, 1970:)* When I enter your system, I move through a series of mental and psychic events. You would interpret these events as space and time, and so often I must use the terms, for I must use your language rather than my own . . . In one way, I translate what I am into an event that you can understand to some extent.[38]

NOTES: Appendix 18

1. Jane discussed Seth Two rather often in *Adventures*. I do plan to write at least briefly about Seth Two in another appendix for this Volume 2 of *"Unknown" Reality*, however, the idea being that such material can be taken as an extension of the Jane-Ruburt-Seth study presented here.

And added later: The opportunity to do so developed much sooner than I thought it would—only a week after the 711th session was held. See Appendix 19 for Session 712.

2. Seth began his material on counterpart selves late next month, in the 721st session. Out of that session grew Appendix 21. The material in Appendix 18, then, is intended to further enrich the counterpart information in Session 721, as well as in its appendix.

3. In Chapter 3 of *The Seth Material* Jane describes our use of the Ouija board in the early sessions. In the 8th session for December 15, 1963,

she began dictating portions of each session; by the 14th session, she was delivering verbally all of Seth's material except for an opening remark or two obtained through the board. A month after that we dispensed with the board entirely.

4. In the 14th session Seth came through with some very valuable remarks about his concepts of time—"It is therefore still a reality of some kind to me," for instance. Because I've always thought those insights well worth repeating, I quoted them in the Introduction for Volume 1 (and, added later, following Session 724 in Volume 2). Now let me further excerpt Seth from that 14th session: "You mentioned earlier, Joseph, that you had the feeling I could refer back to myself almost as if I could turn a later page of a book to an earlier one, and of course this is the case." With a smile: "Viewing a historical moment through your marvelous television, you can refer to much that has passed, [but] one minute of such a referral costs you one minute of present time. Also you end up short-changed: You give up your precious moment in the present, but you do not have a complete (my emphasis) moment in the past to show for it . . . When I refer back to myself, I do not expend an identical moment of time in doing so."

5. See Note 2 for Appendix 12.

6. By the time the 22nd session was held Seth had mentioned the inner senses upon occasion, but had given us a breakdown on just the first one: Inner Vibrational Touch. Consciously, then, we had no way of appreciating what important and interesting parts those "senses leading to an inner reality" were to play in the material over the years. In Chapter 19 of The Seth Material Jane quoted Seth on the nine inner senses he's described so far.

(I should note that Jane's own use of that first inner sense, demonstrated in the example she gives in Chapter 19, reflects a very strong facet of her psychic ability that she seldom indulges. Her reluctance here is closely connected to her deep feelings about personal privacy.)

7. For some related material on patterns and probabilities, see Note 13 for Appendix 12.

8. Even 11 years later, I'm certainly far away from experiencing the concept-essence of any given session, as Seth suggests may be possible. I'm expressing contradictory beliefs, obviously, but it seems unlikely that I can use my abilities in such a fashion, even though I tell myself I'd like to.

I do believe, however, that on occasion Jane has known a stepped-up awareness that almost equates with Seth's concept-essence. One such instance is described in Appendix 7 for Volume 1: her reception of the material for a book called The Way Toward Health. At that time she tuned in to a different "neurological speed," a faster one, so that much of the book was available to her at once. Jane's pleasure at having the ability was strongly tempered, though—for while she "could feel the bulk and immediacy of the book," as I quoted her in Appendix 7, she was "also frustrated that what I've got down is so little and sketchy—WHEN IT'S

ALREADY HERE . . . If I could have immediately *spoken* the whole thing, it would have been done at once . . . I can't tell you how frustrated—how blocked—this made me feel at the time."

(In Volume 1, see the material on neurological speeds in Session 686. In Appendix 5 for the same session, see Jane's own notes on that subject.)

9. Jane produced her manuscript, *The Physical Universe as Idea Construction,* three months before the sessions began. That key event is briefly described in Volume 1. See Note 7 for Session 679.

10. Well, obviously, it's true so far at least that Seth will be "accessible" for the present lifetimes of Jane and me . . .

11. In this appendix, I'm quoting certain portions of the 28th session to make certain points. In Chapter 5 of *The Seth Material,* however, Jane presented much longer excerpts from the same session in order to explain her own views.

12. When Jane began speaking for Seth we checked out the definitions for concepts like dissociation, trance, and so forth, without being particularly influenced by what we found. We merely thought the meanings given were quite incomplete, so we decided to go our own collective way. As the sessions progressed we came to understand that for Jane dissociation simply meant her ability to direct an intense concentration toward certain highly creative goals—Seth and the sessions—so that we could learn from them.

Her "psychic" accomplishments grew outside the session framework too, of course, as can be seen in much of the appendix material in Volume 1 (to mention those examples only); and so to varying degrees, dissociation, or that strong power of concentration, entered into those activities.

13. Following his comments about his reassembly in our reality, Seth went into some analogous material (in that 28th session) that I've always wanted to see published. In part, then: "Condensed time is the time felt or experienced by the entity, while any of its given personalities 'live'— and you had better put that in quotes—on a plane of physical materializations. To go into this a bit further, many men have said that life was a dream. They were true to the facts in one strong regard, and yet far afield as far as the main issue is concerned.

"Individual life, or the life of the present individual, could be legitimately compared to the dream of an entity. While the individual suffers and enjoys his [or her] given number of years, these are but a flash to the entity. The entity is concerned with such years in the same manner that you are concerned with your own dreams . . . And as your dreams originate with you, arise from you, attain a seeming independence and have their ending with you, so an entity's personalities arise from it, attain various degrees of independence, and return to it while never leaving it for an instant.

"The entity organizes its personalities and to some extent

directs their activities while still allowing them what you would call free will. There exist infinities of diversity and opportunity for the personalities.

"The entity itself does not have to keep constant check on its personalities, because in each one there is an inner self-conscious part that knows its origin. I have mentioned before that some part of you knows exactly how much oxygen the lungs breathe, and how much energy it takes to pace a floor, and this is the part of you of which I spoke. It is the self-conscious part that receives all inner data.

". . . the part that translates inner data sifts it down through the subconscious, which is a barrier and also a threshold to the present camou-flage personality. I have said that the topmost part of the subconscious contains personal memories, that beneath these are racial memories, and so forth. Things are simply not layered in the way I speak of them, but continuing with the necessary analogy, on the other side of (or beneath, to you) the racial memories, you no longer exist within your plane; you look out upon another with the face of this other self-conscious part of you. This part receives inner data, is in contact with the entity to some greater degree than you are in contact with your dreams, and actually directs all of the important functions that you think are either automatically or uncon-sciously controlled.

"When such abilities as telepathy occur, this telepathic function is carried on continually by this other self-conscious part of you; but as a rule you act upon those data without the knowledge of the conscious self with which you are familiar.

(With a laugh:) "There is of course an apparent contradiction here, but it is only apparent—your dilemma being this: If you have another self-conscious self, then why aren't you aware of it?

"Pretend that you are some weird creature with two faces. One face looks out upon one world and one looks out upon another. Imagine, further, this poor creature having a brain to go with each face, and that each brain interprets reality in terms of the world it looks upon. Yet the worlds are different, and more, the creatures are Siamese twins.

"At the same time imagine that these creatures are really one creature, but with definite parts equipped to handle two entirely different worlds. The subconscious, therefore, in this ludicrous analogy, would exist between the two brains, and would enable the creature to operate as a single unit.

"At the same time—and this is the difficult part to explain—neither of the two faces would ever see the other world. They would not [usually] be aware of each other, and yet each would be fully self-conscious."

14. Seth discussed many facets of his concept of probabilities in Volume 1, of course. In Volume 2, see Note 16 for Appendix 12.

15. In Volume 1, see Note 3 for Session 679.

16. *Memories, Dreams, Reflections* by C. G. Jung, © 1961 by Random House, Inc., New York, N.Y.

17. For many readers Seth's remarks about the anima and the animus will require a bit of explaining. Carl Jung (1875–1961), the Swiss psychologist and psychiatrist, postulated that the unconscious of the male contains a female, archetypal (or typical, instinctive) figure called the "anima"; the correlative male form in the unconscious of the female Jung called the 'animus." In Session 119, then, Seth comments on how Jane herself has an animus—the hidden male within—and on how Ruburt, that larger "male" entity of which she is a "self-conscious part," contains an anima, or hidden female. (See the excerpts in this appendix from the 83rd session.) The contrasts are most interesting. From this information I infer that the entity or whole self of each of us, regardless of our current, individual sexual orientation, contains its own counterbalancing male or female quality, whichever the case may be. Seth hasn't said so yet—nor have we asked him—but I suspect that an energy gestalt like the entity is much more aware than we can be of its "hidden" opposite-sex form—or forms; for there may be many of them.

Below, I'll quote very short passages from sessions 555–56 in Chapter 13 of *Seth Speaks*, while referring the reader to them at the same time, then present some additional material from the 83rd session that I saved for this note–since in it Seth discussed the theories of both Jung and Jung's famous teacher, Sigmund Freud (1856–1939).

In *Seth Speaks*, Seth developed Jung's ideas about the anima and the animus by stating that such other-sex qualities or personifications within each of us actually represent memories of past lives. (Jung himself thought the questions of reincarnation, and of karma [or, roughly, destiny or fate], to be "obscure"—he couldn't be sure of the existence of such phenomena.) From Session 555 for October 21, 1970: "The anima and the animus . . . are highly charged psychically, and also appear in the dream state. They operate as compensations and reminders to prevent you from overidentifying yourself with your present physical body." And from Session 556: "The reality of the anima and the animus is far deeper than Jung supposed. Symbolically speaking, the two together represent the whole self with its diverse abilities, desires, and characteristics . . . Personality as you know it cannot be understood unless the true meaning of the anima and the animus is taken into consideration."

Two notes in connection with the excerpts from the 83rd session: 1. The famous professional break between Freud and the younger Jung occurred in 1931: Seth's material touches upon the divergent psychological paths taken by each of them.   2. The libido is regarded as the sexual urge or instinct—positive, loving, psychic energy that shows itself in changing ways as the individual matures. Seth:

"There are a few points of a general nature that I would like to make. Ruburt has been reading Jung, though not consistently. The libido does not originate in the subconscious of the present personality. It begins instead in the energy of the entity and inner self, and is directed by means of the inner senses—outward, so to speak, through the deeper layers of the individual subconscious mind, then through the outer or personal areas.

"Your Freud and Jung have probed into the personal subconscious. Jung saw glimpses of other depths, but that is all. There are rather unfortunate distortions occurring in his writings, as well as in Freud's, since they did not understand the primary, cooperative nature of the libido . . .

"We have spoken of the biological interdependence and cooperation among organisms in your physical universe. The appearance of an individual into the physical realm is aided by the psychic collaboration of individuals on your plane. Almost at once the new libido takes up its adopted duty of maintaining the physical universe, along with all others. If it did not do so it would not exist for long. Cooperation on all levels is the necessity on all planes.

"I was somewhat concerned with Ruburt's reading of Jung, simply because while Jung seems to offer more than Freud, in some aspects he has attempted much and his distortions are fairly important: Seeming to delve further and offering many significant results, Jung nevertheless causes conclusions . . . all the more hampering because of his scope.

"It is true that the outward manifestations of the libido are directed toward the physical world, but until its source is seen, not in the topmost subconscious layers of the individual, and not even in the racial subconscious, but within the entity itself, then man will not know himself.

"Basically, Jung feared such a journey because he felt that it led only to the racial source . . . that anyone involved in such a study would end up in the bottleneck of a first womb—but there, there is an opening up into other realms, through which the libido also passed. Figuratively speaking, it squeezed itself through the bottleneck, and there is a lack of limitation on the other side.

"Freud courageously probed into the individual topmost layers of the subconscious, and found them deeper than even he suspected. These levels are indeed filled with what may be termed life-giving differentiated and undifferentiated impulses acquired in the present life of an individual, but when these have been passed there are many discoveries still to be made. After that passage the diligent, consistent, intuitive, and flexible seeker-after-knowledge will find horizons of which Freud never dreamed. Freud merely touched the outer boundaries. Jung, with his eyes clouded by the turmoil set up by Freud, glimpsed some further regions, but poorly."

18. As Jane wrote in Chapter 8 of *The Seth Material,* the Instream tests were very unsatisfactory for us. Since we were never informed as to their results, we were left with no way to judge what proportions of Seth's impressions could be considered hits, near-misses, or failures. Our nine-month involvement under those conditions revealed both our naiveté at the time and our stubbornness in trying to learn. But learn we did, if not always as we'd expected to; for besides gaining valuable insights into Seth-Jane's abilities through our own envelope tests, we discovered much through our dealings with at least some kinds of "authority." Overall, the affair of the tests was most instructive.

19. Seth commented upon some of his own "psychic" abilities

when I asked him if he'd telepathically acquired any information about the test object from me, since I was the one who had chosen it, rather than from the object itself. The results of the second envelope test were obviously more precise than for the first one. At break I told Jane that she'd done well. We were very encouraged.

Two quick reminders: 1. Clairvoyance ("clear-seeing") is the paranormal perception of events or objects regardless of distance, and without help from another mind.   2. Telepathy is the communication of thoughts or emotions between minds, regardless of distance. In actuality, it's often difficult to tell whether clairvoyance, telepathy, or both operated in a given instance. Nor am I noting here how the use of these phenomena may be connected to the perception of the past or future.

20. In this appendix, the presentations from sessions 28 and 83 contain Seth's comments as to whether he's "a secondary or split personality of Ruburt's" (to quote him from the latter). On her own, Jane expressed concern about secondary personalities in Chapter 6 of The Seth Material; see her account of our meetings with Dr. Instream. Additional, related material can be found in Chapter 2 of The Coming of Seth, and in the sessions dealing with "Augustus" in Chapter 6 of Personal Reality.

21. In Volume 1, see Seth's material on man's emerging ego consciousness in sessions 686 (after 10:37), 687, 689, and Appendix 6.

22. I noted at the beginning of this appendix that it was inspired, at least in part, by the material Seth had given in the 711th session on the psychological bridge, or framework, linking Jane and himself. I refer the reader to those passages now; they start at 11:40. Also see the last two paragraphs of the opening notes for Session 705 (in this volume), with Note 2 for that session.

Seth actually initiated his material on the psychological bridge in the last (241st) session. However, I chose to excerpt the 242nd session on the subject because of the information it also contains on the ego and survival personalities in general.

23. The 241st session, mentioned in Note 22, is one of those we hope to publish in full, for in it Seth discussed how the psychological bridge helps Jane "translate" his telepathic material. The information came through in connection with our envelope tests and those for Dr. Instream, both sets of which were in mid-course then, in March 1966. (See the account of Jane's "year of testing" and the excerpts from sessions 179–80.)

Here are a few insights from Seth's material in the 241st session: "This psychological framework is in itself capable of growth. It represents on Ruburt's part an expansion, and indeed on my own part also. It is formed partially by abilities inherent within all personalities—psychic abilities—and it is composed of energy. It is not a secondary personality, for it exists in quite a different dimension than do secondary personalities ...

"The psychological bridge can transmit, you see, and to some extent translate, but not interpret. I am dependent in a large measure upon Ruburt's own knowledge, and lack of it, in that I cannot force from him, from his speech mechanism, concepts with which he is entirely unfamiliar.

I must introduce them step by step . . . as I explained moment points *(see Note 11 for Appendix 12)* to you . . . It is not as simple a thing as it might seem, for there is no coercion involved, Ruburt always consenting to let me push concepts at him, which he interprets speech-wise with my assistance.

"In our experiments, often, I will give him an impression, and he will automatically translate it into visual terms . . . There is sometimes at his end a last tug and pull, so that the vocal mechanism will finally speak the correct interpretation. Of course Ruburt's own associations are used by me, up to a certain point, to lead him to the proper subject or image . . . When we are successful there is a divergence from his associations so that he says the correct word, even though for him personally it may be the wrong word.

"On Ruburt's part this can sometimes be disconcerting. We must always work with psychological organizations, however. The emotions always follow associative lines in this regard.

"The trick is to allow Ruburt's associations free reign to a certain point, and then expertly insert the correct data. This is sometimes difficult. His associations may go, for example, from C, D, E, and F, but precisely where he would say 'G,' we must insert X or Y, and do it so smoothly that he is quite unaware.

"He consents for me; he consents to let me use his associations in such a manner."

24. In the 464th session I made sure that I asked Seth to elaborate upon his statement in the last session: "The slightest perception alters every atom within your body." He came through with his answer just before first break:

"Returning to the material on perception, there are changes in the positive and negative atomic charges, alterations of movement inside the atoms in the smaller particles, a change in pulsation rate. The activity of atoms is actually caused by perceptive qualities. To begin with, atoms do not just move within themselves because they are atoms. The constant motion within them is caused by the unending perceptive nature of any consciousness, however minute in your terms. Does that answer your question?"

"Yes," I said, "but I could ask a lot more of them."

Seth continued: "Each of the particles within the atom is perceptively aware of all of the other particles within that same atom. They move in response to stimuli received from each other, and to stimuli that come from other atoms . . . Each atom within a cell, for example, is aware of the activity of each of the other atoms there, and to some extent of the stimuli that come to the cell itself from outside it.

"Perceptions in general physical terms usually seem to involve information picked up from an arbitrarily designated structure, of an event seemingly occurring in another structure outside of itself. In the entire act of perception, however, there is a oneness and a unity between the seemingly objectively perceived event and the perceiver.

"The entire act has its own electromagnetic reality, and the event is actually electromagnetic motion. The movement within the atoms, mentioned earlier, is therefore basically a part of the entire perceived event. Does this make the issue plainer for you?"

"Yes . . ."

"Egotistically, you make arbitrary designations of necessity, perceiving only portions of any given action: again, the ego attempting to separate itself from overall action, and to see itself as an entirely independent structure." (See the excerpts from the 242nd session.)

"You may take your break."

(To go into modern knowledge of the components of the atom can be a very complicated task, so I'll note only that such particles are regarded as actually being packets of energy, or "probability patterns," that can also manifest themselves as waves; both the particle and the wave aspects are legitimate in space-time. An atom, then, is composed of a "heavy" positively charged nucleus orbited by "lighter" negatively charged electrons. Generally speaking, these positive and negative qualities could be those Seth referred to in the 464th session.

The electron is the lightest particle known to have mass and charge, and its internal structure—whatever it may be—is unknown. The atomic nucleus is largely made up of more massive protons and neutrons, but investigation within the nucleus has either uncovered or produced many other subatomic particles as well—over 200 of these, some of them very unstable, are presently known. According to Seth, of course, all of the particles or probability patterns discussed here would be composed of the much, much smaller CU's, or units of consciousness.

(In Volume 1, see Note 4 for Session 682; in Session 702, see the material on electron spin, and Note 6. Note 5 for that session also contains applicable references.)

25. Jane held her first ESP class on the evening of September 12, 1967, although she didn't let Seth come through within that format until the following December, so cautious was she in taking that psychic step. She had no personal experience or other precedent to go by; her *How to Develop Your ESP Power* had been published in 1966, but she was still experimenting with her own abilities (even as she is now). It could also be said that at issue was the whole question of firsthand public interaction with, and acceptance or rejection of, Seth and his material. Classes were quite small for some time, although they'd grown considerably by the end of 1969. After *The Seth Material* was published in 1970, class became well-known enough to start attracting visitors from various parts of the country. It still does so.

Class Seth material and other events can be found in all of the books by Jane and/or Seth, of course. See, for example, Chapter 13 of *The Seth Material,* the Appendix of *Seth Speaks,* and several chapters in Part One of *Adventures in Consciousness.*

(A note added later: Jane's *ESP Power* was originally issued by Frederick Fell Publishers, Inc. Pocket Books reprinted it in 1976 as a paperback and with a new title: *The Coming of Seth.* In Volume 1, see Note 2 of the *Preface by Seth.*)

26. Although in that 1971 class Seth stressed his experiences

with the human condition through reincarnation, in 1964 he'd had this to say: "To me this [reincarnational and family material] is all so obvious that I almost hesitate to mention it, but this is because I tend to forget what human experience on your plane actually involves." (See the excerpts from the 27th session in this appendix.) In that early session Seth spoke to me alone; in class he faced a large group. I'd say that from his position or focus as an "energy personality essence" both attitudes are true, rather than contradictory—and that one or the other predominated according to the circumstances and subject matter of the session involved. I don't think the time gap between the two sessions—seven years—was a factor.

    27. Concerning reincarnation, as well as books on the subject, here's Seth from the 588th session in Chapter 22 of *Seth Speaks*: "Now when I began contacting Ruburt and Joseph, I hid from them the fact of my numerous lives. *(Smile:)* Ruburt, in particular, did not accept reincarnation, and the idea of such multiple life experiences would have been highly scandalous to him.

    "The times and names and dates are not nearly as important as the experiences, and they are too numerous to list here. However, I will see to it at some time that these are made fully available ... In a book on reincarnation, I hope to have each of my previous personalities speak for themselves, for they should tell their own stories."

    Seth said a lot in that last sentence, of course, but that just means that more questions than usual come to mind. Although Jane and I think his idea for such a book is unique, we haven't done anything to implement it, nor have we asked him to explain further. Just how would Seth propose to have his "previous personalities speak for themselves...."? Since Seth presumably wouldn't simply relay such messages, would Jane find herself giving voice for a host of others, male and female, young and old, from many time periods and of the most diverse nationalities? A long project, and one for which she would use her abilities in new ways.

    28. Seth's remarks here are actually an extension of a long discussion on individual beliefs and spontaneity that he'd initiated in a class session two weeks ago: "Now, my words will not, I hope, be used to begin a new dogma. My dogma is the freedom of the individual *(my emphasis)*. My dogma is the sacrilegious one—that each of you is a good individual. There is nothing wrong with your emotions, or feelings, or being. When you know yourself then you are joyfully—joyfully—responsive, and, being joyfully responsive, you can carry your society to the furthest reaches of its creativity."

    29. See Chapter 17 of *Oversoul Seven,* for instance. In *Personal Reality,* Seth discussed "a sort of reprogramming" of the past; see sessions 653–54 in Chapter 14.

    (A note added later: That January 1975 class session is an excellent one in many respects, and Jane presented much of it in Chapter 15 of her *Psychic Politics.* Although Seth finished his work on both volumes of *"Unknown" Reality* well before Jane was through with *Politics,* the latter was published first—and *that* chronology is treated in my Introductory Notes for Volume 1.

30. In this appendix, see the excerpts from sessions 54 and 58.

31. "In late 1963," Jane wrote in Chapter 2 of *The Seth Material,* "some months before our sessions began, we'd taken a vacation in York Beach, Maine, hoping that a change of environment would improve Rob's health. The doctor didn't know what was wrong with his back and suggested that he spend some time under traction in the hospital. Instead we decided that his reaction to stress was at least partially responsible, hence this trip."

By then I'd lost many months from my job as a commercial artist, which was work I'd returned to several years earlier to help ease our financial pressures. I was 44 years old—and, as I recognized after the sessions began, at a point in life where I greatly needed more penetrating insights into the meaning of existence. So did Jane, even though she was almost 10 years younger. As the sessions became part of our joint reality, we gradually came to understand that the illness I struggled with was a disguised expression of rebellion for both of us. We were very dissatisfied with our status quo: After years of work, Jane had managed to publish but a few poems and a few pieces of science fantasy (several short stories and two brief novels), and in my own view I wasn't making it as the kind of artist I wanted to be. We were driven to know more—about art, about writing, about the human condition, about *everything*. My own need, as well as Jane's, struck deep responses within her psyche.

For an account of what happened to us at York Beach on that trip, see more of Chapter 2 in *The Seth Material.* Also see Note 6 for Session 680, in Volume 1.

32. In Volume 1, see Session 679 (with its Note 4, among others) for material on Jane's early years with her mother. I often remind myself that from her earliest years Jane lived in an atmosphere permeated by the fact of illness, while by contrast my background in that respect was much more ordinary. Growing up, she was "frightened most of the time," Jane told me as I prepared this note: She often lived alone with her bedridden mother, such periods being punctuated by a succession of itinerant housekeepers appointed by the welfare department. She soon became strongly imprinted by human frailty and vulnerability.

Yet, we fully agree with Seth—that like any other personality Jane chose her physical environment before birth, planning to meet certain challenges within that setting.

33. See Seth in the excerpts from the ESP class session for April 20, 1971: "I have a reservoir of personality banks upon which I can draw...."

34. Since Jane and I equate the "bits" of consciousness mentioned in this excerpt with Seth's EE (electromagnetic energy) units and his CU's (units of consciousness), see the references listed in Note 3 for Appendix 12.

35. Seth's material in this excerpt reminded me strongly of certain passages of his (and mine) in the 702nd session in Volume 1: "As long as you think in terms of [subatomic] particles, you are basically off the track—or even when you think in terms of waves. The idea of interrelated fields comes closer, of course, yet even here you are simply changing one kind of term for one like it, only slightly different. In all of these cases you are ignoring the reality of consciousness, and its gestalt formation and manifestations. Until you perceive the innate consciousness behind any 'visible' or 'invisible' manifestations, then, you put a definite barrier to your own knowledge."

Then in my note at 10:20 I wrote: "I thought it very interesting that Seth had talked about subatomic waves and particles in the last paragraph of his delivery tonight. Such ideas involve the physicists' ongoing conception of the duality of nature. For instance: Is light made up of waves or particles? A contemporary accommodation, called complementarity, leads experimenters to accept results that show *either* aspect to be true."

Since Seth obviously sees little real difference between the concepts of fields and wave/particles, I'd say that in the 775th session he cast his material in accord with the latter so as to make it as clear as possible to us, who are so bound by ideas of space and time: "In those terms . . ." But overall the physicists discuss *energy* and Seth talks about *consciousness*—and therein, as I see it, lies the basic contrast between the two approaches to reality.

Apropos of that "reality of consciousness" quoted above (from the 702nd session), Seth also came through with the following more generalized material in Session 775: "You are actually 'reincarnated' many times during one accepted lifetime. There are often great challenges to which you respond. You pick these for your own reasons. In doing so you often change affiliations.

"Consciousness forms patterns of identities. They move faster than the speed of light. They can be in more than one place at one time. *(See notes 5 and 6 for Session 702.)* They can operate in a freewheeling fashion as identities in themselves, or as 'psychological particles.' They can also operate in a wavelike fashion, flowing through other such particles. They can form together into endless, infinite combinations, forming psychological gestalts. Certain portions of these gestalts can then operate as 'psychological particles' in time and space, while other portions operate in a wavelike manner outside of time and space. These represent the unconscious elements of the species, which become 'particleized' in physical existence."

Although these final paragraphs from the 775th session contain many ideas, I want to stress two of them that I find especially evocative: Seth's reference to many reincarnations in one accepted lifetime, and the unconscious elements of the species being represented by its wavelike characteristics.

Since this session was held almost 13 months after *"Unknown"* *Reality* was completed, I can look back and note that Seth developed the statement on reincarnation in his material on counterparts; this begins with Session 721 in Section 5. Appendix 21 grew out of that session. In that same section, the 725th session (with Note 4) contains additional information on particles, identities, and psychological gestalts.

36. Many passages in Appendix 12, and in its notes, could be quoted to illuminate Seth's comments here. Notes 13 and 20 are examples, and their superscription numbers can be used as references to the appropriate paragraphs in the appendix itself. In general, I suggest reviewing the last few pages of Appendix 12, beginning with my own material: "My position after writing this appendix is . . ."

37. In Volume 1, see Session 700. Seth at 9:53: "The true art of dreaming is a science long forgotten by your world. Such an art, pursued, trains the mind in a new kind of consciousness—one that is equally at home in either [exterior or interior] existence, well grounded and secure in each."

And from Session 704: "The dream-art scientist, the true mental physicist, the complete physician—such designations represent the kinds of training that could allow you to understand the unknown, and therefore the known reality, and so become aware of the blueprints that exist beyond the physical universe."

38. Apropos of his quotations from *Seth Speaks,* here's what Seth had to say in a later personal session: "There are rhythms that exist over a period of time, as I have mentioned before, and had you the leisure to check your records you would see that overall we have about the same number of sessions each year. There are many cycles involved—some connected with the two of you, with myself, or with other conditions quite apart.

"Some of these conditions could be called the result of psychological atmospheres that surround the earth, say. I do not travel physically in a UFO *(with amusement),* and yet my mental or psychic journeys must occur in a medium of some kind. There are rhythmic activities in that atmosphere that I count upon and use, as for example a sea captain might use the rhythm of the waves for his voyages. Those inner atmospheric 'waves' have a certain regularity. They are more intense at certain times than others."

APPENDIX 19
(For Session 712)

(I'll preface the abbreviated version to follow of Jane's first slow, or "long sound" session, the 612th for September 6, 1972, with these notes about Seth Two, since this is the ideal place for them.

(Seth Two wasn't dealt with in Volume 1 of "Unknown" Reality. *In Note 1 for Appendix 18, I wrote that I wanted to at least briefly discuss Seth Two in another appendix for this Volume 2, "the idea being that that material can be taken as an extension of the Jane-Ruburt-Seth study presented here." The few references to Seth Two in Appendix 18 were all meant to be resolved below, including my note that "Seth Two exists in relation to Seth in somewhat the same manner that Seth does to Jane, although that analogy shouldn't be carried very far."*

(With Seth's help, Jane first encountered the idea of Seth Two in the 406th session for April 22, 1968. That important development in her abilities took place four and a half years after she began to speak for Seth, and once it opened up Seth Two came through in the next seven twice-weekly sessions. Most of that material hasn't been published, although in Chapter 17 of The Seth Material *Jane described Seth Two to some extent, including "his, hers, or its" intimate connections with Seth: the subjective pyramid or cone effects she experiences just above her head when contacting Seth Two; and the great energy she feels at such times. In Chapter 17 she quoted Seth Two from sessions 406–7, and from a couple of others that were held later in the year. The excerpts show not only something of Seth's connections on the "other side" of Jane, but in one case her violent reactions of surprise and panic when she attempted to translate something of Seth Two's reality in terms of our own camouflage world: She found herself deeply involved in an unexpected experience with "massiveness"—one of the subjects I want to refer to in these preliminary notes. And Seth Two—or our imperfect grasp of what such an energy gestalt can mean or represent— comprises at least one of the sources of the Seth material itself.*

(Unlike Seth, Seth Two has never been physical in our terms, and only partially comprehends our reality even while helping to form it. Very quickly, and perhaps simplifying too much, here's Seth Two from the 407th session, speaking in Jane's high, distant, deliberate and asexual interpretation of what such an energy gestalt's "voice" might sound like:)

Seth is what I am, and yet I am more than Seth is. Seth is, however, independent, and continues to develop as I do . . . Simply as an analogy, and only as an analogy, I am what you would refer to as a future Seth, as Seth in a "higher" stage of development. This is

not to be taken literally, however, since both of us are fully independent and exist simultaneously.

(Following those introductory sessions, Seth Two has spoken at widely spaced intervals. At this writing I think it's been well over a year since I've heard that very complicated personality. Occasionally Jane will speak for Seth Two in class. I do think that she could contact Seth Two at my request. Yet she has to get into a "certain mental climate" in order to reach Seth Two, Jane said, and all of her other trance phenomena—Sumari, and so forth—are also related to that state. [1]

(I've already cited Jane's experience, as given in Chapter 17 of The Seth Material, showing that on rare occasions Seth Two and her feelings of massiveness can go together; but she can also be in an altered, massive state of consciousness without having a session, or she can be speaking for Seth. Seth or Seth Two—obviously, when either of those qualities combine with her massive perceptions, then Jane knows a multifaceted trance state. In Volume 1, Seth devoted much of the 681st session to a discussion of probabilities, or, in sum, All That Is, and interwound Jane's psychic and physical experiences with that material: "The cellular consciousness experiences itself as eternal . . . Part of Ruburt's feeling of massiveness[2] comes from the mass [life-to-death] experience of the body, existing all at once. Therefore to him the body feels larger." Beginning at 11:10 in that session, see also Jane's own comments on her massive responses.

(These two ideas from Seth, which came through in connection with his data on moment points, are to me very suggestive of the concept of long sound. From the 681st session:) In your terms—the phrase is necessary—the moment point, the present, is the point of intersection between all existences and reality. All probabilities flow through it, though one of your moments may be experienced as centuries, or as a breath, in other probable realities of which you are a part. (From session 682:) There are systems in which a moment, from your standpoint, is made to endure for the life of a universe. . . .[3]

(Jane's expressions of long sound and her sensations of massiveness are of course directly related to the multidimensional neurological activity, the "sidepools" of consciousness, that she described in Appendix 4 of Volume 1. Seth also mentioned neurological pulses and/or speeds in various sessions in Volume 1. In the opening delivery for Session 686, for example, see his infor-mation on our species' selection of one "official" series of neurological pulses for physical reality, and, at 12:19 A.M., his remarks on prejudiced perception. Appendix 5 for the same session contains more of Jane's own material on neurological speeds.

(Finally, the excerpt to follow from the 612th session is presented just as received, but I've updated some of the notes for it [beginning with Note 4] *in order to take advantage of later material, including some published in Volume 1.)*

Session 612
September 6, 1972
9:19 P.M. Wednesday

(The first delivery for this session,[4] running until break at 9:47, is deleted here since it contains much personal material. During it Jane spoke for Seth as usual. His last sentence before break was: "I will have something to say concerning Ruburt's experience the other evening. . . ." With that statement he referred to Monday night's session, which had been an entirely personal one. Just before its start, Jane had had the self-conscious idea that she should rub between her eyes with a circular motion—"You know, where the third eye[5] would be. . . ." In the session itself, she came through with material about herself on her "own," without Seth, but in an altered state of consciousness in which she experienced many vivid subjective images, coupled with strong feelings of massiveness. Some of the images reflected internal states of her own body. I thought her very interesting way of acquiring the information represented another step in the development of her abilities.

(Now to recap the situation leading up to tonight's [612th] session: At supper time Jane encountered some relaxation effects[6]—so much so, in fact, that she had to lay down briefly in the midst of preparing the meal. Then not long before the session was due she became aware to some extent of her pyramid sensation, meaning that Seth Two, or possibly a variation of that personality gestalt, was around. And once again she felt like rubbing her forehead where the mythical third eye would be. Many things, it seemed, were developing at once; we expected that after first break tonight Seth would comment upon them, as well as upon Monday evening's session. But events didn't work out that way at all; Seth did not return. Jane carried the rest of the session herself—and a unique one it turned out to be. . . .

(10:09. "I'm getting the feeling of a whole lot of beings or personalities way behind my head," Jane said as she sat in her Kennedy rocker. Her eyes were open; she was very relaxed; she smoked a cigarette as we waited for Seth to return. Then after a pause: "I'm getting stuff but I don't know how I'm supposed to give it—through Seth Two, or what. So I'm just waiting. . . ."

(10:16. Jane's head was lowered, but I could still see various expressions of puzzlement and inquiry move across her face. "I've got that massive feeling again," she said finally, referring to Monday night's session. Her massiveness, among other effects, had been very pronounced for her then; she'd felt herself to be truly giant-sized. Now her eyes slit open. Two minutes later she spoke through lips that hardly moved: "Like in my head this enormous body is out through space—all space as we think of it—"

(10:20. "I can't do it," she said quietly. "I don't think I can do it. . . ." She repeated variations of this idea several times; some of them were less intelligible than others. "I don't understand what I'm getting, and I don't know what to do with it. It . . . doesn't sound logical." Pause. "I don't know . . . but I'll try. . . ."

(10:22. In a voice quite a bit deeper and stronger than usual, but not as overpowering as I've heard it be on occasion, Jane began to express a series of very "long," drawn-out syllables. I'd expected anything from a whisper to a scream. What follows at first are my phonetic interpretations of the sounds she uttered. Her eyes were closed, her head still down. [When Jane reads these typed notes she may not agree with some of my approximations.] Now in a heavy voice, almost grating:)

"Aaaaaaaaahhhhhhhhhhhhhhhhaaaaaaaaa . . . . . . Thhh-hhhhhheeeeeeeuuuuu . . . . . . Mmmmmmmaaaaaaahhhhhhnnnn-nnsssss . . . . . . Eeeeeehhhhhrrrruuuuuuuu . . . . . . Aaaaaahhhhhhh-mmmmmmmnnnn . . . . . . Wwwwwhhhhhheeeeeeuuuuuu . . . . . . Jaaaaahhhhhhhhhhhuuuuuuu . . . . . . Wwwwhhhhhheeeeeeeuuuu-uuuu."

(Pause at 10:26. I couldn't distinguish words or meanings here. I concentrated merely on trying to convert the sounds into letters:) "Wwwwhh-hheeeeeeuuuuuuunnnnn . . . . . . Aaaahhhhhmmmmmmnnn . . . . . . Wwwwhhhheeeeeee . . . . . . Baaaayyyyyeeeeeeeuuuuu . . . . . . Sssseeeeeeuuuuuuuggggghhhheeeee."

(Pause at 10:27. Now I began to make out very drawn-out "long" or slow words. Jane's voice remained on the same deep, even keel:) "Wwwwh-hhhheeeeeeennnnnnnn . . . . . . Wwwwcccccceeeeee . . . . . . Sssspeeee-eeeaaaaakkkkk . . . . . . Wwwwooooorrrrrllllllldssssss . . . . . . Ffffoooo-orrrrrmmmmmmm." *(My interpretation: "When we speak worlds form."*

(10:28. Jane's head vibrated quickly from side to side on a small scale, not at all disruptive, as she continued:) "Wwwweeeeeeee . . . . . . Co-oooooommmmmmmeeeee . . . . . . Wwwweeeeeeeeee . . . . . . Aaaa-hhhrrrrrrr . . . . . . Thhhheeeeeeee . . . . . . Iiiiinnnnneeeeerrrrr . . . . . . Mmmmooooossssshhhhhiiiiioooooonnnnnnnn . . . . . . Sssoooooo-oooot." *("We come. We are the inner motion—" I couldn't decipher the last syllable or word.)*

(10:30.) "Wwwweeeeeeee . . . . . . Aaaaaarrrrreeeee . . . . Thhhheeeeee . . . . . . Ssssssstrrrreeeeeennnnngthhhhh . . . . . . Iiiii-nnnnnnn . . . . . . Mmmmmaaaaaaateeeeeeeerrrrrr." *("We are the strength in matter.")*

(10:32.) "Wwwwwiiiiilllllliiiiinnnnnggllyyyyy . . . . . . Ffff-oooooorrrrmmmmmiiinnnggggg . . . . . . Sssssllllooowwwwweeee-rrrrrr . . . . . . Thhhhaaaaannnnnnnn . . . . . . Lllllliiiiiiighhhhhhhtt . . . . . . Paaaaaaarrrrrrtiiiiiclllleeeeeessss . . . . . . Thhhhhiiiiissssss . . . . .

Iiiiiiiiisssssssss. . . .Oooooonnnnnnneeeee. . . . . . .Aaaaasssssspeeeeect.
. . . . .Oooooofffffff. . . . . .Ooooooooouuuuuurrrrrrr. . . . .Aaaaaaac-
tiiiiivvvvviiiiiiitiiiiieeeeeessssss. . . . . "(Willingly forming slower-than-
light particles. This is one aspect of our activities)."

(10:35. Jane paused briefly, her eyes closed. Suddenly her voice
became high-pitched and, at first, quite incomprehensible to me because of the
rapidity of her speech. The effect was remarkably like that of a tape recording
played too fast: Her voice went way up the scale, issuing from stiffly held lips. After
a few moments I began to understand her:) "—on another level this is
completely unintelligible—at another level the pieces are completely
unintelligible—"

(She repeated variations of this idea again and again, which gave
me time to write down some of them. Her speech was as fast as it could be while
remaining at all explicit. Then at a bit slower rate:) "All of these are aspects
of one reality . . . Atoms are sound. You do not hear them. . . ."

(10:36. Now Jane's place slowed considerably. In the same high
voice she began stressing as separate units many of the syllables of the words she
spoke. This was reminiscent of Seth Two's method of delivery, yet subjectively I
felt differences. Also, Seth Two had usually expressed "itself" in the singular,
whereas tonight's material was coming through under the plural "we":) "All
con-scious-ness has as-pects that are act-i-va-ted and ex-pressed in
all idi-oms or real-i-ties. This is all we can clear-ly com-mun-i-cate
with you now."

(10:38. Jane slumped in her rocker, eyes closed. She had trouble
getting them open. She remembered giving the variations on the sounds and
methods of speech. She told me that "something" wanted to manifest through her
so slowly that it was almost inexpressible; she'd felt deep rolling sounds going
through her, yearning to be translated, yearning to make sense in our terms. "It
would have taken me three hours to do it right." The slow material simply came
out that way when she tried to express it. She couldn't really understand what
"they" wanted her to do, if anything.

(Jane said the high-voiced, rapid delivery reminded her of Seth Two,
then mentioned a point I'd forgotten: She'd experienced a similar effect once
before—last month, while writing poetry, and only mentally. At that time, as
now, she hadn't been able to comprehend what was happening well enough to
translate it, let alone write down anything.[1]

(10:48. After we'd rested for a few minutes, Jane began to speak in
her regular voice. I've purposely refrained from mentioning earlier the rather
extensive material that follows; perhaps the reader, coming upon it unexpectedly, will feel something of my own surprise as Jane started to develop it out
of both the slow and rapid effects she'd already demonstrated:)

"I'm getting something, Rob. Something to do with
atoms. The slow thing, represented by those drawn-out sounds, is in

the center of the atom. Then that's surrounded by faster-than-light particles, represented by the real fast sounds. So the center of this thing—whatever it is—is massive in terms of mass.[8] I don't know whether this means it's <u>heavy</u> or not, but it's tremendous in terms of mass—though it <u>may</u>, underlined, be very small in size.

"Everything is conscious, of course. Atoms and molecules, the whole thing. The massive part is the core. This core is, I believe, not discovered yet [by physicists], and it's so slow to us that no motion is apparent. I don't know whether this is an atom or not. You can call it a dead hole" (Pause.) "Its motion in our terms is so slow as not to be observable, but in terms of time it's a backward motion."[9]

(Pause at 10:50.) ". . . [this core is] always surrounded by these faster-than-light particles. This is a structure . . . but it does cause a pulling-in or wrinkling effect where it appears. There are many of these, I think, in our galaxy as well as others. Nothing can be drawn <u>through</u> the dead hole, though, as things can be drawn through the black hole, because of [the dead hole's] literally impenetrable mass. Now as with atoms alone, and all othe such structures, these also exist as sound.[10] Black holes and white holes do also.[11] The sounds are actually characteristics that act as cohesives, characteristics automatically given off. The slower center por ions of the dead holes themselves move backward into beginnings becoming heavier and heavier."

(11:00.) "In a way of speaking you could say these centers fall through space, but they really fall through th . space of themselves. (Jane shook her head, her eyes closed.) As they fall backward through themselves—I'm getting this—I don't know how to say it—the faster-than-light particles collapse in on top. The dead hole seems to swallow itself, with the real fast particles like a lid that gradually diminishes . . . From our point of view the hole is closed, say, once the faster-than-light particles follow the sl wer core backward into beginnings."

(11:05.) "As the core goes backward—in quotes—'in time,' however, it begins to accelerate. I don't know how to put this. When it emerges in another universe, the faster-than-light particles have slowed down, and the core becomes faster than light. The dead hole is repeated in microscopic size—that's small, isı 't it? Before the emergence of the atom . . . oh, dear . . . as an analogy, you could say that the dead hole we've been talking about emerges as an atom in another universe. But it's the stage <u>before</u> the apı earance, or the stage <u>from which</u> an atom comes.

"Speaking of the dead hole in a galaxy, say ours, it

emerges in what would be to us an atom of fantastic size, but the same thing happens on a different scale as far as the creation of matter is concerned within our own system."[12]

(11:12.) "As mentioned, sound is connected here also, and each one of these phenomena has consciousness that does express itself, and is aware of the stages through which it passes. In certain terms, dead holes connect past and present; also future. In practical terms, they have to do with the seeming permanence of an object. They are the invisible portions of the atom. There are giant-sized atoms, as well as the ones you're familiar with."

(11:17.) "I—I know there's more there . . . I want to find out more. I don't get their [the 'consciousnesses' behind tonight's material] purpose. *(Jane looked tired and disheveled now, and I suggested she end the session. She sat with her eyes closed. She had trouble enunciating the next sentence, and had to repeat it:)* Dead holes turn into live holes . . . where the motion and impetus, in your terms, would be toward the future . . . I can't get any more. . . . *(Once again I urged her to quit.)* I'm almost finished. In this case, the core appears as matter-to-be. I guess I'll stop. I can't follow it. This whole thing has to do with those voice effects earlier. . . ."

(11:19.) "I was getting images through the whole thing. *(Jane rested briefly.)* I was trying to explain what *they* meant. It's something when you don't know what you're trying to say. . . . *(She described the images to some extent—delineating stars, a series of circles, condensing matter, imploding galaxies and other such effects—but they didn't mean as much to me as her material in the session itself.)* I just got tired receiving the stuff. That was really a workout. There's a lot more there to be had, too. . . ." *(She likened her dissertation to the way she often gets impressions concerning people; the information "just comes," and she recites it.*

(I'd maintain that Jane has been on a creative upsurge for a year now. During that time she finished Seth Speaks *and helped me proofread it, wrote her novel,* Oversoul Seven, *and worked on another* Seven *book [still unfinished], as well as* Personal Reality *and* Adventures. *These activities meant keeping to her schedule of two regular sessions a week for the most part, although I do the work of transcribing her trance material. Jane also held her weekly ESP classes and writing classes, and continued her work on poetry and an autobiography [also unfinished]. With all of this, we also went through the flood caused by Tropical Storm Agnes in June 1972. Jane's daily predictions have been working out exceptionally well. Recently she was informed that impressions she gave for certain people as long as two years ago have been proving correct in large measure—a very heartening development. . . .*

(The day after this session, Jane greatly enlarged upon her original estimate—three hours—of the time she'd need to interpret the long or slow

sounds. Now she felt that "to do proper justice to them would take years—centuries perhaps." Because of our ordinary time sense the sounds were actually so slow to us that they appeared to be motionless, or "dead," she told me, leading us to speculate that this may be one of the reasons why in usual terms we call inanimate matter—rocks, for instance—"dead." But Jane couldn't really define any sources behind last night's material, beyond calling them "consciousnesses, or beings—but maybe not personalities as we think of that term." Then, again increasing her estimate, she said that if "they" tried to communicate with us through sound, through our sensual equipment, "it would take forever."

(After reading my typed interpretations of the long sounds she'd started to deliver at 10:22, Jane wrote: "I knew what the drawn-out words were at the beginning, and thought Rob had understood them. Now I haven't the slightest idea of what they said."

(I want to conclude this appendix with a poem Jane wrote during the summer of 1963, a few months before she began the sessions. To me her long-sound material, given nine years later in the 612th session, simply represented her psychic way of "catching up" with, and developing, deeply intuitive knowledge that she'd possessed all along:)

Long Is the Light

Long is the light
Of the moth and the willow.
Long is the journey
Of the root and the stem.
Deep is the cry
Of the tree bark and blossom.
The leaf hears its growing,
And life sings its truth.

Sweet is the depth
Of air to the swallow.
Long is the still breath
Of the stone and the pebble.
Deep is the trance
Of the mountain and meadow.
The leaf hears its growing,
And stones speak their truth.

NOTES: Appendix 19

1. In Appendix 3 of *Adventures* Jane listed and described the altered states of consciousness that she's attained so far in her psychic

development. She also considered Seth Two in various other parts of *Adventures*. In Chapter 2, for instance, the Seth Two quotations are cast in the editorial "we," the guise in which that energy gestalt often comes through: "We are trying to appreciate the nature of your present existence . . . For you there may seem to be an unbearable loneliness, because you are so used to relating to the warm victory of the flesh, and [here] there is no physical being . . . Yet beyond and within that isolation is a point of light that is consciousness. It pulses with the power behind all the emotions that you know . . . This is the warmth that . . . is born from the very devotion of our isolation . . . that creates the reality that you know, without itself experiencing it."

Seth Two is mentioned but a few times in *Personal Reality*. Those who are interested can also refer to the Seth Two descriptions and excerpts in Chapter 22 of *Seth Speaks*; see Session 588 from 11:35 P.M., and Session 589.

2. Jane's earliest experiences with the phenomenon of massiveness are described in the 39th session for March 30, 1964; in Volume 1, see the excerpts in Appendix 3 (for Session 681).

(I remind the reader that Appendix 3 also contains a reference to Jane's extraordinary adventure with—and in—massiveness on April 4, 1973. She described it herself in the 653rd session for Chapter 13 of *Personal Reality*.

3. In Note 9 for the 712th session, see the two analogies to long sound that I drew from the 514th session in *Seth Speaks*.

4. By the time the 612th session was held we were finally getting back into our old rhythms of work; they'd been seriously disrupted by the flood caused by Tropical Storm Agnes in June 1972. Just before the flood materialized (over two months ago), Seth-Jane had completed the Preface and the first session for Chapter 1 of *Personal Reality*; see the opening notes for Session 613 in that work.

5. I was surprised to hear Jane's somewhat embarrassed references to the third eye, since I couldn't remember her mentioning it before in the sessions. The third eye (sometimes called the "back eye") is the legendary organ of psychic perception, supposedly located behind the forehead. In occult science it's been connected with the pineal body, or gland; that mysterious member of the endocrine system is buried deep within the brain, and through the centuries has been considered by many—including the French philosopher and mathematician, René Descartes (1596–1650)— to be the seat of the soul.

Many are familiar with the Hindu discipline of Yoga. In that ascetic system of breathing, meditation, and postures, the third eye corresponds to the sixth chakra, as one starts counting the positions of those seven nonphysical wheels of psychic energy from the base of the spine to the brain's cerebrum.

Consciously Jane knows very little about the history of the third eye, so-called. I wouldn't say that either of us believes in it particularly, so it's interesting, then, to consider what intuitive knowledge she might possess that led her to talk about it now.

6. In Chapter 6 of *Adventures,* Jane described how we rented a second apartment across the hall from our first one in order to have more living and working space. (The apartments are on the second floor.) Jane's psychic identification with the leaves of the great oak tree, growing so close beside the second apartment's kitchen windows, marked the beginning of a different kind of relaxation for her; the kitchen became her evocative "tree house." Several years later, I asked her to write for this note her own account of the relaxation effects that grew out of the hours she spent in contemplation with that massive tree:

"That particular kind of relaxation seems to repeatedly come upon me over a period of several months or even a year, then to vanish for the same amount of time. I first felt it right after we moved into the new apartment in June 1971, and when it started I knew it was a different kind of feeling. It's a sort of superrelaxation; almost profound, and mental and physical at once. A completely different thing than just yawning, even though I might *be* yawning.

"The relaxation involves a curious sense of dropping down inwardly, of going slowly beneath the realities we usually recognize. It's a smooth transition in which perception is slowed down topwise, but deepened so that usually unperceived stimuli seem to rise from an underside of consciousness and bodily sensation. In that kind of relaxation the body itself perceives differently; *that's* what I'm trying to emphasize. Looking at a leaf while in that state, I easily feel myself as part of the leaf, and I think this is a biological as well as a psychic perception. At certain levels the body feels that way itself, although ordinarily we aren't aware of it. Such a relaxation, then, is almost an extension of biological insight."

7. From Jane's notebook: "I was writing poetry one day early in August 1971, when suddenly I mentally heard the oddest sounds—incredibly fast, too quick to follow. Instantly I 'knew' that these faster sounds were objects coming into material focus. They slowed down to become physical. I sensed this neurologically, though how that was possible, I don't know. . . ."

Perhaps this mental event was Jane's way of "practicing" for the physical one that was to follow a month later, in the 612th session. In my opinion, she offers a most important insight here toward understanding the formation of our mundane physical reality. Besides Jane's material in appendixes 4 and 5 for Volume 1 of *"Unknown" Reality,* see Seth's deliveries on inner sound, light, and electromagnetic patterns in the four sessions (623–26) making up Chapter 5 of *Personal Reality.*

8. Since Jane has just referred to them, in this note I'll touch upon atoms (and, incidentally, molecules), faster-than-light particles, and mass. The reader can use the definitions below to make his or her own associations with Jane's material. (The other sources given will also add extra dimensions to this 612th session.)

In conventional terms, atoms are regarded as the submicroscopic entities making up all objects and substances in our world. Each atom consists of a nucleus of protons, neutrons, and other subatomic particles, around all of which move a complicated system of much lighter electrons. (An atom of hydrogen, however, is made up of but one proton and one electron.) All is in balance: The number of positive charges on the nucleus equals the number of negatively charged electrons. Note 24 for Appendix 18 contains a short discussion of the particle-wave duality involving the components of the atom. In Note 35 for the same appendix, I quoted Seth from the 702nd session in Volume 1; he advanced his own idea of interrelated fields versus particle-wave theory.

Atoms combine to form molecules. If the assembled atoms are all alike, an element results; if two or more different kinds of atoms combine into molecules, a compound is created.

In Note 1 for Session 709 I wrote that "Tachyons ... are supposed faster-than-light particles that are thought to be possible within Einstein's special theory of relativity." (In the session itself Seth makes some intriguing references to related possibilities: "In out-of-body states, consciousness can travel faster than light—often, in fact, instantaneously." Also see Note 2.) In the 682nd session for Volume 1, while discussing his CU's, or.units of consciousness, Seth told us: "Of course they move faster than light." Then see notes 3 and 4 for that session.

The 581st session for Chapter 20 of *Seth Speaks* not only contains notes on tachyons, but Seth's own material on superspeed entities: "Some of these in your terms share the same space as your own universe. You simply would not perceive such particles as mass." And: "There are many ranges and great varieties of such units, all existing beyond your perceivable reach."

I remind the reader of a remark Seth made in the 702nd session for Volume 1, when Jane was delivering material for him on electron spin and related concepts: "Ruburt's vocabulary is not an official scientific one. Nor, for our purposes should it be—for that vocabulary is limiting." Jane has only the sketchiest of scientific backgrounds, but a very strong intuitive grasp of the qualities involved. By choice, even in trance she attempts to relay specialized information in ordinary verbal terms, without the use of formulas, equations, or highly technical language. The material in this session is a good example of her approach. We've never tried to get her—or Seth—to deliver mathematical or chemical formulas during a session; it's not her thing. However, she thinks that if she were to motivate herself she could accomplish something through the formalized language of mathematics, say, but that in the beginning at least she'd acquire the information visually; then she would write it down, even while the session was in progress. . . .

Ordinarily we think of mass as meaning the bulk and/or weight of an object. In classical physics the amount of matter in a given object is measured according to its relation to inertia, which in turn is the tendency of matter to keep moving in the same direction, if moving, or to stay at rest if at rest. An object's mass is arrived at through dividing its weight by the acceleration caused by gravity.

In his special theory of relativity, however, Albert Einstein showed that mass is a highly concentrated form of energy. Any object contains energy "on deposit" in its mass, then. The masses of colliding subatomic "particles," for instance, can be transferred into both energy and new particles. In Volume 1, see the material on Einstein in Session 701, with notes.

9. In the physics of elementary particles, time reversal, or symmetry, is a basic concept. I'll make two references to Volume 1: In Session 682, after 9:47, Seth told us that in our terms his CU's, or units of consciousness, "can move forward or backward in time. But they can also move into thresholds of time with which you are not familiar." In Session 702, Seth discussed relationships involving electron spin and the direction, or flow, of time; also see Note 6 for that session.

10. Sound, and various symbolic attributes of that phenomenon, are uniting factors in back of much of Seth-Jane's material, and I could list many instances. I'm not referring here only to "outside" developments like Jane's powerful Seth voice, her speaking and singing in Sumari, or her slow and fast sounds as produced for this session, but to inner, audible and inaudible manifestations or translations of sound.

In the 24th session for February 10, 1964, Seth explained how a recent vision I'd had, involving a ladderlike series of heads opening and closing their silent mouths, had really been my attempt to cast inner data into a more familiar outer-sense kind of perception. "You felt sound," Seth told me. After my initial unease over this new type of experience, I found it most intriguing; I've had my own little adventures embodying that feeling-perception of sound ever since. In the same session, Seth discussed Jane's periodic feeling of sound; in her case, she often hears music internally.

Seth, from the 154th session for May 12, 1965: "Basically, the physical body has the potential for perceiving stimuli on a generalized basis. By this I mean that although the eyes are for seeing, the ears for hearing, and so forth, the potentials of the physical body include the capacity to hear, for example, through any given portion of the bodily expanse . . . Sound, then, can be felt as well as heard, although in such cases you may say that the sound is heard in the depths of the tissues; this, however, being an analogy . . . Ruburt, in feeling sound, merely experienced it from a different perspective.

"Within your system colors may be perceived as sound (chromesthesia, or 'colored hearing'). Their connections with human moods are only too apparent. Concerning Joseph's point about sound: Sound, alone, entering the body, instantaneously changes it . . . Any perception instantly changes the perceiver. It also changes the thing perceived. . . ."

For some other material on sound see the 572nd session for Chapter 18 of Seth Speaks, for instance, or the already mentioned sessions (in Note 7) that make up Chapter 5 of Personal Reality.

And added later: Many people undergo some form of chromesthesia—that is, certain colors or color patterns are seen upon hearing certain sounds. Occasionally Jane will experience one of her own variations of such an ability. A good example for this note can be found in her material at 10:47 in the 714th session: "Wait a minute . . . What I'm getting is a fantastic sound that's imprisoned in a crystal, that *speaks* through light, that's the essence of personality. I'm getting almost jewel-like colored sounds. . . ."

11. According to modern cosmology, a black hole consists of the remains of a very massive star (one much larger than our own sun, for example) that's suffered complete gravitational collapse after the death of its nuclear fires. Such an object is very small and unimaginably dense; within it, time and space are interchangeable. It's also quite invisible, because its surface gravity is so enormous that not even light can escape from it. (Yet, in Volume 1, see the comments in Note 4 for Session 688, on the possibility of light radiation from the "event horizon" of the black hole.) So far just two black holes have been tentatively located, although many of them are believed to exist.

Since the matter surrounding a black hole would also be drawn into it, some astrophysicists have suggested that this might emerge into another universe through its opposite—a white hole—where it would be seen as an extremely brilliant quasar, or quasi-stellar radio source. So there would be an exchange of matter-energy between universes or realities.

Interestingly enough, several very distant quasars have been linked to certain observed faster-than-light effects, thus contradicting current physical theory that nothing can exceed the speed of light. For science this is a very uncomfortable situation that has yet to be resolved. But I'm sure that in scientific terms (quite aside from Seth's material in Note 1 for the 712th session) there are many discoveries to be made in this area. The faster-than-light effects may be the results of observations that are simply not understood in some as-yet-unexplained way. . . .

In trance or out, Jane likes to "take off" in her own creative ways from concepts like that of the tachyon, or the black hole or the white hole—so in this session she came up with the "dead hole." Then, from another angle, she explored related ideas in *Adventures*; see Chapter 19, "Earth Experience as a White Hole," in which she wrote, "What kind of a structured universe could explain both the inner and exterior worlds? If we consider the universe as a white hole—our exterior universe of sense—we at least have a theoretical framework that reconciles our inner and outer activity, our physical and spiritual or psychic experience; and the apparent dilemma between a simultaneous present in which all events happen at once, and our daily experience in which we seem to progress through time from birth to death."

In closing: See the 593rd session in the Appendix of *Seth Speaks* for Seth's material on black holes, white holes, and coordination points: "A black hole is a white hole turned inside out . . . The holes, therefore, or coordination points [points of double reality, or where realities merge], are actually great accelerators that reenergize energy itself." In the 688th session for Volume 1, Seth presents an analogy in which his basic units of consciousness, or CU's, operate as minute but very powerful black holes and white holes.

12. A note added over a year later: For some time I've intuitively felt connections between Jane's material in this paragraph and ideas we first read about some six months after this 612th session was held in September 1972: that for various reasons (having to do with gravitational waves, mass, et cetera) many galaxies, including our own, could have been formed out of matter accumulating around black holes at their centers.

APPENDIX 20
(For Session 713)

(Seth hasn't often talked about UFO's—unidentified flying objects— in the sessions. He thinks they have various states of origin. Occasionally he'll mention them in connection with another subject; as an example, see the two paragraphs about "saucers" and the pulsating nature of atoms and molecules in the ESP class session for January 12, 1971, in the Appendix of Seth Speaks.

(That material actually flows from a session held seven years earlier: the 16th for January 15, 1964, which still contains Seth-Jane's longest delivery on such craft. We found the information in the session quite intriguing because we thought it offered a fresh approach to a very controversial puzzle. We still think so. [In the early sessions, incidentally, Seth used the word "plane" often, but not long afterward began the general changeover to "reality," which for the most part we like better. However, note at the end of these excerpts from the 16th session the meanings and delineations he found within that word "plane"— even though he regarded it as our term.])

The strange thing about your flying saucers is not that they appear, but that you can see them. As science advances on various planes the inhabitants learn to travel between planes occasionally, while carrying with them the [camouflage] manifestations of their home stations . . .

I am quite sure—I know for a fact—that beings from other planes have appeared among you, sometimes on purpose and sometimes completely by accident. As in some cases humans have quite accidentally blundered through the apparent curtain between your present and your past, so have beings blundered into the apparent division between one plane and another. Usually when they have done so they were invisible on your plane, as the few of you who fell into the past, or the apparent past, were invisible to the people of the past.

This sort of experience involves a sudden psychic awareness, straight from the entity, that all boundaries are for practical purposes only. However, there are indeed many kinds of science. There are a number of sciences dealing just with locomotion. Had the human species gone into certain mental disciplines as thoroughly as it has explored technological disciplines, its practical transportation system would be vastly different, and yet by this time even more practical than it is now. *(With amusement:)* I am making this point because I want it made plain—this, dear Joseph, is a pun— that when I speak of science on another plane I may not speak of the plain old science that you know.

Now back to the point. When sciences progress on various planes, then visitations become less accidental and more planned. Once the inhabitants of a plane have learned mental-science patterns, then they are to a great degree freed from the more regular camouflage [physical] patterns. This applies to "higher" planes than mine, generally speaking, although mine is further along in these sciences than your own.

[Many of] the flying saucer appearances come from [such] a plane, [one] that is much more advanced in technological sciences than earth at this time. However, this is still not a mental-science plane. Therefore the camouflage paraphernalia appears, more or less visible, to your own astonishment. Now, so strong is this tendency for vitality to change from one apparent form to another, that what you have here in your flying object is something that is actually, as you view it, not of your plane or of [whatever] plane of its origin . . . The atoms and molecules that structurally compose the UFO, and which are themselves formed by vitality, are more or less aligned according to the pattern of its own territory. Now as the craft enters your plane a distortion occurs. Its actual structure is caught in a dilemma of form . . . between transforming itself completely into earth's particular camouflage pattern, and retaining its original pattern. The earthly viewer attempts to correlate what he sees with what he supposedly knows or imagines possible in the universe.

What he sees is something between a horse and a dog, that resembles neither. The flying saucer retains what it can of its original structure and changes what it must. This accounts for many of the conflicting reports as to shape, size, and color. The few times the craft shoots off at right angles, it has managed to retain functions ordinary to it in its particular habitat.

I do not believe you will have any saucer landings for quite a while, not physical landings in the usual sense of the word. These vehicles cannot stay on your plane for any length of time at all. The pressures that push against the saucer itself are tremendous . . . The struggle to be one thing or another is very great on any plane. To conform to the laws of a particular plane is a practical necessity, and at this time the flying saucer craft simply cannot afford to stay betwixt and between for any indefinite period.

What they do is take quick glimpses of your plane—and hold in mind that the saucer or cigar shape [often] seen on your planet is a bastard form having little relation to the structure as it is at home base.

At a later date I may go into the inhabitants of [those planes] more thoroughly, but as it is I am not very much acquainted with them myself.[1]

There are so many things you do not understand that I hope to explain to you. There are other things you do not understand that I cannot explain to you, simply because they would be too alien now for your regular mode of thought . . .

One note along these lines. A plane—and I am using your term; I will try to think of a better one—is not necessarily a planet. A plane may be one planet, but a plane may also exist where no planet is. One planet may have several planes. Planes may also involve various aspects of apparent time—this particular matter being too difficult to go into right now, although I will continue it later.

Planes can and do intermix without the knowledge of the inhabitants of the particular planes involved. I want to get away from the idea of a plane being a place. It may be in some cases but is not always. A plane may be a time. A plane, believe it or not, may be only one iota of vitality that seems to exist by itself. A plane is something apparently divided from the rest of the universe for a time and for a reason. A plane may cease to be. A plane may spring up where there was none. A plane is formed for entities as patterns for fulfillment on various levels. A plane is a climate conducive to the development of unique and particular capacities and achievements. A plane is an isolation of elements where each one is given the most possible space in which to function.

Planets have been used as planes and used again as other planes. A plane is not a cosmic location. It is oftentimes practical that entities or their various personalities visit one plane before another. This does not necessarily mean that one plane must be visited before another. A certain succession is merely more useful for the entity as a whole.

In other terms, you could say that an entity visits all planes simultaneously, as it is possible for you to visit a certain state, county, and city at one time. You might also visit the states of sorrow and joy almost simultaneously, and experience both emotions in heightened form because of the almost immediate contrast between them.

In fact, the analogy of a plane with an emotional state is much more valid than that between a plane and a geographical state—particularly since emotional states take up no room.

NOTES: Appendix 20

1. A note added a decade later: So far, Seth has failed to volunteer information on the inhabitants of any of the "saucer" planes—but neither have we asked him to do so.

APPENDIX 21
(For Session 721)

(Jane and I consider Seth's concept of counterparts to be an intriguing psychological framework, spacious enough to serve as a workable thematic structure in which the social and nationalistic characteristics of our species can be studied, as well as the components of the individual psyche. That is, the private person is here seen as interacting with others because there is, beneath our awareness, an inner "person-to-person" relationship connecting each individual with his or her physical counterparts, though they may well be living in other parts of the globe while sharing the same historical period. It follows, then, that one may or may not ever meet a counterpart "in the flesh"— may or may not even suspect the existence of such relationships.

(The material on counterparts emerged from Seth's treatment of reincarnation. Along with his addition of simultaneous time, I'd say that the concept of counterparts provides reincarnation with a novel approach indeeed; and that our awareness of both has always been latent within the reincarnational framework, whether in simultaneous or linear terms.

(Now I'd like to present a batch of notes, ideas, and excerpts from sessions about reincarnation, counterparts, and related data, pulling them together into a coherent picture. Although reincarnation and its variations has been discussed by Seth almost from the very beginning of our sessions, the subject didn't represent one of our own main concerns. For that matter, Jane almost actively resisted such information in the past. She still says comparatively little about reincarnation on her own, although Seth shows no such reservations.

(Actually, we've had two recent indications that Seth was going to initiate something like the counterpart thesis, even though he hadn't used the term itself. The first clue came in a private, or deleted, session held a week ago on Monday night [November 18, 1974]; the second hint was given in ESP class on the following evening.

(In our private session, Seth commented on my "quite legitimate" reincarnational data involving the black woman, Maumee or Mawmee, who'd lived on the Caribbean island of Jamaica early in the 19th century. He went on to say:) You helped that woman. Your present sense of security and relative detachment gave her strength. She knew she would survive, because she was aware of your knowledge. I will say more about it, but for now that is the end of the session. Ruburt has had enough for a night.

(Jane was tired by the session's end. Without thinking, I casually remarked that currently I had three things going reincarnationally[1]—involving

the Roman soldier, the black woman, and Nebene—and that if I could untangle their time sequences, I could use them as part of a chronological list of my "past" lives.

("I wish you hadn't said that, Rob," Jane answered, somewhat ruefully. "Now I've got a whole bunch of stuff on reincarnation and time. So let's get it down."

(I humorously protested, knowing that she was really tired, and told her not to say anything that later she'd wish we had recorded. I refused to get out my notebook and pen again. It was obvious that Jane wanted only to sleep, even though she was willing to continue the session after trying to wake up by drinking a cup of coffee.

("All right," she said finally. "I'll just tell you this: The whole idea of reincarnation is all screwed up. To unscramble it would really be confusing. What I'm getting is that the idea of just one life in any given time is bullshit—the psyche is so rich that it can have more than one life in one time period, like your Nebene and Roman soldier living together in the first century. But if you tell people that, you'll just get them all mixed up."

("Well, assuming that my intuitions were reasonably accurate when I picked up on those two personalities," I said, "there have to be explanations."

("Sure," Jane replied. "There's a whole lot there I could give you right now—"

("Okay. I really want to know all about it. But at some other time."

(After that, we gave up and went to bed. In ESP class the following night, Seth indicated that he was ready to expand his concepts of personality still further—though, again, he didn't mention counterparts per se. He started by commenting on my experience with Maumee once more. Then he continued:)

Now: a footnote to our [private] session of last night. Ruburt was correct: Lives <u>are</u> simultaneous. You can live more than one life at a time—in your terms now—but that is a loaded sentence. You are neurologically tuned in to one particular field of actuality that you recognize.[2] In your terms and from your viewpoint only, messages from other existences live within you as ghost images within the cells, for the cells recognize more than you do on a conscious level. That is, for a brief time, Joseph *(Rob)* was consciously able to perceive a portion of another existence.

<u>You could not be consciously aware of those other realities all of the time, and deal with the world that you know.</u> You have several time and space tracks in operation at once, then, but you acknowledge only certain neurological messages physically. Yet there is more to the body than you perceive of it, and this is difficult to explain to you . . . If you can think of a multidimensional body

existing at one time in various realities, and appearing differently within each one while still being whole, then you can get some glimpse of what is involved.[3]

Now our friend Joseph here was able to handle another reality while still being involved in this one. *(To me:)* Neurologically, you crossed your messages. You were aware of ghost images that you usually do not recognize, and those were translated into ghost sense data. *(To the class:)* That is, he knew the black woman was not in the physical room with him in this space and time, running through his studio [where he had the experience]. But in other terms, she was indeed running in another environment that our friend was able to see, and to superimpose over the reality he knew, while keeping both intact.

(Here I asked Seth if the strong thrilling sensations I'd repeatedly felt at the time had anything to do with my perceptions of the "ghost images" of Maumee and her surroundings. Seth answered:)

Those were the result of the neurological changeover, and they are your particular symbol that this is occurring. Others will have symbols of their own.

But such pictures are there for any of you who want to view them. When you are ready to see them, you will. Many of you are not ready to meet those kinds of data . . . for a certain kind of finesse is required—a balance that you are learning. And each of you knows intuitively when you are open to such encounters.

There are, of course, future memories as well as past ones . . . As Joseph often says, "When you think of reincarnation, you do so in terms of past lives." You are afraid to consider future lives because then you have to face the death that must be met first, in your terms. And so you never think of future selves, or how you might benefit from knowing them. . . .

(The material in these recent excerpts rather prepared us for Seth's introduction of counterparts, then, in Session 721. In ESP class the next evening [on November 26], Seth began contending with some of the questions that instantly arose as a result of his new material. I'd just read aloud portions of the 721st session when one longtime student, whom I'll call Florence, commented that there "has to be a balance between each of us and our counterparts." Speaking strongly and humorously, Seth immediately took over the discussion.

(To Florence:) Far be it from me to disturb your ancient ideas of yin and yang, or Jung, or good and evil, or of right and wrong, or of good and bad vibrations! I was beginning a new body of material, and so we have not finished with it by a long shot! What I

hope to say is that your world exists in different terms than those you recognize, and that reincarnation is indeed a myth and a story that stands for something else entirely.

Each of you takes part in your world—and in your time as you understand it, and in your terms, all the creatures of the earth participate in the century. You work out creative challenges and possibilities. You are born into different races, into different cultures, with different—but the same—desires . . . There are many things that you are learning. And so, if you will forgive me, my dear Florence, I will use you as an example.

For there is also a version of our Florence, a young man in China, who does not weigh even 70 pounds, and who is 26 years old. *(Florence is in her late 40's.)* He has starved for years. He feels very vulnerable. It does not particularly help that young man when our Florence piles on weight because <u>she</u> then feels less vulnerable, and more protected from her world.

On the other hand, our young man sometimes dreams of being overweight, and it is one of his most satisfying dreams. Now those dreams are going to help him in his own manner, for he is already working on some concepts involving the planting of fields that will benefit the people in his village.

In his particular village, the elders believe that there is some merit to being underweight. Our young man hates the Americans. He believes that this is an opulent, luxurious, and wicked society, and yet he yearns toward it with all his heart.

Now our Florence is working with her own ideas of good and evil, searching for what she <u>thinks</u> of as an aesthetic and moral code that she can rely upon. Her counterpart had that code, but found that he could <u>not</u> count upon it. Each is working on the same series of challenges. There are also two other counterparts. Between the four of them, the century is being covered. *(To Florence, smiling:)* I will tell you about that at another time. It is not <u>my</u> suspense story— it is your own![4]

(Florence: "What you said about my counterpart in China makes perfect sense to me."

(Then Seth came through with this aside, as he referred to a guest:) One small note to our astrologer-in-spirit over there. One tiny, wicked hint! Each of you has a birthday that you recognize—<u>one</u> birthdate—but there are hidden variables, because of what I am saying here tonight, that do not apply in those charts because you have not thought of them.

Now in your terms only, these other counterparts are like latent patterns within your mind. Echoes. How many of you have actually thought of what the unconscious may be? Or, the voices that you hear within your mind or heart? Are they yours? To what counterparts do they belong? And yet each of you, in your own identity, has the right to do precisely as you wish, and to form your own reality. . . .

(And, later in the session:) I will give you an example. There is a member of the class—and (with obvious amusement) I will close my innocent eyes so that I do not give the secret away—but there is a class member who is indeed a fine Jesuit, handling problems of great weight, having to do with the nature of religion. There is a renegade priest who has been in this class, and who ran off to California; he likes to put the boot to theology and "do his own thing." There is also an extremely devout woman who lives in England. All of these counterparts are dealing with the nature of religion. They are experiencing versions of religion because it interests them.

[Each of] you will create the attributes of reality that interest you and work with them in your own way. If you want to study the nature of religion and do a good job of it, then you must be among other things a skeptic and a believer, and an Indian and a Jew, say. Otherwise you will not understand anything at all, and have a very lopsided picture. And (to a black student) you cannot know what it is like to be black in this culture—you may not agree here—unless you are also white in it. . . . Now I return you to yourselves and to your counterparts.

("Well," I said to Jane after class, as we discussed the Chinese-American situation cited by Seth, "I don't know about counterpart relationships in other kinds of realities, but it's certainly obvious that at least some physical counterparts can hate each other . . ." So the larger self, I thought, would be quite capable of seeking experience through its parts in every way imaginable. Although it might be difficult for us to understand, let alone accept, the whole self or entity must regard all of its counterparts as sublime facets of itself—no matter whether they loved, suffered,[5] hated, or killed each other or "outsiders." Within its great reaches it would transform its counterparts' actions in ways that were, quite possibly, beyond our emotional and intellectual grasp. At the same time, the self would learn and be changed through the challenges and struggles of its human portions.

(On more "practical" levels, we thought that behavior among nations might be changed for the better if the idea of counterparts were understood, or at least considered—if, for instance, many of the individuals making up a country realized that they could actually be acting against portions of themselves [or of their whole selves] in the persons of the "enemy" country, and so modified the virulence of their feelings. The nations of the world would benefit greatly from even a small improvement in their relationships with each other.

And if an individual strongly disliked a counterpart in another land, wouldn't this quality of emotion be detrimentally reflected in the person doing the hating?

(So far we've been dealing with the idea of counterparts in our own physical reality. By way of contrast, however, Seth stated last month in the 713th session, after 10:32:) Nothing exists outside the psyche, however, that does not exist within it, and there is no unknown world that does not have its psychological or psychic counterpart. *(Before that, from Session 712:)* To some extent or another, there are counterparts of all realities within your psyche.

(Continuing to trace such references back through the material, I'd like to direct the reader to several passages from the 683rd session for Volume 1 of "Unknown" Reality; in them Seth contends with variations on the counterpart theme as they're developed in certain other probable realities:)

(1.) It is quite possible, for example, for several selves to occupy a body, and were this the norm it would be easily accepted. That implies another kind of multipersonhood, however, one actually allowing for the fulfillment of many abilities of various natures usually left unexpressed. It also implies a freedom and organization of consciousness that is unusual in your system of reality, and was not chosen there.

(2.) In some systems of physical existence, a multipersonhood is established, in which three or four "persons" emerge from the same inner self, each one utilizing to the best of its abilities those characteristics of its own. This presupposes a gestalt of awareness, however, in which each knows of the activities of the others, and participates; and you have a *different* version of mass consciousness. Do you see the correlation?

("Yes," I said.)

In the systems in which evolution of consciousness has worked in that fashion, all faculties of body and mind in one "lifetime" are beautifully utilized. Nor is there any ambiguity about identity. The individual would say, for example, "I am Joe, and Jane, and Jim, and Bob."[6] There are physical variations of a sexual nature, so that on all levels identity includes the male and female. Shadows of all such probabilities appear within your own system, as oddities. Anything apparent to whatever degree in your system is developed in another.

(Seth's material on counterparts did make us wonder about Jane's and his earlier uses of the word and its concepts. Checking backward through past sessions and Jane's poetry, I soon learned that her intuitive grasp of the term had always been truer than mine, for I'd carried the idea that "counterpart" implied a status of opposites rather than the complementary one it really does. Seth also used the term in its correct sense.[7]

(The entire poem, Dear Love, *which Jane wrote for me in December 1973, can be found in Note 3 for the 713th session. I want to repeat the first verse of it for obvious reasons, although all of the poem is an excellent creative exposition of counterpart ideas:*

> *Dear love,*
> *what times unmanifest*
> *in our lives reside*
> *beneath our nights and days?*
> *What counterparts break*
> *within our smiles,*
> *what cracks appear in other skies*
> *as we talk and drink coffee*
> *in quiet domestic grace?*

(In Chapter 19 of Personal Reality, *I found this line of Seth's in the 667th session for May 30, 1973:)* For reason and emotion are natural counterparts.

(Ten sessions earlier, there's a particularly evocative reference to counterparts in the 657th session for April 18, 1973, in Chapter 15 of Personal Reality. *In retrospect that material seems to be a clear indication of the later development of the counterpart concept—and one passage could well refer to* "Unknown" Reality *long before that project was ever thought of as far as Jane and I were concerned. Seth:)*

In a way that will be explained in another book for those interested in such matters, there is a kind of coincidence with all of these present points of power[8] that exist between you and your "reincarnational" selves. There are even biological connections in terms of cellular "memory."

... those selves are different counterparts of yourself in creaturehood, experiencing bodily reality; but at the same time your organism itself shuts out the simultaneous nature of experience.

(During that same month in 1973 Jane wrote Apprentice Gods, *a long poem that's included in Chapter 16 of* Adventures in Consciousness. *In the poem she probed for the origins of our personified gods, and referred to counterparts as follows:)*

> *... for how like us these earth gods are,*
> *yet next to us, superstars,*
> *bigger than life counterparts,*
> *dramatizing us beyond degree*
> *and running off with the show*
> *as vicariously we watch*
> *them play our parts.*[9]

(Also consider these two still-earlier excerpts from the 520th session for March 20, 1970, in Chapter 3 of Seth Speaks:)

Quite literally, the "inner" self forms the body by magically transforming thoughts and emotions into physical counterparts . . .

Now whenever you think emotionally of another person, you send out a counterpart of yourself, beneath the intensity of matter, but a definite form.

(And from a far older session, the 44th for April 15, 1964:)

. . . the so-called laws of your camouflage physical universe do not apply to the inner universe . . . However, the laws of the inner universe apply to all camouflage universes . . . Some of these basic laws have counterparts known and accepted in various camouflage realities.

(Appendix 12 contains lengthy quotations from the 44th session, including the whole of the passage just cited.

(And what about the very first counterpart references in our sessions? In Chapter 1 of The Seth Material, *Jane described how we began these sessions [on December 2, 1963] through our use of the Ouija board. During the first three sessions the material came from a Frank Withers—who, it developed in the 4th session, was one of the "personality fragments" making up the Seth entity, or whole self. Just before Seth announced his presence to us in that same session, Frank Withers spelled out a remark through the board that meant little to Jane and me at the time: "One whole entity may need several manifestations, even at simultaneous so-called times."*

(Though Frank Withers never used the word "counterpart," we see now that this can be a reference to the concept of simultaneous reincarnations, to that of counterparts, or to both.

(Seth himself first used "counterpart" in the 6th session for December 11, 1963. At the time—and for a long while afterward—his employment of the word meant little, if anything, to Jane and me. The newly begun sessions already contained a number of unfamiliar terms and ideas: In the 4th session three days earlier, for instance, Seth had just given us our entity names [Ruburt for Jane, Joseph for me], and touched upon the psychic links connecting the three of us. Any subtleties afforded by concepts like counterparts would have quite escaped us. For that matter, at the time we didn't know whether or not the sessions would continue. Nor were we particularly concerned about the issue.

(In the 6th session, however, I made quite an intuitive remark: I told Jane I had the notion that Ruburt had once been Joseph. It took me a while to recognize that this had simply been my way of groping toward the realization that Seth, Jane and I did have a strong psychic relationship. Though we'd started these sessions with the Ouija board, Jane had made such a rapid progression that she was already giving some material vocally. However, at the

time we still used the board to obtain answers to most of our questions. After I made my statement about Ruburt and Joseph, Seth spelled out his reply through the board's pointer as it moved quickly beneath our fingertips:)

Part of same entity or counterpart.

(And so 11 years were to pass before Seth began his outright discussion of his very provocative concept of counterparts.)

NOTES: Appendix 21

1. For material on the Roman soldier, see the first notes for sessions 715–16; on Maumee and Nebene, see notes 1 and 9, respectively, in the 721st session.

I could list a few other past lives I'm supposed to have known, and so could Jane. Some of those we've picked up on our own. Over the years Seth has also come through with a modest number of reincarnational experiences involving the three of us, as well as others concerning any two of us. Examples are given in Appendix 18. But Jane and I are more intrigued by passages in Appendix 18 like this one, from the 398th session for March 11, 1964: "Personalities are not static things. Entities are eternal. They are not as nicely nor as neatly packaged out, one to a body, as your psychologists believe."

A published relationship in which Seth, Jane, and I took part, one that's innocent of counterpart overtones as far as our material indicates, happened in Denmark in the 1600's. In *Seth Speaks*, see Session 541 for Chapter 11.

2. I've directed the reader to them before—but in Volume 1 of *"Unknown" Reality* see Jane's information on neurological speeds in appendixes 4 and 5. As I wrote in Note 19 for Appendix 12: "My personal opinion is that although many may find it difficult reading, Appendix 4 contains some of the most important material in Volume 1." Jane also referred to her ghostly "Saratoga experience" in that appendix: Both she and Seth dealt with it in sessions 685–86.

3. In the opening notes for the 718th session, I wrote that I'd just finished a series of diagrams for Jane's *Adventures*. In Diagram 1 for Chapter 10, I tried to show schematically the same idea Seth mentions here, but with the terminology Jane used in her own book. She wrote about a series of Aspect selves orbiting a nonphysical source self, then continued: "Imagine a multidimensional Ferris wheel, each separated section being an Aspect self. As our 'seat' approaches the ground level, we're the Aspect who intersects with the space-time continuum, and life starts. But this Ferris wheel moves in every possible direction, and its spokes are ever-moving waves of energy, connecting the Aspects with the center source. Each other position intersects with a different kind of reality in which it is, in turn, immersed."

4. Seth never did tell Florence any more about her other

counterparts, though. Nor did she ask him to; she worked with the information he'd already given her, plus whatever she could divine for herself.

5. I thought of Seth's material on pain and suffering, as presented in Appendix 12. See the excerpts from the 580th session for *Seth Speaks*, and the 634th session for *Personal Reality*.

6. Perhaps I should have briefly discussed it in Volume 1, but ever since Seth originally gave his "Joe, Jane, Jim, and Bob" material (as I call it) in the 683rd session, I've wondered about possible connections between the probabilities described in that session and our own reality: How much of our species' distorted, intuitive knowledge of those probable realities may appear as myth and oddity in our camouflage universe? I'm thinking about androgyny, of course, which is the concept of both male and female in one, and/or of hermaphroditism, wherein a person or animal possesses the sexual organs of both the male and the female. Considering our personal lack of conscious knowledge about androgyny and such related concepts at the time, Jane and I think it most interesting that Seth came through with that particular material in the 683rd session.

A little investigation gave us glimpses into numerous instances in which blended masculine and feminine qualities are contained in the gods of our very ancient myths. The same principles of androgyny can be found in much of the literature of our own century. Whether scientific or not, myths may contain the deepest truths of all for our species, at least in conventional terms: Jane and I are intrigued to think that the sources for those verities could spring partly from other realities.

Much could be written here—volumes, easily. I'll simply add that in religious terms alone Christ can be seen as androgynous, in that he's obviously a symbol of the unification of opposites—whether of the conscious and the unconscious, the feminine and the masculine, this reality and others, the mystical and the "practical," and so forth. And a number of old disciplines thought that before the creation of Eve from his body, Adam, the first, original man, was really male and female.

All of which reminds me that to many viewers the "portraits" I paint are balanced equally between the masculine and feminine, regardless of whether the subject in any one of them is male *or* female. The paintings are of personalities I see mentally rather than physically; they do represent, I believe, my efforts to unify in any particular image my intuitive appreciation of the male/female qualitites embodied within each of us.

7. See Note 10 for the 721st session.

8. A longer version of this material from the 657th session is presented in Note 3 for Session 683, in Volume 1; I wanted to tell readers a little about counterparts then—not only to get them interested in Volume 2 before it was published, but to show the direction in which Seth's material was headed.

That same 657th session contains Seth's extremely useful statement: "The Present Is the Point of Power." From it he proceeds to show how all that we are—whatever our individual belief systems may be—stems from the brilliant focus of our physical, mental, and spiritual abilities in "present" experience.

       9. It's interesting to see how Jane's *Apprentice Gods* echoes and enlarges upon the following lines from another long, but quite youthful and dramatic poem that she wrote in 1949, when she was 19 years old:

> *Return o my brother, counterpart of heaven,*
> *For I am permitted to cry only through your voice . . .*

APPENDIX 22
(For Session 724)

(The day before the 724th session was held on December 4, I had another experience involving internal perceptions of myself as a Roman soldier in the first century A.D. As far as I can tell, however, this latest episode was not a continuation of my three visions of last October, in which I saw the end of my life while I was an officer in the armed forces of Imperial Rome[1]—yet this time also I confronted circumstances surrounding my own death. The little adventure certainly fits in with Seth's idea of counterparts, as he introduced it in the 721st session, but it raises a number of questions, too. Jane discussed my previous "visits" to the first century in Chapter 4 of her Psychic Politics, *but [I can add later] she never did deal with this one. I don't mind noting that I wish she had.[2] She might have been able to offer insights about it that I couldn't come up with, especially concerning the seemingly endless abilities of the psyche—call it personalized energy, consciousness, or what-have-you—to travel through its own space and time.*

(With some elaborations, the following account of my "fourth Roman" is directly from the description I wrote upon awakening. The notes, added later, are intended to give a minimum of "ordinary" background material, and to explore a few of the questions referred to above.)

"December 3, 1974. 4:50 P.M. Tuesday.

"As I lay down for my usual nap this afternoon, I reminded myself that Jane was to hold her ESP class this evening. Jokingly, I thought, I'd probably 'get something' just when I'd have the least amount of time to write it up afterward, make any drawings I could, and just plain take a while to think about it. (On class night we eat supper by 6:00; students often begin to arrive by 7:15, although class doesn't begin until 8:00.) So what happened? I experienced two long-lasting mental images before I slept. Was I happy with them? I didn't know, for they not only rearoused old questions, but brought up some new ones.

"Not long after I closed my eyes I saw, almost in silhouette, a Roman soldier standing on the top of a square, crenelated tower that formed a corner or angle in a massive stone wall. My position was at ground level. I'd lost all sensation of my body lying on the cot. The scene was very faint, so much so that it might almost be called more of an idea than an image. The sky behind the soldier was darkly overcast; I was aware of very little color. I 'knew' that the tower I faced marked the southeastern corner of Jerusalem, and I 'knew' that the wall itself was an enormous fortification that had

surrounded that ancient city sometime during the first half of the
first century A.D.

"As I looked up at the soldier's head and shoulders, I
believe (with some hesitancy) that I confronted another version of
myself. The whole thing was so nebulous—I was almost a disinter-
ested observer, as I'd been while perceiving my first three Roman
episodes. Perhaps this affair was engendered by a book I've just
started to read; it contains descriptions of the long seige that
Imperial Rome, whose military forces had occupied Palestine for 60
years, began against a rebellious Jerusalem in the year 66. I don't
know whether or not the city had a wall surrounding it earlier in that
century, but assume it did.[3]

"There was something very contradictory about the affair:
The soldier-self I saw atop the tower was a *Roman*—whereas, according to the little I know of those times, such a position should
have been occupied by a native Jew, who was perhaps a lookout for
the city behind him. I saw, dimly, the outline of the typical Roman
helmet, what seemed to be a leather vestment or short-sleeved
garment, the upper portion of the shaft of a spear. I don't think the
'me' I watched was an officer, as had been the case in my third
Roman, of October 30.

"What would a Roman soldier be doing up there?, I
wondered. For below, on the flat ground outside the wall, were the
hordes[4] of the Roman army. I don't know whether they were
preparing for an attack, or had some other reason to be assembled
there. I saw only a forest of helmets and spears pointing upward,
with light glinting dully on metal here and there. I write 'saw,' yet it
would be just as accurate to note that I sensed these figures. They
were turned toward the soldier on the tower.

"A sound effect was involved here that was unique for
me—doubly so, actually. First, until now my internal perceptions
have staged themselves like old silent films; second, the sound itself
was quite unusual: The clustered troops on the ground were emitting
a low rhythmic chanting or wailing. This was no happy occasion.
This sound, rising and falling in such mournful cadences, was
unintelligible to me.

"Somehow, without being able to see them, I knew that
stone or clay steps rose up the back of the tower, clear to the top
where the soldier posed. He didn't move. Try as I would, I couldn't
make his image any clearer or closer, or induce it to change in any
other manner. What I did perceive was remarkably steady and lasted
for several minutes, at least. I can still summon it to my mind's eye
when I want to. It came to me that the soldier was 43 years old and

had two male children—where they were, I didn't know. Like an echo in the background lingered a woman, but I couldn't get anything about her.

"Now the scene changed, as one might change a slide in a projector. In another little drama, motionless like the first one, I saw my Roman soldier suspended in the act of falling from the tower. He had, in truth, been thrown off it, and I believe that he was either dead or mortally wounded from stab wounds. He had a bandage wrapped around the biceps of his left arm. Now I knew that a 'task force' of other Roman soldiers had carried out this assault, reaching 'me' by climbing the steps already described. I saw no sign of others on the tower, though. I kept this second image in mind for some time before allowing myself to realize that the victim fell amid a group of his fellows. One of them, I believe, ran a spear into the body.

"My only touch of emotion was involved with this second image; as I first saw it, I felt light thrillings in my body, coupled with a somewhat fearful reaction. I trust the thrilling sensations, since over the years I've learned that they signify something psychically legitimate for me;[5] their onset now at least reinforced my suspicion that the tumbling figure *was* me. Yet, I'm not sure. I slept.

"When I got up half an hour later I hurriedly typed the first version of this account. I also tried to capture the overcast mood of the entire episode in a couple of quick drawings done on typing paper with a ballpoint pen. First I drew my Roman soldier standing half-visible behind the squared crenelations on top of the tower; then I drew him falling, poised face up against the tower wall.[6]

"Several interesting—and frustrating—questions are raised by today's episode. As stated, this makes the second time that I've had an experience involving the violent death of a Roman soldier in the earlier part of the first century A.D. (I never did arrive at names for those two militant individuals.) Perhaps both instances are merely my own psychological reflections of present concerns or challenges, although I think that more is involved. Given Seth's concept of simultaneous time, the best connection I've made so far between the two soldiers is that as counterparts of mine they explore questions having to do with authority. As I rebel against authority now—a characteristic remarked upon by Seth in the 721st session—so do my Roman selves in their times.

"My own defiance is a peaceful one having to do with ideas. I see my two Romans physically undergoing an exploration of the opposite sides of rebellion or subversion, within the context of a much closer, more oppressive military authority: For whatever reasons, the Roman *officer* is turned upon and thrown into the

Mediterranean to drown (as described in Note 1 for the 715th session)[7]; my Roman *soldier,* a man of lesser rank, has evidently betrayed his sworn position of trust, and is caught in authority's vice. I think all of this could be counterpart action, all right, personified by two selves living in the same narrow time period, in close proximity in the same geographical area of the Middle East.[8]

"However, more questions arise from the fact that over three years ago, long before any of my Roman experiences surfaced, I'd obtained vivid information on another life I'd known in the same part of the first century. And not only that—as a man called Nebene I'd spent part of my life in Rome itself. Seth referred to Nebene in the 721st session also.[9] Here too, through that individual, the ramifications of authority are confronted again; if in a way less drastic than one involving death, still certainly in a very dogmatic manner, as expressed through Nebene's rigid personality. The list grows. Counterparts all—three simultaneous lives in which I seemed to play a part, although, as explained below, I insist that I participated in each one of those existences in my own way.

"Seth's data and my own on counterparts make sense to me. I feel (as Seth mentioned in the 721st session) that I wasn't Nebene, or two different Roman soldiers *per se*, but rather that my whole self chose to manifest such personalities together; that I, too, am such a manifestation at a "later" time, then, and that from my own vantage point I can tune in to those other lives. But I question, at least provisionally, any idea of past or counterpart lives that *I* lived one hundred percent. At this writing, I think that *I* am living my only one hundred percent life now, with the privilege of occasionally being able to focus upon scattered portions of those other existences emanating from my whole self, which has its basic reality outside of our space-time concepts.[10]

"Assuming that my internal data about those three lives are reasonably correct, it may be, as Jane said recently, that the psyche is so incredibly rich that *anything* is possible. Is that true? Humorously: I'll have a hell of a time with my list of chronological lives (which I have yet to work on, by the way) if I start turning up a whole group of them in one historical period. What if I happen to list half of the Roman army? I need to know more—lots more."

(Jane held her ESP class that same evening. Long after class break, toward the end of the night, I presented my fourth Roman by reading from the notes just given. Class members passed my sketches around. Almost immediately Seth came through with further elaborations on his ideas about counterparts. He also cleared up a few points for me. Seth:)

You have heard terms like "The Brotherhood of Man," or,

as Ruburt might say, "The Brother-Womanhood of Women" *(humorously)*. But at any given time, in your terms—at any given time—the population of the earth is made up of counterparts . . . and so when you kill an enemy, you are killing a version of yourself . . . For as you are members of a physical species, you are also members of a psychic kind of counterpart reality; and this membership straddles races or countries, or states or politics.

You form your history. You form your reality, and so no one is thrust into a position which first was not accepted as a challenge. So you work out your problems and challenges in whatever way you choose, historically. In your terms, again, you and the Roman are connected; and the Arab and the American; and the African and the Chinese; and so are your identities intermixed with others who may seem to be strangers, but others who speak with your own voice—others who communicate with you in their dreams as you communicate with them. You have comrades, and you come to this earth at a given time and place of your choice, and so do you reap and form the great challenges of your age.

But the world is not filled with strangers, and so our friend here, Joseph, glimpsed a counterpart of himself who lived—in your terms, now—in one particular era.[11] In deeper terms that era still exists, and that is something you should not forget. For as you view a painting and it has a frame, so do you view the centuries and put separate frames around them. . . .

(Seth's delivery, only partly quoted here, was very forceful. It will help the reader to refer back to the 724th session itself, in order to correlate Seth's material given there with this class session, and with other data on reincarnation and counterparts.

(I was in for a surprise as the students discussed Seth's remarks. One class member, a close friend whom I'll call Peter Smith, is an artist and sculptor; after studying my Roman sketches, he had a note passed across the crowded room to me:)

"Rob: In one of my own 'past-life' memories, I was a guard or sentry on a tower like the one in your drawings. Or I was the sentry's enemy, who came up the steps and attacked him. I was overcome and pushed off the tower, falling backwards in the position your drawing shows. It was night or semi-dark."

(Peter's statement was soon confirmed by another longtime friend of ours, Sue Watkins,[12] who also knows Peter well. He'd related the entire affair to her some months ago; his original perceptions had taken place over seven years ago, long before Sue had introduced him to Jane and me in 1973. Peter told me after class that my sketches had instantly rearoused his memories, although in his experience he'd seen the event from different angles. Yet, even with those

discrepancies, and a few others, Peter believed that the walls in Jerusalem, the battlemented tower, the soldiers that I'd just described and depicted, were all the same as those he'd seen in his own visions of so much earlier.

(In the 724th session the following night, Seth remarked upon such circumstances, saying that while Peter and I weren't counterparts, we're "closely enough allied so that in certain terms you 'share' some of the same psychic memories, like cousins who speak about old dimly remembered brothers.")[13]

(And—almost too much—another strange incident was mentioned in the same class. A student I'll call Mary told me about just having met a black woman [in a most prosaic night-school class] who looked "exactly like" my drawing of Maumee,[14] the woman in my Jamaica experience of three weeks ago. Mary's new classmate had no upper teeth, the state in which I'd pictured Maumee.

(In view of these two separate instances, involving Peter and Mary, I wonder: Aside from whatever intrinsic validity they may have, does each of us telepathically pick up on the experiences of others and weave such information into personal psychological dramas? If so, do we do this frequently, so that our private fantasies have an inner coherence with those of our fellow human beings—and connections with them—that quite escapes our usual notice?

(Our questions are without end, and Jane and I don't really think many of them will be answered within our lifetimes. I'll close this appendix with two more queries that psychically are much more personal and very intriguing: Had Peter Smith viewed the same events on that tower in Jerusalem from the vantage point of the soldier who killed my soldier? Were the slain and the slayer meeting now once more, under different circumstances?)

NOTES: Appendix 22

1. See the first notes for sessions 715–16.

2. As he or she has probably done while going over some of the other notes for *"Unknown" Reality,* the reader might wonder why we don't just ask Seth to comment upon a point of interest as soon as it happens. Not as convenient as it sounds, however: The next scheduled session may lie several days ahead; book dictation always comes first when Seth does speak, and at session's end it may be too late for "extra" questions, or we may be tired; even though any given event *is* interesting, it can easily be pushed out of immediate awareness by succeeding ones that are equally intriguing. Before we know it, often, our best chance to ask about a certain happening has passed. We may not return to it for some time; even years can pass in the interim.

3. Yes, I learned from several reference works containing photographs, drawings, and maps, Jerusalem before A.D. 50 had been

walled in. Not once but several times, and in various peripheries enclosing various portions of that ancient site: the old city, the new city, the upper and lower cities, and so forth. Aerial photos show that now, at least, there's more than one southeastern corner of the city formed as the battlemented, meandering southern wall turns north in a series of steps or right angles. I could see no recent indications of towers there. However, the situation way back then would have depended on what walls existed (as well as upon my own psychic "vantage point"). There could have been other southeastern corners, with or without towers: Not all of the authors I consulted agreed upon the location of certain of Jerusalem's fortifications (in the first century or any other), or when they had been built or destroyed.

4. A literal interpretation of "flat ground" and "hordes" would be very questionable, however. I discuss what I mean in Note 6.

5. I experienced much stronger thrilling sensations two and a half weeks ago, during my perceptions of myself as Maumee, the black woman who lived in Jamaica in the early 1800's. See the opening notes for the 721st session, with its Note 1. In Appendix 21, Seth remarked that those suffusing feelings are my personal sign that I've made a "neurological changeover." When that happens I seem able to at least glimpse other time periods, other realities.

6. My ruminations in notes 3 and 4 should indicate how difficult it can be for the conscious mind to interpret psychic data arising from other "layers" of itself. Jane and I haven't been to Jerusalem, although we'd like to make the trip some day, but even if we did I don't think it would be easy to identify the physical site of my "fourth Roman." To do so would take much cautious study. For one thing, I'm sure that my imagery—and drawings—of Jerusalem's fortifications would turn out to be much too meager in scale; surely those "real" works would be far more overpowering in height and mass. To insist upon interpreting my mental information in literal terms only might lead into a labyrinth of supposition, then.

For another thing, what was my nameless Roman self doing on that tower? I didn't "see" the reasons and actions leading to his presence there, and I doubt if I ever will. In my reference works I read accounts describing how Pontius Pilate, the Procurator (or governor) of Judea from approximately A.D. 26 to A.D. 36, had organized hunts for members of the Zealots, the Jewish political-religious sect that had consistently rebelled against the rule of the Roman Empire. This is the correct general time period for my visions, I think, and I felt a surge of thrilling sensations as I learned about certain subversive Zealot activities. Then I "picked up" that my soldier-self was killed by his countrymen because he'd traitorously sought to warn Zealot leaders of a planned search of the lower city of Jerusalem by Roman troops. My thrills deepened considerably—and those feelings of rightness were what I settled for; I could carry my wonderings no further, nor did I want to.

As best I can interpret the objective information at hand, the physical locale of my subjective experience is a precarious one, since outside the eastern and southern boundaries of Jerusalem the terrain quickly drops away into valleys close and steep enough to protect the city from large-scale attack—with hardly enough room there for the "hordes" of Roman soldiers I saw on the "flat ground." I cannot explain my terminology or choice of locations, except to say that I expressed just what I wanted to. I trust the elements of those perceptions, and my reactions to them, but their conscious understanding and integration remain beyond my abilities at this time. Obviously (as will be explained), I think it wise to ascribe as much of the episode's validity to its symbolic meanings as to its physical ones.

For those who may wonder: I'll close here by noting that historically the time period within which my impressions took place would embrace the reputed visits of Jesus Christ to Jersualem during Pilate's tenure, including Christ's crucifixion around A.D. 30—but that my experience *per se* had nothing to do with the Messiah.

7. See Note 12 for Session 721, in which I quote Seth about my Roman officer's querulous attitudes toward authority.

8. Much could be written about the ageless conflicts the individual feels between society's demands and his or her urges toward personal freedom. It seems to me that no matter what role in any life the individual decides upon before birth (to incorporate Seth's ideas here), that individual will carry consciousness's innate drive toward personal expression—but still within the protection furnished by social organization. This applies even to my Roman selves in their restrictive military environments (which are also protective), and even if their chosen courses of action result in demands or challenges they cannot surmount. . . .

9. See Note 9 for Session 721.

10. I note with some amusement that my rather vehement statement may simply reflect the natural, protective attitude of my currently focused consciousness: Even though I find them fascinating, I may be quite reluctant to embrace other equally valid portions of what I conveniently call *my* whole self. Yet that whole self may not consider that any more than a tiny segment of itself "belongs" to me!

11. It's of interest here to note that although he referred to my three Roman-officer perceptions of last October in the 721st session (which itself was held a month after I'd experienced them), Seth didn't mention that I had a *second* Roman-soldier counterpart living in the same time and area of the world in the first century A.D. I didn't ask about any such possibility, either. I don't attach any special meaning to these observations, although we may ask Seth to comment upon them eventually (see Note 2). If his material on counterparts is correct, any of us could have many such relationships going in a given century—too many to conveniently uncover, perhaps, considering the physical time that would be necessary to do the psychic work.

12. For some material on Sue Watkins in Volume 1 of *"Unknown" Reality,* see the opening notes for Session 692, along with Note 2 for that session.

This isn't the first time Peter Smith has been able to comment upon one of my Roman experiences from his own viewpoint. He's traveled a good deal. In Chapter 4 of *Politics,* Jane described how Peter offered some interesting present-day "correlations" with portions of my third Roman, of the first century A.D. Peter's information concerned the Spanish fishermen he saw hauling large nets ashore along certain beaches of the Mediterranean Sea; I'd seen similar actions during my internal perceptions that day.

13. Early in this appendix I wrote that I added these notes later, to give "ordinary background material" for my fourth Roman. So now, what do I make of the considerable similarities between my Jerusalem episode and Peter's? Although his internal data reinforce mine to some extent, he can be no more specific about a physical location in the city for his visions than I can be for mine. (See Note 6.) I've also written about the conflicts involving authority that I believe my two Roman soldiers are expressing. Here I feel on more "solid ground" symbolically than physically. Just as I do, Peter rebels in his own peaceful ways against conventional authority, preferring to go his individual route in the arts, no matter how dubious his rewards may be.

To me, this fact alone lends a credence to his visions that bolsters my own in the most meaningful way: I think our tower experiences of so long ago (in terms of linear time), plus our mutual artistic backgrounds *now,* with their corresponding social implications, are too closely allied to be explained as "coincidence" in the objective fact world. Peter's surprising material, then, helps me tentatively recognize the physical connections those motionless visions of mine may have in our space and time.

14. Can it be a coincidence that that Maumee self of mine had *also* been—indeed, still was—in rebellion against authority? See the notes at the beginning of the 721st session, as well as Note 1.

APPENDIX 23
(For Session 724)

(Seth's material here in the 724th session, given on December 4, 1974, at once reminded me of an informal session he'd held on a Friday evening some 10 months ago. Thirteen of us had gathered in our living room for one of the weekly get-togethers that Jane and I enjoy so much. Some of those present were members of Jane's ESP class; all had heard Seth speak at one time or another.

(We talked about many things, as usual. When our conversation began to range over psychic phenomena, leadership, history, and language,[1] Jane went into trance; then Seth came through strongly. This unexpected kind of session rarely develops these days, but, as Jane said later, the subjects under discussion were "emotionally charged" for her—and for others present, too, I might add. [Incidentally, Seth began Volume 1 of "Unknown" Reality on February 4, 1974—three days after this session was held.]

(Fortunately, class member Sue Watkins managed to tape all but the first few paragraphs of the session, but even the sense of those was taken down in longhand by another student while Sue got our recorder going. [I really enjoyed letting someone else do all the work for a change!] Later that week, Sue transcribed Seth's material, wrote all of the notes for the session, and prepared mimeographed copies for everyone. Only portions of the session are given here, and I've rearranged them—and Sue's notes—a bit for convenience's sake. From her transcript, then:)

Unscheduled Session
February 1, 1974
9:56 P.M. Friday

(A group of us—Alex, Warren,[2] and others—had come over to Jane and Rob's for a casual get-together, and also to talk about that week's class, which seemed to be one of the "milestone" classes that happen occasionally.[3] During the conversation, Alex said that the rise of literacy in the world would spread Seth's ideas on a scale that had never previously been possible. In the discussion of "primitive" and "civilized" man that followed, Warren presented his opinion that some civilizations, such as those of Babylonia, Egypt, the Incas, and so forth, had been founded by initiate groups from Atlantis[4] . . . that while "primitive" man may have had a kind of gestalt consciousness, he had no individual consciousness. As Warren made similar remarks about the development of individual consciousness through historical times to our point of civilization, Seth suddenly and unexpectedly came through loudly and forcefully:)

(To Warren:) Now, when you learn to communicate with the gracious ease with which those primitive people communicated, then you can call yourself civilized. You [as a member of the human species] do indeed see yourself as the supreme flower of history so far, yet when you can know what is going on clearly and concisely on the other side of Elmira, and can communicate it also, then you will be as primitive and as civilized as some of those primitive people.

(Warren: "Well, I was only expressing—")

You were expressing beliefs.

(Warren: "But isn't this stuff all about the development of ego consciousness?")

No indeed—and that is your error. And I will return you to your group and yourselves.

(Jane came out of trance—briefly—and Warren began explaining what had gone on. "I wasn't referring to regular history," he said, "but to esoteric history—"

(Loudly:) And that is the worst kind of history of all! It has nothing to do with the people!

Now, I have tried to tell you this before. The experience of the guru[5] who sits in opulence, bejeweled and begowned, has nothing to do with the peasant who works in the field and whose belly is empty. And so it has been through the centuries.

In your terms, your histories were not written by the people who worked the earth. They were created by the priests and the elite, who made up their own histories to suit their purposes—to hold down the masses, for reasons that I will someday discuss, for they are important. Those histories never spoke of the vast, massive emotions and needs of the human beings involved, who listened, because their hearts and survival depended upon their doing so, to the voices that speak within the earth that your instruments even now cannot perceive. Those histories did not tell of the human beings who had to know what insects would crawl or fly from one end of a continent to another, so that they could be captured and roasted and eaten. They did not speak of the human beings who had to know what migrations of animals would roam through their land—and <u>when</u> and <u>where</u>, and at what phase of the moon—lest they starve . . .

And so those people lifted up their minds and hearts and heard the voices of the earth speak to them, as they still do. The elite did not hear those voices. They wrote histories in which in their own memories they annihilated races of people with emotions as strong and as real as theirs. The elite leave you records and methods, telling you of kings and queens, of gurus and prophets and gods, in whose eyes the masses of the people vanished. The magic that the people had, those gurus never learned. They learned techniques, but the techniques did not bring them magic, did not allow them to really hear and understand the voice of one leaf.

(*Still to Warren:*) So forget all of the histories, my dear friend, and listen to your own thoughts, which are today as alive and vital as those of any man ever born, in whatever time. Forget the dusty old records and feel your reality in the moment as you are. In that moment can you hear the insects sweeping across the continents and the voices of the leaves speak, and feel their echoes in your blood—and that blood lives, beyond the time. It throbs beyond destiny, even as the masses of those people live beyond the beliefs of those gurus.

I return you, as always, to the vitality of your present being, and to the authenticity of yourself. Do not let me make you uneasy.

Now, the session in the last class (*see Note 3*) was a combination of the most sophisticated and the most primitive, for the English words, in your terms, are understood by the proud intellect that rises above the shoulders so securely. Yet the sounds upon which those words ride are far more sophisticated than the language of which you are all so proud. For they are indeed the sounds of insects through the centuries, of stars swirling through the universe, of the blood pounding through your veins.

Now I return the room to all of you—and remember, I am using you (*Warren*) to make the point only because you asked the question. I smile and rejoice in your present vitality. Then surely you should do the same, and not bow down before dusty gurus and histories.

(*Here, Rob asked if Seth would "shed some light" on why all those masses of people had chosen to allow the eradication of their histories by the elite.*)

In one of our books (*Rob grimaced—much laughter*), I will take many chapters to answer.

(*Rob: "How about a little hint?"*)

I cannot give you a little hint.

(*Rob: "Medium-sized?" Laughter. Someone says, "Do you get this sort of thing all the time?"*)

It has to do with the mass beliefs that people chose at various times, and the different roads that were taken in your reality. Any road taken in your reality should—but does not—tell you one thing: By the very fact that you have chosen a particular road, you can be sure that other roads, entirely different, have also been taken.

(*Rob: "Yeah, well, say a group of people chose that type of existence, where their history was essentially obliterated by never being recorded. Could reincarnational reasons be involved, probabilities, or what?")*

As you know, my dear Joseph, there is a difference between probable realities and reincarnational ones. To keep the discussion simple, I will answer you in reincarnational terms; but as Ruburt is discovering as he writes his *Adventures in Consciousness,*[6] many more elements are involved.

According to your intent, your desire, and your beliefs, your ideas intersect with the reality that you know, with physical space and physical time—they become real, in historic terms. In other realities there are different historical terms. A war won here, with a treaty, is not won somewhere else, and there is a different treaty. Even wars seemingly won here are not nearly as clear-cut as would appear; you make history as you go along. You use, in your terms now only, the past as source material. You rewrite it as you go along. As records are lost, you do not even realize that you have rewritten the past.

It did not serve your species' purposes at this time to work with the mind—with telepathy, with the feeling for the earth that you could have developed.

(To Rob:) Remember the private session I gave you the night before last, in which I told you that you could have developed very well as a sportsman[7]—considering the athletic qualities involved—instead of as an artist or writer. In this life, however, you used [the elements of] your personal environment as tools for the artist. The sportsman that you might have been would have used the same tools far differently.

Now in this reality people chose—and I am speaking in very simple terms—people chose to develop in a very different way. Therefore, that world-probability in which telepathy and clairvoyance[8] would have been common, well-known facts of life, self-evident in any civilization—that probability became latent while the species followed another route.

Now, as Ruburt has also written in his *Adventures*—with some help from me now and then!—there are points, again speaking simply and in your terms, where probabilities meet: intersections with space and time that occur in your minds while you change directions, where new probabilities that once lay latent suddenly emerge.[9] And in terms of your civilization and your time, such a time is now.

(To Rob:) So that is a very partial hint as to the direction the material will take when I <u>begin</u> to answer your question!

(After Seth had answered questions from some of the others present,

Jane came out of trance and we discussed what had been said . . . eventually getting into the question of whether or not Seth's ideas were "old" or "new." Several people said they thought his material was old, given many times before and forgotten. Others thought it was new, or at least totally original with the Seth material as such.[10] *Then Seth returned:)*

Now, the material is new, as you yourselves are new. It is old, as the heritage of your selves is old. There is no old knowledge, however![11]

Now, listen to a portion of last Tuesday's class session and follow it with the transcript. See what your mind learns from the words. See what you learn that is not in the words. Hear, again, because several of you liked those sounds so well, the insects creeping across the forests of Europe and Africa. But hear also the voices of acknowledgment of your living cells as they grope and grow in the sacred continents of your own physical beings. See the oneness, and the ancient newness that is never repeated!

(Very forcefully:) One sentence repeated is not the same sentence that it was before! One breath is not another! You are never repeated, and what you know is always new. Because you know it, and because you are the one who knows it, it is never what another one knows. So all knowledge is public—and sacred. And ancient and new.

(End, around midnight.)

NOTES: Appendix 23

1. See Note 4 for the 723rd session.

2. I've given fictitious names to Jane's students, "Alex" and "Warren."

3. The session given in last Tuesday's class (for January 29, 1974) had indeed been one of Seth's best. It was also a long one; the typewritten transcript ran to five and a half single-spaced pages. Seth discussed many of his basic concepts, the wedding of the intellect and the intuitions, his reality and our camouflage physical one, Seth Two, language, myth, and so forth. We'd like to publish it as a chapter in an appropriate book. Here's how he closed out the session:

"I am the voice of your world in its past and its future, and because of that I am your own voice in its past and future. The rocks cannot speak words that you hear, and you do not listen when your cells speak to you, and so I speak humbly for them, and translate for you the archaeology of your own being.

"And I show to you the castles of your past and your future, and the mental civilizations that are your heritage and your birthright. Hear, then, the fossilings within your spirit speak."

4. See Appendix 14.

5. See Appendix 15.

6. When this session was held, on the first of February, 1974, Jane was ready to begin the final draft of her manuscript for *Adventures.* In Volume 1 of *"Unknown" Reality,* see Note 3 for Seth's Preface.

7. See Appendix 2 in Volume 1.

8. See the brief definitions of telepathy and clairvoyance in Note 19 for Appendix 18. In Note 3 for Session 723, I quoted Seth on the relationship between telepathy and language.

9. In *Adventures,* see Chapter 13, with diagrams 4 and 5.

10. In terms of linear time, and in keeping with Seth's material in this session, Jane and I obviously think his concepts are both old and new—while being "totally original," as Sue Watkins noted.

The question of Seth's originality intrigues many who write. Even as I worked on this note Jane received a most enthusiastic letter of approval from a young woman who had just read *Seth Speaks* and Volume 1. To paraphrase a few lines: "Why isn't the whole world reverberating with these fantastic ideas? I'm stunned by the material . . . I can't understand how it took me so long to even hear of the Seth books. . . ."

In turn, the young lady's letter reminded me of certain passages Seth had delivered in the 34th session for March 11, 1964. I asked him why the material he was giving wasn't common knowledge to most people. Seth replied:

"How many people? Very few would take this amount of their camouflage time to deal with it. A peculiar set of abilities and interests is required for work like this to be even partially successful, or accepted by the personalities involved. For many it would be difficult to maintain discipline and balance, while allowing for the necessary freedoms that are involved. That is, this is a controlled experiment, with both of you allowing yourselves certain freedoms of control in some instances and not in others. This is no easy trick. Is that what you meant?"

I told Seth that it could be—but that I also wondered why over the centuries the species couldn't have slowly accumulated a body of knowledge like that he was giving us now.

"It did. But that knowledge has been taken into various religions and doctrines that have grown up about it until it is almost unrecognizable. Bits of it appear here and there, scattered, distorted, and misleading. It comes naked, and everyone must put clothing on it. This means that it usually ends up as either nonsense or armored dogma."

With a smile: "Your particular conscious and subconscious viewpoints are fluent enough so that they do not hamper the basic material, or cover it with the rock of dogmatism so that it becomes impossible to find . . . Actually, what I needed were personalities who were not fanatics along <u>any</u> line—including scientific fanatics who would object as forcibly to the reincarnational data as religious fanatics would object to some of the other material.

      "All religions are distortive. For that matter, much of your science is distortive. Both arrive at approximations, at best, of reality. Religion has been the cause of much prejudice and cruelty, but the bombs over Hiroshima were not caused by the Catholic Saint Teresa showering down any roses. Science is apt to turn into another religion, if it has not done so already. The distortions in science and religion have been truly disastrous. Any fanaticism is vicious, one-sided, and limiting, causing an alarming shrinkage of focus that is explosive and dangerous.

      "I will go into all of these things on other occasions. . . ."

APPENDIX 24
(For Session 725)

(In Session 725 Seth discussed the spiritual aspects of our biological nature, and in Note 4 for that session I presented brief excerpts from the material he'd given in ESP class the night before, on the truly limitless "ceilings to the self," or identity.

(In that same class, however, Seth also brought our biological nature "down to earth" in most literal terms. His material was hilarious, provocative, and profound—all at once. I know one thing: Seth's delivery won't be soon forgotten. It's also one that may startle those who are used to quiet and proper "spirit guides."

(Earlier that evening, class members had been discussing some of the letters they'd been answering for Jane.[1] One young man mentioned "feeling like shit" in connection with another matter—a remark that Seth must have overheard. He began the session by telling the students that they also learned as they attempted to answer the questions asked by correspondents. Then, with much emphasis:)

Now many of you here use the word "shit." You apply the term in a derogatory manner to yourselves, and you think: "I am full of shit." And where does the great spectacular reality, the physical reality of your earth, spring from? Why is shit not considered sacred and blessed and glorious? You think of shit, unfortunately, as the antithesis of good; and when you play around it or with it, you think you are being childish at the best, and wicked at the worst.

A child sits, perhaps three years old, with his finger stuck up his ass, feeling the shit that warmly runs down, and that child knows that shit is good. Then, give him credit!

You think that the soul is a white wall with nothing written upon it, and so your idea of sacrilege is to shit upon it, not realizing that the shit and the soul are one, and that the biological is spiritual; and that, again—if you will forgive my homey concept—flowers grow from the shit of the earth. And in a true communion, all things of this life return to the earth, and are consumed and rise up again in a new life that is never destroyed or annihilated, though always changing form.

So, when you shrink from such words or such meanings, why do you shrink? Because you do not trust the biology of your being or the integrity of your soul in flesh. You are people. You are made of the stuff of the earth, and the dust from the stars has formed into the shit that lies in piles—warm piles that come from the beasts and the creatures of the earth. And that shit fertilizes the flowers and the ground, and is a part of it.

How dare any of you, therefore, set yourselves against that, or in conflict with it? *(Here, Seth's voice was powerful and emphatic indeed. He looked at one student and said:)*

This does not mean, my dear young friend, that you need to go about speaking [the word] to those who do not like it, and saying "Fuck you." *(To the class, with deep humor:)* He wanted me to use that word *(fuck)* on tape. But again: This does not mean that you should use such a word to make other people uncomfortable.

Your soul and your flesh are wedded together. One is not "better" than the other. Both are good. Both <u>are</u>, and you <u>are</u> both. The heritage of the earth, in your terms, is ancient and yet ever new, and when you write your letters *(to correspondents)* you write . . . with your intelligence and your wit. Yet if it were not that you shit once or twice a day, you would not be writing any letters!

(Class members laughed, of course, and Seth said:) Yet when you laugh, you laugh because you still think the word is beneath you, and you are being sneaky or smart-alecky—or you think <u>I</u> am—by speaking so freely.

When I say "soul," you do not snicker.

(Seth has always cautioned us against being too self-righteous; warned us against considering silence, seriousness, or piety as synonymous with goodness or "truth." Above all, he's insisted upon the exuberance and "rightness" of the physical world. He put the same idea across beautifully, of course, in Session 725 without ever using the word "shit." But when dealing directly with people, Seth is— direct, and most perceptive. For many people will accept the same philosophy when expressed as it was in the 725th session, and yet be quite upset when those ideas are discussed in the vernacular, in language that certainly cannot be considered ambiguous in any fashion.)

NOTES: Appendix 24

1. See the closing notes for Session 725.

APPENDIX 25
(For Session 732)

(I began this short appendix a couple of weeks after the 732nd session was held, but didn't finish certain parts of it until some time later. Seth's naming a good number of class members as counterparts came as no great surprise to Jane and me—but it did make us more than a little suspicious at first. We've been thinking about counterpart ideas since Seth introduced the concept two months ago; see the opening notes for the 721st session. Then, in the 726th session, Seth named Jane and me as counterparts of each other. Although we keep the power of suggestion in mind, on one level we found Seth's associations quite pleasant for the most part, and, once given, somewhat as we might have expected them to be. Yet I felt no strong surge of emotion, for instance, to learn that Norma Pryor [whom I've met but a few times], Peter Smith, and Jack Pierce are counterparts of mine—nor did they when I read Seth's material to them during ESP class six nights later. Jane's feelings were pretty similar to mine, when Seth named three students as her counterparts: Sue Watkins, Zelda, and "the young man from Maryland. . . ."

(Our suspicions entered in, however, when Jane and I realized that between us [and including each other] we were personally acquainted with nine counterparts: All but one of them [Alan Koch] were class members. As Jane wrote:

"We're so used to thinking that our encounters with others are caused by chance—except for those we purposely bring about through choice, such as marriage partners—that Seth's comments about my students seem a bit outrageous at first: So many counterparts in one room?

"Yet," she continued, "second thoughts make us question old assumptions: Granted the existence of counterparts to begin with, certainly their common goals, though differently expressed, *would* bring them together when possible. *And,* according to Seth, the same would apply to any group. So beneath such gatherings there would be hidden dynamics, psychological activities that could explain the behavior of crowds, political parties, and so forth. . . ."

(I suppose that one can find all sorts of variations within counterpart situations, all sorts of reasons for such affiliations, so I can merely hint at a few here as they rise out of the class framework, or orbit around it:

(Student Bill Herriman is a professional pilot who flies a considerable distance to Elmira for class; his counterpart in class, Carl Jones, lives in Elmira each summer while giving instructions in sailplane flying; the third member of the counterpart trio, Bill Granger, is not a member of class, lives in

786

Elmira, has always had a deep interest in aircraft, and is now learning to pilot sailplanes. Carl Jones knows Bill Herriman and Bill Granger well—but Bill Herriman and Bill Granger have never met; all three are obviously males; all bear a general physical resemblance; all fall within a certain rather broad age bracket. The close observer could, I think, find among the three men more physical and psychological correlations [some having to do with illness], as well as meaningful opposing features, so that in this instance the counterpart relationships can be seen as quite apropos.

(My counterpart, Peter Smith, and I are both professional artists; we're roughly of an age, with strong interests in other forms of creativity, such as writing, and in myth and fantasy.[1] A number of the similarities and differences between Jane and me should be obvious to our readers; she also does quite a lot of painting. Both of my other class counterparts, Norma Pryor and Jack Pierce, are themselves of a younger generation than Jane, Peter, and I. Jack writes novels, as yet unpublished. Norma does not. Both are very quiet and unassuming.

(Jane's own counterparts, Sue, Zelda, Alan Koch, "Maryland," and myself, are all committed to the dissemination of Seth-type ideas, either through professional writing, classes, and/or lecture appearances that extend from one end of the country to the other.

(I found it very interesting to consider my class counterparts with that general designation of them in mind. Peter and I had rather idly speculated that because of our common interests we could have reincarnational ties.[2] Seth's naming Norma as being psychically affiliated with me was unexpected, however. Norma is a new member of class. She's from out of town, and I hardly know her [she's also so quiet]; but even so, I could see how it was possible that she could be embarked upon her own series of lifetime challenges while expressing certain qualities of the entity, or whole self, from which we both emerged. Some of her characteristics, which I've just begun to glimpse, complement some of mine; others are opposing. And Norma, of course, would turn all of this around and examine it from her own very independent viewpoint.

(But individual reactions to a given idea or event can vary tremendously, from the most withdrawn behavior to the most explosive. Jane and I saw Norma socially one evening, along with a few other students as well as some people who were not class members. Psychic matters weren't stressed, and counterpart ideas weren't even mentioned. That is, I made no effort to bring up the subject, nor did Norma as I waited somewhat curiously through the evening. Still, it's worth noting that being in the presence of a relative stranger who may also be one's counterpart does make some sort of interior difference in response or attention. I wondered about the countless times counterparts had unwittingly gathered on similar occasions, and what sort of numberless exchanges had taken place on unconscious levels between those who were psychically related in some fashion.

(How different human relations would be, I thought after all of our

guests had left, if the counterpart thesis could gain a more general acceptance on conscious levels.)

NOTES: Appendix 25

     1. I can add that my counterpart, Peter Smith, has also enjoyed some double dreams, as I call them. See the material on the double dreams of Sue Watkins, Lee R. Gandee, and myself in Session 692, with its Note 2, for Volume 1 of *"Unknown" Reality.*
     2. See Note 8 for the 732nd session.

APPENDIX 26
(For Session 734)

(It happened that in ESP class last night Seth came through with material pertaining to the nine families of consciousness he'd begun discussing a week ago; see the 732nd session. These class excerpts, which I've rearranged somewhat for easy reference, may be used when considered with book material still to come, since Seth will occasionally use the class format to supplement his dictation in our "regular" sessions. The quotations also lead us back to the circumstances surrounding Seth's delivery of his first session on the Sumari.)

Now *(Seth told us last night),* you can expand the functions of any particular family group, or you can cut it down, by deciding how precise you want to be. If one family deals with the nature of healing, then you can slice it down to the healing of a toe . . . an ear . . . an eye.

The categories [healing, teaching, or whatever] are general descriptions of the families of consciousness. You can split them up also and make further distinctions, if you choose. You can cut those divisions down. They merely represent interpretations that you can understand in your reality. In the most mundane of terms, some families are travelers, and some prefer to stay at home. But generally speaking, I have simply given you an outline which follows the characteristics of consciousness as it is embarked in physical form. I am not giving you these groups to set up divisions, but to help you understand that consciousness is diversified—that usually each of you falls, because you want to, into a certain family. And there you acquire friends, alliances, and counterparts.

Besides the physical relationships that each of you know, therefore, you have other brothers and sisters, mothers and fathers, on a psychic level; and to that degree, you are not alone. I am telling you this to give you greater leeway. If you do not like the families that you have, you have others to choose from.[1]

Now these families fall generally into certain groups. In greater terms you can "cut the pie" however you want to, but you will still share an emotional and psychic feeling of belonging with the family of which you are a part. And *(with broad amusement)* most of you here are Sumari, and it demands great discipline for Sumari to take down lists—even of psychic families!

The Sumari experience began when one family, the Sumari, learned that some class members felt alone in this world— bereft of family, often. A class member lost a father. Ruburt *(Jane)* lost a parent also. And because of that emotional and quite human experience, Ruburt <u>allowed</u> the Sumari development to show itself. . . .

(I shouldn't have been surprised last evening to hear Seth say that such an impetus had triggered Jane's Sumari abilities, for today, when I reread the 598th session for November 24, 1971, I was reminded that he'd said the same thing then. The death of the student's father had taken place on Thursday, November 11 of that year; Jane's father, Delmer, died without forewarning on the following Tuesday, November 16; Jane came through with Sumari in class one week later, on November 23; and the next night, in the 598th session, Seth discussed Sumari for the first time.

(Part of my surprise stemmed from what I'd taken to be my knowledge of Jane's relationship with her father. Her parents had divorced when she was two years old, and since her mother did not remarry Jane grew up without a father.[2] Jane and "Del" met again, briefly, when she became 21 years old in 1950. After Jane and I married a few years later we occasionally visited her father in various parts of the country—but still, we hadn't seen him for several years before his death. Yet now it seemed that even beneath that scattered performance Jane's psyche had felt stronger ties of some kind—at least with Del, if not with her mother—than either of us had suspected; that at least some part of her had sensed a sort of biological or creature loss upon the death of a blood relative. I'd never heard her express such attachments or feelings. Even now she could only link the release of her very creative Sumari attributes, the singing, poetry, and prose [as embodied in her novel, Oversoul Seven, *for instance], with Seth's reference to psychic families as well as physical ones.*

(And to me, the whole Sumari thing speaks of some kind of compassionate observation or knowledge of the human condition . . . or in lieu of putting it that way, of an opening up of human awareness to embrace more of the possibilities of consciousness.)

NOTES: Appendix 26

1. I can note a good deal later that Seth's material on our making further distinctions in the families of consciousness, beyond the nine he's already named for us, is certainly related to the passages from a private session that I quoted in the last three paragraphs of Note 8 for the 732nd session: Seth stated that Peter Smith and I "are and are not counterparts"—that with another in this life each of us may often come together, then part, "forming a counterpart relationship when it suits your purposes. . . ."

2. In Volume 1 of *"Unknown" Reality* there are several sources of information on Jane's parents and her early background in general. See, for example, Session 679 with Note 4; Appendix 1 for that session; the opening notes for Session 696, and so forth.

APPENDIX 27
(For Session 739)

(Jane's ESP class for Tuesday evening, February 25, took place the day after the 739th session was held, and was her last one before we began preparing for our move to the hill house. Sue Watkins was present. During class I read aloud Seth's material from the 738th session on the Grunaargh family of consciousness,[1] which Sue had tuned in to during the 598th session for November 24, 1971. After class, Sue told us that she believed she'd been associated with the Grunaargh family—in Europe—through printing processes dating from the 1400's, or possibly somewhat earlier. Since Sue herself is a Sumari, like Jane and me, I asked her to write an account of her feelings, thinking it would furnish a good example of one person's emotional and intellectual involvement with a family of consciousness other than their own— and yes, of their reincarnational memories of those activities.

(Within the week Sue came through with the following paper, offered in a slightly abridged form and with a few annotations:)

"When I first mentioned the family name, Grunaargh (as Seth spelled it out for us in that session over three years ago), I knew that its members had something to do with printing, or the promulgation of printed material. Since at the time I was working as a typesetter,[2] I figured my impression had derived from that. However, after that session my impression 'grew' in such a way that I knew this family had something to do in a more direct way with the printing process—with the fascination of putting ideas down on paper through the use of typefaces that would, as much as the language involved, express the ideas behind the words themselves. In the plant where I worked at the time, I 'recognized' several people in the Grunaargh family—all were printers—and with a feeling quite as strong as the recognition I had for Sumari.

"When Seth listed the families of consciousness last January,[3] but didn't include the Grunaargh, Rob asked him about it in the 738th session. In Jane's final class, Rob read Seth's explanation having to do with family 'mergings.' Right away, right there in class, I knew what was behind the feeling I'd had about this family: Members of the Grunaargh, and I personally, were involved in the invention of movable type. I write 'were' out of habit, because I have this delightful feeling that my printing, writing, and newspaper interests now are what led me to be drawn to the same things back then, even as my work there caused me to be interested in the same things now—an exchange across the board.

"It seems so hilariously logical that the Sumari, who are creators, would want to 'merge' with a family more prone to organization,[4] to come up with what they would need to spread ideas: movable type. Otherwise, how would they ever get up the gumption to sit around and carve out all those damn little characters? Too exasperating!

"I see myself, then, as one of the people involved in the thinking-up and making-of the typefaces. I see a large, sort of beefy man with a red face, sitting at a piece of furniture like a drafting table, carefully cutting out these characters. He had fingers like sausages; people in town were always amused that he was so big and worked with such small pieces. He made them out of wood, I think, and they served as molds or models that ended up cast in metal. He rubbed a substance on the wood grain to protect it. But using these models gave the alphabets some kind of standardization.[5]

"My heavyset friend was filled with the thrill of knowing that now words would spread faster. This is hard to specify, but he had the same feeling I have now about newspapers—the daily spreading out of ideas, and the kind of tremendous power behind that ability . . . I can see that corner of his shop/work area clearly in a half-light, illuminated by a candle in an enclosed mesh lantern sitting on a tabletop. This man had several apprentices, and he was a real artisan, putting ideas across in the form of movable type. I know that Gutenberg is credited with this invention, and probably rightly so; but I also feel this as one of those discoveries that appeared in several places at once, and that my beefy fellow's shop was in the general vicinity of Gutenberg's—in Germany? I can't recall. This idea was 'shared' in many places at once, then.[6]

"It all gives me this feeling of great hilarity that I often have about these ideas. And the thought of families of consciousness merging for different reasons—even while I accept that all of this is put in very limited terms—seems to have such perfect inner logic and delightful playfulness about it that I launch into the mergings notion with all kinds of questions, and impressions exploding outward.

"I think my beefy gentleman, by the way, also wrote editorials. . . ."

(That was the end of Sue's paper. She hasn't read any history of printing, per se. Actually, she told us, the material available to her from that time "could go on" indefinitely. She went on to answer my question:)

"Sure, I was a Sumari then, too. I've always been one. I've always had the knowledge of Sumari, I think . . . Funny—I don't know how to describe it, really, but I feel that through all of my lives at least one of my functions has been to act as a sort of catalyst between the Sumari and other families of consciousness. I seem to have played roles where I'd get involved with people in other families, then lead them over to the Sumari. At least that way different groups made contact and learned from each other."[7]

NOTES: Appendix 27

    1. See the notes on Sue and the Grunaargh at the start of the 737th session.
    2. And Sue is still involved with "the promulgation of printed material." Now she's co-editor of a weekly newspaper published in a small town north of Elmira. (Again, see the opening notes for Session 737.)
    3. See the 732nd session.
    4. The Grunaargh family of consciousness is a variation of the Gramada family—the organizers. See Note 6 for the 737th session.
    5. "My friend wanted nothing but plain, simple letters—nothing fancy," Sue told Jane and me as we discussed her material. She drew some of the typefaces either designed or approved by that large, male, "earlier" creation of her whole self. In all cases the letters were of the cleanest simplicity, both for esthetic reasons and ease in carving and casting.
    6. Sue could well be correct here. It's believed that Johann Gutenberg (1400?–1468) was experimenting with movable metal type in Strasbourg, Germany, before 1448–but there's also possible evidence of printing from such type in Holland by 1430, for instance. (And typography itself was known, but not much used, in China and Korea in the 11th century.) In about 1448 Gutenberg became a citizen of Mainz, Germany, where he continued his work. By then, of course, the news about printing was spreading throughout Europe.
    7. In Session 692 for Volume 1 of *"Unknown" Reality* see the material on Sue's double dreams in the opening notes and in Note 2. Personally, at least, I see strong connections between the idea of double dreams and the kind of conscious reincarnational memory—or knowledge—detailed by Sue in this appendix.

EPILOGUE

In the 82nd session, which was held on the evening of August 27, 1964, Seth said: "When man realizes that he, himself, creates his personal and universal environment in concrete terms, then he can begin to create a private and universal environment much superior to the [present] one, that is the result of haphazard and unenlightened constructions.

"<u>This</u> is our main message to the world, and this is the next line in man's conceptual development, which will make itself felt in all fields, and in psychiatry perhaps as much as any."

In one way or another all of Seth's book are elaborations of that basic message, stated nine months after his sessions with us began in December 1963. It should be obvious that the two volumes of *"Unknown" Reality* are further ramifications of that thesis, for here Seth shows us the usually invisible psychological dimensions that underlie the known world. He reveals the very structure upon which our free will rests: for if events were immutable or fated, no free will would be possible.

As far as we can see, Seth's reincarnational, counterpart, and probable selves, and his families of consciousness, suggest the varied, complicated structure of human personality—and hint of the invisible psychological thickness that fills out the physical event of the self in time.

The two volumes of *"Unknown" Reality* hardly tie truth up in neat packages, though, so that after completing them the reader can claim to know all of the answers. In fact, Seth's material always raises more questions to stimulate the intellect and intuitions, and these two books are no exception. In a sense, they *are* incomplete and complicated at times, with new terms, for the unknown reality they attempt to describe will, I fear, always elude us to some extent; and new terms are needed as old ones become stereotyped and worn.

Seth told us ahead of time, of course, that *"Unknown" Reality* would follow an intuitive and inner organization rather than a linear one, and that this writing method would itself arouse the creative, revelatory characteristics of the psyche. Material on any given subject may start, go on for a while, then either stop almost in mid-sentence or "evolve" into another topic. Yet underneath, the books ride securely upon rhythms that reflect the psyche's deep resources.

Now it seems that my own purposes in preparing these volumes were too gargantuan to ever accomplish more than partially. I wanted to show the ever-widening vital reactions that Seth's dictation of *"Unknown" Reality* had on our personal lives, and how those effects rippled outward. It's almost impossible to describe the creative frustration I sometimes felt—for no matter how fast I worked to record the sessions themselves, noted our day's activities, hunted down the references pertinent to a given discussion, I couldn't truly keep up: Reality kept splashing over the edges of my notes. New events kept happening, surfacing from usually hidden dimensions.

It seems clear now that Seth knew all along that this would happen. The creative explosions begun with these books still erupt, for *"Unknown" Reality* does seem to have a life of its own, one that defies definition, and that even now serves as a springboard for new psychic and creative experience. Talk about probable realities! This manuscript seems to possess dimensions that place it—and Jane and me—in many probabilities at once. As I type its pages for the final time, I'm back at our old Water Street apartments, and in our new "hill house" at once; I'm referring to 1975 sessions and recording Seth's dictation on his latest book as well. Sometimes I feel like saying: "One reality at a time, please."

In vital ways, Seth's material itself *is* timeless, yet its production, of course, is tied to the events of our lives. I hope my notes provide that "living story"—the narrative that gives the material its flesh in our time. The material itself can stand on its own, though, and we trust it will continue to do so when Jane and I are through with this particular joint physical adventure. Then Seth's work will fall back upon the timeless quality that always illuminates it.

In any case, I feel that the entire production, Seth's dictated work and my running commentaries and references, adds up to extra dimensions of creativity that can be sensed, if not described. When I get *that* feeling of psychological multiplicity, I realize that the goal I had in mind was at least somewhat realized.

Then also, I remember what Seth said about being reckless in the pursuit of the ideal. (See the Introductory Notes.) I don't know that I was that daring, but I was persistent despite the hesitations and misgivings. So along with Seth's work, we tried to share our reality with the reader, and to provide a platform in time for knowledge that must basically straddle our ideas of time and reality alike.

Long before I finished my part of *"Unknown" Reality,* Seth and Jane had started their next book: *The Nature of the Psyche: Its Human Expression.* I recorded those sessions, of course, while keeping up with my own work. Jane finished her *Psychic Politics,* and began some new poetry and world-view material. She was taking calls from readers in all parts of the country, trying to keep up with the mail, participating in an occasional radio interview, and, for most of that time, conducting her classes. And oh, yes, both of us also did a lot of ordinary living, such as moving and getting settled in our new home and entertaining friends now and then. Yet none of those "outside" events were fully removed from *"Unknown" Reality.* They found their way into the pages, the sessions, somehow, even if only by *feel* or inference. For how could any one event not jostle all of the others in lives so closely bound?

Yet we think now that such extensive notes have served their purposes for Seth's material, at least for some time, so those books-in-the-works will carry minimum notes—as they do, say, in *Seth Speaks.* For one thing, as I write this Epilogue, Seth has finished *The Nature of the Psyche,* and has already begun still *another* book. *Psyche,* as Jane and I call it, contains some excellent new material, such as Seth's first discussions of sex—including lesbianism, homosexuality, and bisexuality—as well as other related subjects that we know, from our correspondence, to be of intense general concern. By using simple session notes only, we can get that next book to the public in a minimum of time, and it should be published shortly after this second volume of *"Unknown" Reality*—perhaps within just a few months.

Also, Jane has long since completed *The World View of Paul Cézanne: A Psychic Interpretation,* which was published in 1977; and she's finished *The Afterdeath Journal of an American Philosopher: The World View of William James*—both books growing out of the world-view material given by Seth in *"Unknown" Reality.*

The luxurious creativity displayed by Seth's and Jane's work raises more questions about the abilities of the psyche than it seems we can ever hope to answer. Despite the different lights in which Seth may be regarded, despite the varying degrees of reality his existence may be granted by others, there can be no doubt of his individuality or productivity as it's displayed in his books.

And again, at latest count Jane has written three books (including *Psychic Politics*) since Seth began *"Unknown" Reality*—and worked on several others—so what is the relationship between the human psyche and such "other" sources of creativity and knowledge?

No one, whether that individual is a psychic, a mystic, a writer, a poet, or even if he or she combines all of those qualities (as I think Jane does), can encompass all of the incredible differences within the human species. I believe that thick, sprawling works like *"Unknown" Reality* offer some important answers, but beyond that it's up to the multidimensional, multitudinous, over four billion *multinational* individuals on this planet to follow their own intuitions and seek answers in their personal ways. Lots of those people will never hear of the Seth material—nor, as Seth himself has said, will they ever *need* to—but then, Jane and I know that some *will*, and so we proffer what we can.

We have so much to learn about our inner and outer worlds that once an attempt is made to discuss those large issues, a host of questions arise. What I for one finally get down on paper, then, must be very incomplete when compared to what I *don't* write, or don't know. Jane and I, for instance, have never particularly cared for the term "ESP," or *extra*sensory perception (my emphasis), since to us it implies misleading conceptions about certain inner abilities. We hardly think those attributes are "extra" at all, although they're obviously more developed or consciously available in some individuals than in others—but then, so is a "gift" for music, or baseball or whatever. (I'll add here that Jane calls her class an ESP class for the obvious reason that the term has become so well known that most people understand something of its implied meaning.)

After making those points, however, I note with some amusement that I find it difficult indeed to believe that many millions of people must wait for a handful of their "superior" peers—philosophers, scientists, psychologists, parapsychologists— to tell them it's *all right* to believe in at least a few of the inner abilities that each of us possesses, to whatever degree. Obviously, numerous individuals simply refuse to wait for the official light of recognition to shine forth.

That wait could be a very long one. Who is to help initiate meaningful changes in our psychological and social orders? Surely Jane feels the necessity to turn aside from the selected dogmas of our time. For to her, and to me, our world's present definitions of personality are as limited as the conventional meaning implied by the term ESP. We hope that Jane's work can help expand such concepts.

We also think science is "objective" enough in its own terms of serial time and measurement, as it claims to be, but that eventually it must *choose* to look inward as thoroughly as it does outward. To us, much of the turmoil in the world results from our steadfast refusal to accept a major portion of our natural heritage. We project our inner knowledge "outward" in distorted fashion; thus on a global scale we thrash about with our problems of war, overpopulation, and dwindling natural resources, to name but a few.

According to Seth, each of us chose such a course at this time—but now, we think, a time of imperative change is necessary if we are to continue our progress as a species. A new blending of inner and outer consciousnesses—a new, more meaningful coalition of intellectual and intuitive abilities—will be the latest step in the process of "consciousness knowing itself," as Seth has described it.

I don't think our conventional social systems, including our scientific ones, are going to resolve our questions within Jane's and my personal lifetimes. I'm not putting down our cultures and science either, since they very accurately reflect the collective lives and conditions that we've chosen to create. But Jane and I *do* want to know more; we're sure that Seth can help us here.

Whatever or whoever Seth is, or whatever the nature of the Seth-Jane relationship, we long ago decided that we could learn from it. No need to dogmatically insist upon reincarnation as being a "fact," or upon the existence of Seth's counterparts or the families of consciousness. In the material as a whole there are bound to be significant clues as to the nature of the human animal: creative clues that can't help but enlighten us in many—and sometimes unexpected—ways. I deal with some of the material we've acquired about the Seth-Jane relationship in Appendix 18 for Session 711, in Section 4; but here I want to stress our overall interest in knowledge, whatever that knowledge may be, and wherever it may lead us.

As I've joked with Jane more than once: "If there's life after death, each of us in turn will find it out—including the nonbelievers. And if there isn't—well, no one will ever know *that*. Either way, there's absolutely nothing to worry about. . . ." So in the meantime the search can be fun, and intriguing—even a passion—but at the same time, without absolutism or any Messianic drive to change the world.

But if Seth-Jane are at all right, then consciousness is more than encompassing enough to embrace all that we are, and everything that each of us can even remotely conceive of doing or being. Try as we might, we'll not exhaust or annihilate consciousness: Whatever we accomplish as people will still leave room for—indeed, *demand*—further ramifications and development. And in the interim we can always look at nature with its innocent, spontaneous order to sustain us. We can at least observe, and enjoy, the behavior of other species with whom we share the world.

For in closing, I'd like to return to one of my favorite happenings: the migration of geese. I wrote the following notes in October 1975, some seven months after Jane and I had moved into our "new" house:

> "The view of sky sweeping over our hill makes it much easier to see the great flights of geese heading south for the winter. Twice this week in the daytime, and once at night, large flocks have passed over. On each occasion I heard them while I was working inside the house, then rushed out into the yard. The geese seem to be more numerous on cloudy days and clear nights.
>
> "One late-afternoon gaggle reached nearly from horizon to horizon, in three long and very noisy V-formations. And always, one bird led each V, with the two sides of the bird 'lettering' trailing back quite unevenly—wobbling, flexing, shifting. What free sociable claques, I thought. Amazing, the way their honking carried back to Jane and me as we stood in the driveway. We watched the geese fly toward the hills on the far side of the valley; we could still hear them even when they'd become practically invisible."

In its way the nighttime visitation was even more mysterious, for that time I looked up at a starlit but moonless sky that didn't have a cloud in sight—and heard this multitudinous *sound* moving across it. The night was chilly. Jane was sleeping. All of the qualities of the birds' flight were heightened for me by its very invisibility, for while I actually saw no geese at all, that sound was everywhere. And what guided those creatures, I wondered—magnetic lines of force, genes, innate knowledge—or what? And I knew that no objective reasoning processes alone could explain their magnificent flight.

Somehow the twice-yearly, north-and-south migrations of the geese have become symbols for me of the known and unknown qualities of life—sublime and indecipherable at the same time, enduring yet fleeting, and almost outside of the range of human events. For me, those migrations have become portents of the seasons and of the earth itself as it swings around "our" sun in great rhythms. The one consciousness (mine) stands in its body on the ground and looks up at the strange variations of itself represented by the geese. And wonders. In their own ways, do the geese wonder also? What kind of hidden interchanges between species take place at such times? If the question could be answered, would all of reality in its unending mystery lie revealed before us?

Robert F. Butts
September 1978

Index